The Night Marchers

and Other Oceanian Stories

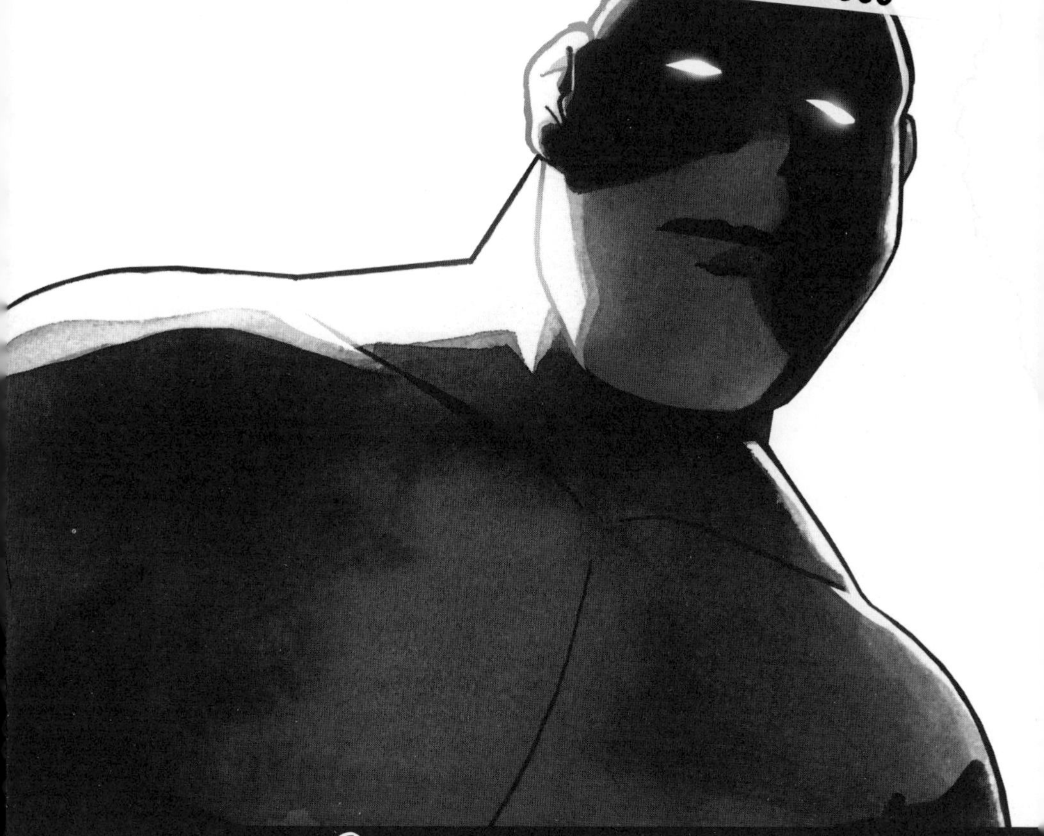

A Cautionary Fables & Fairytales Book

editors
Kel McDonald, Kate Ashwin & Sloane Leong

cover artist
Nick Iluzada

publisher
C. Spike Trotman

art director
Matt Sheridan

print technician & book design
Beth Scorzato

published by
Iron Circus Comics
329 West 18th Street, Suite 604
Chicago, IL 60616
ironcircus.com

first edition: April 2021

ISBN: 978-1-945820-79-3

10 9 8 7 6 5 4 3 2 1

Printed in China

strange and amazing
inquiry@ironcircus.com   www.ironcircus.com

The Night Marchers and Other Oceanian Stories

Publisher's Cataloging-In-Publication Data
(Prepared by The Donohue Group, Inc.)

Names: Ashwin, Kate, editor. | Leong, Sloane, editor. | McDonald, Kel, editor.
Title: The night marchers, and other Oceanian stories / [edited by Kate Ashwin, Sloane Leong, and Kel McDonald].
Other Titles: Night marchers, & other Oceanian stories | Cautionary fables & fairytales (Series) ; 4.
Description: First edition. | Chicago, IL : Iron Circus Comics, 2021. | Series: A cautionary fables & fairytales book ; [4] | Interest age level: 010-012. | Summary: An anthology of folktales from the Pacific Islands reimagined with a modern twist.
Identifiers: ISBN 9781945820793 (trade paperback)
Subjects: LCSH: Pacific Islanders–Folklore–Comic books, strips, etc. | Fairy tales–Islands of the Pacific–Comic books, strips, etc. | CYAC: Pacific Islanders–Folklore–Fiction. | Fairy tales–Islands of the Pacific–Fiction. | LCGFT: Folk tales. | Fairy tales. | Fables. | Graphic novels.
Classification: LCC PZ7.7 .N535 2021 | DDC [Fic] 398.2099–dc23

TABLE OF CONTENTS

Tabi Po *(Philippines)*
Iole Marie Rabor 5

Pele and Poliahu: A Tale of Fire and Ice *(Hawaii)*
DJ Keawekane & Kel McDonald 22

The Dancing Princess *(Philippines)*
Mariel Maranan 42

The Night Marchers *(Hawaii)*
Jonah Cabudol-Chalker & Kate Ashwin 61

The Legend of Apolaki and Mayari *(Philippines)*
Kim Miranda 67

Nanuae the Sharkboy *(Hawaii)*
Gen H. 85

Thousand Eyes *(Philippines)*
Paolo Chikiamco & Tintin Pantoja 108

The Story of Benito *(Philippines)*
Nicole Mannino 122

The Legend of the Coconut Tree *(Fiji)*
Yiling Changues 141

The Turtle and The Lizard *(Philippines)*
Cy Vendivil 154

Let's Learn Baybayin
Cy Vendivil 174

Kapo'i and the Owl *(Hawaii)*
Sloane Leong, Kate Ashwin & Meredith McClaren 176

The Tyrant has Horns (Philippines)
Diigii Daguna 184

The Ibalon Epic: a Retelling of Baltog (Philippines)
Mark Gould 203

Left in the Canefields (Hawaii)
Brady Evans 218

The Alan and The Hunters (Philippines)
Rob Cham 233

The Hula Manō (Hawaii)
Sloane Leong 249

About the Artists 250

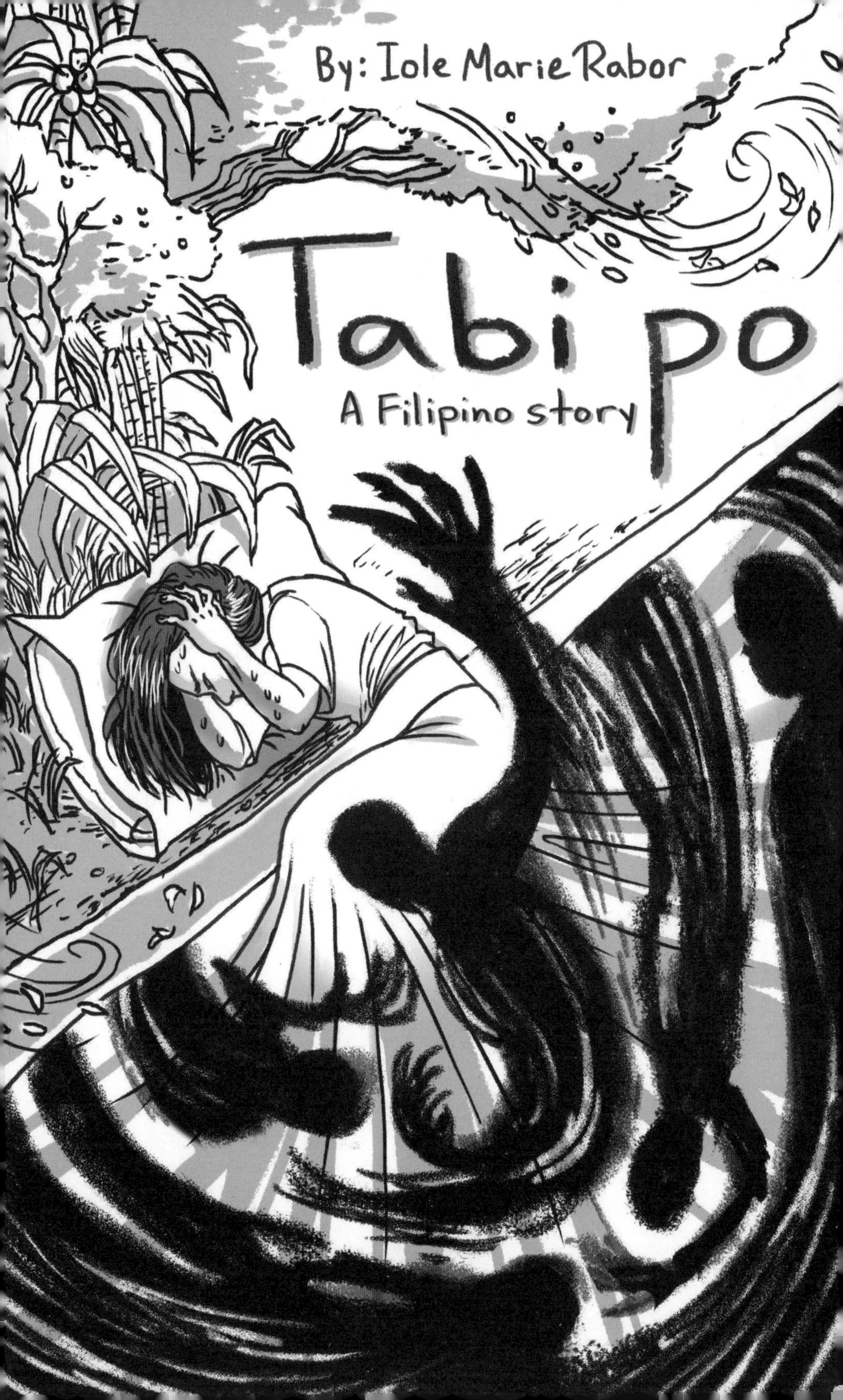
By: Iole Marie Rabor
Tabi po
A Filipino story

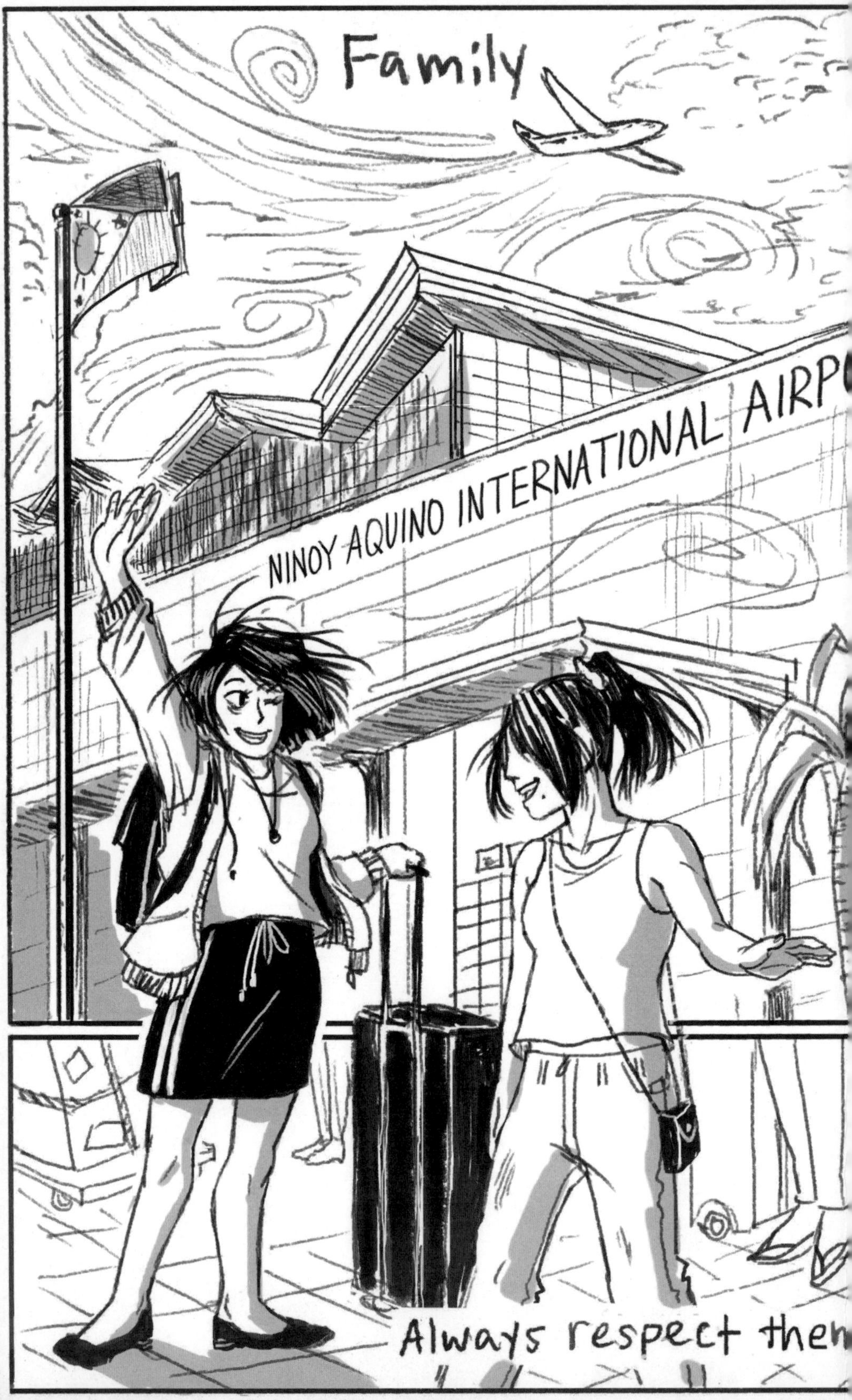
Family
NINOY AQUINO INTERNATIONAL AIRP
Always respect them

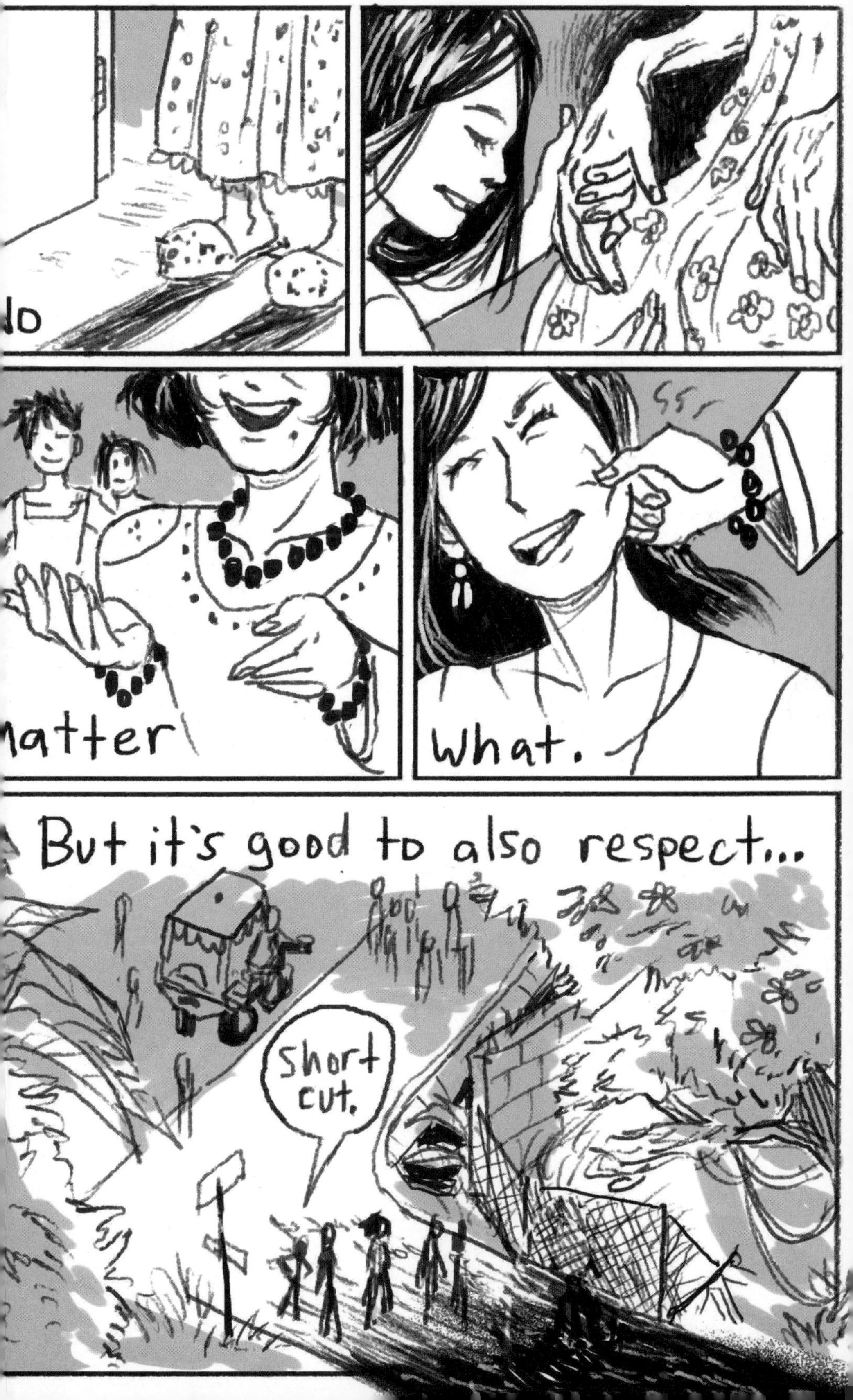

lo
atter
What.
But it's good to also respect...
Short cut.

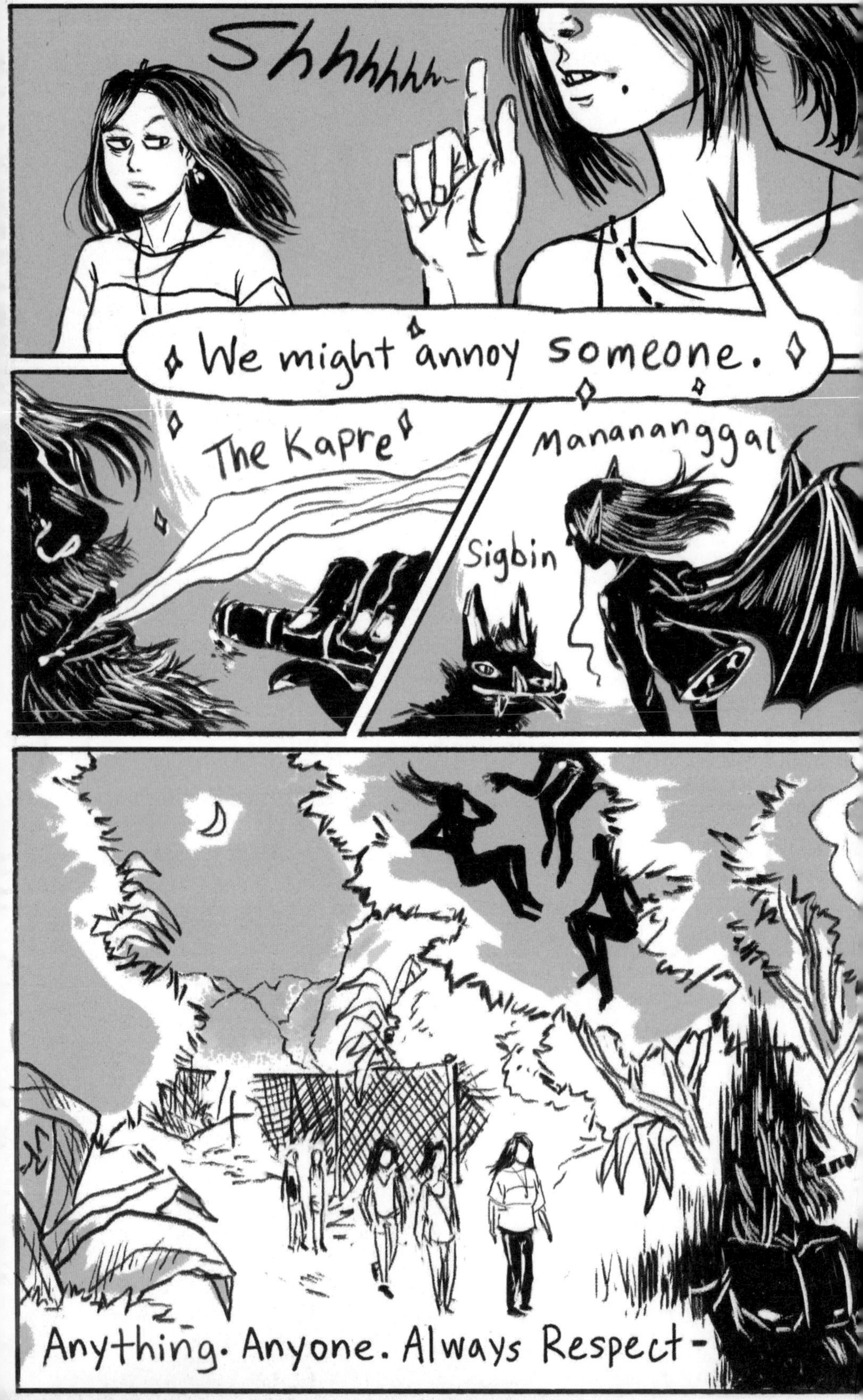
Shhhhhh
We might annoy someone.
The Kapre
Manananggal
Sigbin
Anything. Anyone. Always Respect-

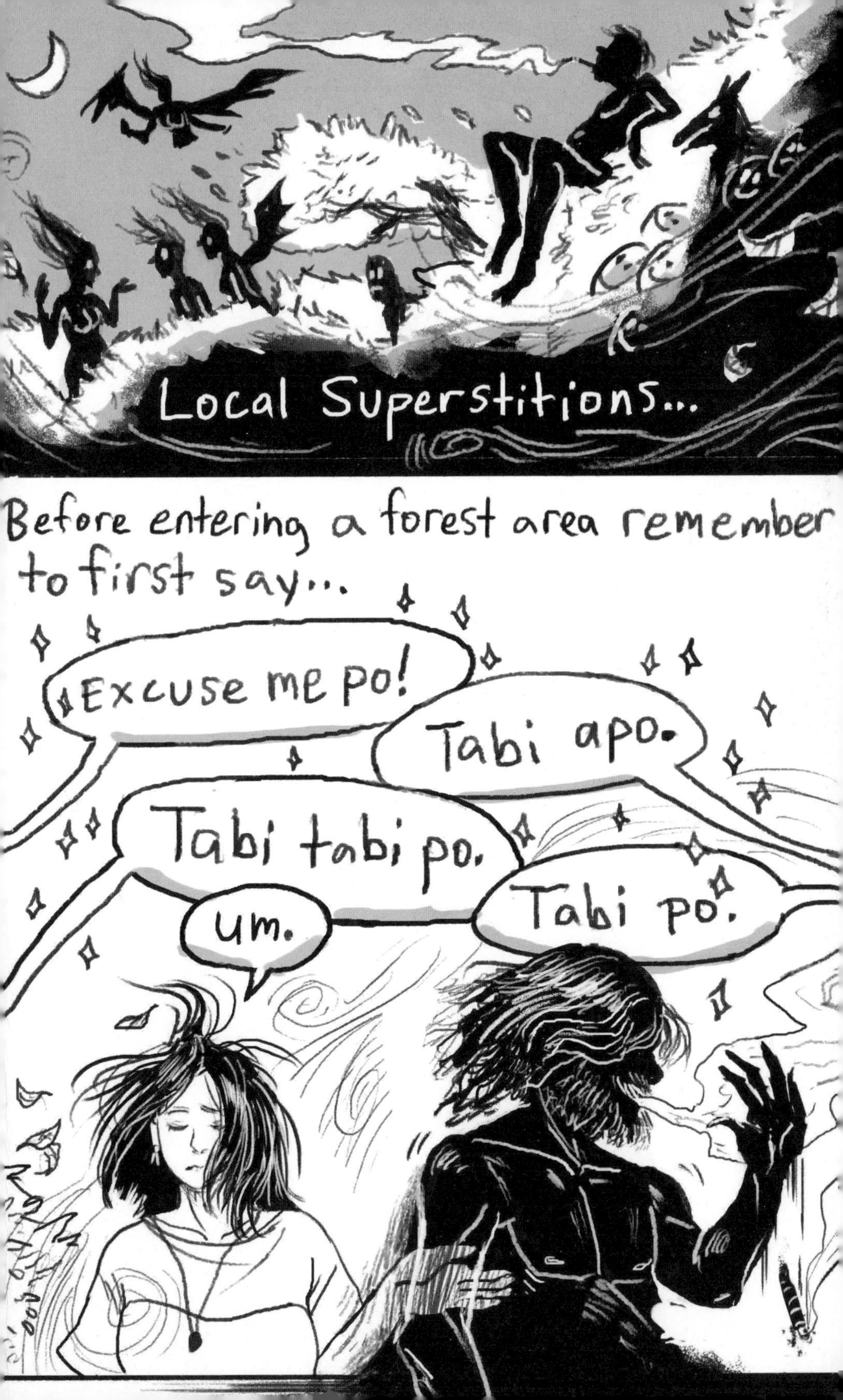
Local Superstitions...
Before entering a forest area remember to first say...
Excuse me po!
Tabi apo.
Tabi tabi po.
Tabi po.
um.

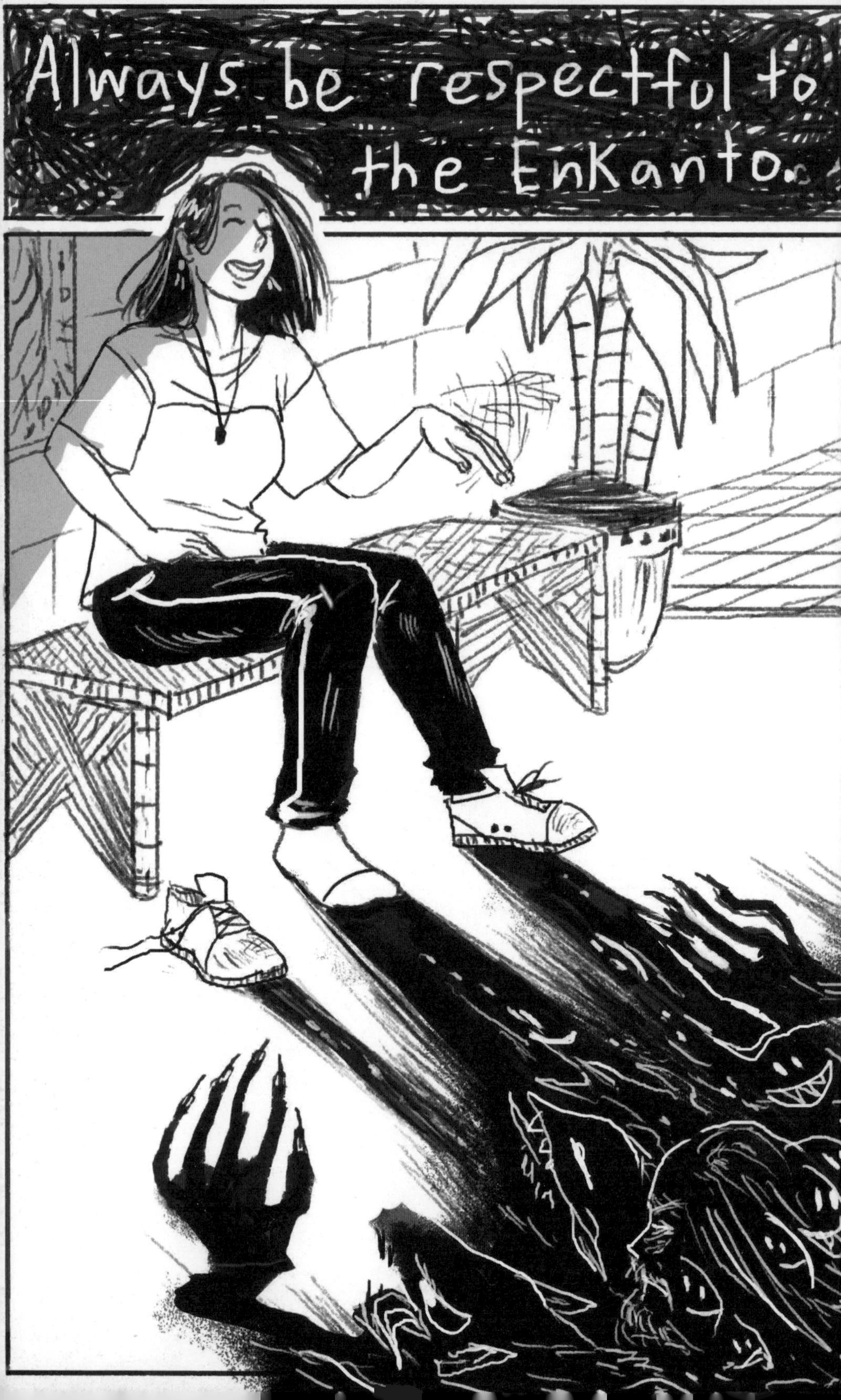
Always be respectful to the EnKanto.

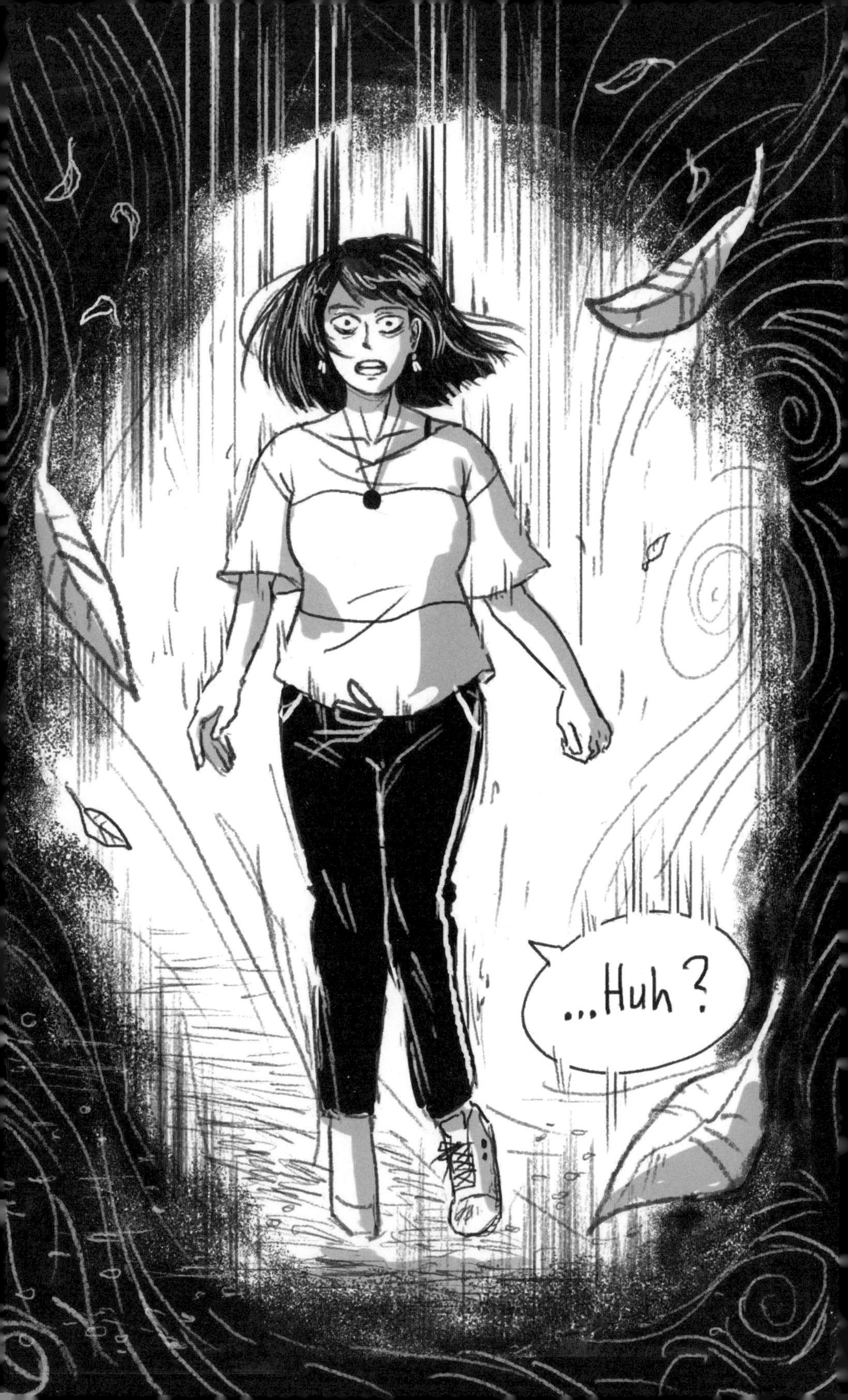
...Huh?

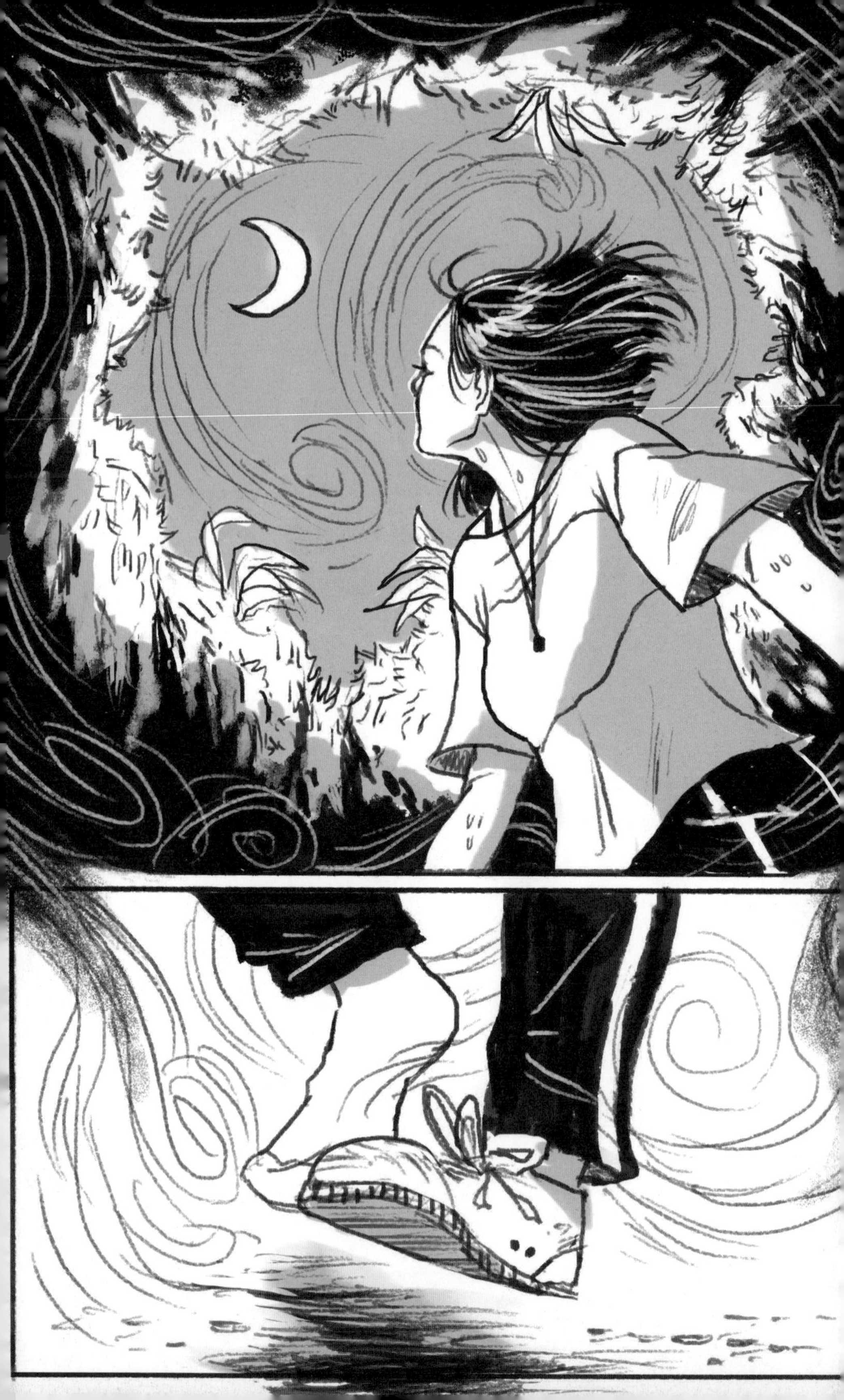

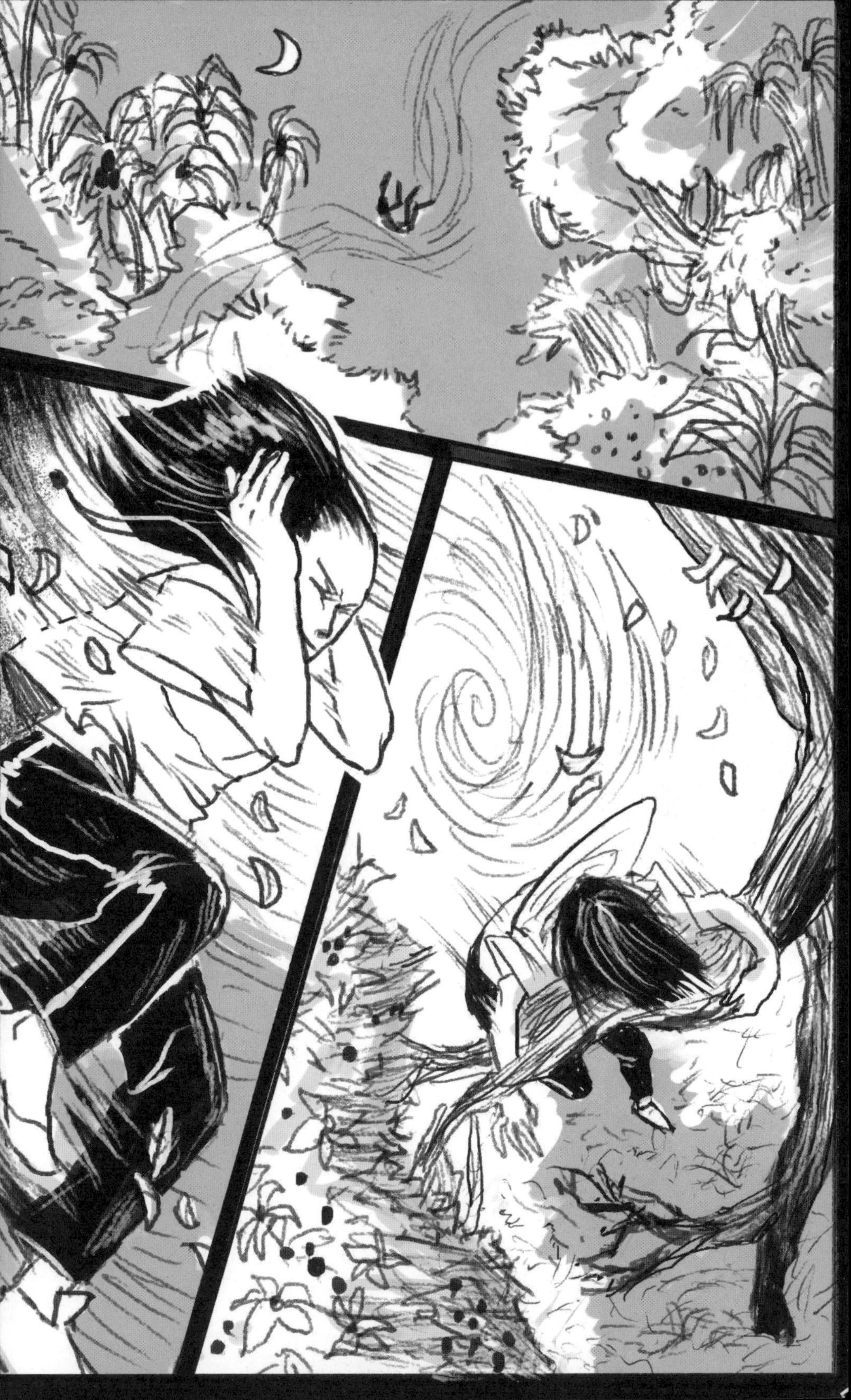

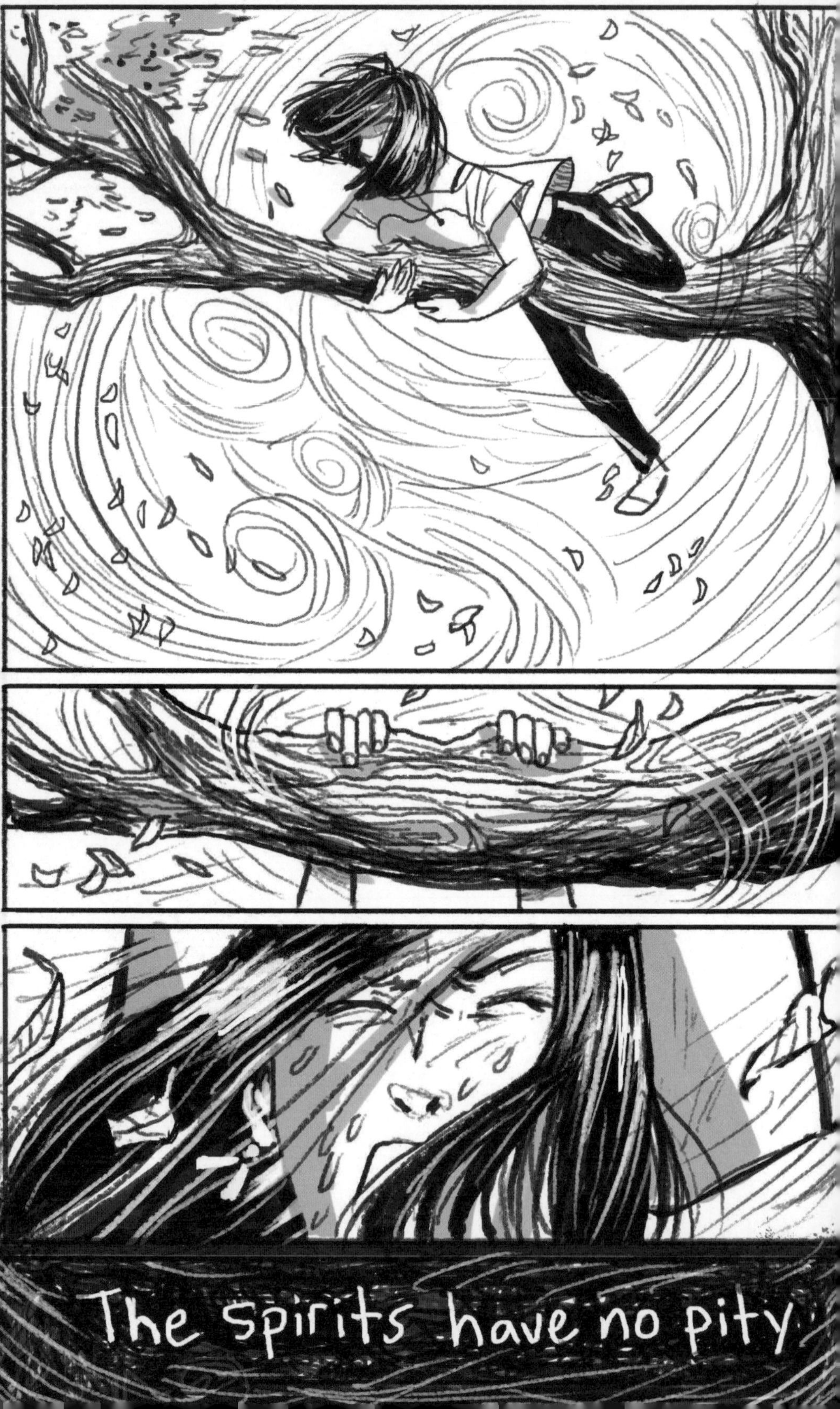
The spirits have no pity

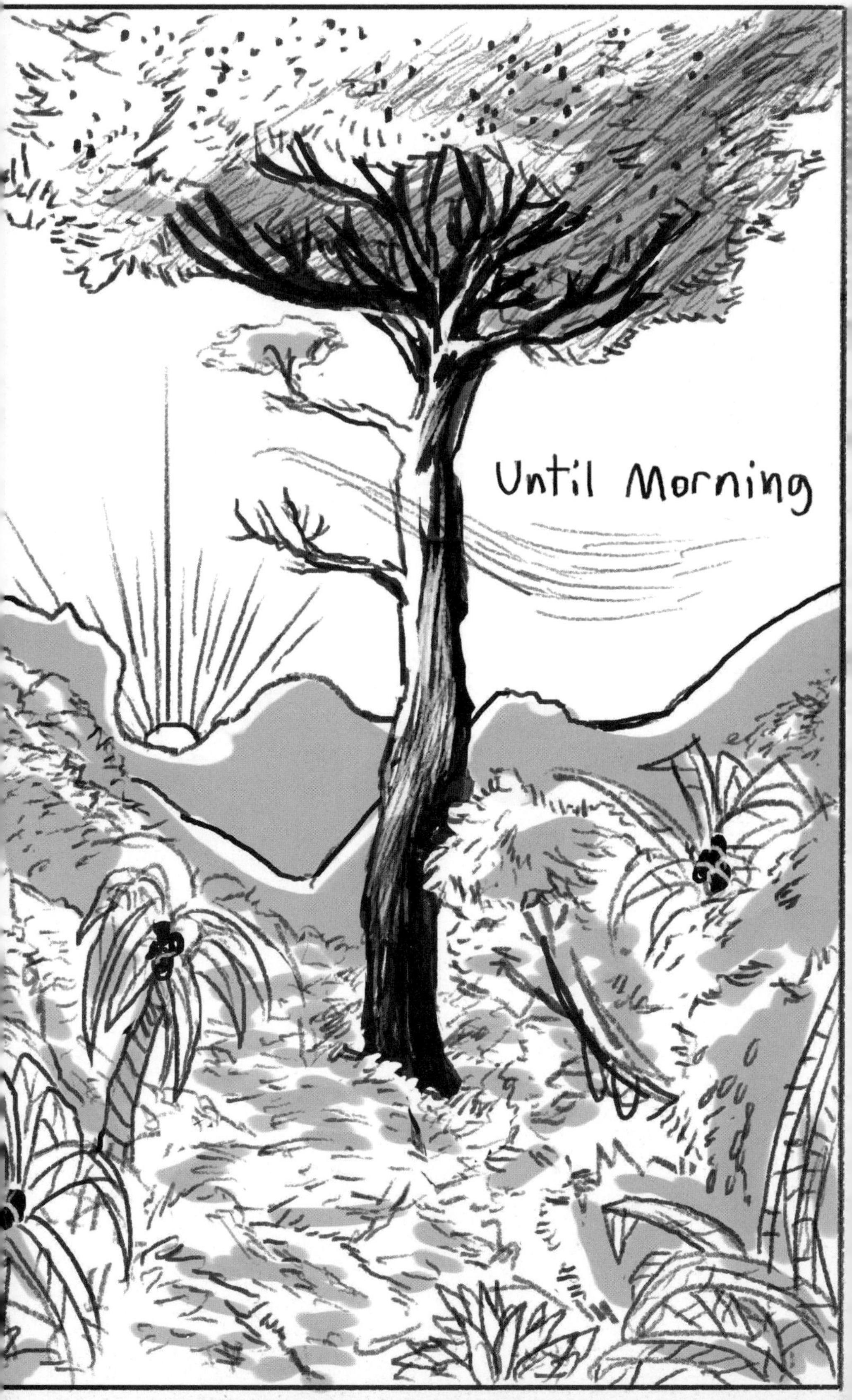
Until Morning

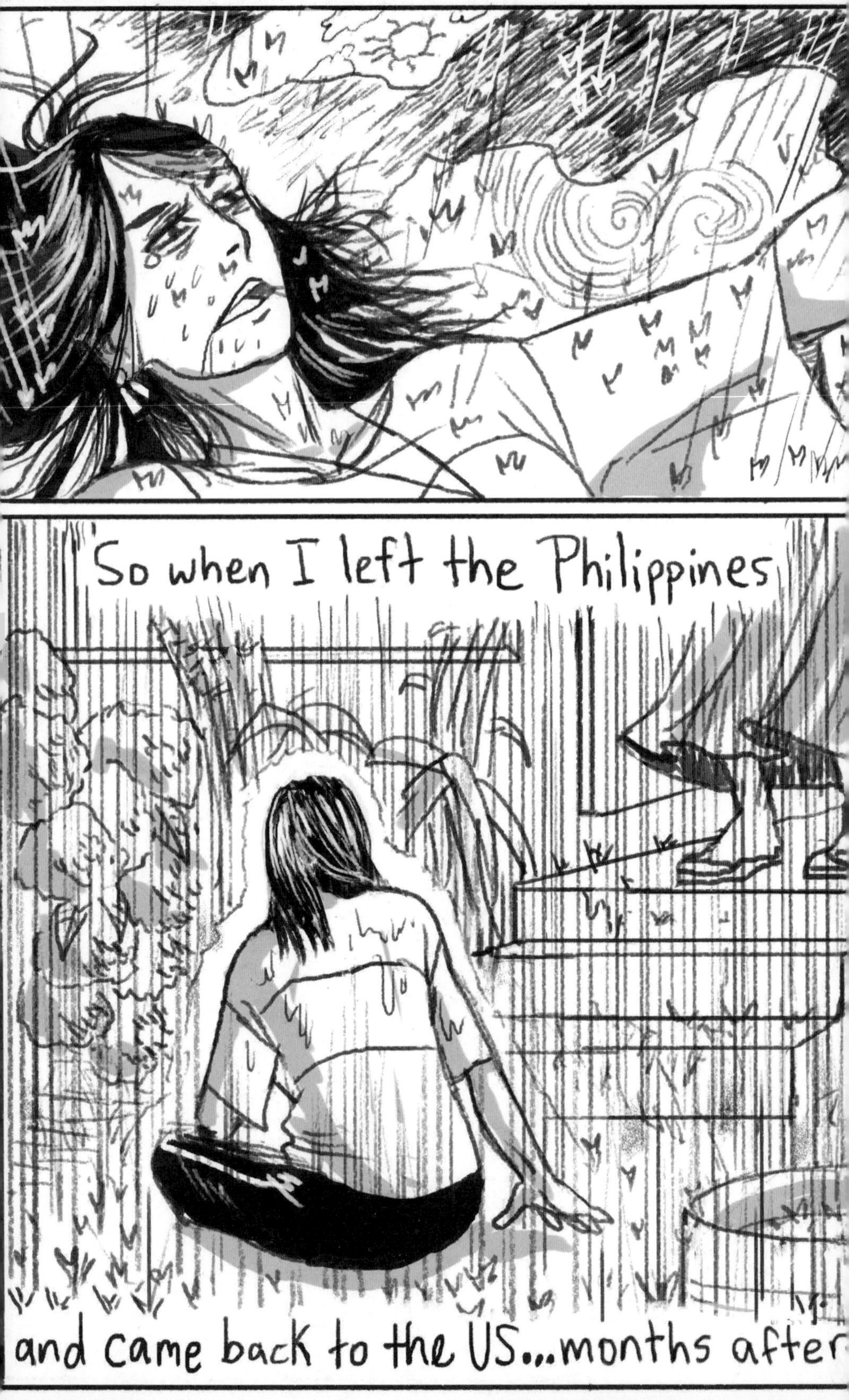
So when I left the Philippines
and came back to the US...months after

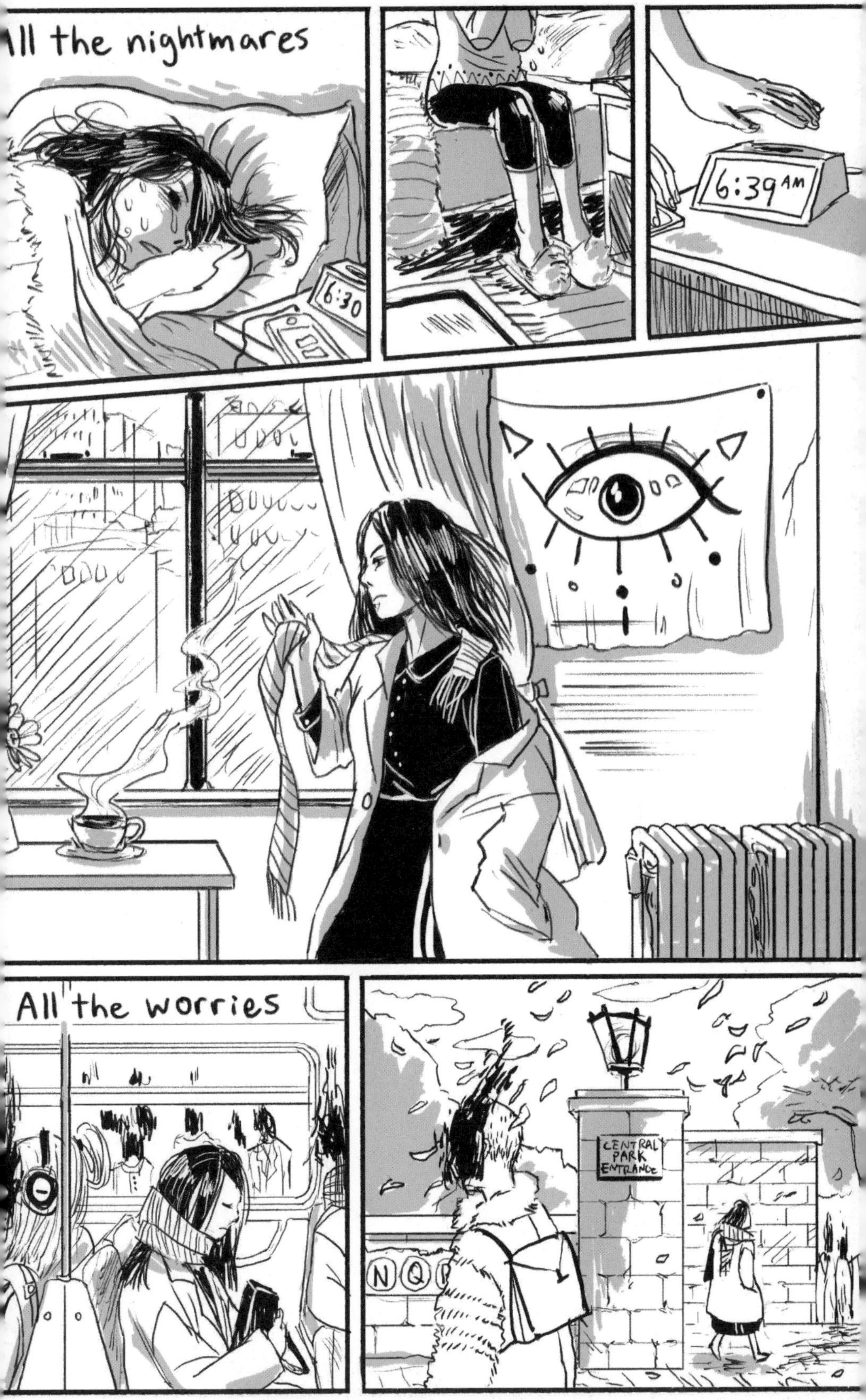
All the nightmares
6:30
6:39 AM
All the worries
CENTRAL PARK ENTRANCE
N Q

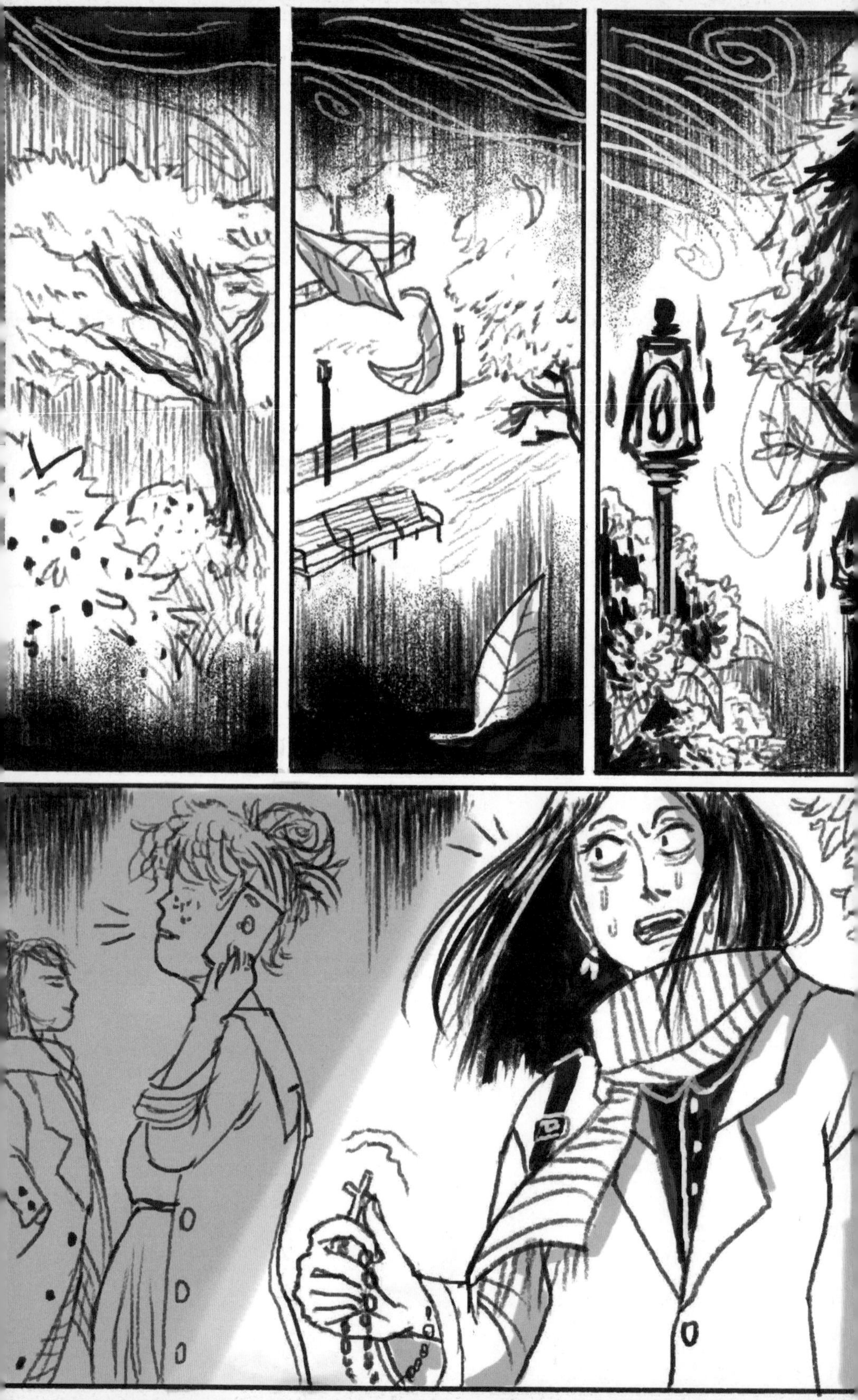

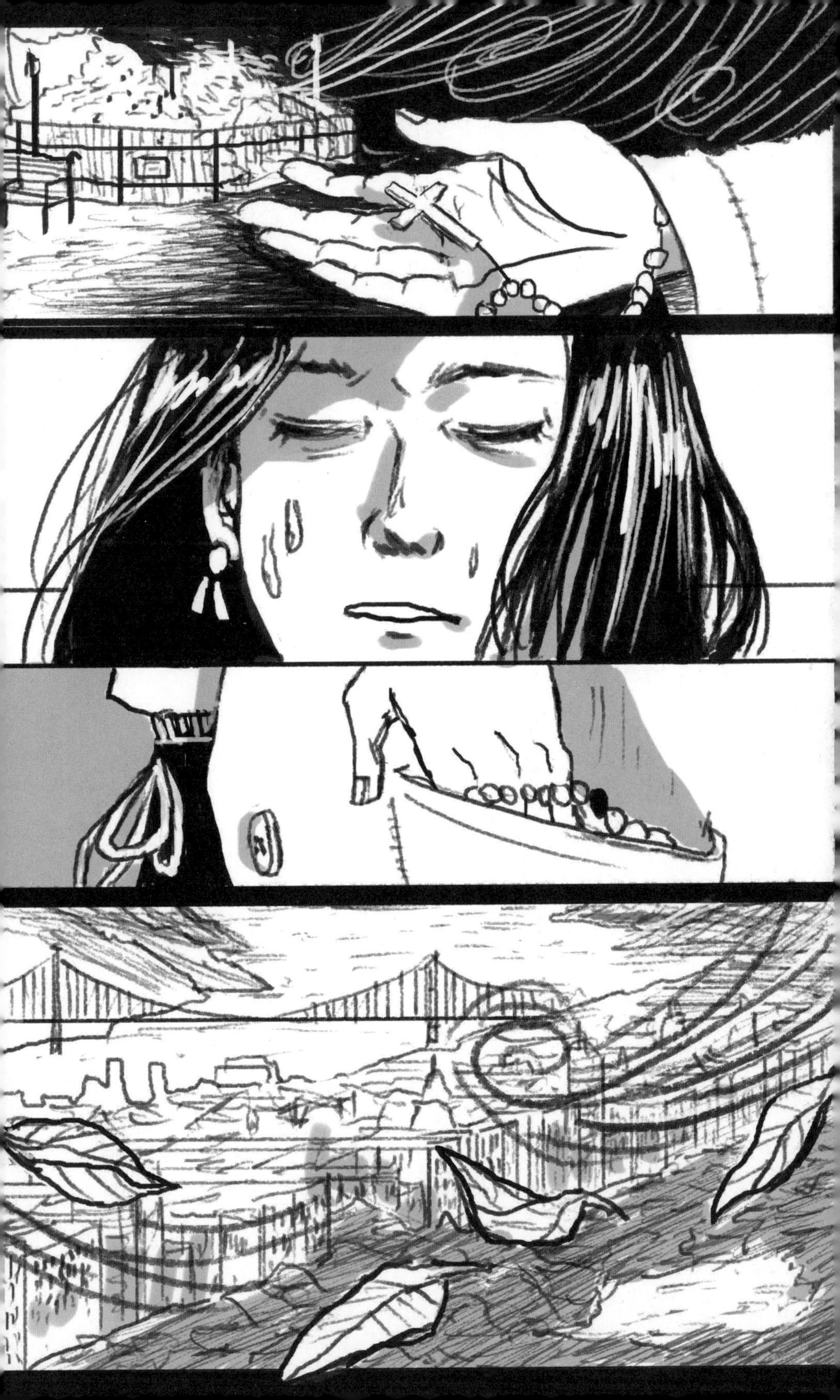

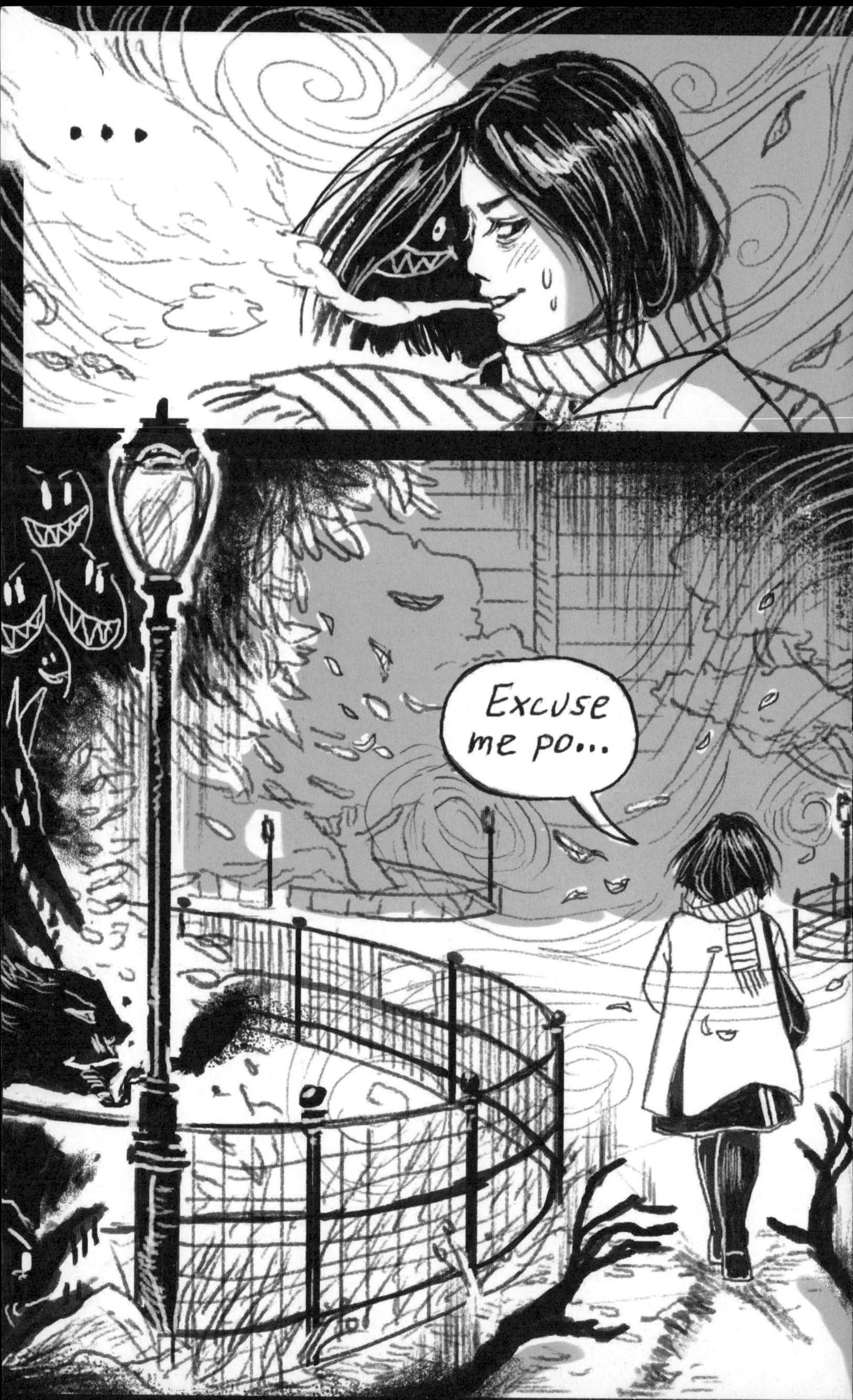
...
Excuse me po...

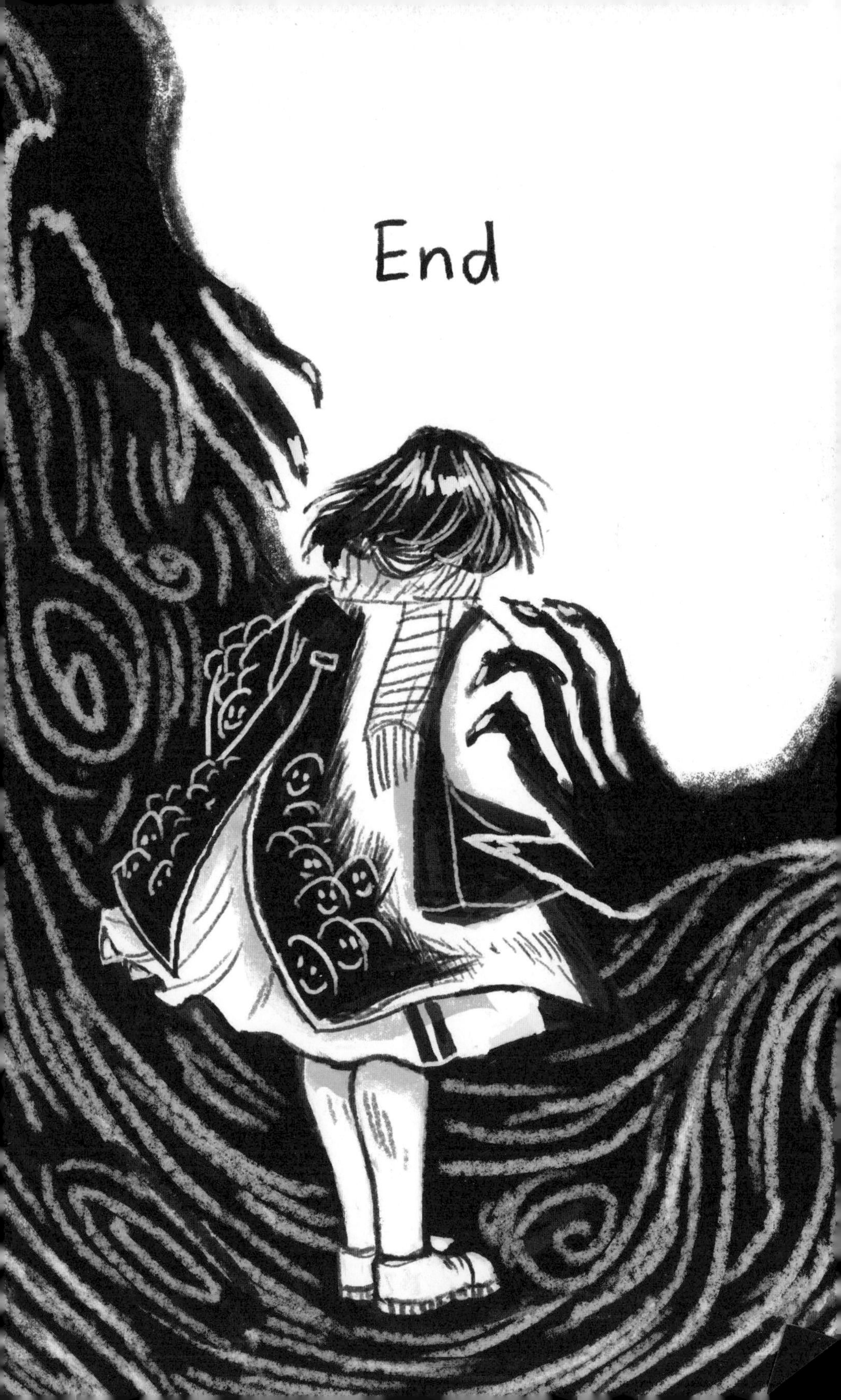
End

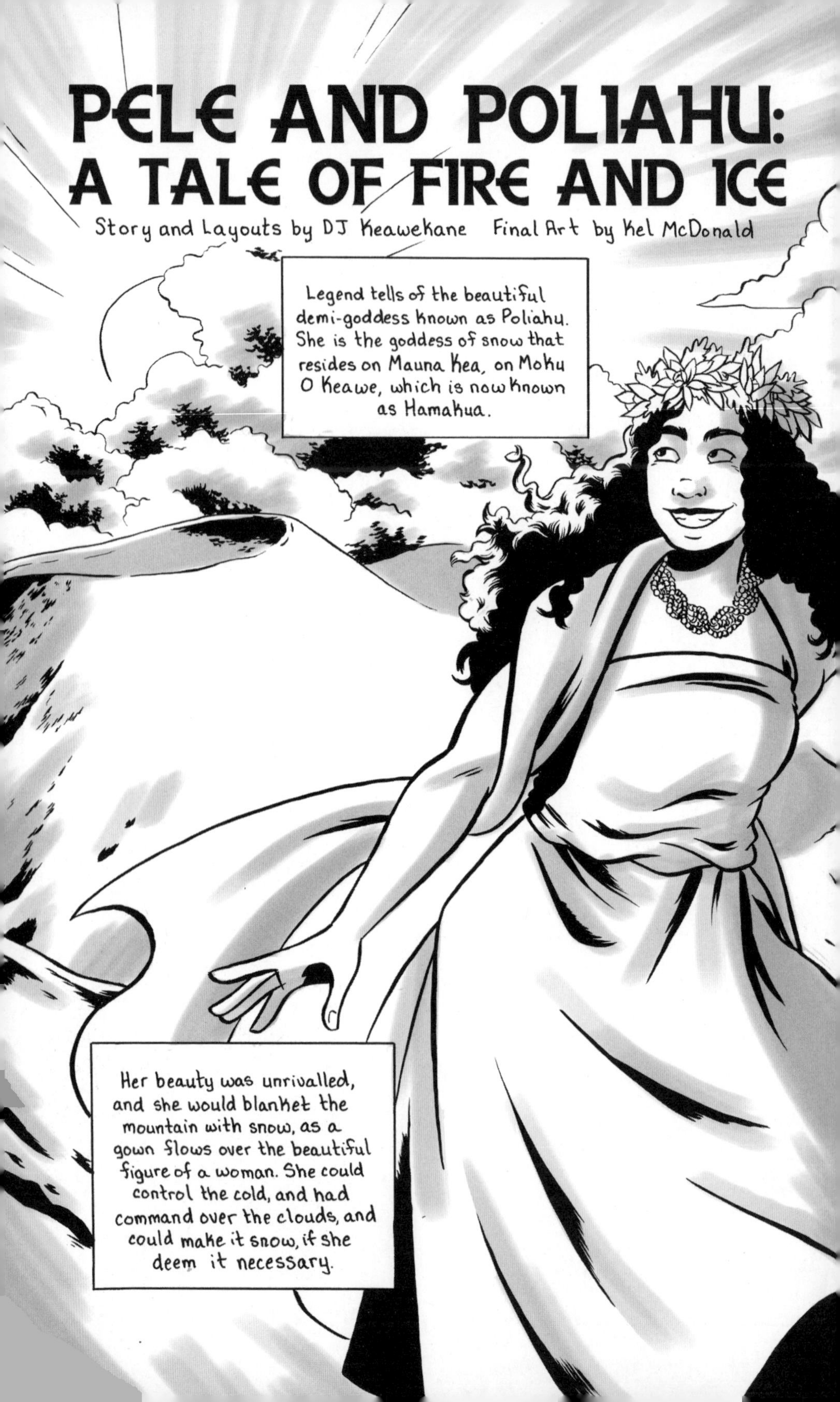
PELE AND POLIAHU:
A TALE OF FIRE AND ICE
Story and Layouts by DJ Keawekane Final Art by Kel McDonald
Legend tells of the beautiful demi-goddess known as Poliahu. She is the goddess of snow that resides on Mauna Kea, on Moku O Keawe, which is now known as Hamakua.
Her beauty was unrivalled, and she would blanket the mountain with snow, as a gown flows over the beautiful figure of a woman. She could control the cold, and had command over the clouds, and could make it snow, if she deem it necessary.

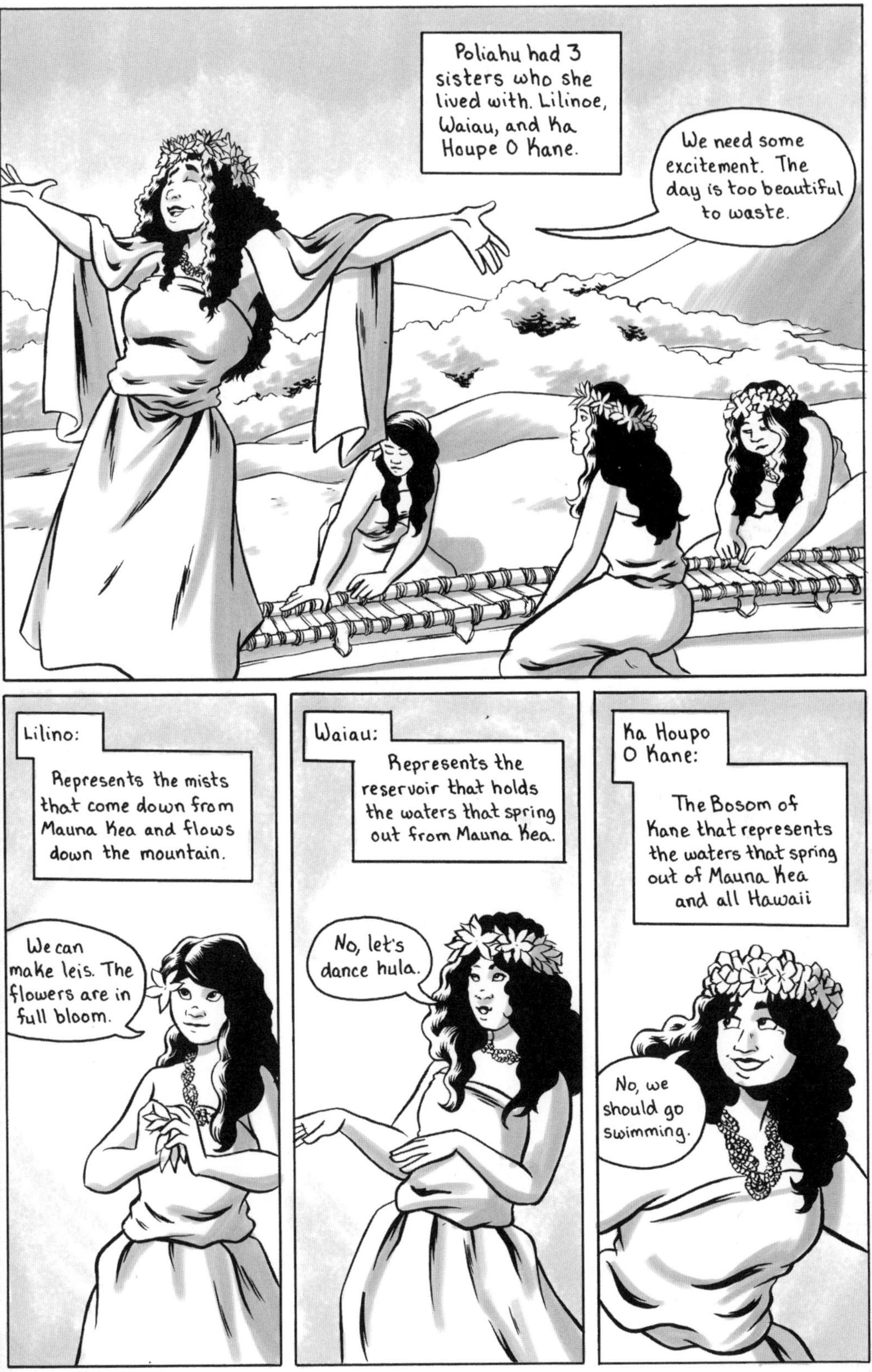
Poliahu had 3 sisters who she lived with. Lilinoe, Waiau, and Ka Houpe O Kane.
We need some excitement. The day is too beautiful to waste.
Lilino:
Represents the mists that come down from Mauna Kea and flows down the mountain.
We can make leis. The flowers are in full bloom.
Waiau:
Represents the reservoir that holds the waters that spring out from Mauna Kea.
No, let's dance hula.
Ka Houpo O Kane:
The Bosom of Kane that represents the waters that spring out of Mauna Kea and all Hawaii
No, we should go swimming.

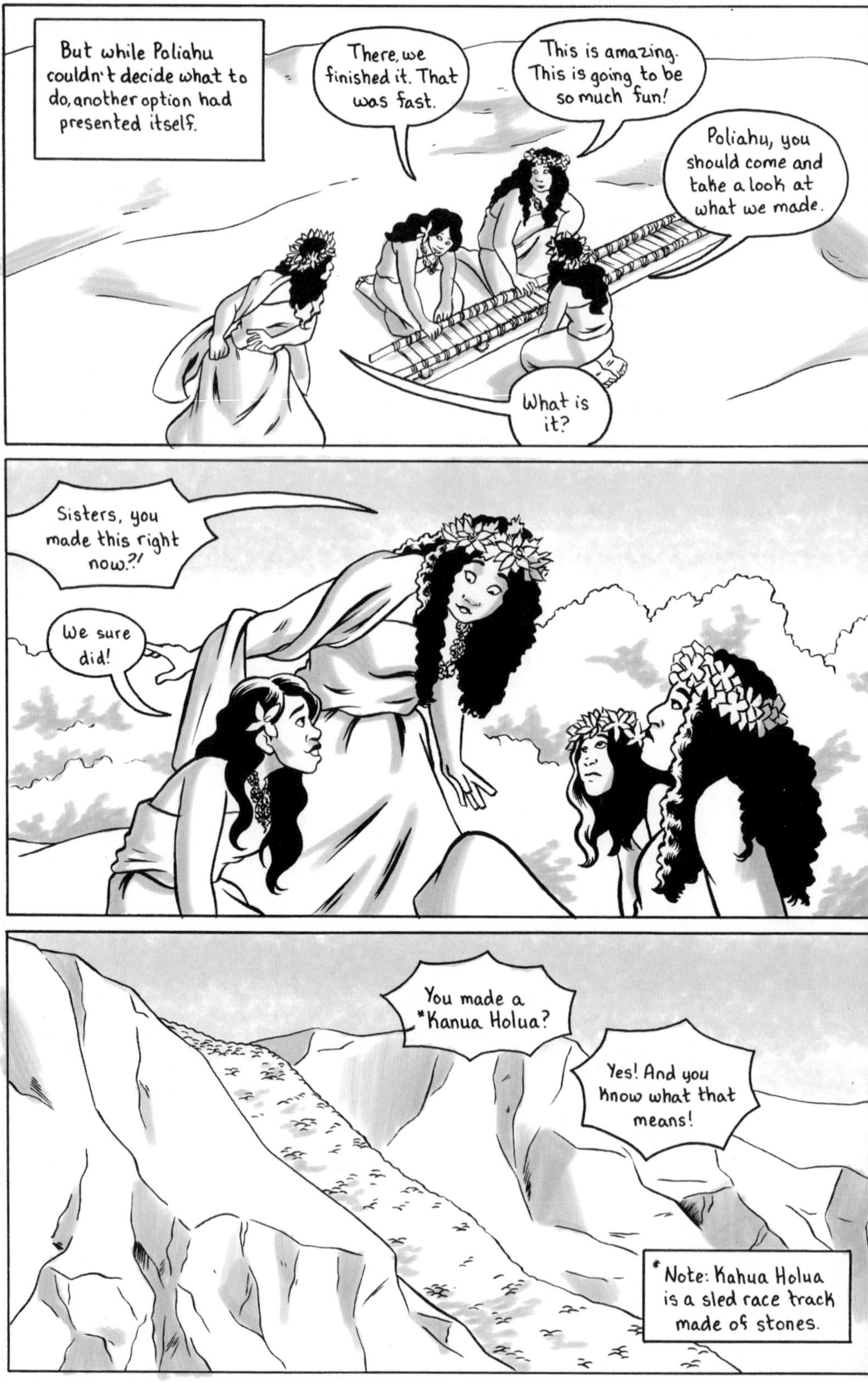

But while Poliahu couldn't decide what to do, another option had presented itself.
There, we finished it. That was fast.
This is amazing. This is going to be so much fun!
Poliahu, you should come and take a look at what we made.
What is it?
Sisters, you made this right now?!
We sure did!
You made a *Kanua Holua?
Yes! And you know what that means!
*Note: Kahua Holua is a sled race track made of stones.

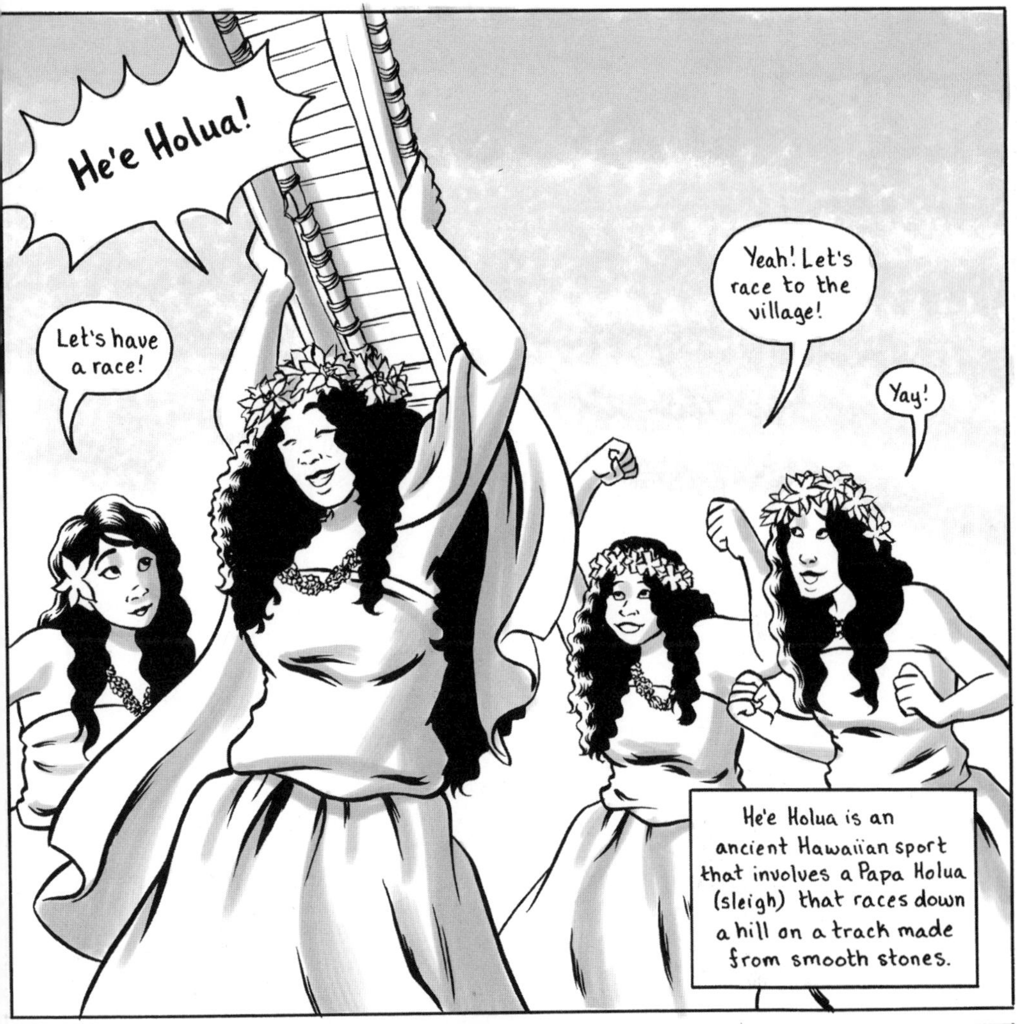
He'e Holua!
Let's have a race!
Yeah! Let's race to the village!
Yay!
He'e Holua is an ancient Hawaiian sport that involves a Papa Holua (sleigh) that races down a hill on a track made from smooth stones.

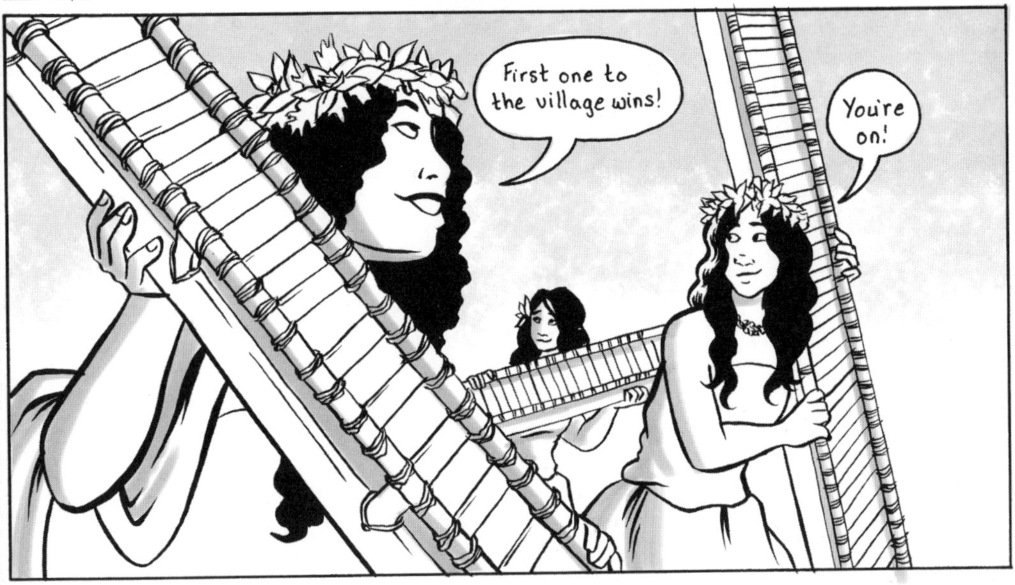
First one to the village wins!
You're on!

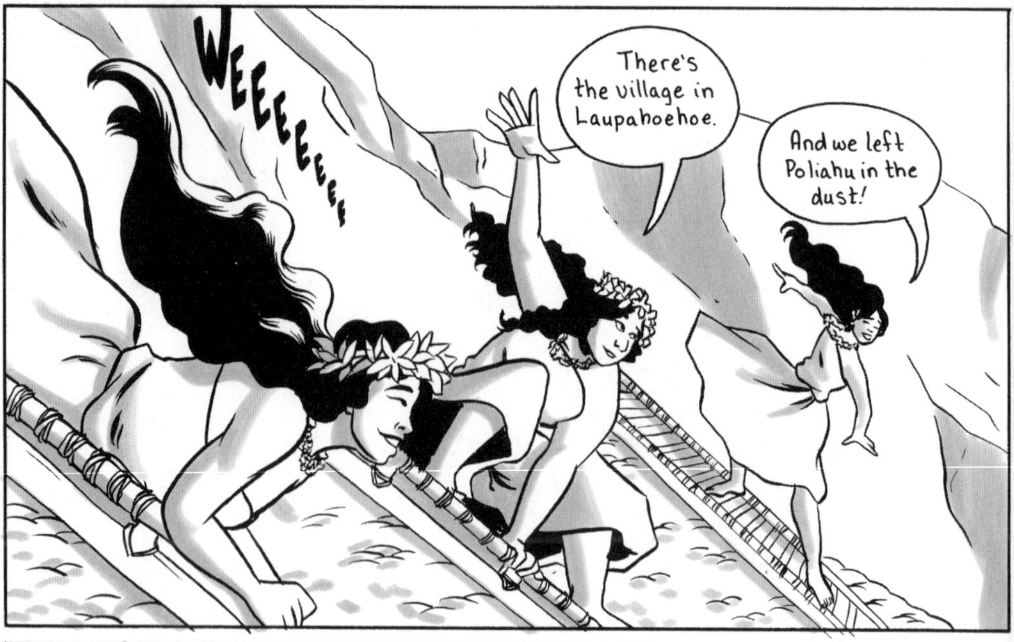
WEEEEEEEE
There's the village in Laupahoehoe.
And we left Poliahu in the dust!

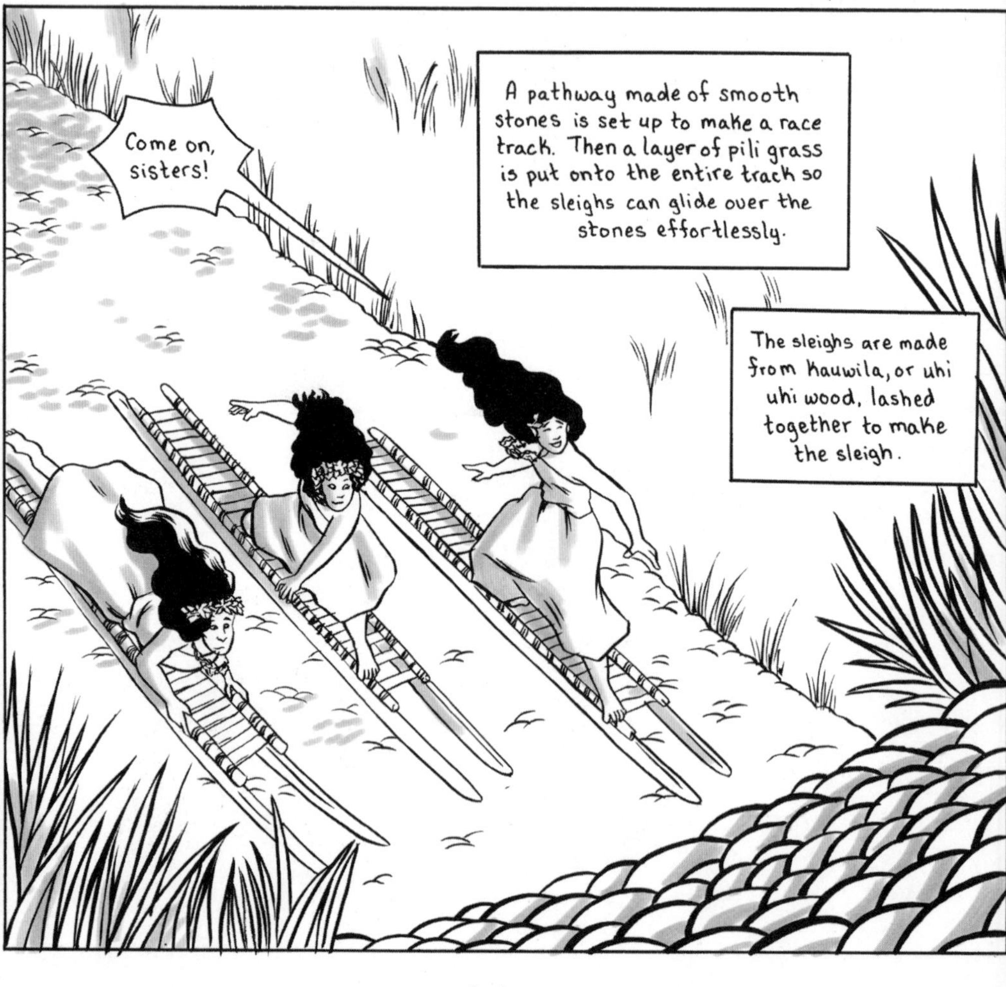
Come on, sisters!
A pathway made of smooth stones is set up to make a race track. Then a layer of pili grass is put onto the entire track so the sleighs can glide over the stones effortlessly.
The sleighs are made from kauwila, or uhi uhi wood, lashed together to make the sleigh.

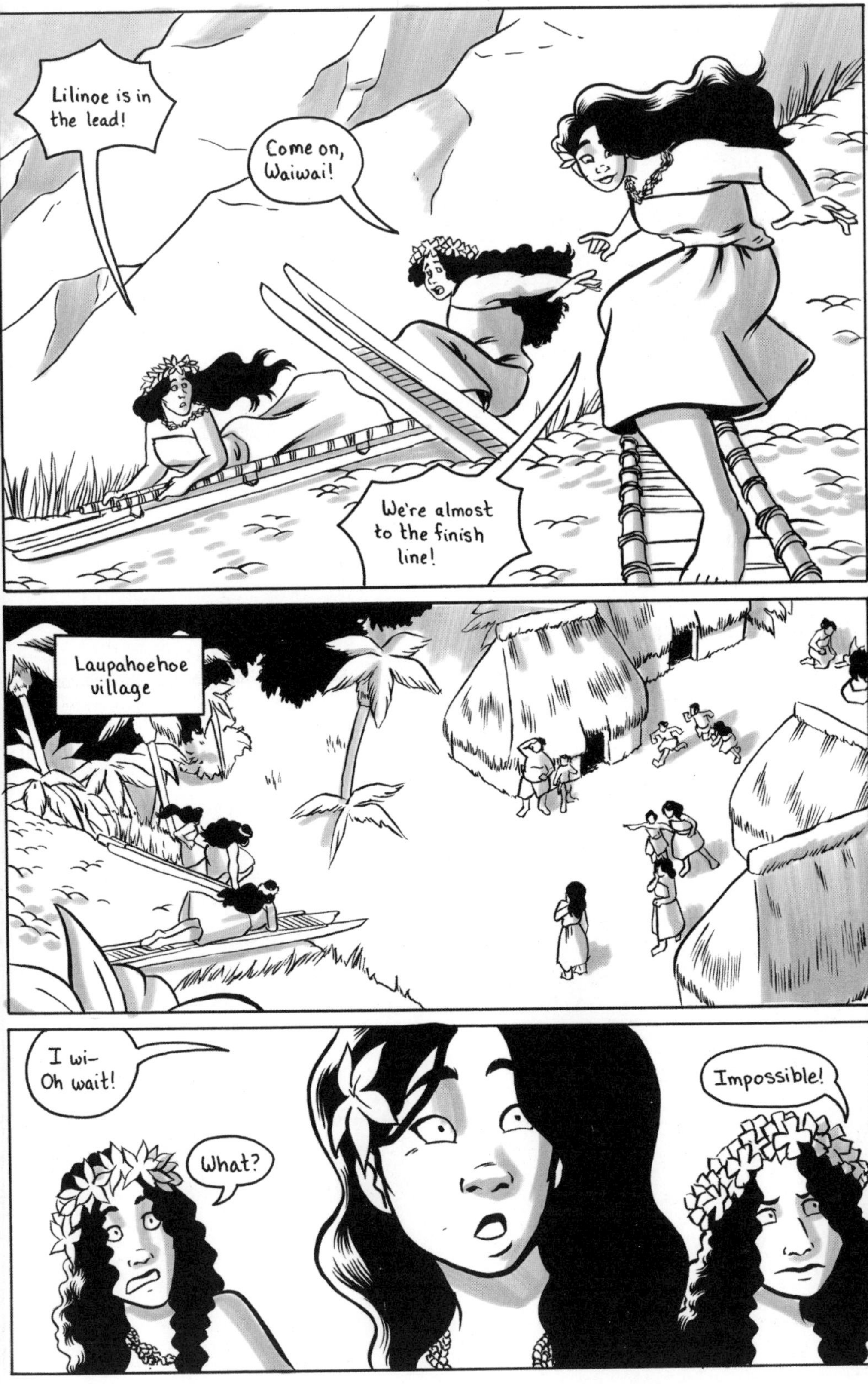
Lilinoe is in the lead!
Come on, Waiwai!
We're almost to the finish line!
Laupahoehoe village
I wi– Oh wait!
What?
Impossible!

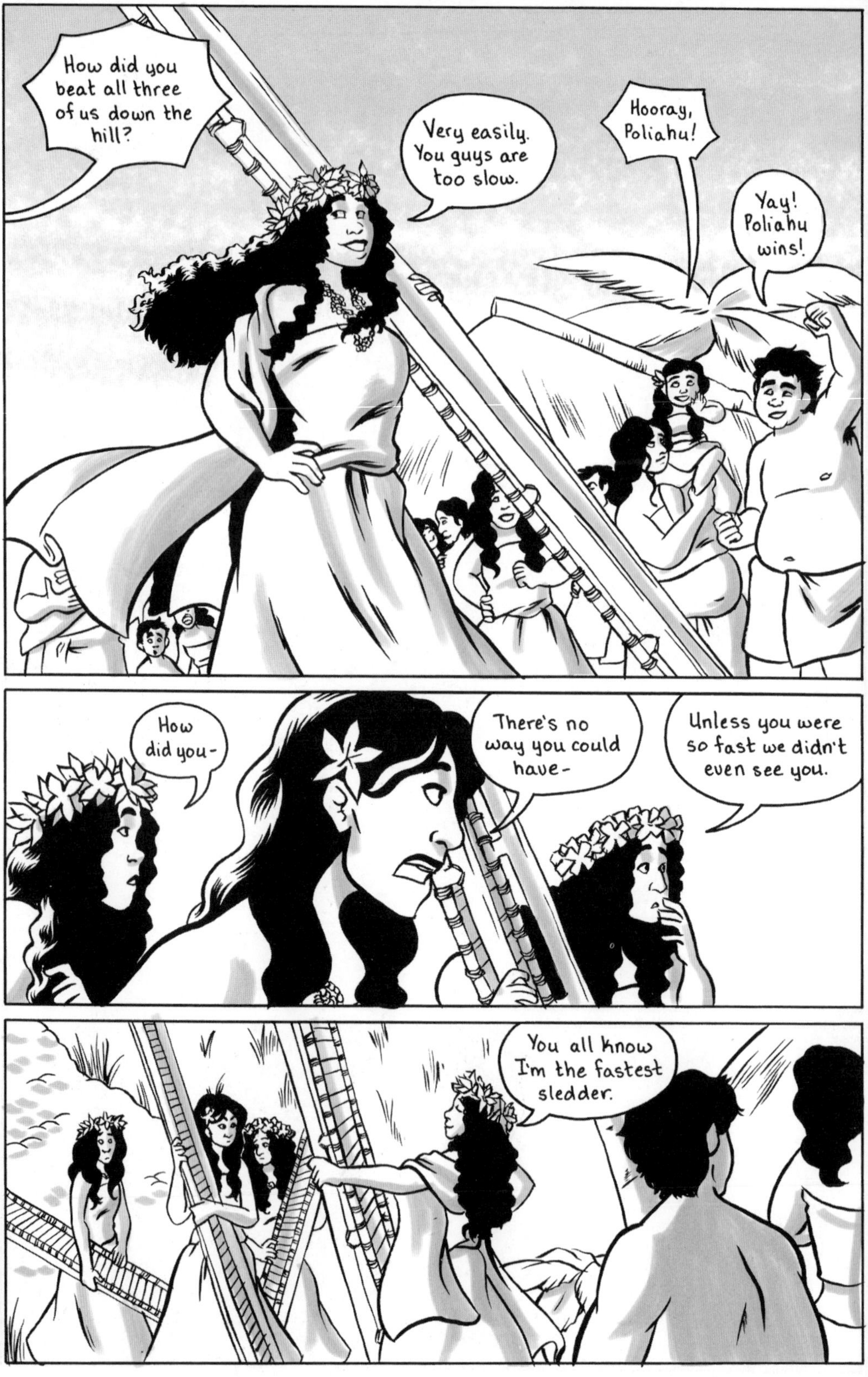
How did you beat all three of us down the hill?
Very easily. You guys are too slow.
Hooray, Poliahu!
Yay! Poliahu wins!
How did you-
There's no way you could have-
Unless you were so fast we didn't even see you.
You all know I'm the fastest sledder.

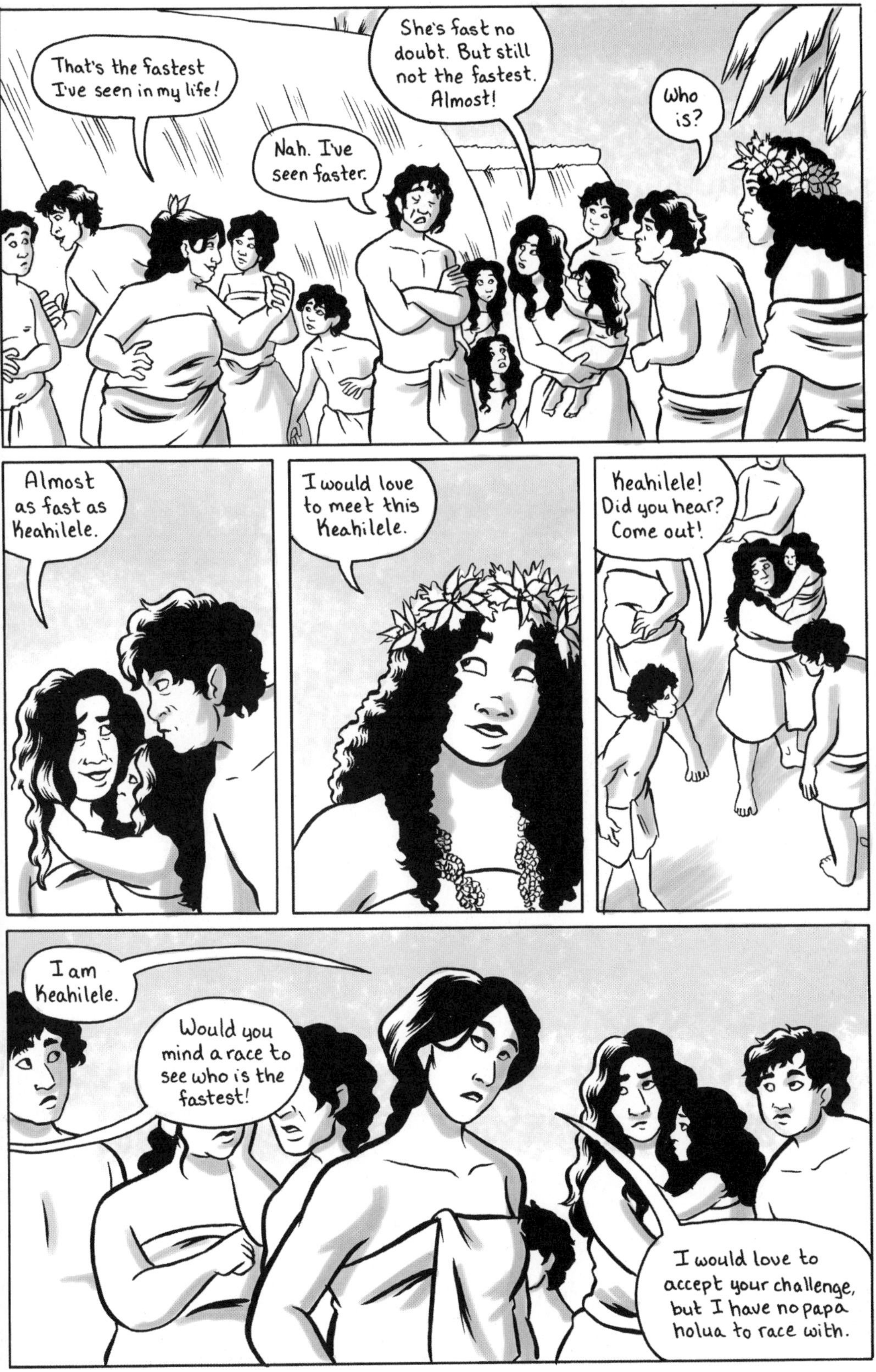
That's the fastest I've seen in my life!
Nah. I've seen faster.
She's fast no doubt. But still not the fastest. Almost!
Who is?
Almost as fast as Keahilele.
I would love to meet this Keahilele.
Keahilele! Did you hear? Come out!
I am Keahilele.
Would you mind a race to see who is the fastest!
I would love to accept your challenge, but I have no papa holua to race with.

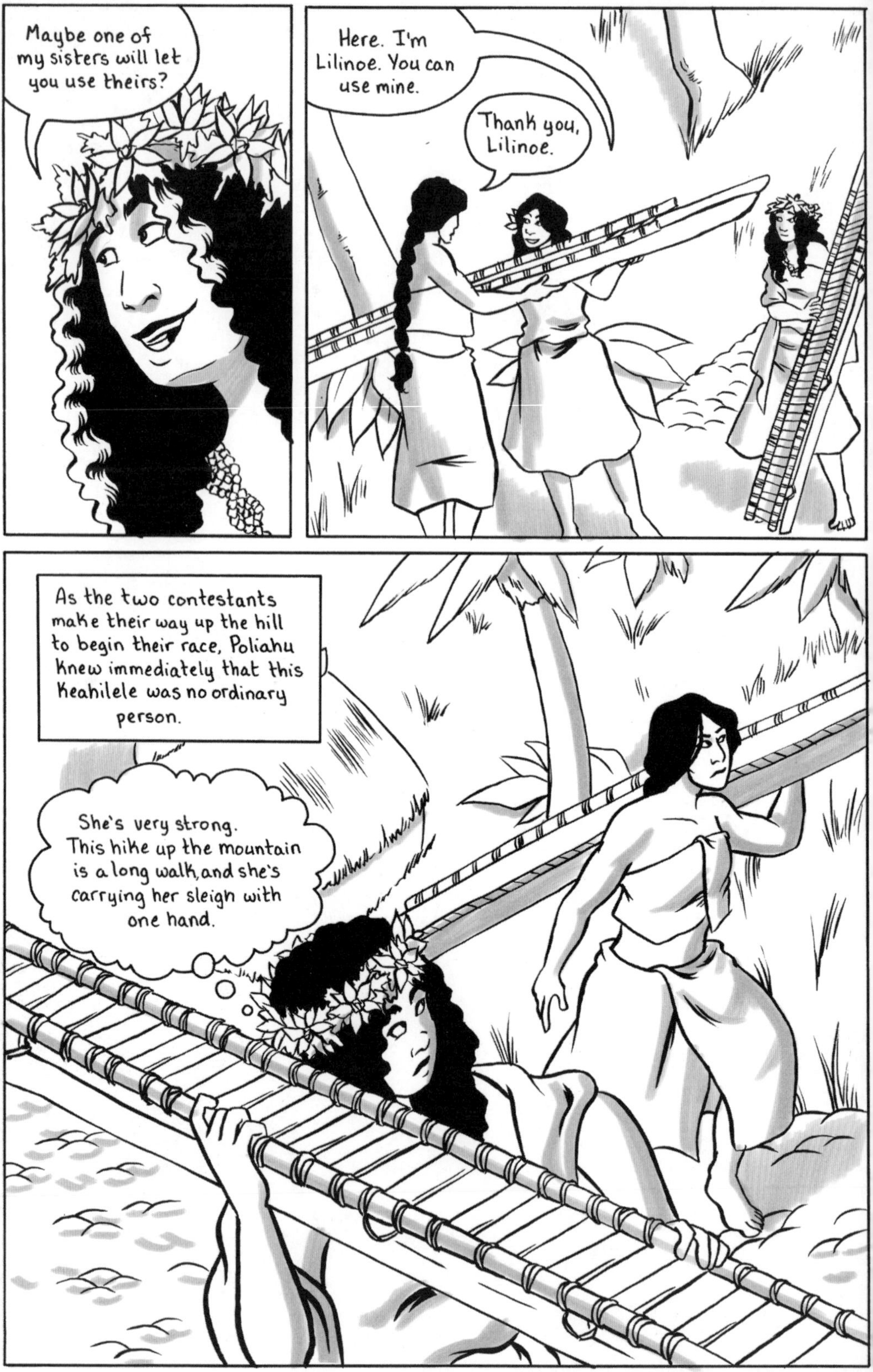
Maybe one of my sisters will let you use theirs?
Here. I'm Lilinoe. You can use mine.
Thank you, Lilinoe.
As the two contestants make their way up the hill to begin their race, Poliahu knew immediately that this Keahilele was no ordinary person.
She's very strong. This hike up the mountain is a long walk, and she's carrying her sleigh with one hand.

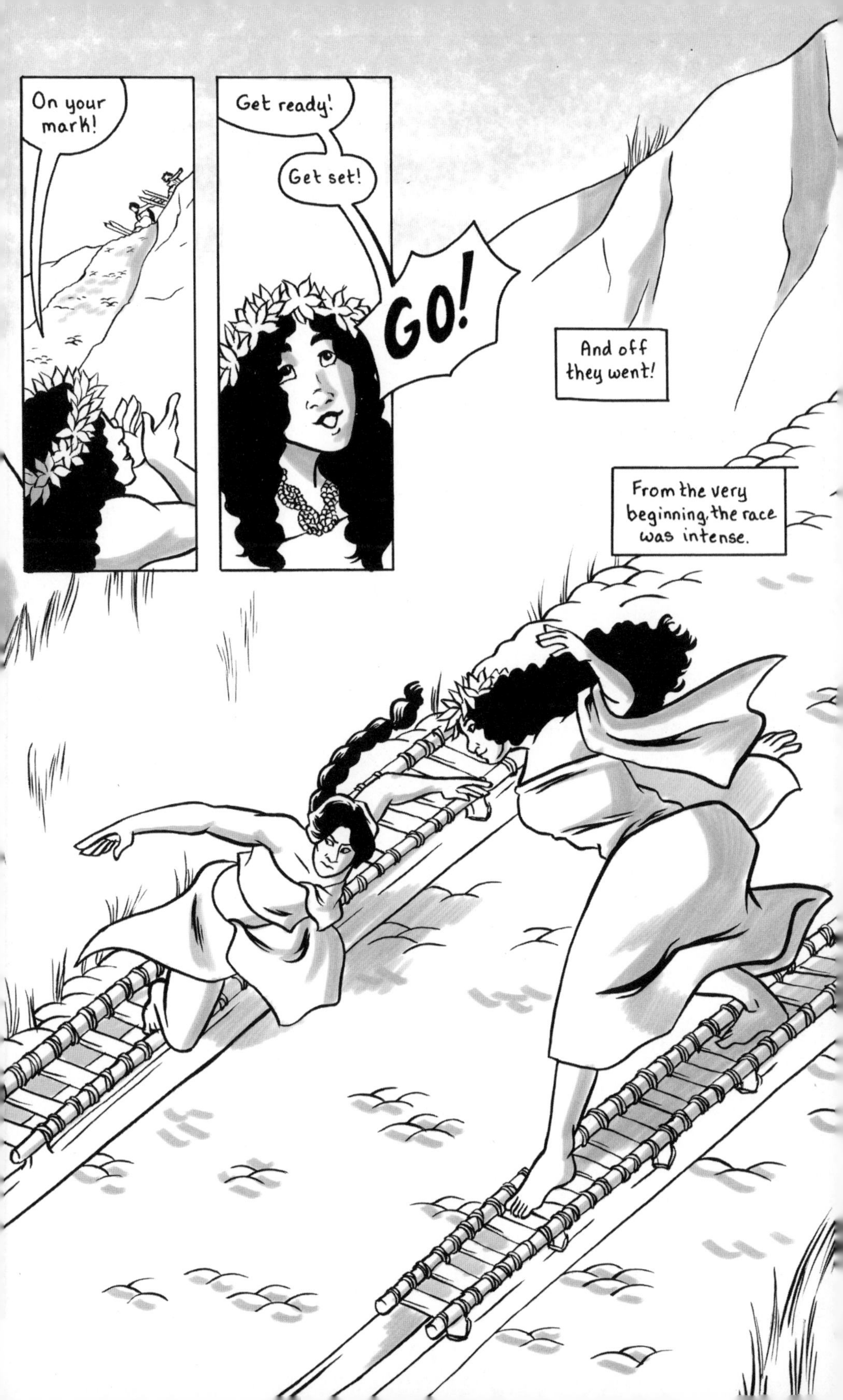
On your mark!
Get ready!
Get set!
GO!
And off they went!
From the very beginning, the race was intense.

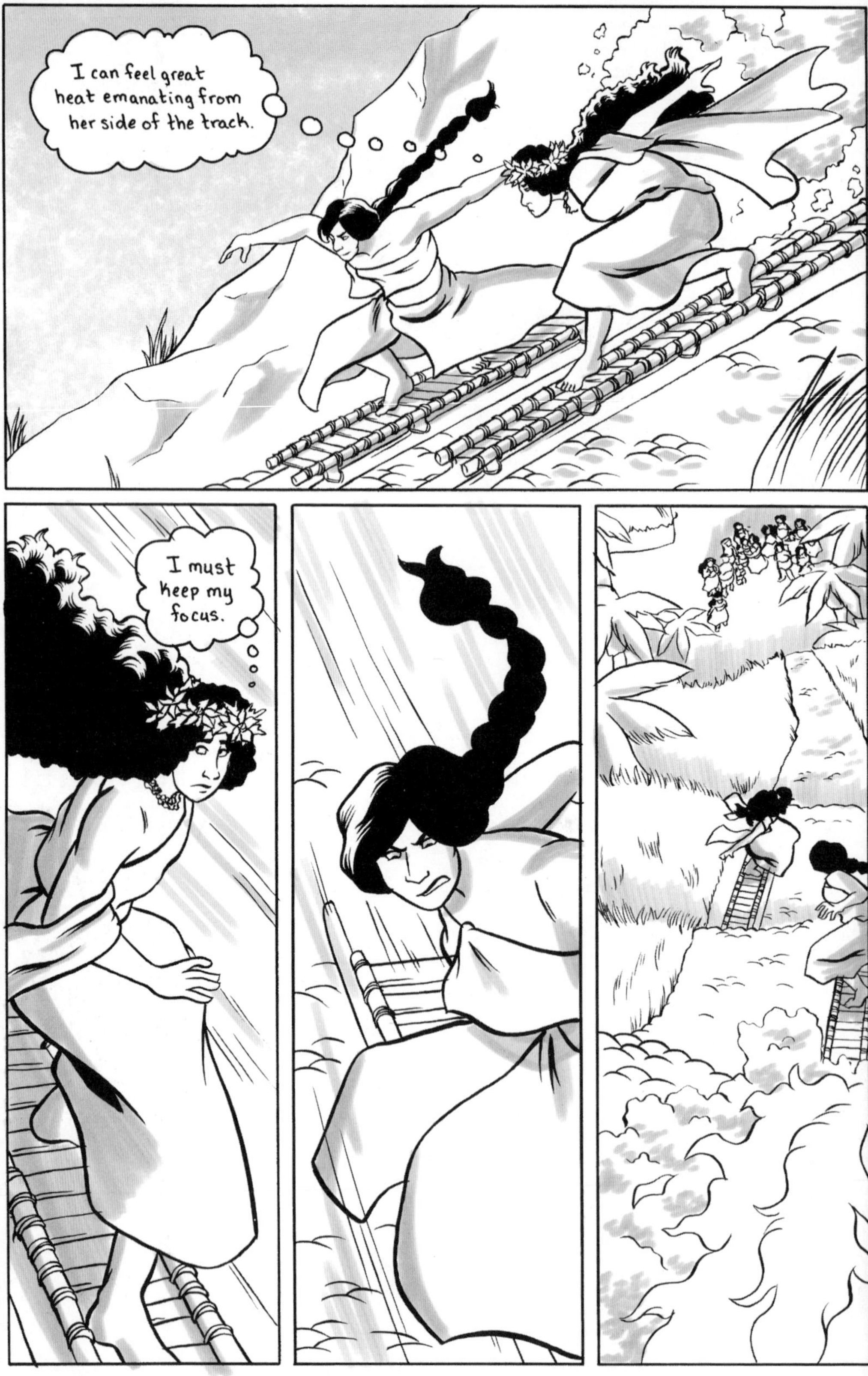

I can feel great heat emanating from her side of the track.
I must keep my focus.

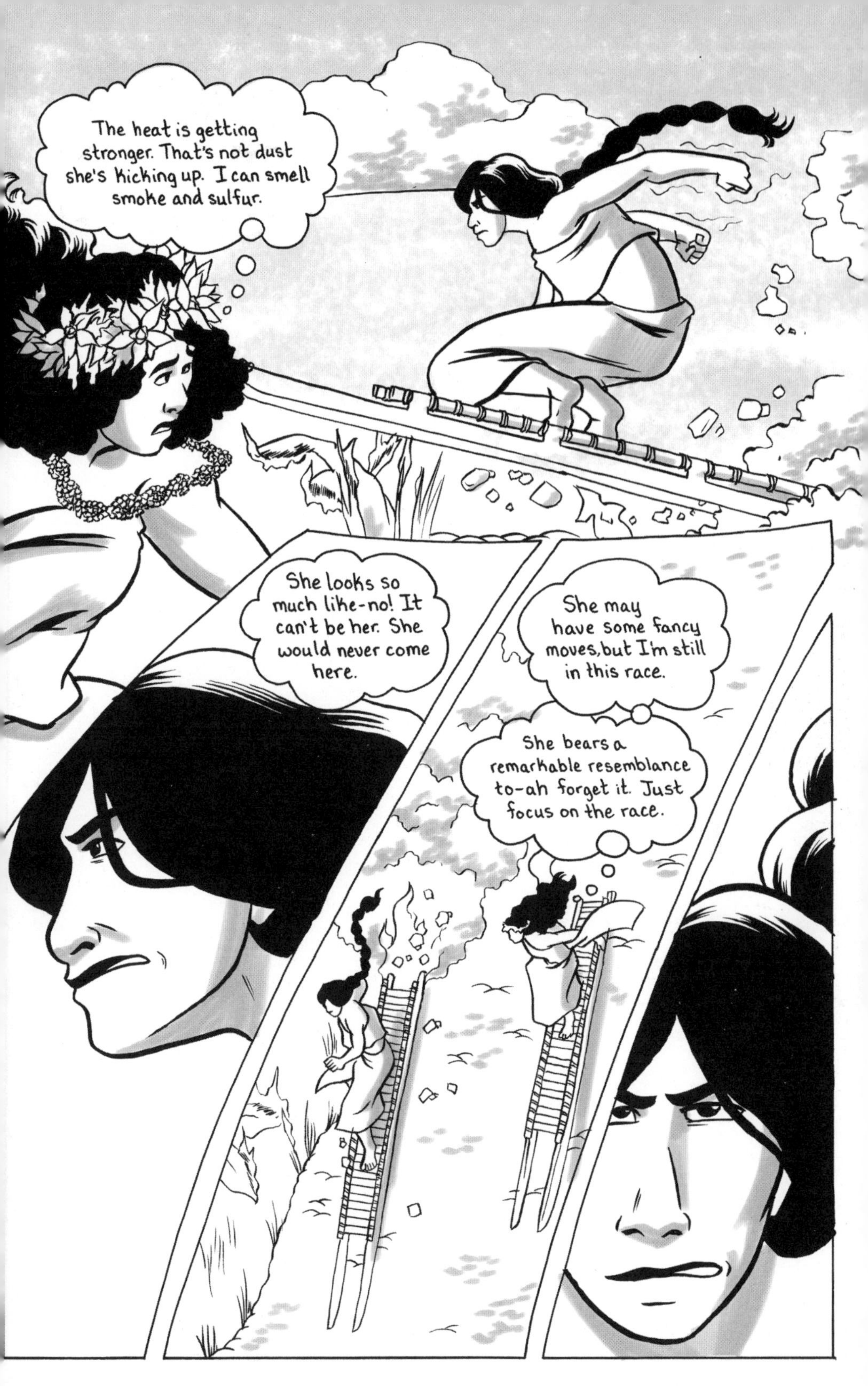

The heat is getting stronger. That's not dust she's kicking up. I can smell smoke and sulfur.
She looks so much like-no! It can't be her. She would never come here.
She may have some fancy moves, but I'm still in this race.
She bears a remarkable resemblance to-ah forget it. Just focus on the race.

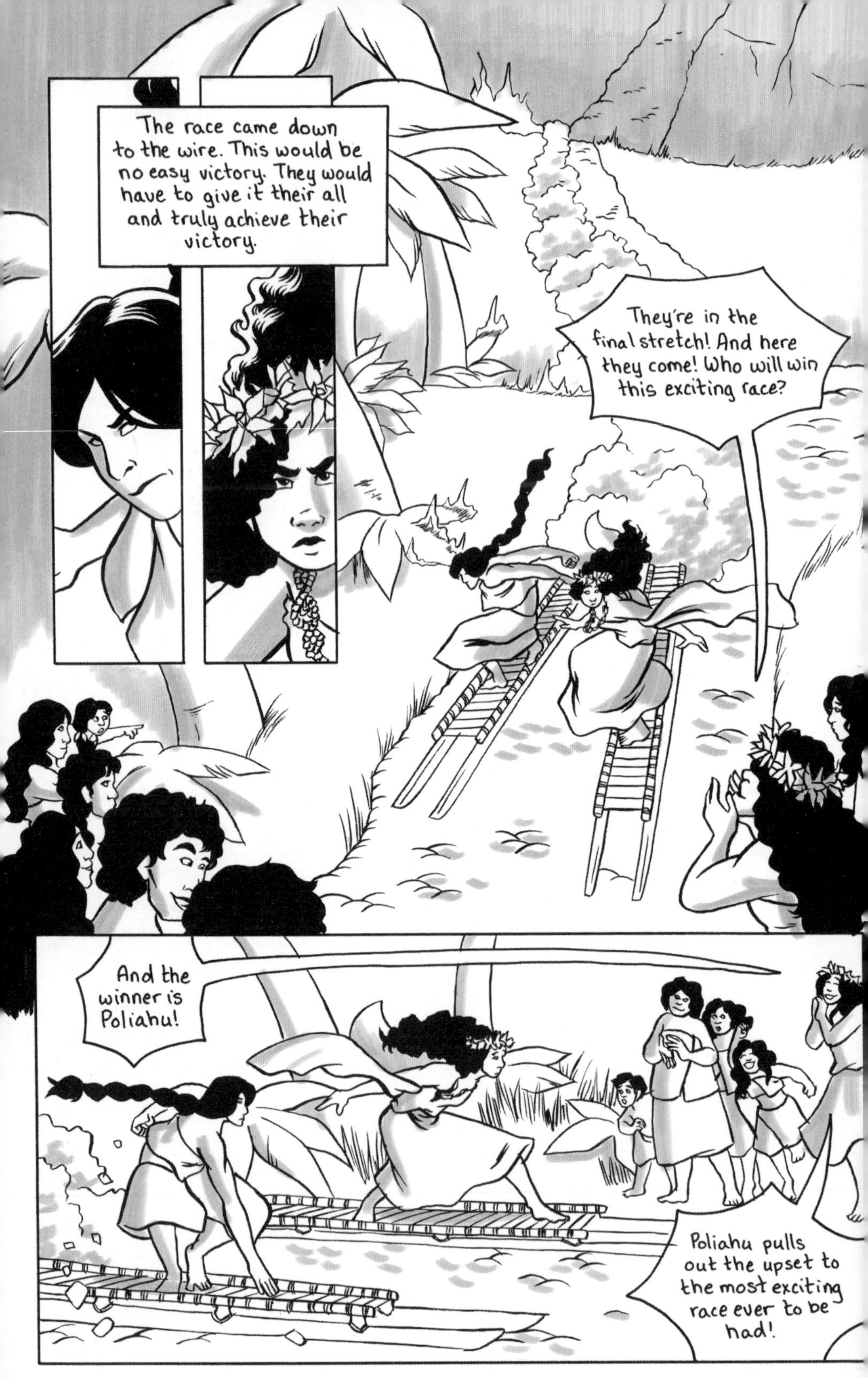
The race came down to the wire. This would be no easy victory. They would have to give it their all and truly achieve their victory.
They're in the final stretch! And here they come! Who will win this exciting race?
And the winner is Poliahu!
Poliahu pulls out the upset to the most exciting race ever to be had!

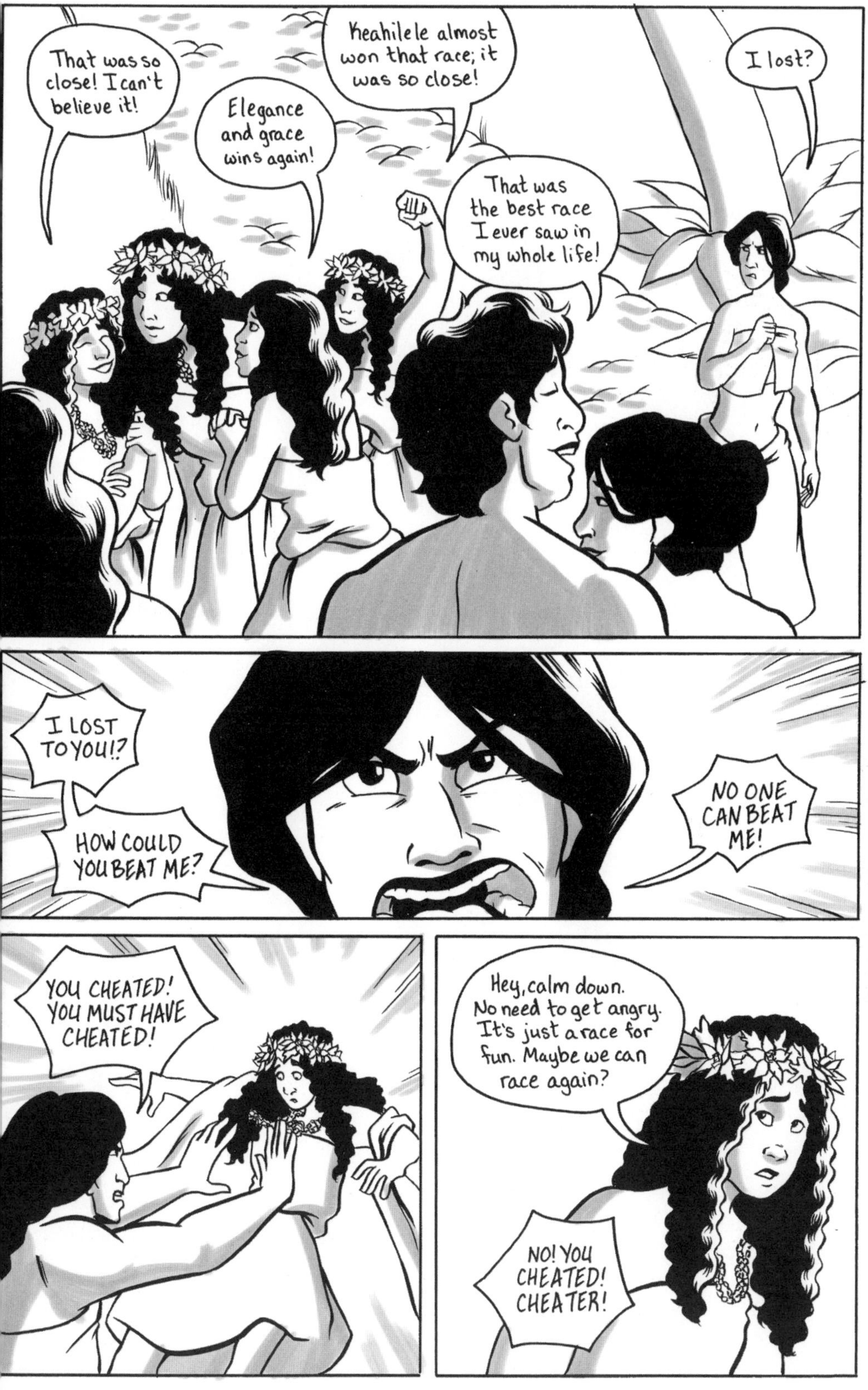

That was so close! I can't believe it!
Elegance and grace wins again!
Keahilele almost won that race; it was so close!
I lost?
That was the best race I ever saw in my whole life!
I LOST TO YOU!?
HOW COULD YOU BEAT ME?
NO ONE CAN BEAT ME!
YOU CHEATED! YOU MUST HAVE CHEATED!
Hey, calm down. No need to get angry. It's just a race for fun. Maybe we can race again?
NO! YOU CHEATED! CHEATER!

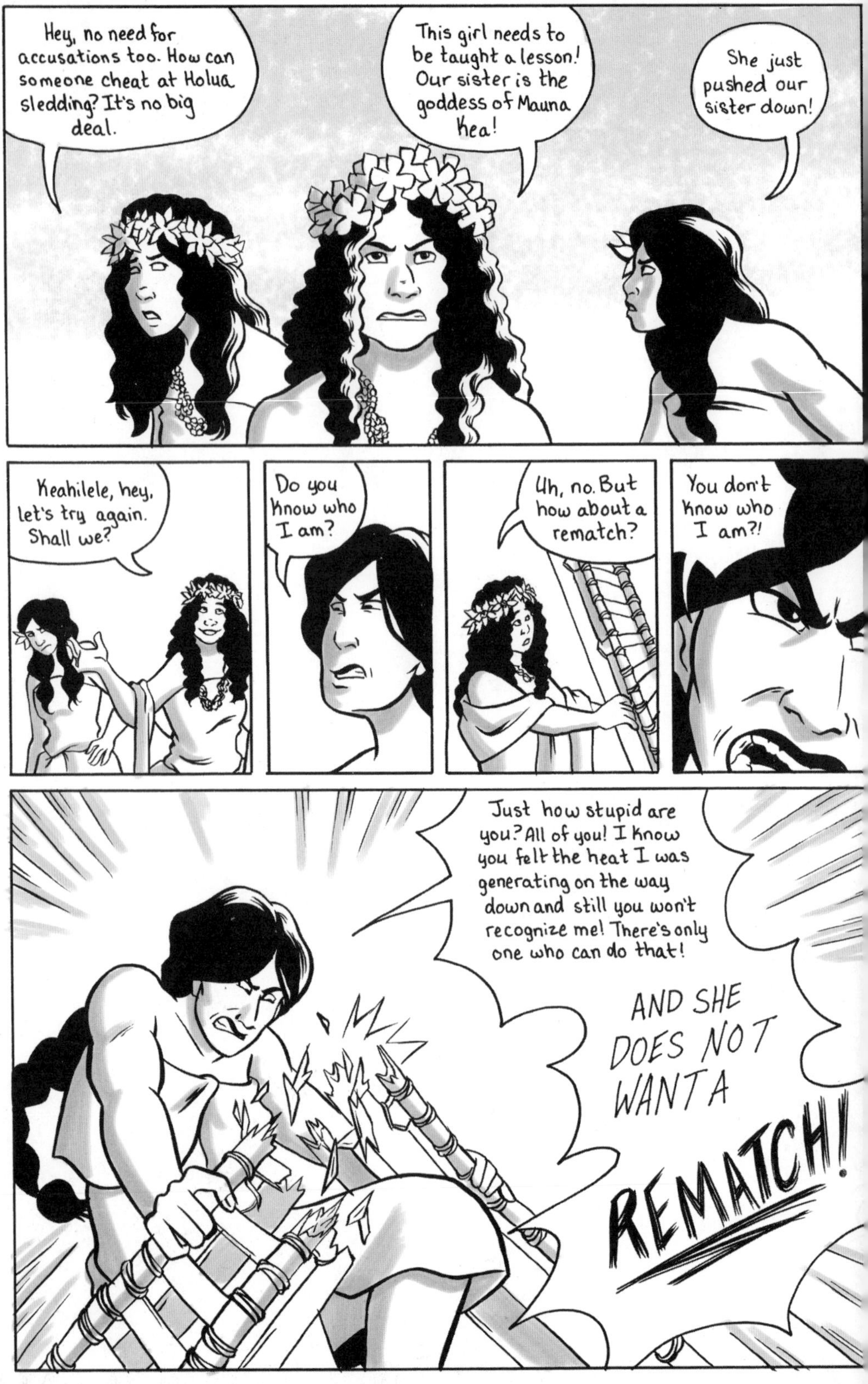

Hey, no need for accusations too. How can someone cheat at Holua sledding? It's no big deal.
This girl needs to be taught a lesson! Our sister is the goddess of Mauna Kea!
She just pushed our sister down!
Keahilele, hey, let's try again. Shall we?
Do you know who I am?
Uh, no. But how about a rematch?
You don't know who I am?!
Just how stupid are you? All of you! I know you felt the heat I was generating on the way down and still you won't recognize me! There's only one who can do that!
AND SHE DOES NOT WANT A
REMATCH!

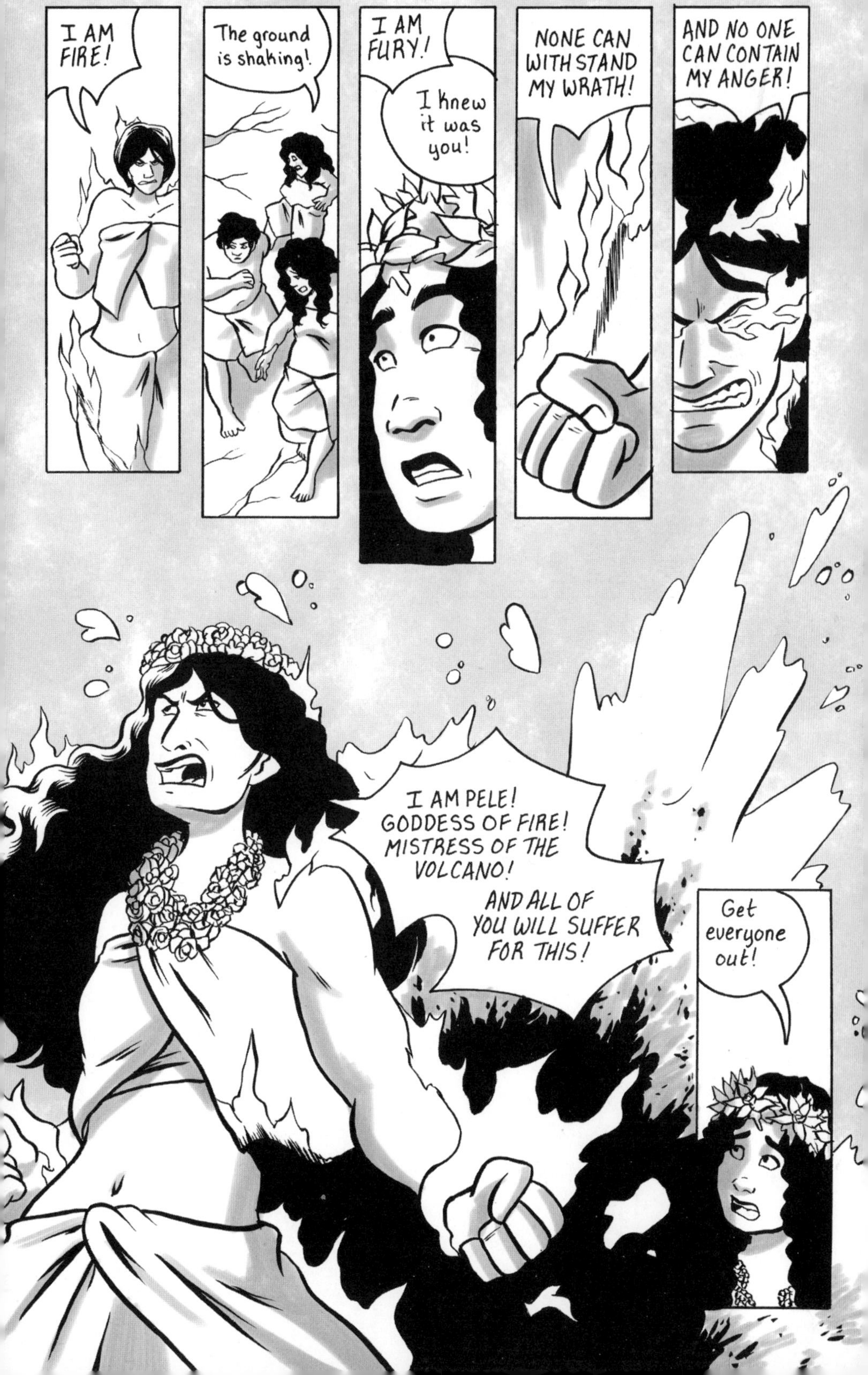
I AM FIRE!
The ground is shaking!
I AM FURY!
I knew it was you!
NONE CAN WITHSTAND MY WRATH!
AND NO ONE CAN CONTAIN MY ANGER!
I AM PELE! GODDESS OF FIRE! MISTRESS OF THE VOLCANO!
AND ALL OF YOU WILL SUFFER FOR THIS!
Get everyone out!

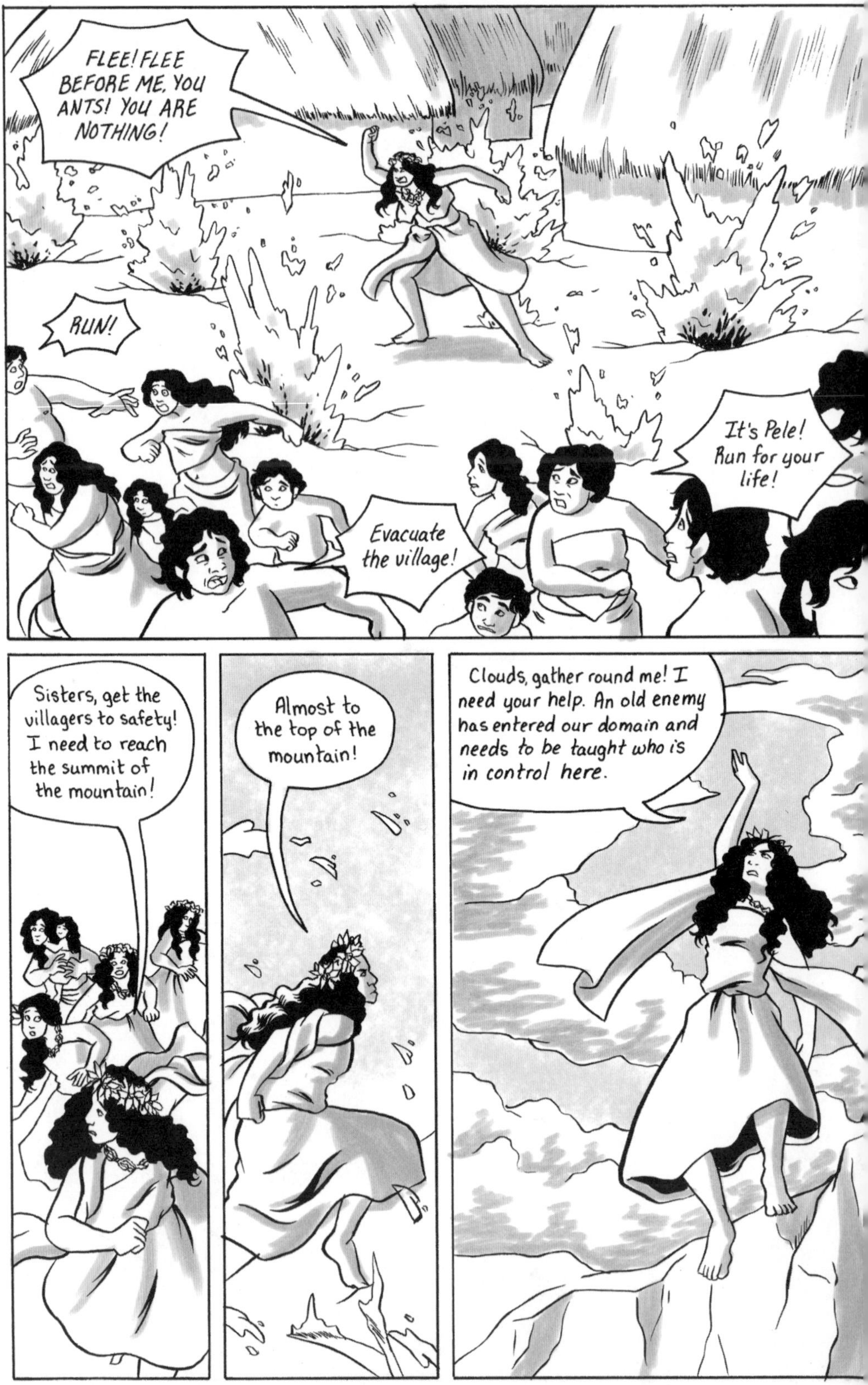
FLEE! FLEE BEFORE ME, YOU ANTS! YOU ARE NOTHING!
RUN!
Evacuate the village!
It's Pele! Run for your life!
Sisters, get the villagers to safety! I need to reach the summit of the mountain!
Almost to the top of the mountain!
Clouds, gather round me! I need your help. An old enemy has entered our domain and needs to be taught who is in control here.

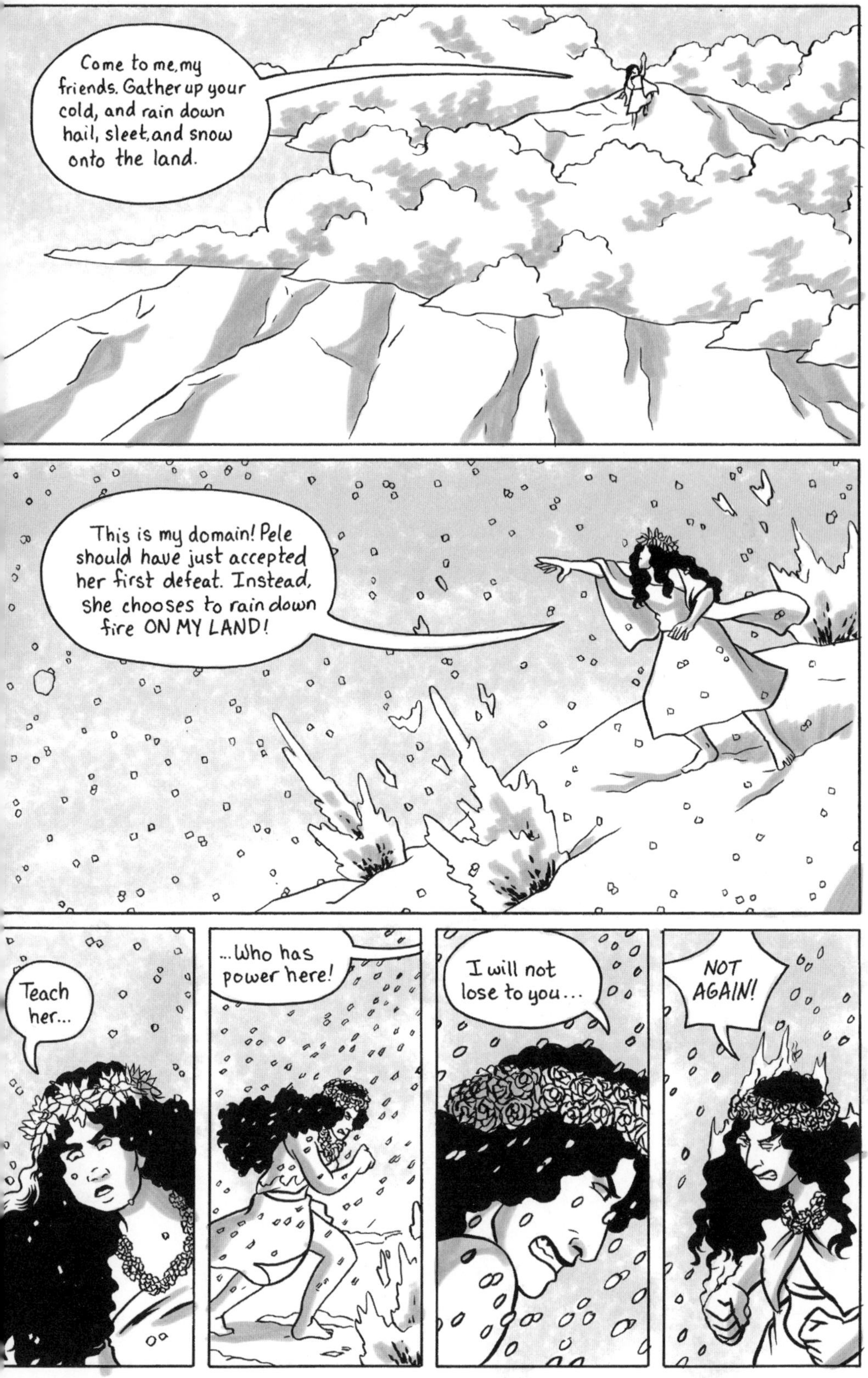
Come to me, my friends. Gather up your cold, and rain down hail, sleet, and snow onto the land.
This is my domain! Pele should have just accepted her first defeat. Instead, she chooses to rain down fire ON MY LAND!
Teach her...
...Who has power here!
I will not lose to you...
NOT AGAIN!

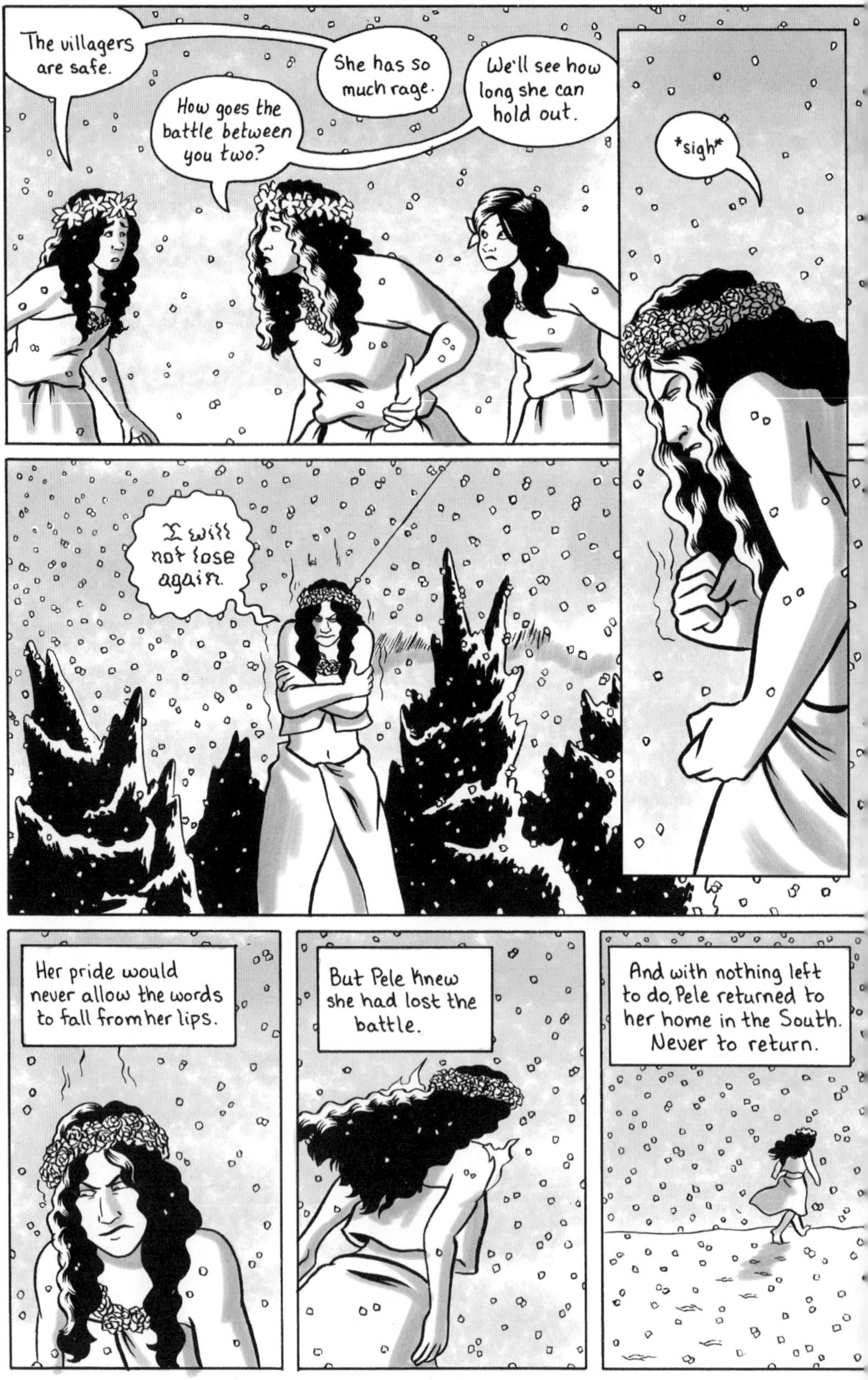
The villagers are safe.
How goes the battle between you two?
She has so much rage.
We'll see how long she can hold out.
sigh
I will not lose again.
Her pride would never allow the words to fall from her lips.
But Pele knew she had lost the battle.
And with nothing left to do, Pele returned to her home in the South. Never to return.

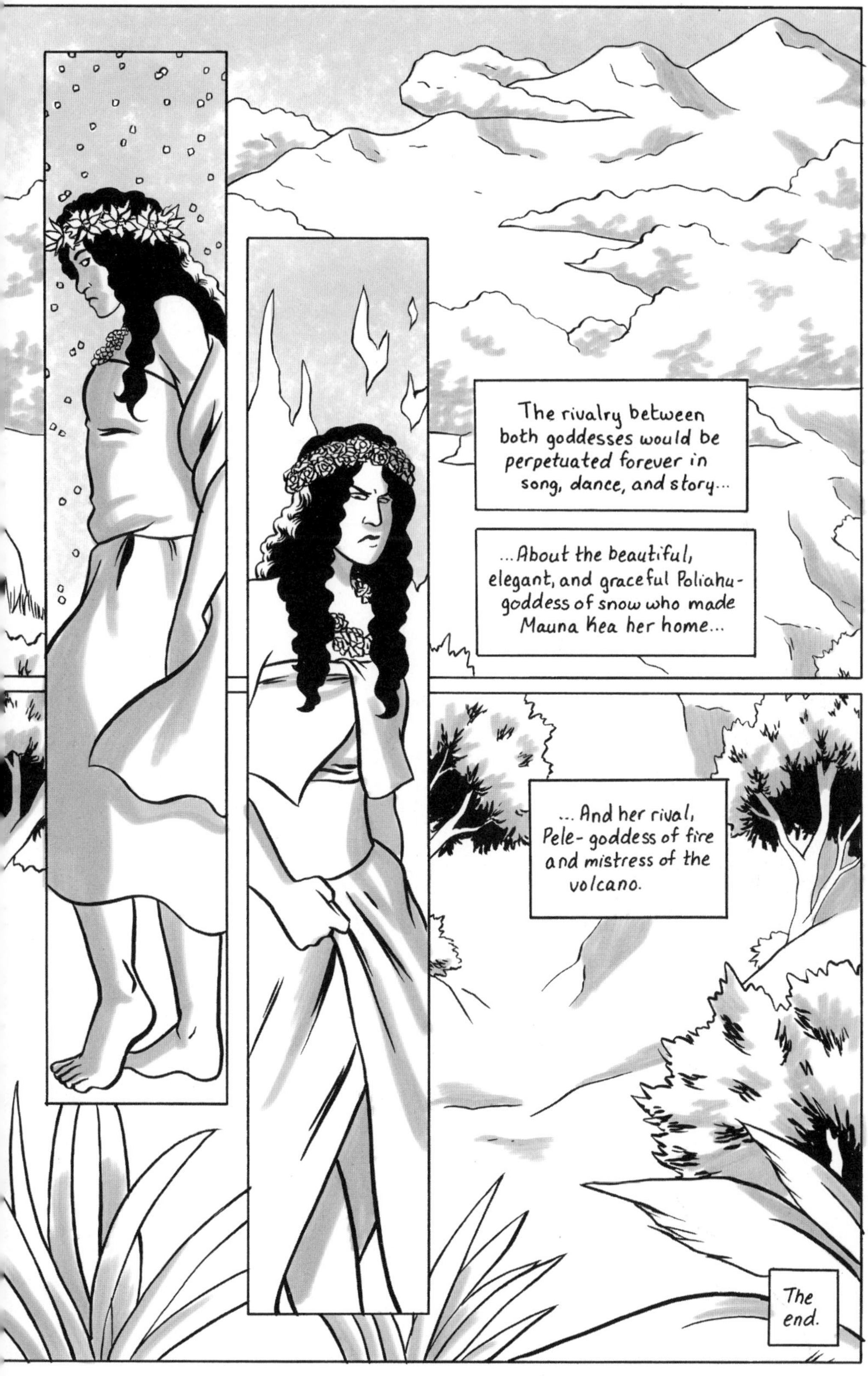
The rivalry between both goddesses would be perpetuated forever in song, dance, and story...
...About the beautiful, elegant, and graceful Poliahu- goddess of snow who made Mauna Kea her home...
... And her rival, Pele- goddess of fire and mistress of the volcano.
The end.

The Dancing Princess

by Mariel Maranan

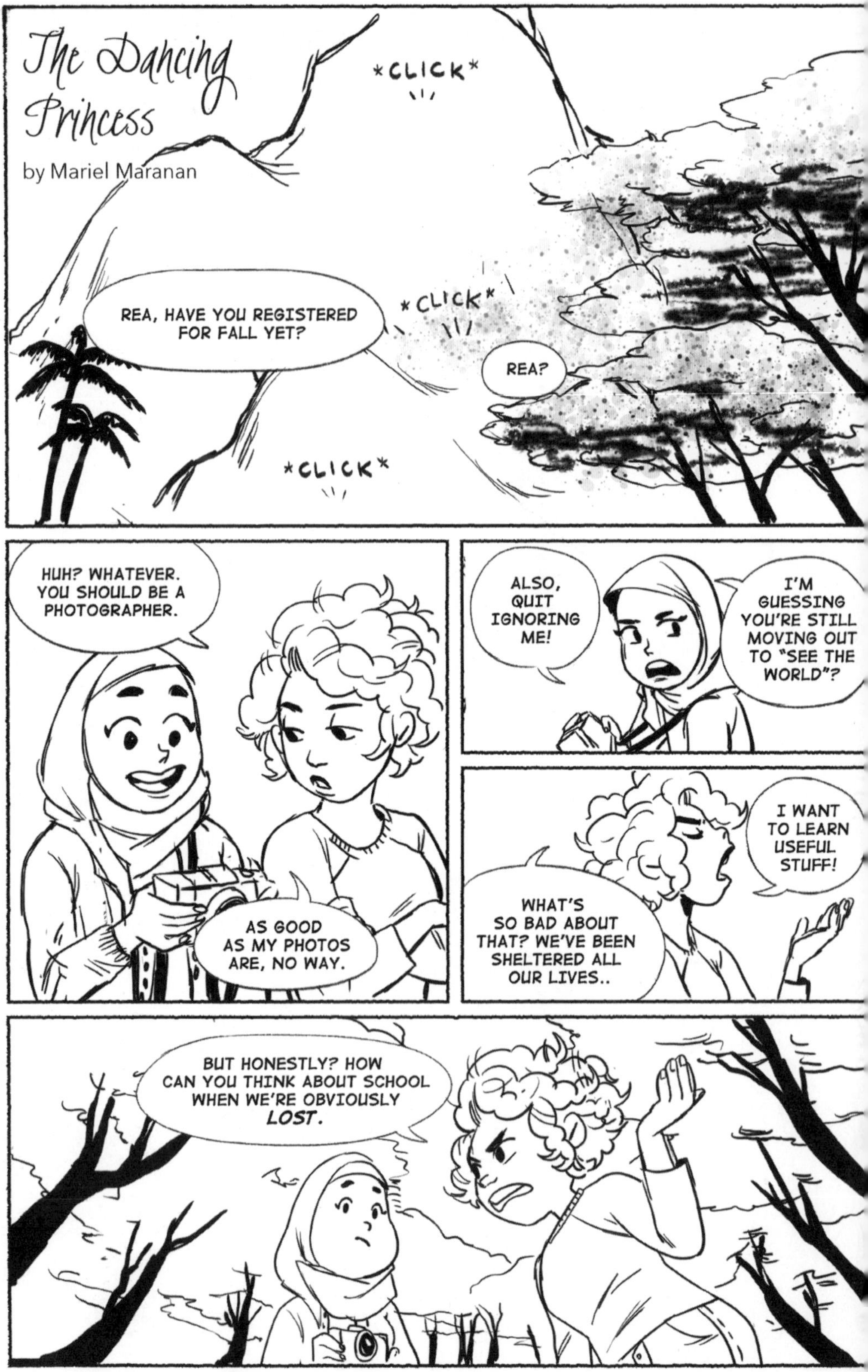
CLICK
REA, HAVE YOU REGISTERED FOR FALL YET?
CLICK
REA?
CLICK
HUH? WHATEVER. YOU SHOULD BE A PHOTOGRAPHER.
AS GOOD AS MY PHOTOS ARE, NO WAY.
ALSO, QUIT IGNORING ME!
I'M GUESSING YOU'RE STILL MOVING OUT TO "SEE THE WORLD"?
I WANT TO LEARN USEFUL STUFF!
WHAT'S SO BAD ABOUT THAT? WE'VE BEEN SHELTERED ALL OUR LIVES..
BUT HONESTLY? HOW CAN YOU THINK ABOUT SCHOOL WHEN WE'RE OBVIOUSLY *LOST*.

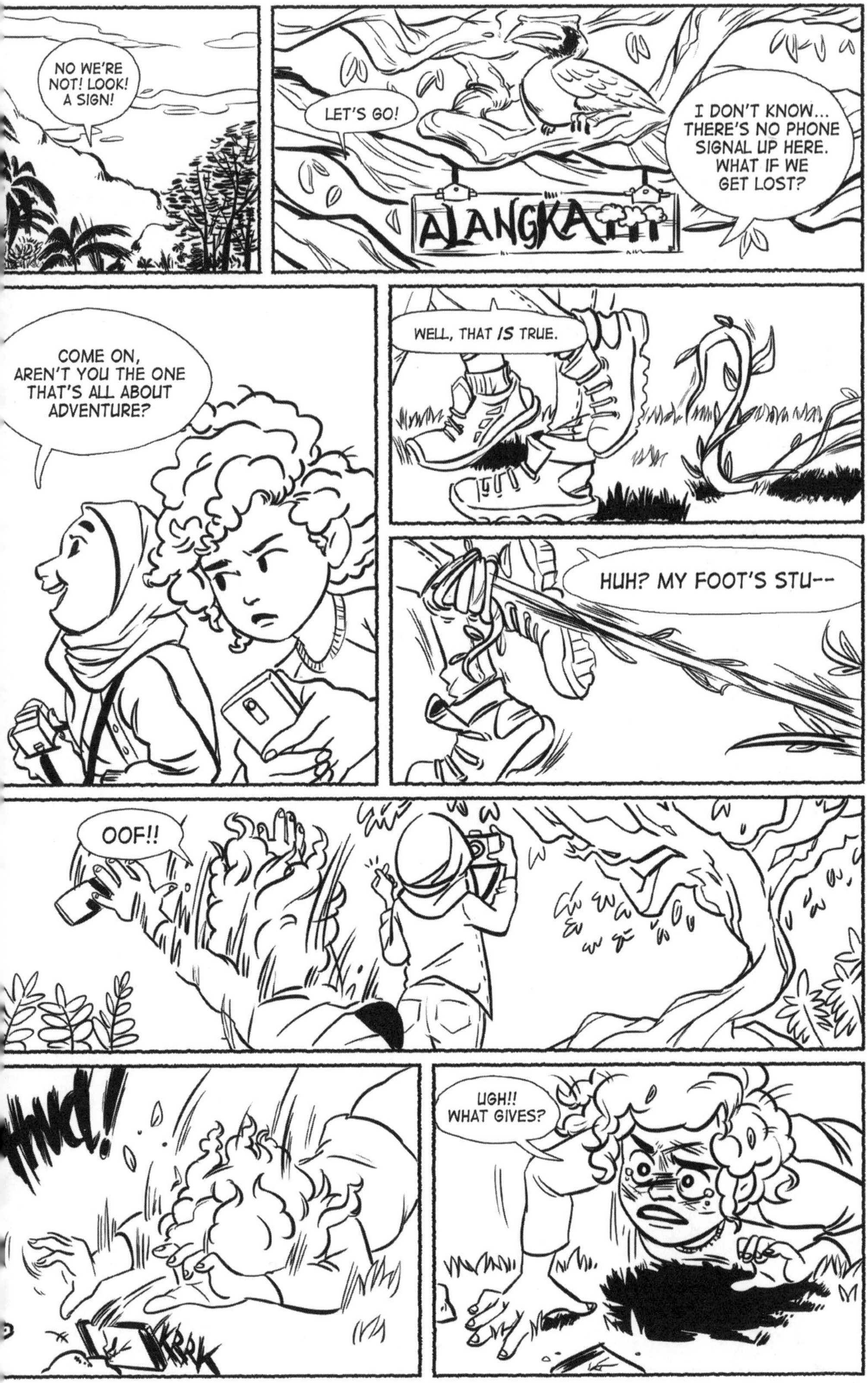
NO WE'RE NOT! LOOK! A SIGN!
LET'S GO!
I DON'T KNOW... THERE'S NO PHONE SIGNAL UP HERE. WHAT IF WE GET LOST?
ALANGKA
COME ON, AREN'T YOU THE ONE THAT'S ALL ABOUT ADVENTURE?
WELL, THAT IS TRUE.
HUH? MY FOOT'S STU--
OOF!!
KRRK
UGH!! WHAT GIVES?

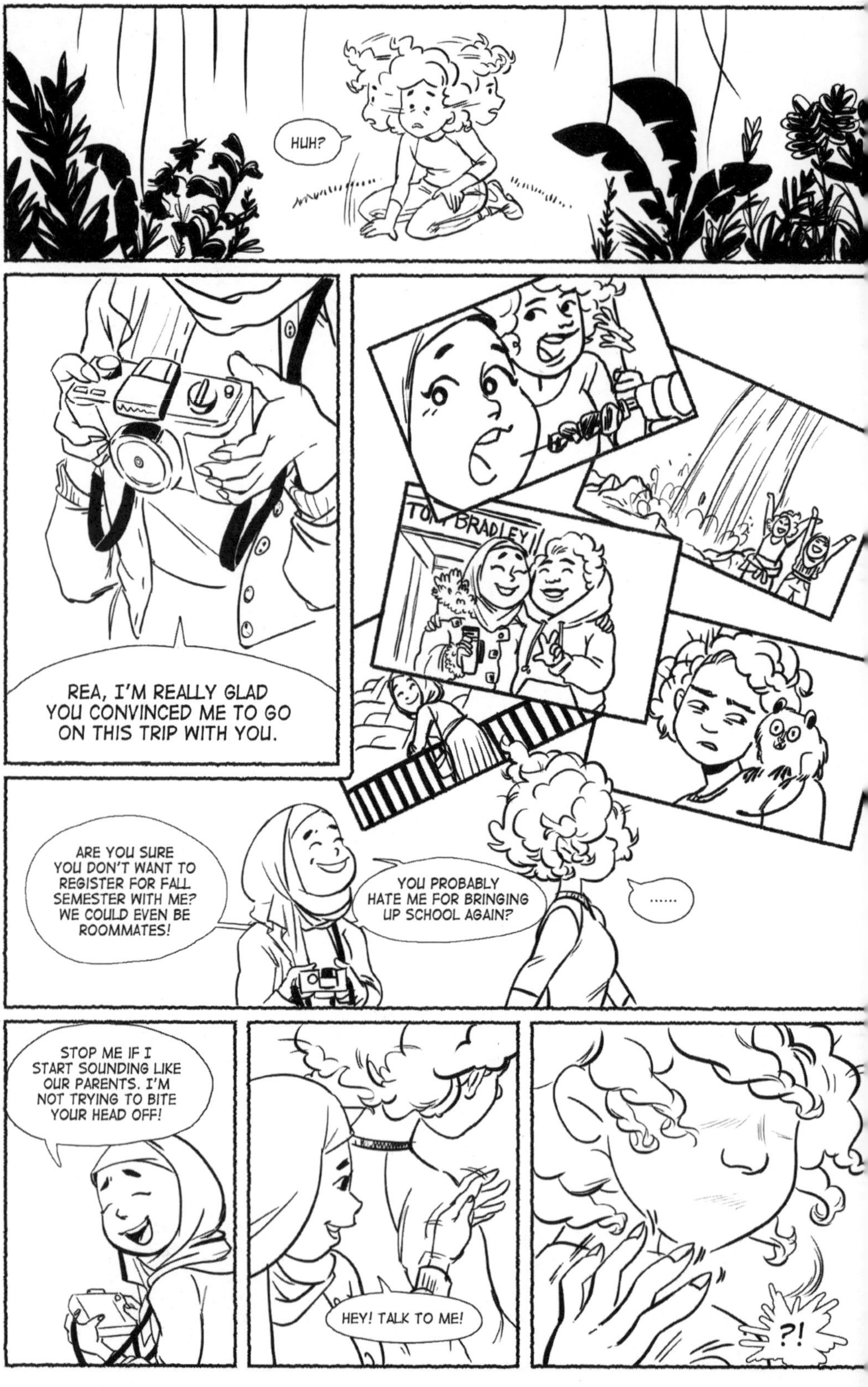

HUH?
REA, I'M REALLY GLAD YOU CONVINCED ME TO GO ON THIS TRIP WITH YOU.
TOM BRADLEY
ARE YOU SURE YOU DON'T WANT TO REGISTER FOR FALL SEMESTER WITH ME? WE COULD EVEN BE ROOMMATES!
YOU PROBABLY HATE ME FOR BRINGING UP SCHOOL AGAIN?
......
STOP ME IF I START SOUNDING LIKE OUR PARENTS. I'M NOT TRYING TO BITE YOUR HEAD OFF!
HEY! TALK TO ME!
?!

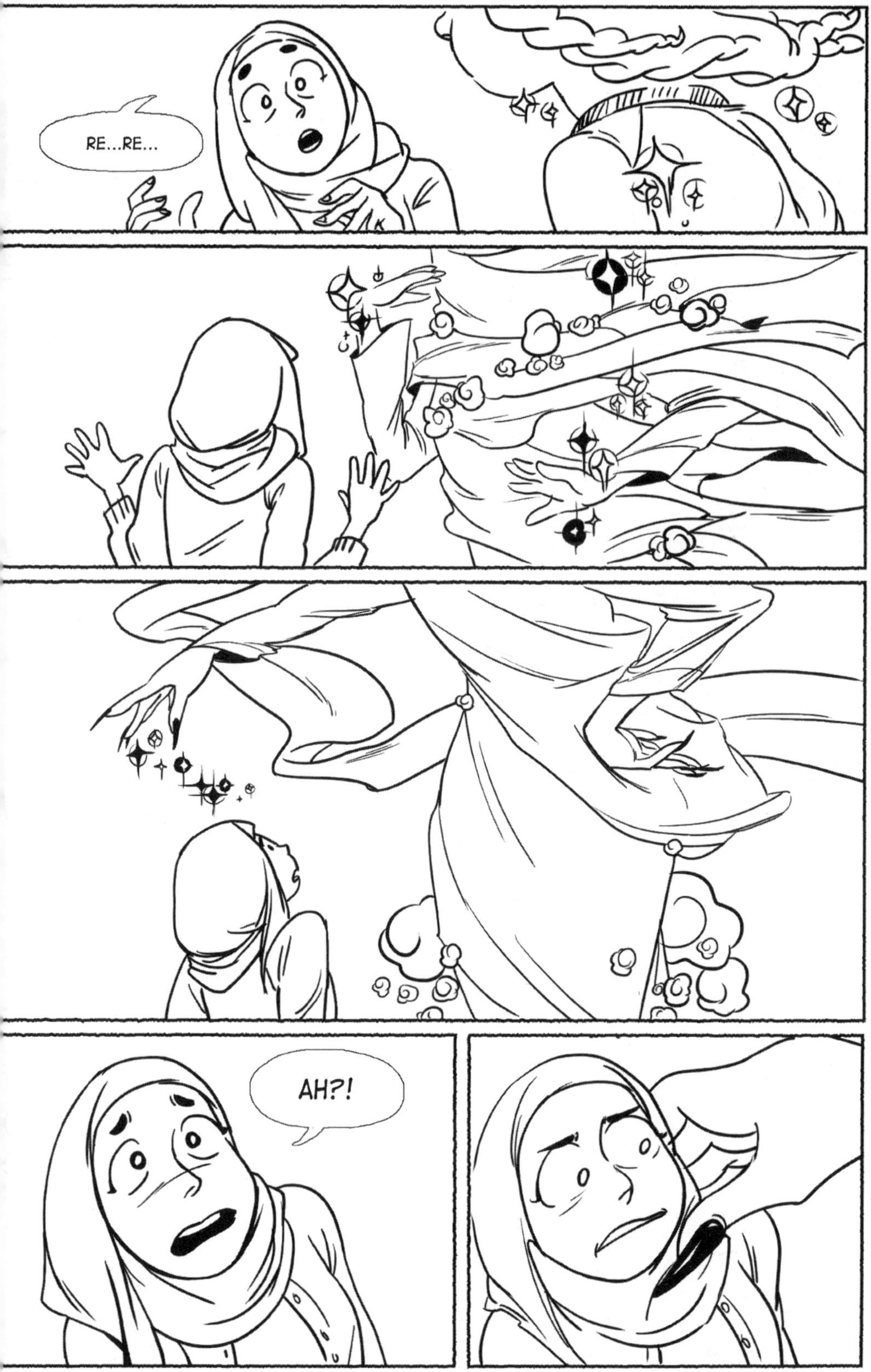
RE...RE...
AH?!

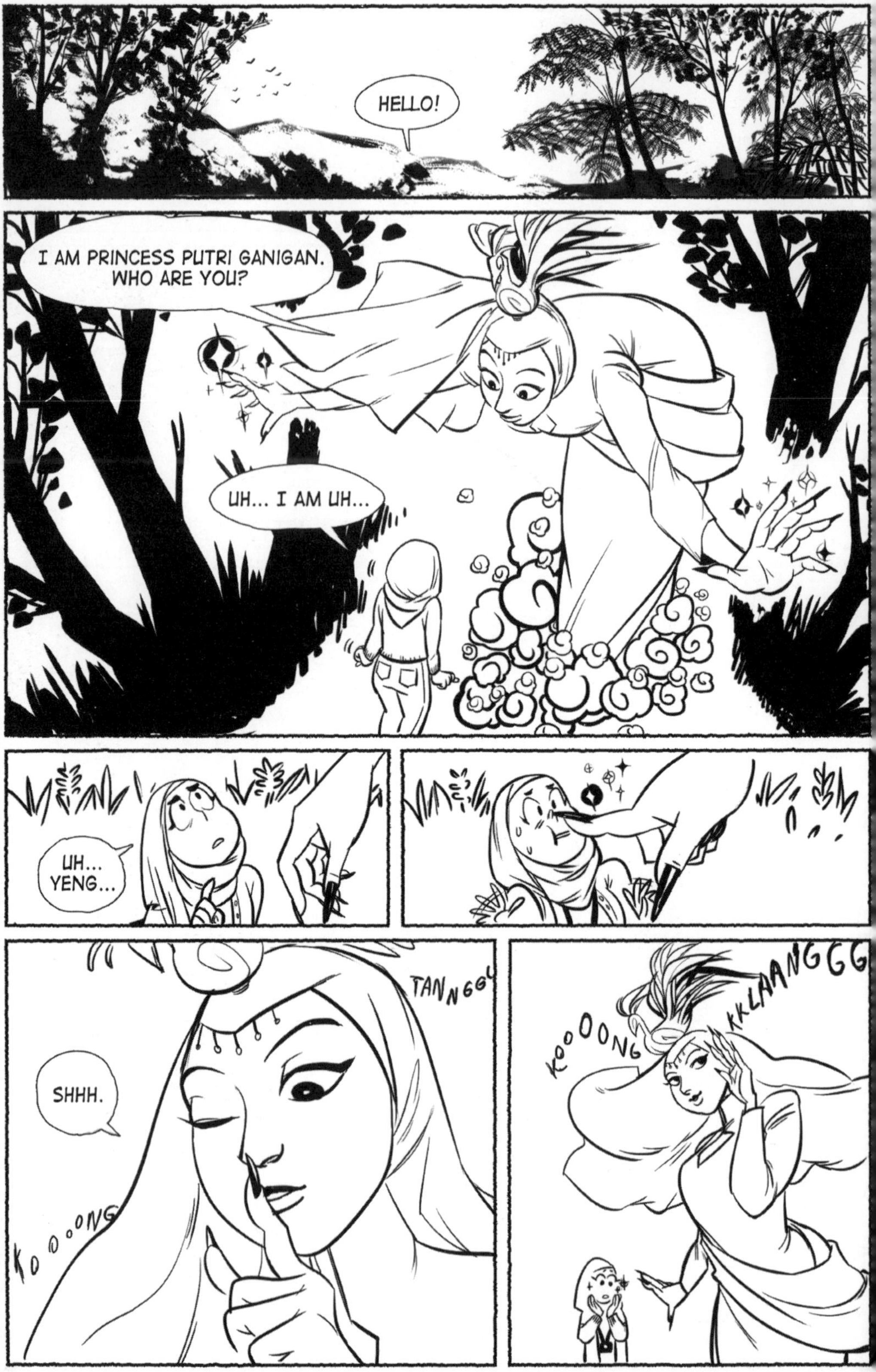
HELLO!
I AM PRINCESS PUTRI GANIGAN. WHO ARE YOU?
UH... I AM UH...
UH... YENG...
SHHH.
TANNGG
KOOOOONG
KOOOONG
KKLAANGGG

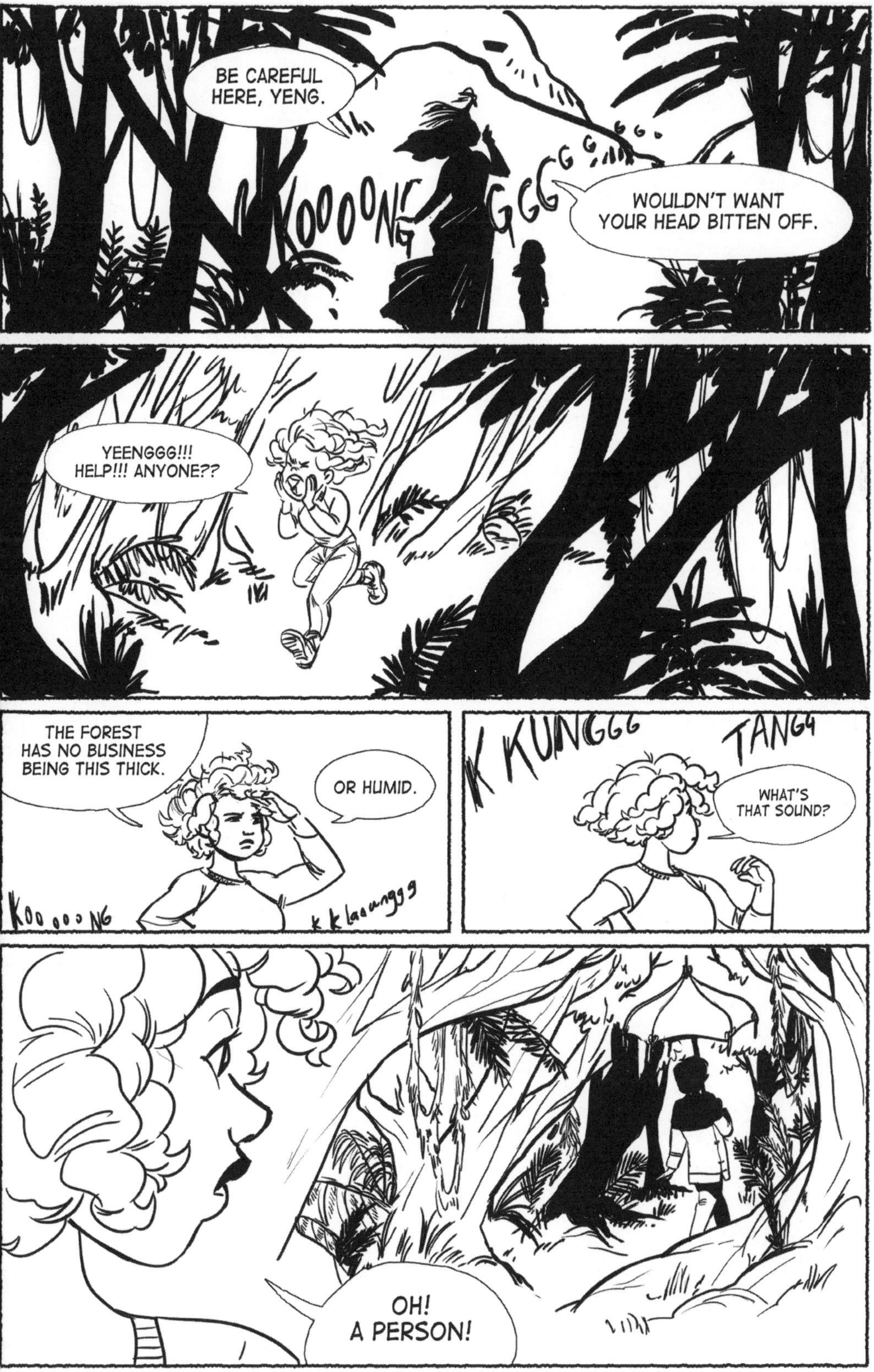
BE CAREFUL HERE, YENG.
WOULDN'T WANT YOUR HEAD BITTEN OFF.
YEENGGG!!! HELP!!! ANYONE??
THE FOREST HAS NO BUSINESS BEING THIS THICK.
OR HUMID.
K KUNGGG
TANGG
WHAT'S THAT SOUND?
OH! A PERSON!

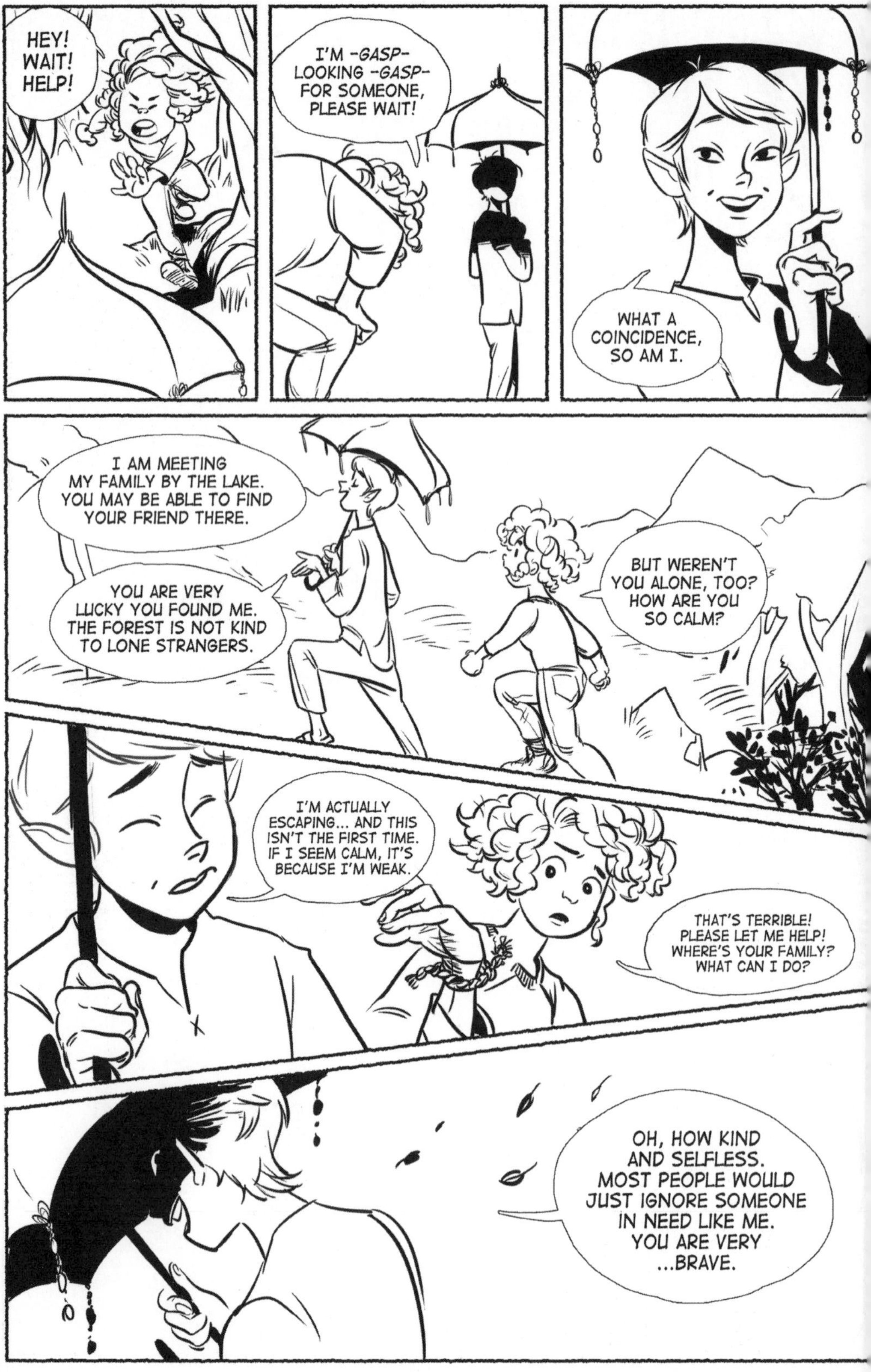

HEY! WAIT! HELP!
I'M -GASP- LOOKING -GASP- FOR SOMEONE, PLEASE WAIT!
WHAT A COINCIDENCE, SO AM I.
I AM MEETING MY FAMILY BY THE LAKE. YOU MAY BE ABLE TO FIND YOUR FRIEND THERE.
YOU ARE VERY LUCKY YOU FOUND ME. THE FOREST IS NOT KIND TO LONE STRANGERS.
BUT WEREN'T YOU ALONE, TOO? HOW ARE YOU SO CALM?
I'M ACTUALLY ESCAPING... AND THIS ISN'T THE FIRST TIME. IF I SEEM CALM, IT'S BECAUSE I'M WEAK.
THAT'S TERRIBLE! PLEASE LET ME HELP! WHERE'S YOUR FAMILY? WHAT CAN I DO?
OH, HOW KIND AND SELFLESS. MOST PEOPLE WOULD JUST IGNORE SOMEONE IN NEED LIKE ME. YOU ARE VERY ...BRAVE.

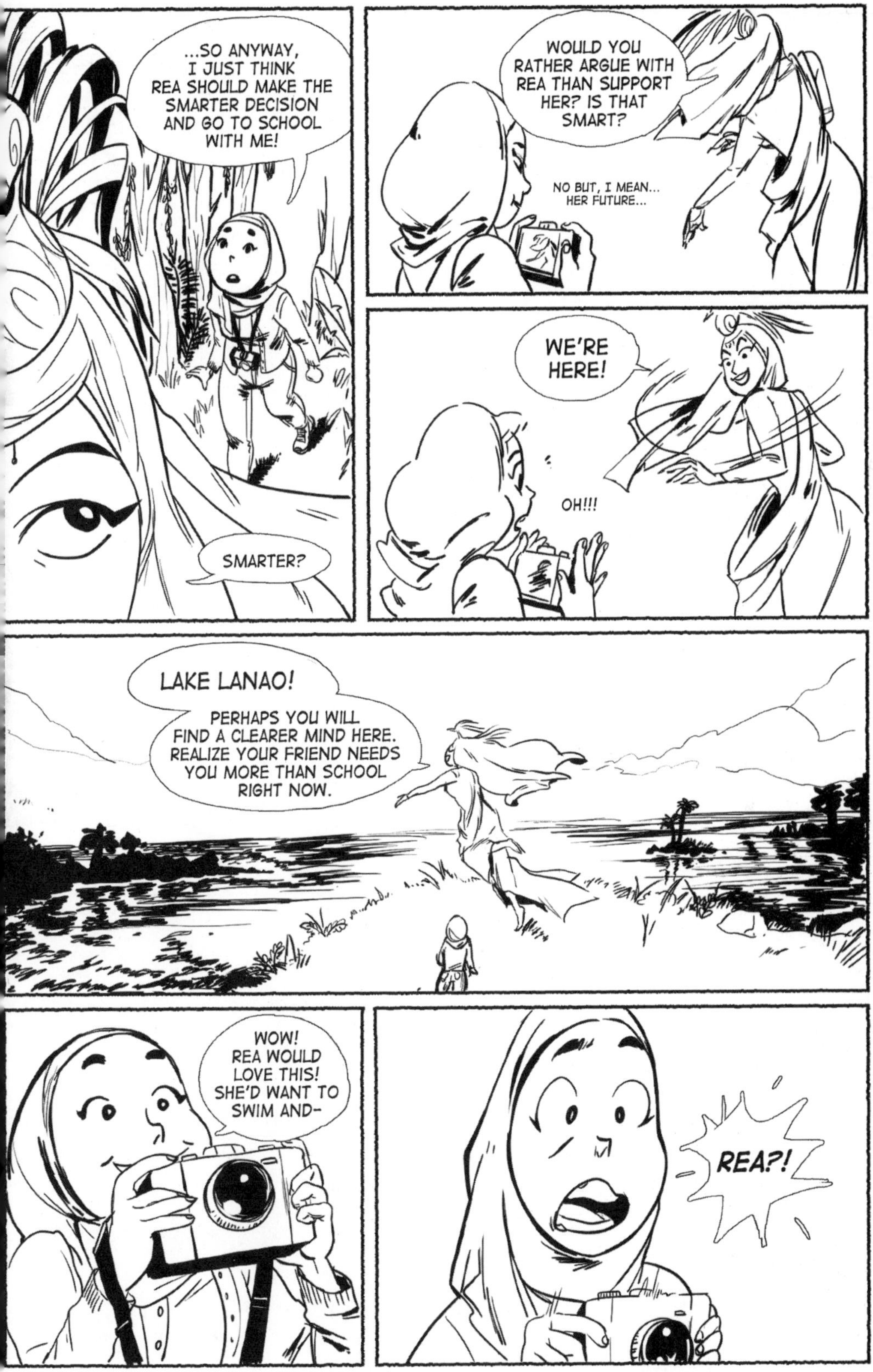
...SO ANYWAY, I JUST THINK REA SHOULD MAKE THE SMARTER DECISION AND GO TO SCHOOL WITH ME!
SMARTER?
WOULD YOU RATHER ARGUE WITH REA THAN SUPPORT HER? IS THAT SMART?
NO BUT, I MEAN... HER FUTURE...
WE'RE HERE!
OH!!!
LAKE LANAO!
PERHAPS YOU WILL FIND A CLEARER MIND HERE. REALIZE YOUR FRIEND NEEDS YOU MORE THAN SCHOOL RIGHT NOW.
WOW! REA WOULD LOVE THIS! SHE'D WANT TO SWIM AND-
REA?!

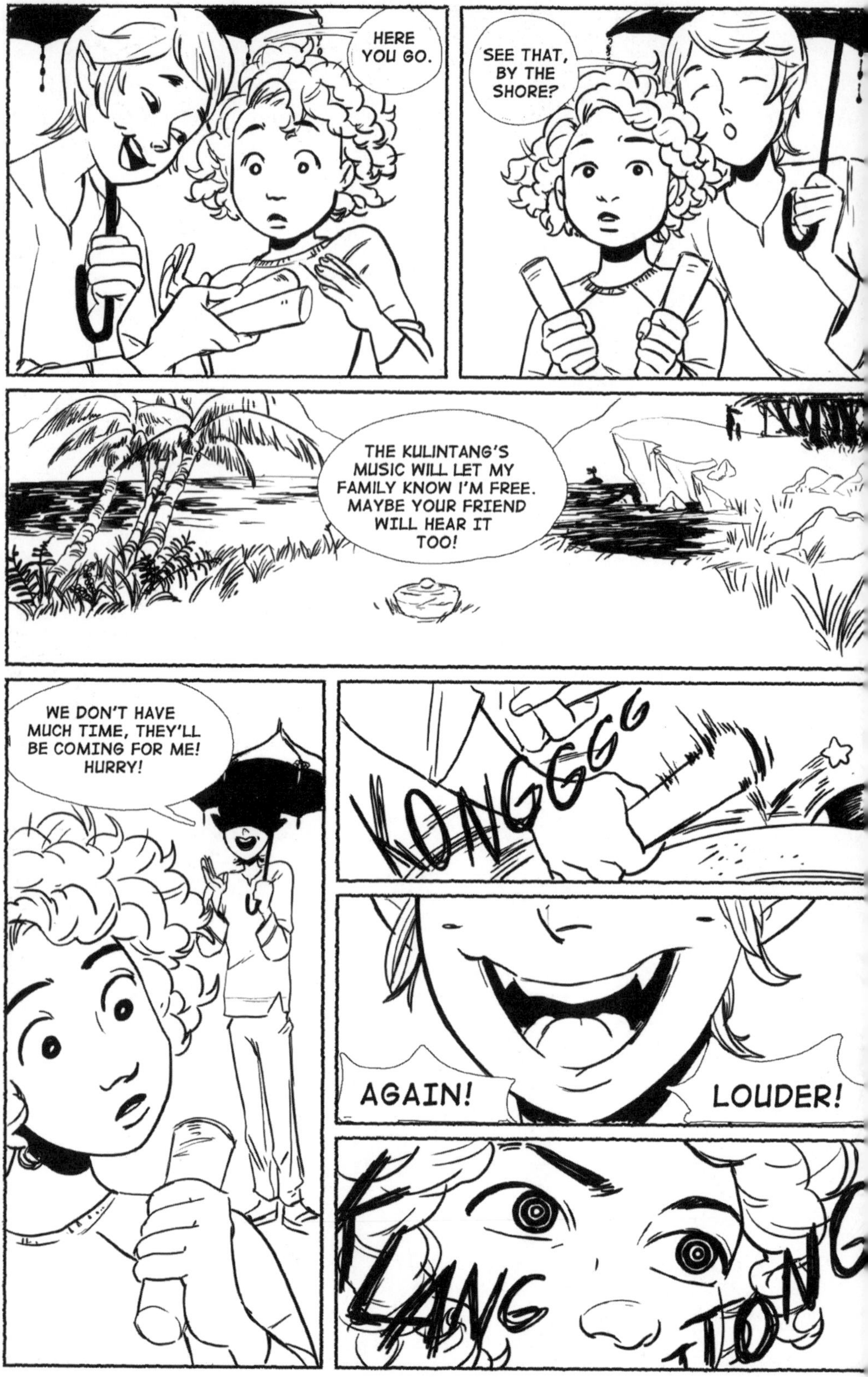
HERE YOU GO.
SEE THAT, BY THE SHORE?
THE KULINTANG'S MUSIC WILL LET MY FAMILY KNOW I'M FREE. MAYBE YOUR FRIEND WILL HEAR IT TOO!
WE DON'T HAVE MUCH TIME, THEY'LL BE COMING FOR ME! HURRY!
KONGGGG
AGAIN!
LOUDER!
KLANG
TONG

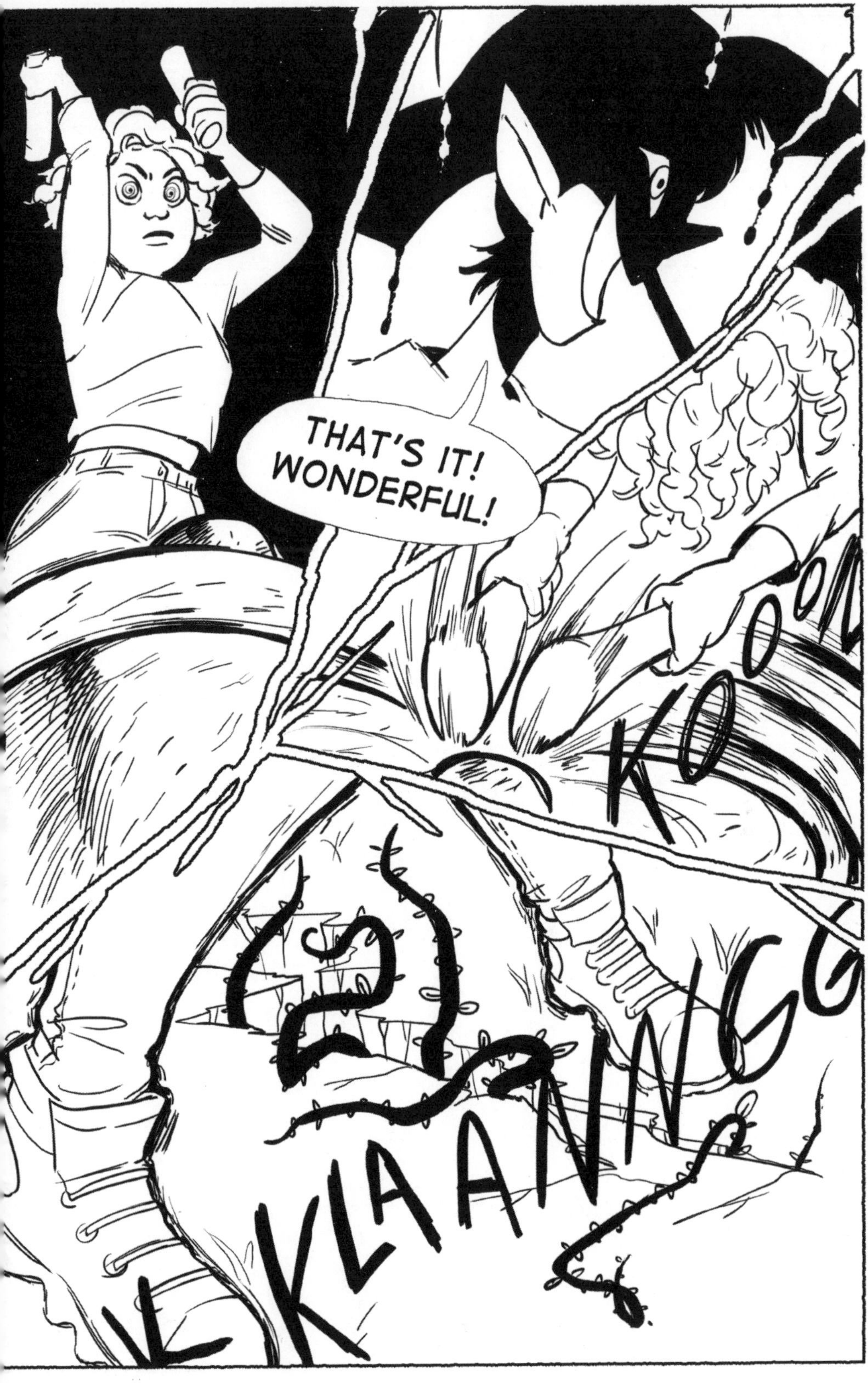
THAT'S IT! WONDERFUL!
KLAANNGG
KOOOO

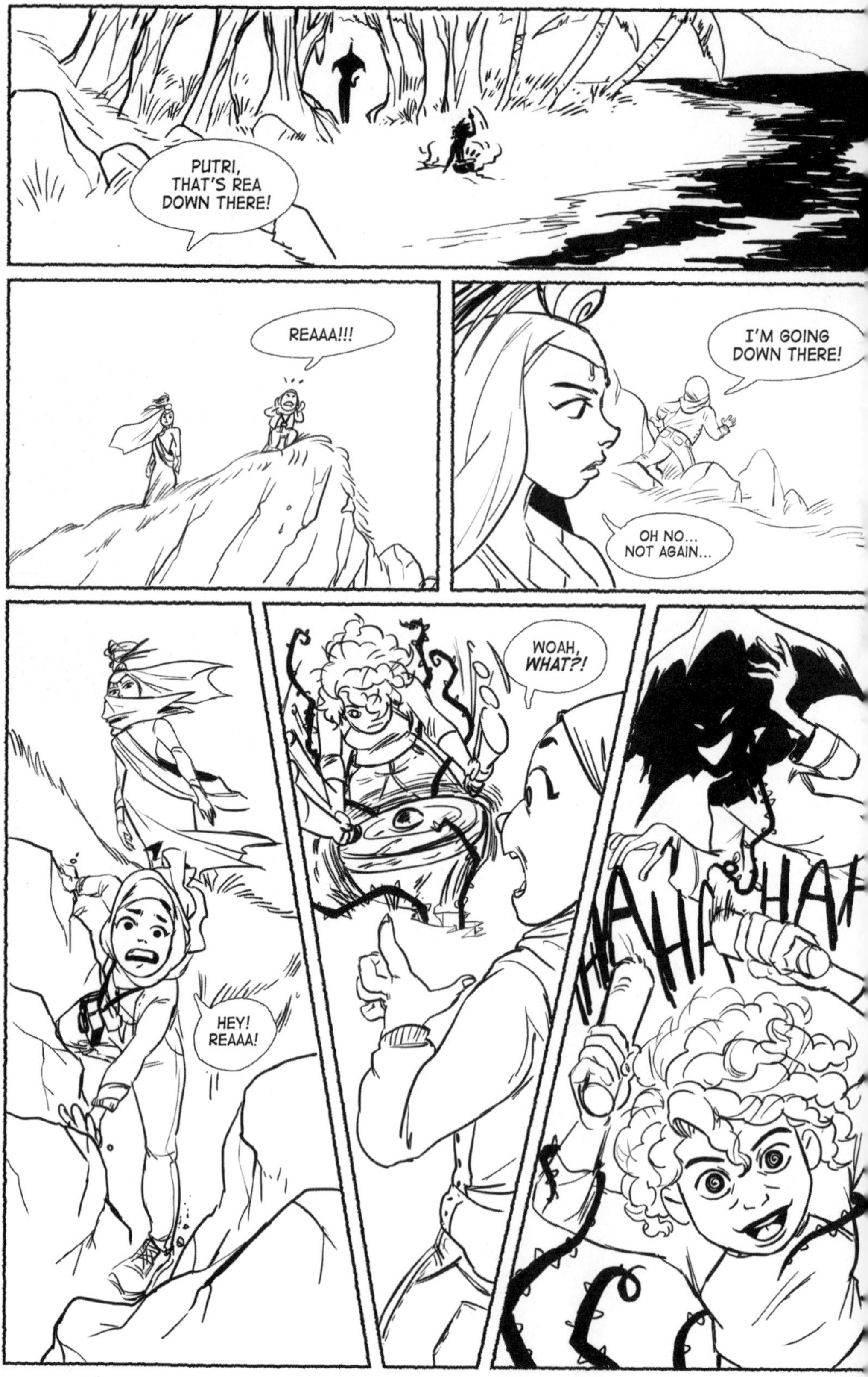
PUTRI, THAT'S REA DOWN THERE!
REAAA!!!
I'M GOING DOWN THERE!
OH NO... NOT AGAIN...
HEY! REAAA!
WOAH, WHAT?!
HA HA HA HA

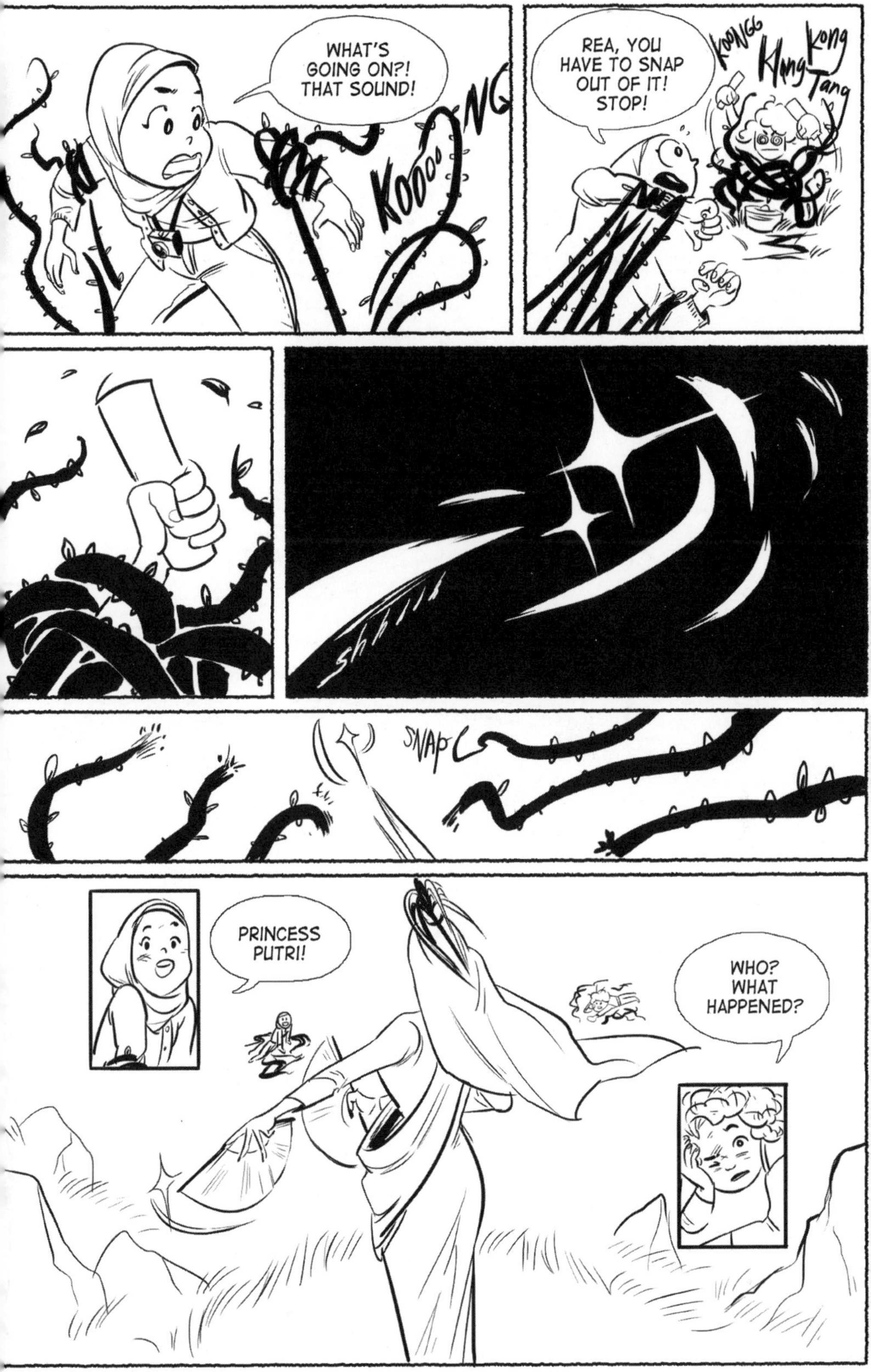
WHAT'S GOING ON?! THAT SOUND!
REA, YOU HAVE TO SNAP OUT OF IT! STOP!
Klang
Kong
Tang
SNAP
PRINCESS PUTRI!
WHO? WHAT HAPPENED?

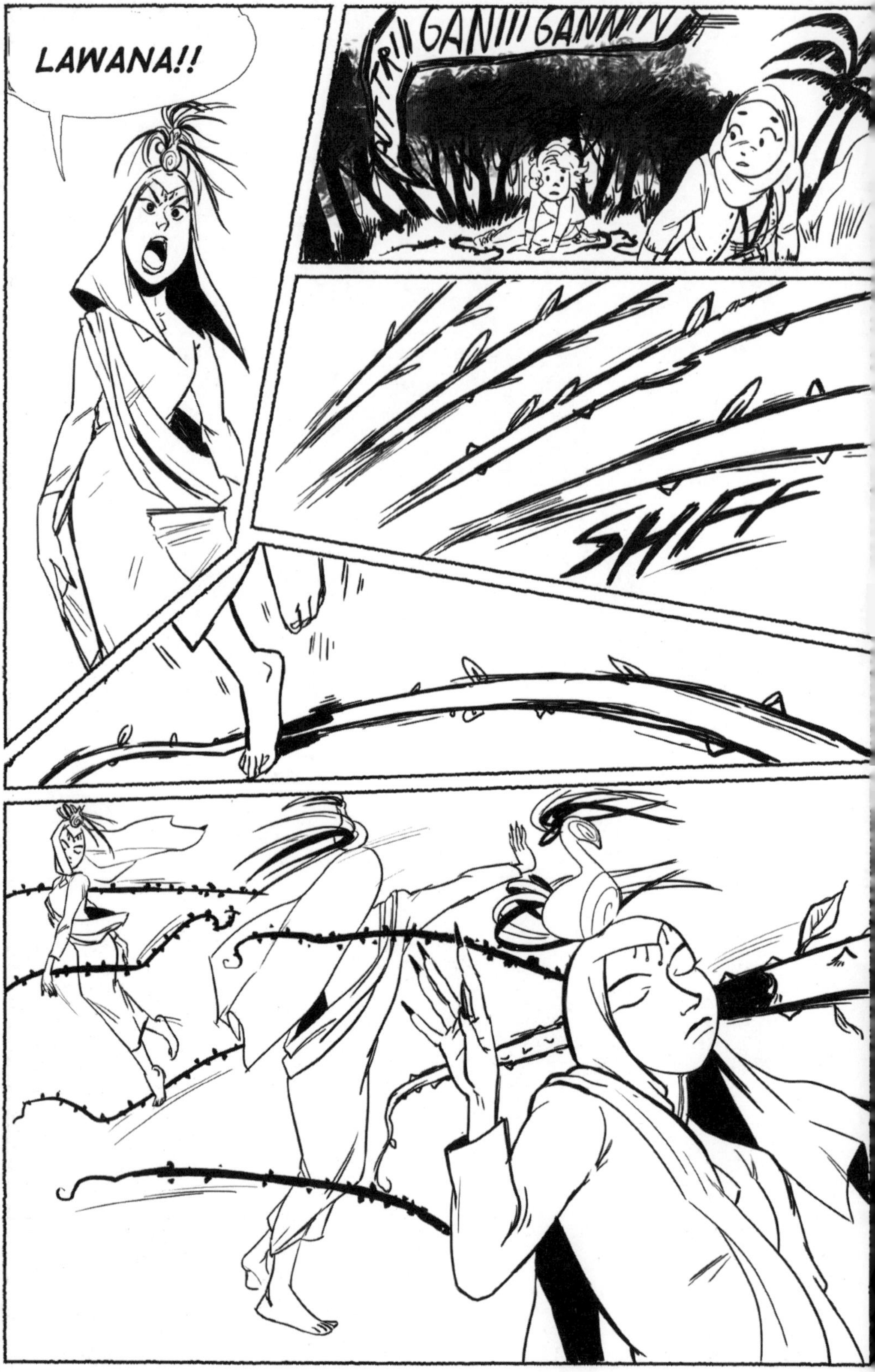

LAWANA!!
TRII GANIIII GANNNN
SHFF

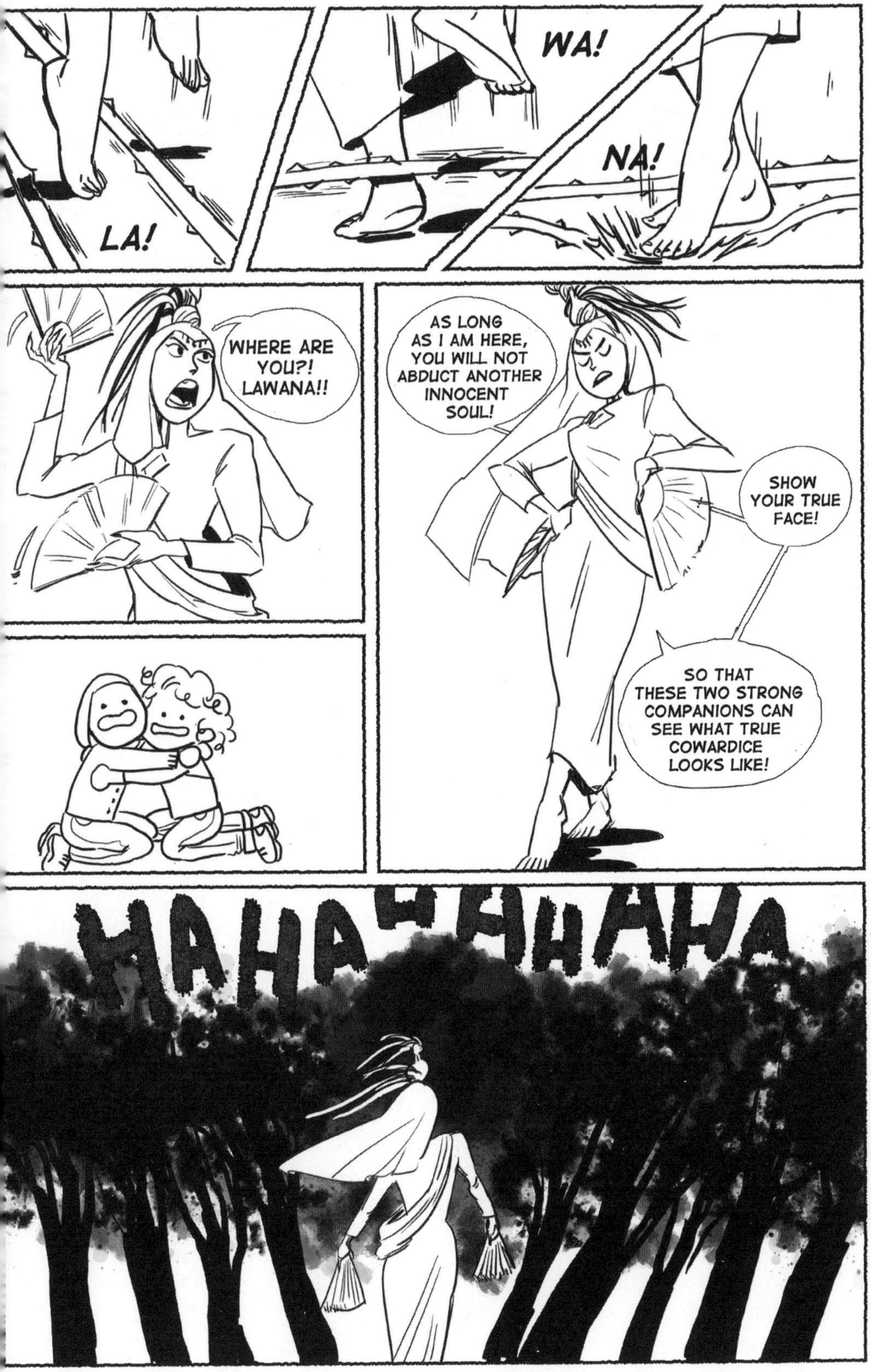
LA!
WA!
NA!
WHERE ARE YOU?! LAWANA!!
AS LONG AS I AM HERE, YOU WILL NOT ABDUCT ANOTHER INNOCENT SOUL!
SHOW YOUR TRUE FACE!
SO THAT THESE TWO STRONG COMPANIONS CAN SEE WHAT TRUE COWARDICE LOOKS LIKE!
HAHAHAHAHAHA

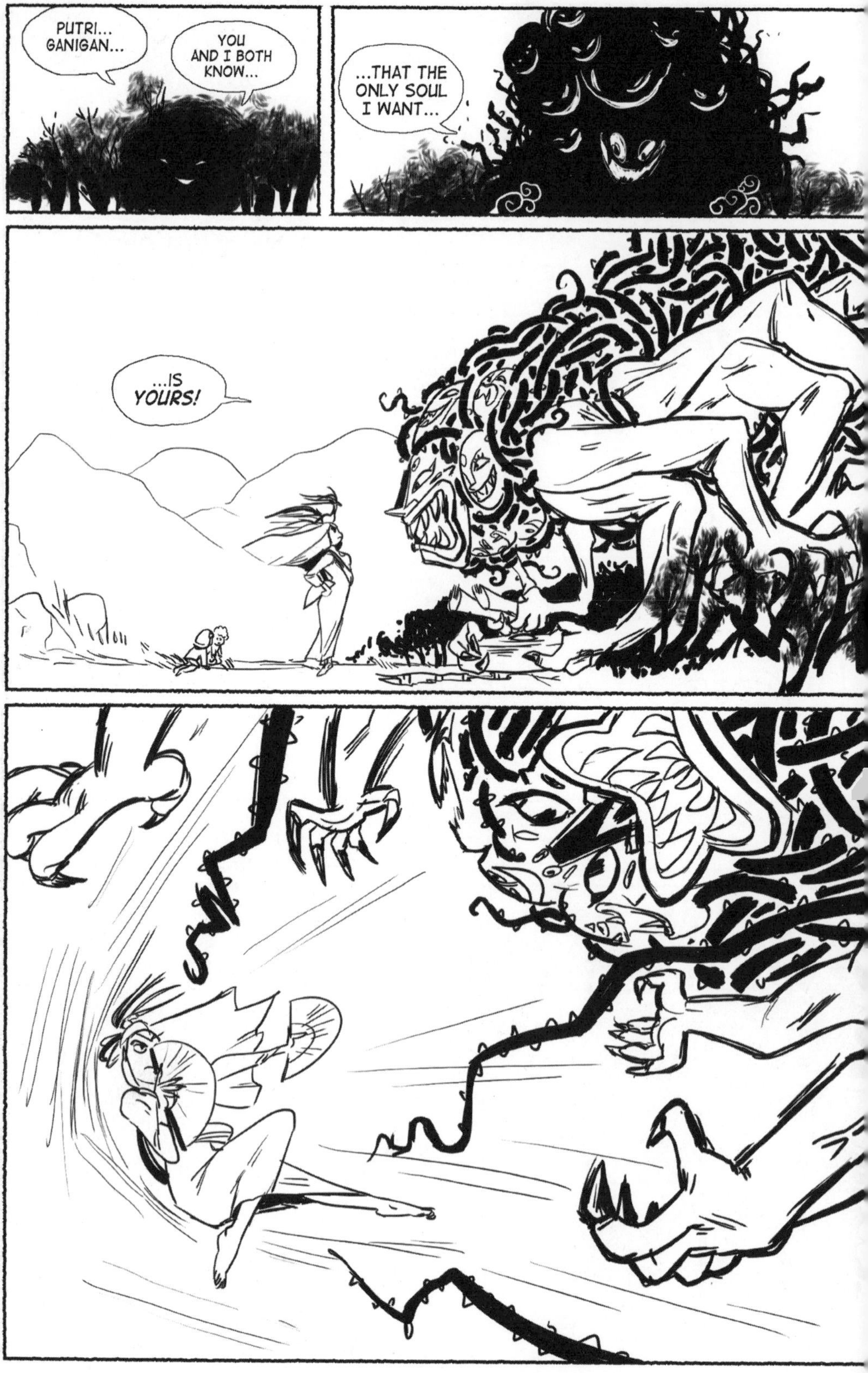
PUTRI... GANIGAN...
YOU AND I BOTH KNOW...
...THAT THE ONLY SOUL I WANT...
...IS *YOURS!*

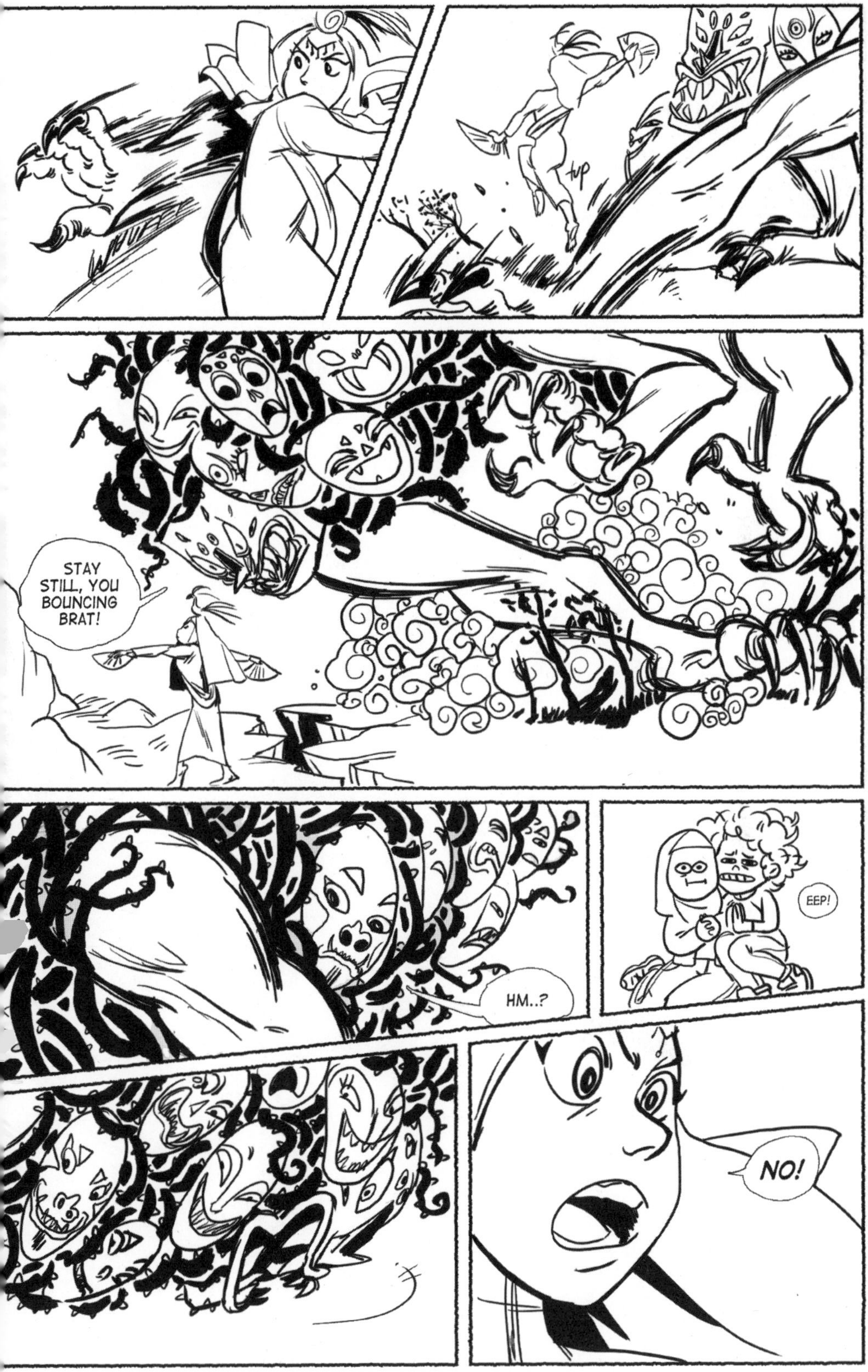
TUP
STAY STILL, YOU BOUNCING BRAT!
HM..?
EEP!
NO!

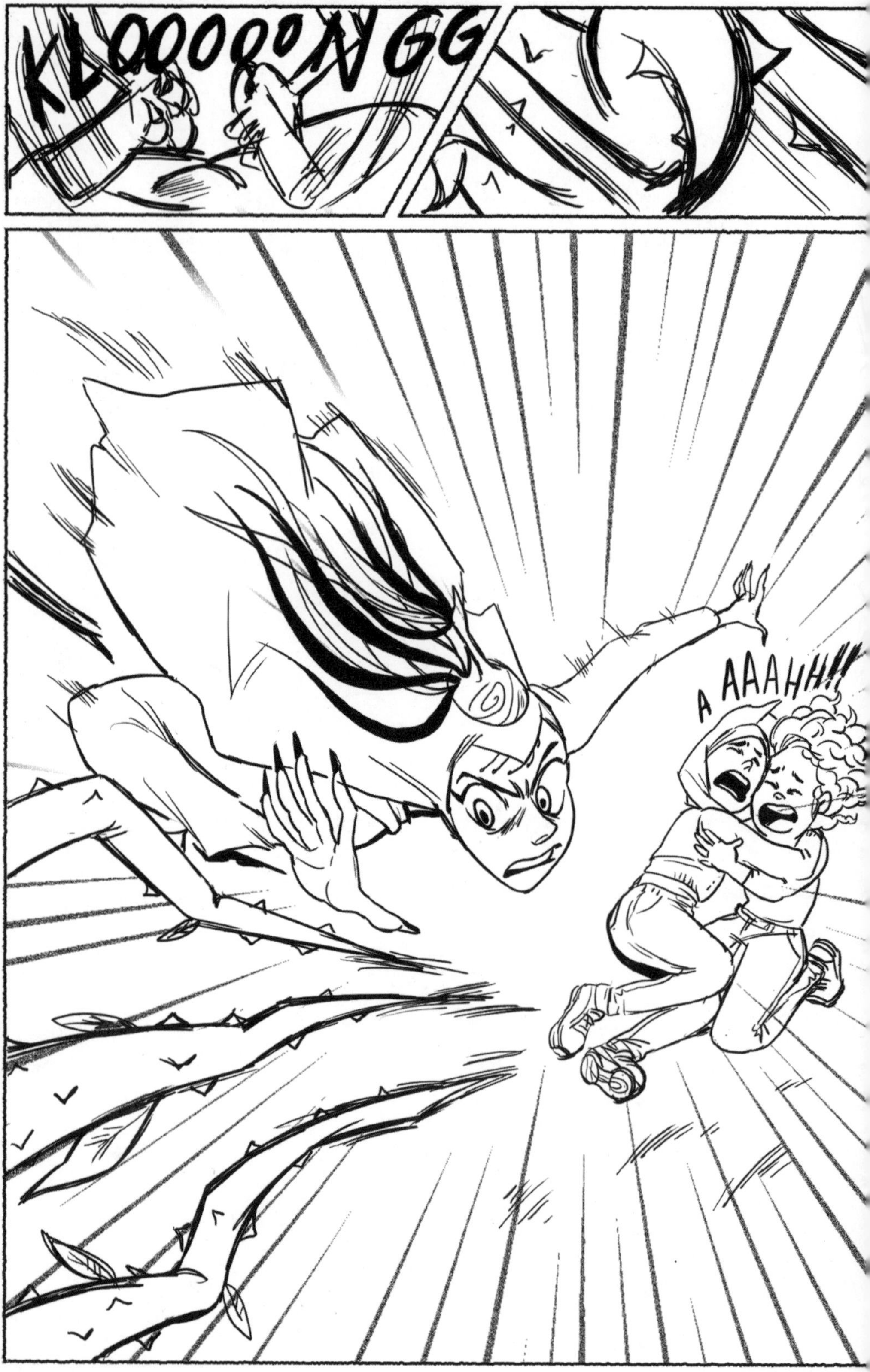
KLOOOOOONGG
A AAAHH!!

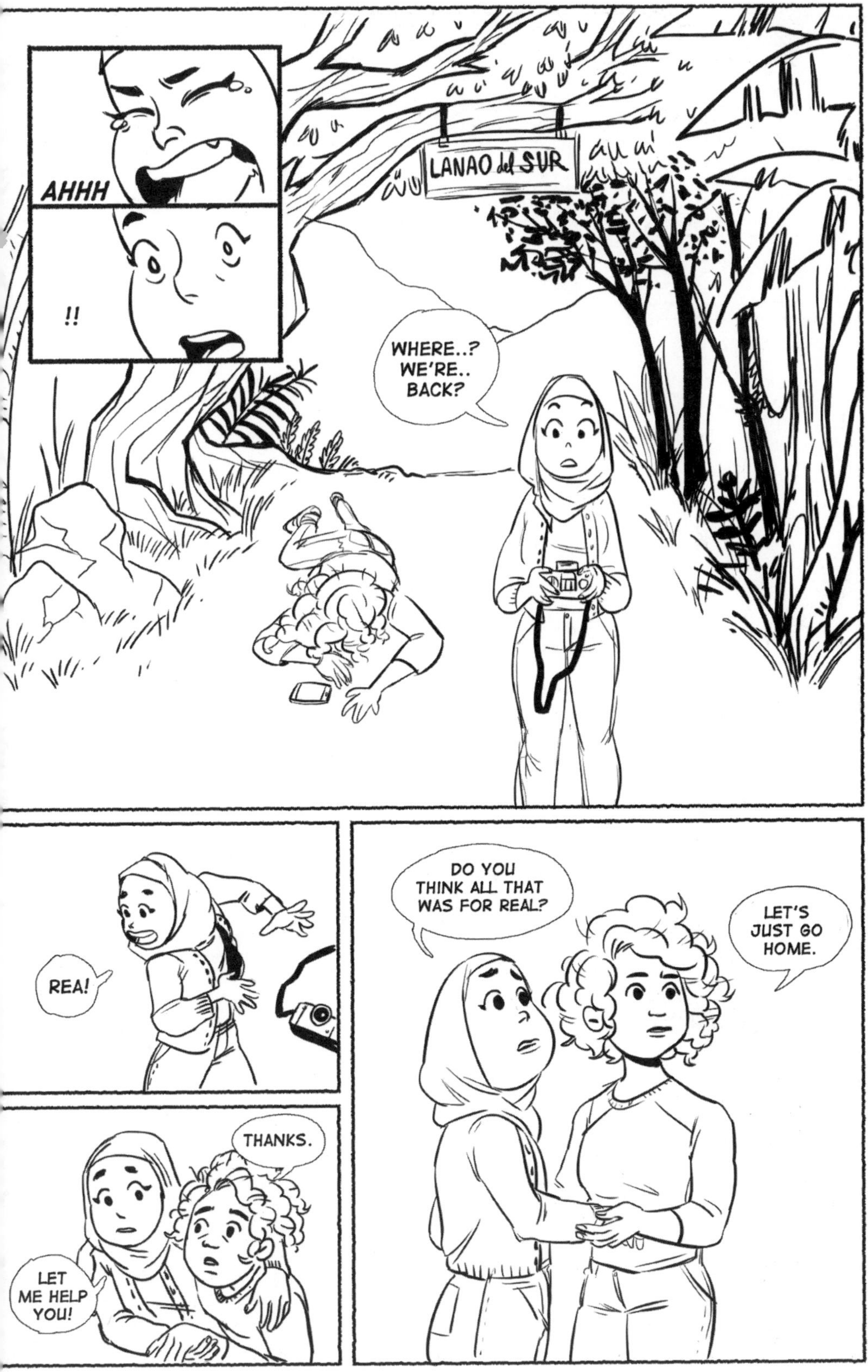
AHHH
!!
LANAO del SUR
WHERE..? WE'RE.. BACK?
REA!
LET ME HELP YOU!
THANKS.
DO YOU THINK ALL THAT WAS FOR REAL?
LET'S JUST GO HOME.

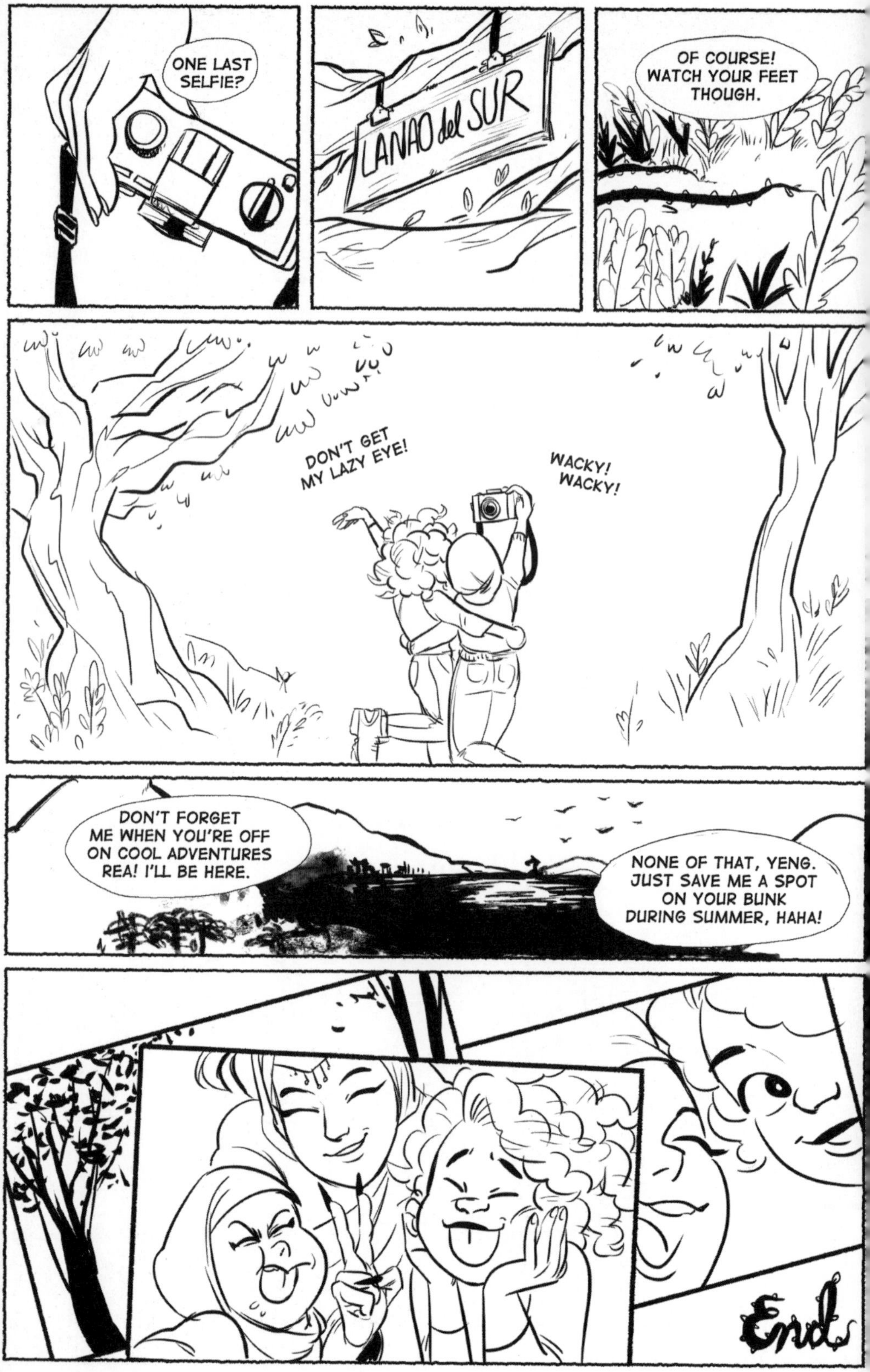
ONE LAST SELFIE?
LANAO del SUR
OF COURSE! WATCH YOUR FEET THOUGH.
DON'T GET MY LAZY EYE!
WACKY! WACKY!
DON'T FORGET ME WHEN YOU'RE OFF ON COOL ADVENTURES REA! I'LL BE HERE.
NONE OF THAT, YENG. JUST SAVE ME A SPOT ON YOUR BUNK DURING SUMMER, HAHA!
End

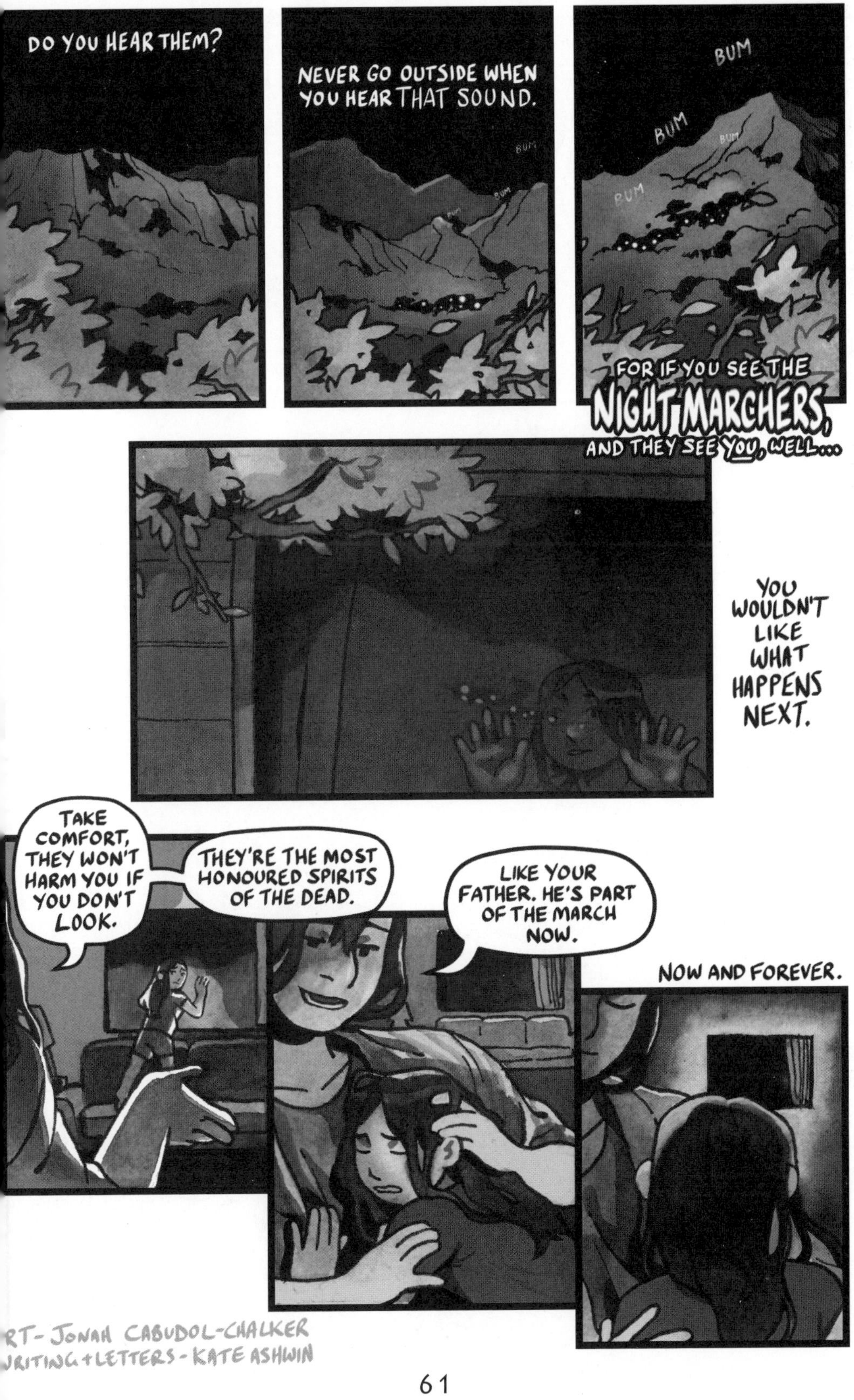
DO YOU HEAR THEM?
NEVER GO OUTSIDE WHEN YOU HEAR THAT SOUND.
BUM
BUM
BUM
BUM
BUM
BUM
BUM
FOR IF YOU SEE THE NIGHT MARCHERS, AND THEY SEE YOU, WELL...
YOU WOULDN'T LIKE WHAT HAPPENS NEXT.
TAKE COMFORT, THEY WON'T HARM YOU IF YOU DON'T LOOK.
THEY'RE THE MOST HONOURED SPIRITS OF THE DEAD.
LIKE YOUR FATHER. HE'S PART OF THE MARCH NOW.
NOW AND FOREVER.

RT- JONAH CABUDOL-CHALKER
RITING + LETTERS - KATE ASHWIN

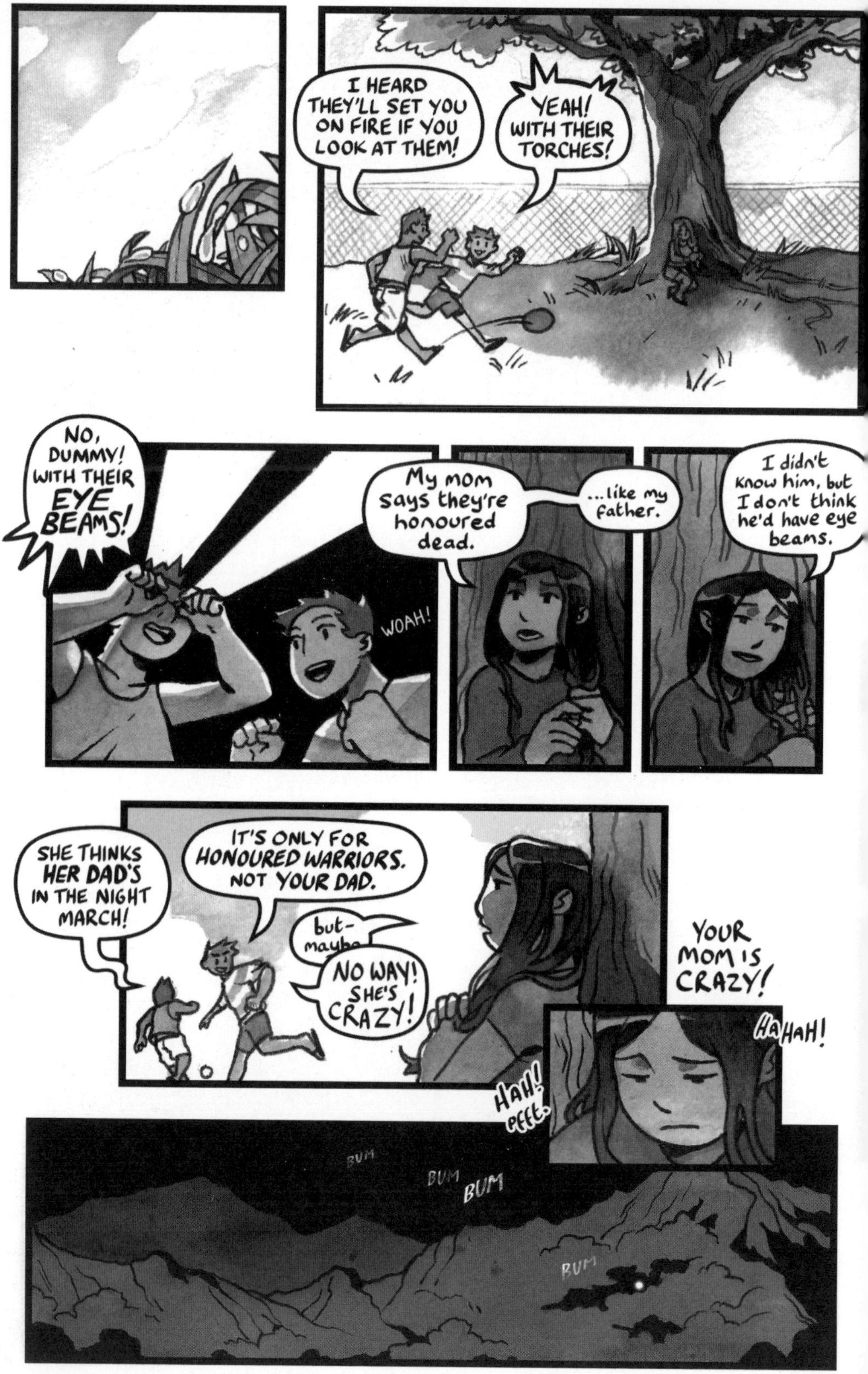

I HEARD THEY'LL SET YOU ON FIRE IF YOU LOOK AT THEM!
YEAH! WITH THEIR TORCHES!
NO, DUMMY! WITH THEIR EYE BEAMS!
WOAH!
My mom says they're honoured dead.
...like my father.
I didn't know him, but I don't think he'd have eye beams.
SHE THINKS HER DAD'S IN THE NIGHT MARCH!
IT'S ONLY FOR HONOURED WARRIORS. NOT YOUR DAD.
but- maybe
NO WAY! SHE'S CRAZY!
YOUR MOM IS CRAZY!
HAHAH!
HAH! PFFT.
BUM
BUM
BUM
BUM

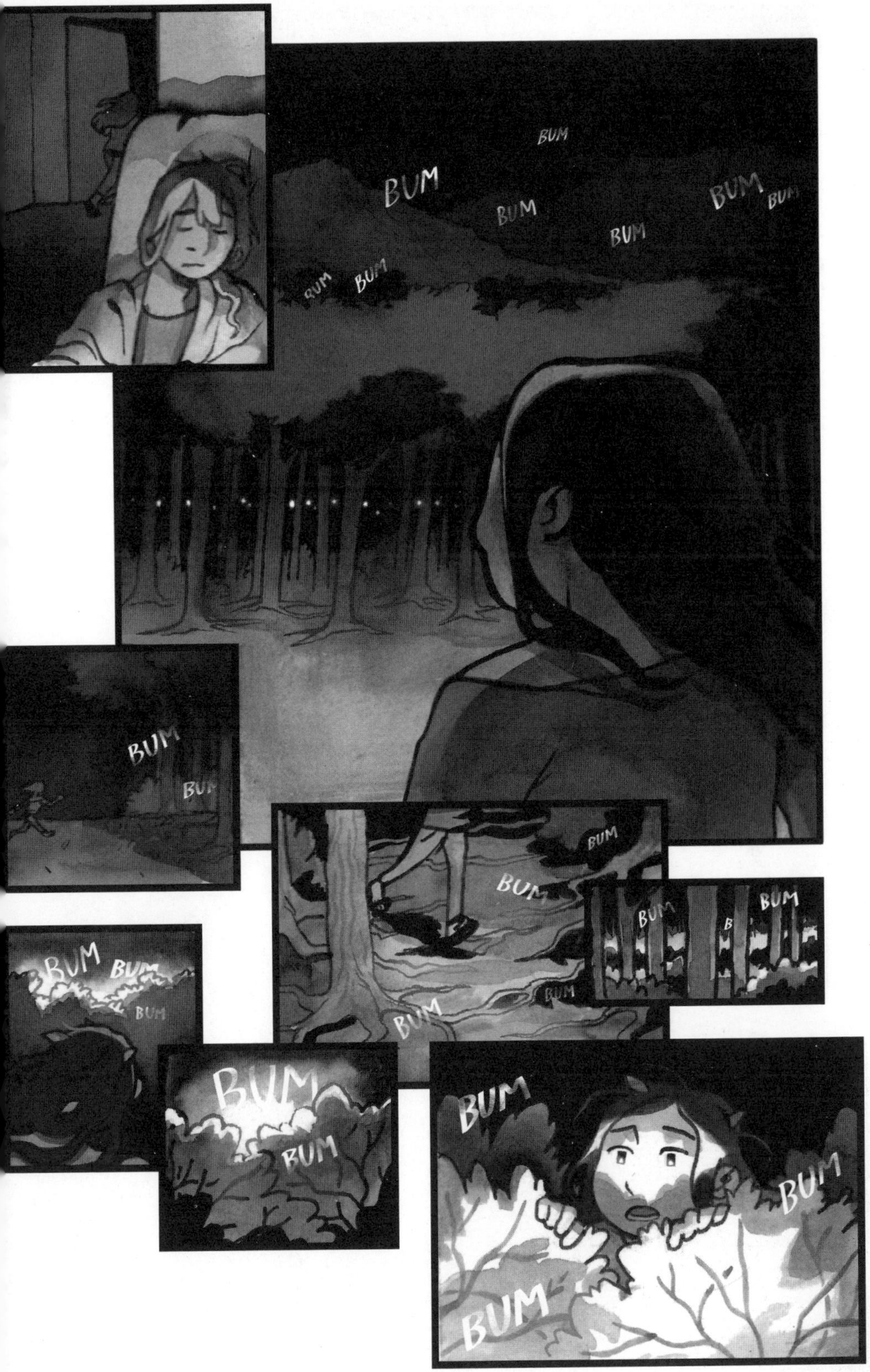
BUM
BUM
BUM
BUM
BUM
BUM
BUM
BUM
BUM
BUM
BUM
BUM
BUM
BUM
BUM
BUM
BUM
BUM
BUM
BUM
BUM
BUM
BUM
BUM

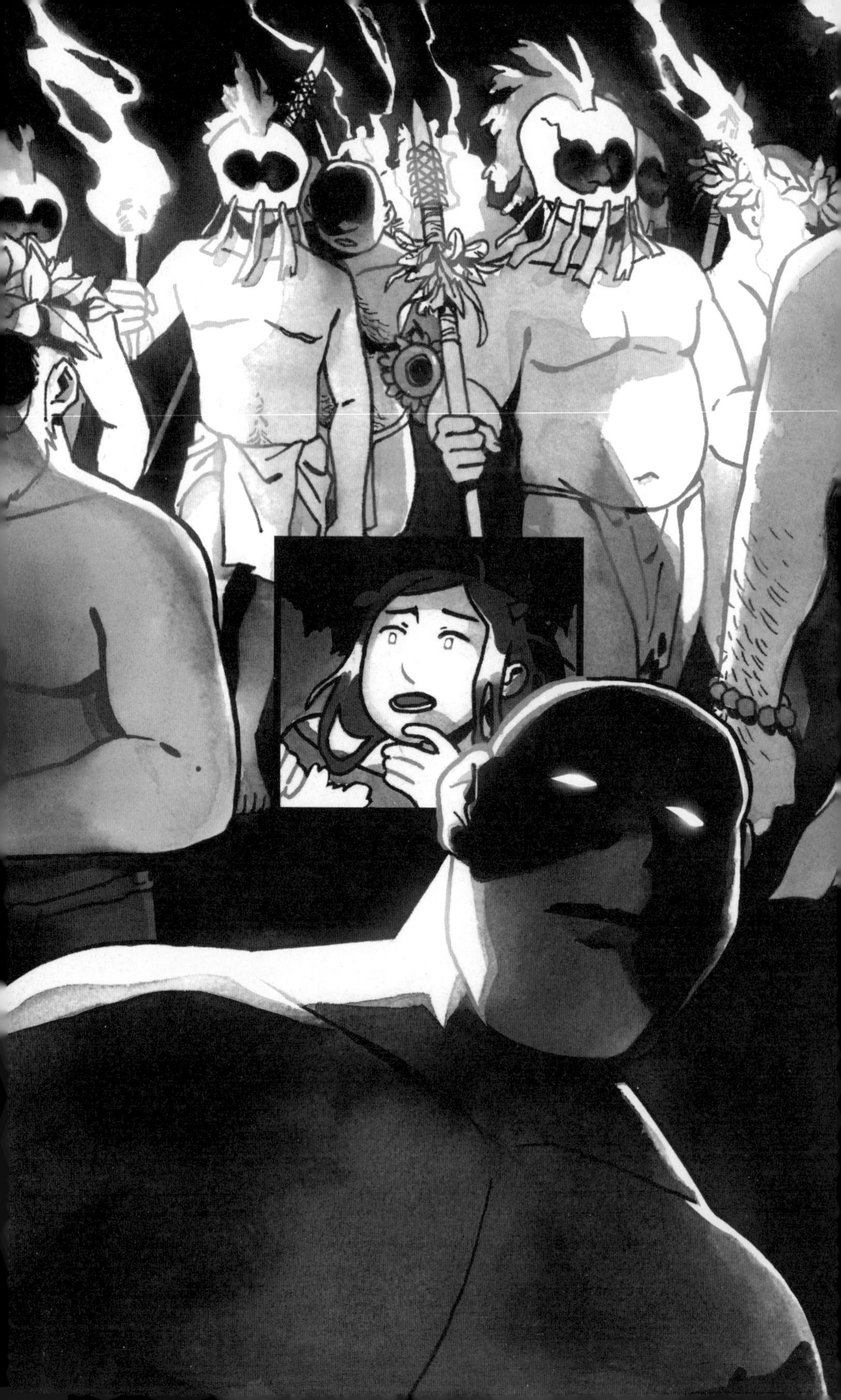

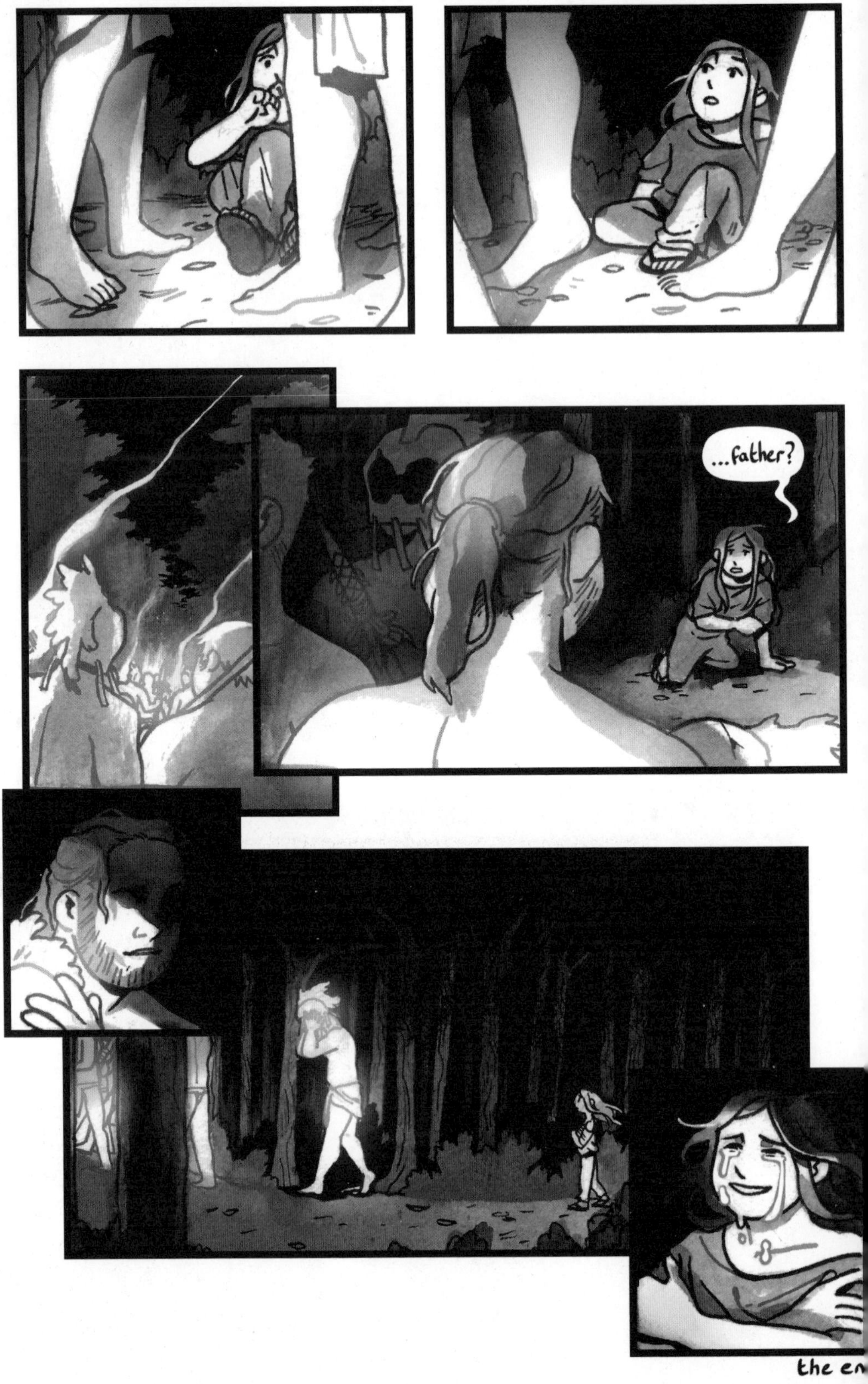
...father?
the en

THE LEGEND of APOLAKI & MAYARI

Based on the Filipino Myth

Art by Kim Miranda

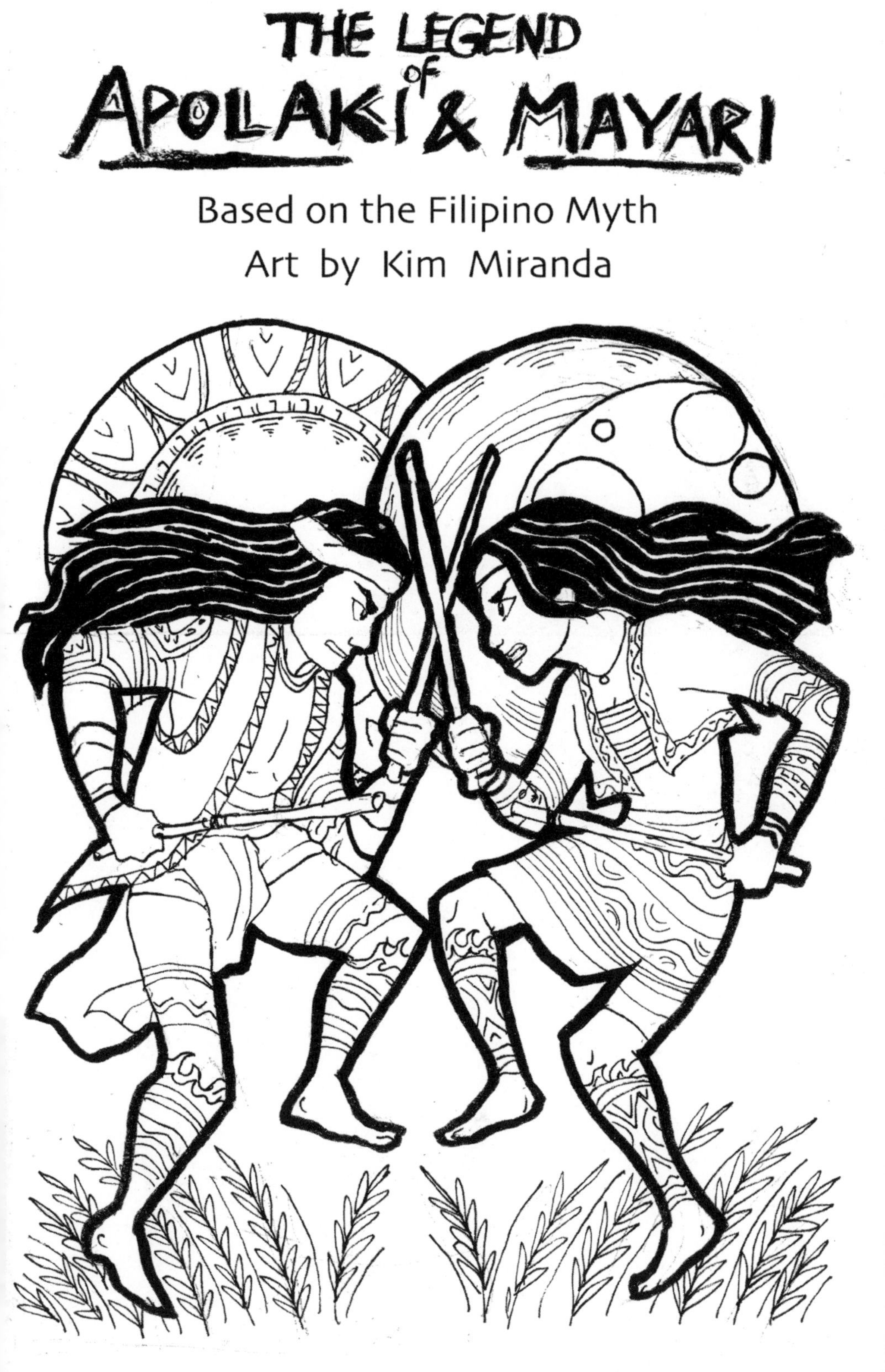

My brother and I usually get along.

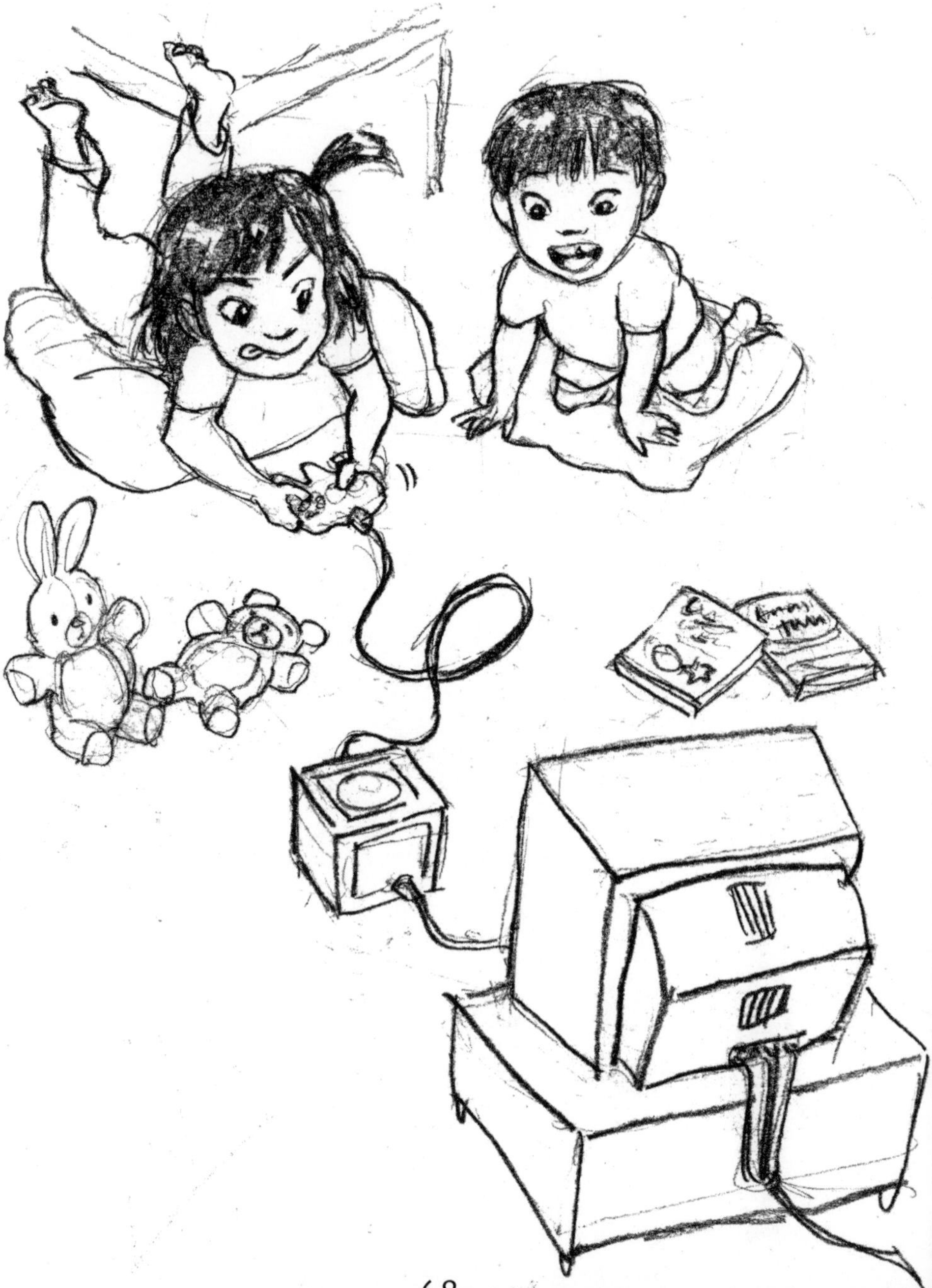

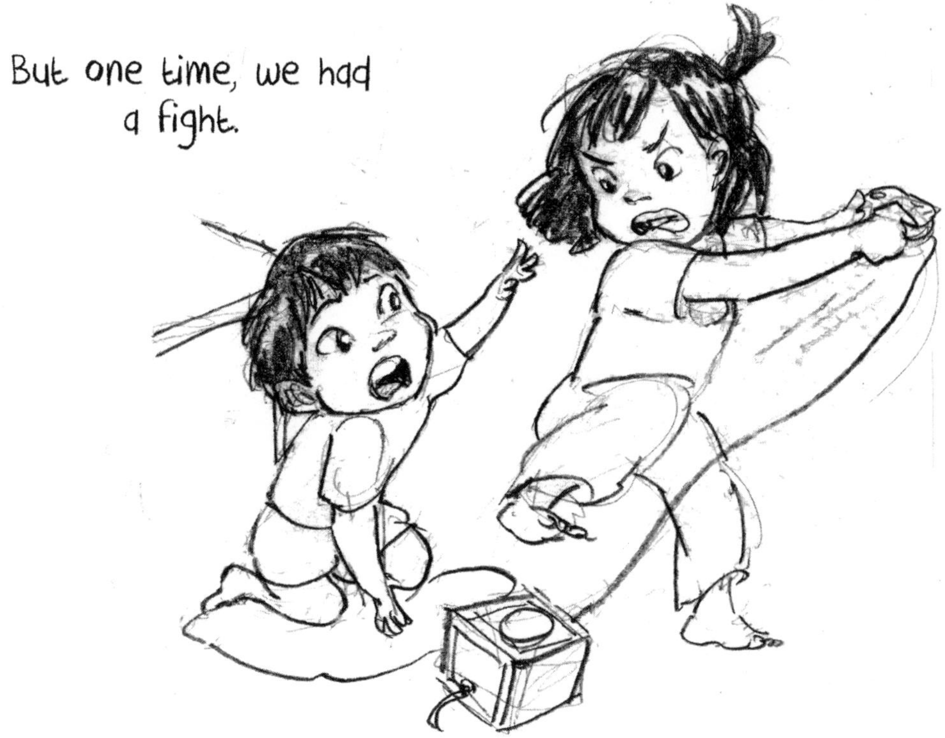
But one time, we had a fight.

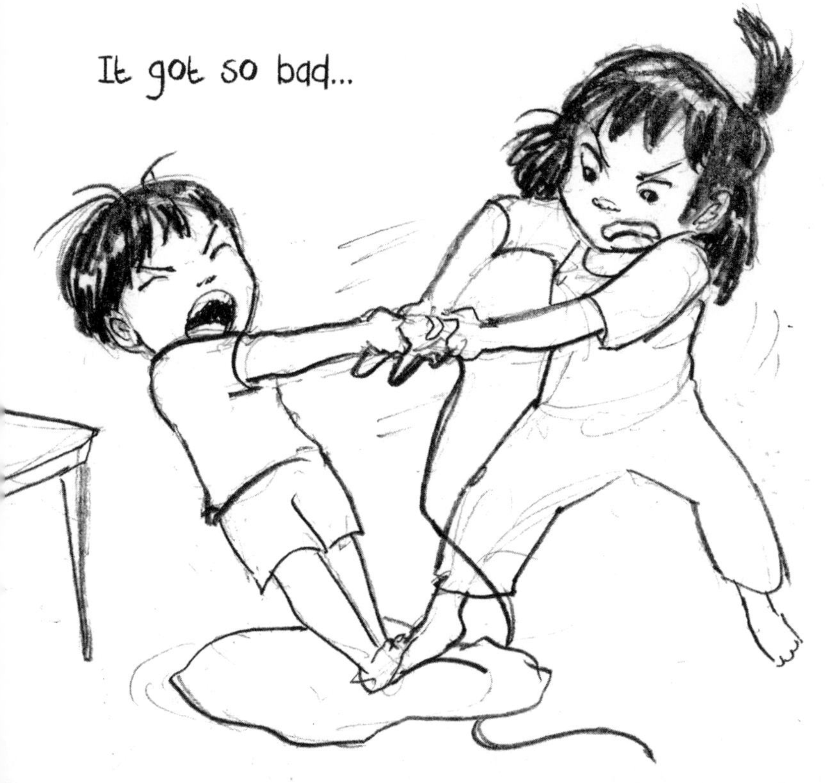
It got so bad...

I let my brother get hurt!

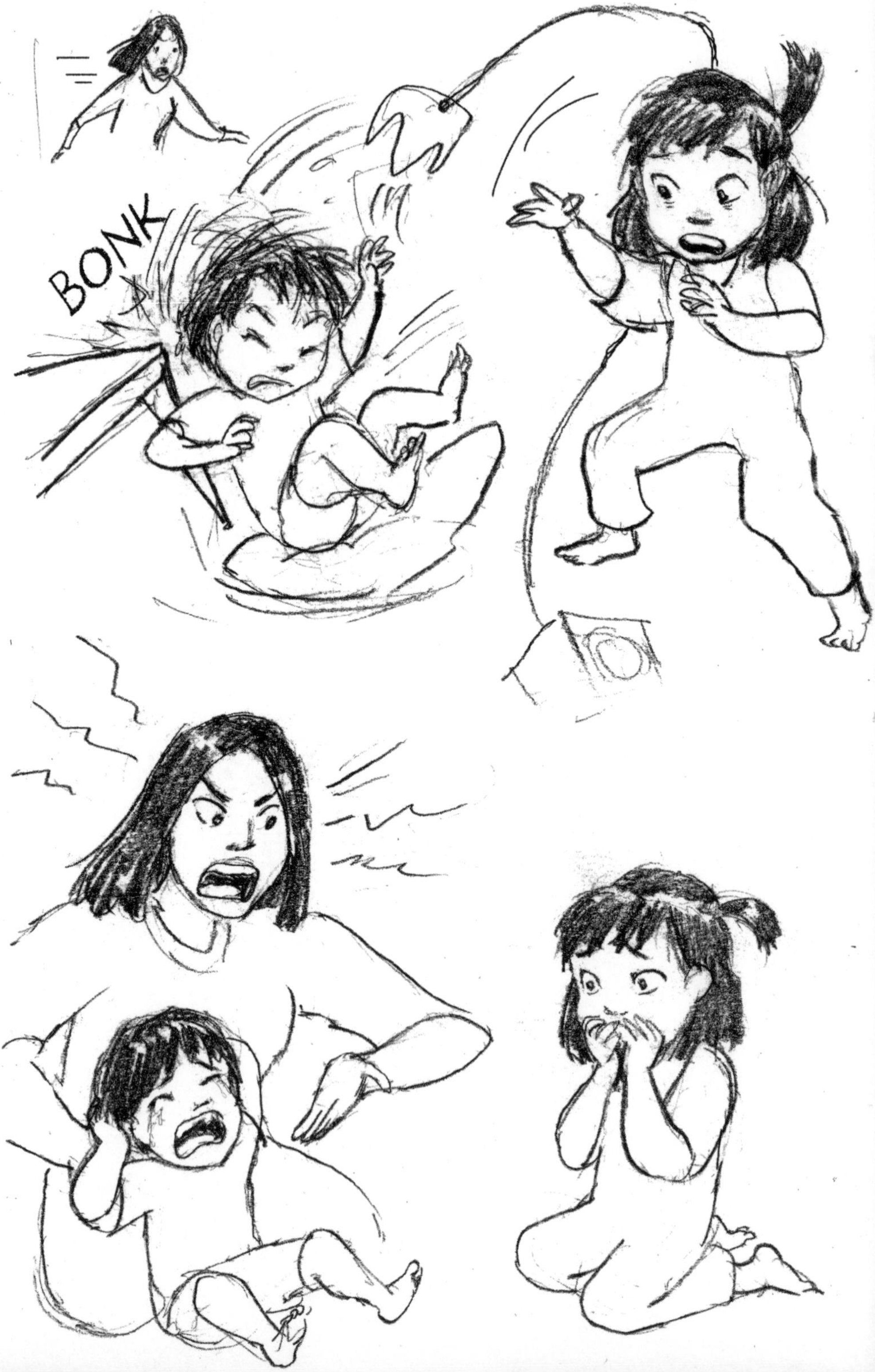
BONK

My mother was angry and disappointed.

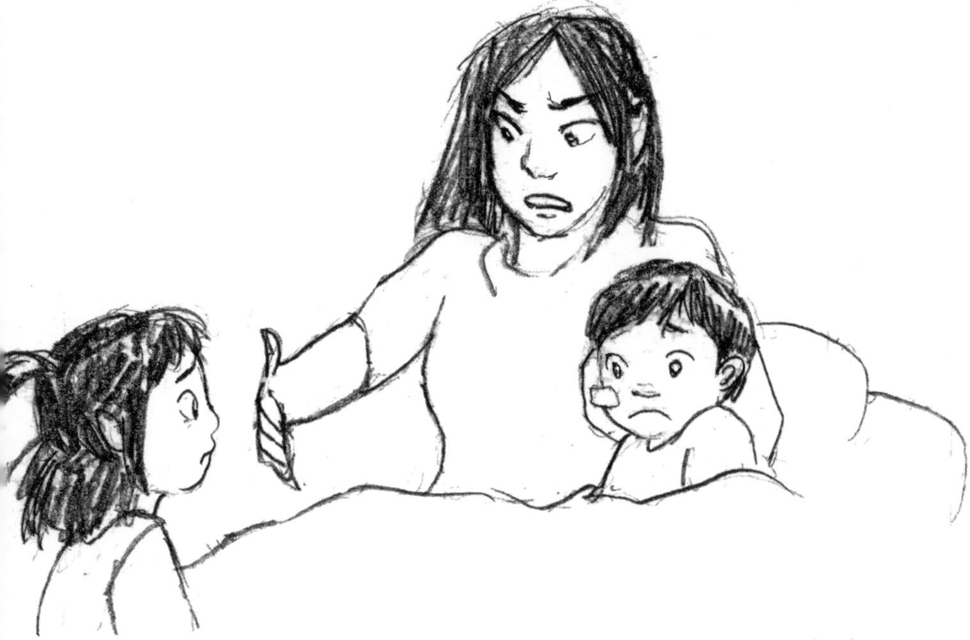

But she wanted us to make it right.

So she told us both a story so we could learn why.

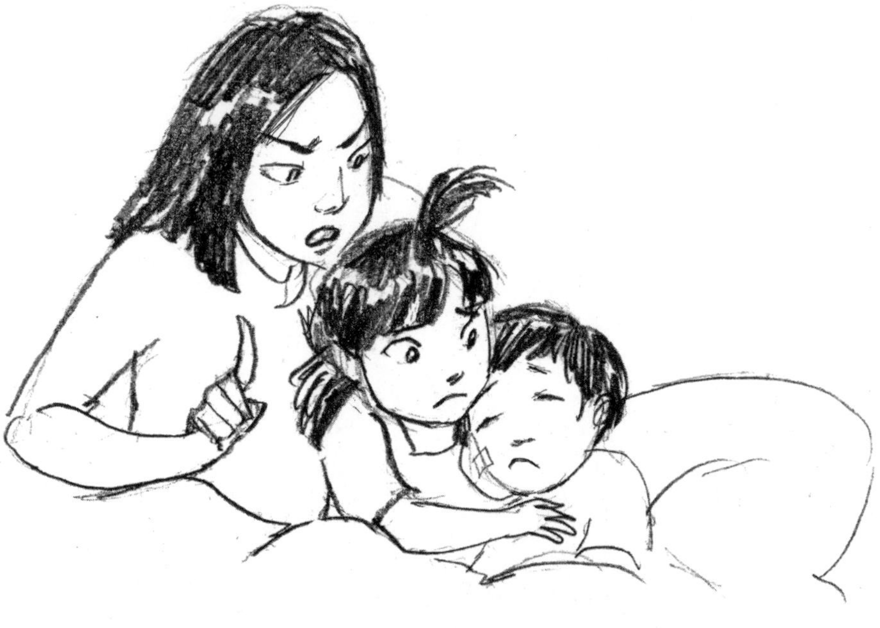

"Long ago, the god Bathala had two beautiful children.

A sister named Mayari and her brother, Apolaki ."

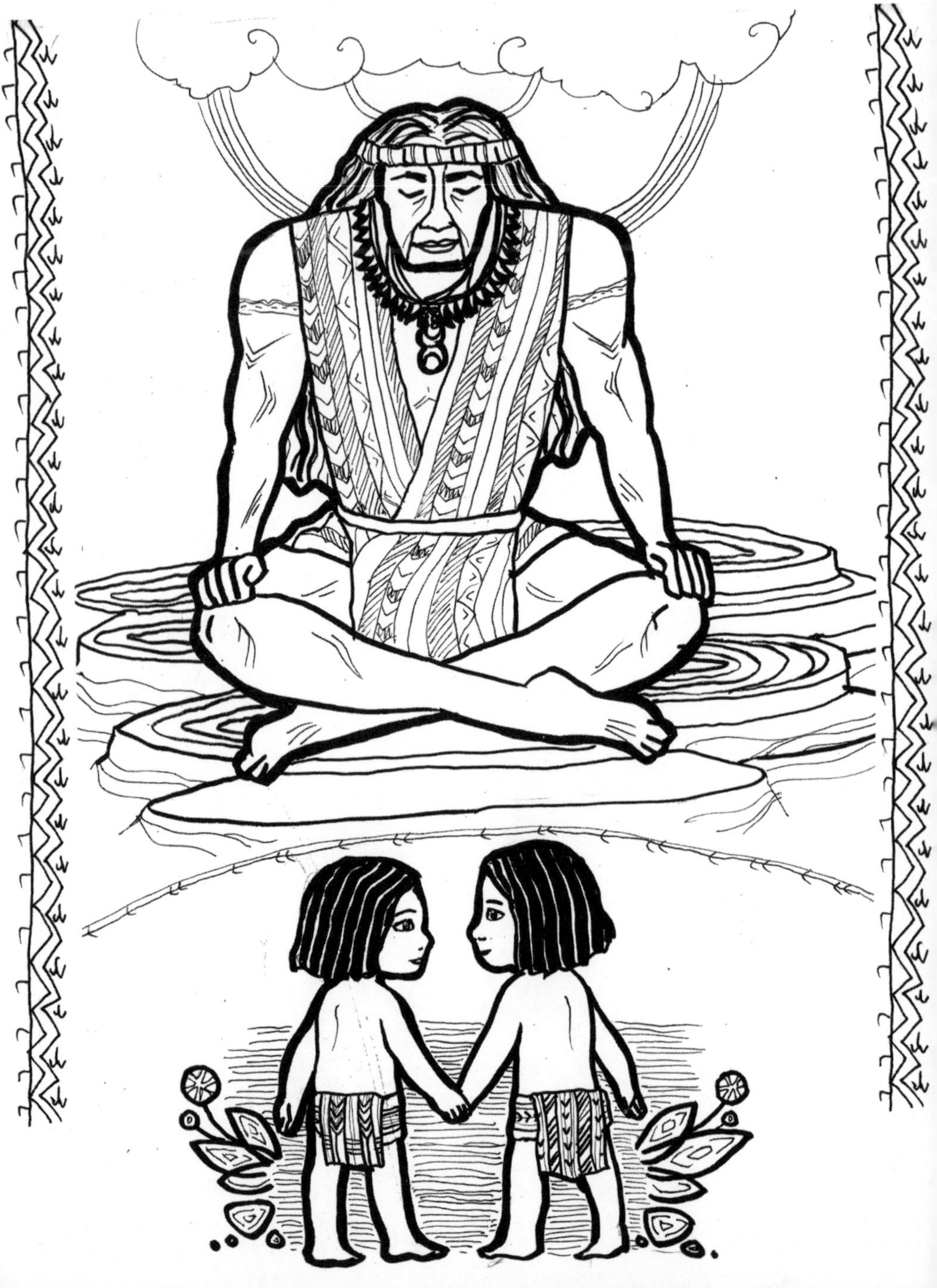

"Apolaki and Mayari
were both equal
in mind and strength."

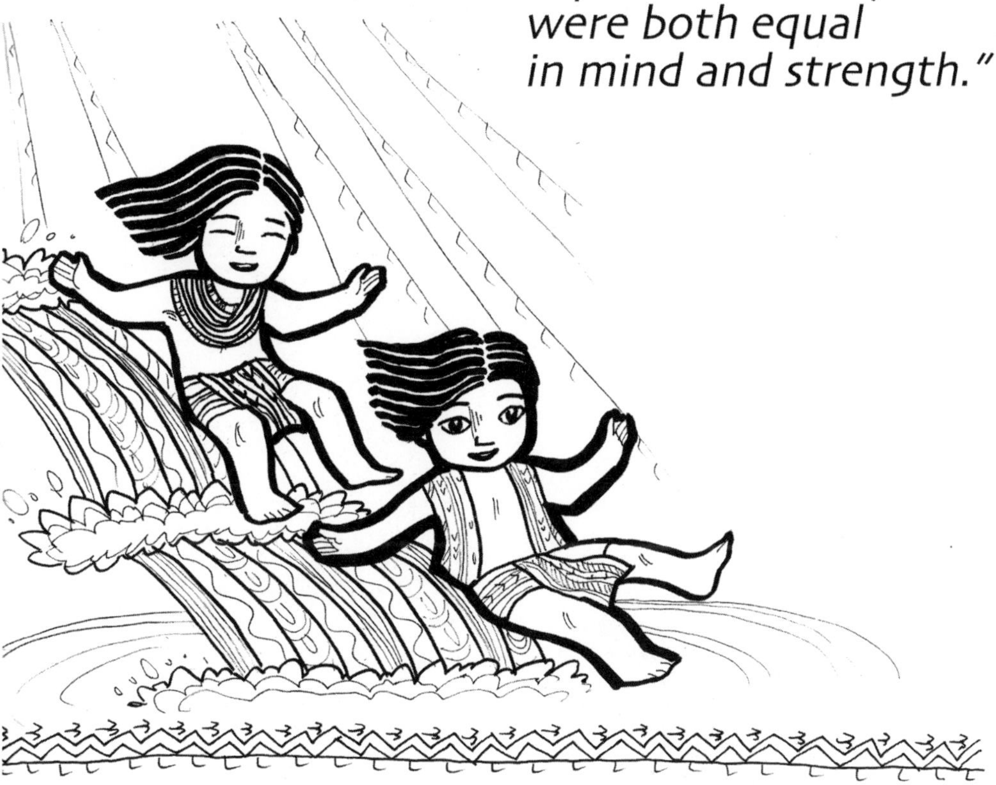

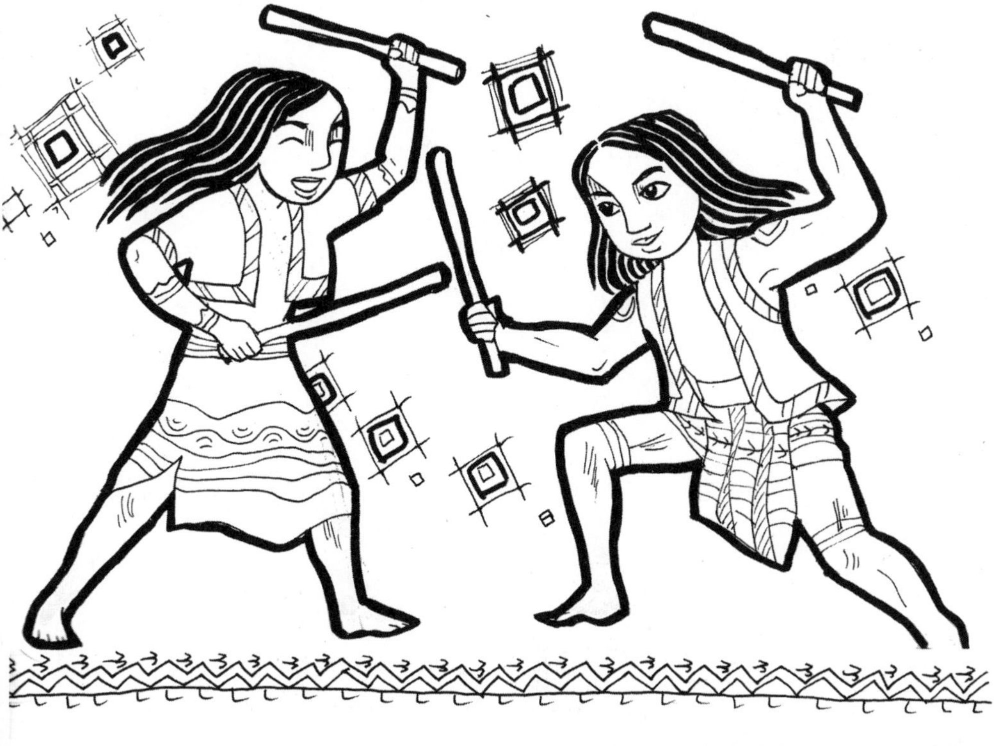

"But then, the god Bathala passed away. He had left no will to his children. Neither knew who would continue to rule his kingdom and people."

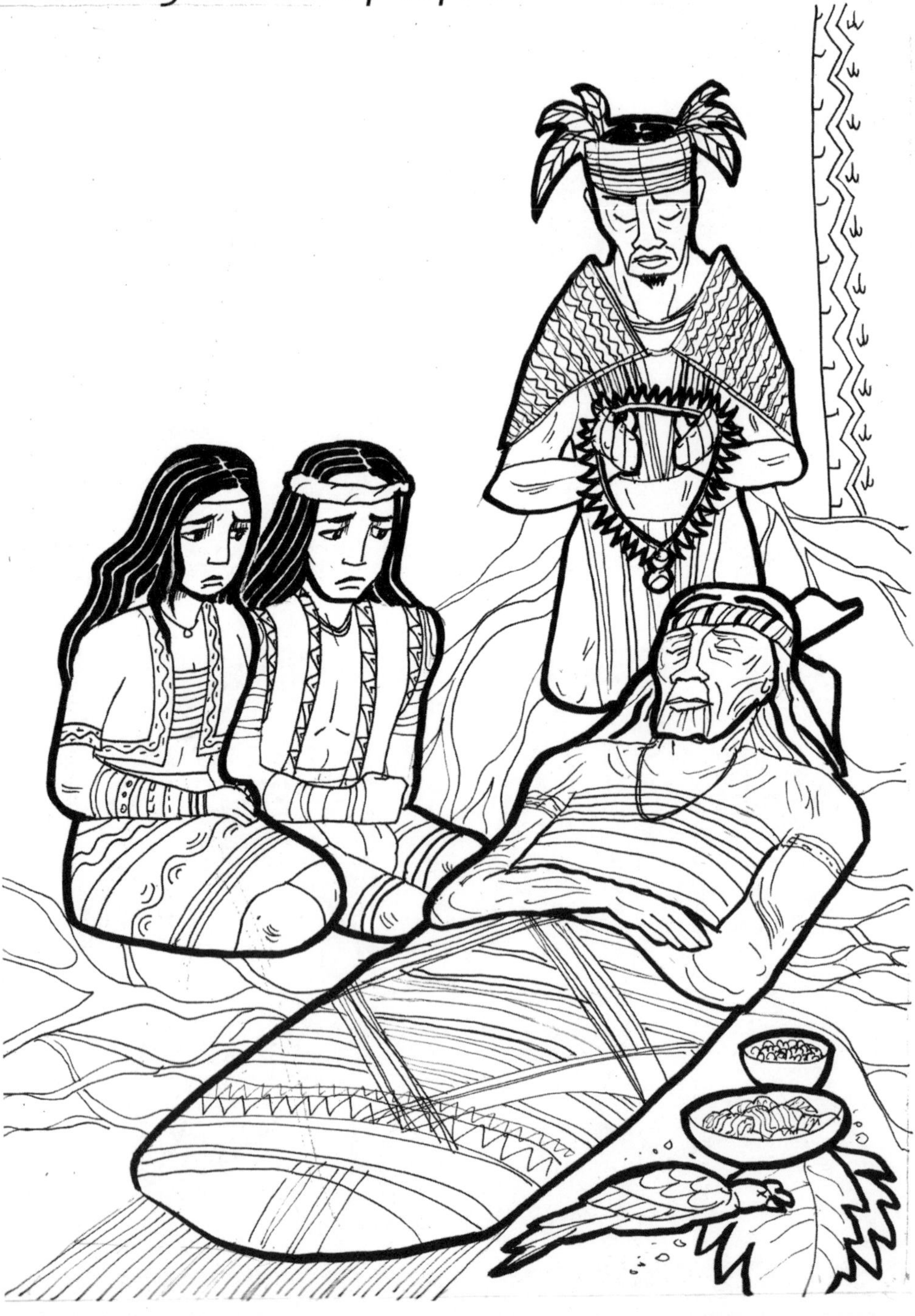

"Apolaki stepped up and decided to be the one to rule his father's kingdom.

But Mayari disagreed."

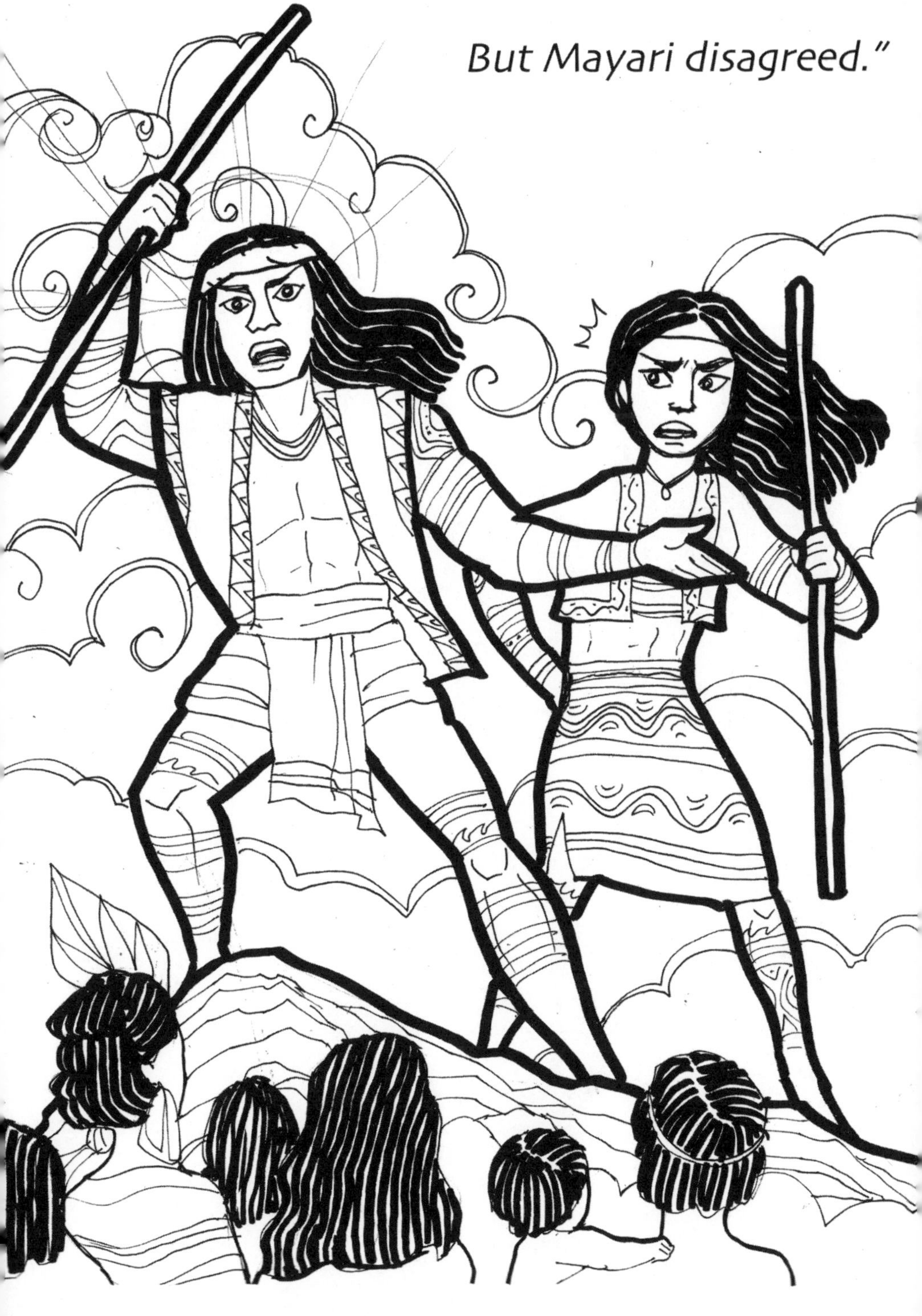

"Mayari deemed it unfair that Apolaki should decide he rule by himself.

She shouted that they both should rule the kingdom equally.

Apolaki refused."

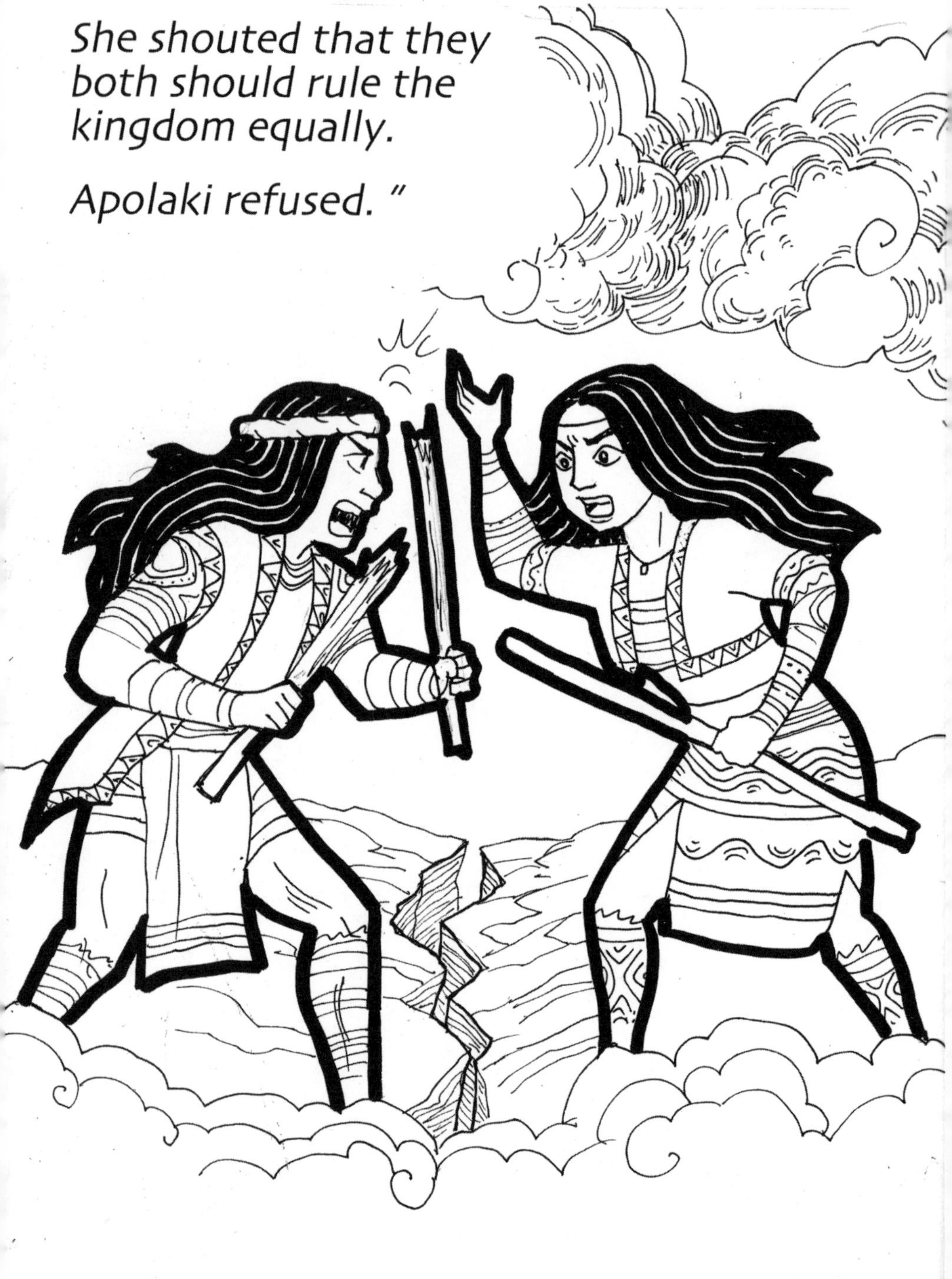

"Their anger and resentment towards each other grew.

They furiously began to fight using their bamboo sticks.

Suddenly, Mayari lunged towards her brother."

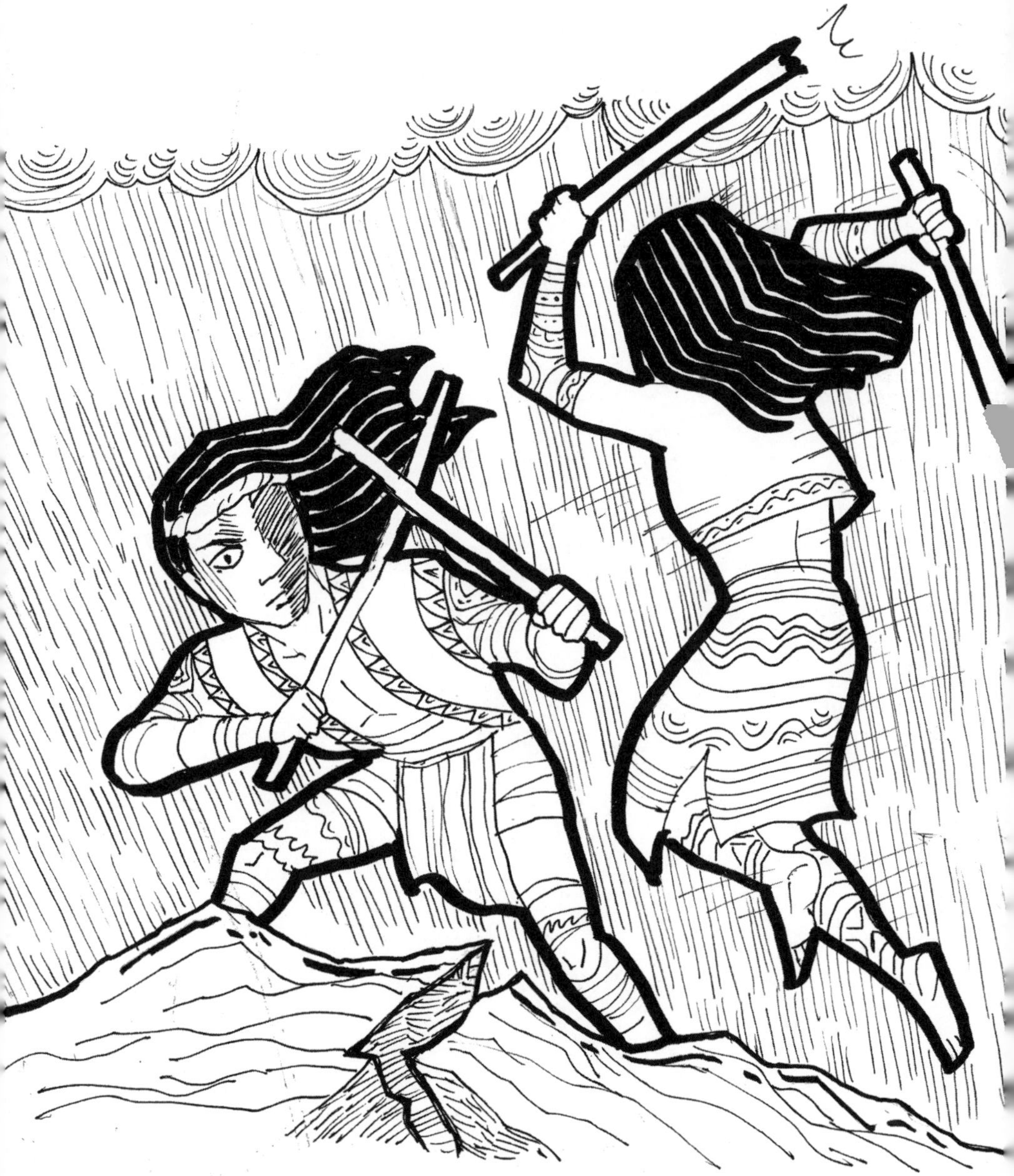

"In an attempt to protect himself,
Apolaki swung his weapons,
striking Mayari in the
face!"

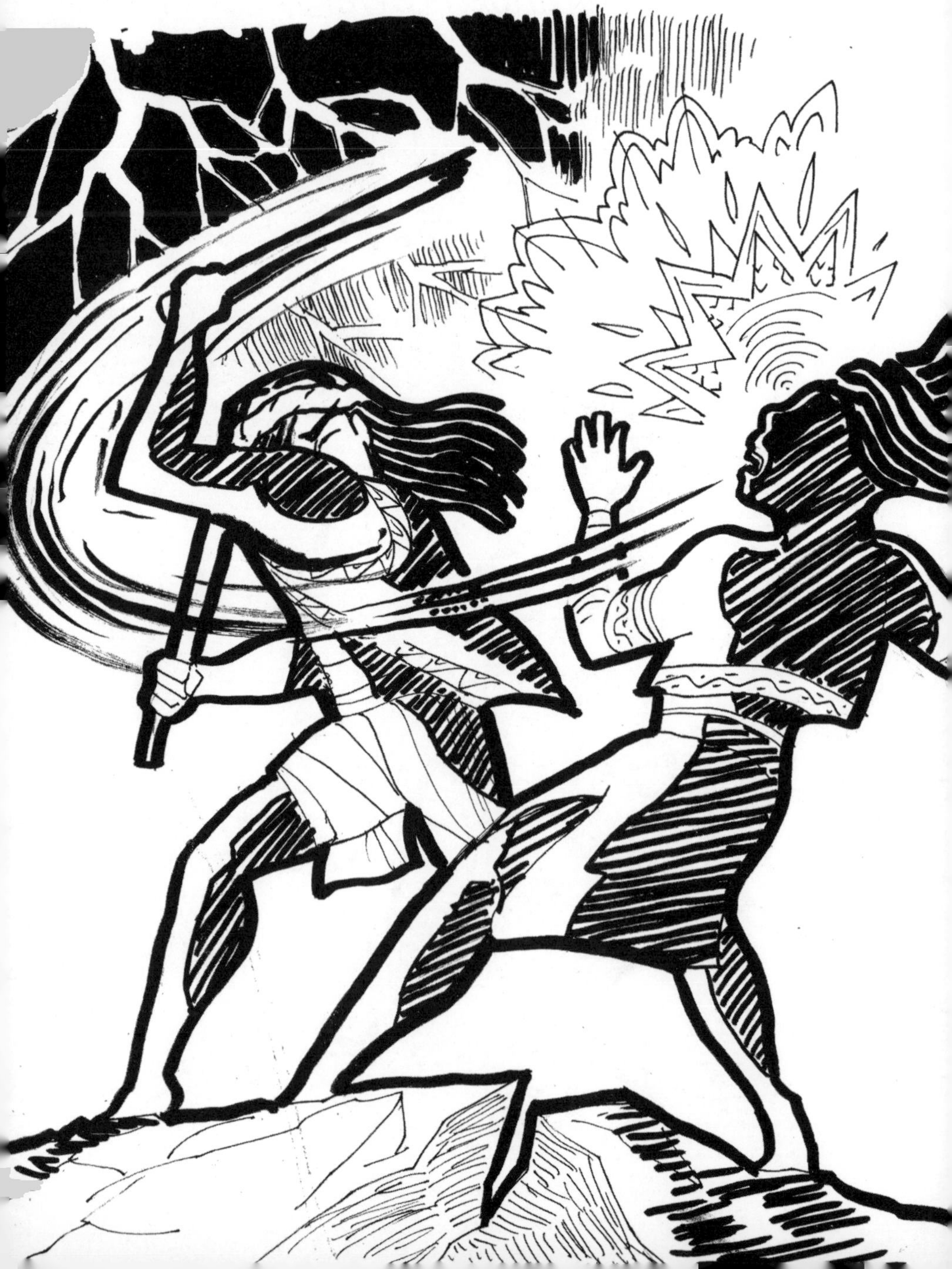

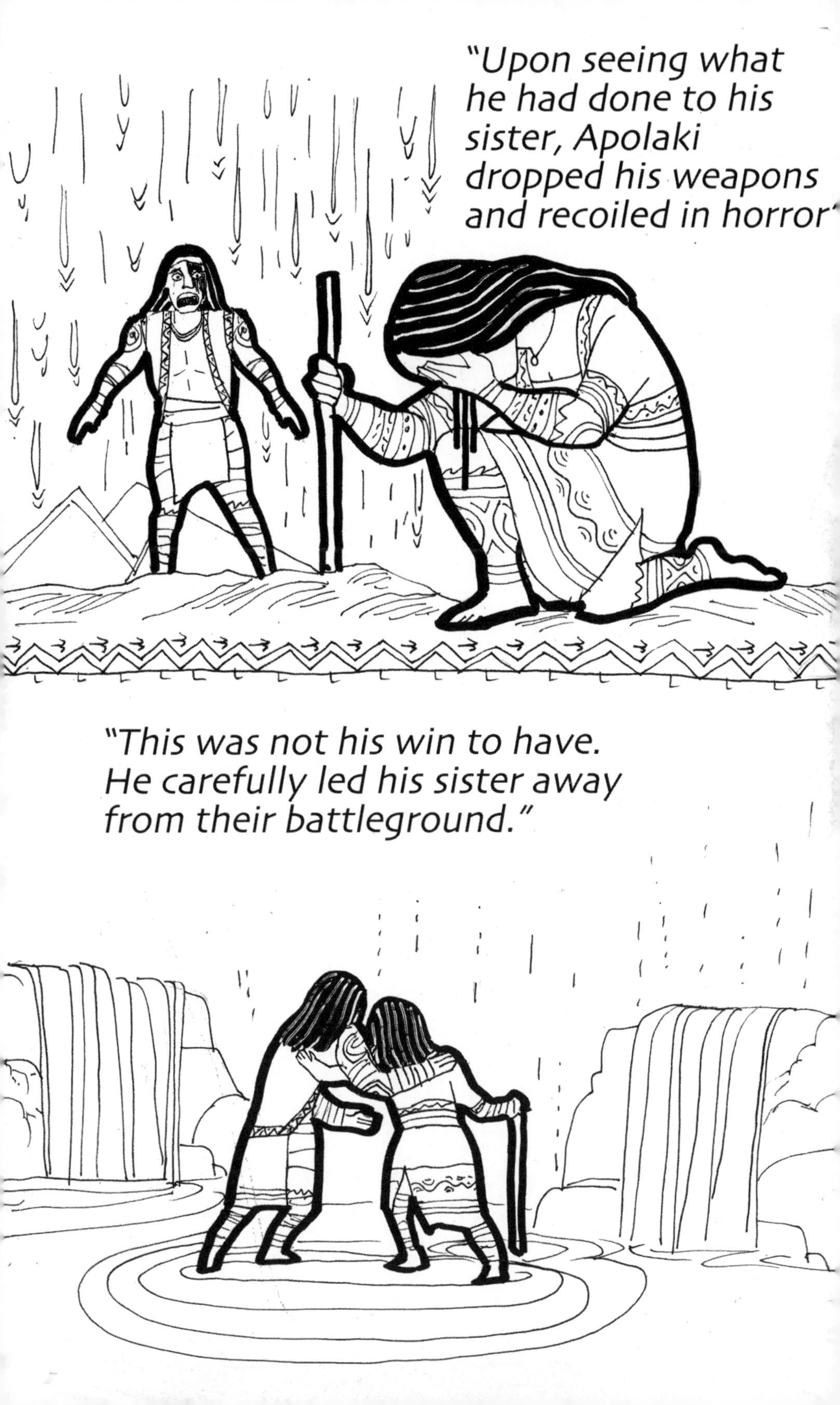
"Upon seeing what he had done to his sister, Apolaki dropped his weapons and recoiled in horror"
"This was not his win to have. He carefully led his sister away from their battleground."

"Mayari had lost one of her eyes. Apolaki begged for her forgiveness, which she gave.

No longer bitter towards each other, the two mended their bond.

They decided to rule their father's kingdom together."

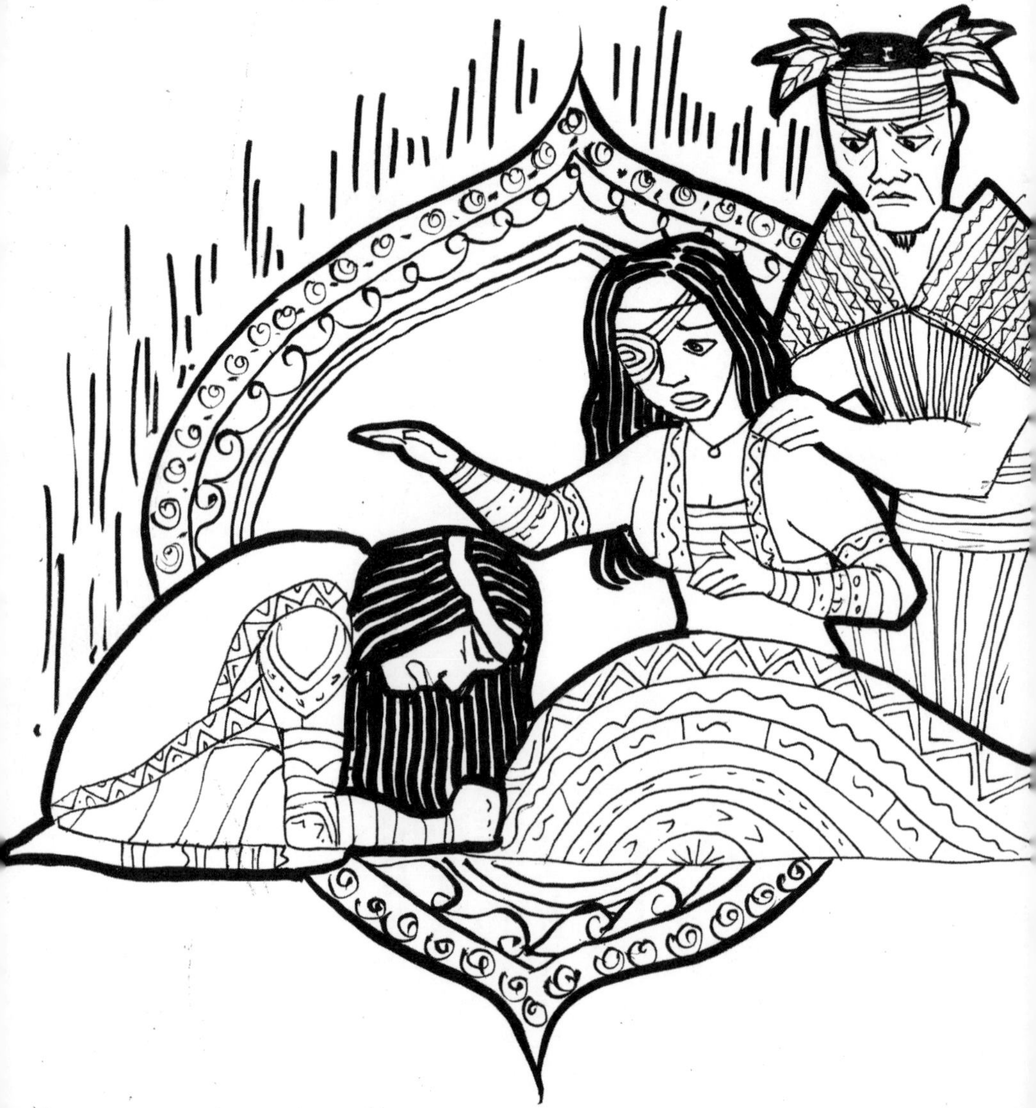

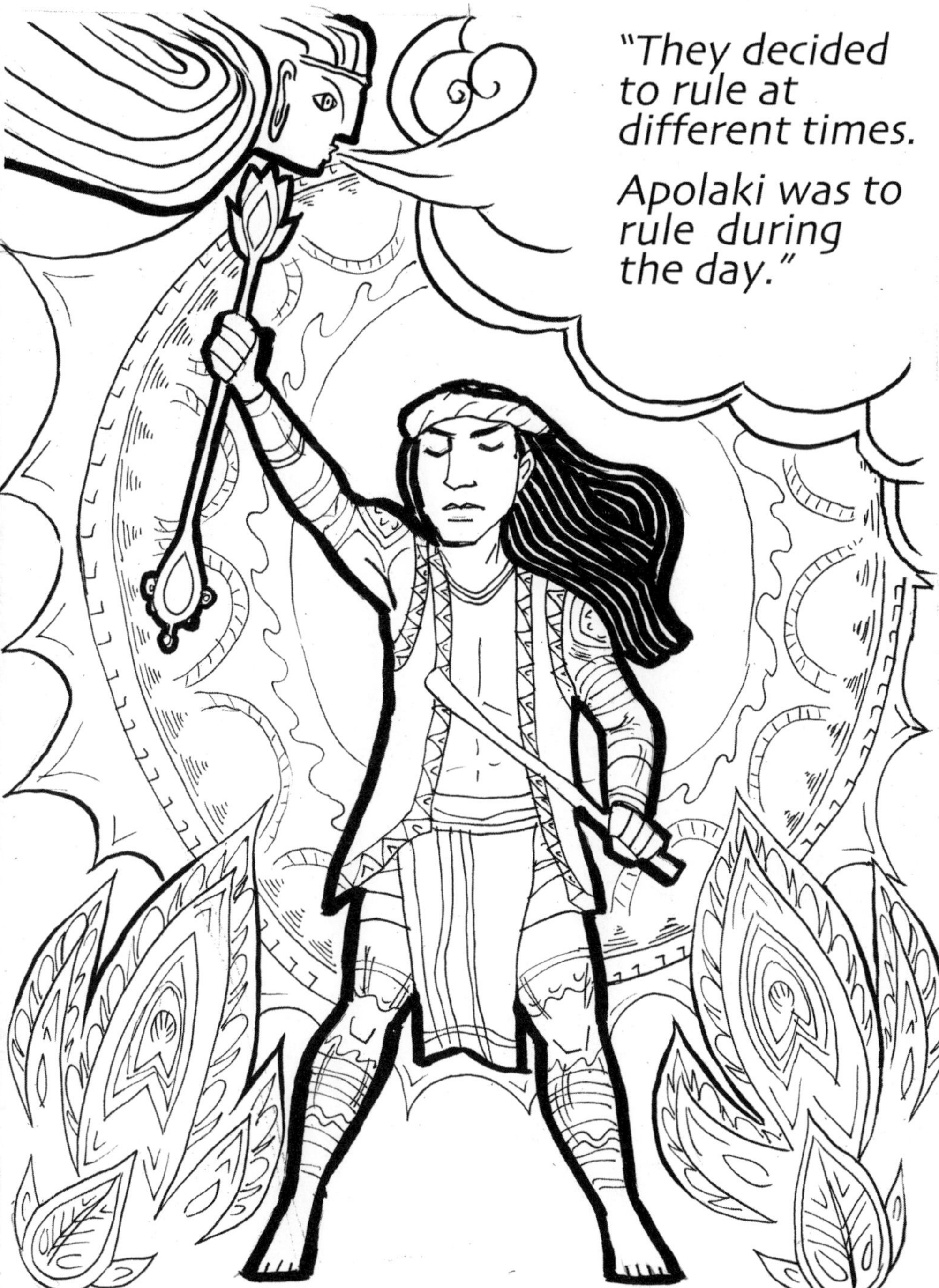
"They decided to rule at different times.
Apolaki was to rule during the day."

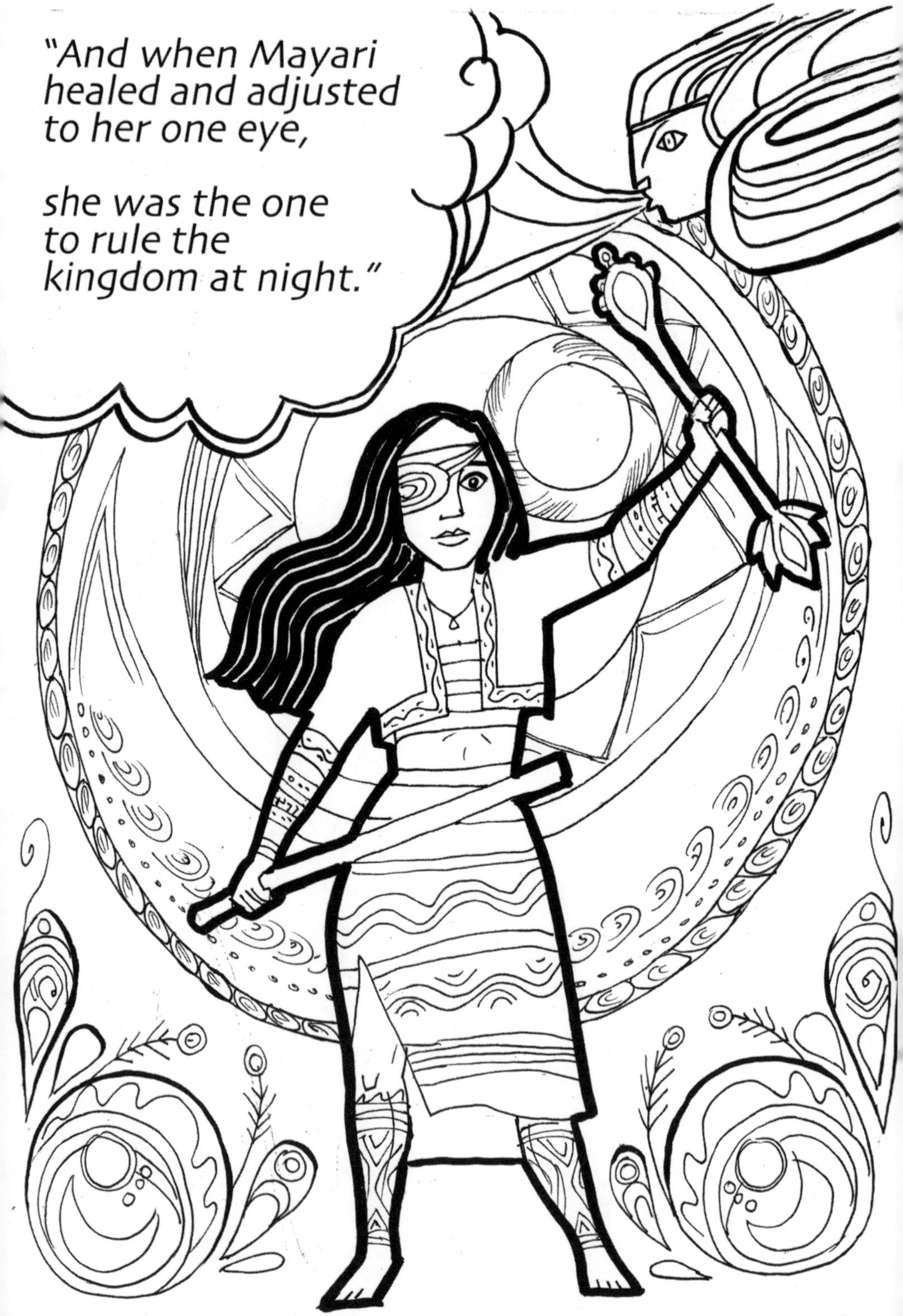
"And when Mayari healed and adjusted to her one eye,
she was the one to rule the kingdom at night."

"Together they continue to rule the kingdom.

Mayari, the goddess of the Moon

and Apolaki, the god of the Sun."

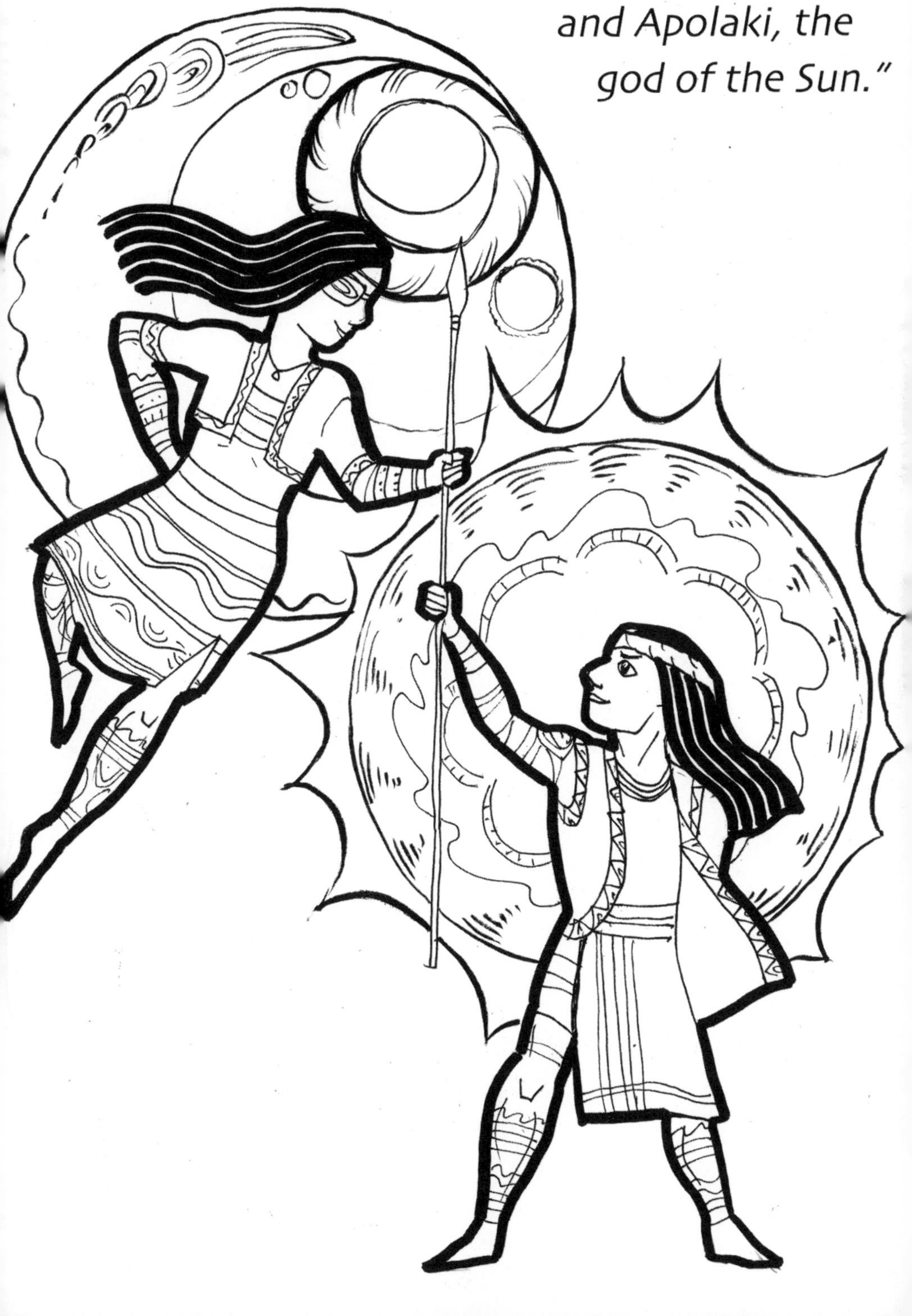

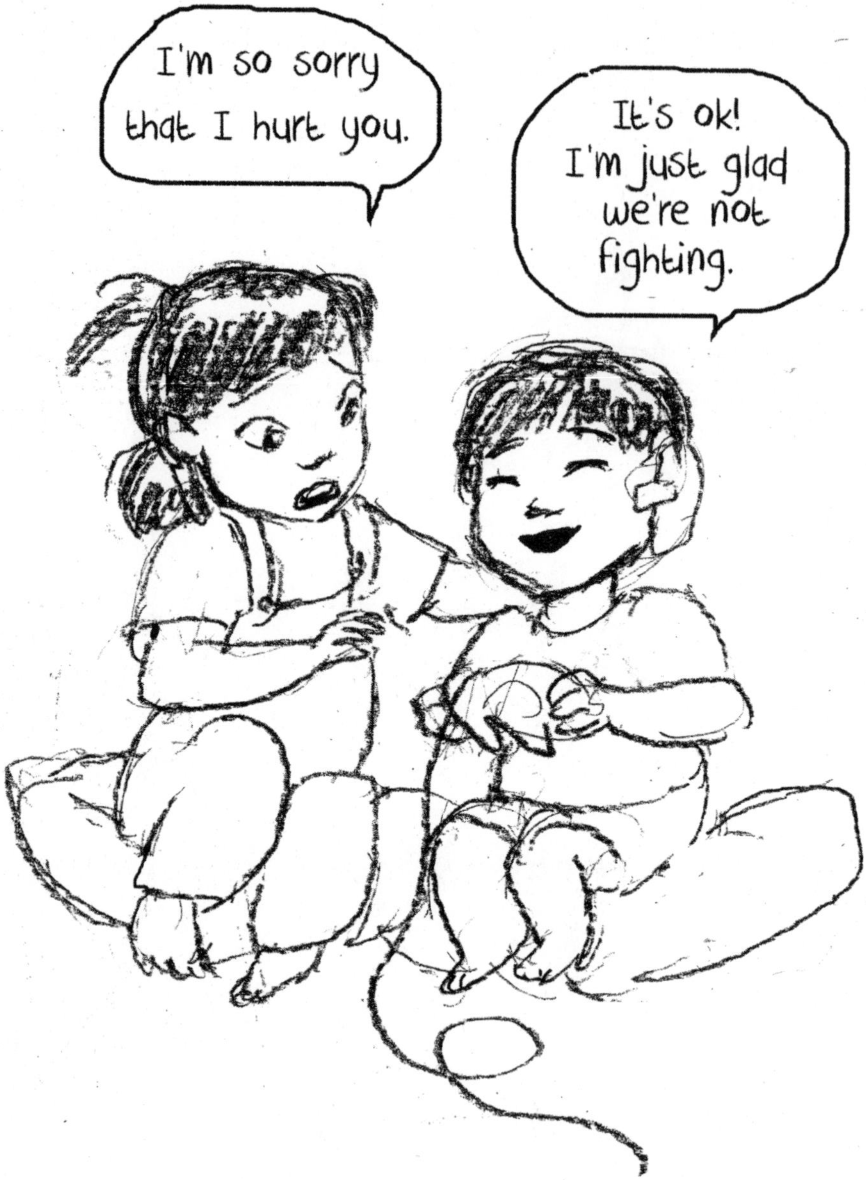
I'm so sorry that I hurt you.
It's ok! I'm just glad we're not fighting.

My brother and I decided to share the video game.

THE END.

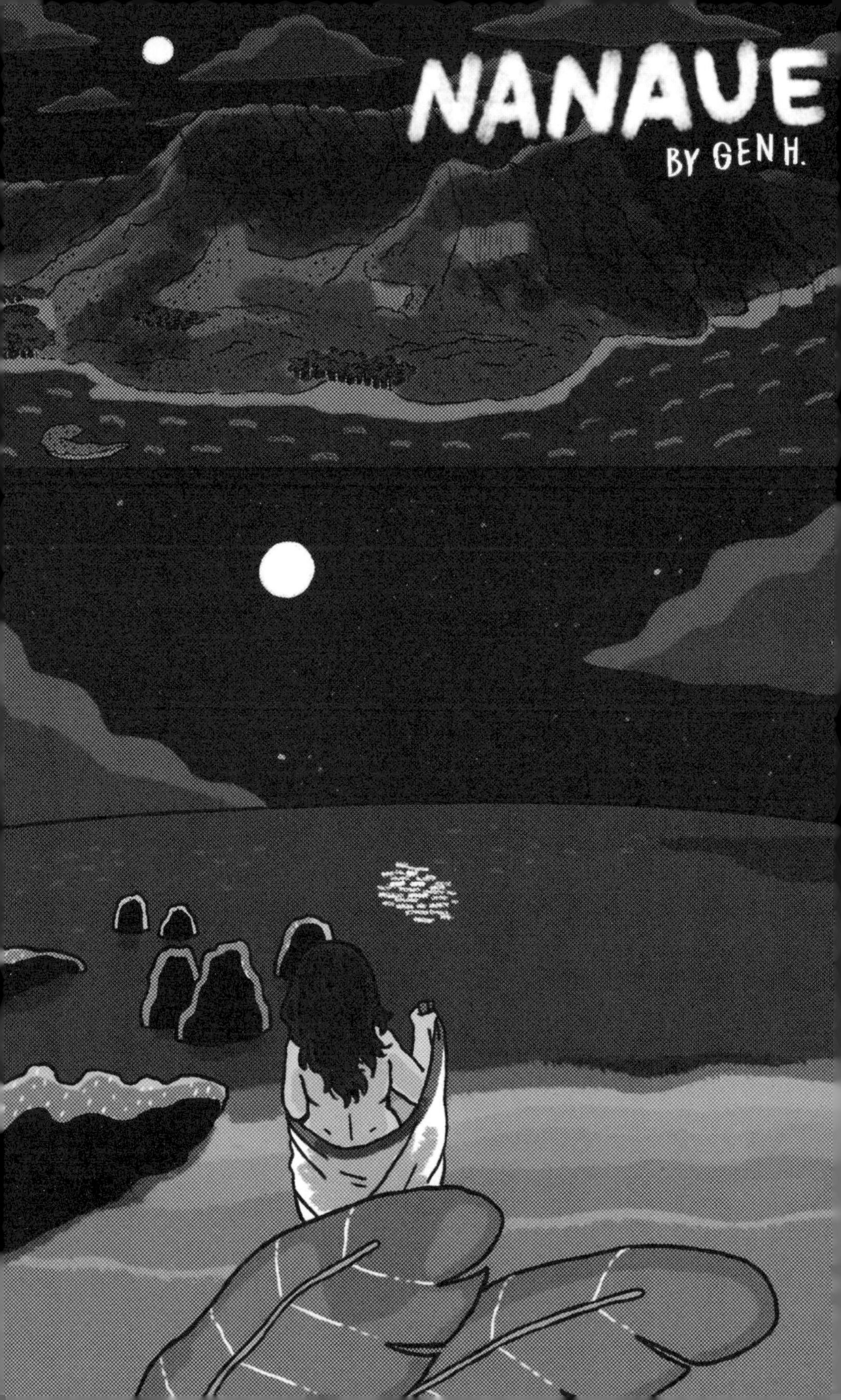
NANAUE
BY GEN H.

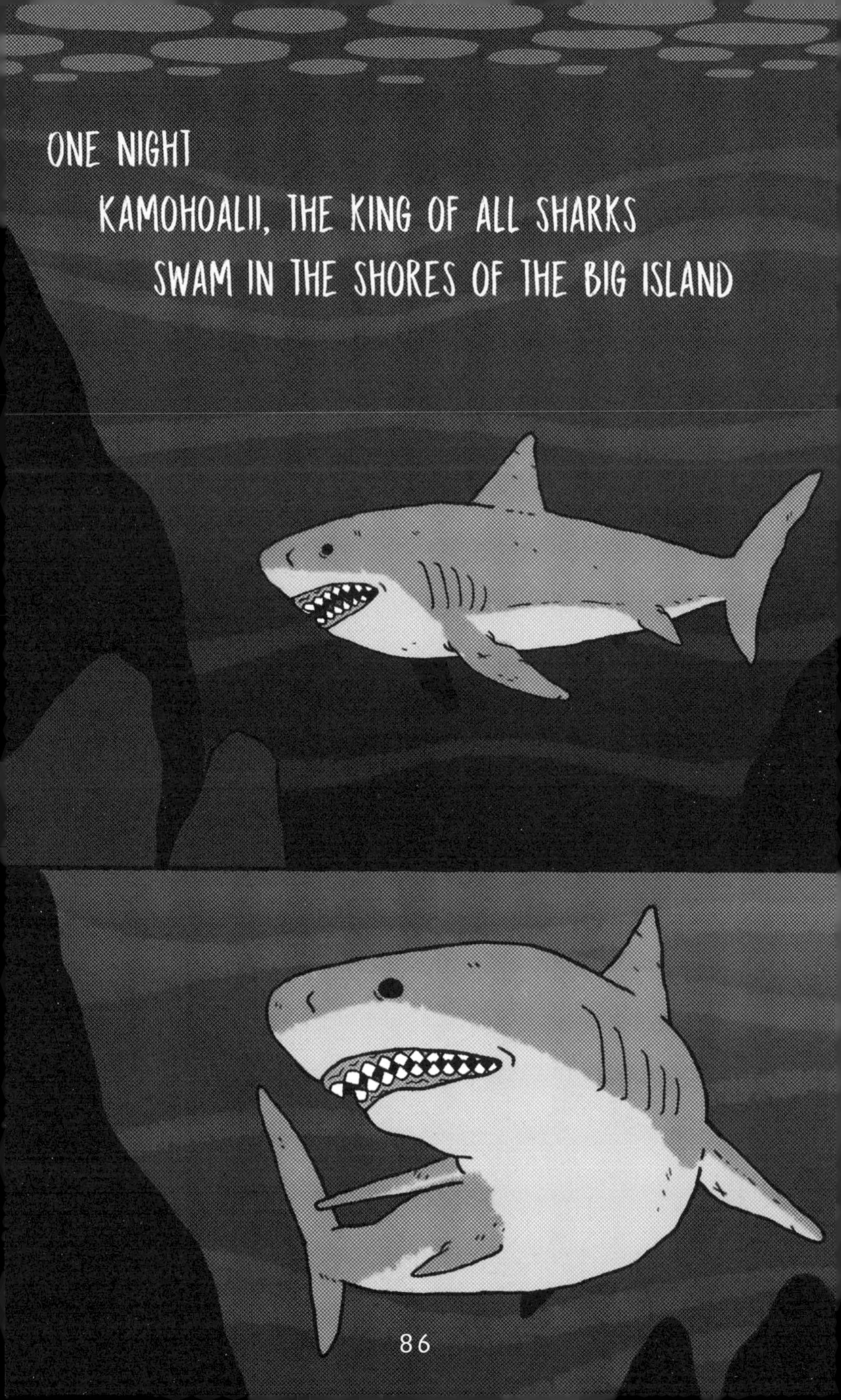
ONE NIGHT
KAMOHOALII, THE KING OF ALL SHARKS
SWAM IN THE SHORES OF THE BIG ISLAND

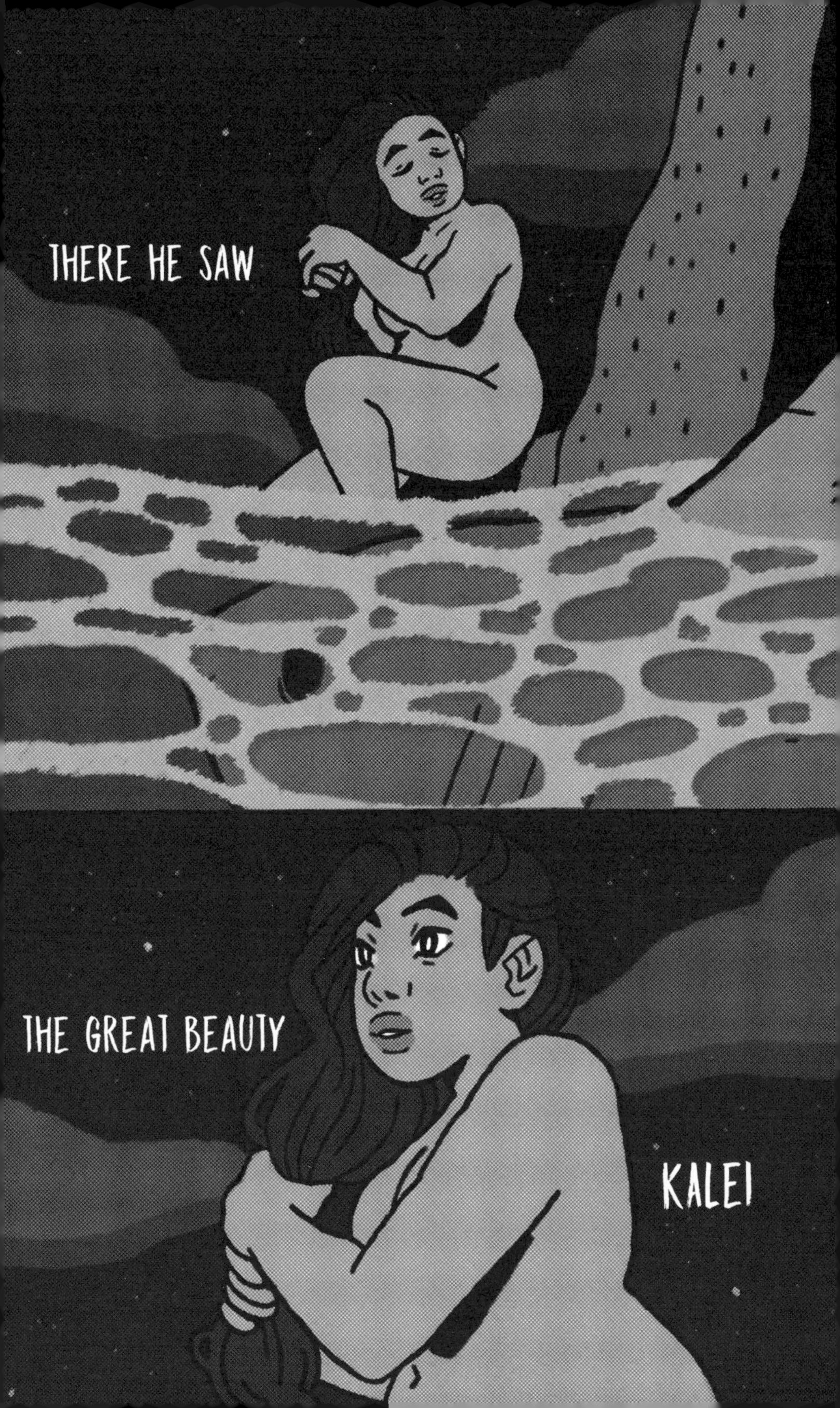
THERE HE SAW
THE GREAT BEAUTY
KALEI

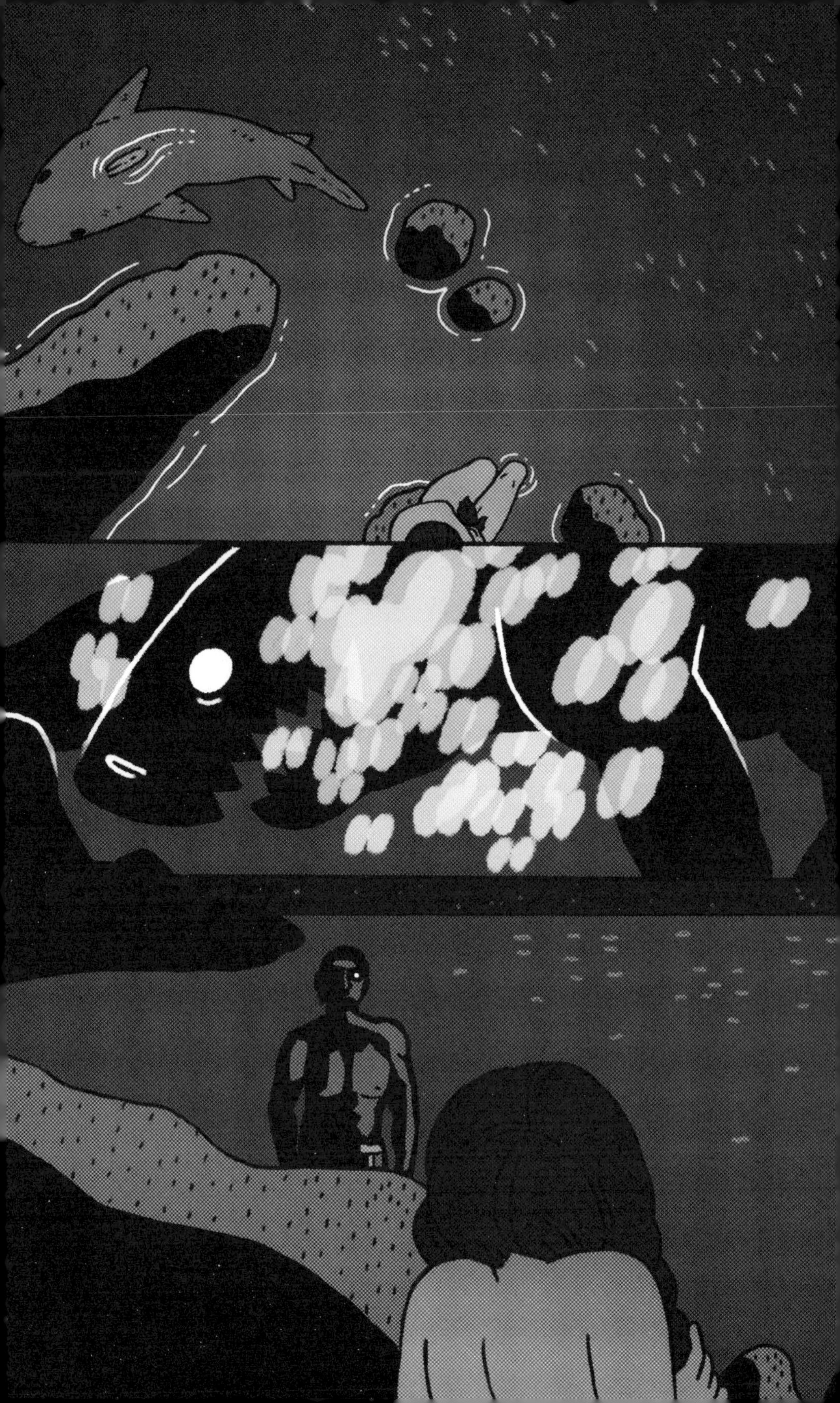

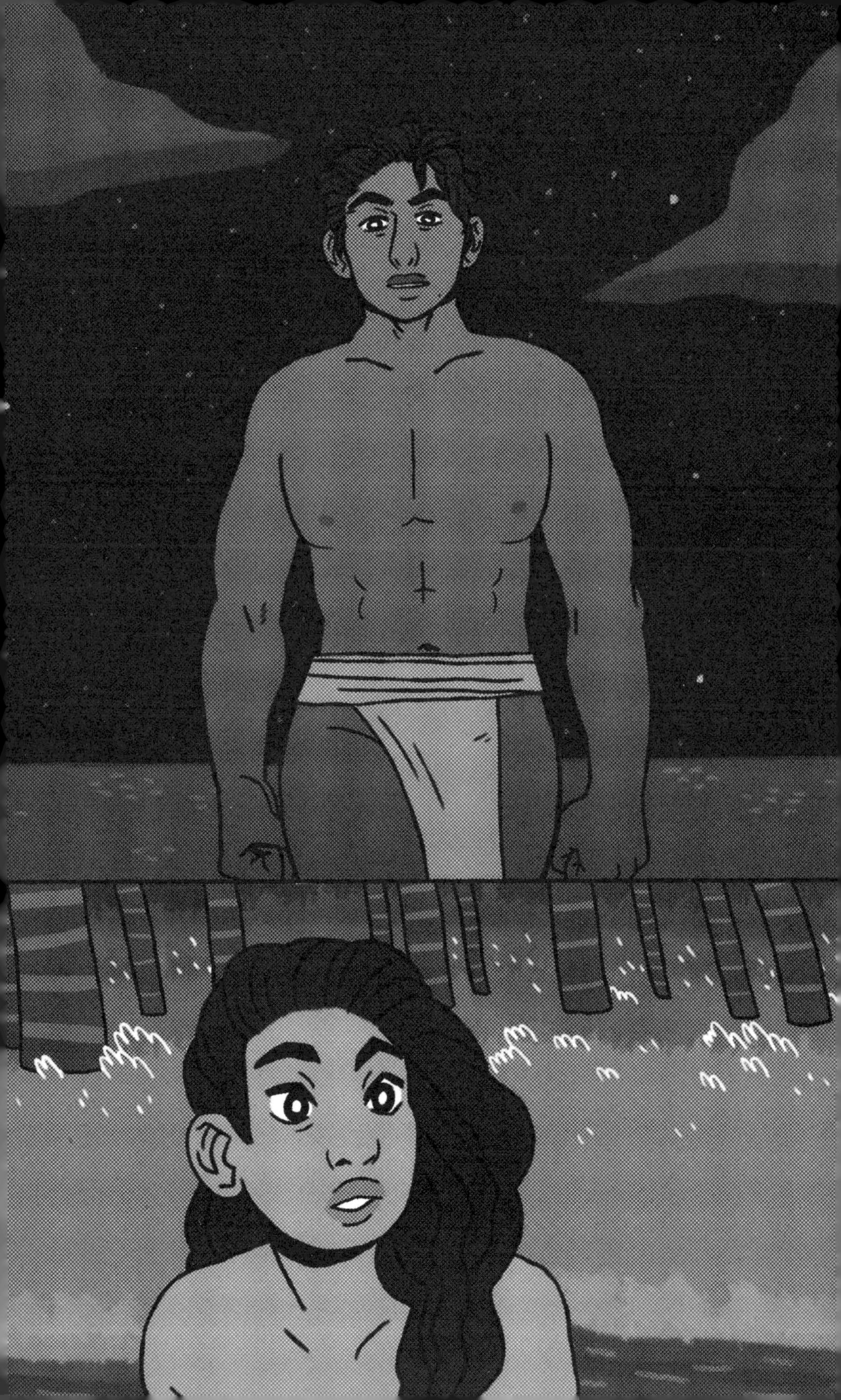

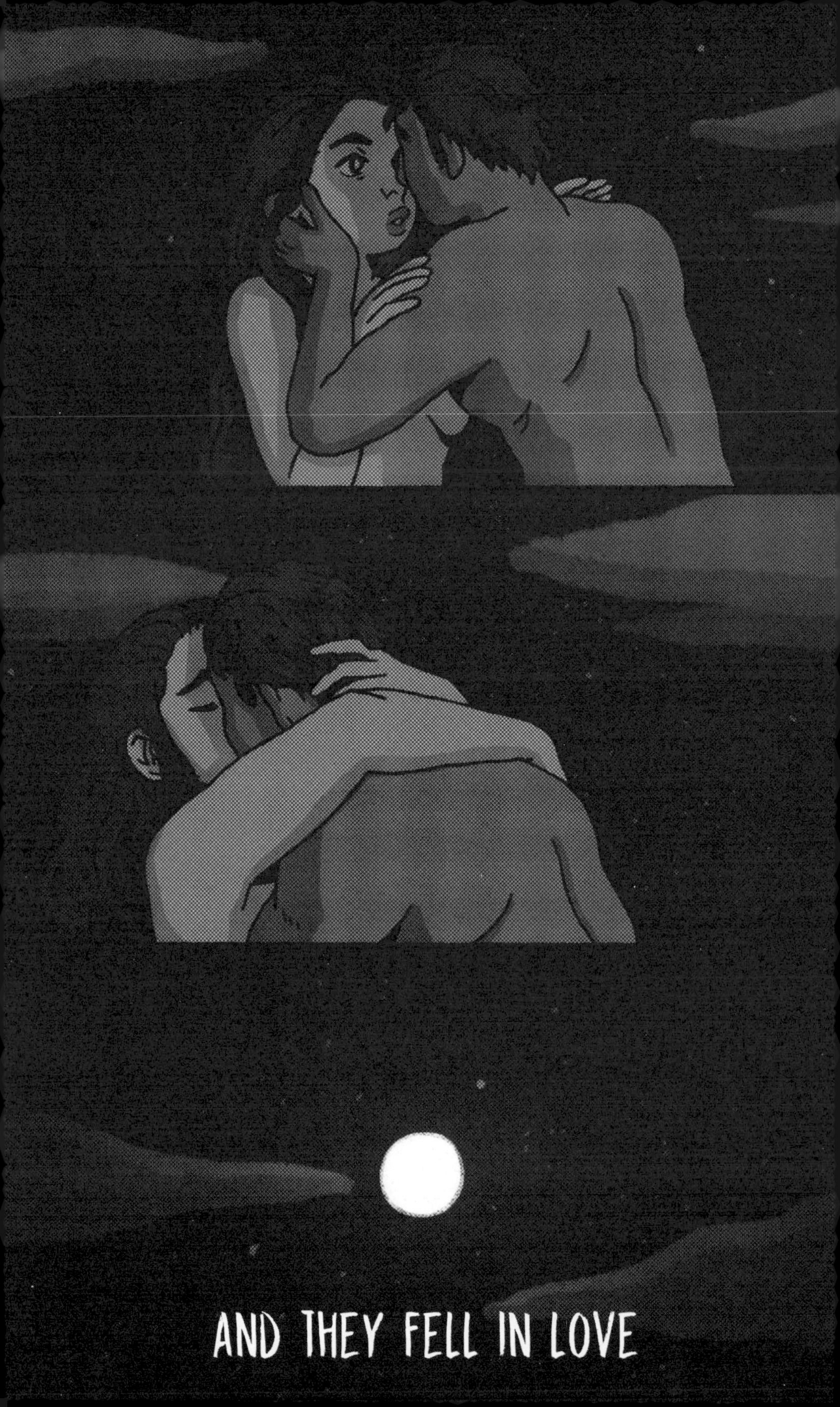
AND THEY FELL IN LOVE

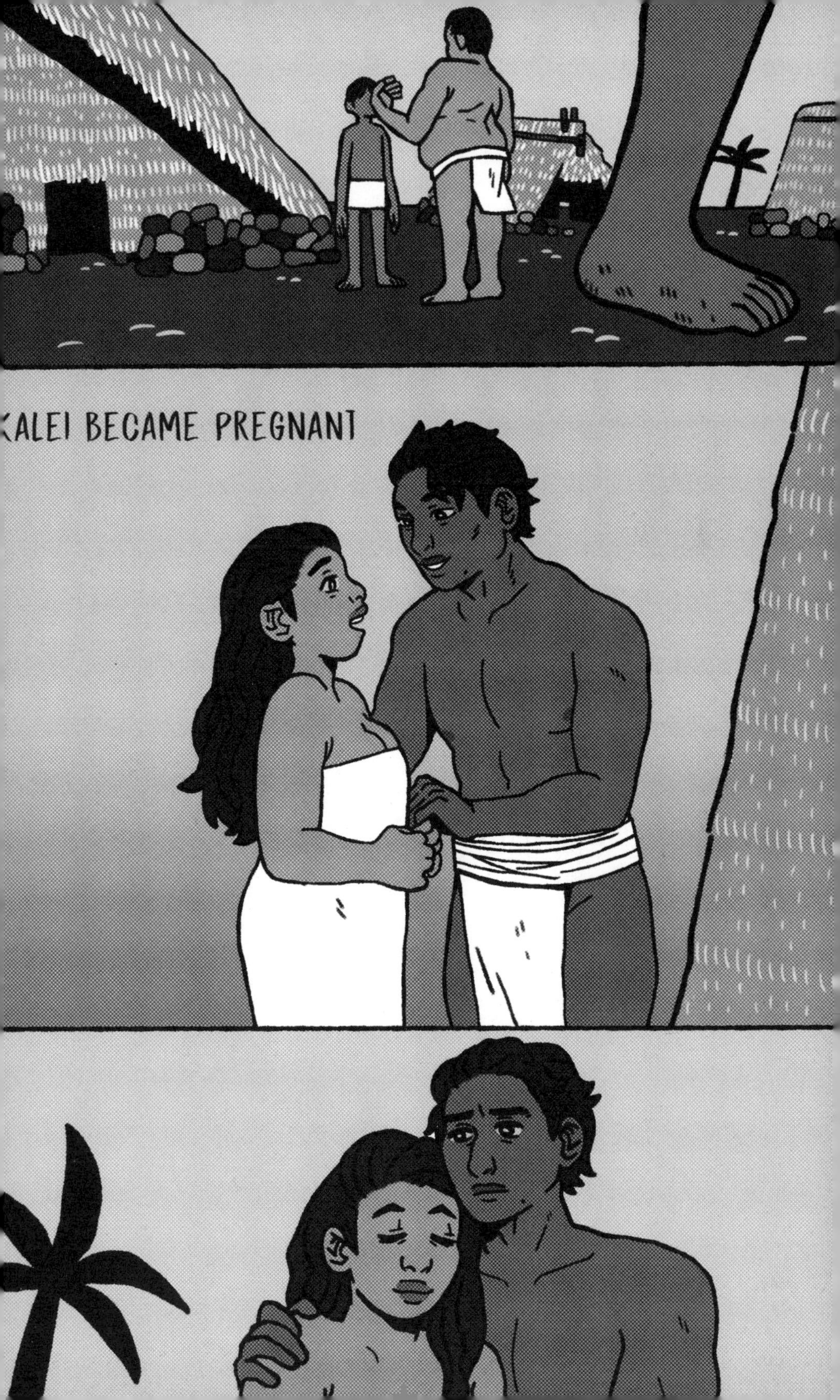

ALEI BECAME PREGNANT

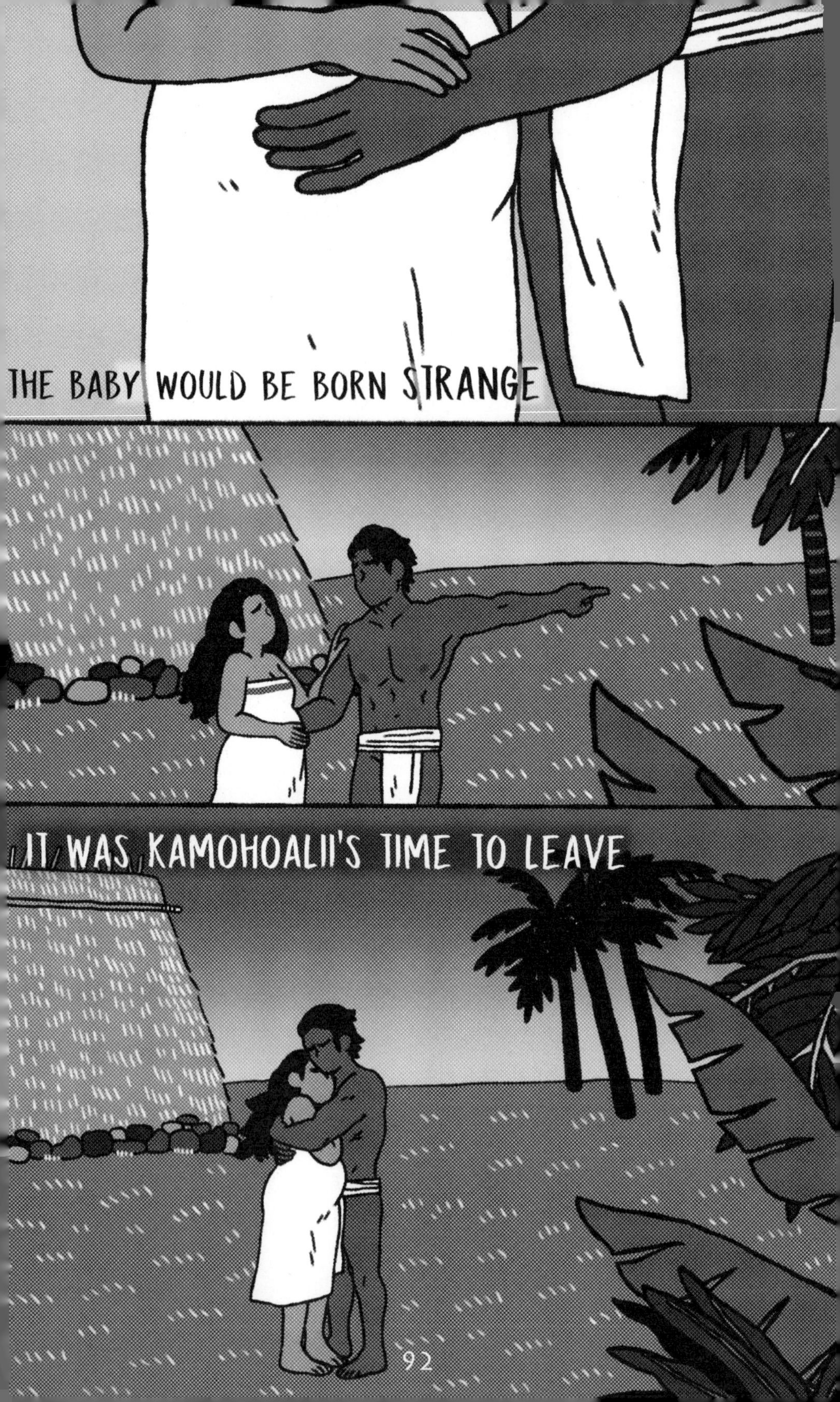
THE BABY WOULD BE BORN STRANGE
IT WAS KAMOHOALII'S TIME TO LEAVE

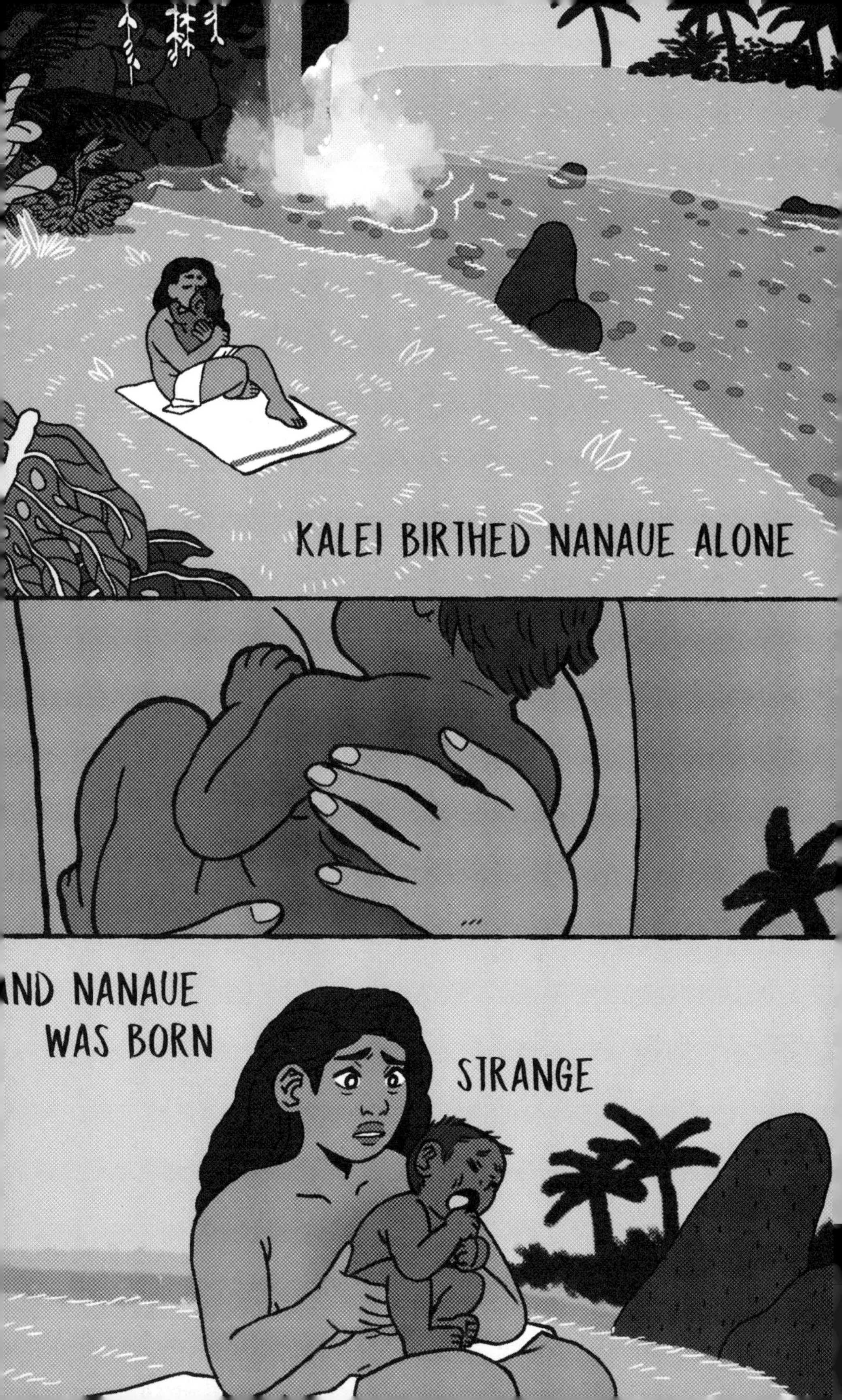
KALEI BIRTHED NANAUE ALONE
ND NANAUE WAS BORN
STRANGE

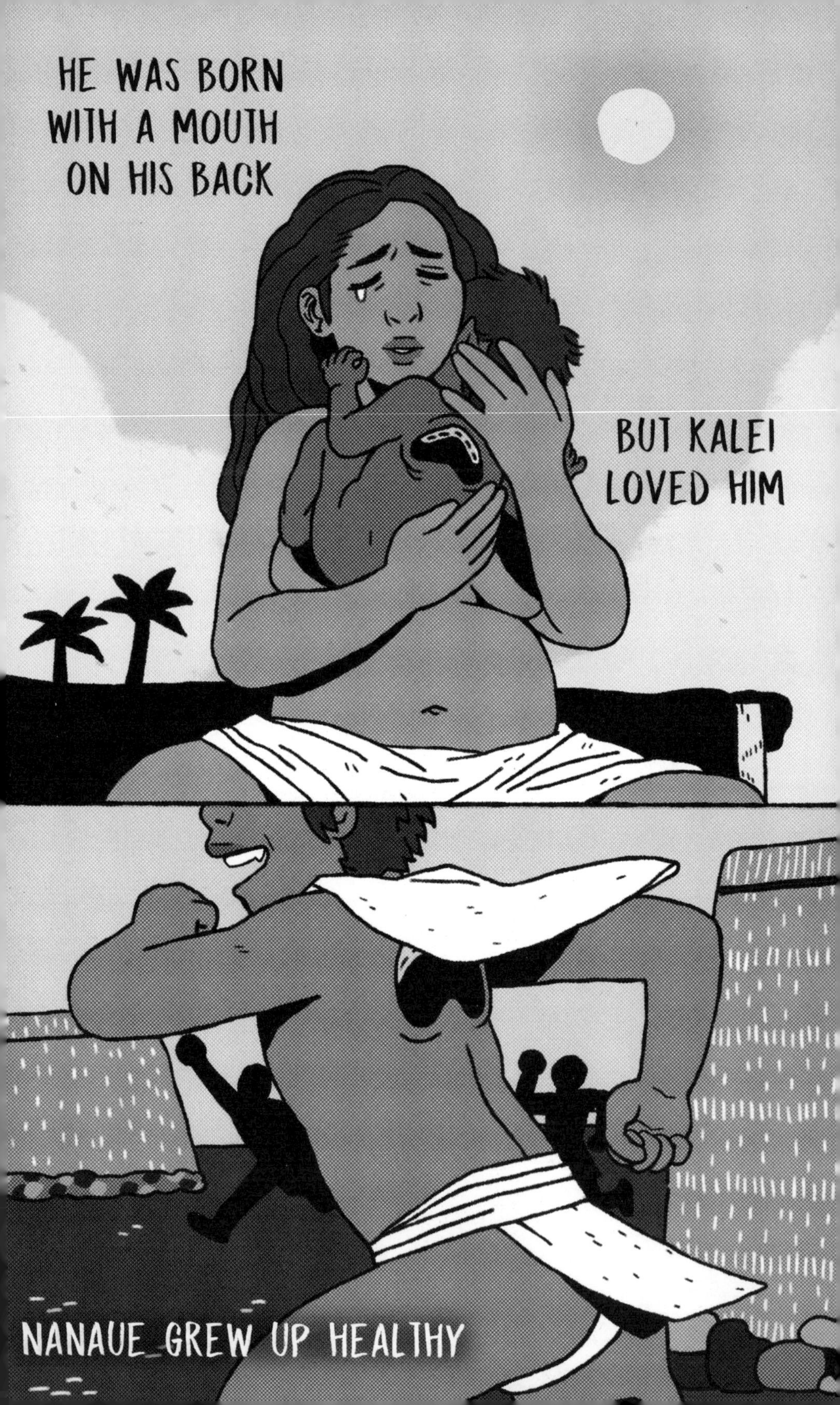
HE WAS BORN
WITH A MOUTH
ON HIS BACK
BUT KALEI
LOVED HIM
NANAUE GREW UP HEALTHY

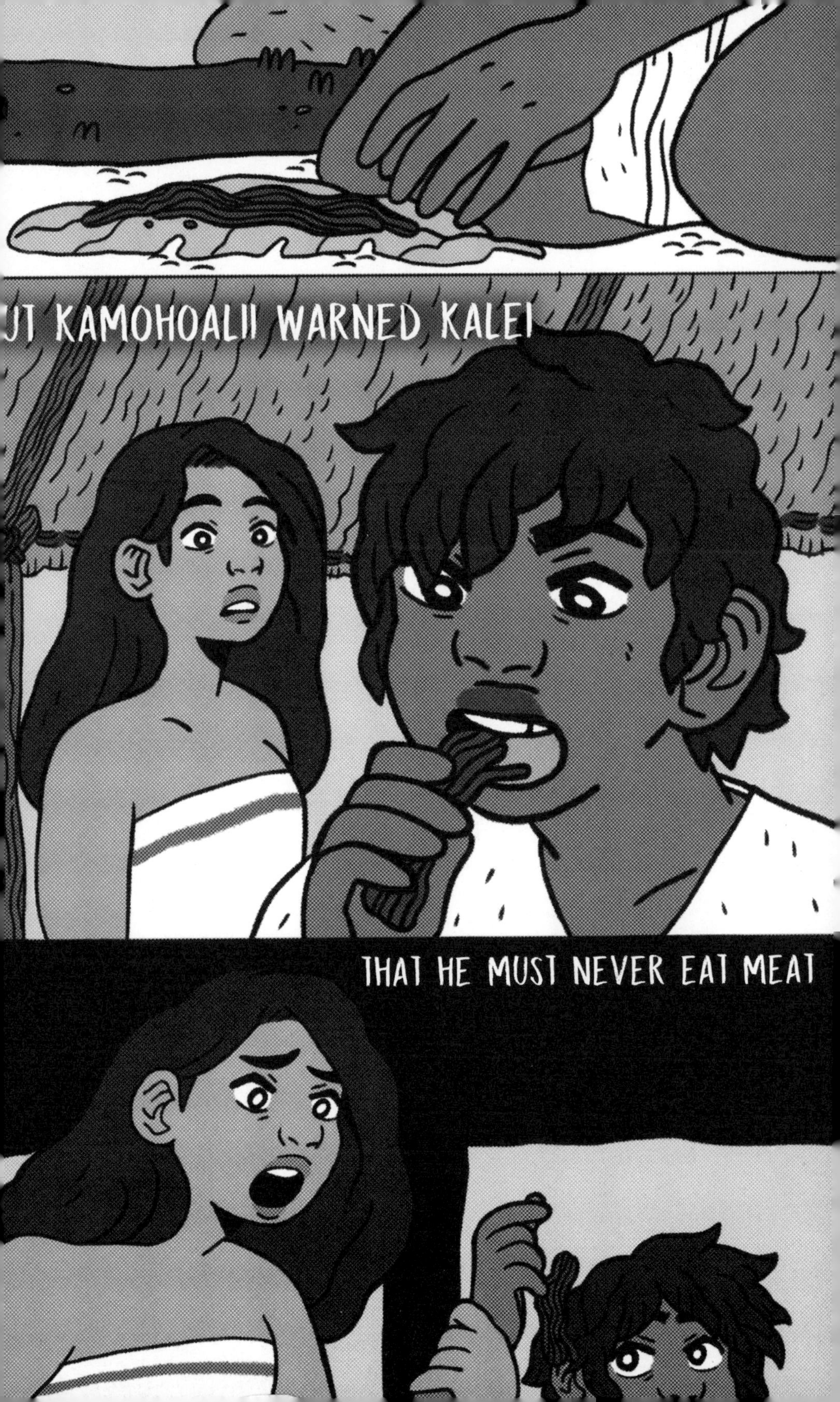
UT KAMOHOALII WARNED KALEI
THAT HE MUST NEVER EAT MEAT

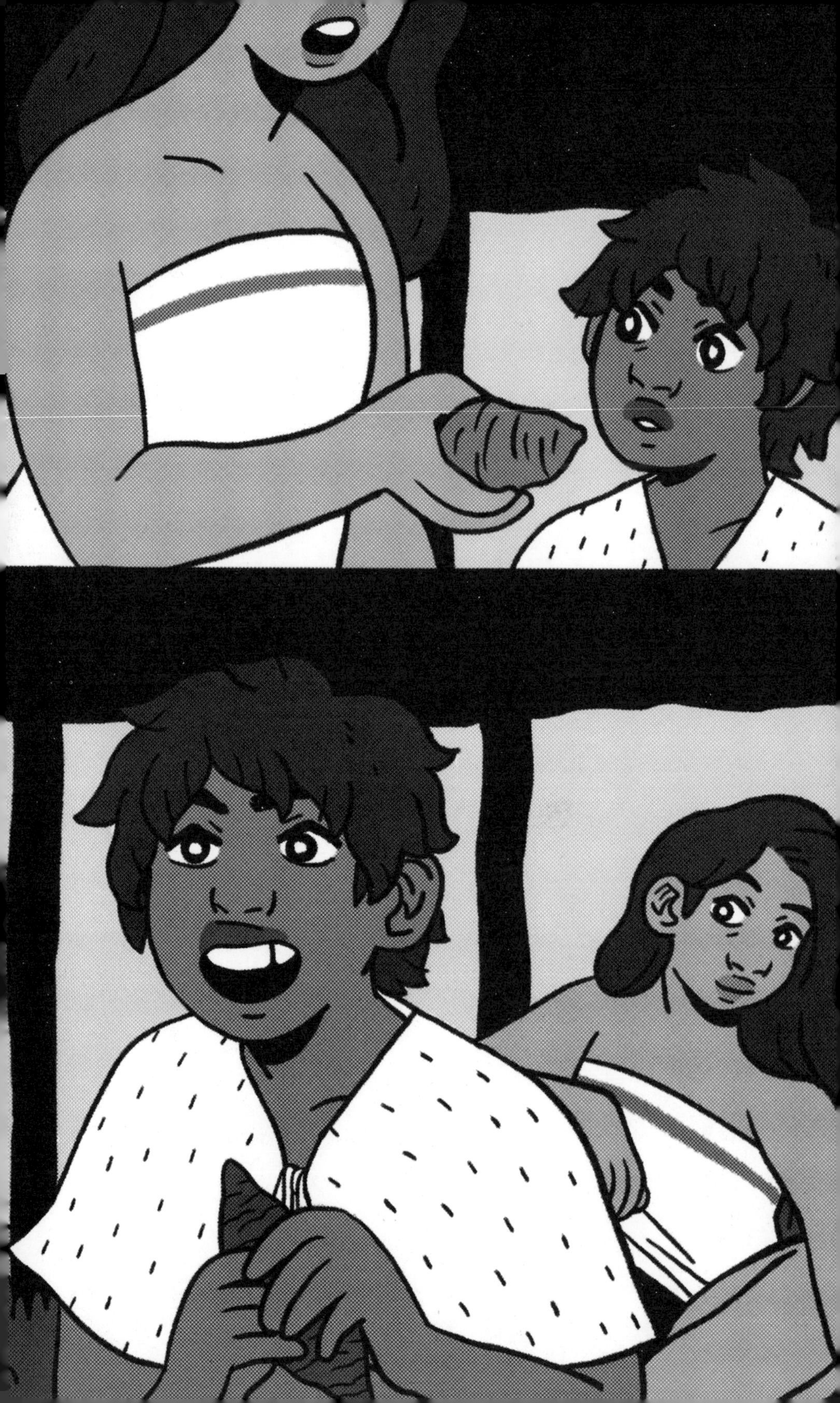

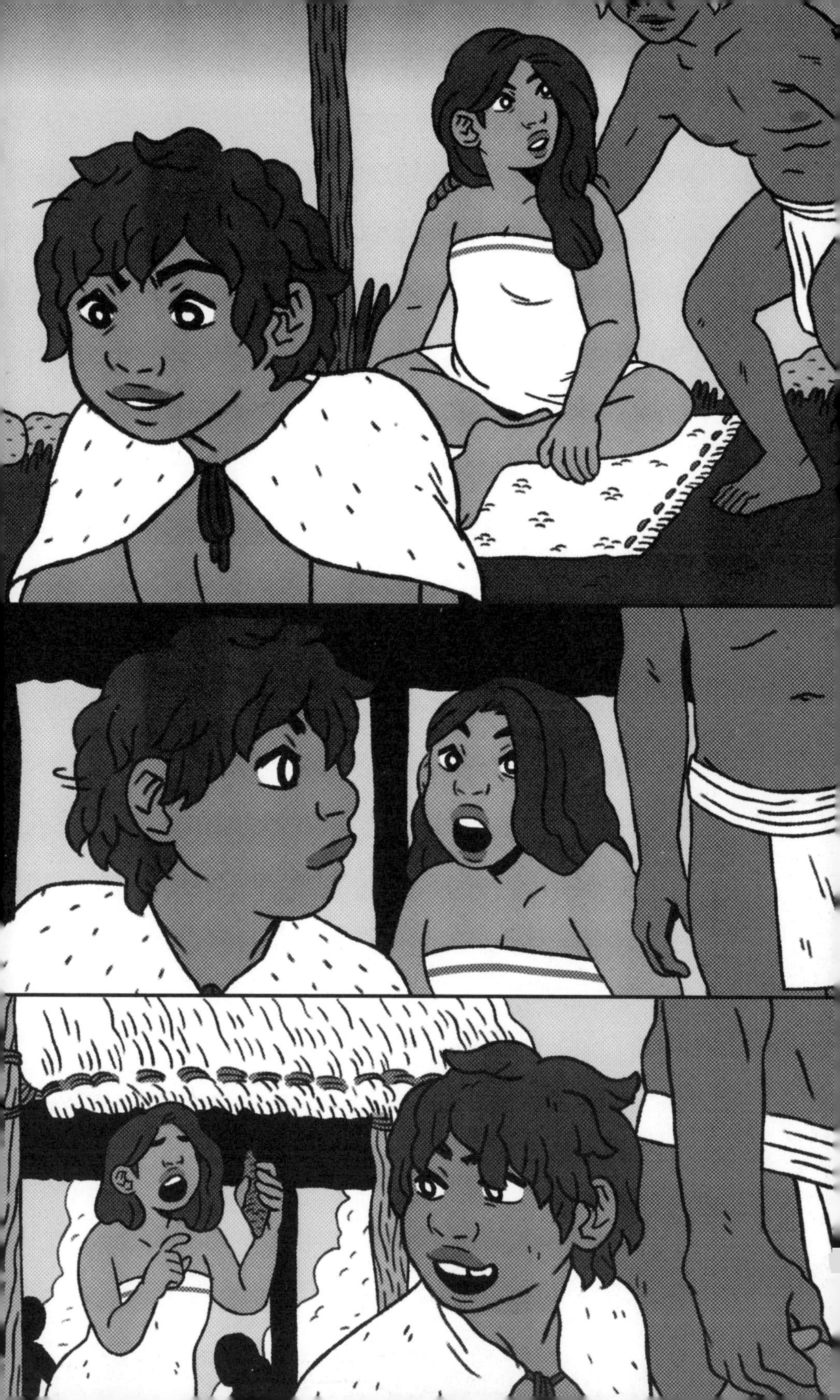

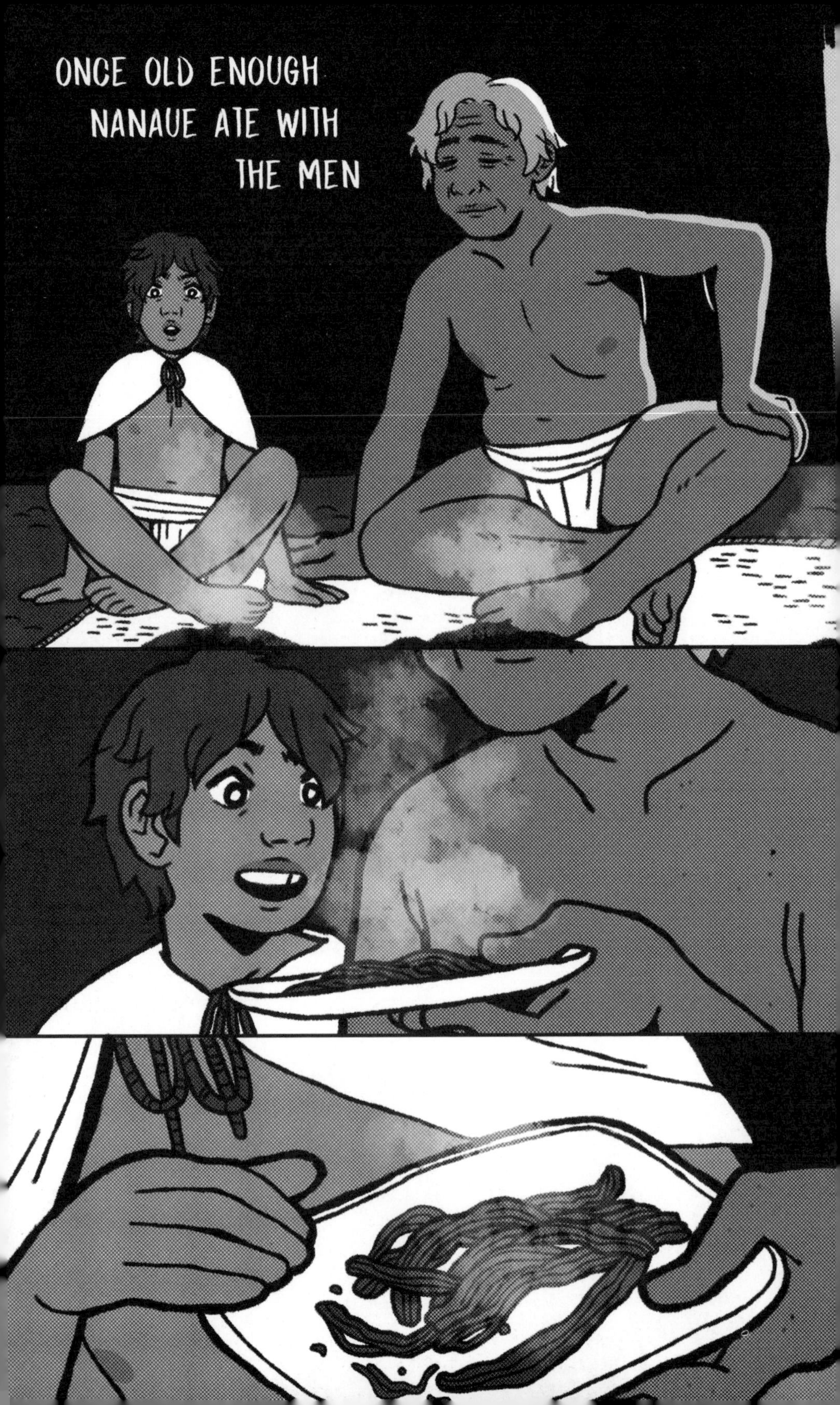
ONCE OLD ENOUGH NANAUE ATE WITH THE MEN

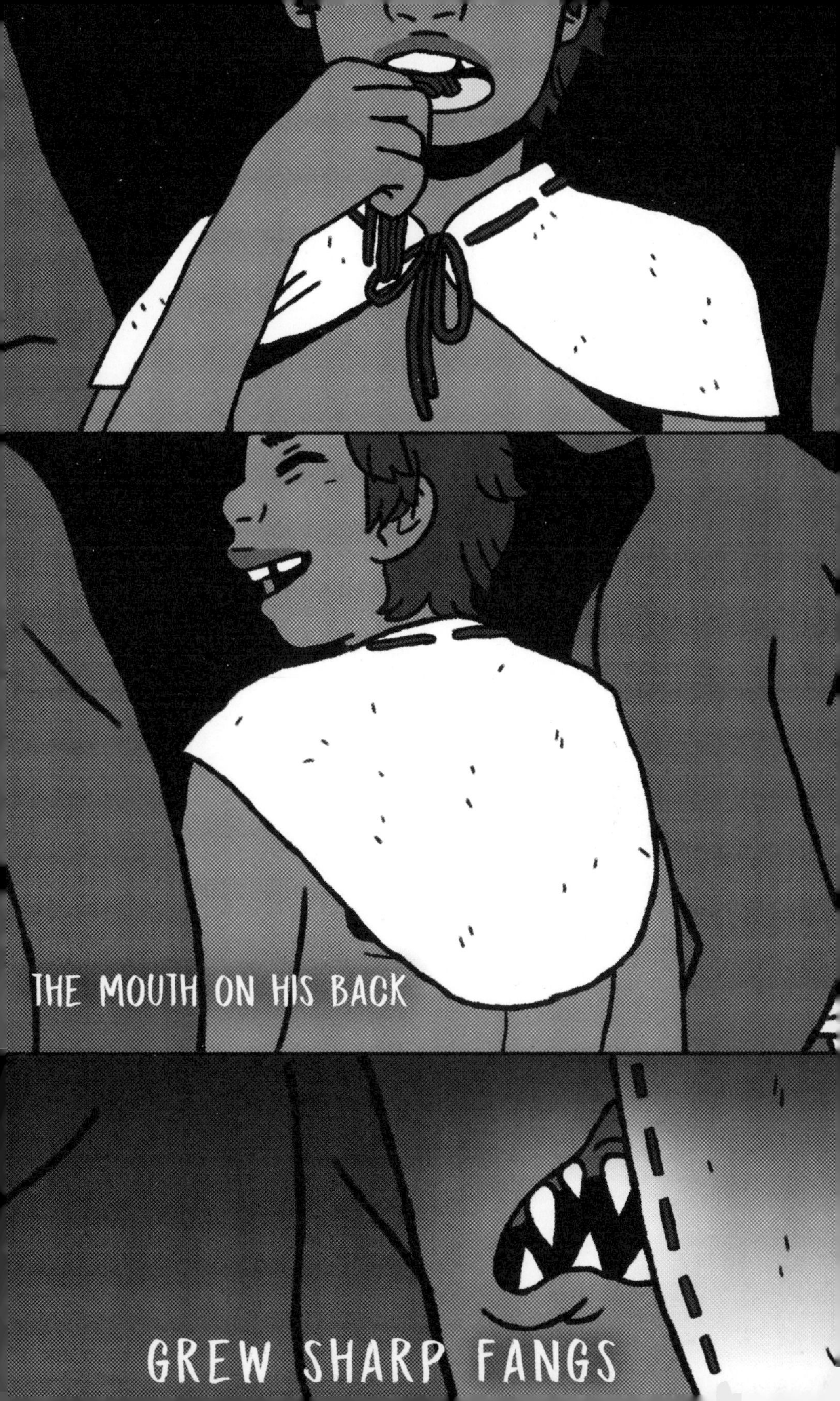
THE MOUTH ON HIS BACK
GREW SHARP FANGS

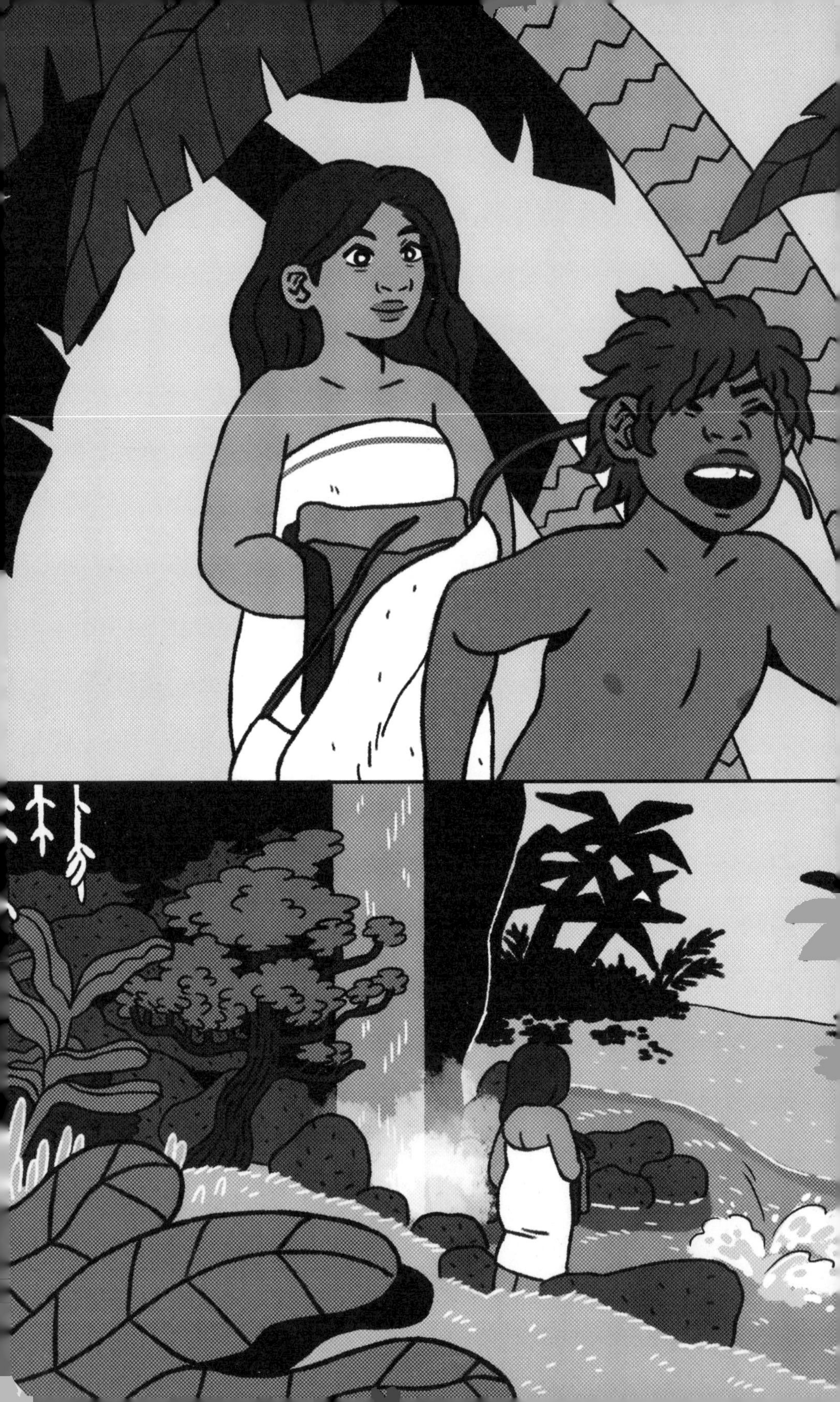

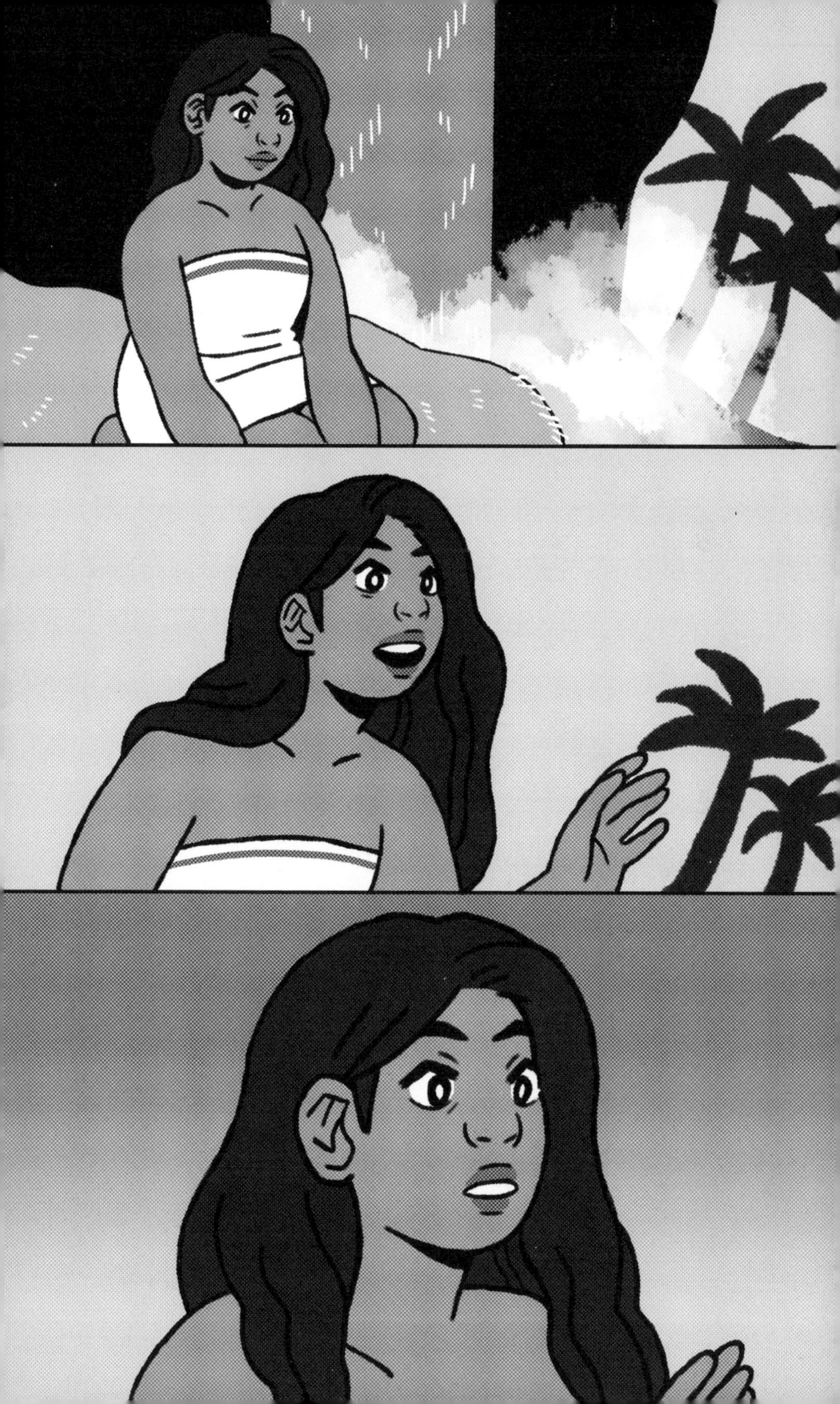

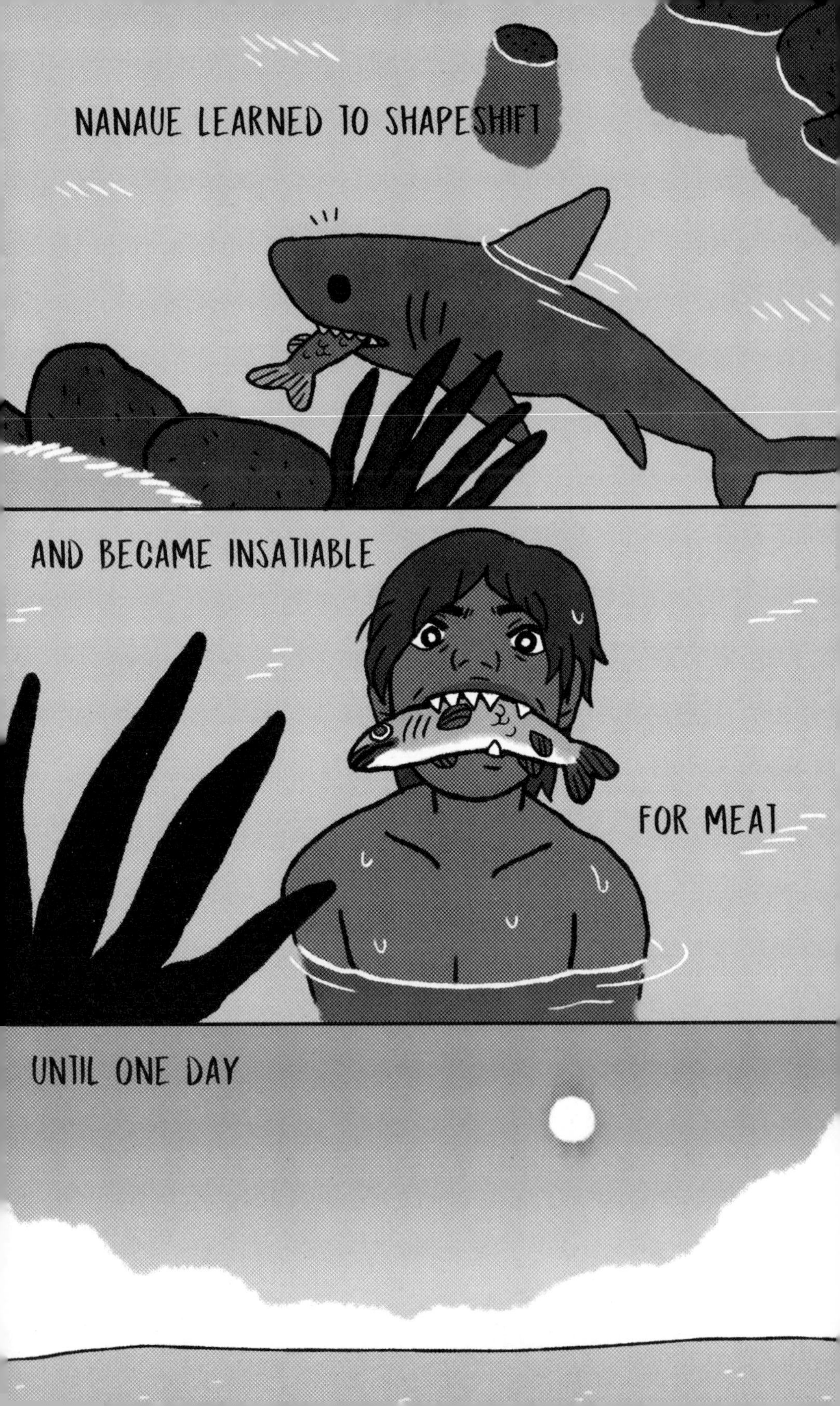
NANAUE LEARNED TO SHAPESHIFT
AND BECAME INSATIABLE
FOR MEAT
UNTIL ONE DAY

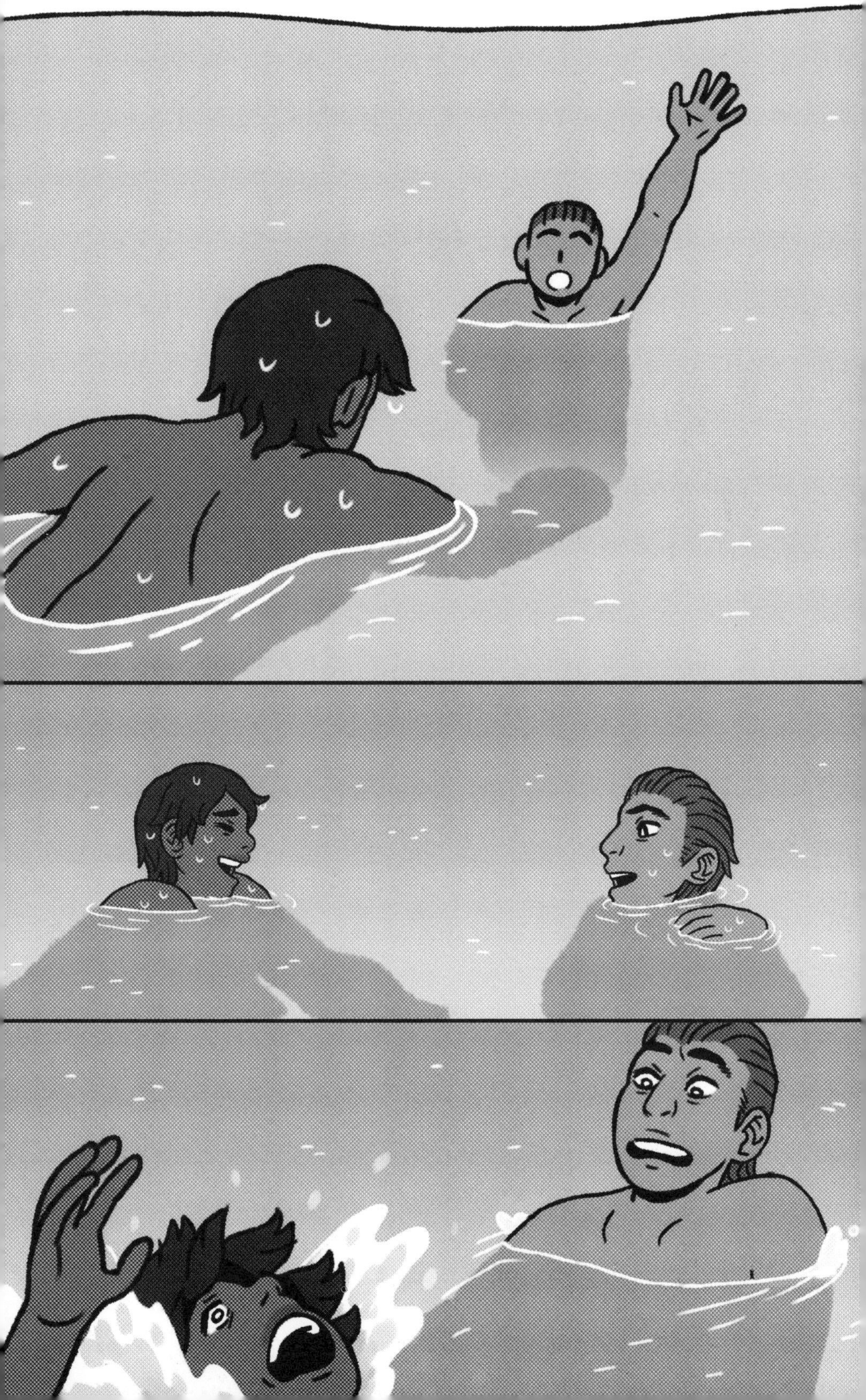

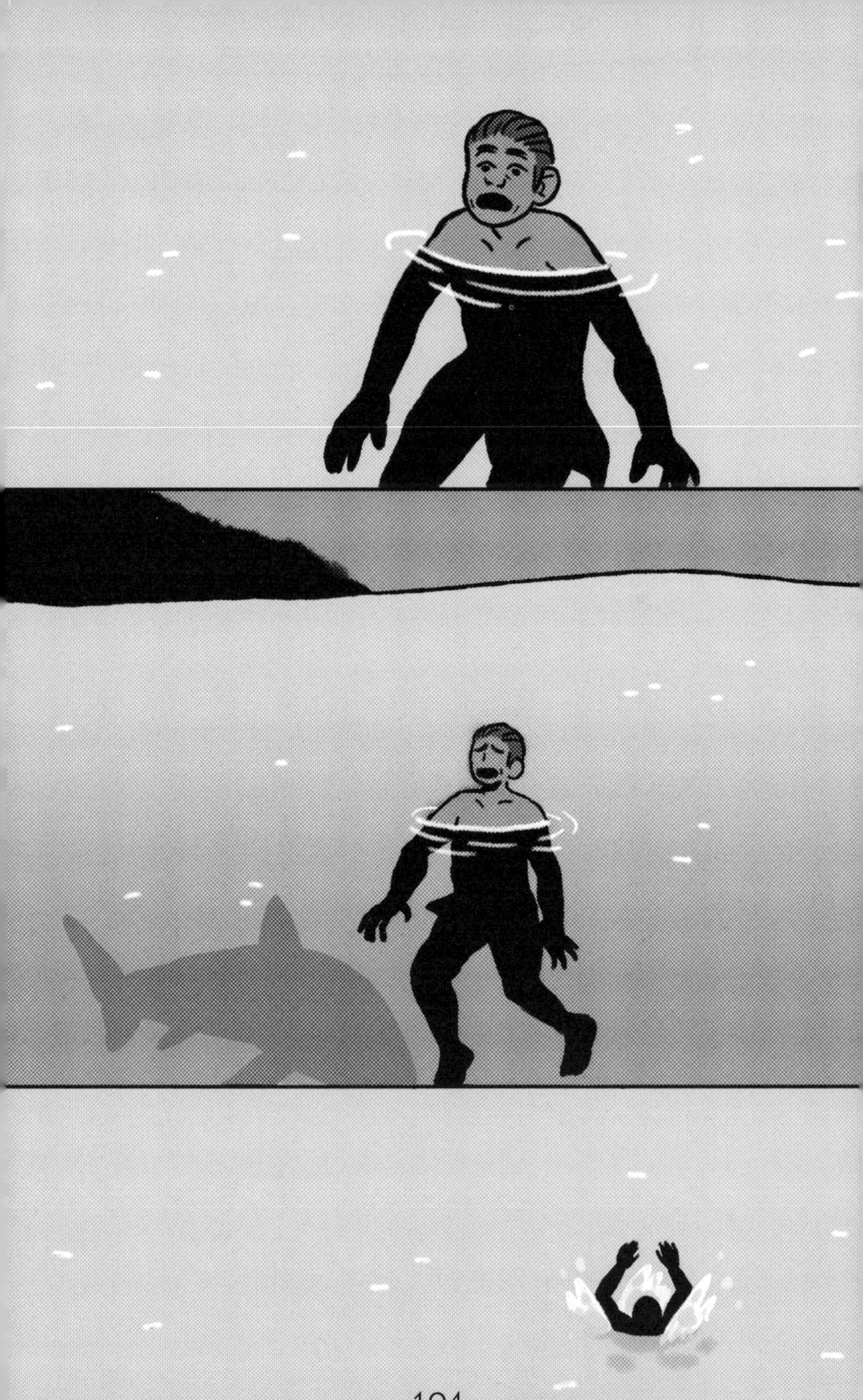

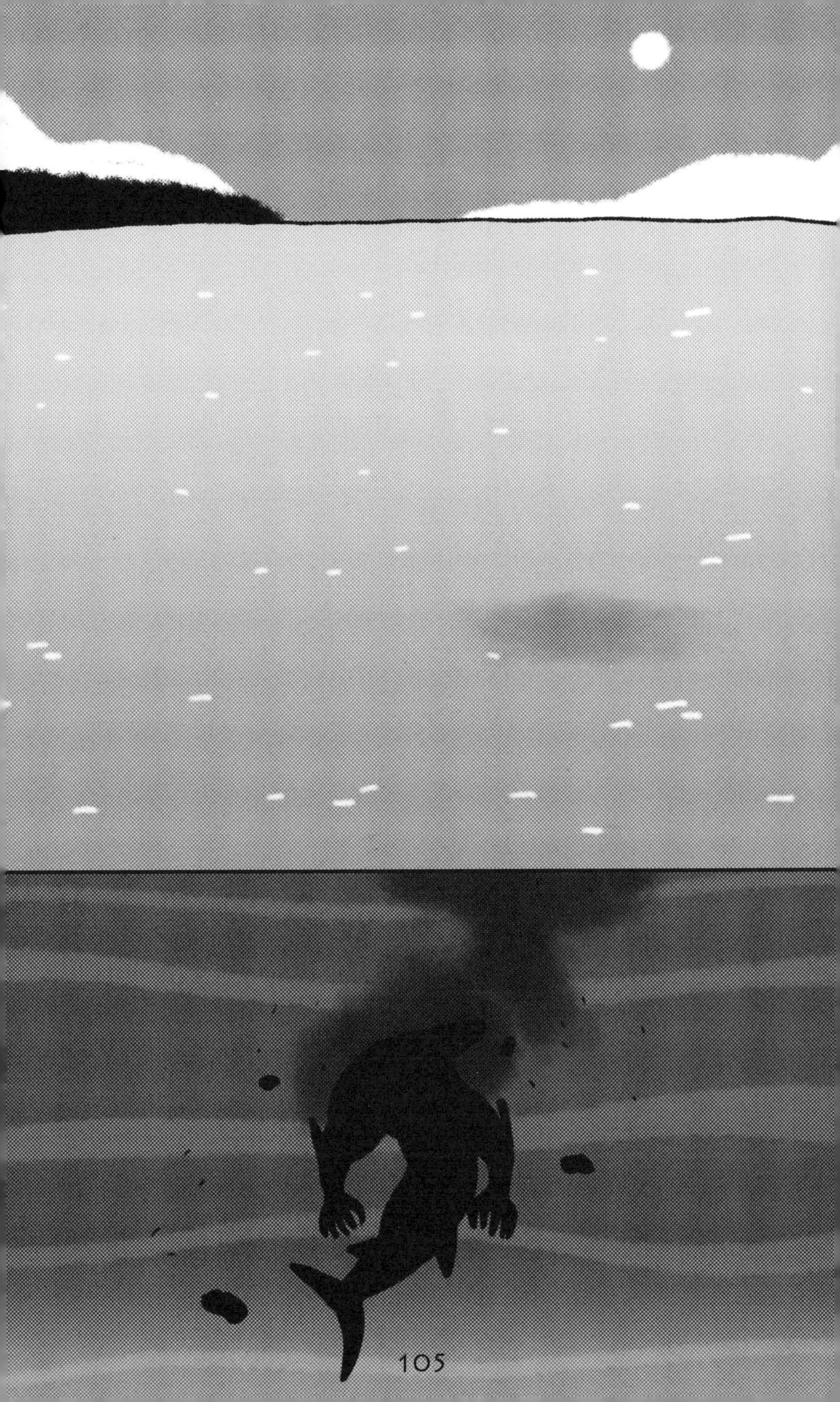

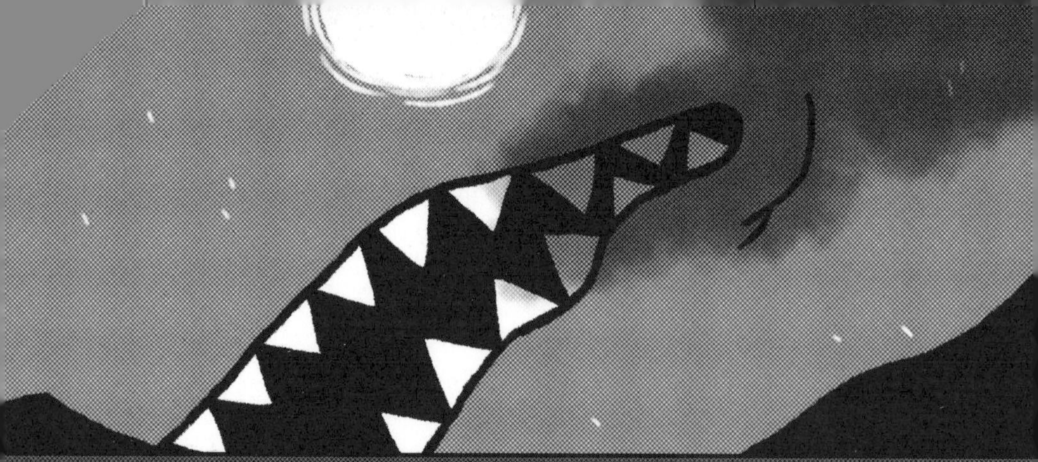
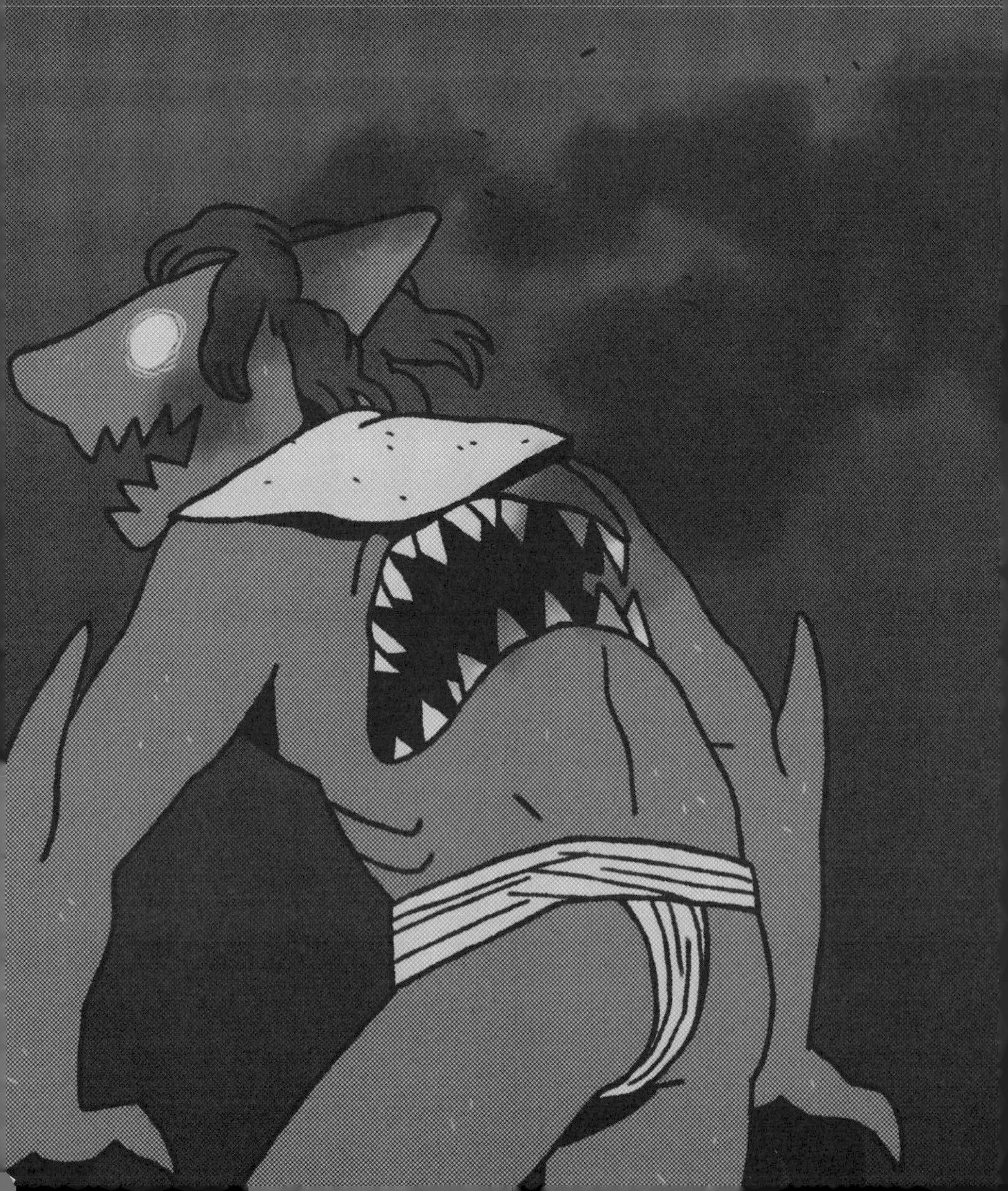

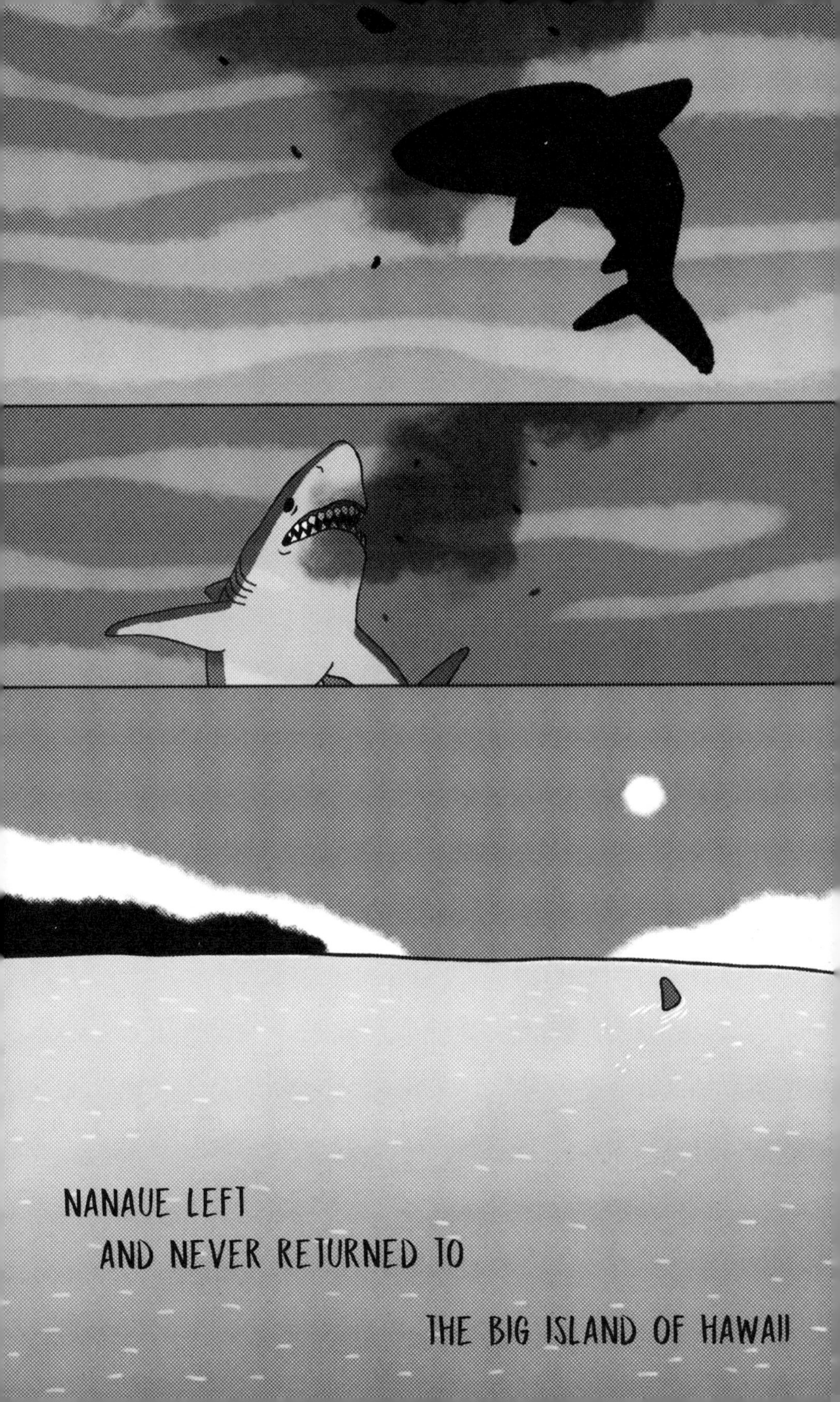
NANAUE LEFT
AND NEVER RETURNED TO
THE BIG ISLAND OF HAWAII

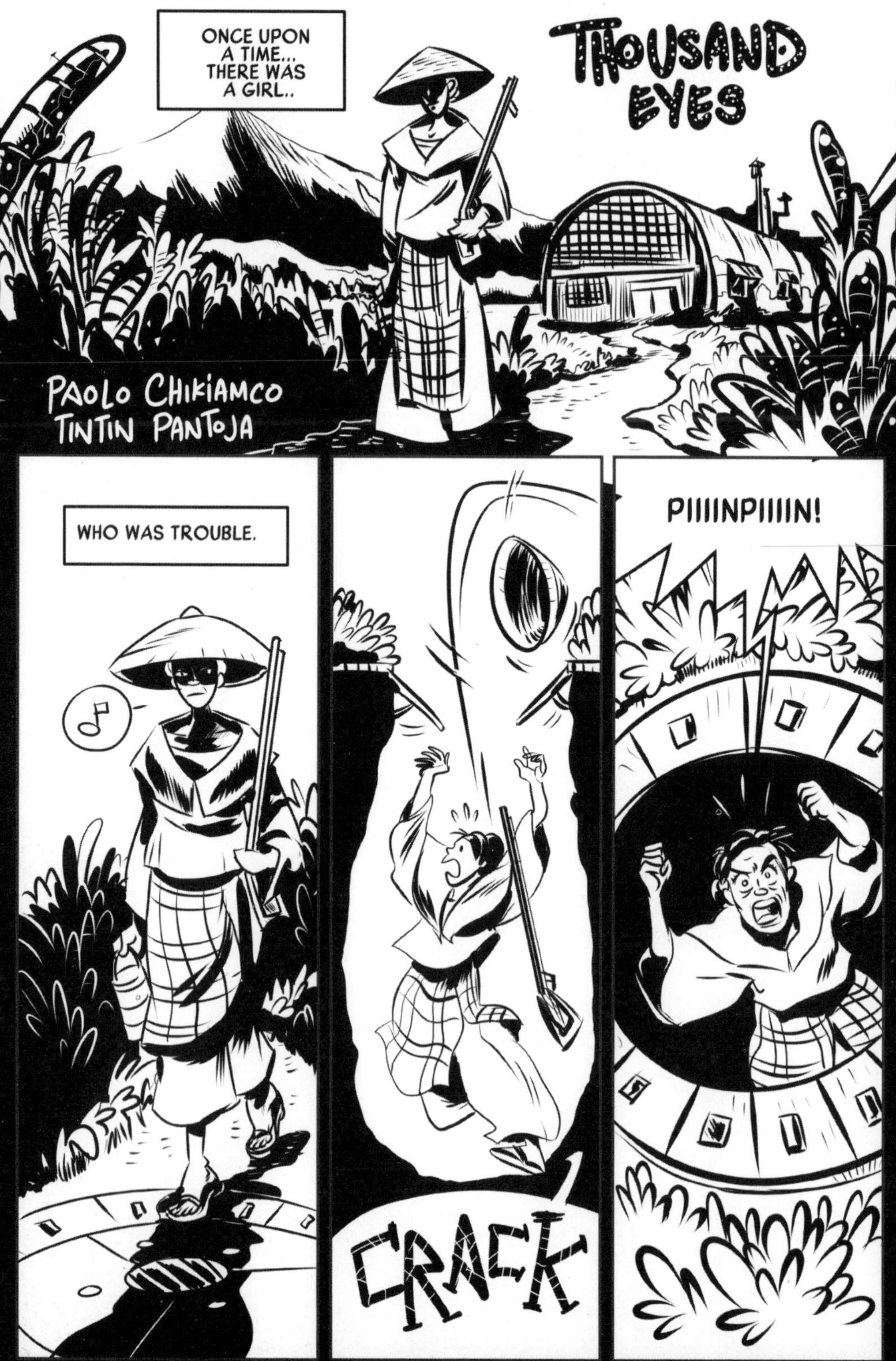
ONCE UPON A TIME... THERE WAS A GIRL..
THOUSAND EYES
PAOLO CHIKIAMCO
TINTIN PANTOJA
WHO WAS TROUBLE.
CRACK
PIIIINPIIIIN!

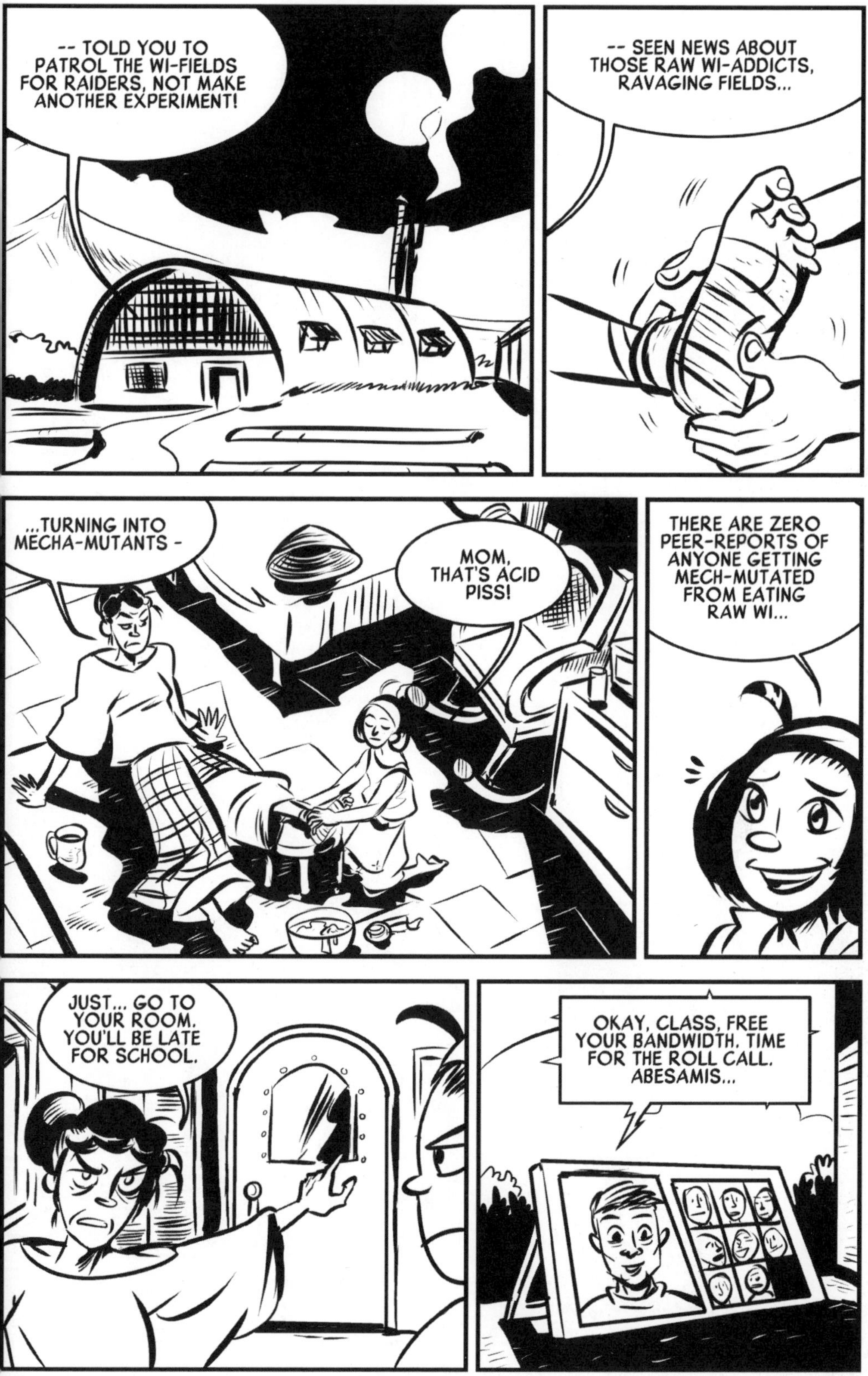
-- TOLD YOU TO PATROL THE WI-FIELDS FOR RAIDERS, NOT MAKE ANOTHER EXPERIMENT!
-- SEEN NEWS ABOUT THOSE RAW WI-ADDICTS, RAVAGING FIELDS...
...TURNING INTO MECHA-MUTANTS -
MOM, THAT'S ACID PISS!
THERE ARE ZERO PEER-REPORTS OF ANYONE GETTING MECH-MUTATED FROM EATING RAW WI...
JUST... GO TO YOUR ROOM. YOU'LL BE LATE FOR SCHOOL.
OKAY, CLASS, FREE YOUR BANDWIDTH. TIME FOR THE ROLL CALL. ABESAMIS...

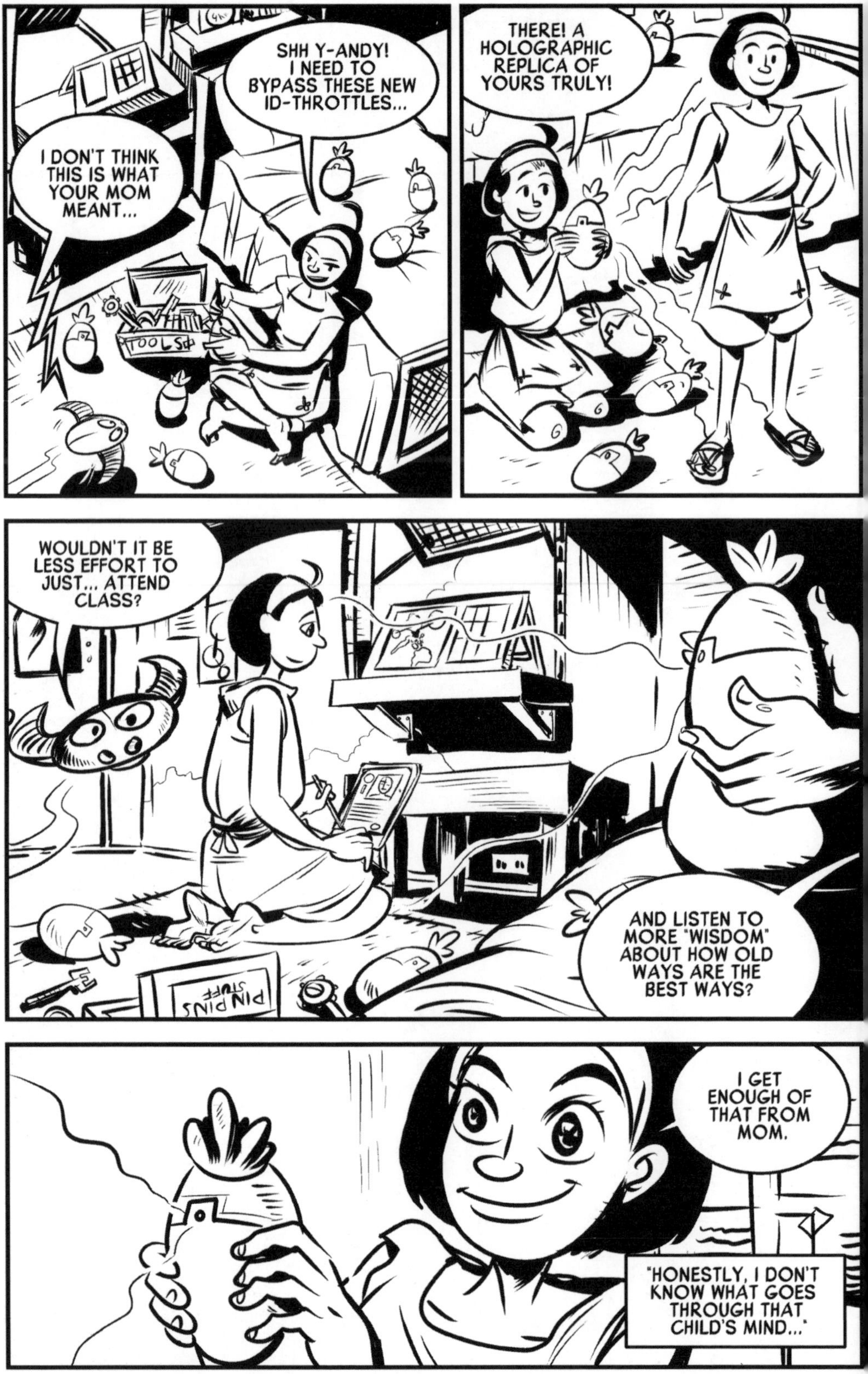

I DON'T THINK THIS IS WHAT YOUR MOM MEANT...
SHH Y-ANDY! I NEED TO BYPASS THESE NEW ID-THROTTLES...
TOOLS
THERE! A HOLOGRAPHIC REPLICA OF YOURS TRULY!
WOULDN'T IT BE LESS EFFORT TO JUST... ATTEND CLASS?
AND LISTEN TO MORE "WISDOM" ABOUT HOW OLD WAYS ARE THE BEST WAYS?
PIN PINS STUFF
I GET ENOUGH OF THAT FROM MOM.
"HONESTLY, I DON'T KNOW WHAT GOES THROUGH THAT CHILD'S MIND..."

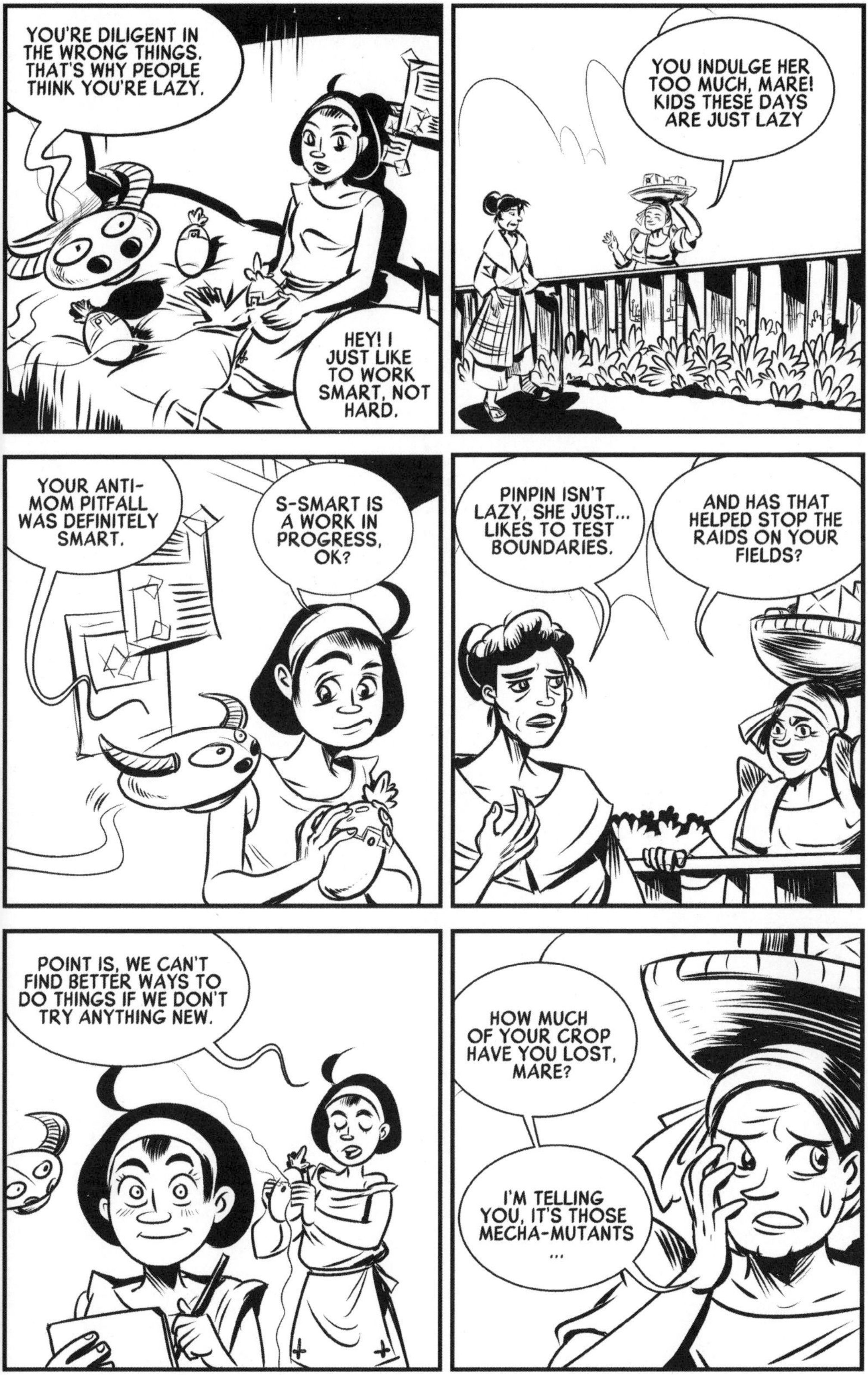
YOU'RE DILIGENT IN THE WRONG THINGS. THAT'S WHY PEOPLE THINK YOU'RE LAZY.
HEY! I JUST LIKE TO WORK SMART, NOT HARD.
YOU INDULGE HER TOO MUCH, MARE! KIDS THESE DAYS ARE JUST LAZY
YOUR ANTI-MOM PITFALL WAS DEFINITELY SMART.
S-SMART IS A WORK IN PROGRESS, OK?
PINPIN ISN'T LAZY, SHE JUST... LIKES TO TEST BOUNDARIES.
AND HAS THAT HELPED STOP THE RAIDS ON YOUR FIELDS?
POINT IS, WE CAN'T FIND BETTER WAYS TO DO THINGS IF WE DON'T TRY ANYTHING NEW.
HOW MUCH OF YOUR CROP HAVE YOU LOST, MARE?
I'M TELLING YOU, IT'S THOSE MECHA-MUTANTS ...

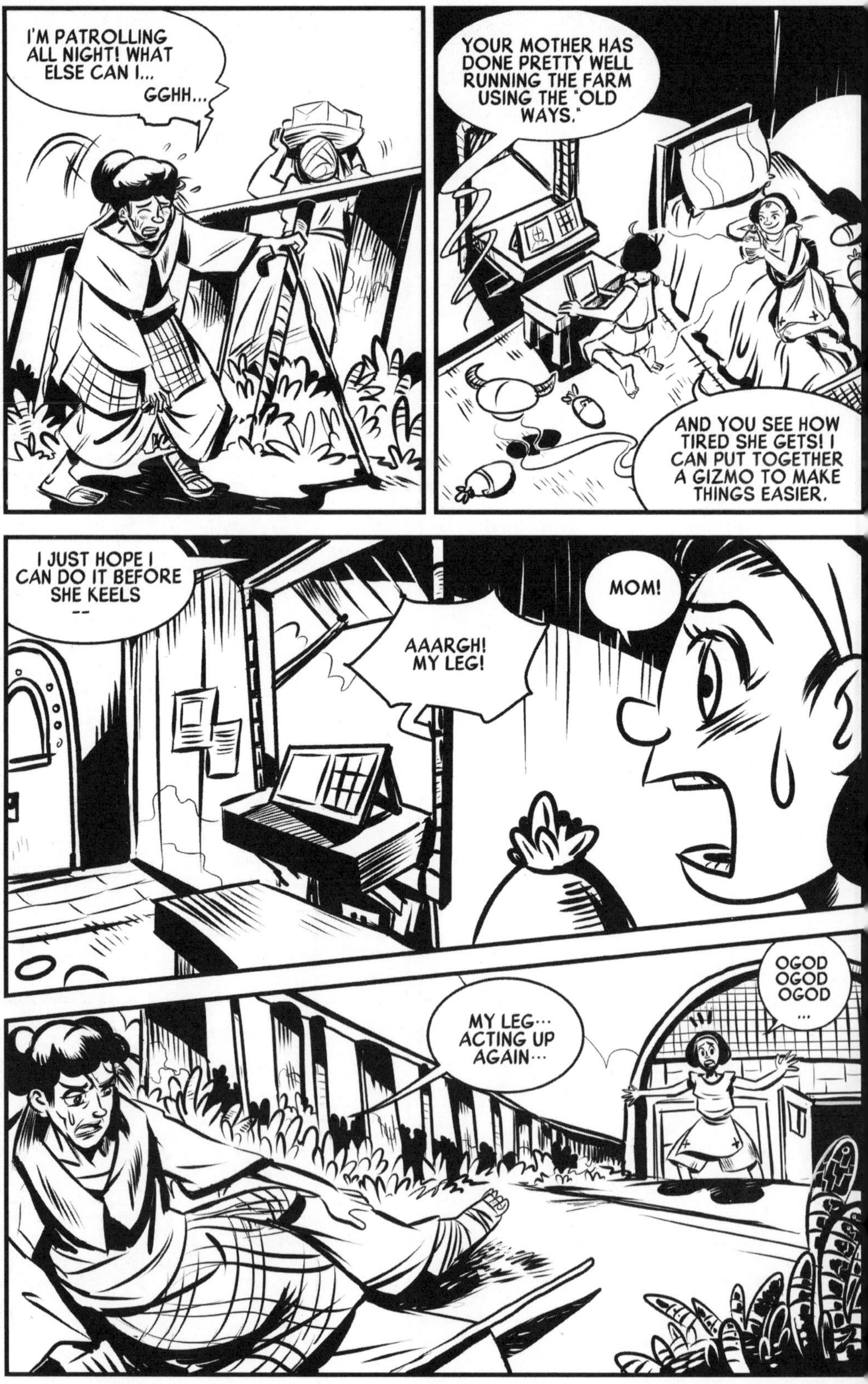
I'M PATROLLING ALL NIGHT! WHAT ELSE CAN I... GGHH...
YOUR MOTHER HAS DONE PRETTY WELL RUNNING THE FARM USING THE "OLD WAYS."
AND YOU SEE HOW TIRED SHE GETS! I CAN PUT TOGETHER A GIZMO TO MAKE THINGS EASIER.
I JUST HOPE I CAN DO IT BEFORE SHE KEELS --
AAARGH! MY LEG!
MOM!
MY LEG... ACTING UP AGAIN...
OGOD OGOD OGOD ...

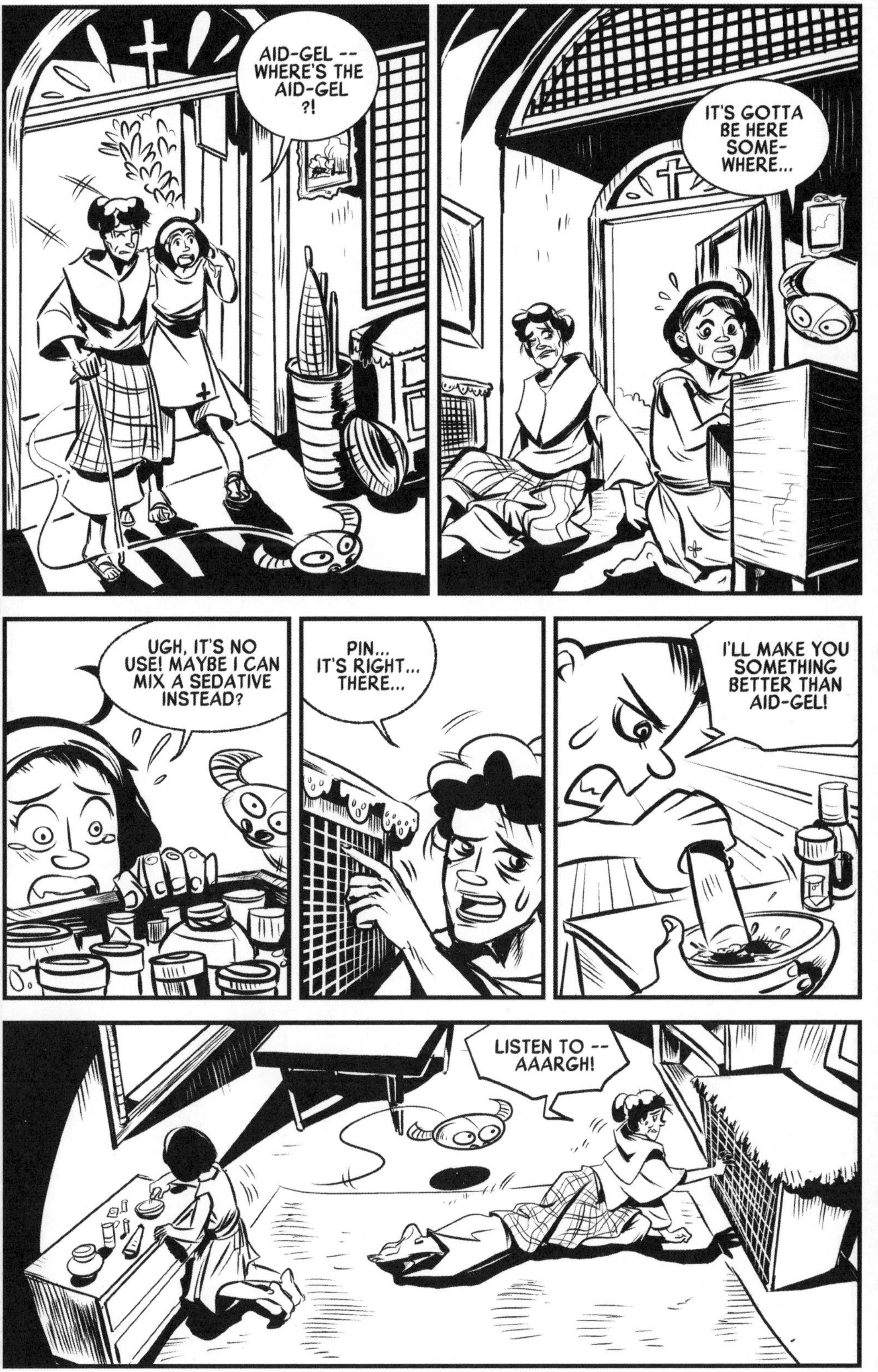
AID-GEL -- WHERE'S THE AID-GEL ?!
IT'S GOTTA BE HERE SOME-WHERE...
UGH, IT'S NO USE! MAYBE I CAN MIX A SEDATIVE INSTEAD?
PIN... IT'S RIGHT... THERE...
I'LL MAKE YOU SOMETHING BETTER THAN AID-GEL!
LISTEN TO -- AAARGH!

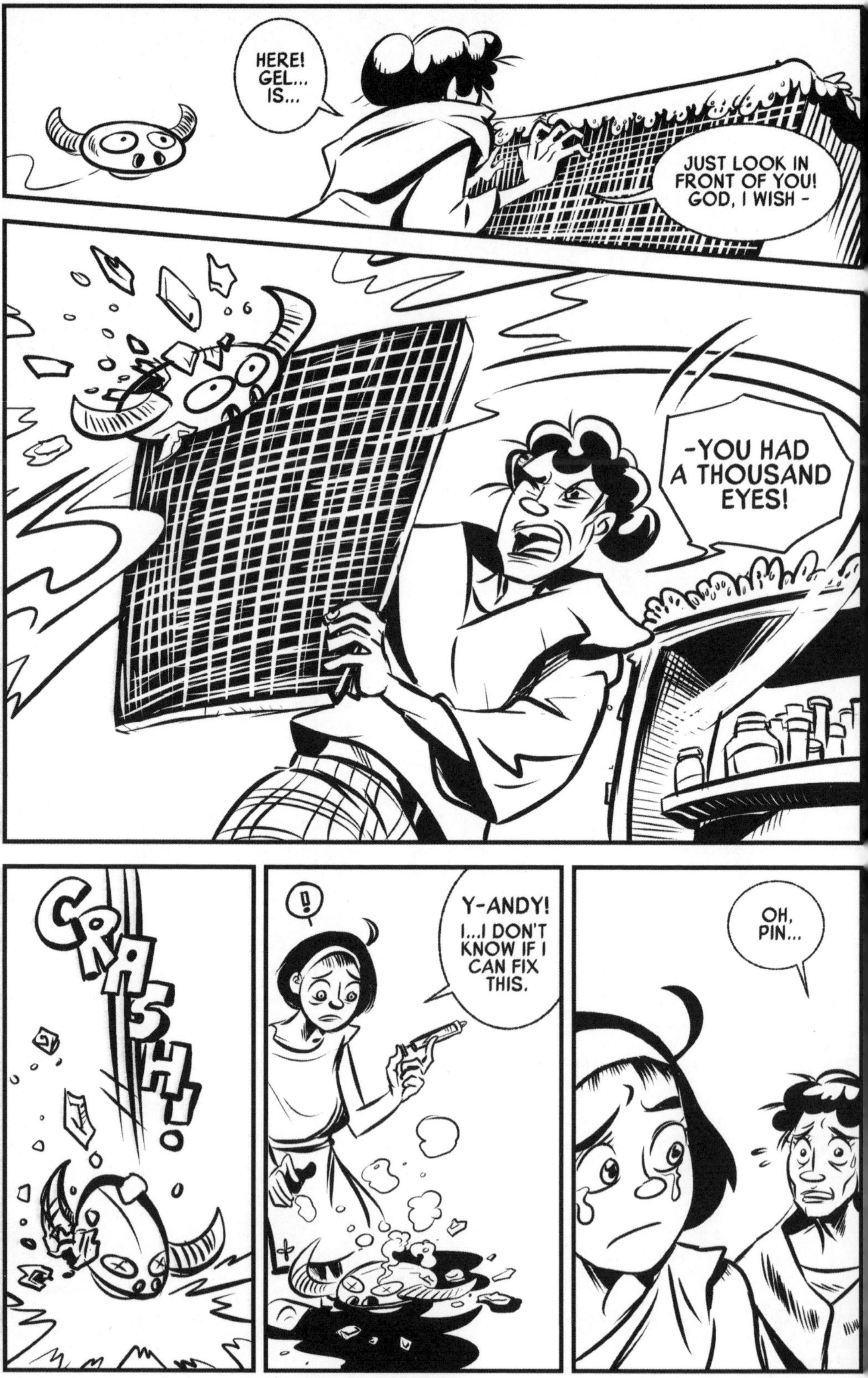
HERE! GEL... IS...
JUST LOOK IN FRONT OF YOU! GOD, I WISH -
-YOU HAD A THOUSAND EYES!
CRASH!
!
Y-ANDY! I...I DON'T KNOW IF I CAN FIX THIS.
OH, PIN...

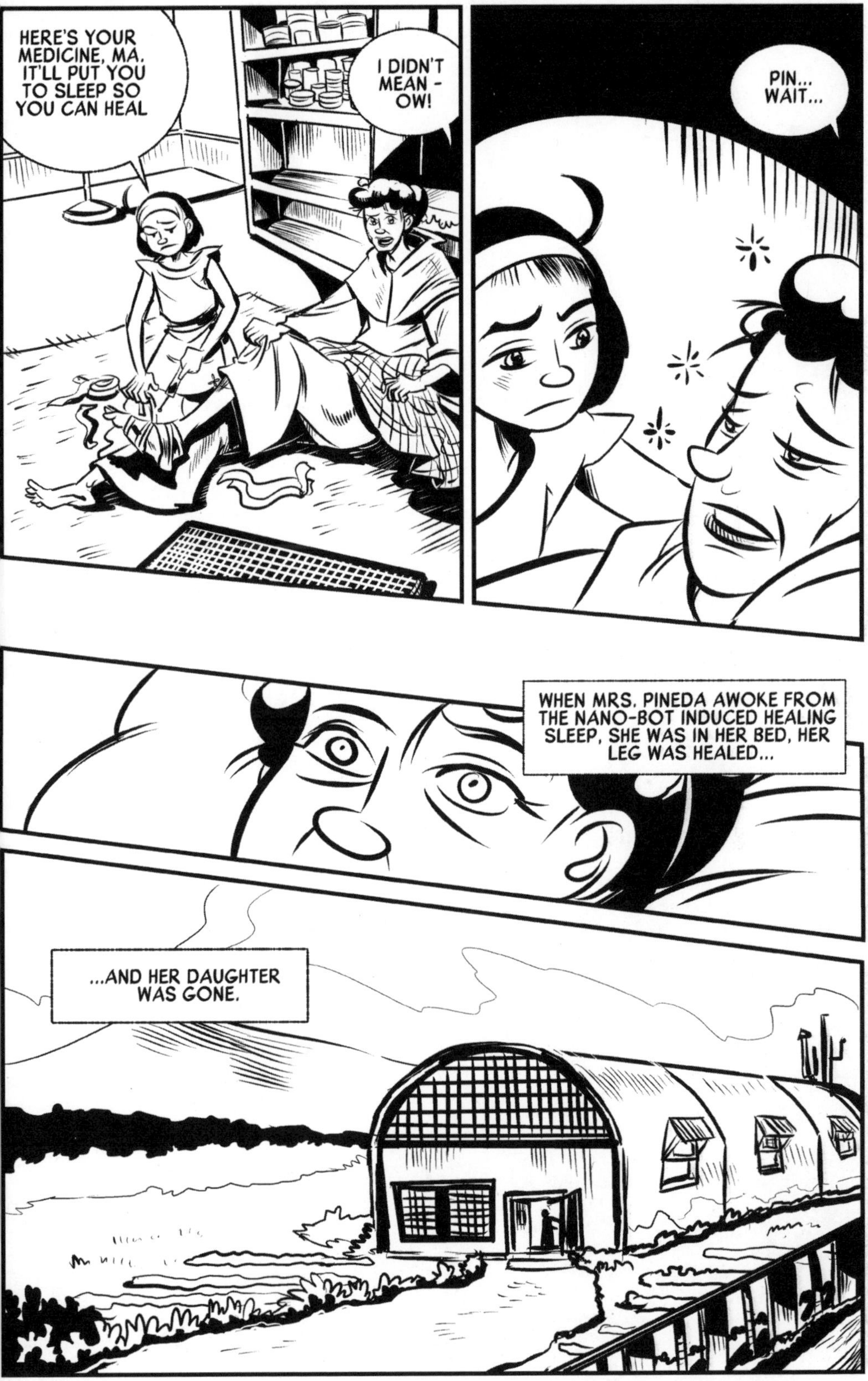
HERE'S YOUR MEDICINE, MA. IT'LL PUT YOU TO SLEEP SO YOU CAN HEAL
I DIDN'T MEAN - OW!
PIN... WAIT...
WHEN MRS. PINEDA AWOKE FROM THE NANO-BOT INDUCED HEALING SLEEP, SHE WAS IN HER BED, HER LEG WAS HEALED...
...AND HER DAUGHTER WAS GONE.

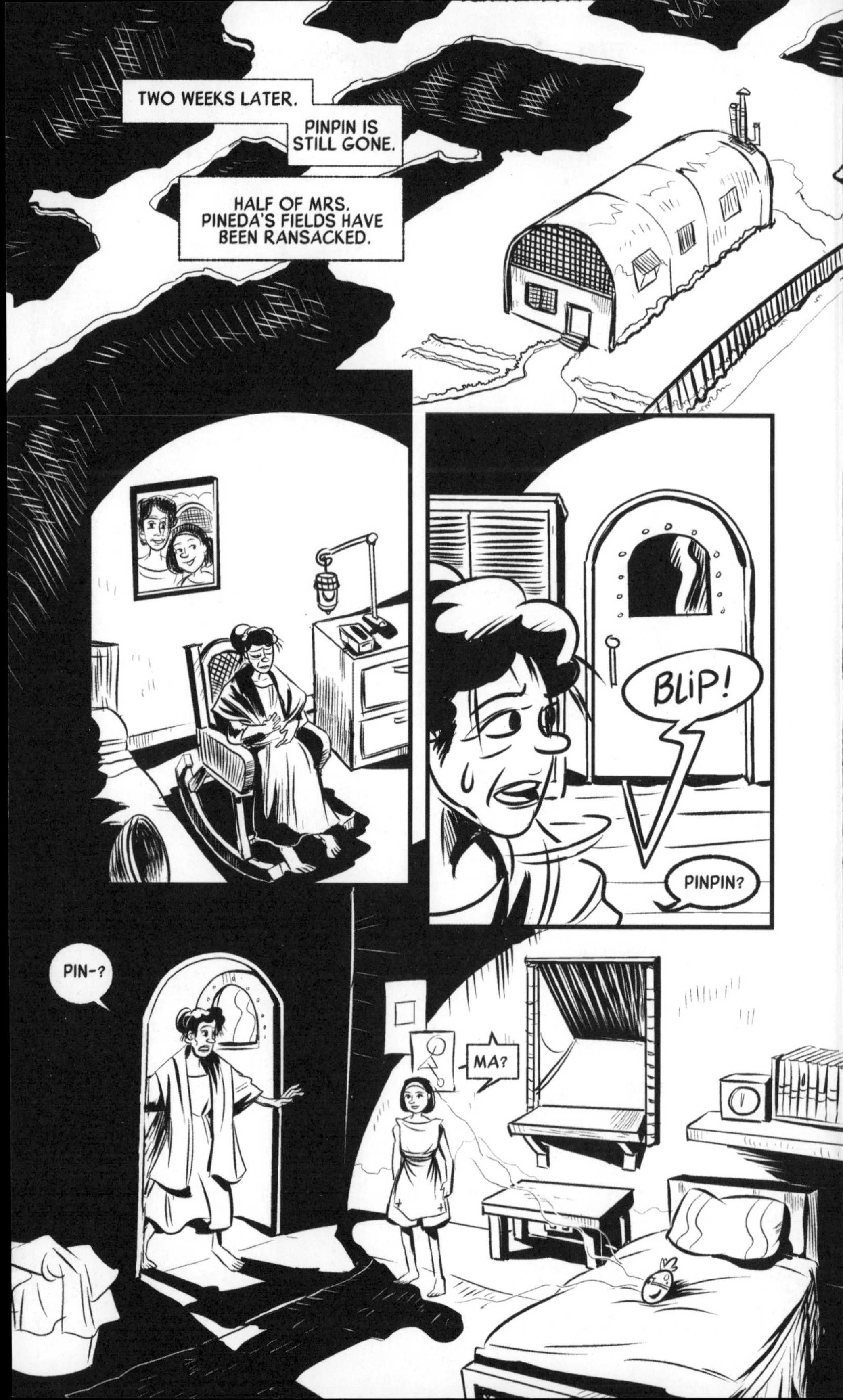
TWO WEEKS LATER.
PINPIN IS STILL GONE.
HALF OF MRS. PINEDA'S FIELDS HAVE BEEN RANSACKED.
BLIP!
PINPIN?
PIN-?
MA?

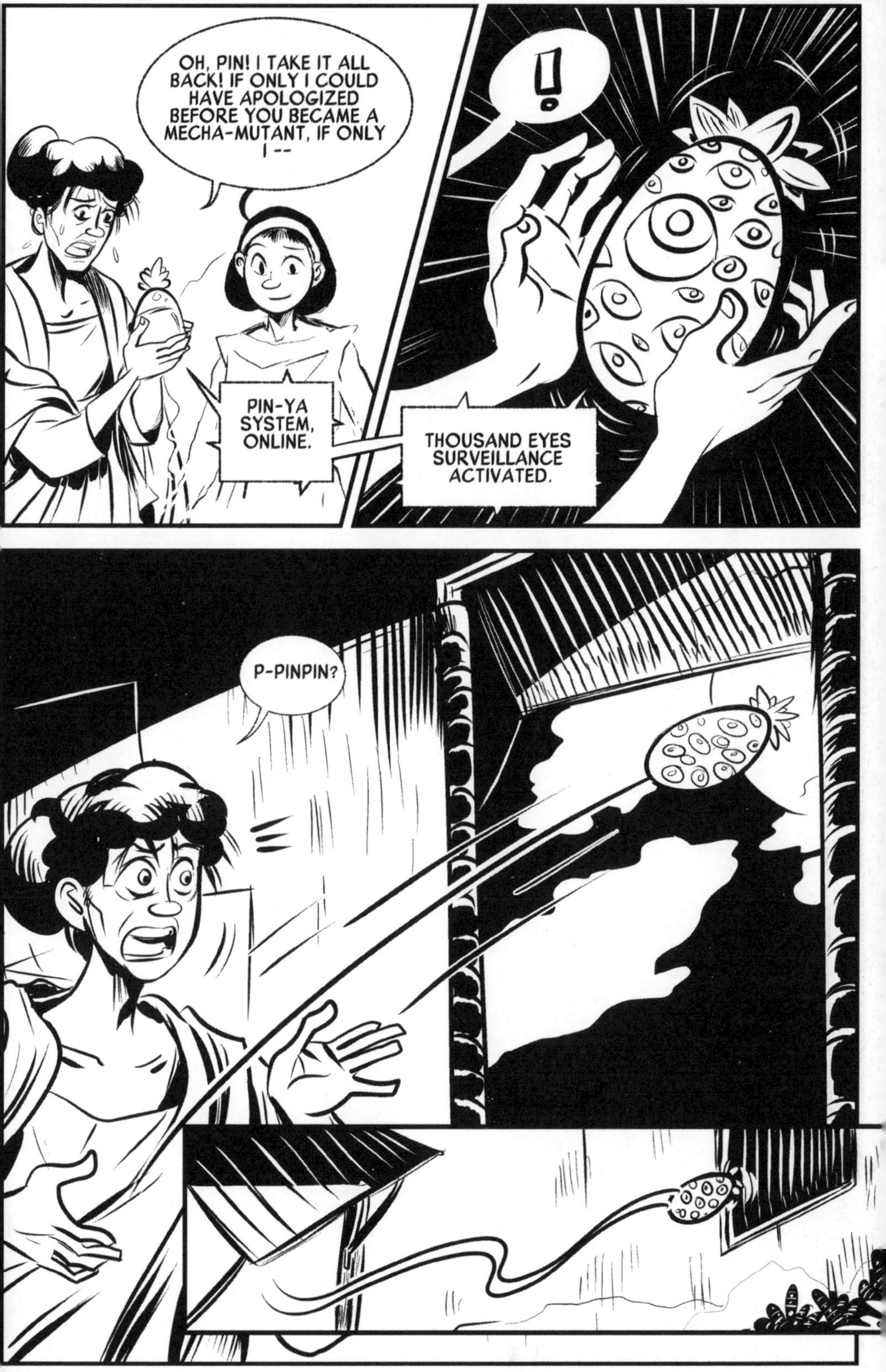
OH, PIN! I TAKE IT ALL BACK! IF ONLY I COULD HAVE APOLOGIZED BEFORE YOU BECAME A MECHA-MUTANT, IF ONLY I --
PIN-YA SYSTEM, ONLINE.
!
THOUSAND EYES SURVEILLANCE ACTIVATED.
P-PINPIN?

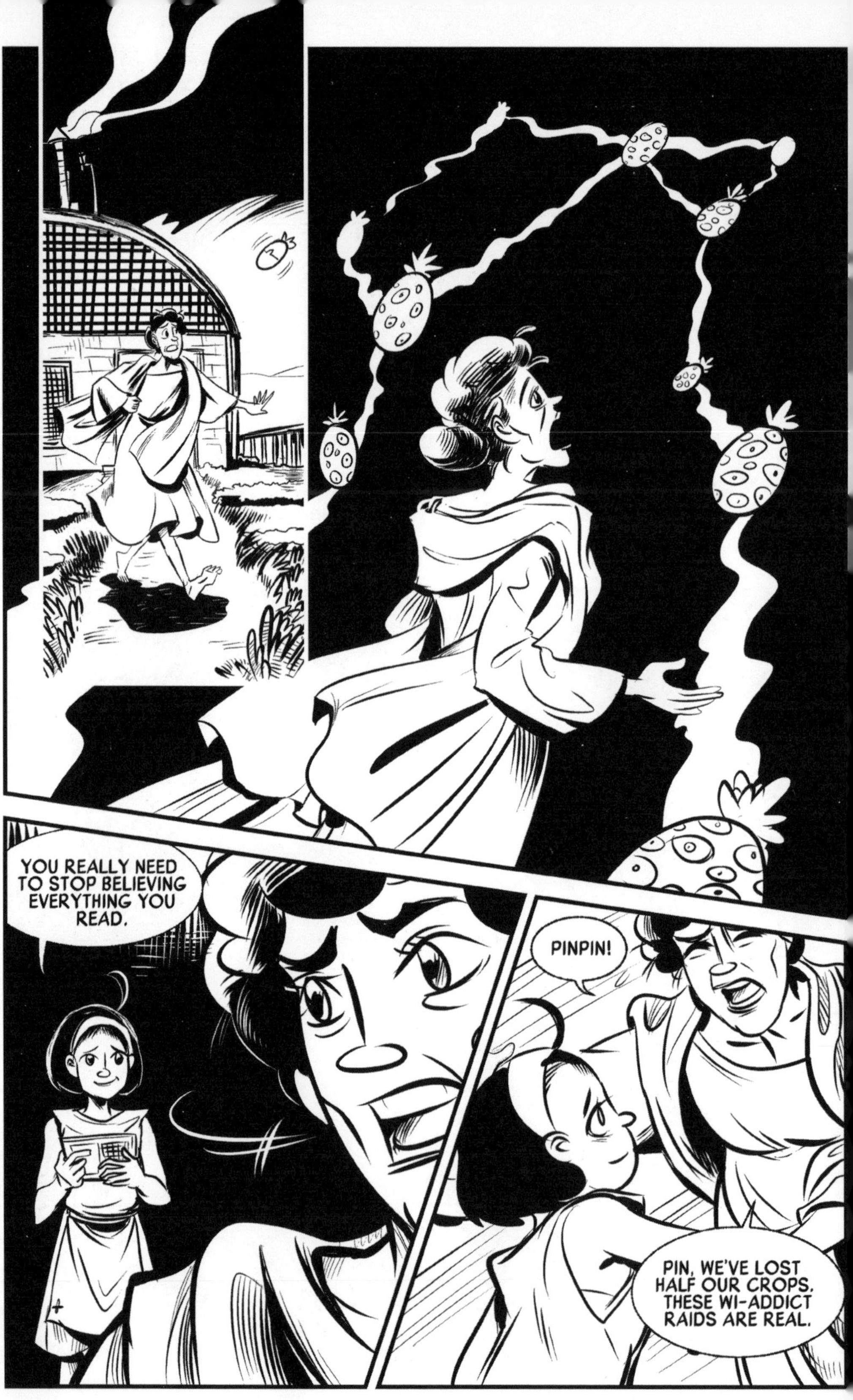
YOU REALLY NEED TO STOP BELIEVING EVERYTHING YOU READ.
PINPIN!
PIN, WE'VE LOST HALF OUR CROPS. THESE WI-ADDICT RAIDS ARE REAL.

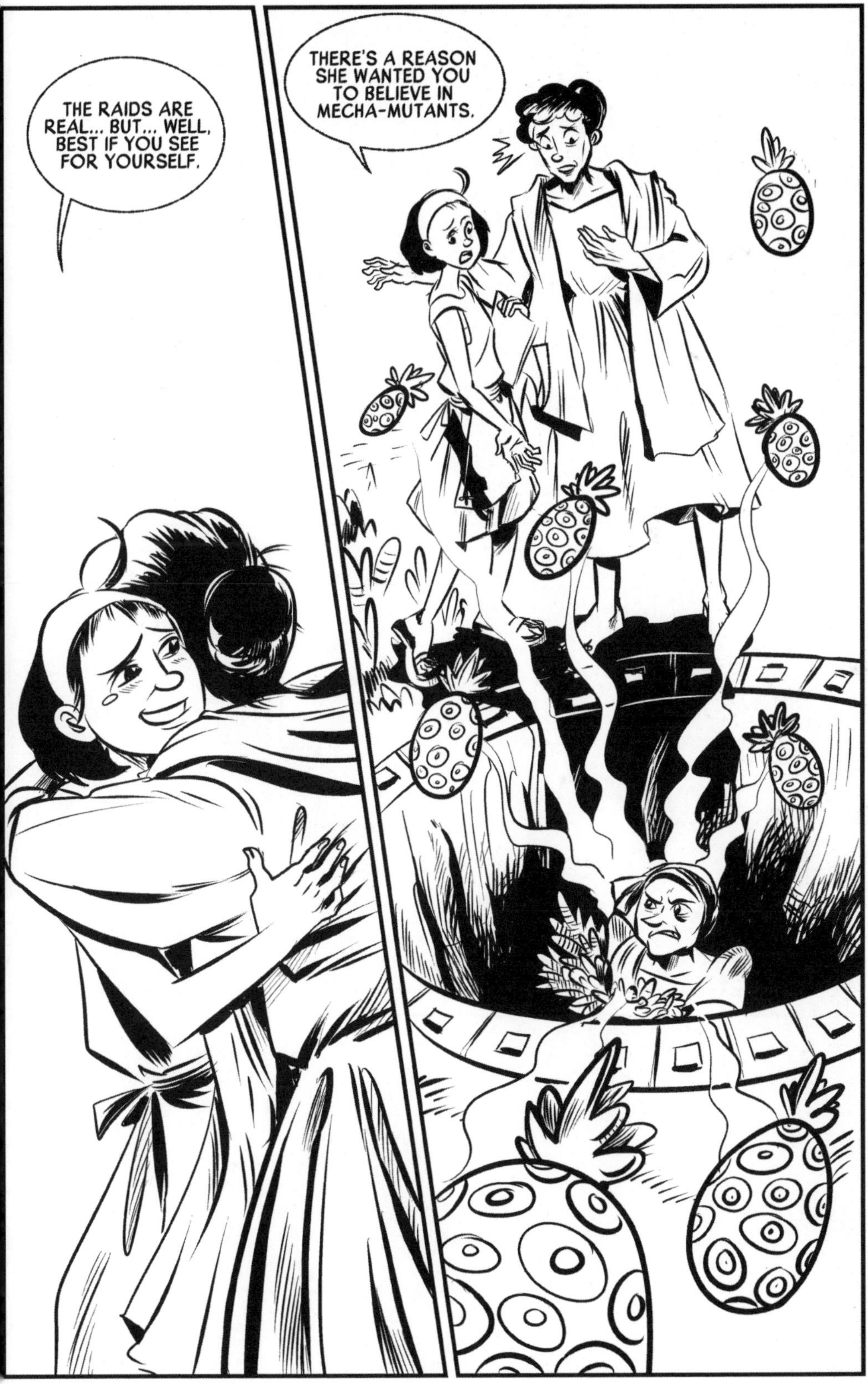
THE RAIDS ARE REAL... BUT... WELL, BEST IF YOU SEE FOR YOURSELF.
THERE'S A REASON SHE WANTED YOU TO BELIEVE IN MECHA-MUTANTS.

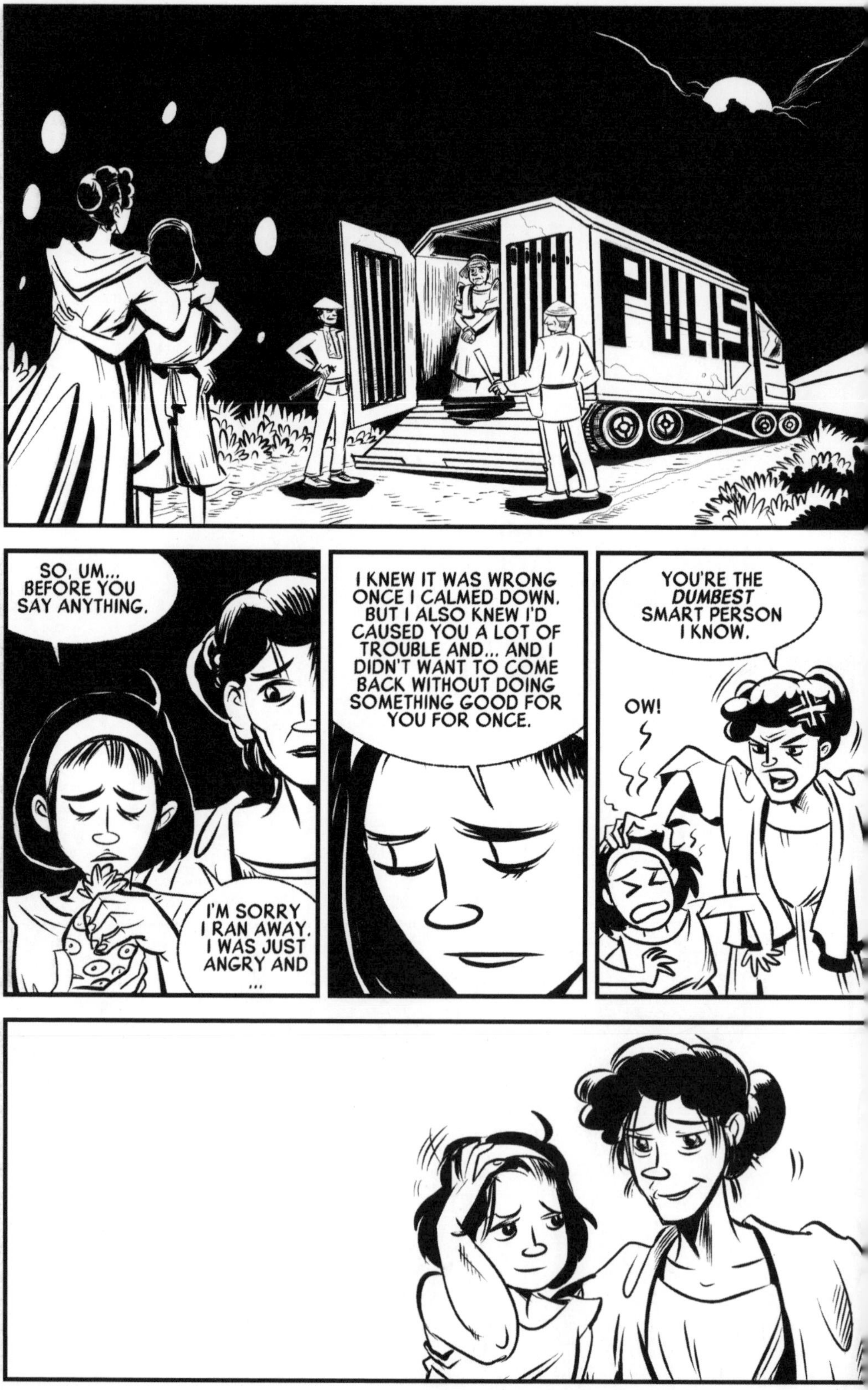
PULIS
SO, UM... BEFORE YOU SAY ANYTHING.
I'M SORRY I RAN AWAY. I WAS JUST ANGRY AND ...
I KNEW IT WAS WRONG ONCE I CALMED DOWN. BUT I ALSO KNEW I'D CAUSED YOU A LOT OF TROUBLE AND... AND I DIDN'T WANT TO COME BACK WITHOUT DOING SOMETHING GOOD FOR YOU FOR ONCE.
YOU'RE THE *DUMBEST* SMART PERSON I KNOW.
OW!

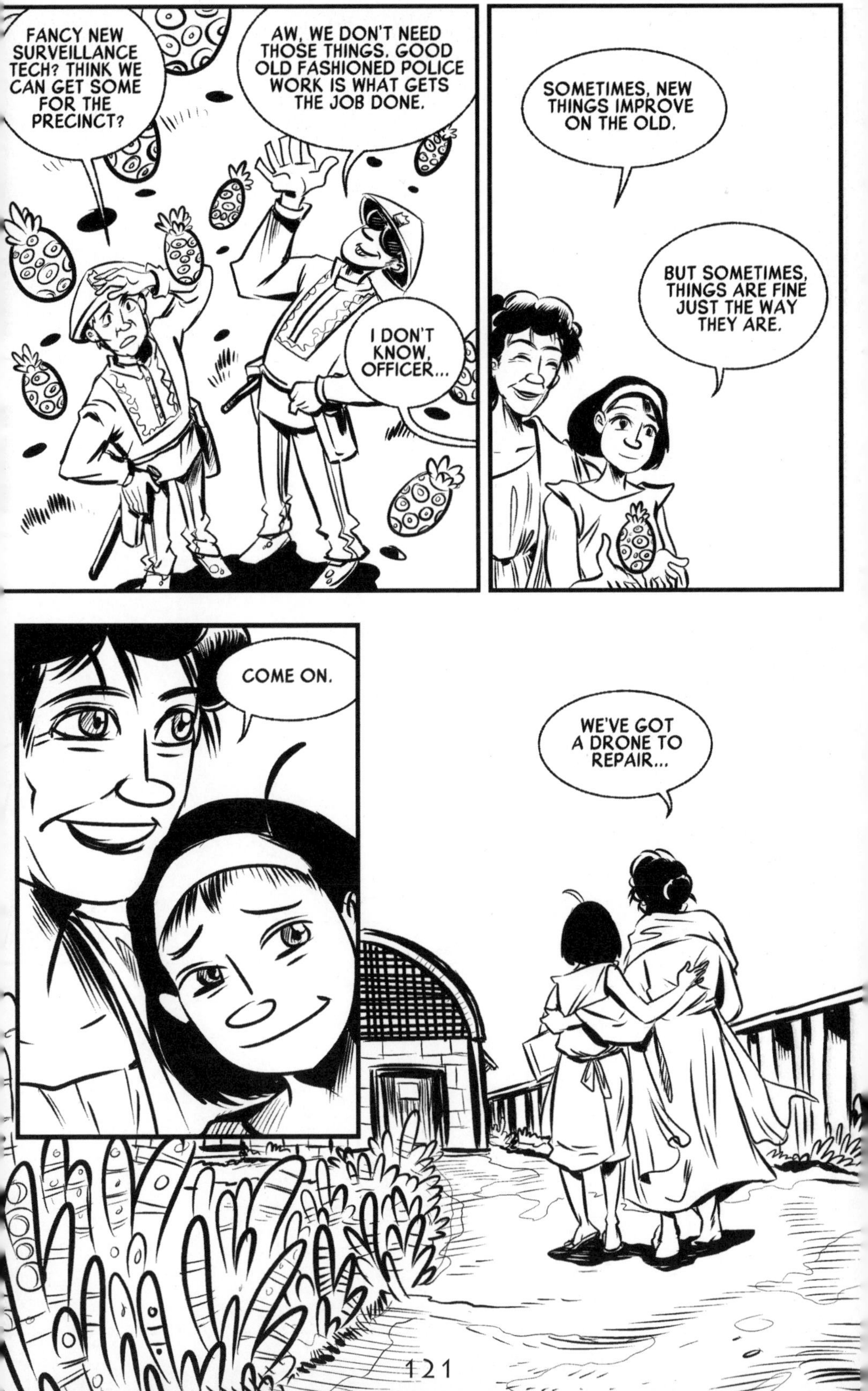
FANCY NEW SURVEILLANCE TECH? THINK WE CAN GET SOME FOR THE PRECINCT?
AW, WE DON'T NEED THOSE THINGS. GOOD OLD FASHIONED POLICE WORK IS WHAT GETS THE JOB DONE.
I DON'T KNOW, OFFICER...
SOMETIMES, NEW THINGS IMPROVE ON THE OLD.
BUT SOMETIMES, THINGS ARE FINE JUST THE WAY THEY ARE.
COME ON.
WE'VE GOT A DRONE TO REPAIR...

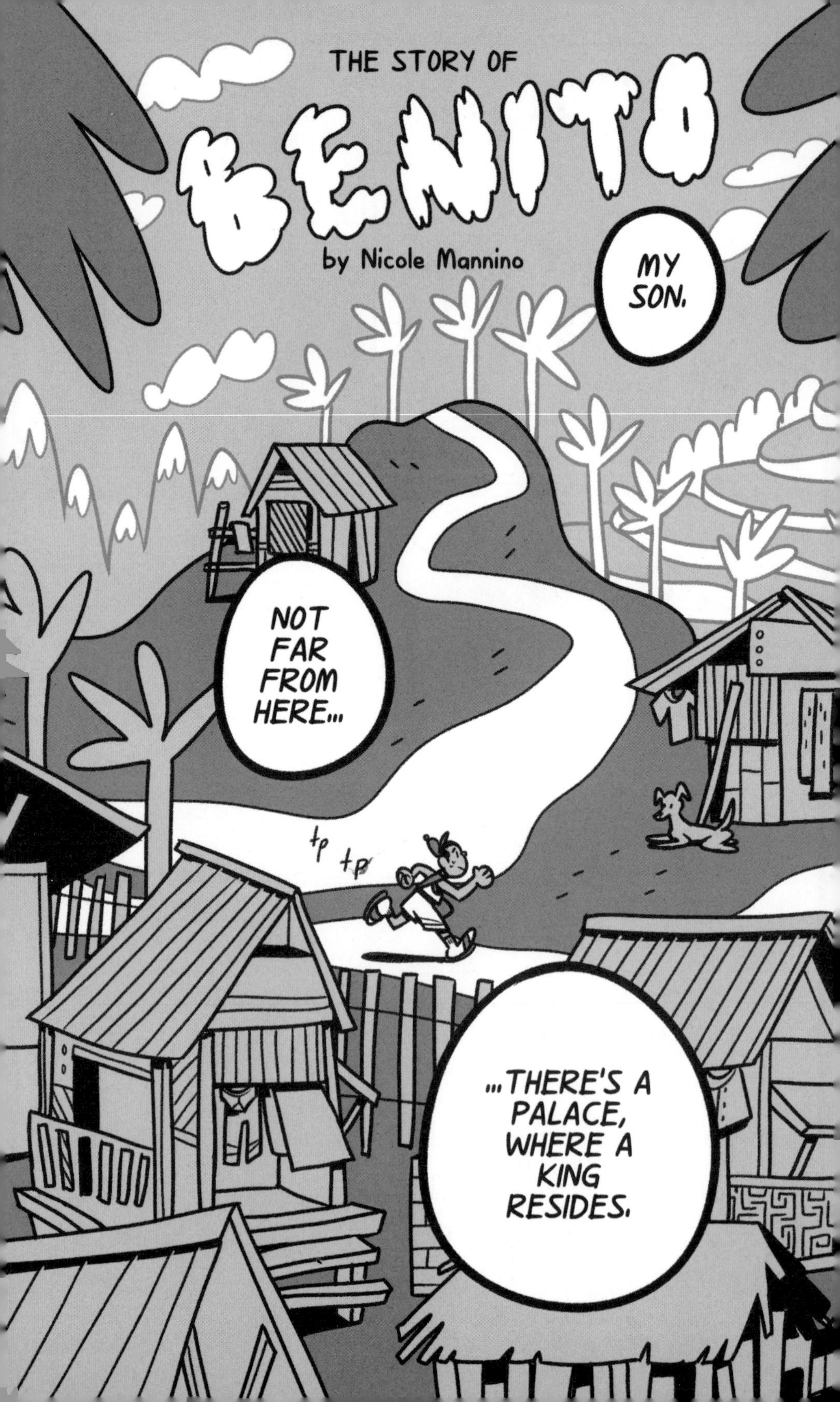
THE STORY OF
BENITO
by Nicole Mannino
MY SON.
NOT FAR FROM HERE...
tp tp
...THERE'S A PALACE, WHERE A KING RESIDES.

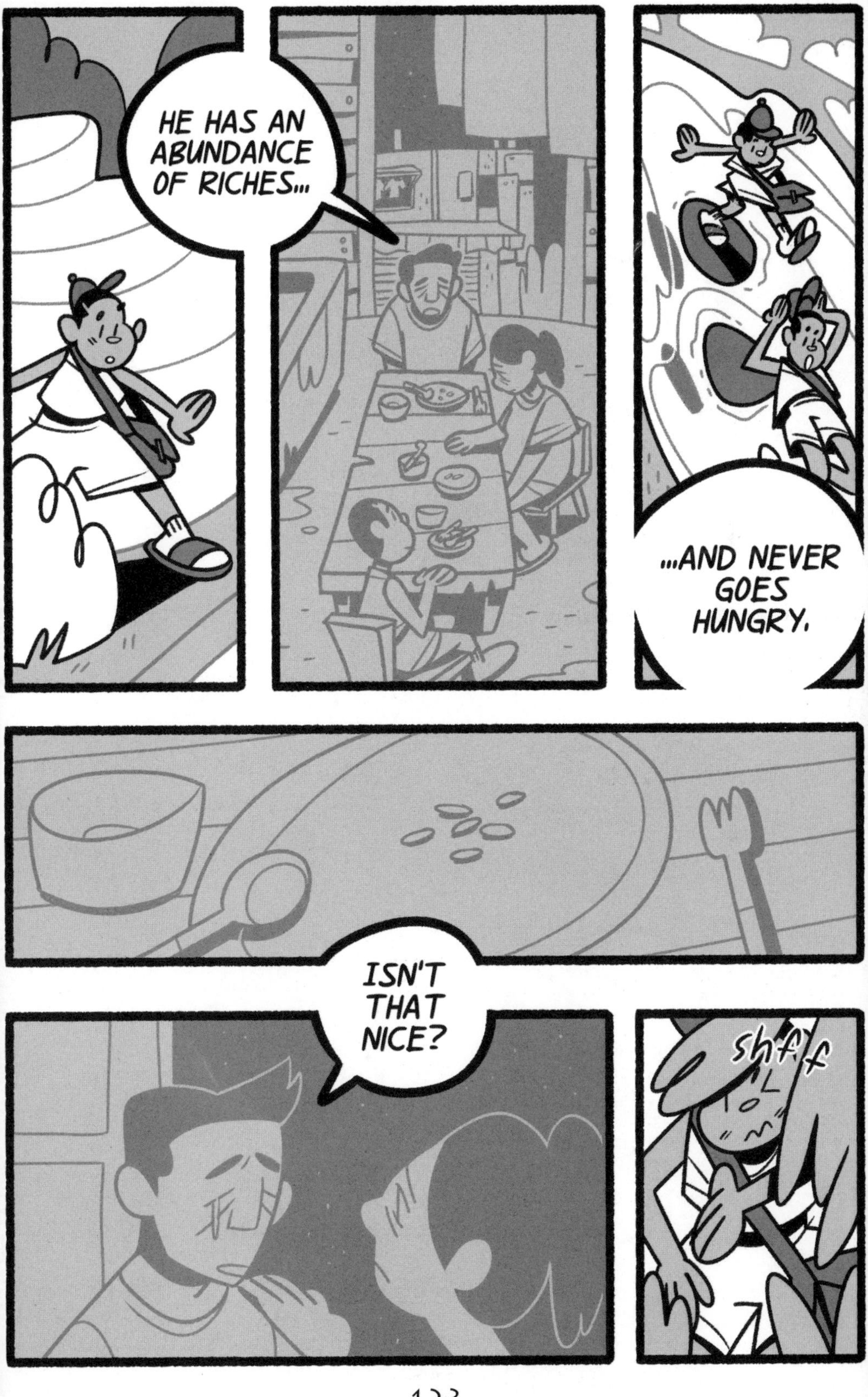
HE HAS AN ABUNDANCE OF RICHES...
...AND NEVER GOES HUNGRY.
ISN'T THAT NICE?
shfff

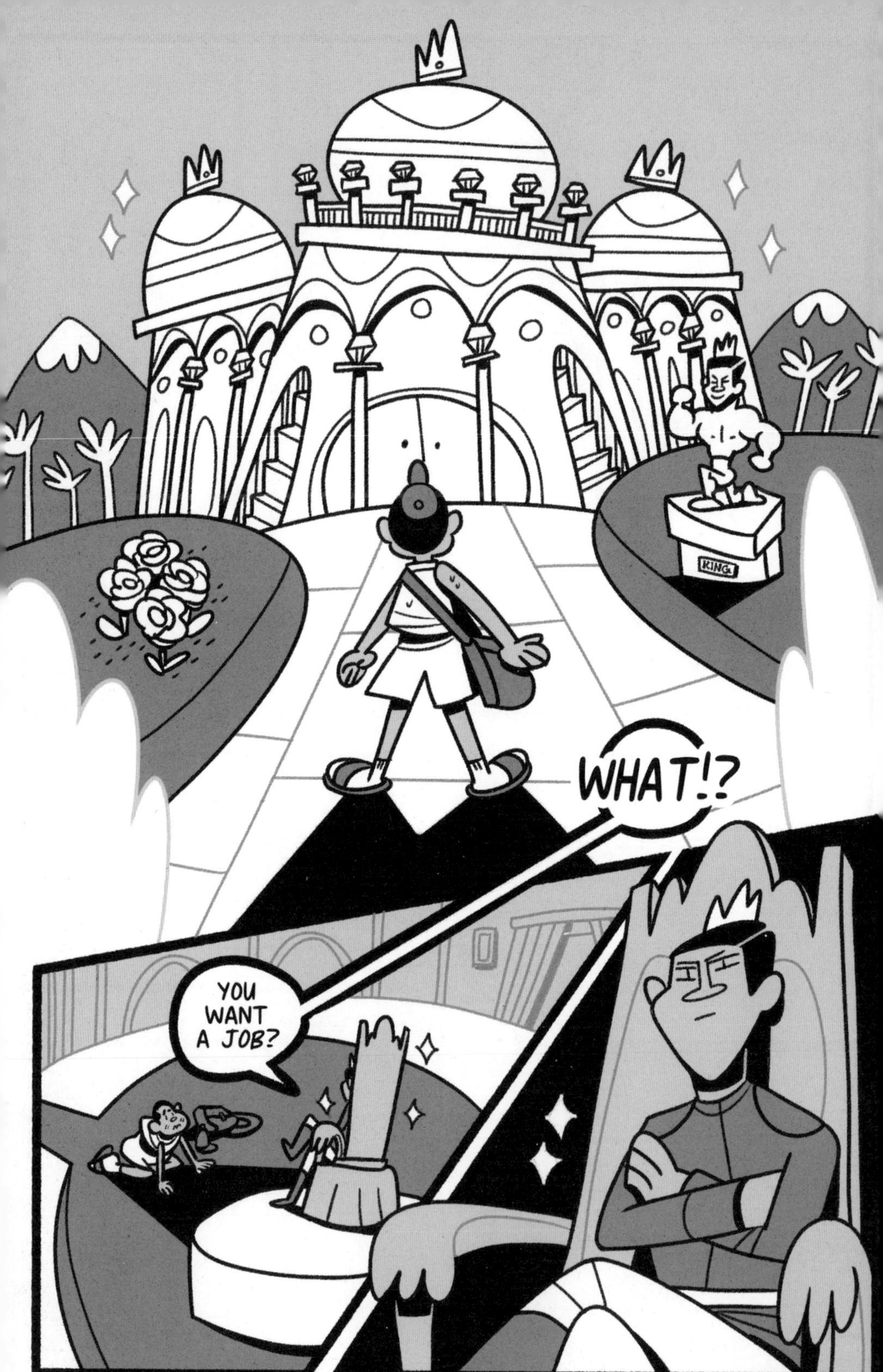
KING
WHAT!?
YOU WANT A JOB?

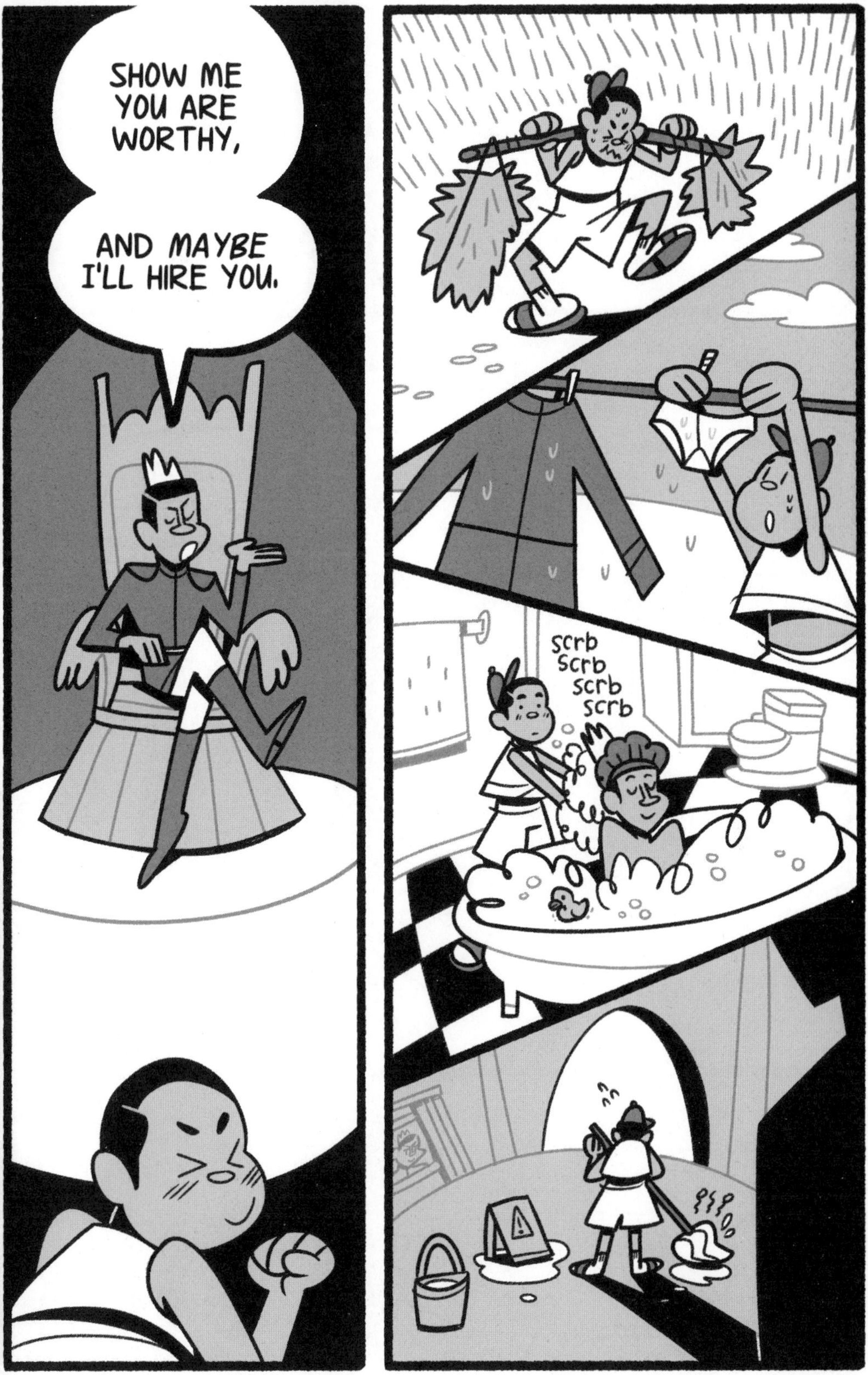
SHOW ME YOU ARE WORTHY,
AND MAYBE I'LL HIRE YOU.
scrb scrb scrb scrb

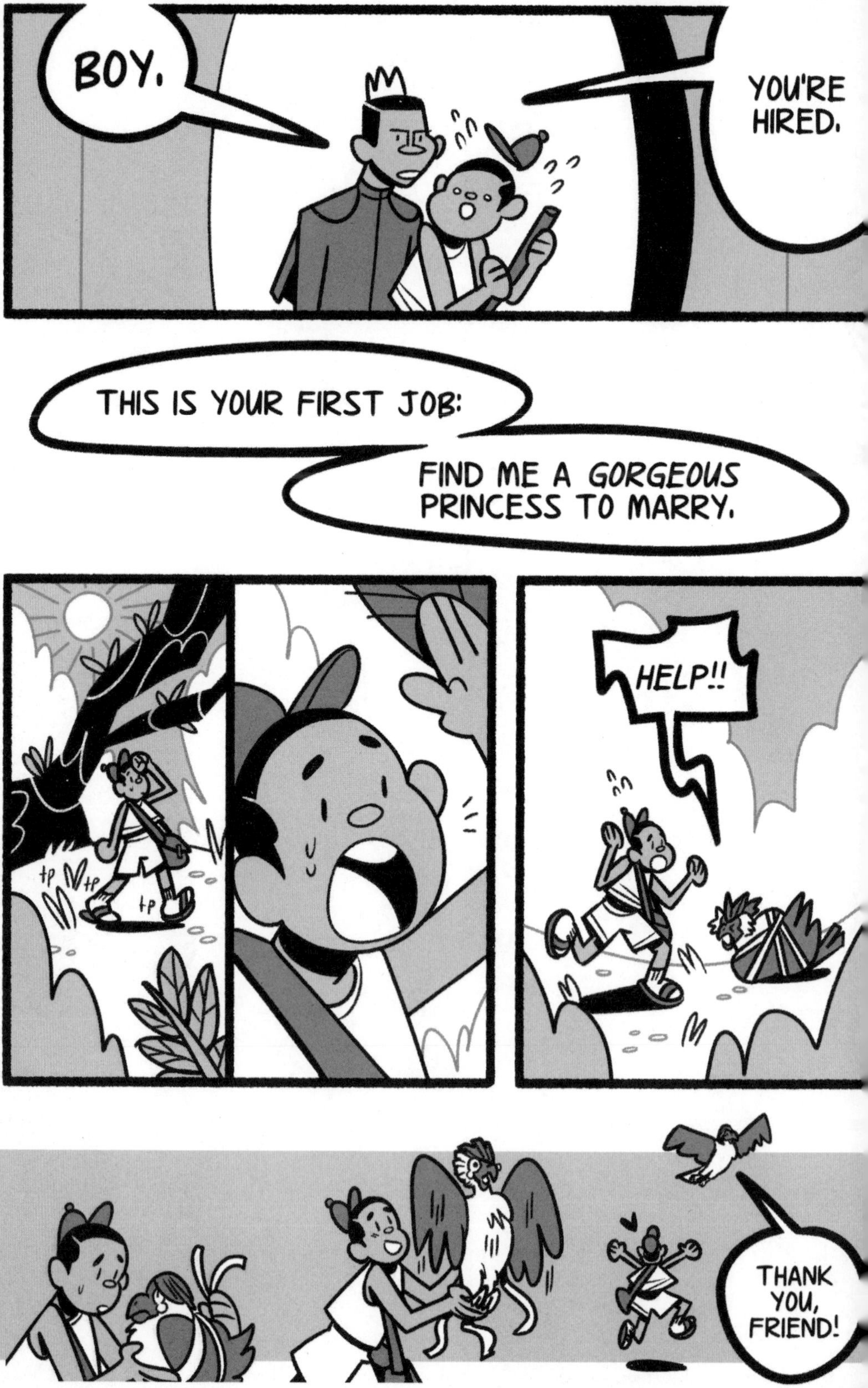
BOY.
YOU'RE HIRED.
THIS IS YOUR FIRST JOB:
FIND ME A *GORGEOUS* PRINCESS TO MARRY.
tp tp tp
HELP!!
THANK YOU, FRIEND!

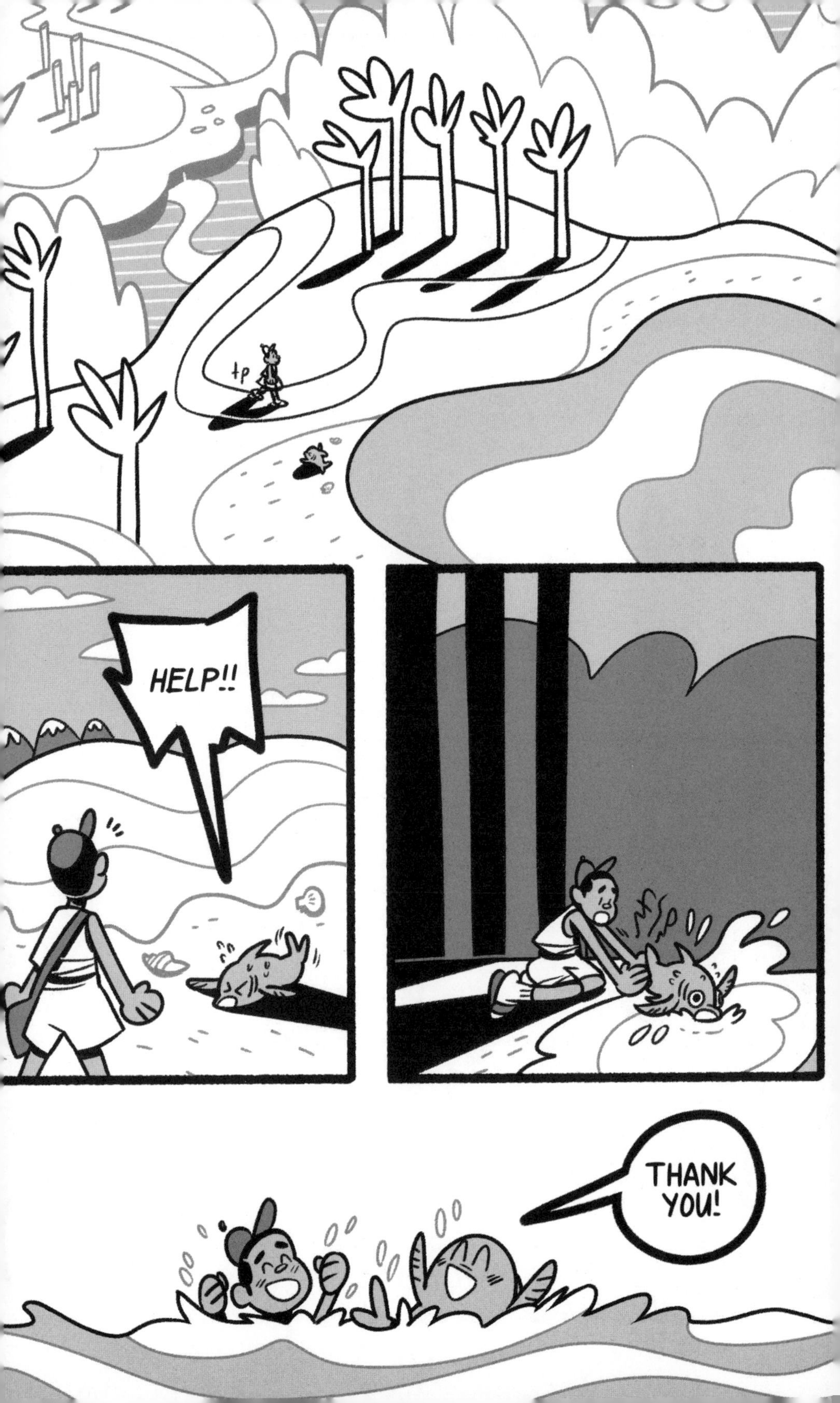

tp
HELP!!
THANK YOU!

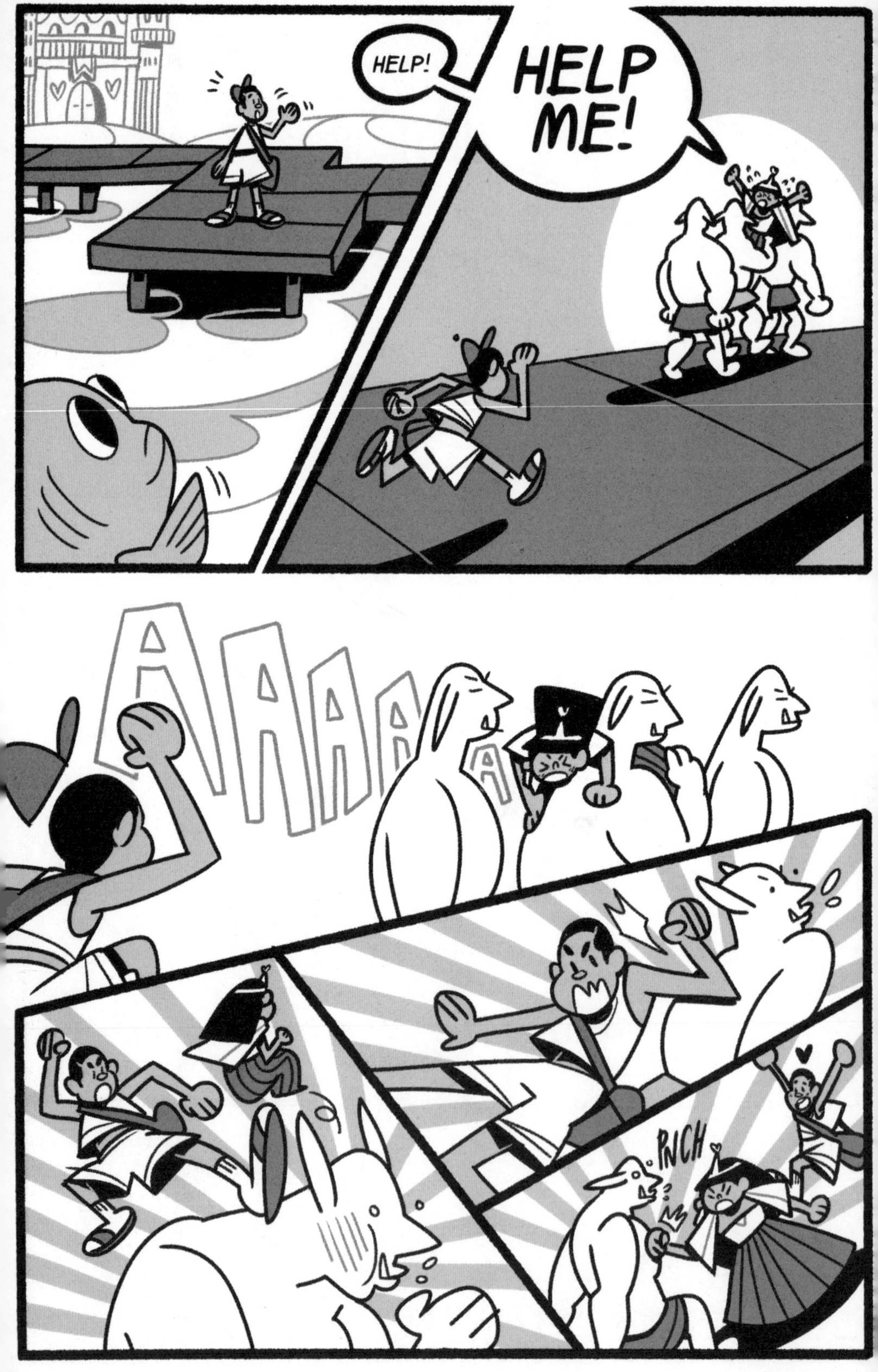
HELP!
HELP ME!
AAAAAA
PNCH

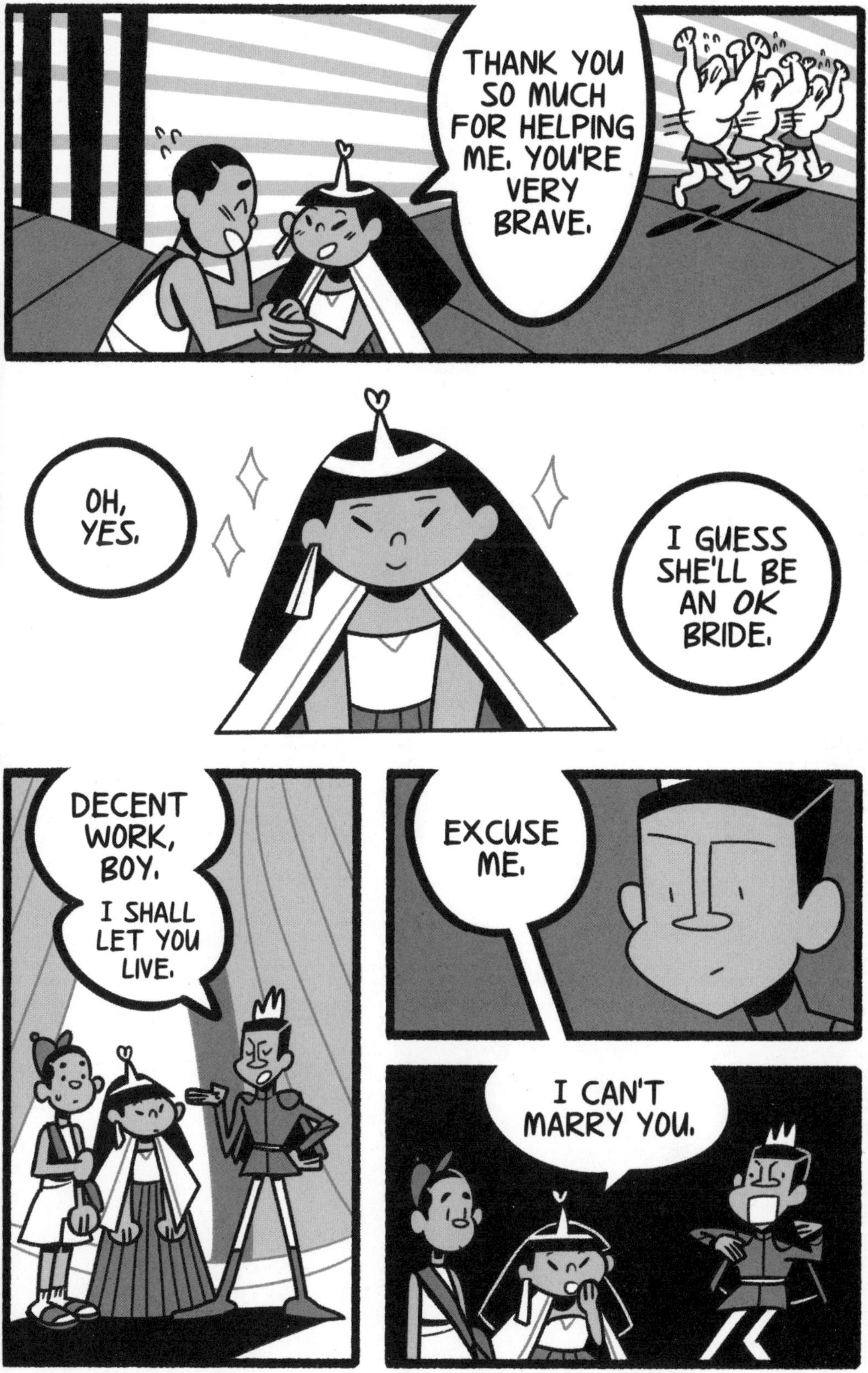
THANK YOU SO MUCH FOR HELPING ME. YOU'RE VERY BRAVE.
OH, YES.
I GUESS SHE'LL BE AN OK BRIDE.
DECENT WORK, BOY.
I SHALL LET YOU LIVE.
EXCUSE ME.
I CAN'T MARRY YOU.

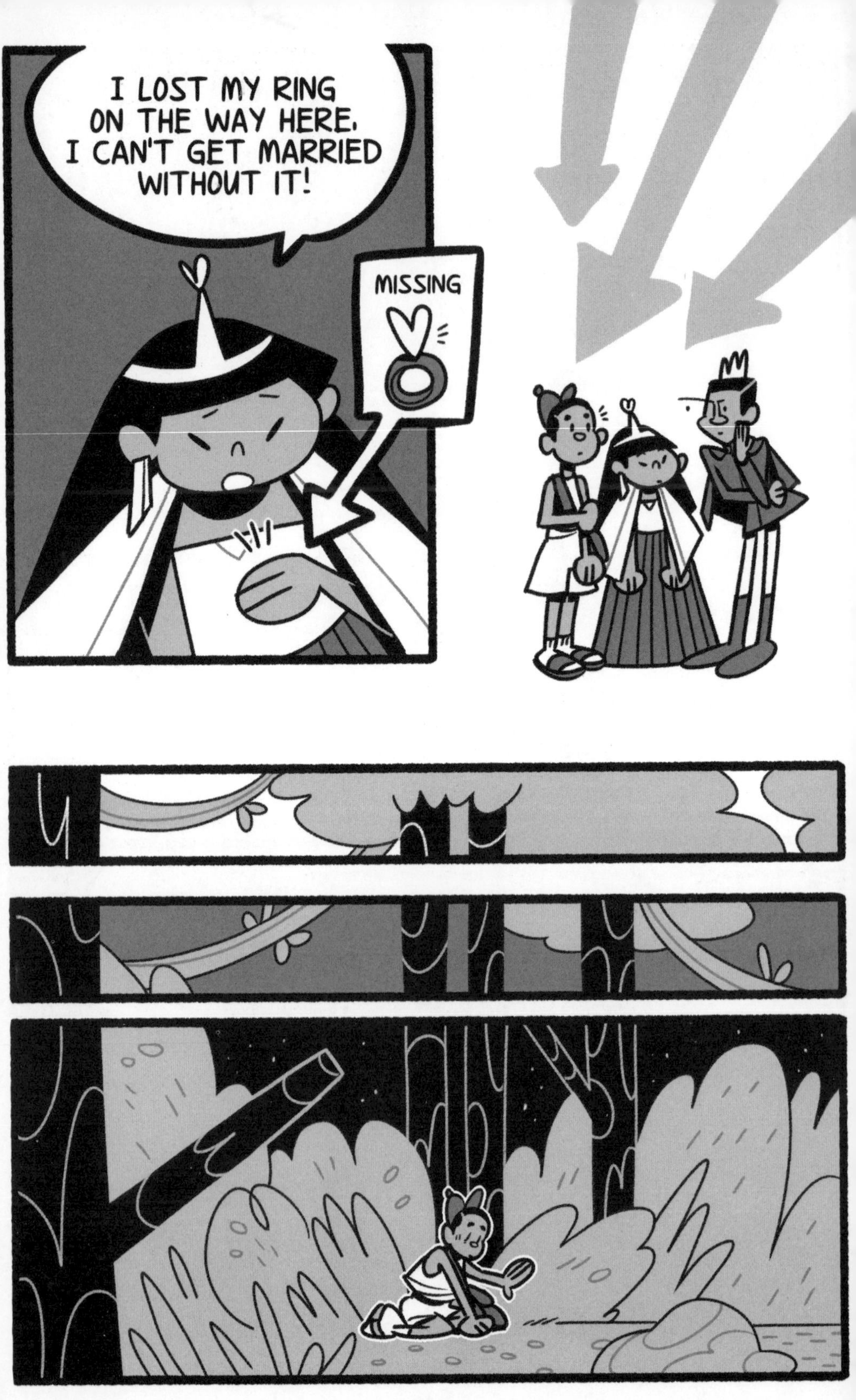
I LOST MY RING ON THE WAY HERE. I CAN'T GET MARRIED WITHOUT IT!
MISSING

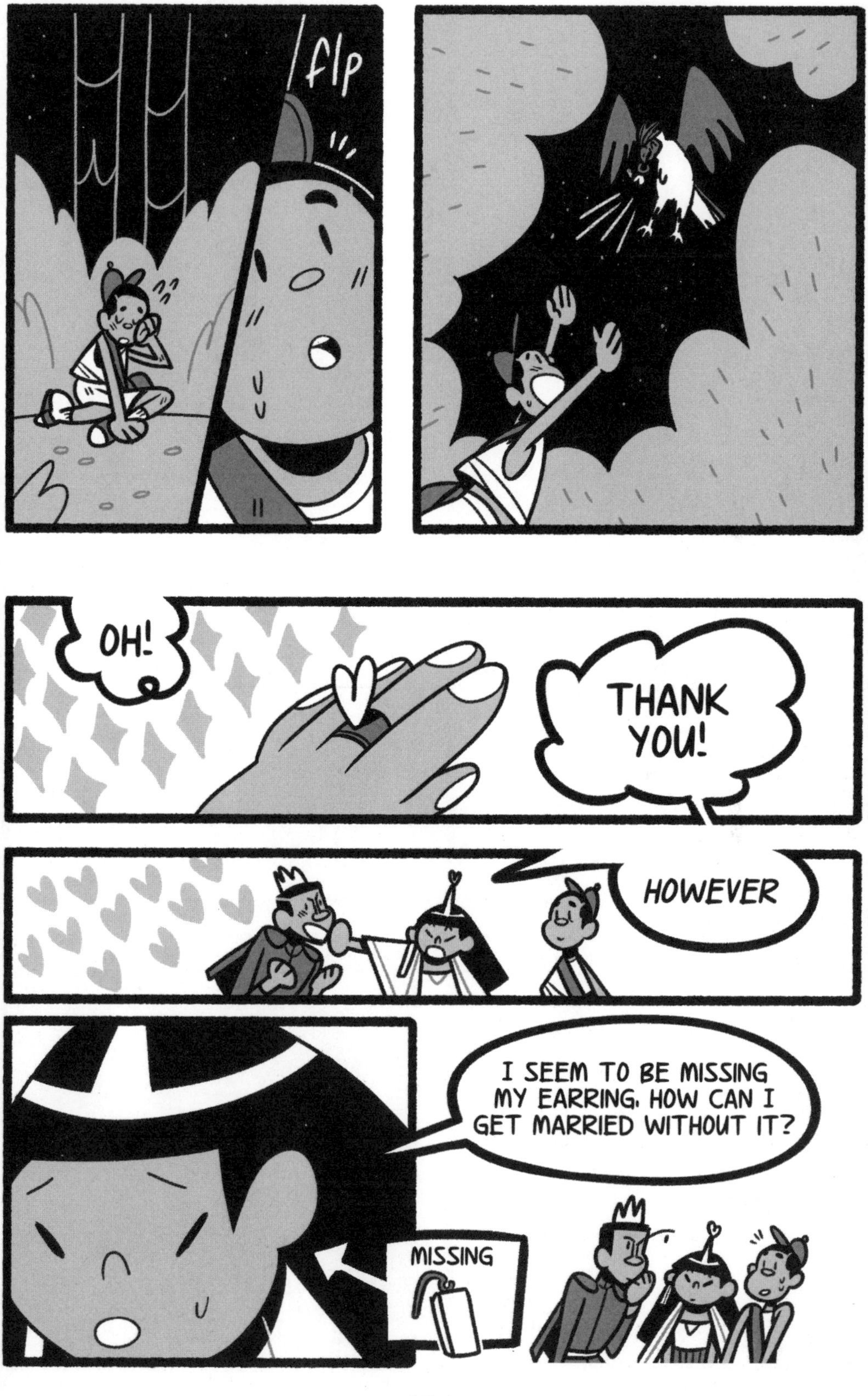
flp
OH!
THANK YOU!
HOWEVER
I SEEM TO BE MISSING MY EARRING. HOW CAN I GET MARRIED WITHOUT IT?
MISSING

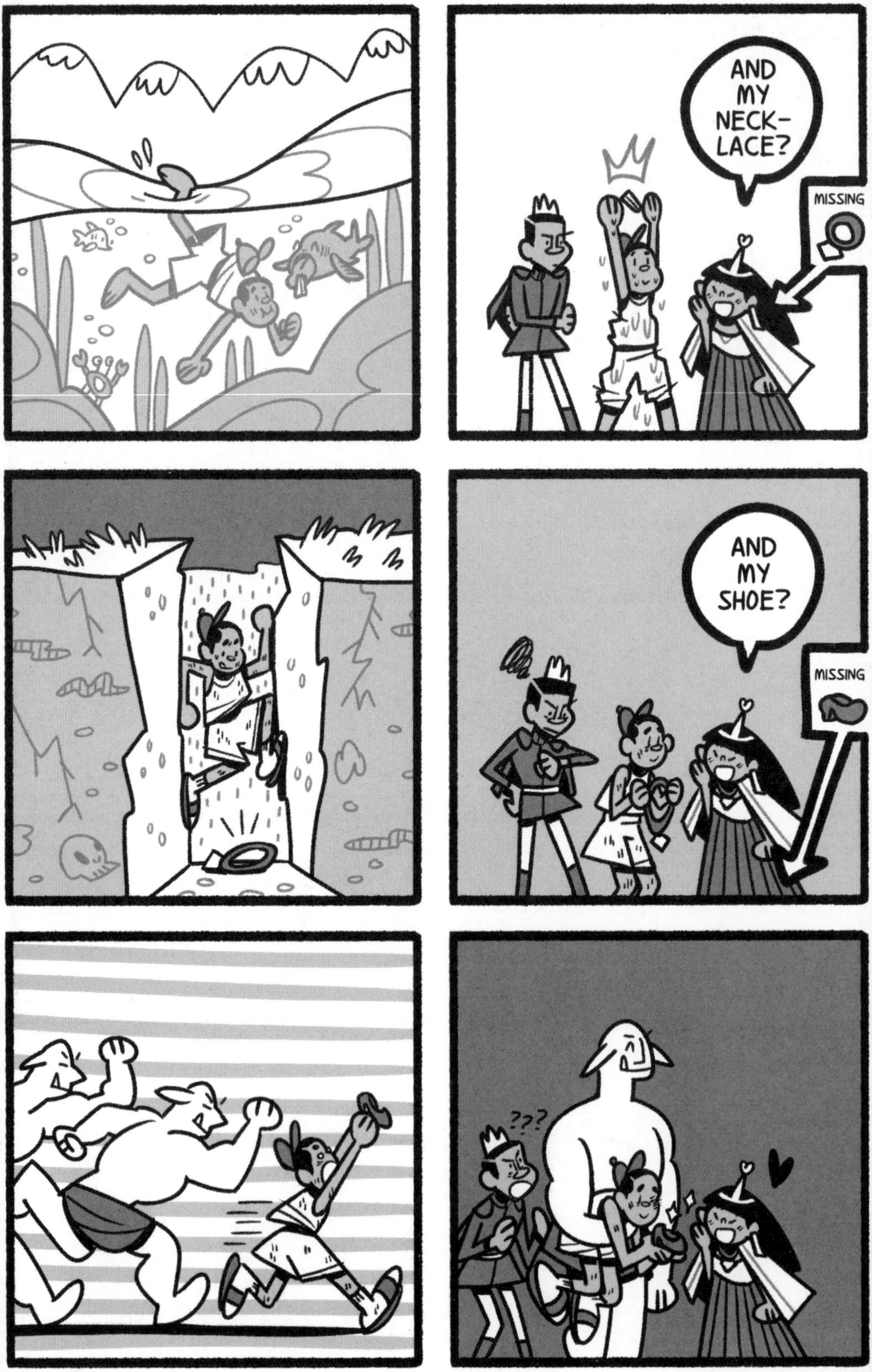
AND MY NECK-LACE?
MISSING
AND MY SHOE?
MISSING
???

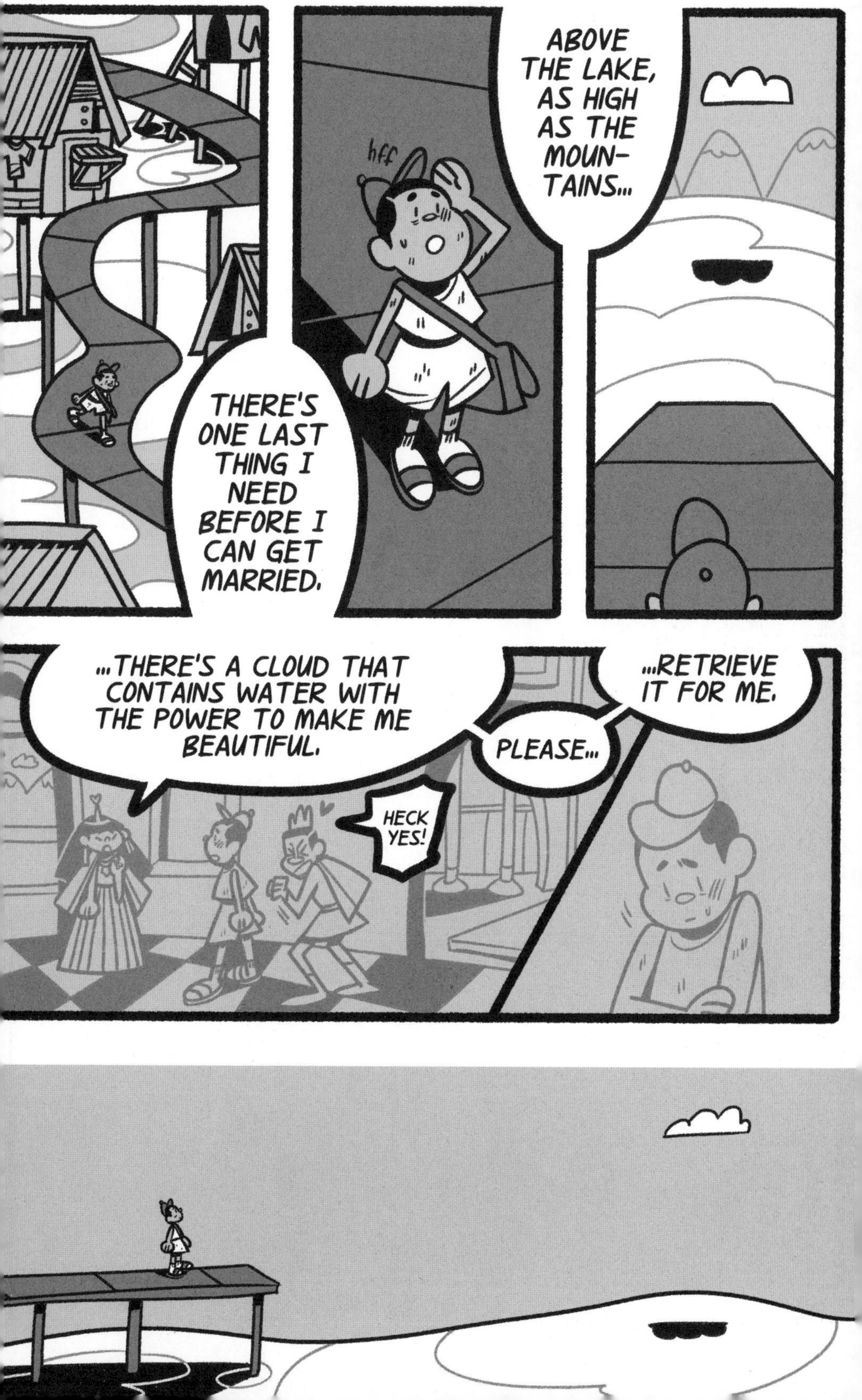
hff
THERE'S ONE LAST THING I NEED BEFORE I CAN GET MARRIED.
ABOVE THE LAKE, AS HIGH AS THE MOUN-TAINS...
...THERE'S A CLOUD THAT CONTAINS WATER WITH THE POWER TO MAKE ME BEAUTIFUL.
HECK YES!
PLEASE...
...RETRIEVE IT FOR ME.

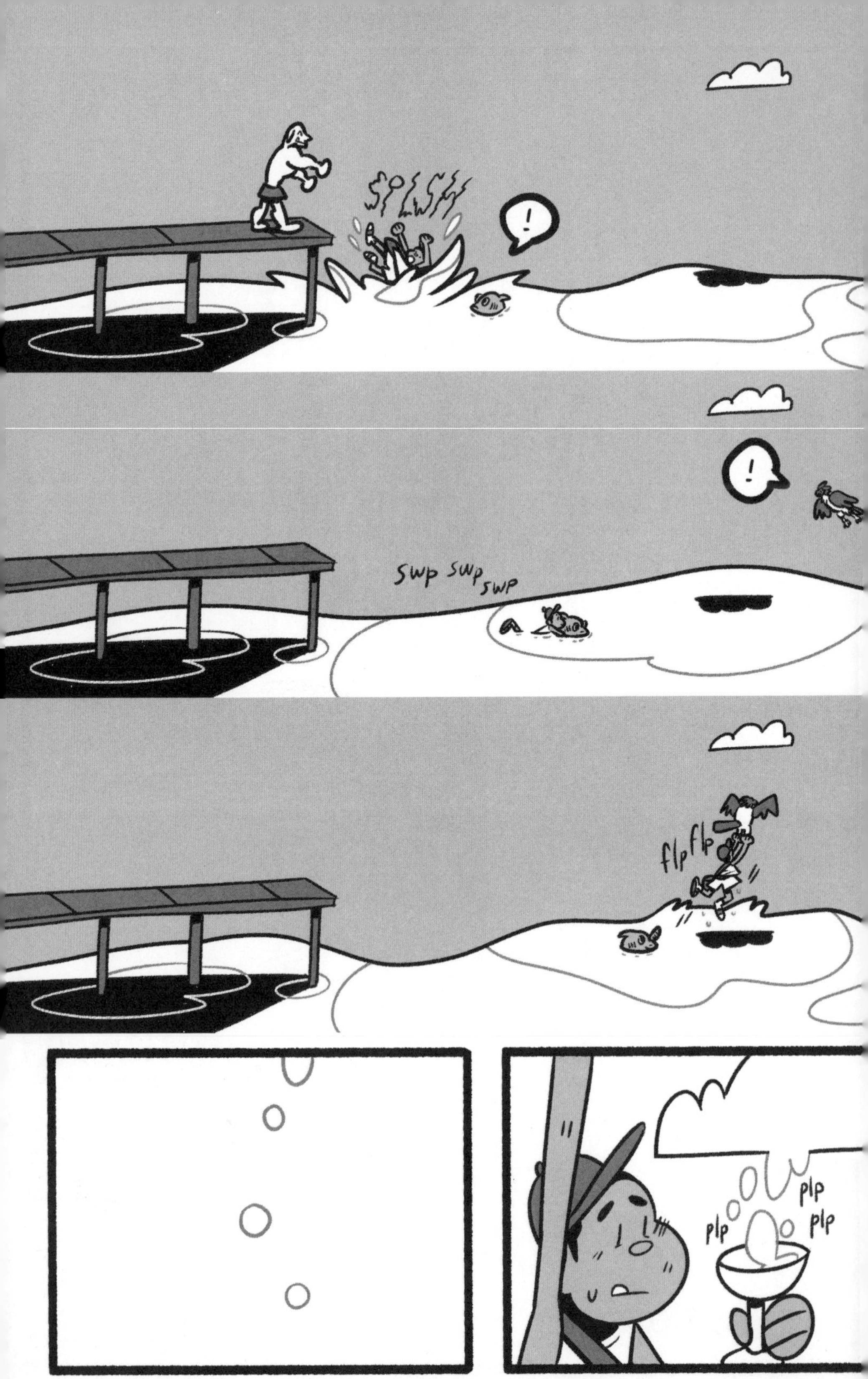
!
!
swp swp swp
flp flp
plp
plp
plp

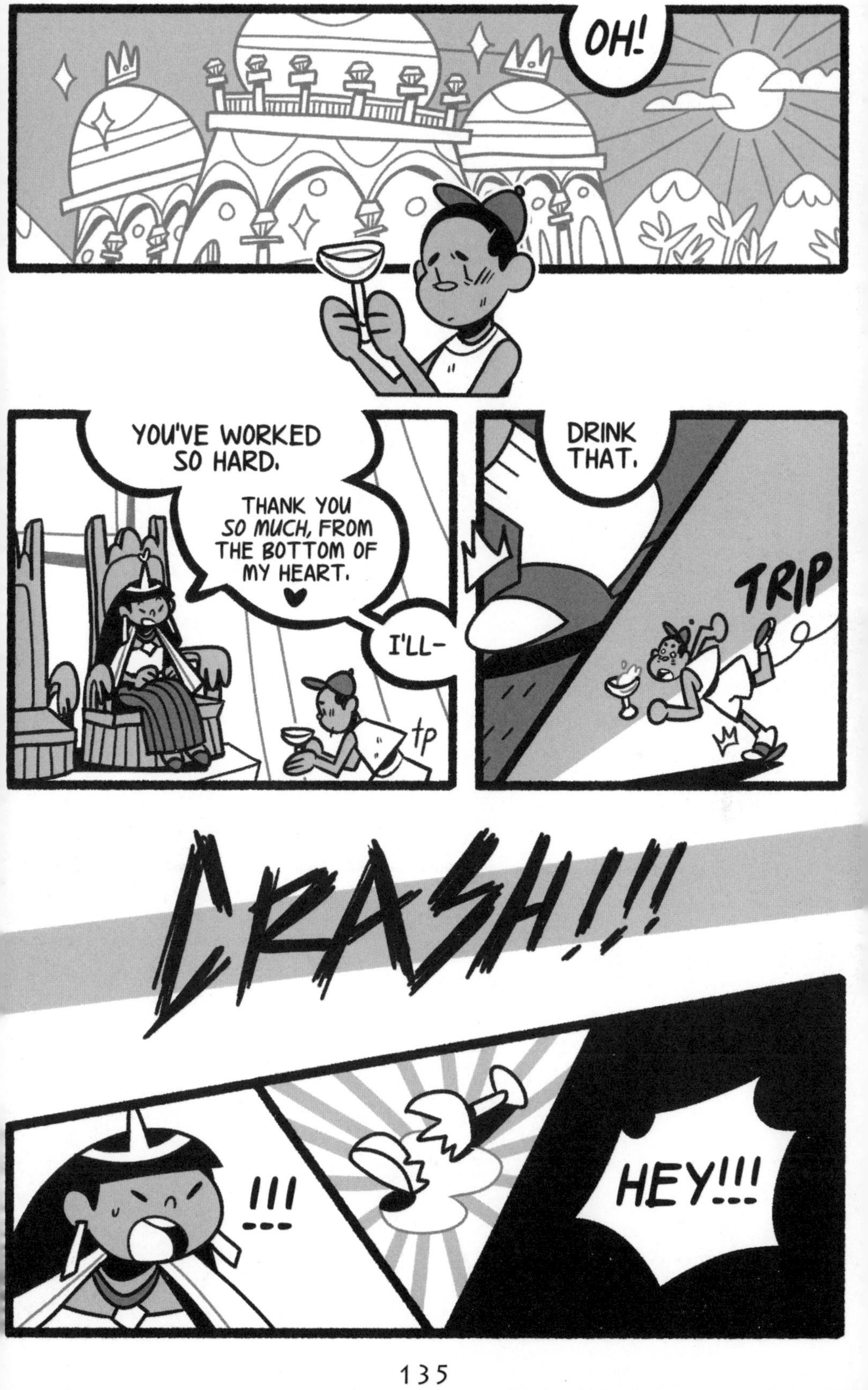
OH!
YOU'VE WORKED SO HARD.
THANK YOU SO MUCH, FROM THE BOTTOM OF MY HEART.
I'LL-
tp
DRINK THAT.
TRIP
CRASH!!!
!!!
HEY!!!

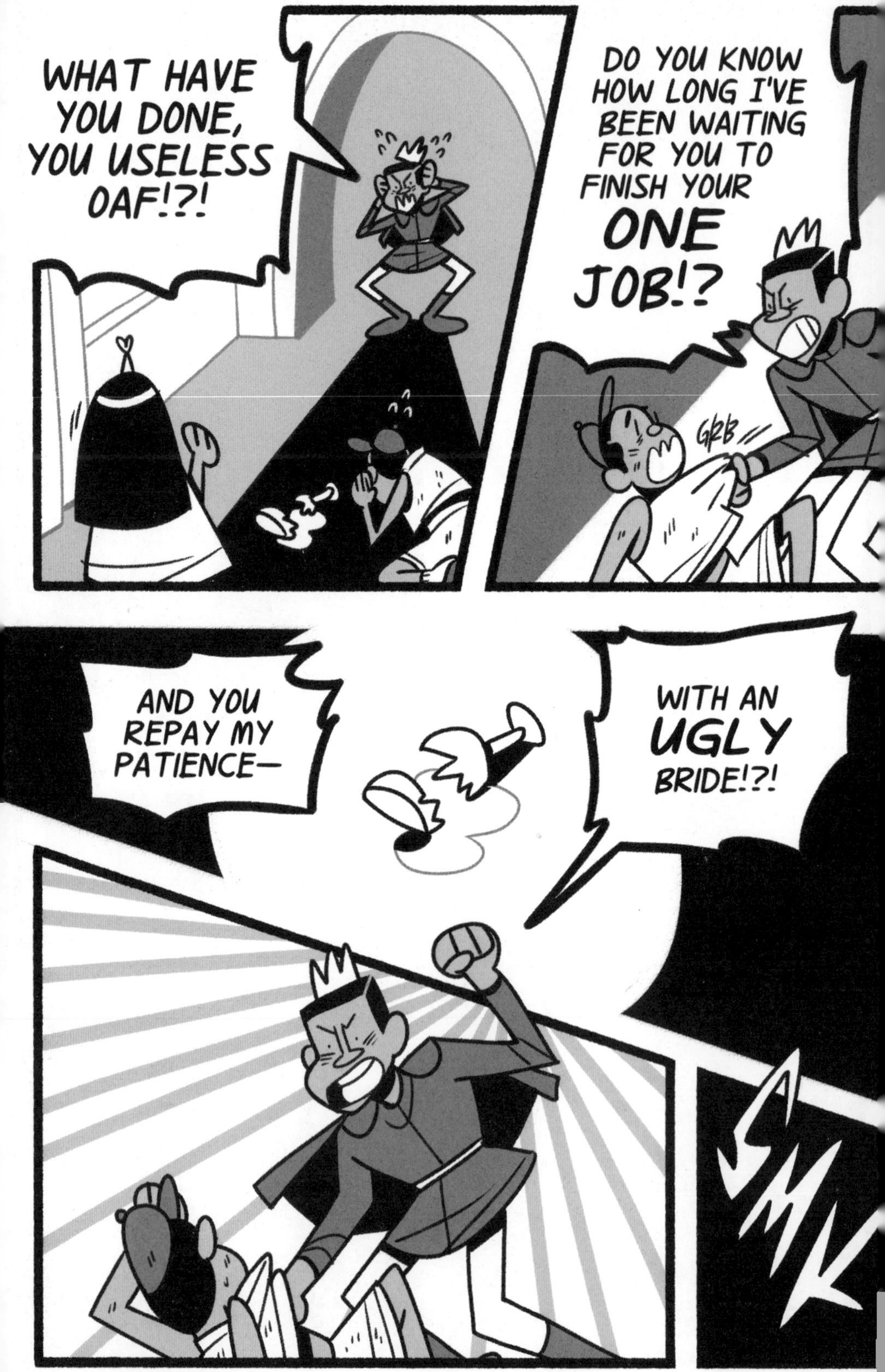
WHAT HAVE YOU DONE, YOU USELESS OAF!?!
DO YOU KNOW HOW LONG I'VE BEEN WAITING FOR YOU TO FINISH YOUR ONE JOB!?
GRB
AND YOU REPAY MY PATIENCE—
WITH AN UGLY BRIDE!?!
SMK

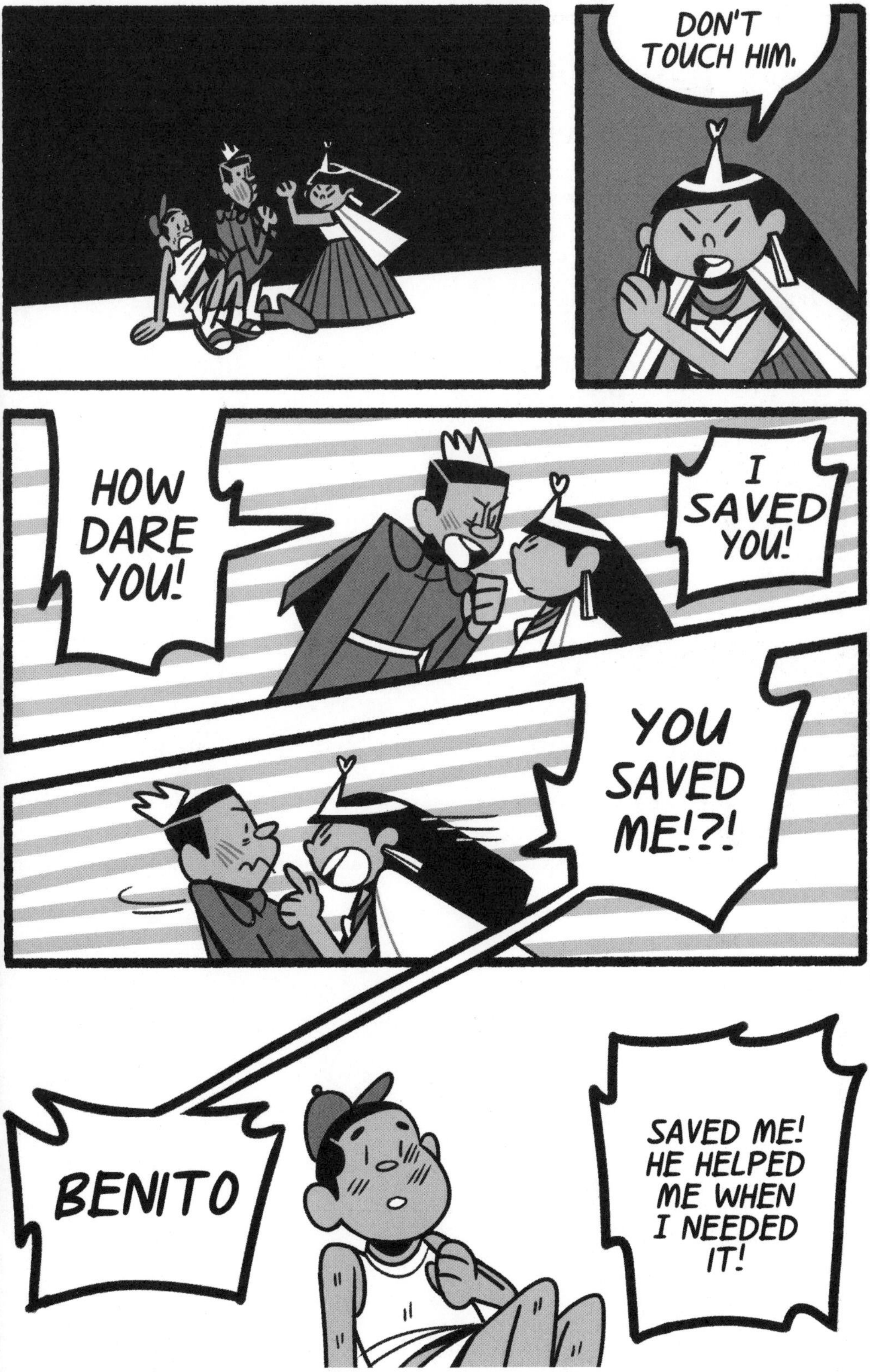

DON'T TOUCH HIM.
HOW DARE YOU!
I SAVED YOU!
YOU SAVED ME!?!
BENITO
SAVED ME! HE HELPED ME WHEN I NEEDED IT!

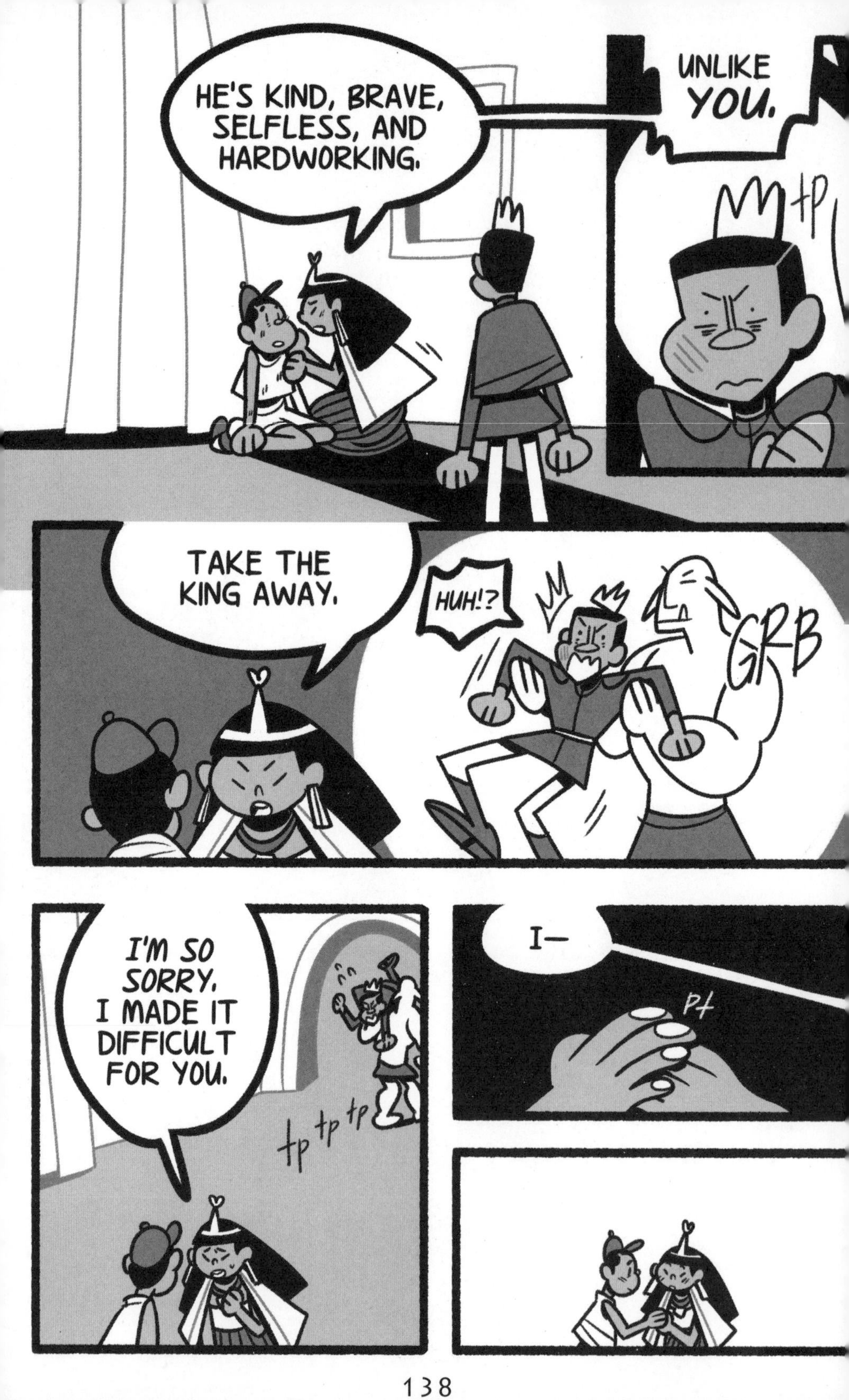
HE'S KIND, BRAVE, SELFLESS, AND HARDWORKING.
UNLIKE YOU.
tp
TAKE THE KING AWAY.
HUH!?
GRB
I'M SO SORRY. I MADE IT DIFFICULT FOR YOU.
tp tp tp
I—
pt

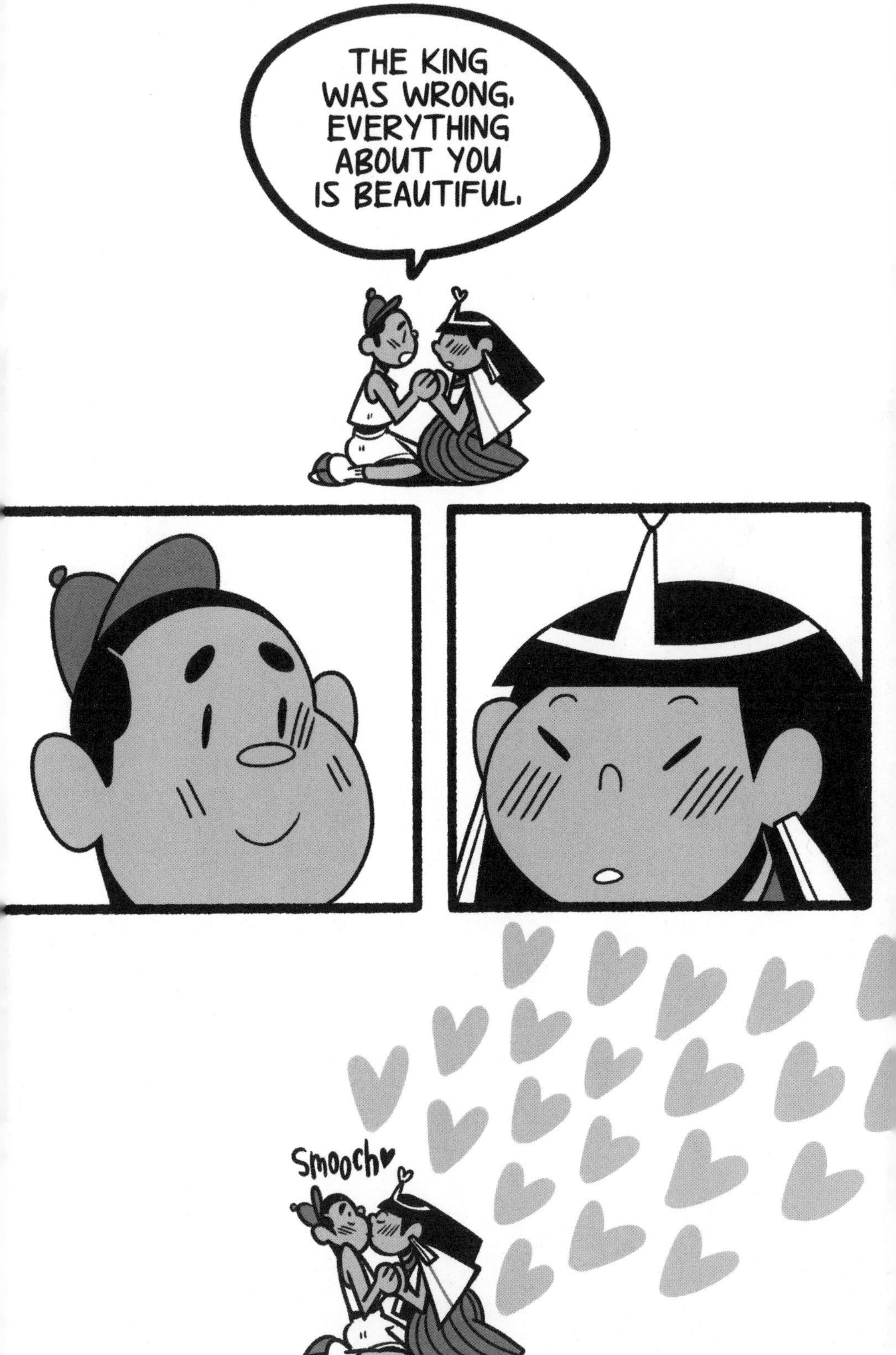
THE KING WAS WRONG. EVERYTHING ABOUT YOU IS BEAUTIFUL.
Smooch♥

NOT FAR FROM HERE, THERE'S A PALACE
WHERE A KING RESIDES.
HE HAS AN ABUNDANCE OF RICHES
AND NEVER GOES HUNGRY.

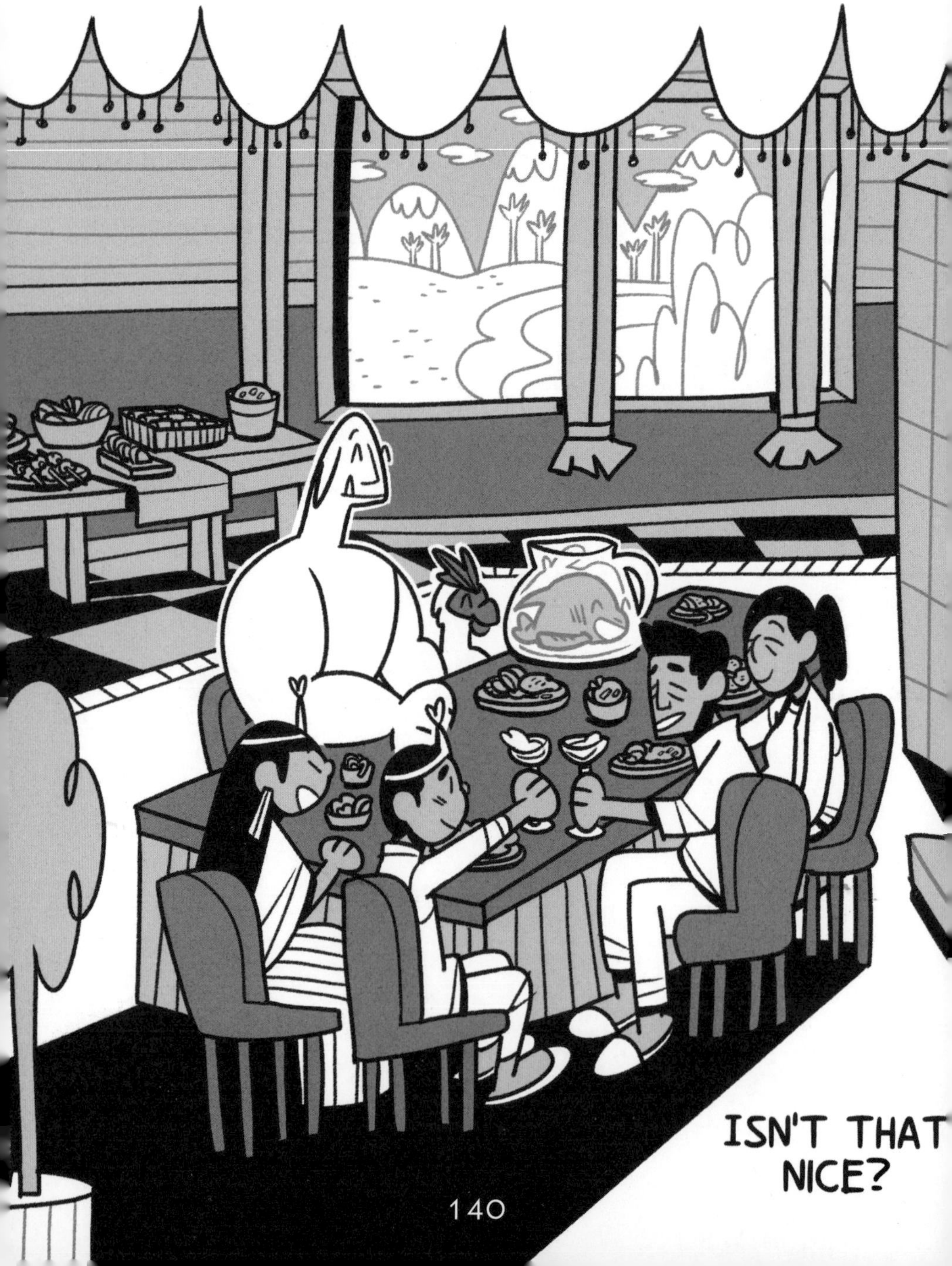
ISN'T THAT NICE?

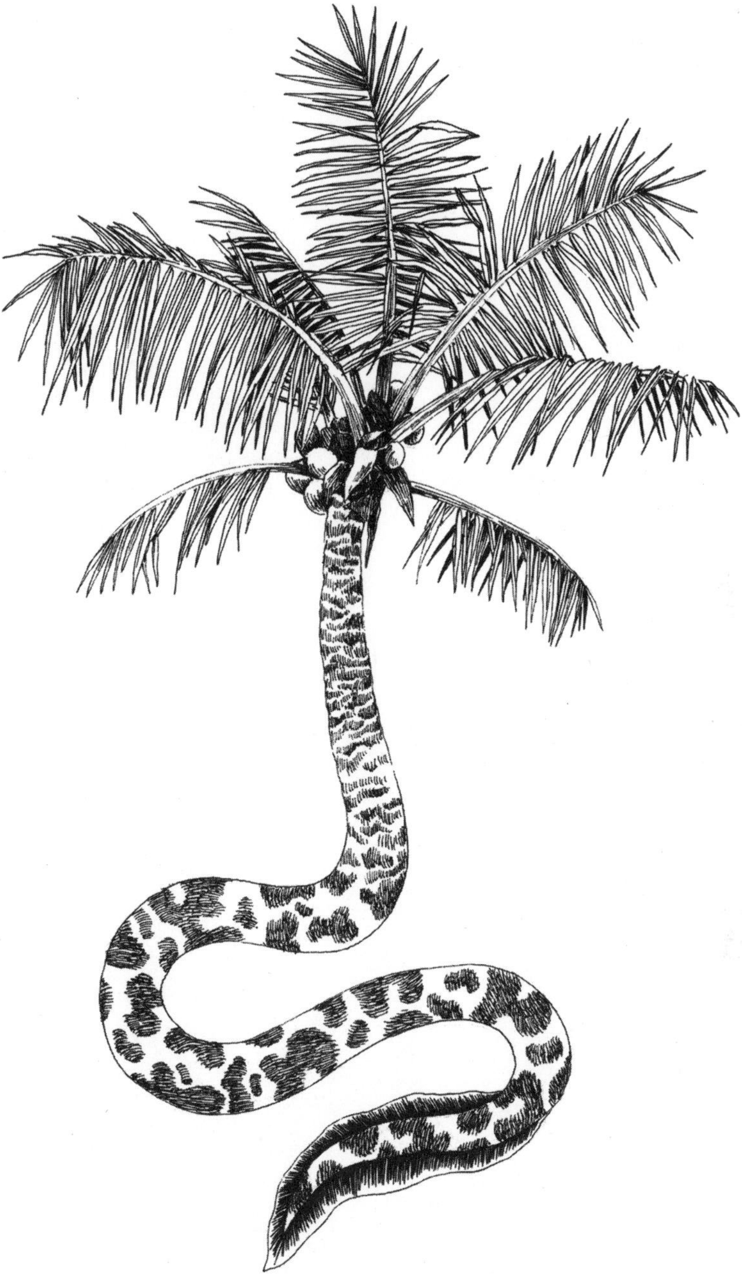

THE LEGEND OF THE COCONUT TREE

By Yiling Changues

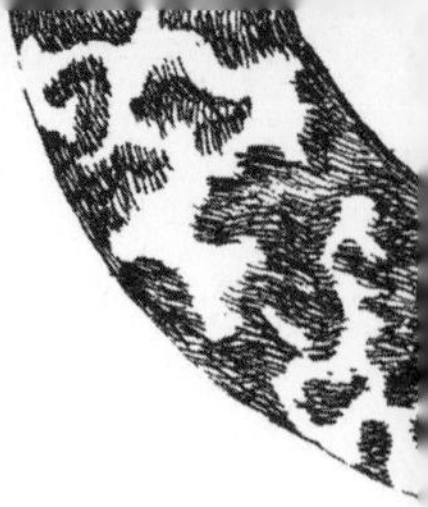

SHE WAS BEAUTIFUL

*TIARE** IN HER LONG DARK HAIR
COPPER TONE SKIN

SHE WAS TO MARRY
TO ME

A PRINCESS
OF LAND BEAUTY
FOR THE KING
OF LAKE VAIHIRIA

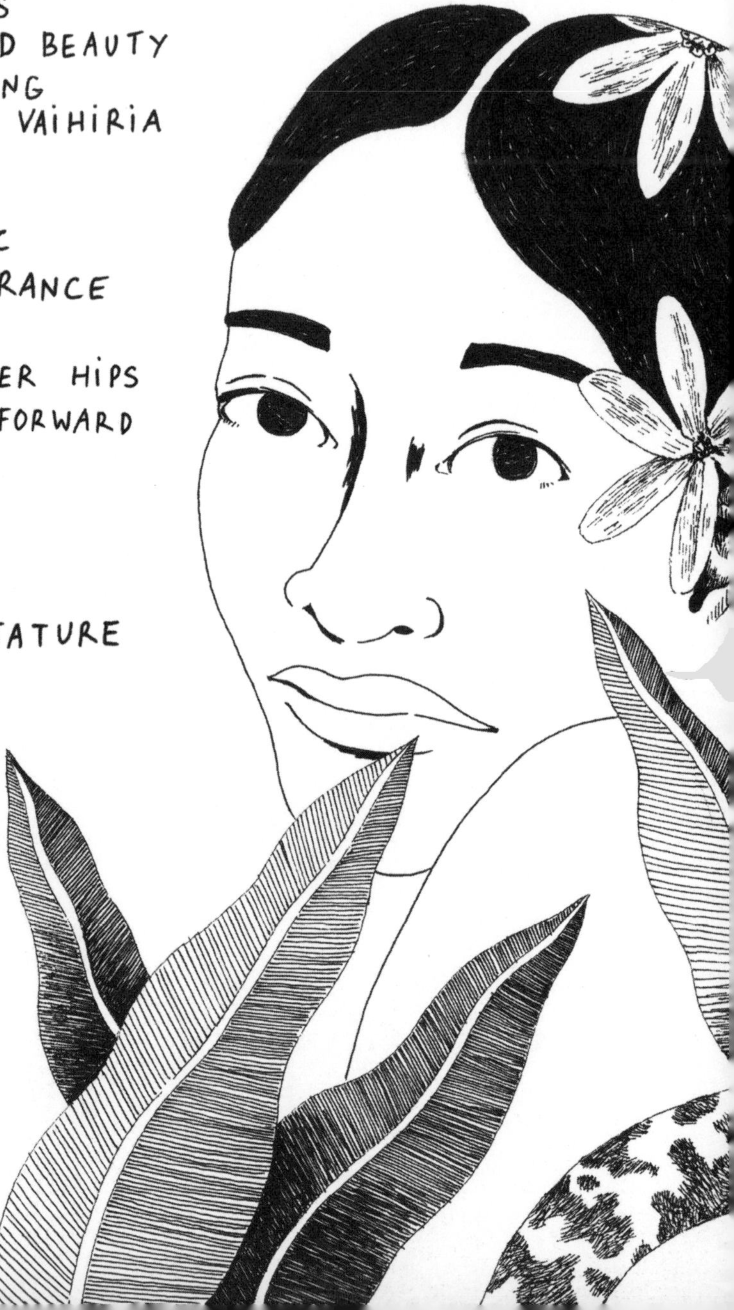

HER HYPNOTIC
FRAGRANCE
THE *TAPA**
WAVING ON HER HIPS
AS SHE CAME FORWARD

DEEP EYES
FULL LIPS
PROUD STATURE

MY FUTURE
WIFE

* *Tiare : tahitian flower*
Tapa : traditional cloth made out of tree bark

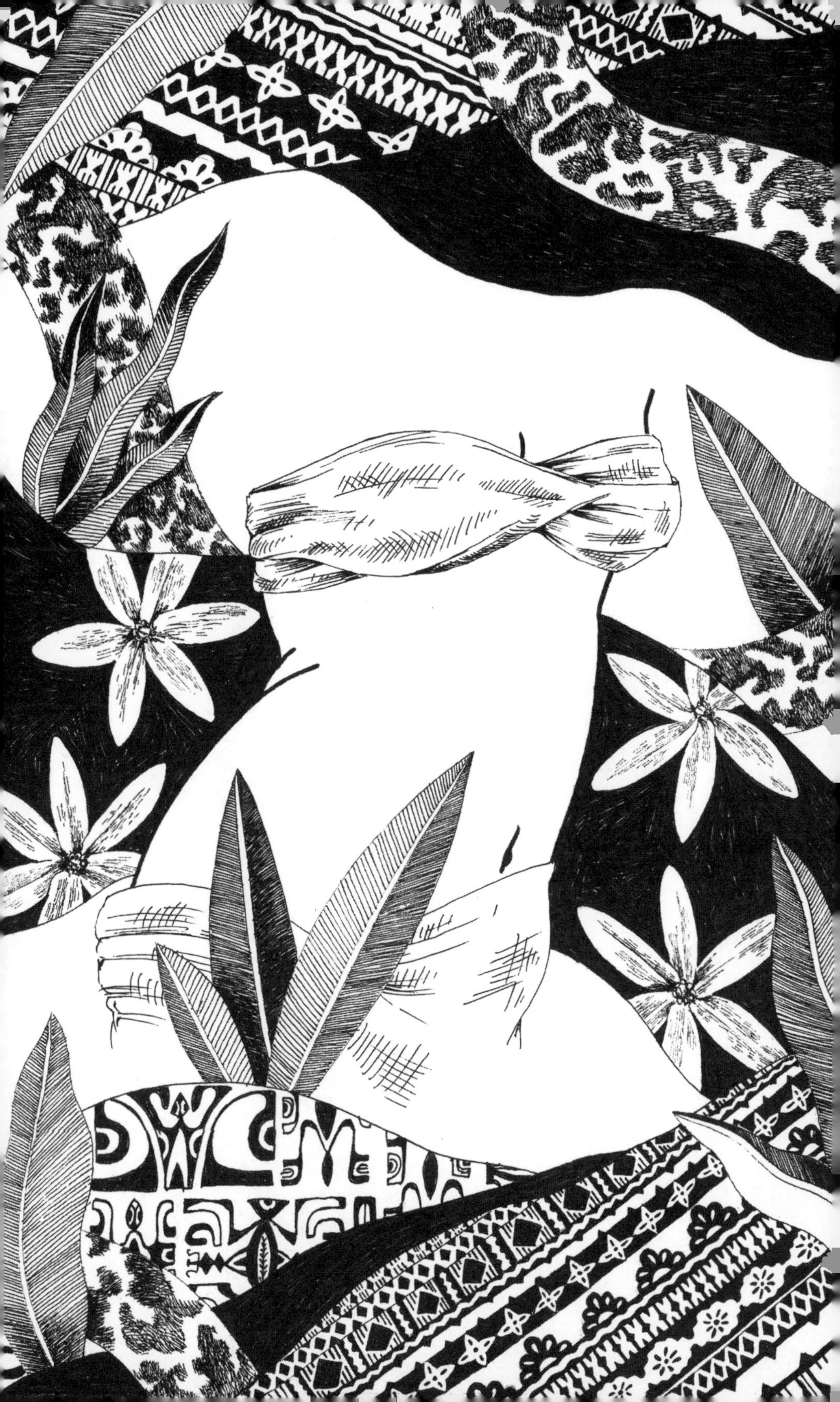

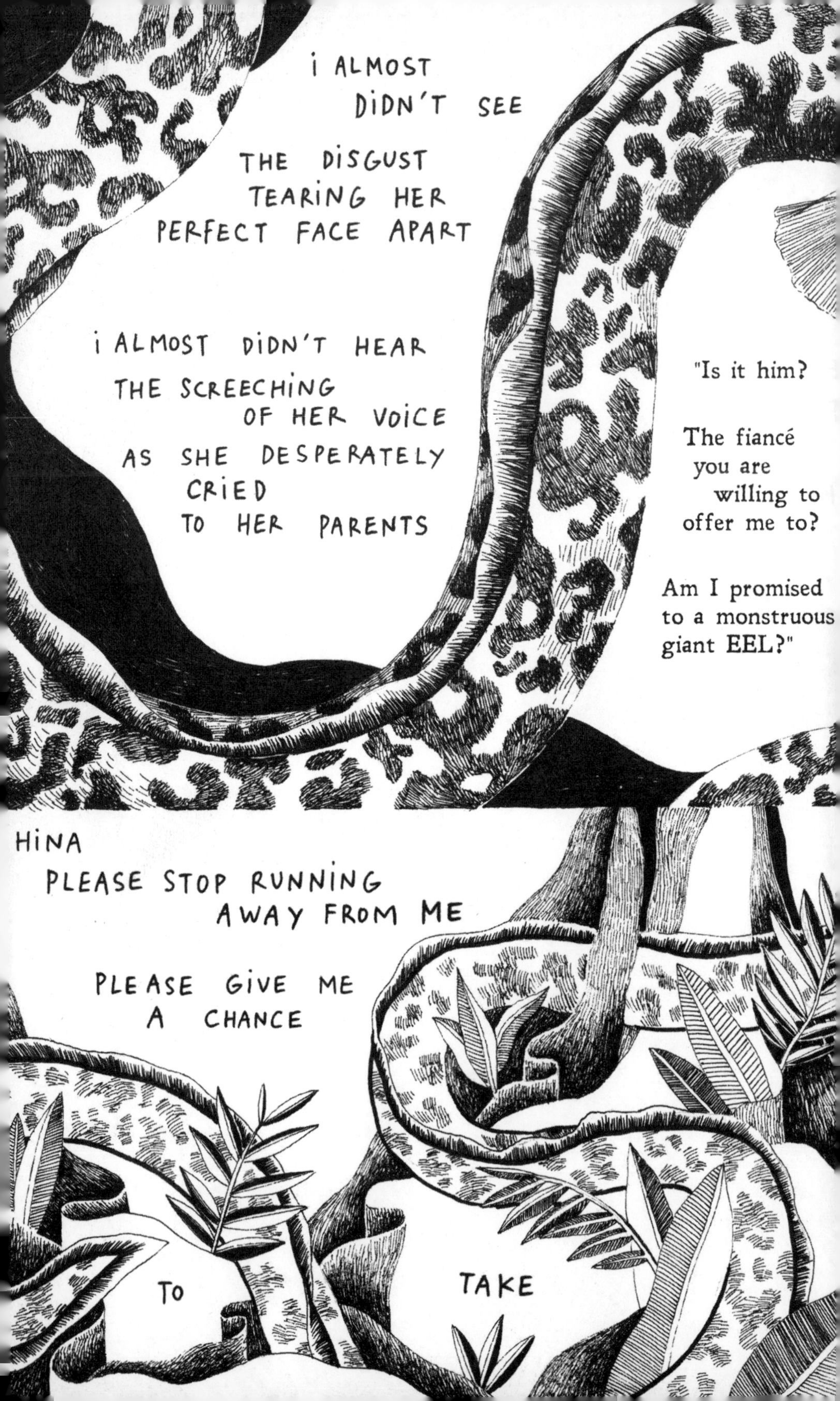
I ALMOST DIDN'T SEE
THE DISGUST TEARING HER PERFECT FACE APART
I ALMOST DIDN'T HEAR THE SCREECHING OF HER VOICE AS SHE DESPERATELY CRIED TO HER PARENTS
"Is it him?
The fiancé you are willing to offer me to?
Am I promised to a monstruous giant EEL?"
HINA PLEASE STOP RUNNING AWAY FROM ME
PLEASE GIVE ME A CHANCE
TO
TAKE

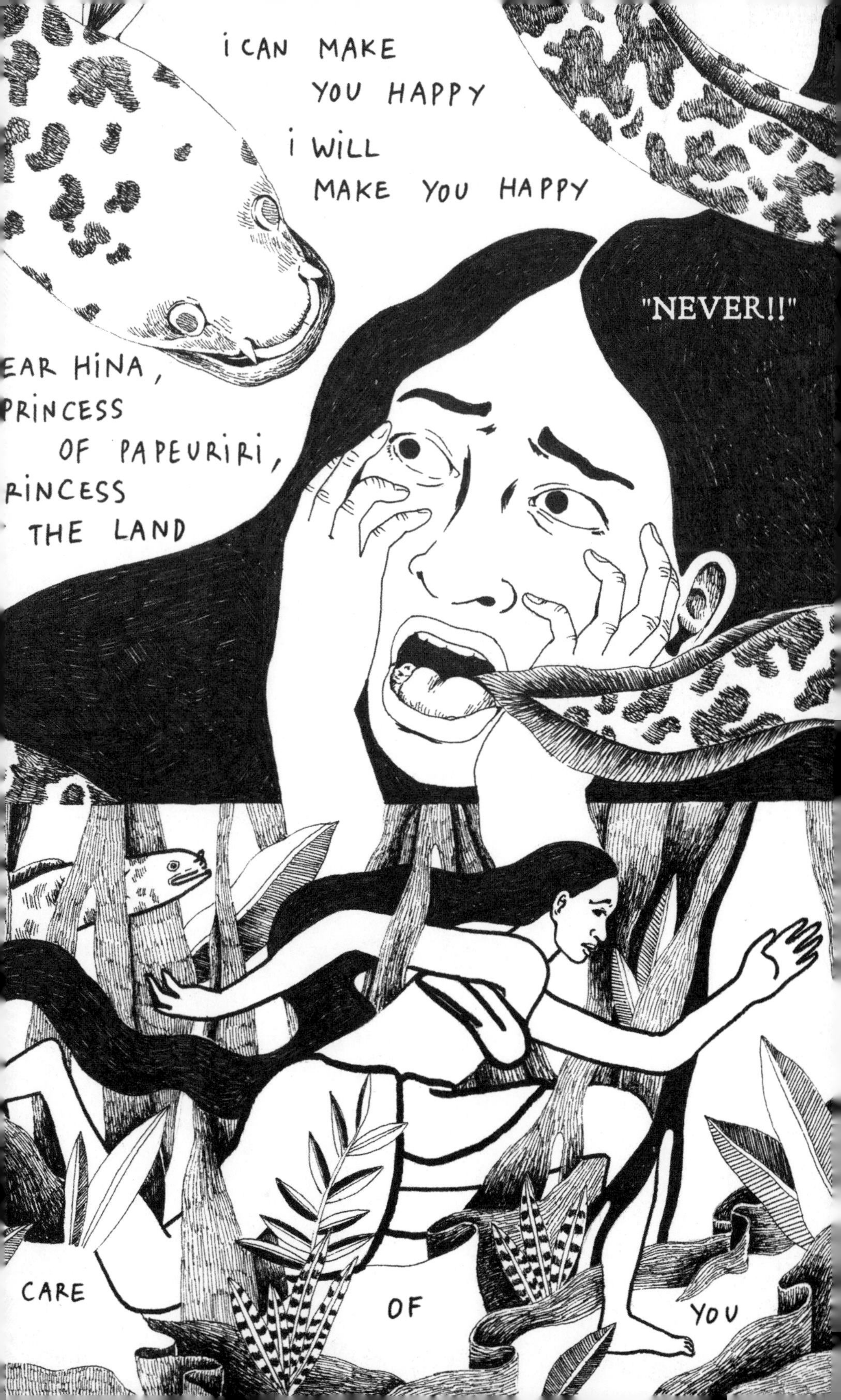
I CAN MAKE YOU HAPPY
I WILL MAKE YOU HAPPY
"NEVER!!"
EAR HINA, PRINCESS OF PAPEURIRI, RINCESS THE LAND
CARE
OF
YOU

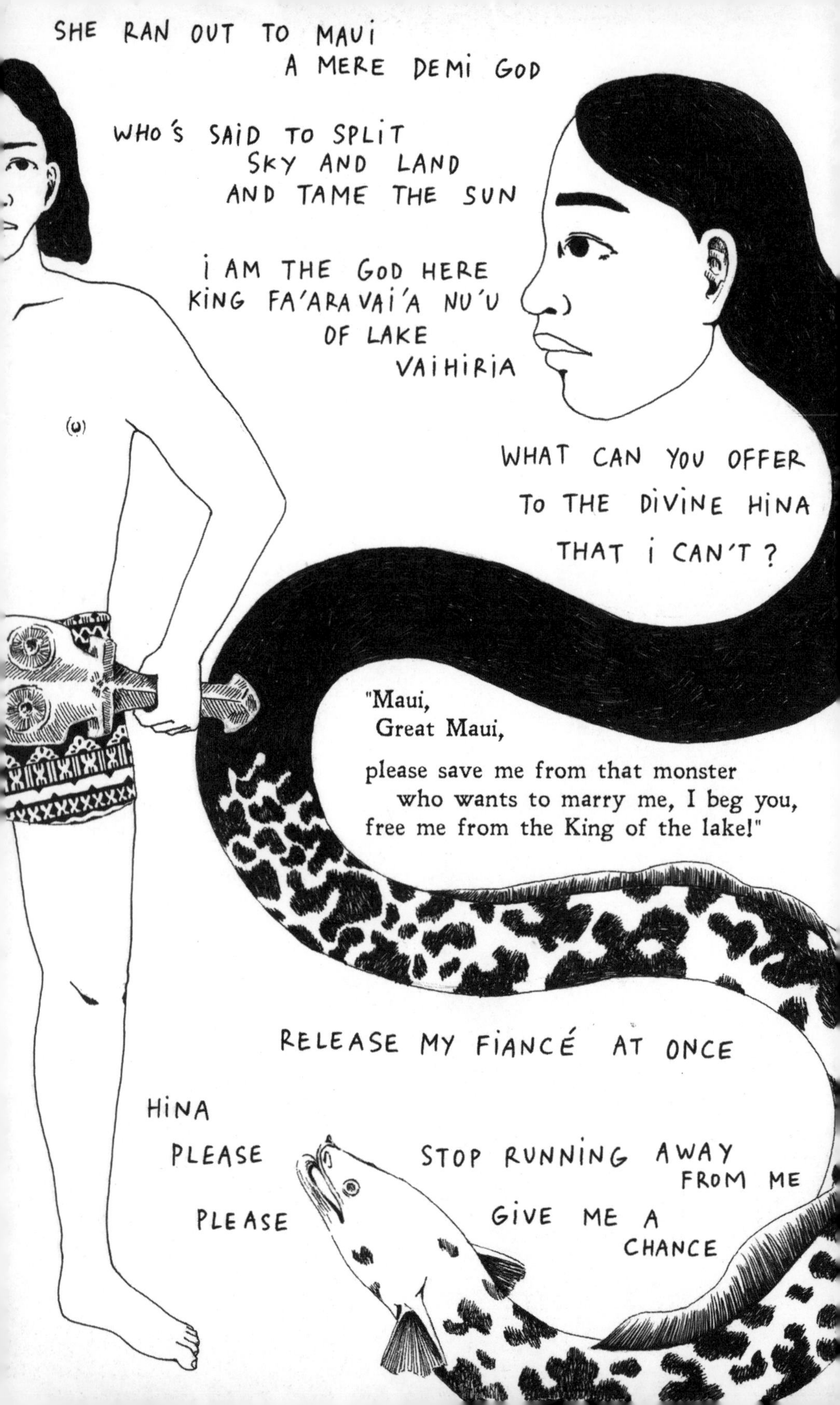
SHE RAN OUT TO MAUI
A MERE DEMI GOD
WHO'S SAID TO SPLIT
SKY AND LAND
AND TAME THE SUN
I AM THE GOD HERE
KING FA'ARAVAI'A NU'U
OF LAKE
VAIHIRIA
WHAT CAN YOU OFFER
TO THE DIVINE HINA
THAT I CAN'T?
"Maui,
Great Maui,
please save me from that monster
who wants to marry me, I beg you,
free me from the King of the lake!"
RELEASE MY FIANCÉ AT ONCE
HINA
PLEASE
STOP RUNNING AWAY
FROM ME
PLEASE
GIVE ME A
CHANCE

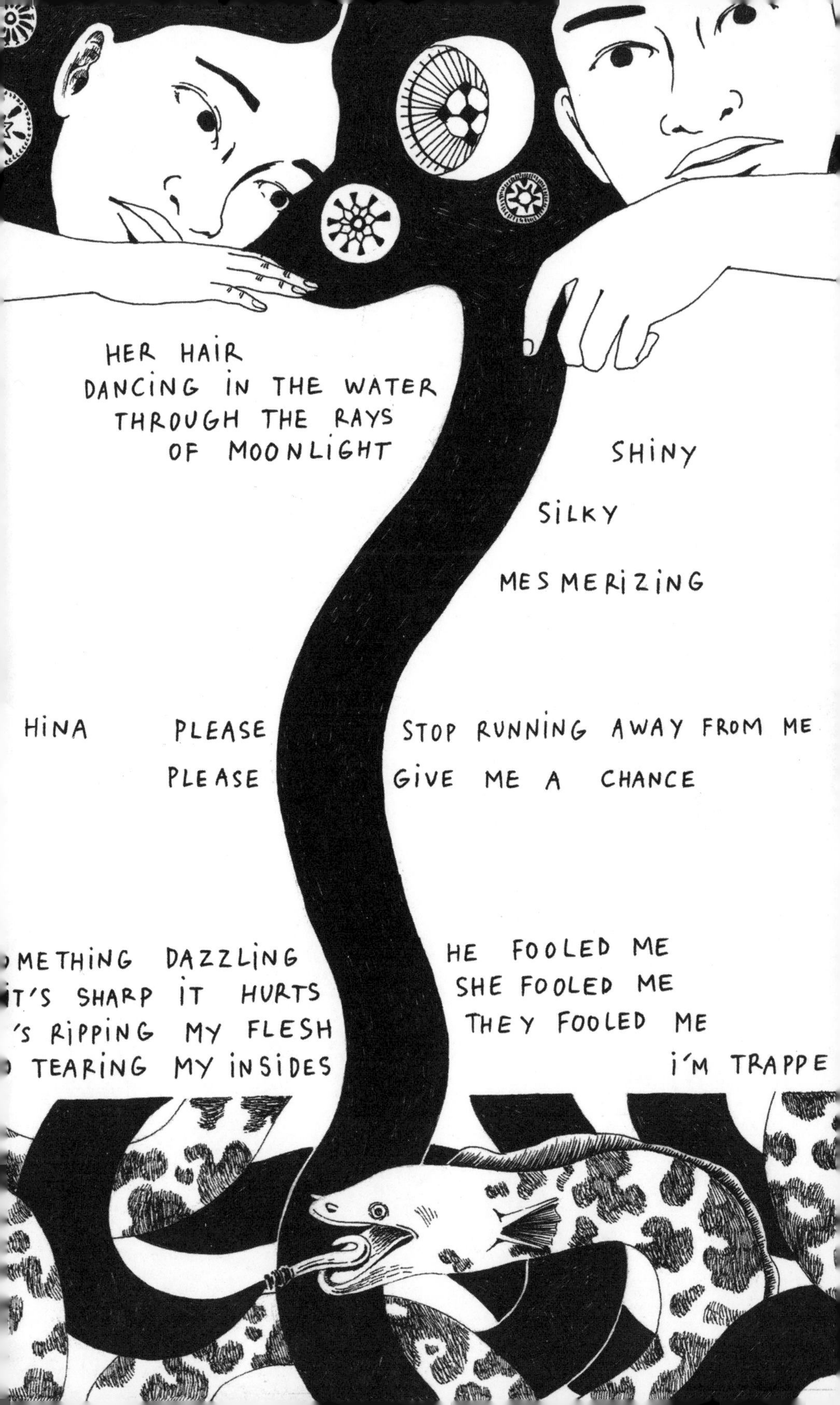
HER HAIR
DANCING IN THE WATER
THROUGH THE RAYS
OF MOONLIGHT
SHINY
SILKY
MESMERIZING
HINA PLEASE STOP RUNNING AWAY FROM ME
PLEASE GIVE ME A CHANCE
METHING DAZZLING
T'S SHARP IT HURTS
'S RIPPING MY FLESH
TEARING MY INSIDES
HE FOOLED ME
SHE FOOLED ME
THEY FOOLED ME
I'M TRAPPE

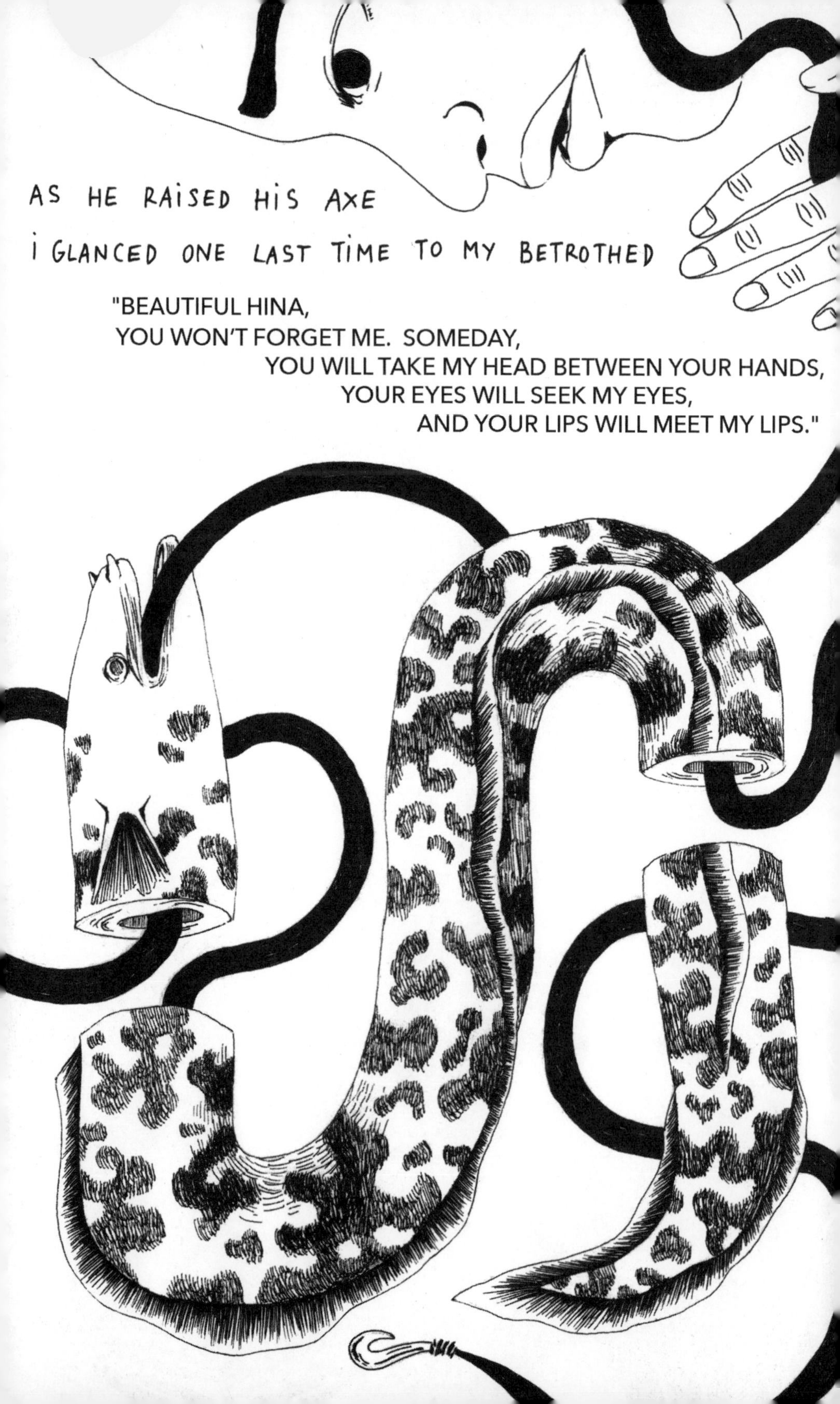

AS HE RAISED HIS AXE
I GLANCED ONE LAST TIME TO MY BETROTHED
"BEAUTIFUL HINA,
YOU WON'T FORGET ME. SOMEDAY,
YOU WILL TAKE MY HEAD BETWEEN YOUR HANDS,
YOUR EYES WILL SEEK MY EYES,
AND YOUR LIPS WILL MEET MY LIPS."

"TAKE THE HEAD, DEAR HINA, AND GO HOME. ONCE ARRIVED, BURY IT IN FRONT OF YOUR *MARAE**, IT HOLDS GREAT TREASURES.
DO NOT SET IT DOWN UNTIL YOU'VE ARRIVED...
GO NOW, AND REMEMBER MY WORDS."

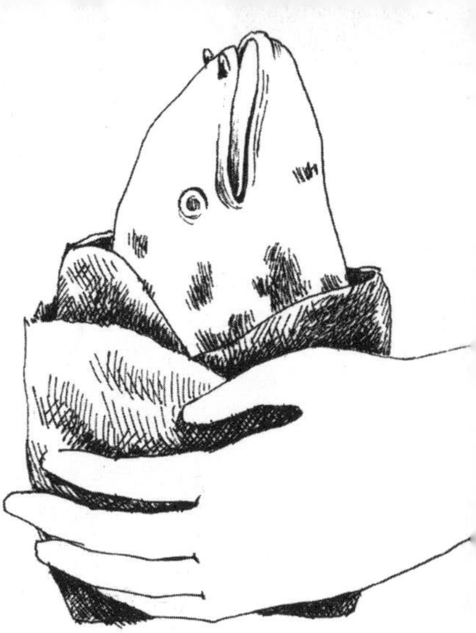

* *Marae : sacred altar*

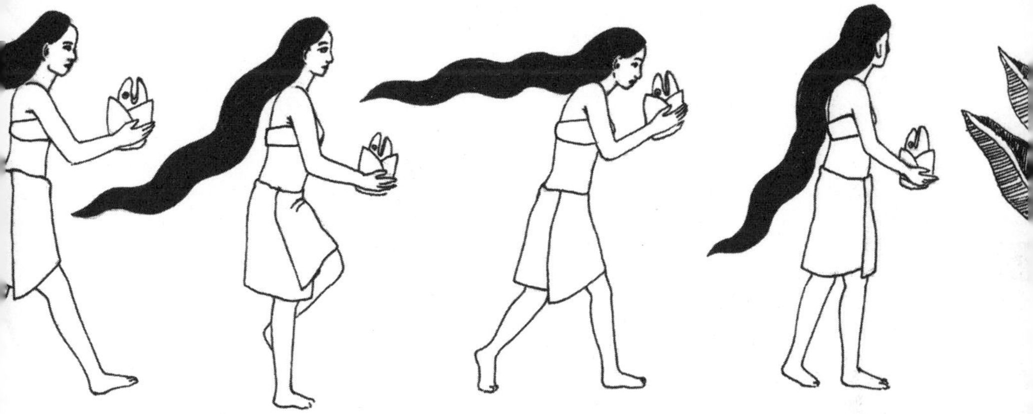

"So hot..."

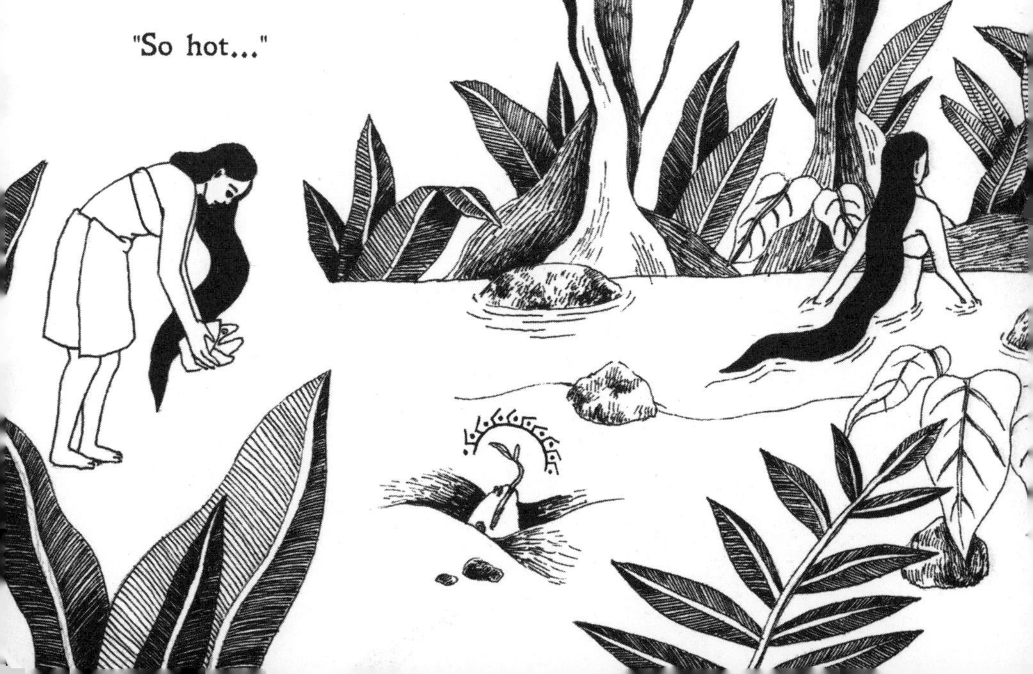

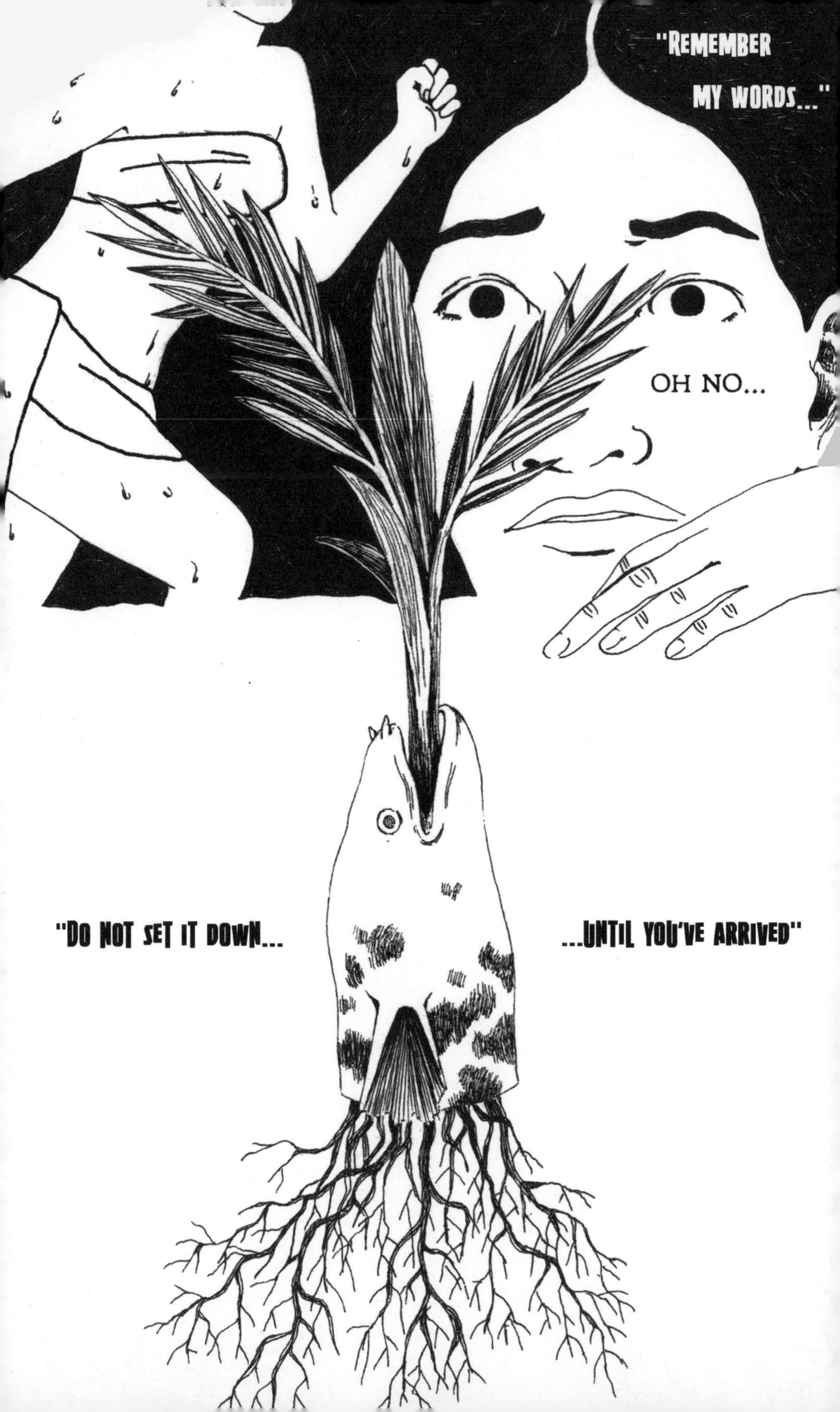
"REMEMBER MY WORDS..."
OH NO...
"DO NOT SET IT DOWN...
...UNTIL YOU'VE ARRIVED"

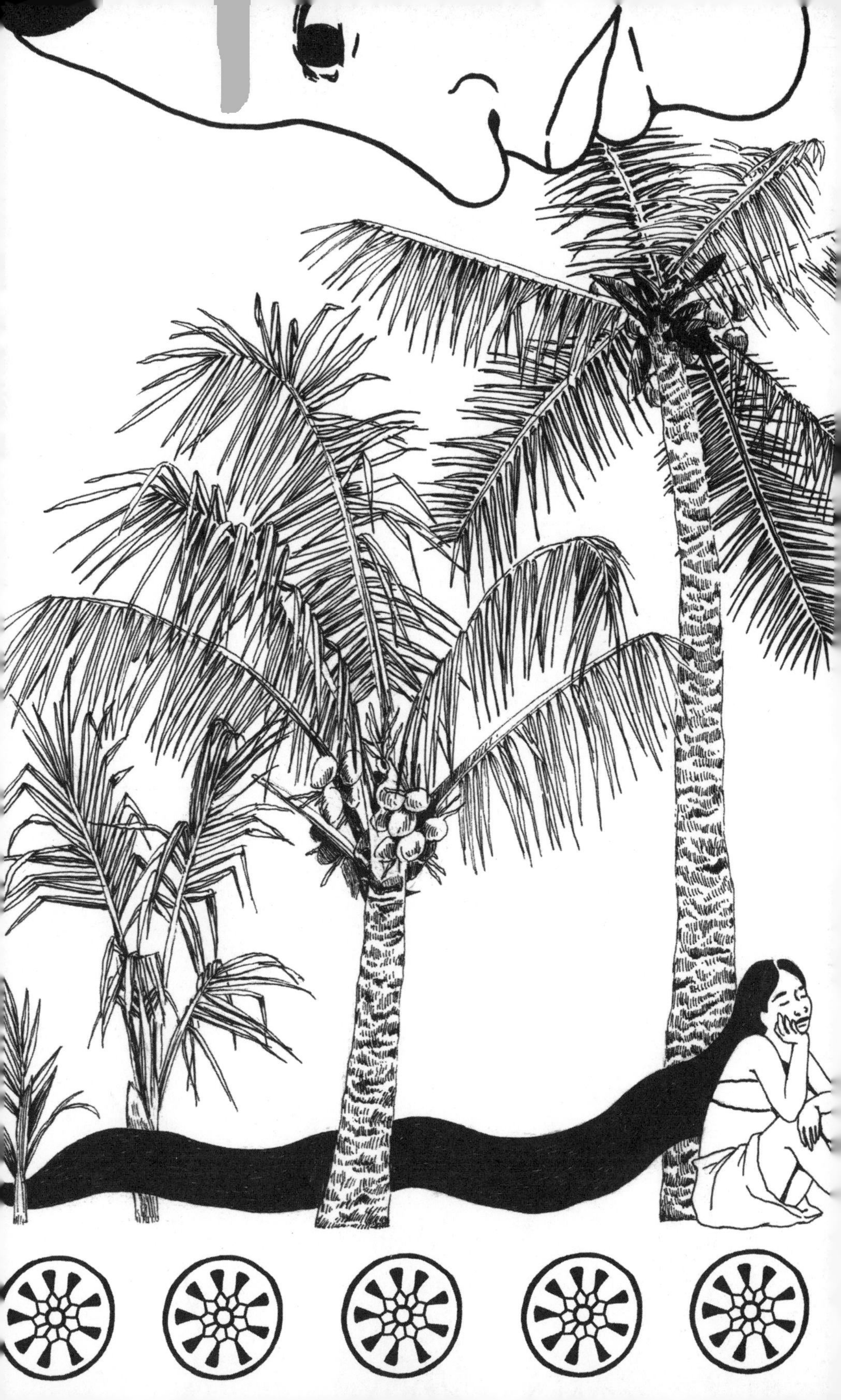

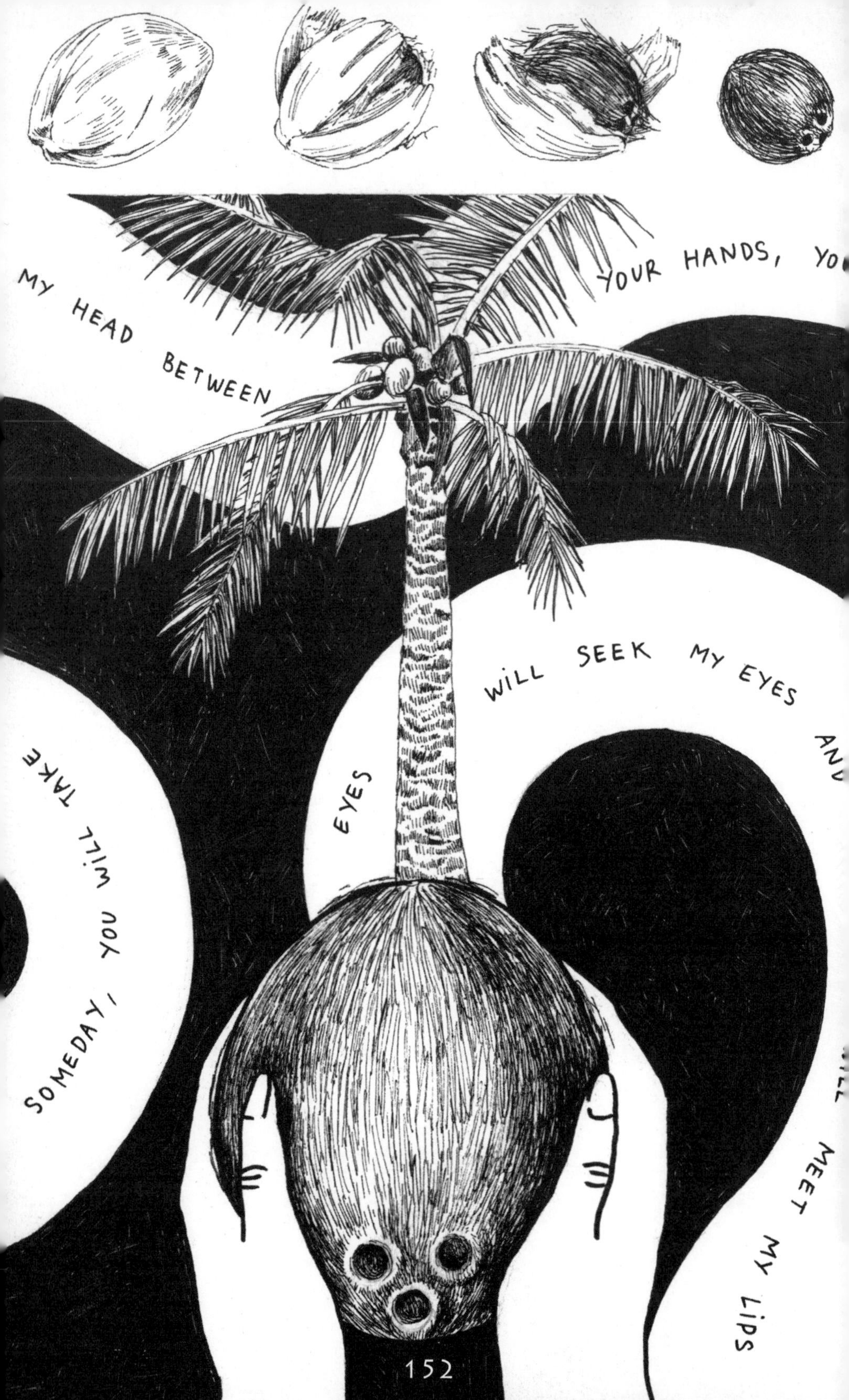
SOMEDAY, YOU WILL TAKE
MY HEAD BETWEEN
YOUR HANDS, YO
EYES
WILL SEEK MY EYES
AN
MEET MY LIPS

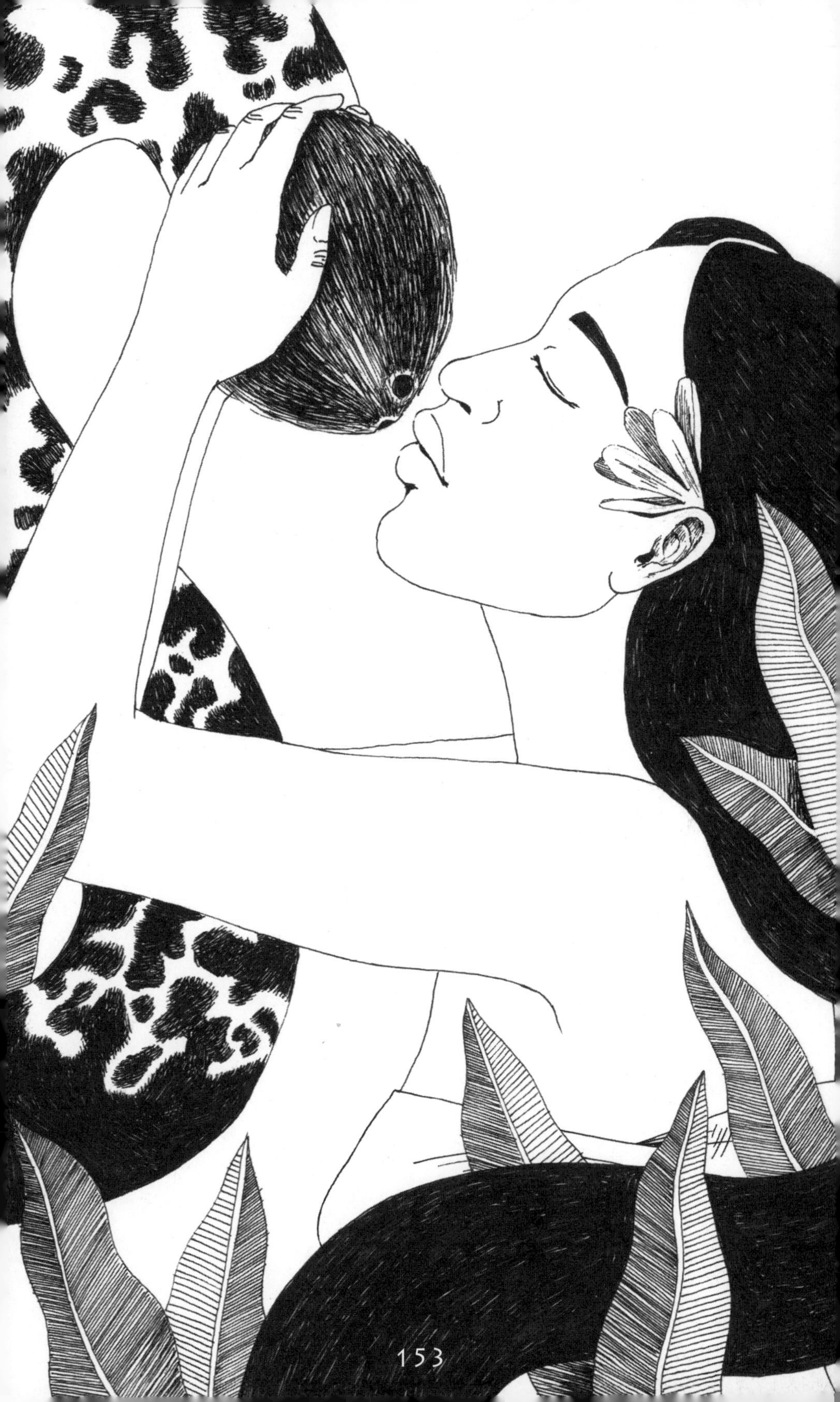

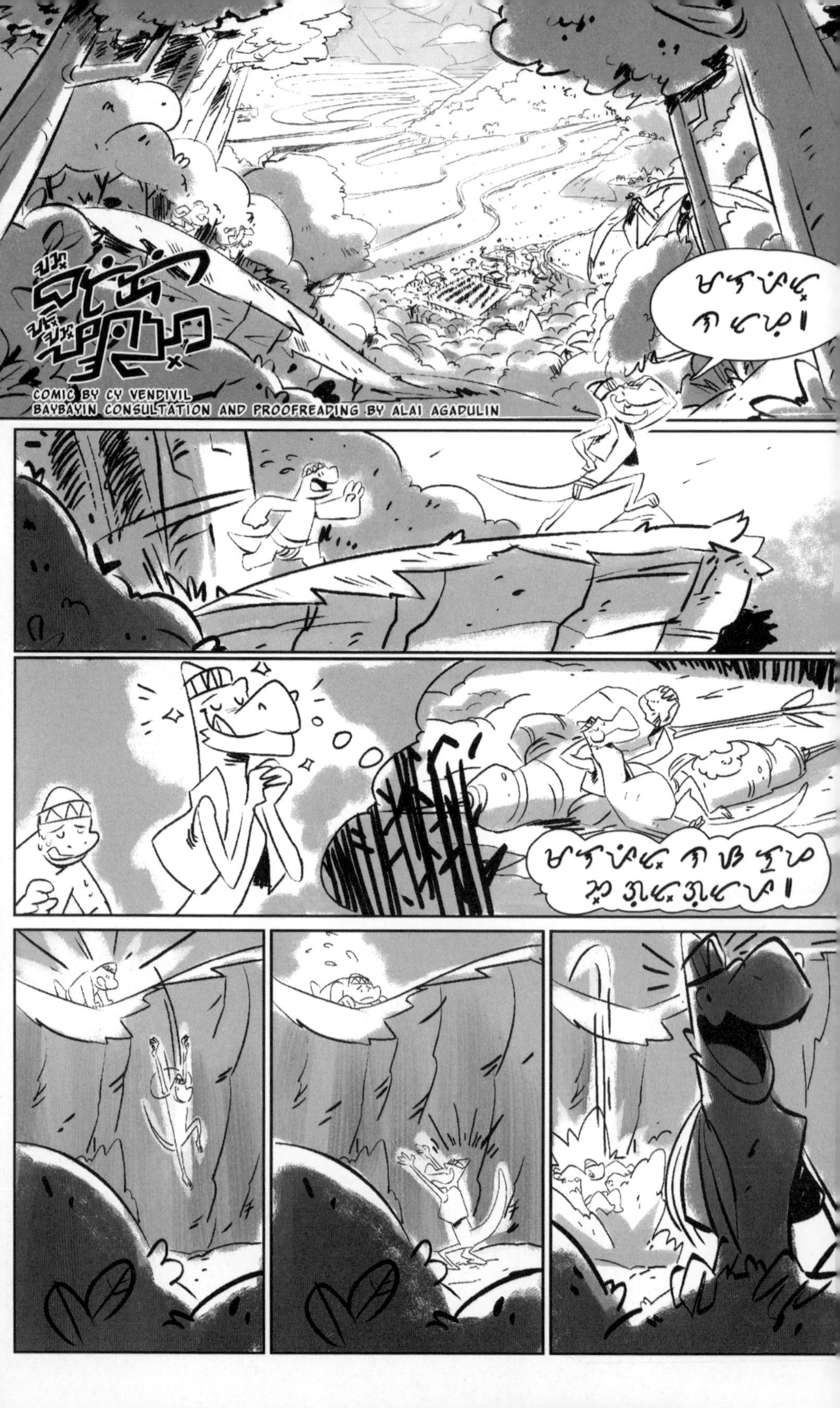
COMIC BY CY VENDIVIL
BAYBAYIN CONSULTATION AND PROOFREADING BY ALAI AGADULIN

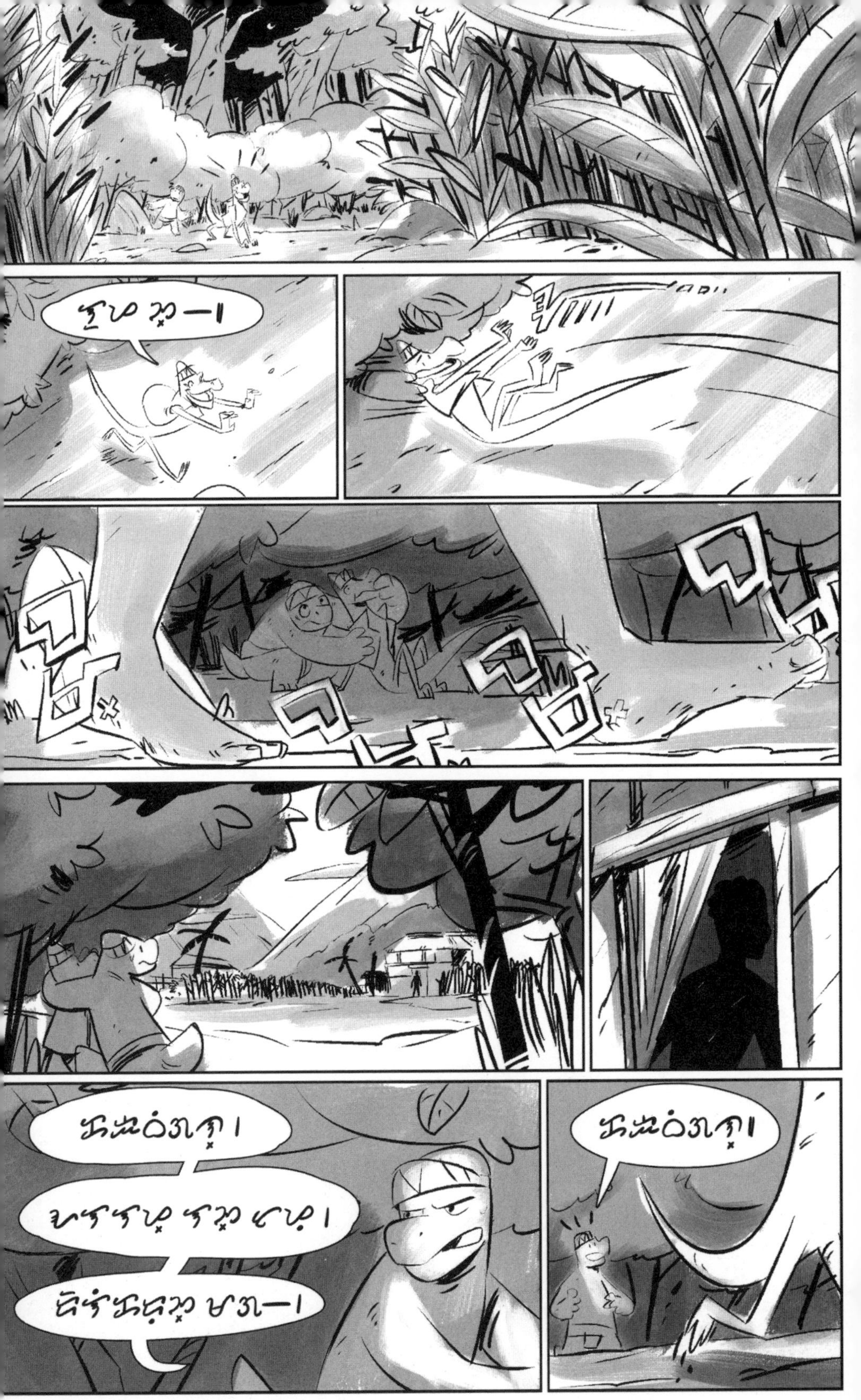

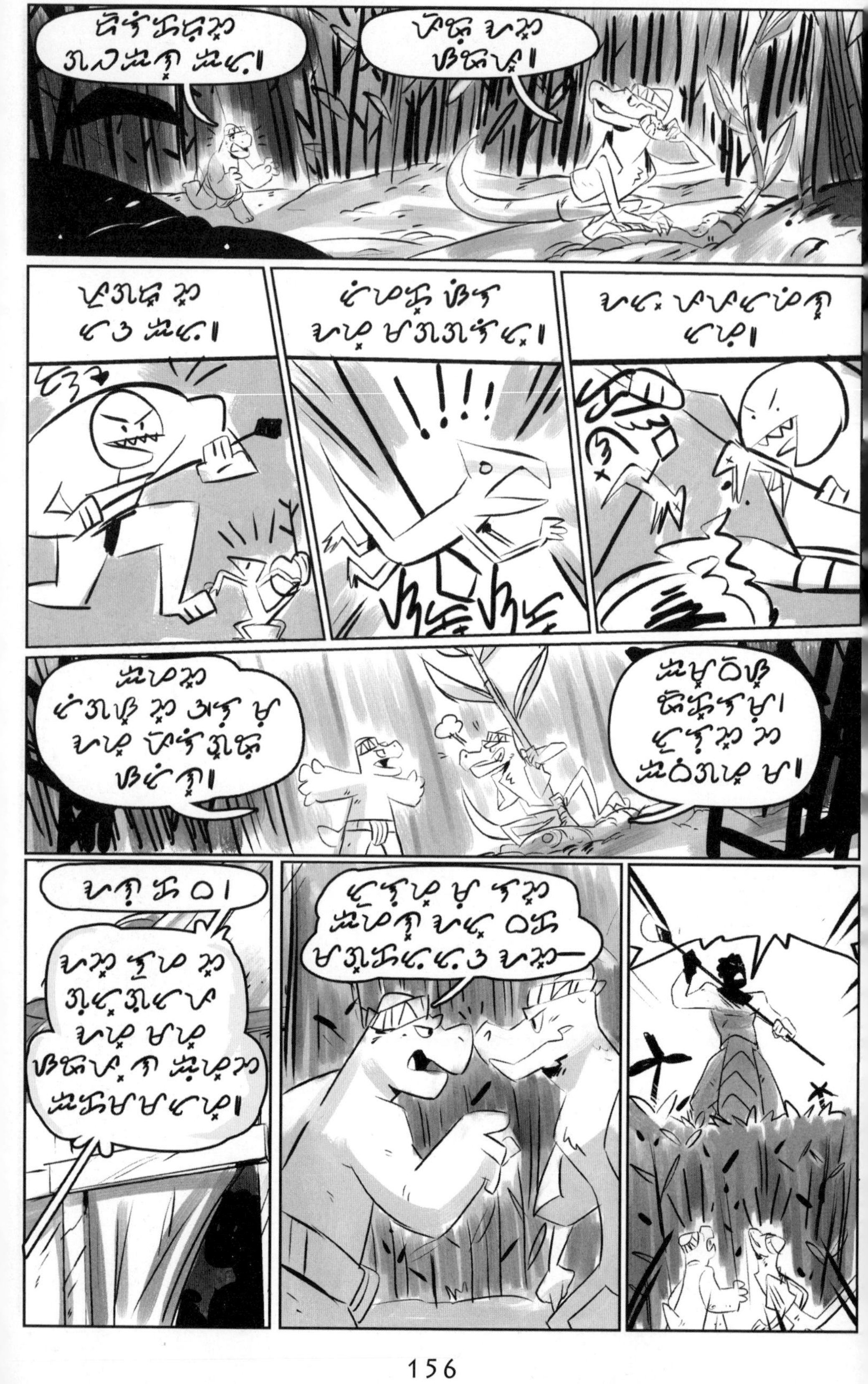

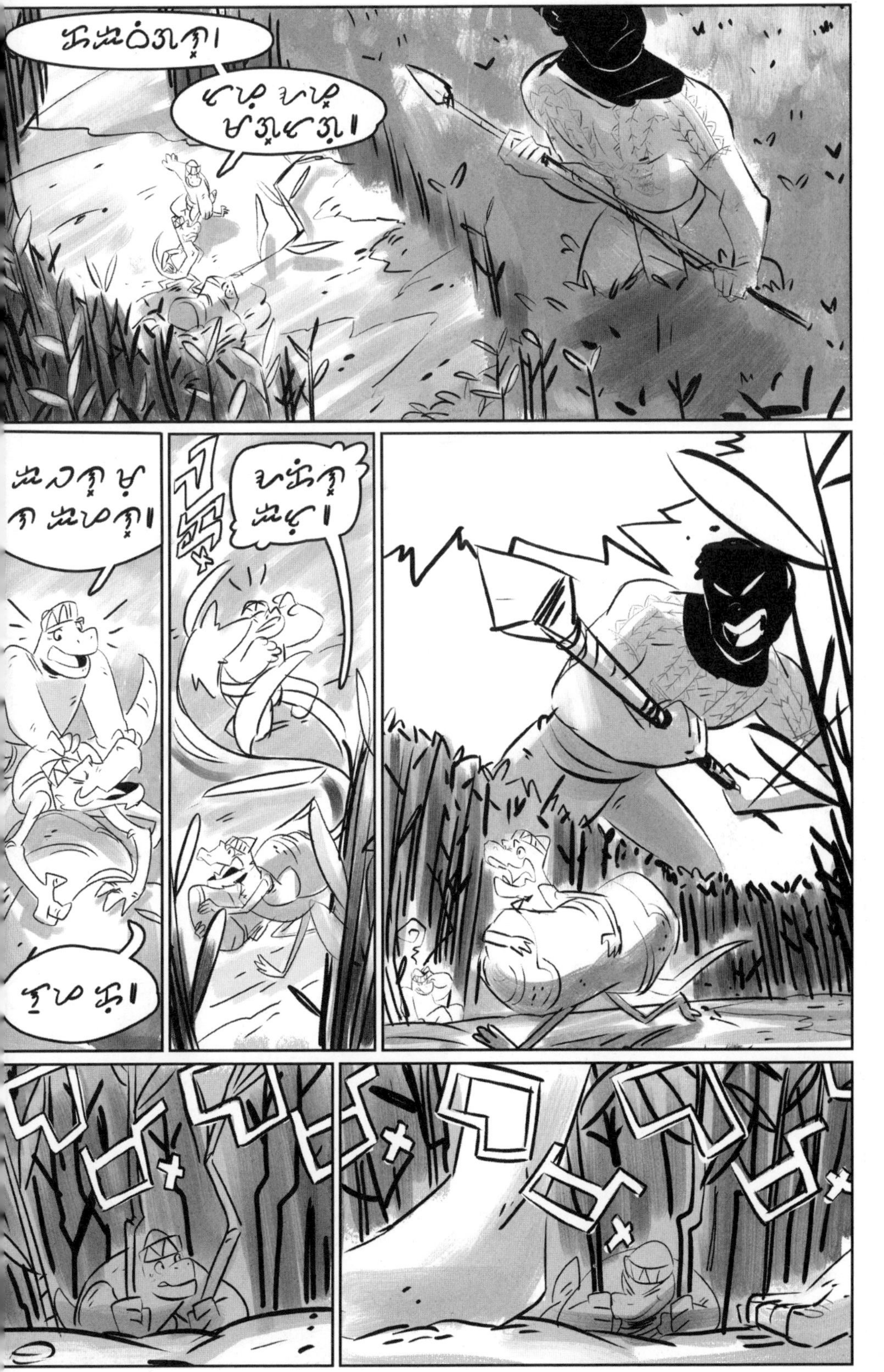

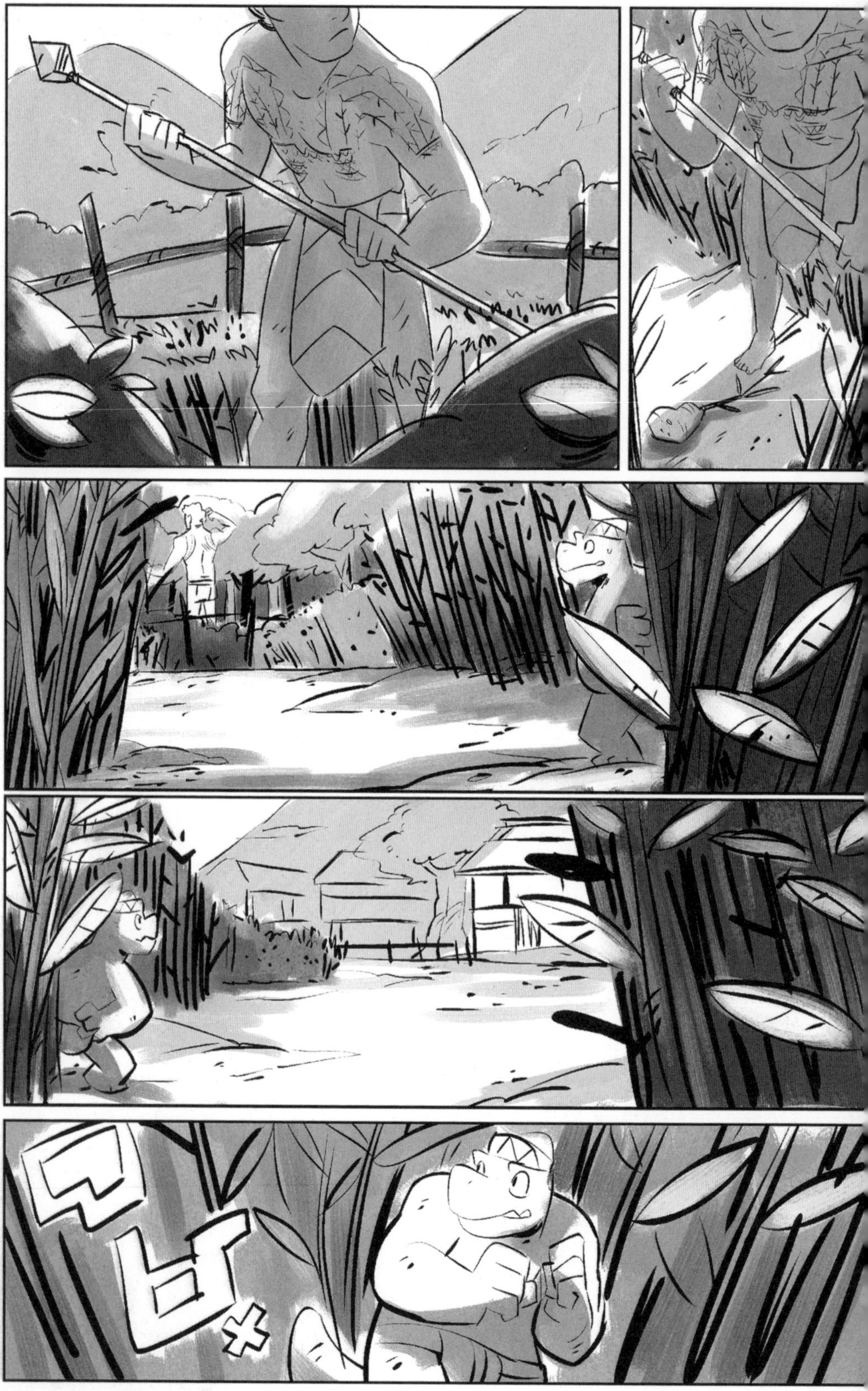

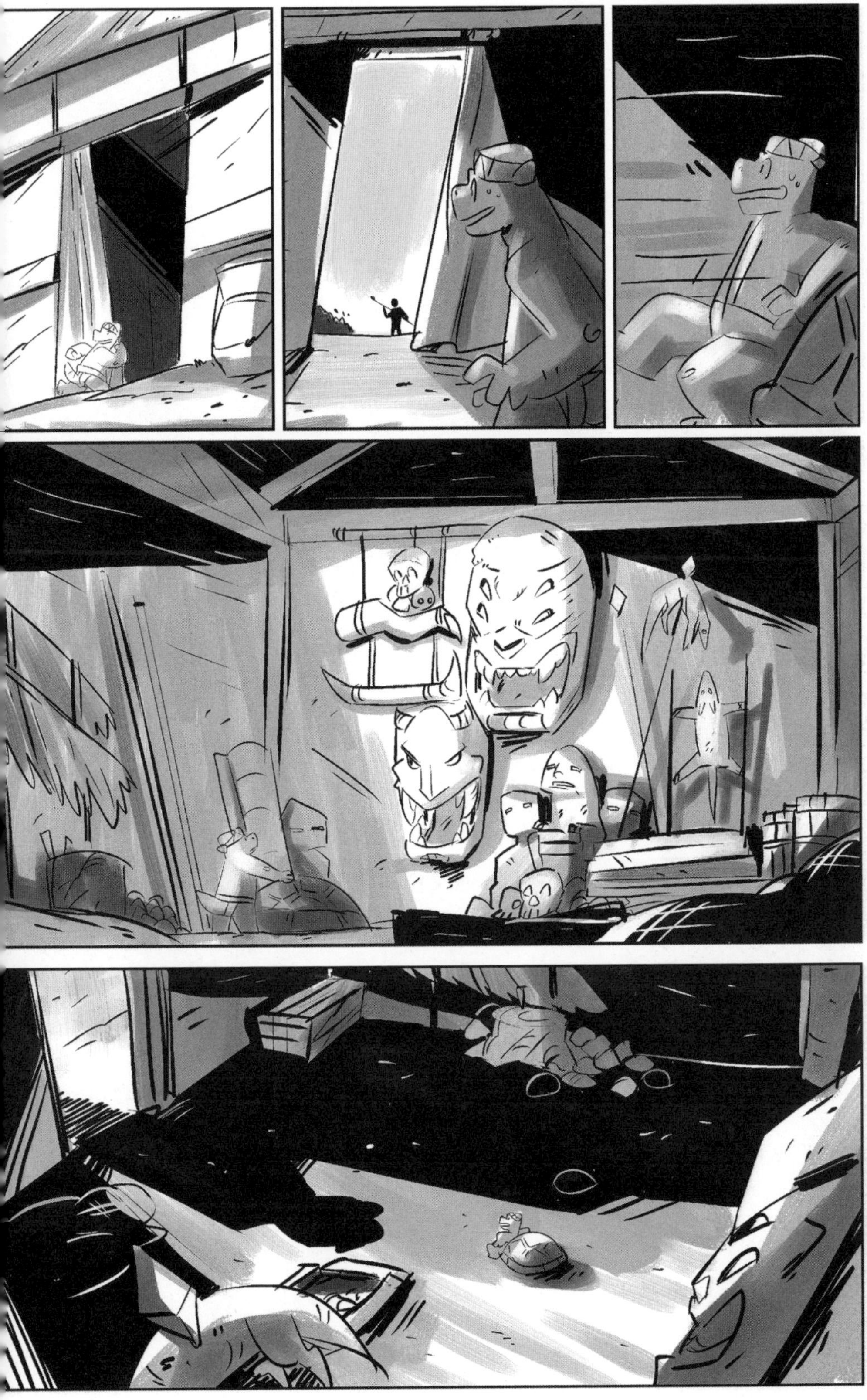

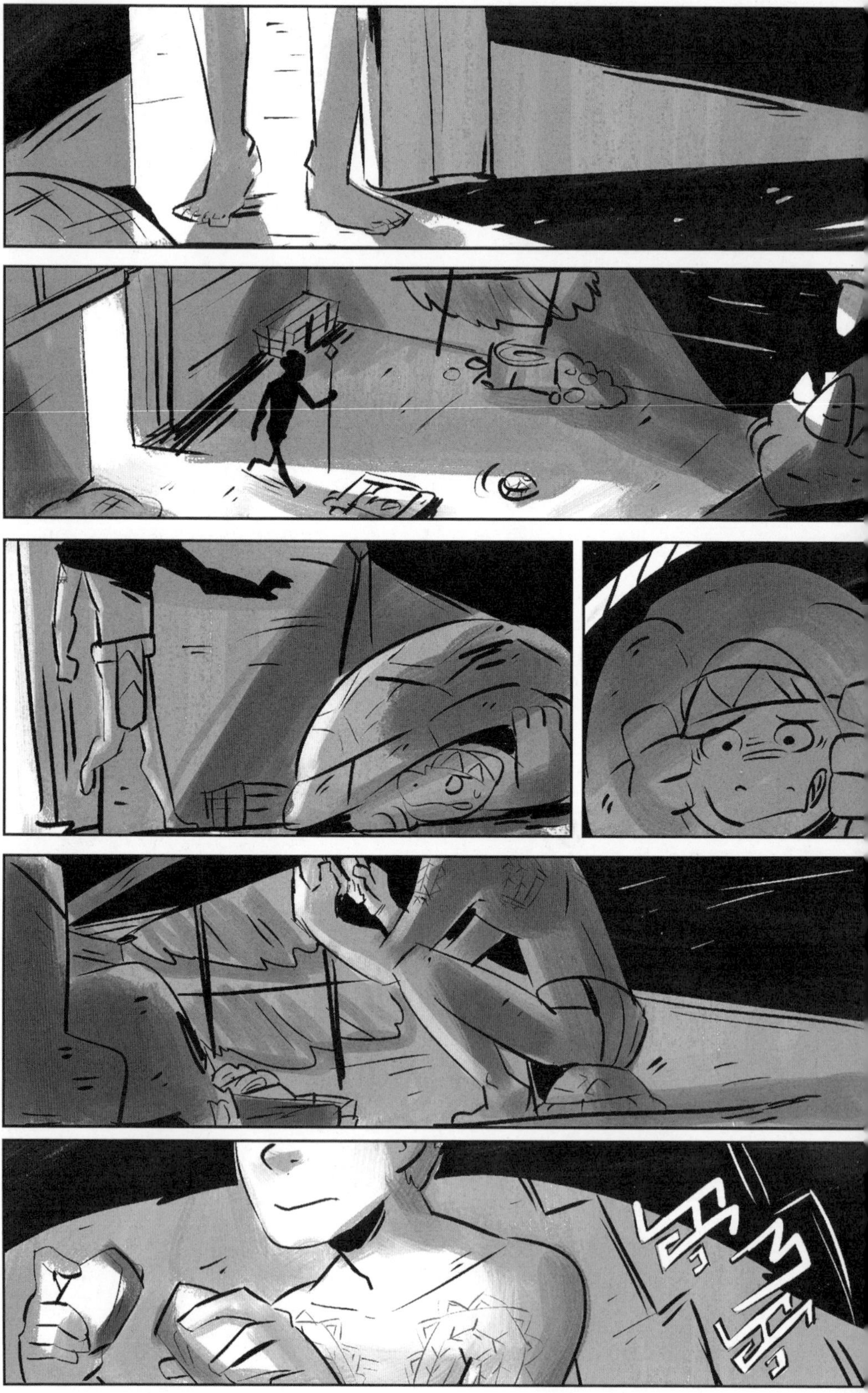

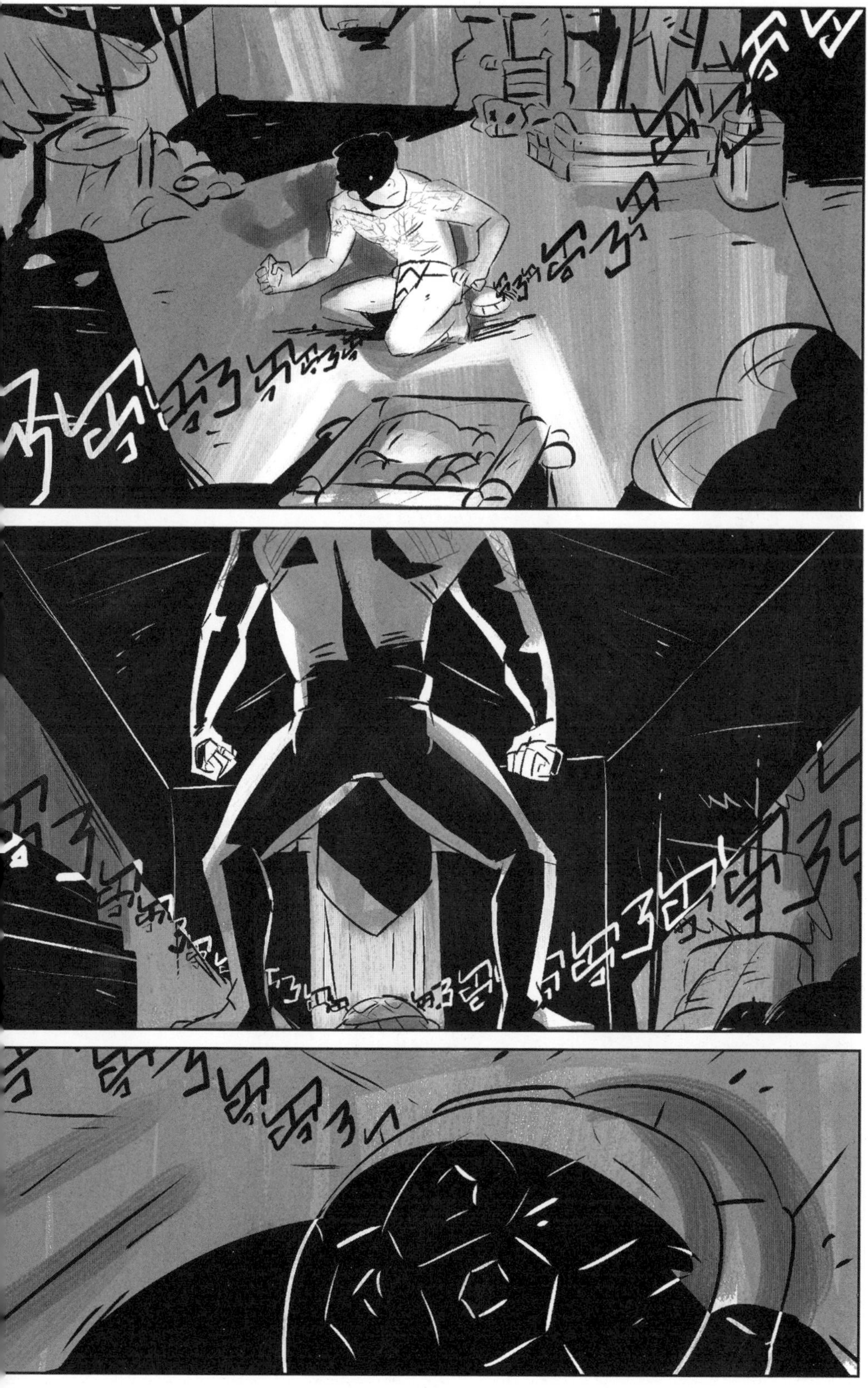

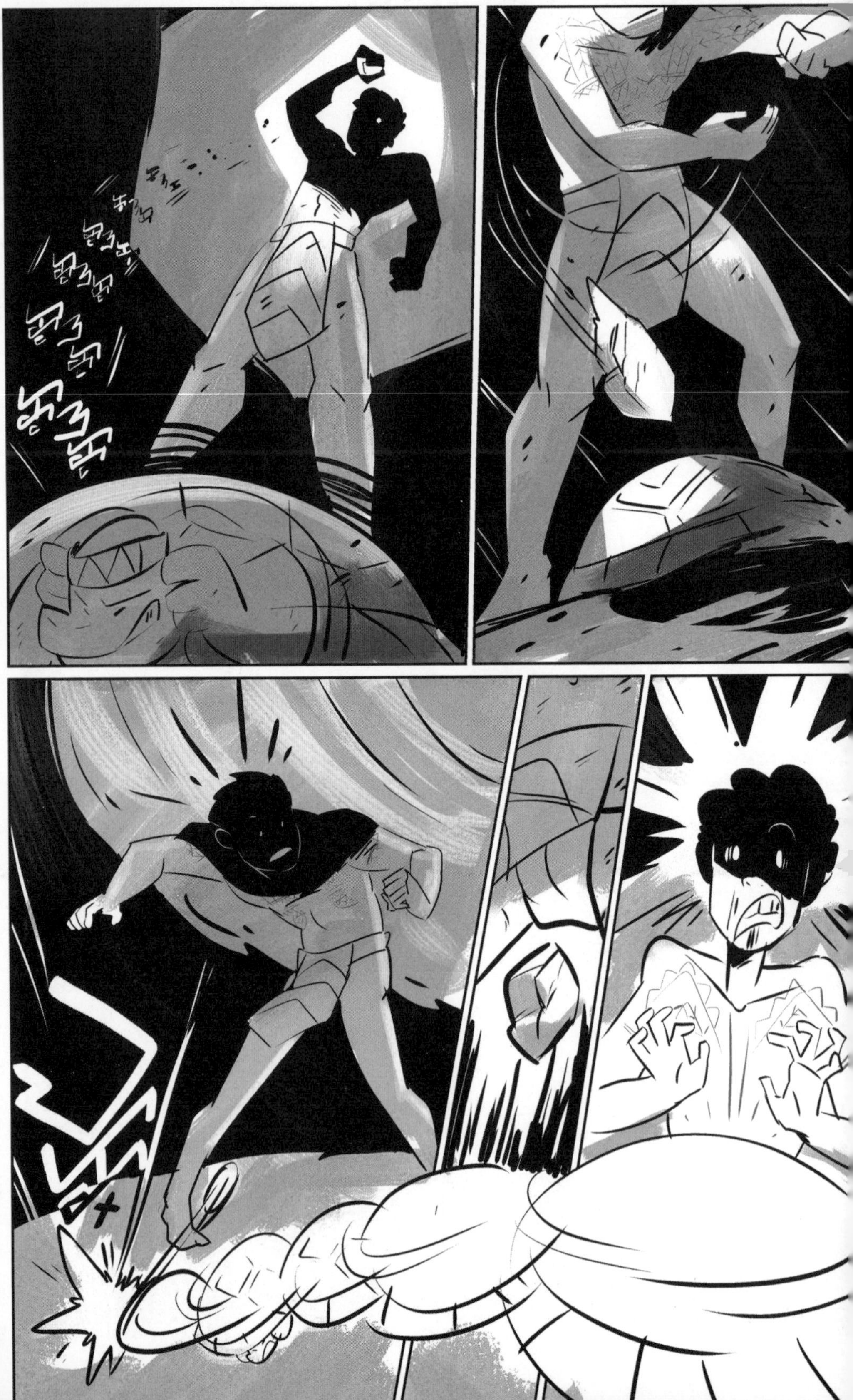

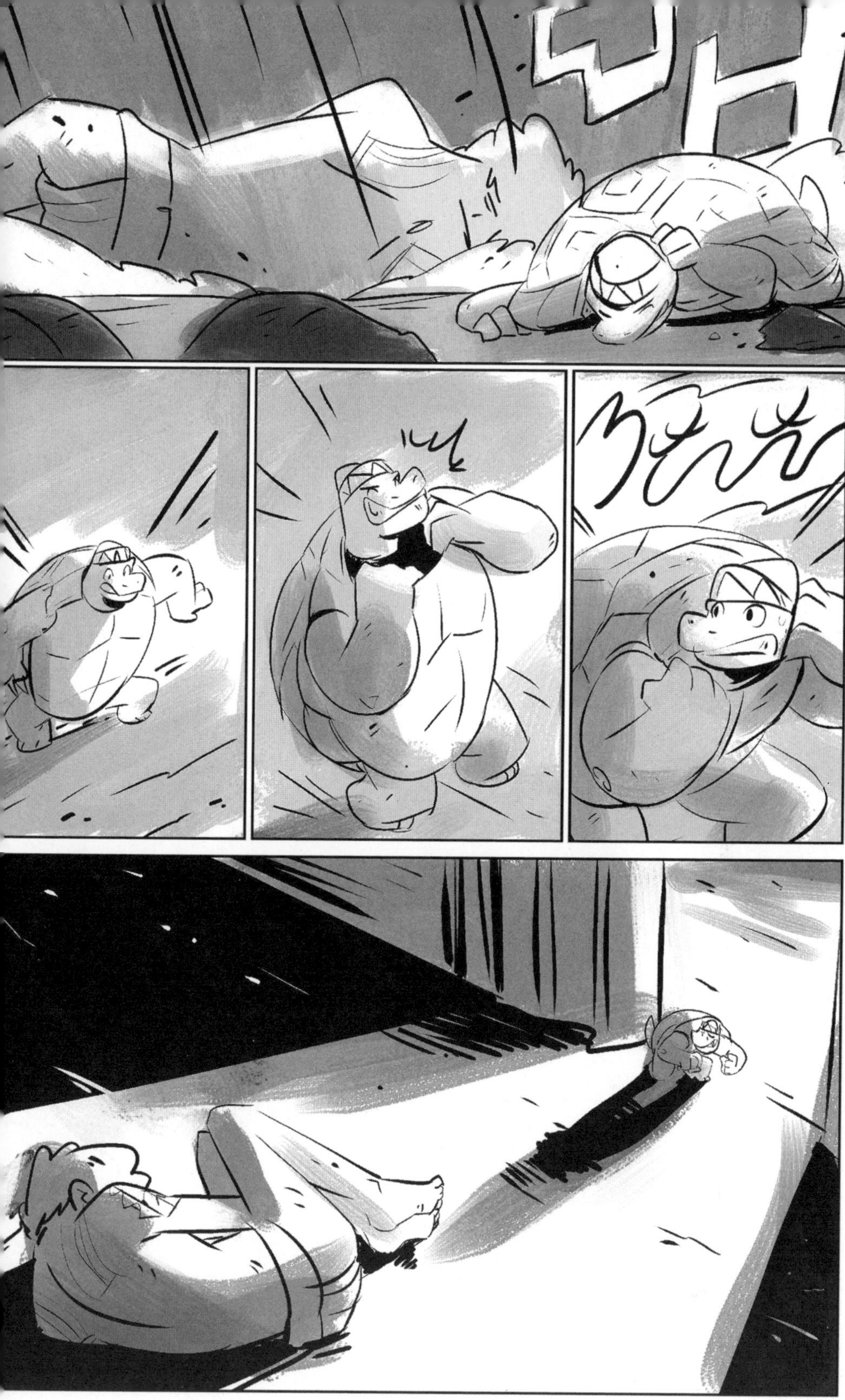

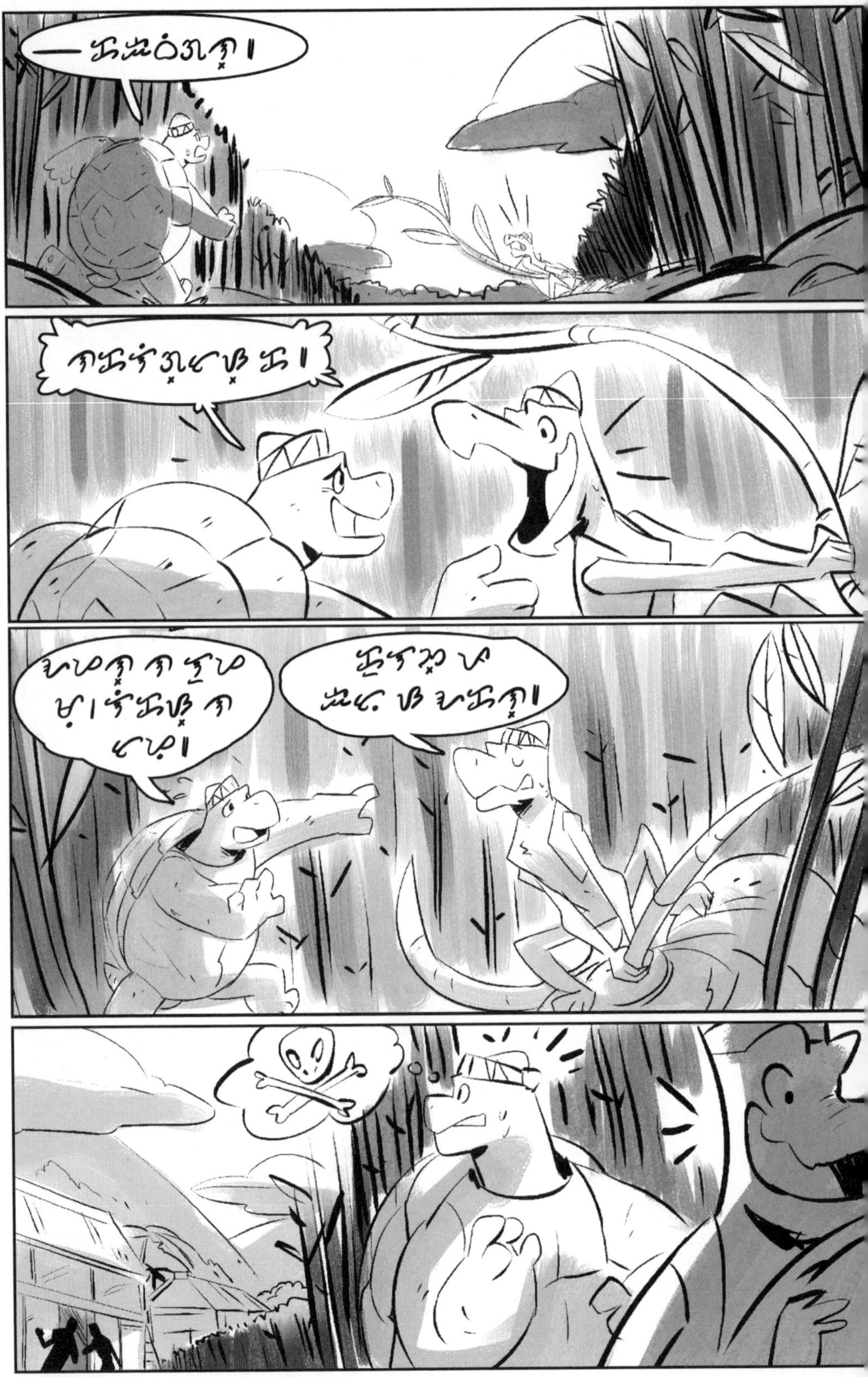

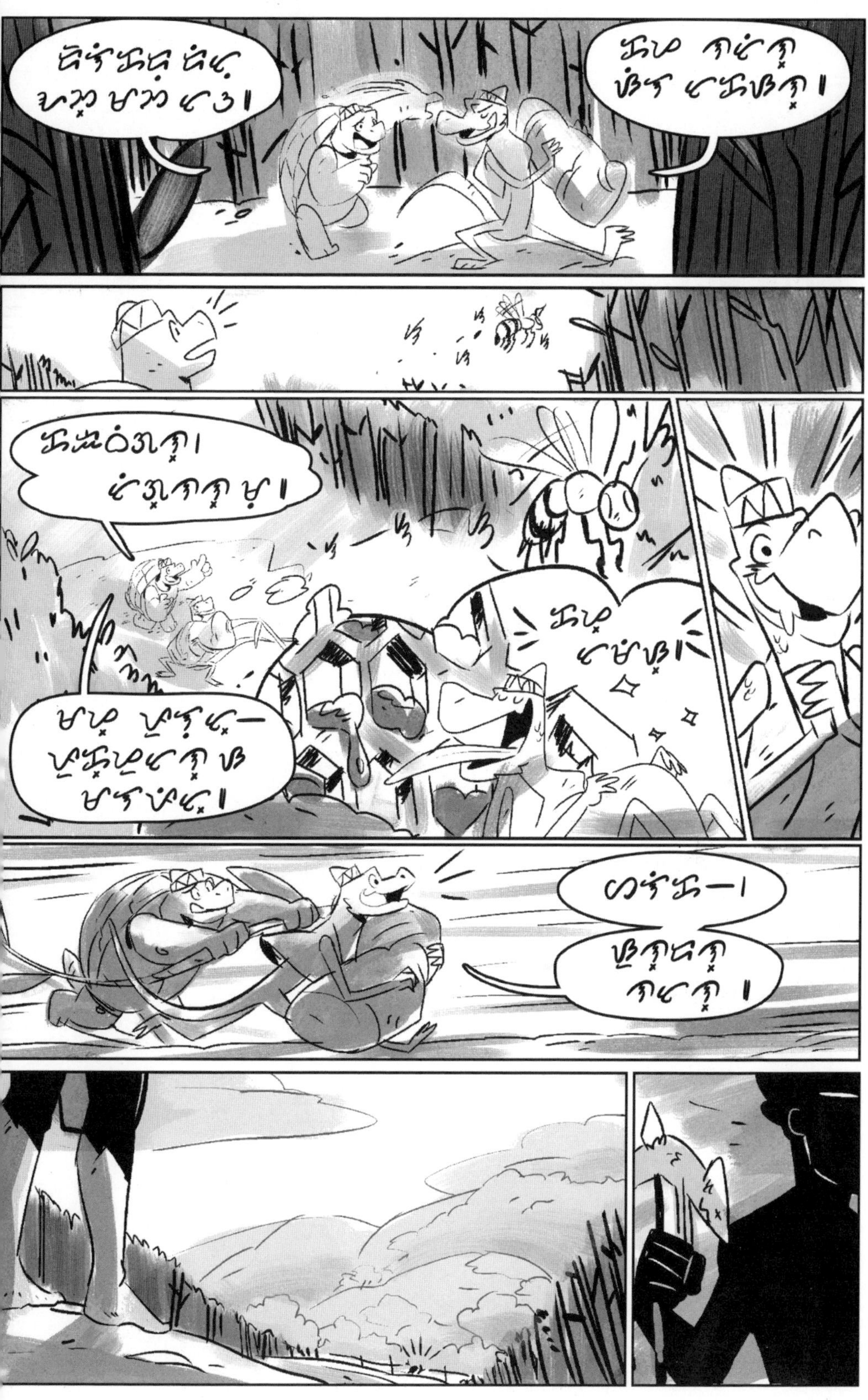

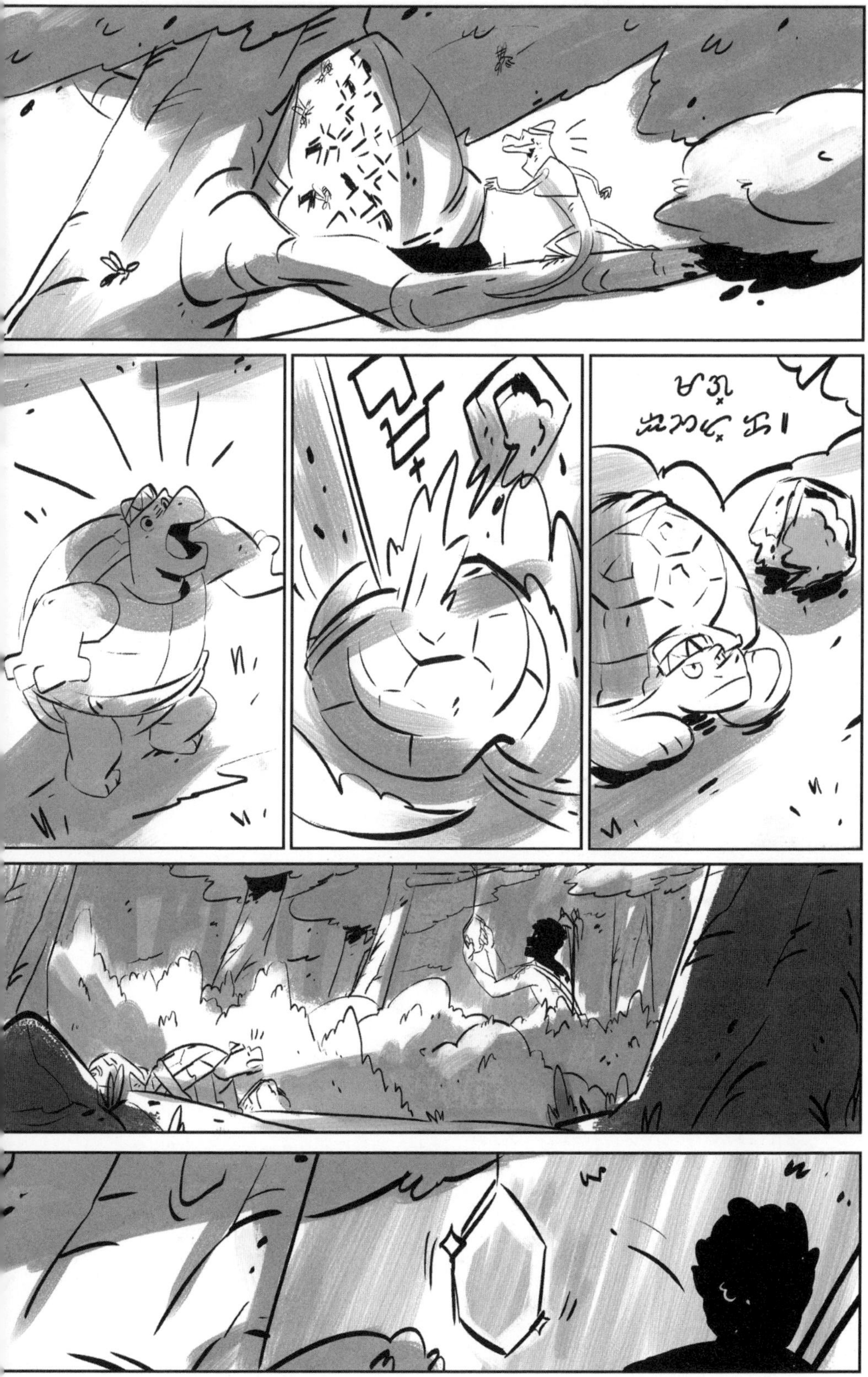

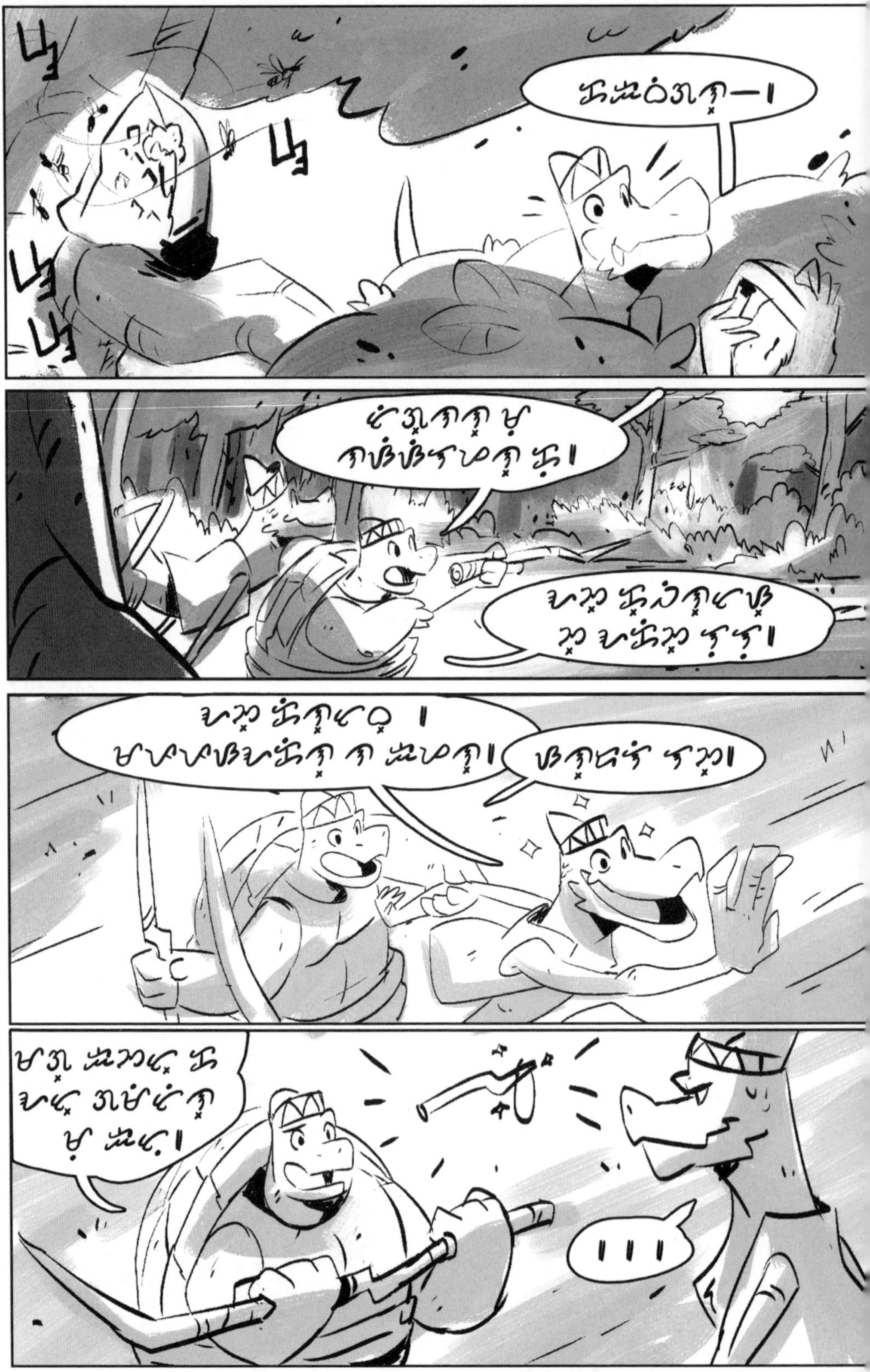

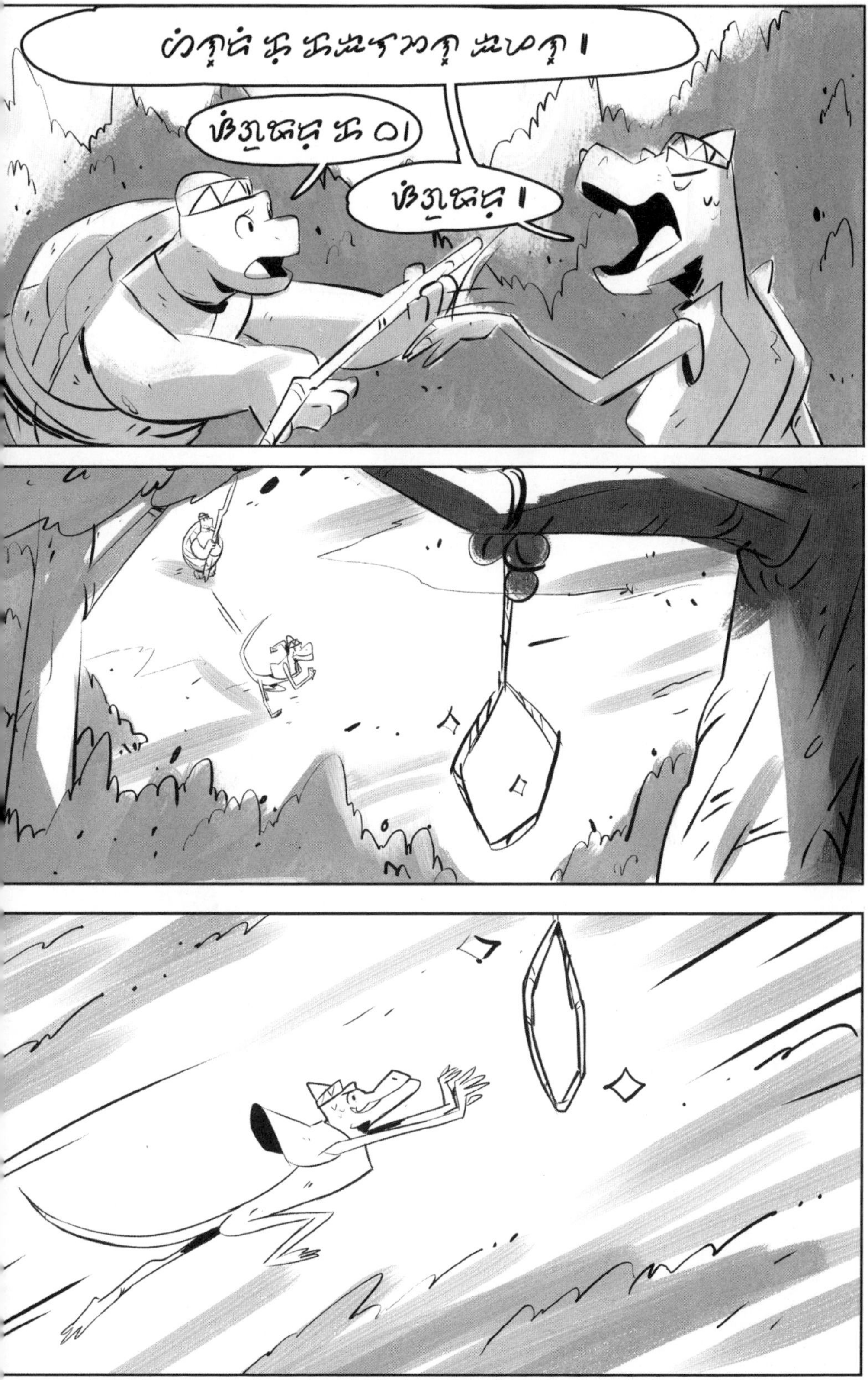

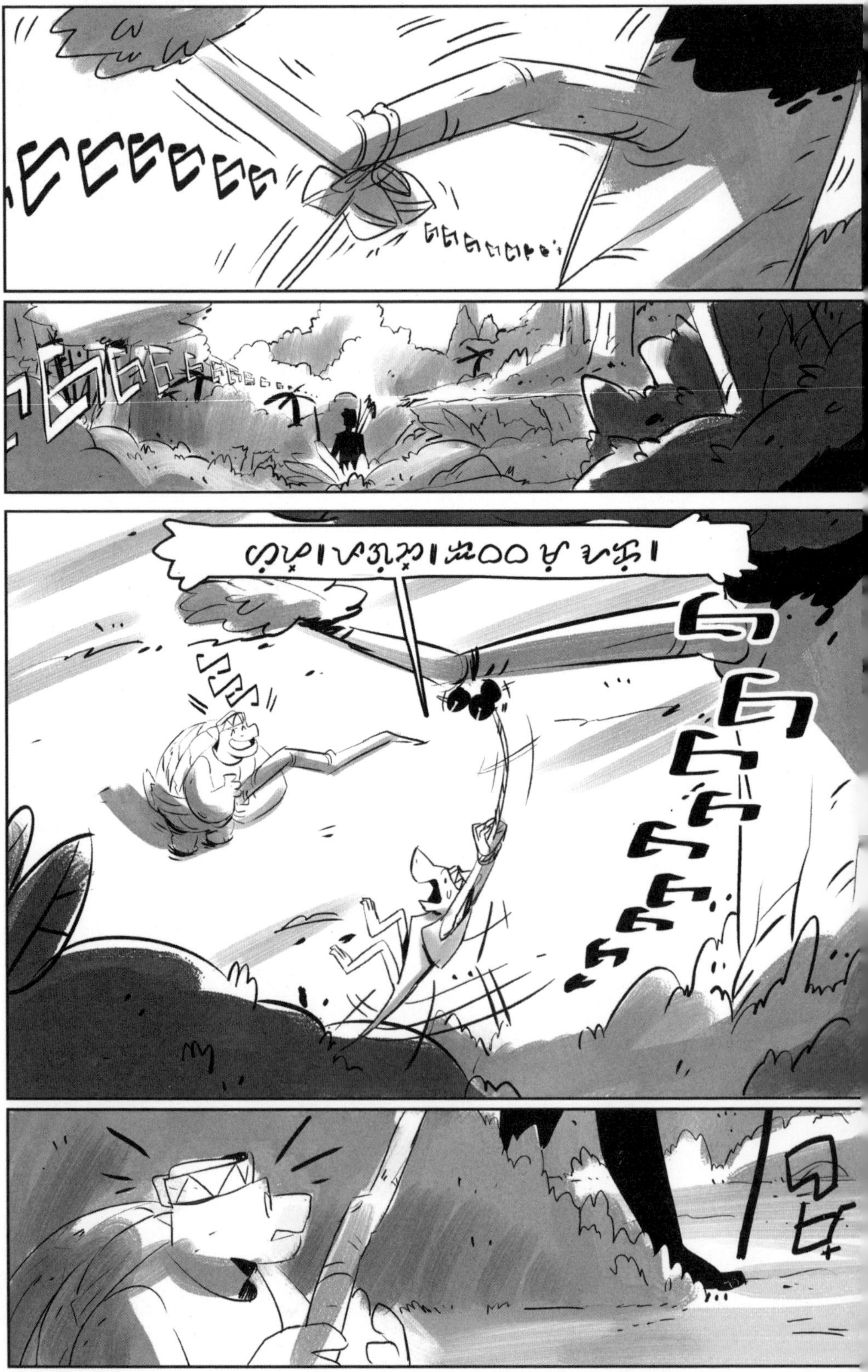

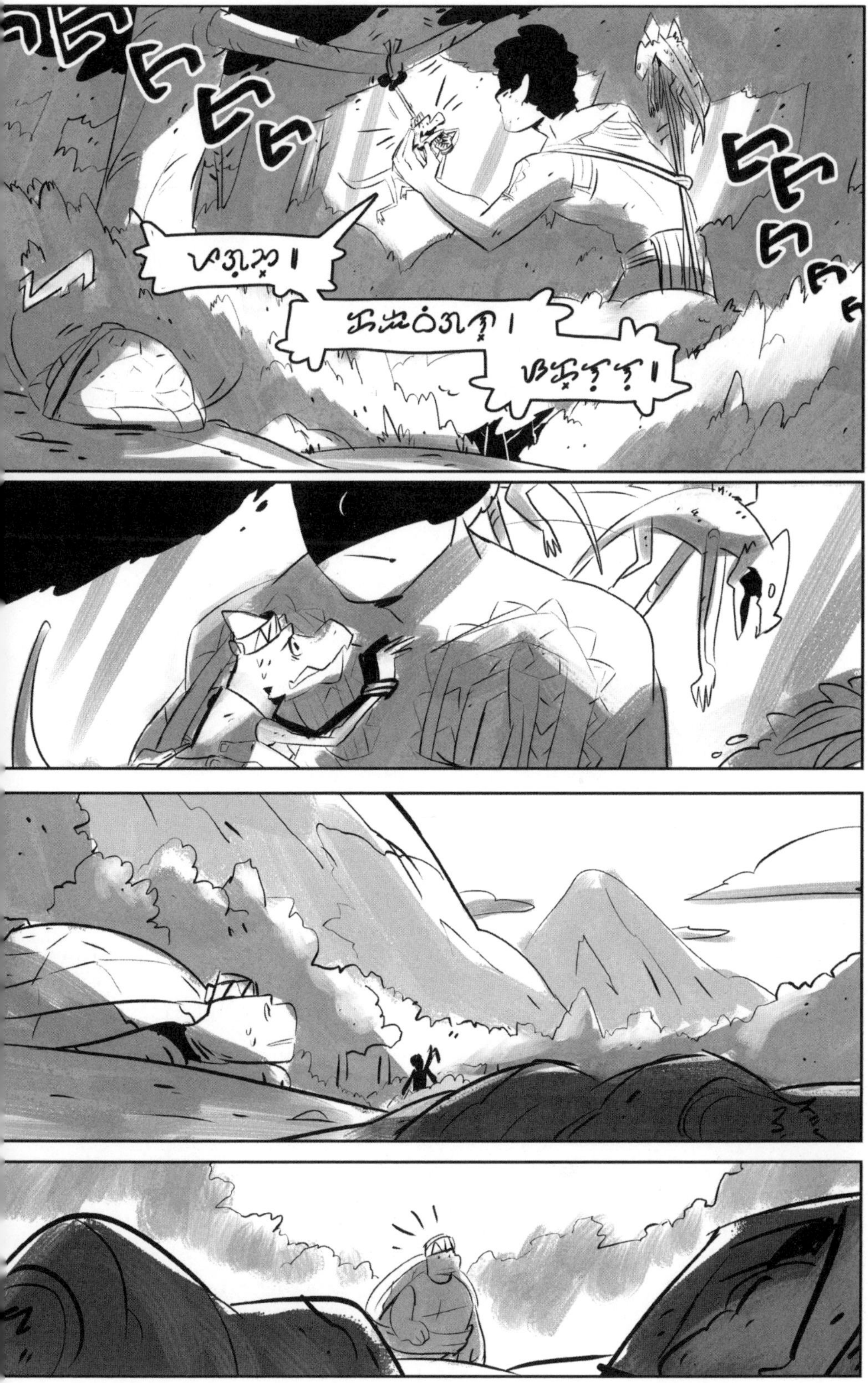

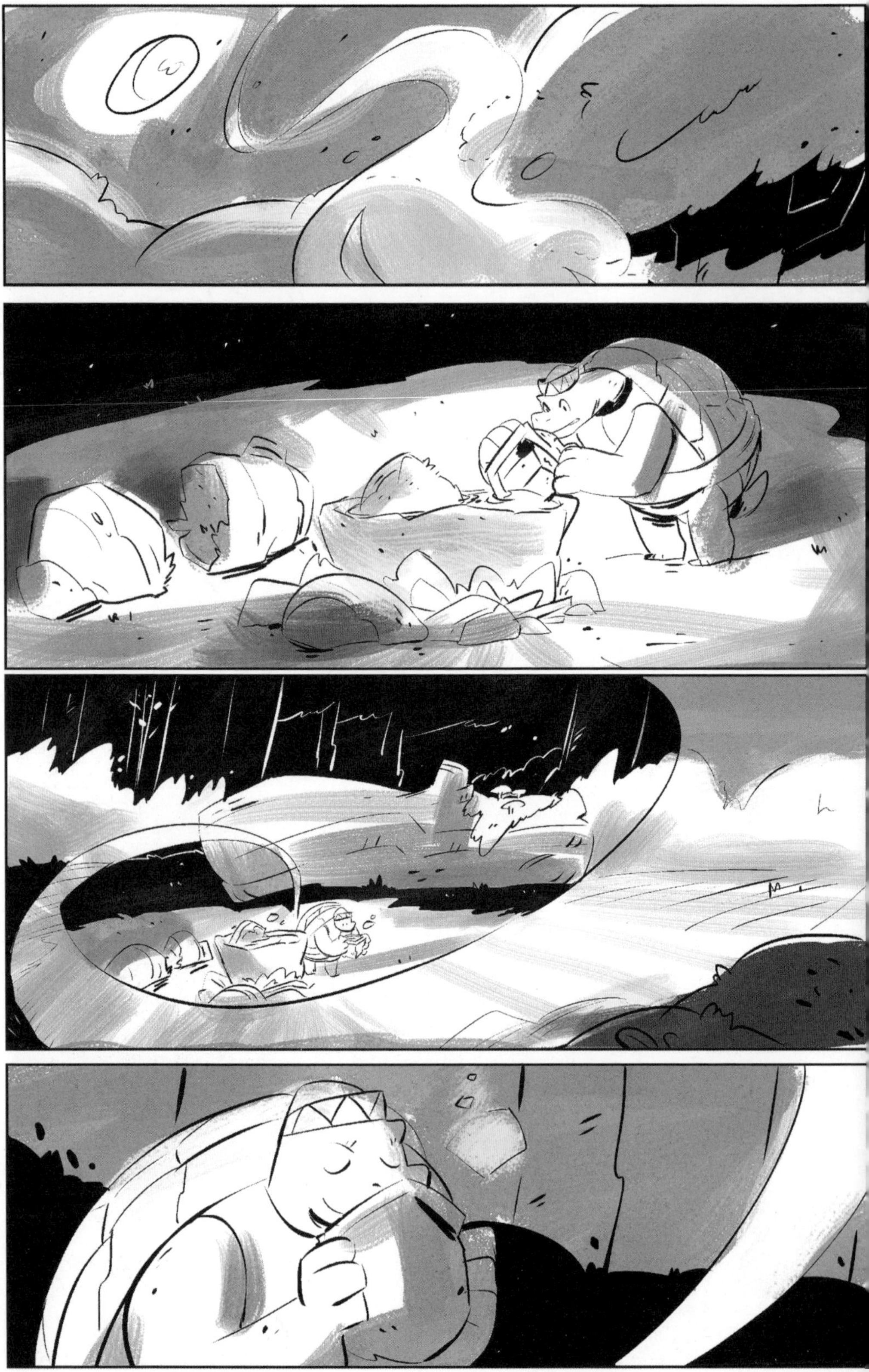

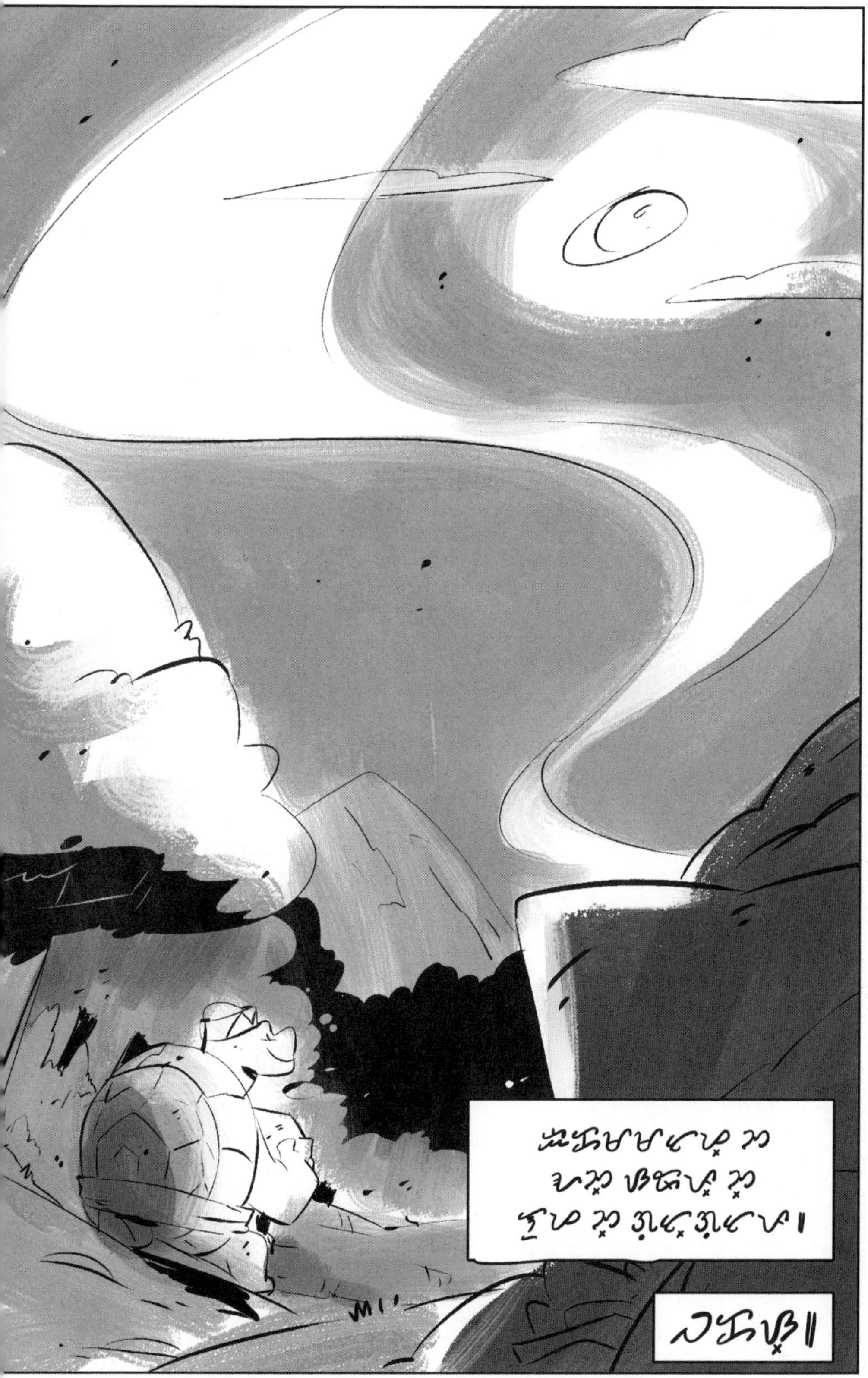

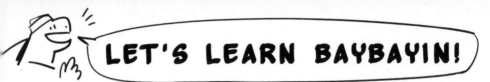

LET'S LEARN BAYBAYIN!

THE CHARACTERS IN THE COMIC, "THE TURTLE AND THE LIZARD" SPEAK IN FILIPINO, AND THE ANIMALS' DIALOGUE IS WRITTEN WITH AN OLD TAGALOG SCRIPT CALLED BAYBAYIN.

AS A SYLLABIC SCRIPT, LETTERS ARE READ AS A SYLLABLE SOUND OF EITHER A SINGLE VOWEL OR A CONSONANT/VOWEL PAIR.

AND SINCE IT'S FALLEN OUT OF USE, ATTEMPTS TO MODERNIZE THE SCRIPT HAVE BEEN INTRODUCED SO LETTERS CAN BE EASILY READ WITHOUT RELYING ON CONTEXT. DO NOTE THERE IS NO OFFICIAL ONE YET!

LET'S START WITH THE VOWELS:

A
E
U
MODERN ADDITION
I
O

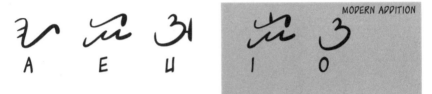

NEXT ARE THE CONSONANT/VOWEL PAIRS WHICH ARE PAIRED BY DEFAULT WITH THE VOWEL "A."

BA
KA
DA
GA
HA
LA
MA
NA
NGA
PA
SA
RA
TA
WA
YA

MODERN ADDITION
FA
JA
LLA
ÑA
VA
ZA
TSA
CA
QUA
XA

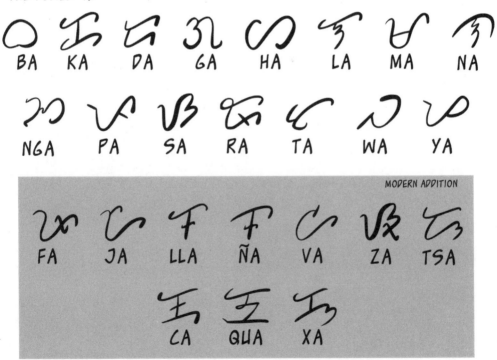

NOTES AND REFERENCES:

* BAYBAYIN MODERNIZATION REFERENCED FROM MODERN BAYBAYIN (HTTP://MODERNBAYBAYIN.BLOGSPOT.COM/)
* COVER FONT BY BAYBAYIN MODERN FONTS (HTTP://NORDENX.BLOGSPOT.COM/)
* ONLINE VERSION AND FULL TRANSCRIPT OF THE COMIC IN TAGALOG AND ENGLISH AT BIT.LY/BAYBAYINCOMIC
* SPECIAL THANKS TO ALAI AGADULIN WHO SERVED AS CONSULTANT AND PROOFREADER FOR THE BAYBAYIN.

CONSONANTS CAN BE PAIRED WITH OTHER VOWELS BY ADDING A MARK CALLED KUDLIT(.) EITHER ON TOP OR BENEATH THE LETTER. A WAVY LINE KUDLIT (–) IS ADDED TO MAKE DISCTINCTIONS BETWEEN E/I AND O/U.

WHILE ADDING A DIFFERENT MARK CALLED A VIRAMA (+ OR X) WILL CANCEL OUT THE VOWEL SOUND.

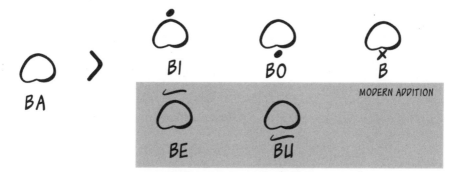

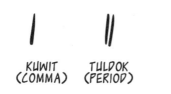

* NOTE: THE VIRAMA WAS ONLY LATER INTRODUCED IN 1620 AS AN AID TO TRANSLATION ATTEMPTS OF FOREIGN TEXT TO TAGALOG.

AND FINALLY, BAYBAYIN USES THE FOLLOWING FOR PUNCTUATION:

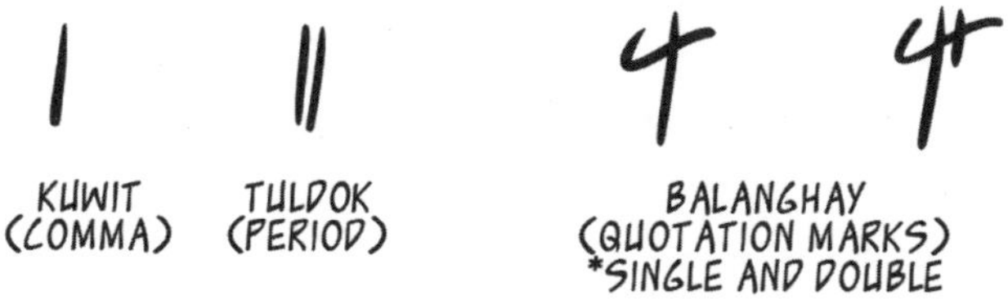

KUWIT (COMMA)	TULDOK (PERIOD)	BALANGHAY (QUOTATION MARKS) *SINGLE AND DOUBLE

THAT'S ALL FOR THE BASICS. NOW TRY TO DECIPHER SOME OF THE TAGALOG WORDS YOU MAY FIND IN THE STORY!

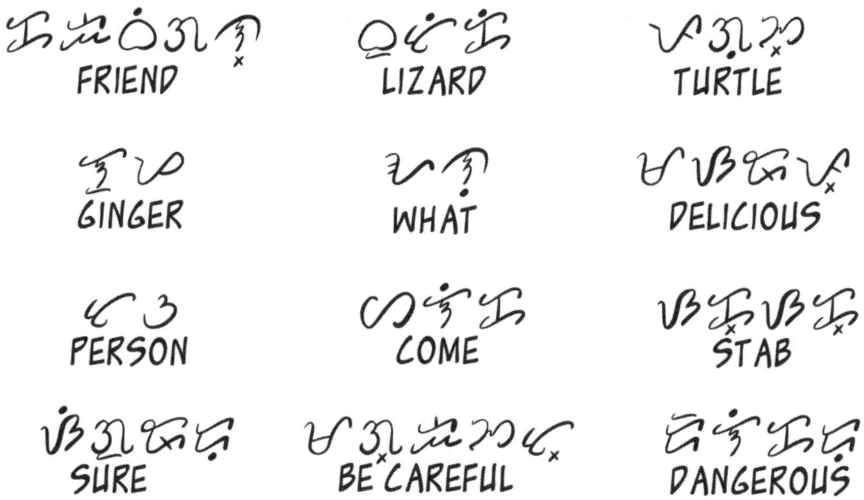

FRIEND

LIZARD

TURTLE

GINGER

WHAT

DELICIOUS

PERSON

COME

STAB

SURE

BE CAREFUL

DANGEROUS

KAPO'I AND THE OWL

SLOANE LEONG
KATE ASHWIN
MEREDITH MCCLAREN

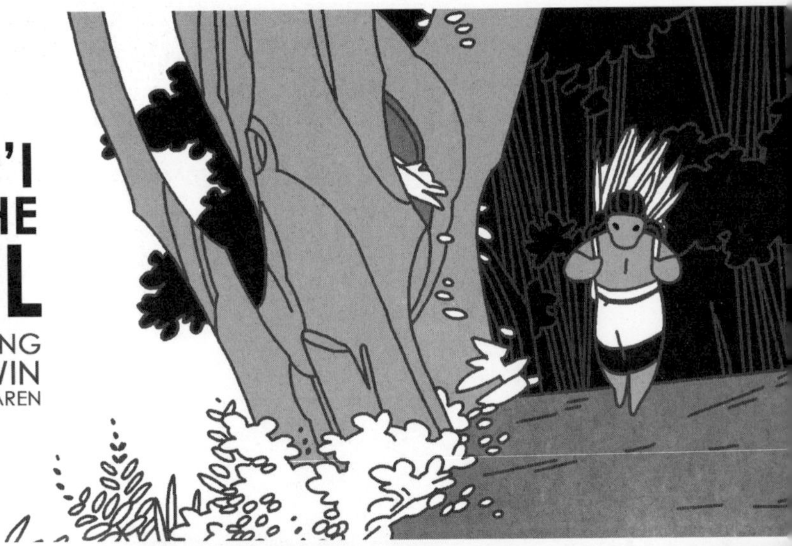

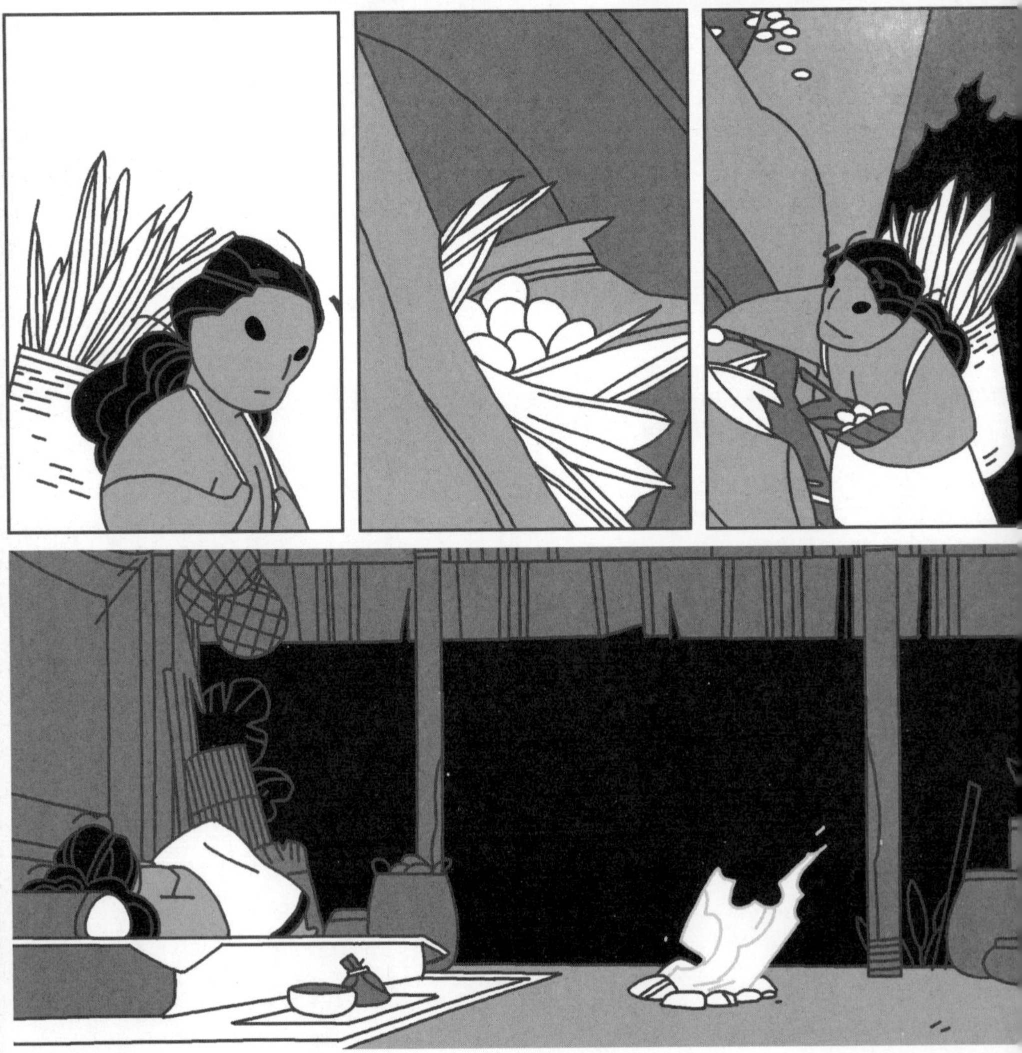

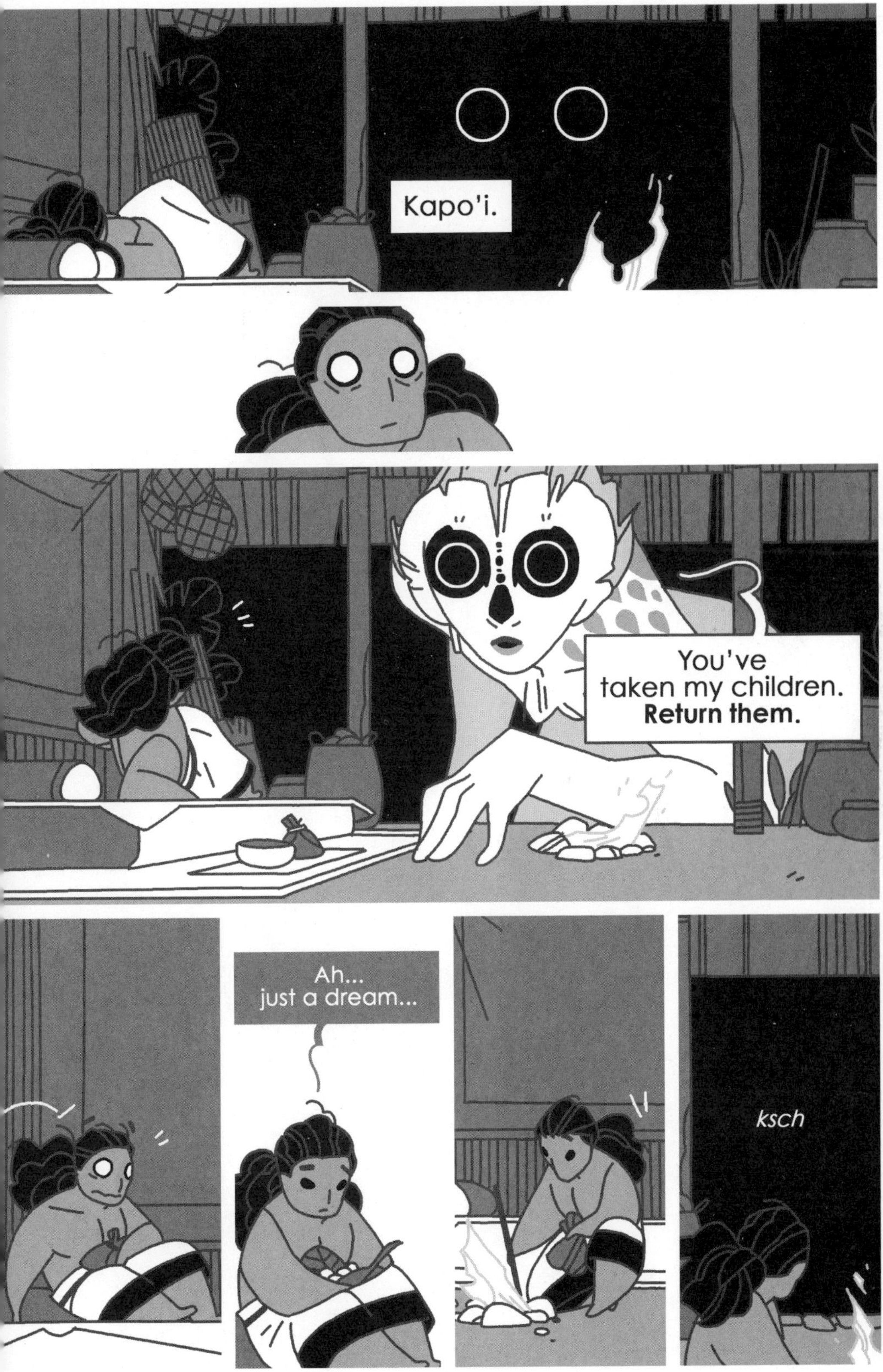
Kapo'i.
You've taken my children. **Return them.**
Ah... just a dream...
ksch

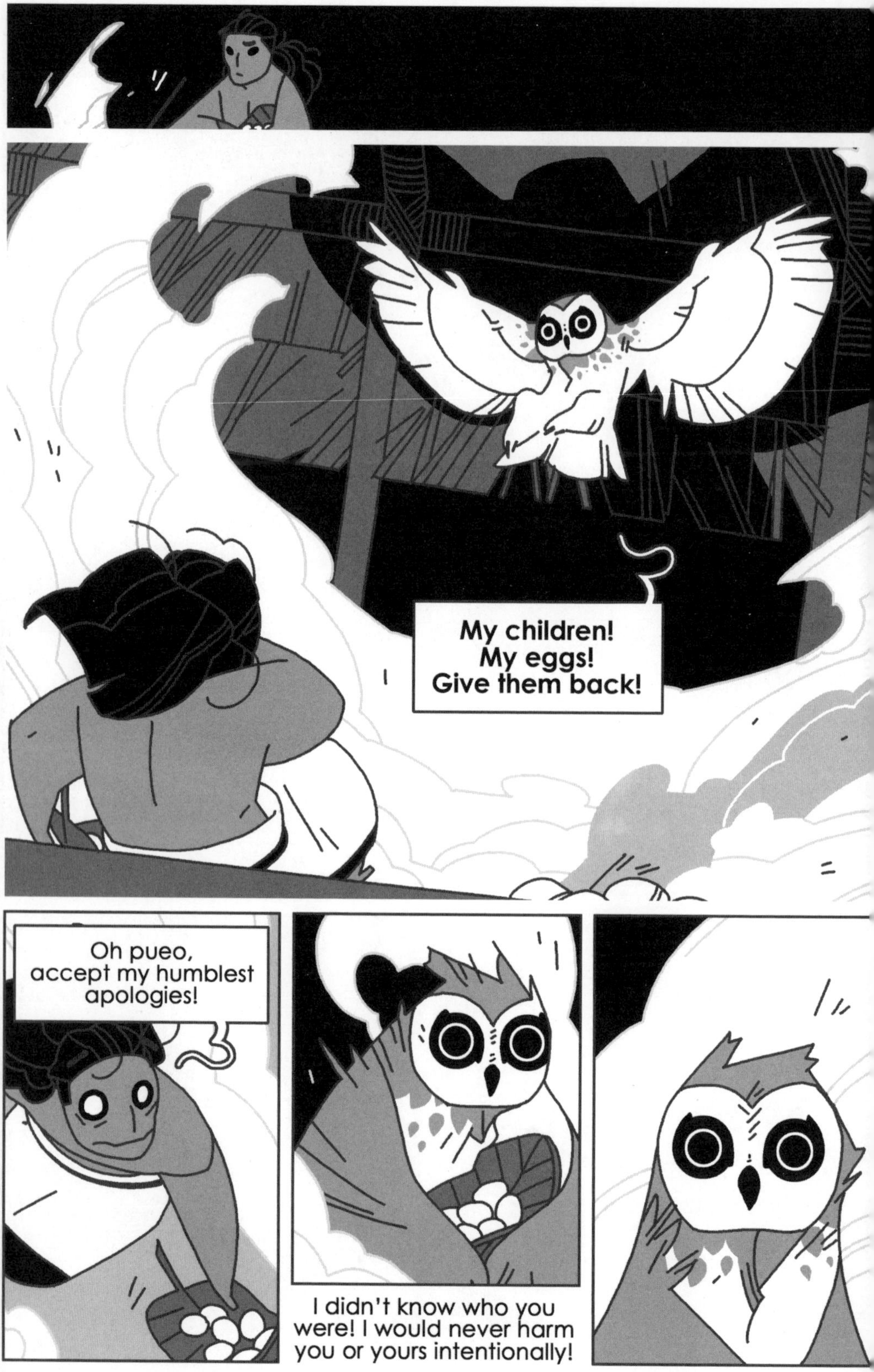
My children!
My eggs!
Give them back!
Oh pueo,
accept my humblest
apologies!
I didn't know who you
were! I would never harm
you or yours intentionally!

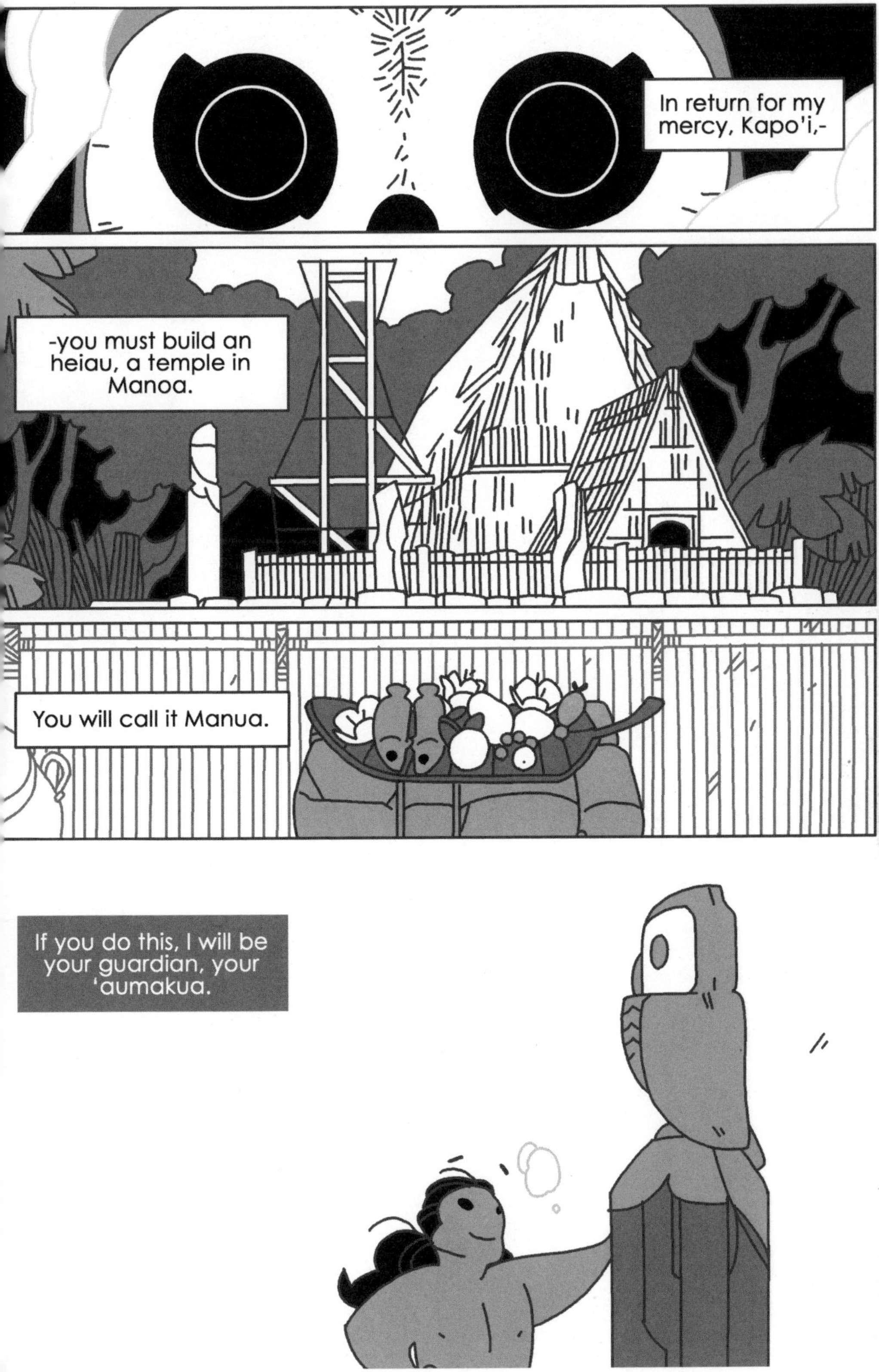
In return for my mercy, Kapo'i,-
-you must build an heiau, a temple in Manoa.
You will call it Manua.
If you do this, I will be your guardian, your 'aumakua.

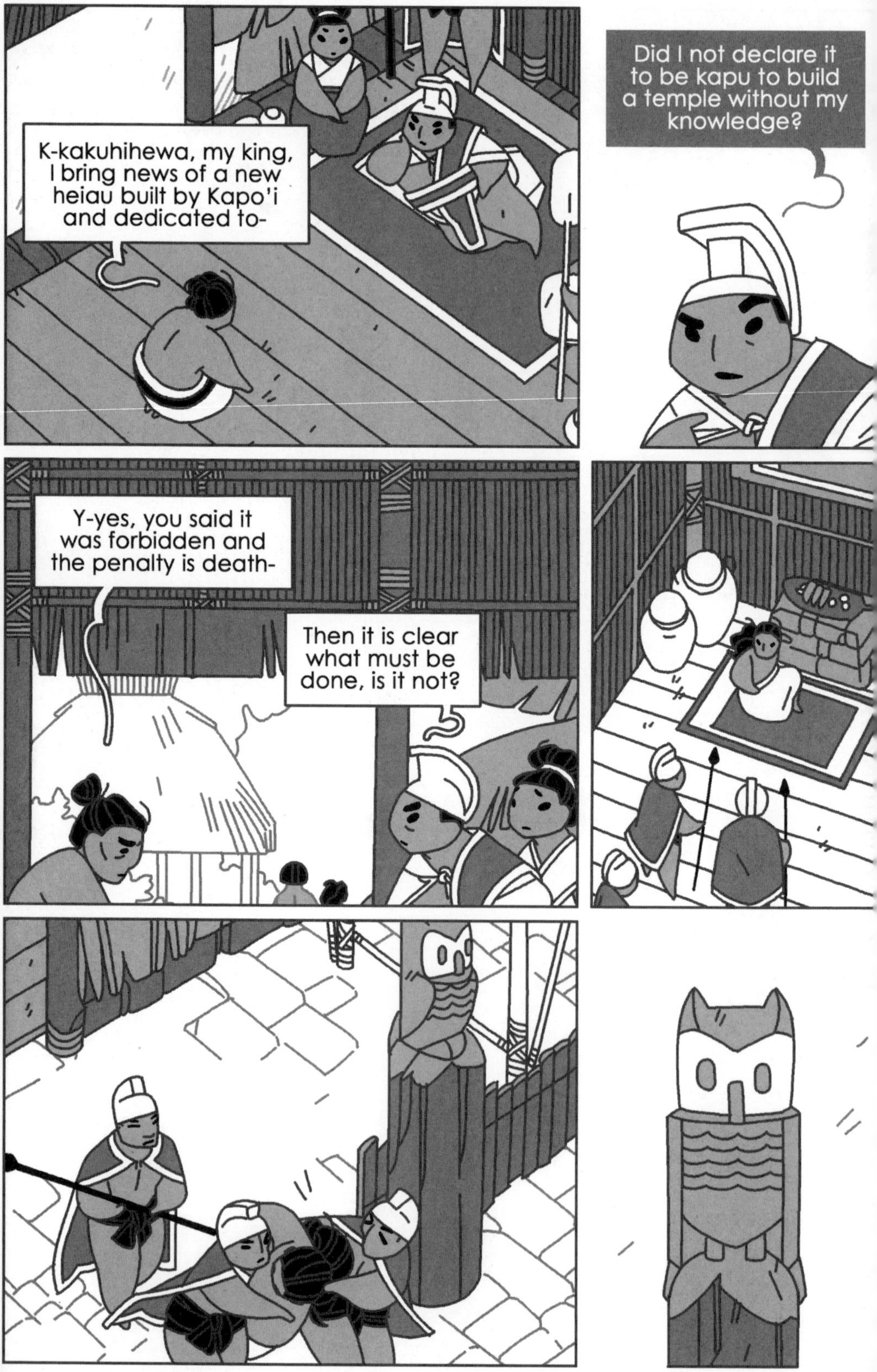
K-kakuhihewa, my king, I bring news of a new heiau built by Kapo'i and dedicated to-
Did I not declare it to be kapu to build a temple without my knowledge?
Y-yes, you said it was forbidden and the penalty is death-
Then it is clear what must be done, is it not?

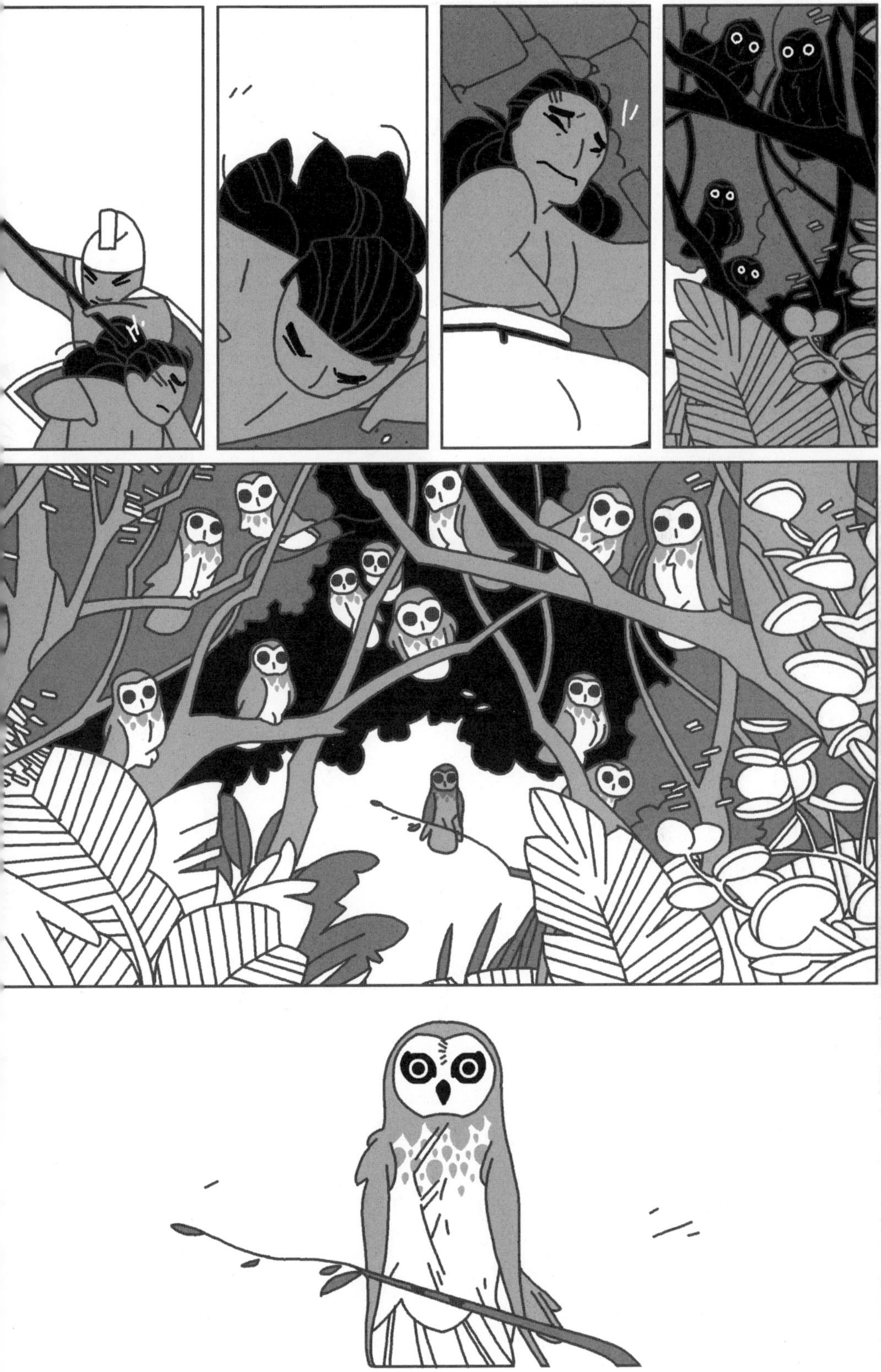

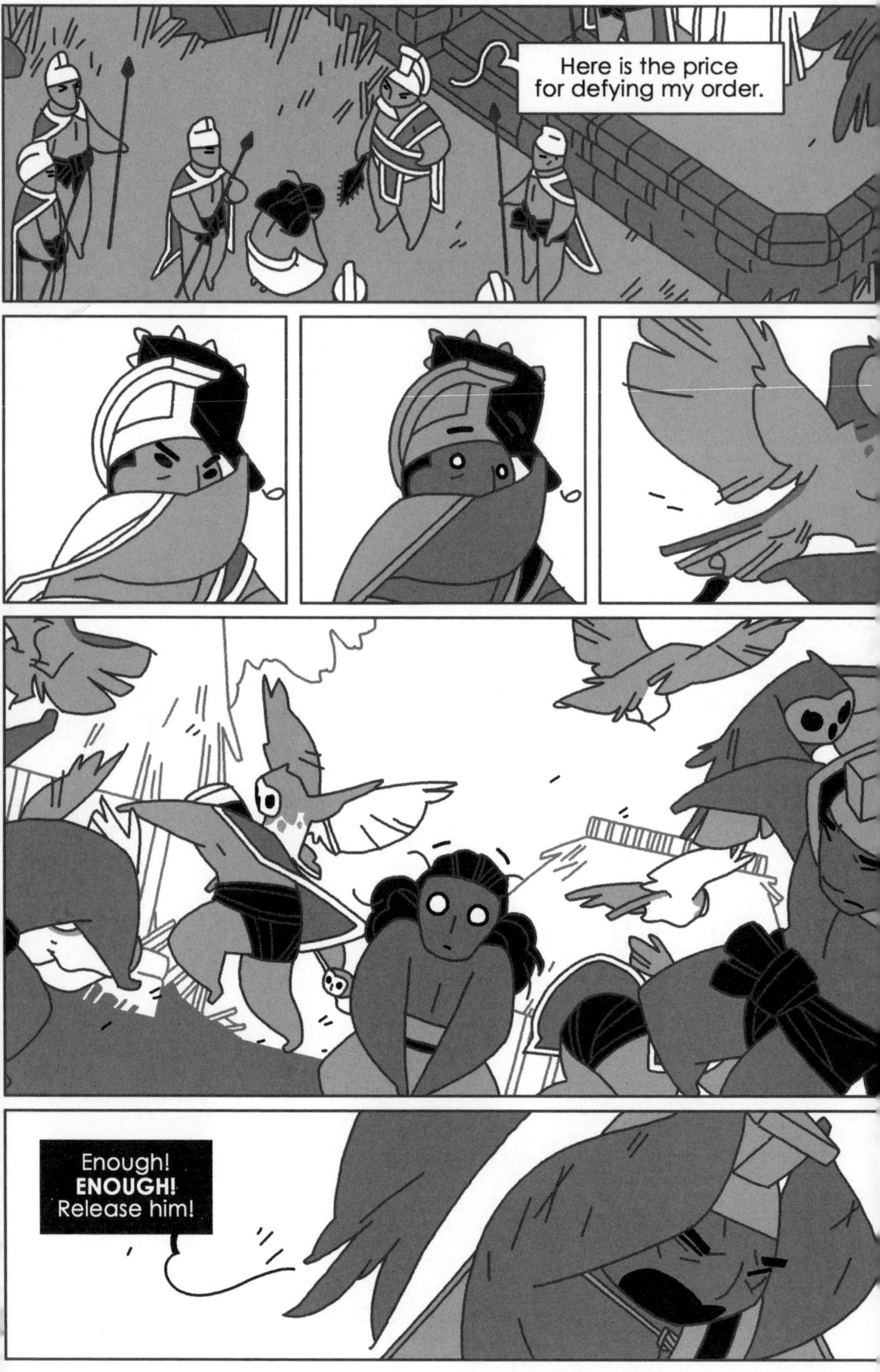
Here is the price
for defying my order.
Enough!
ENOUGH!
Release him!

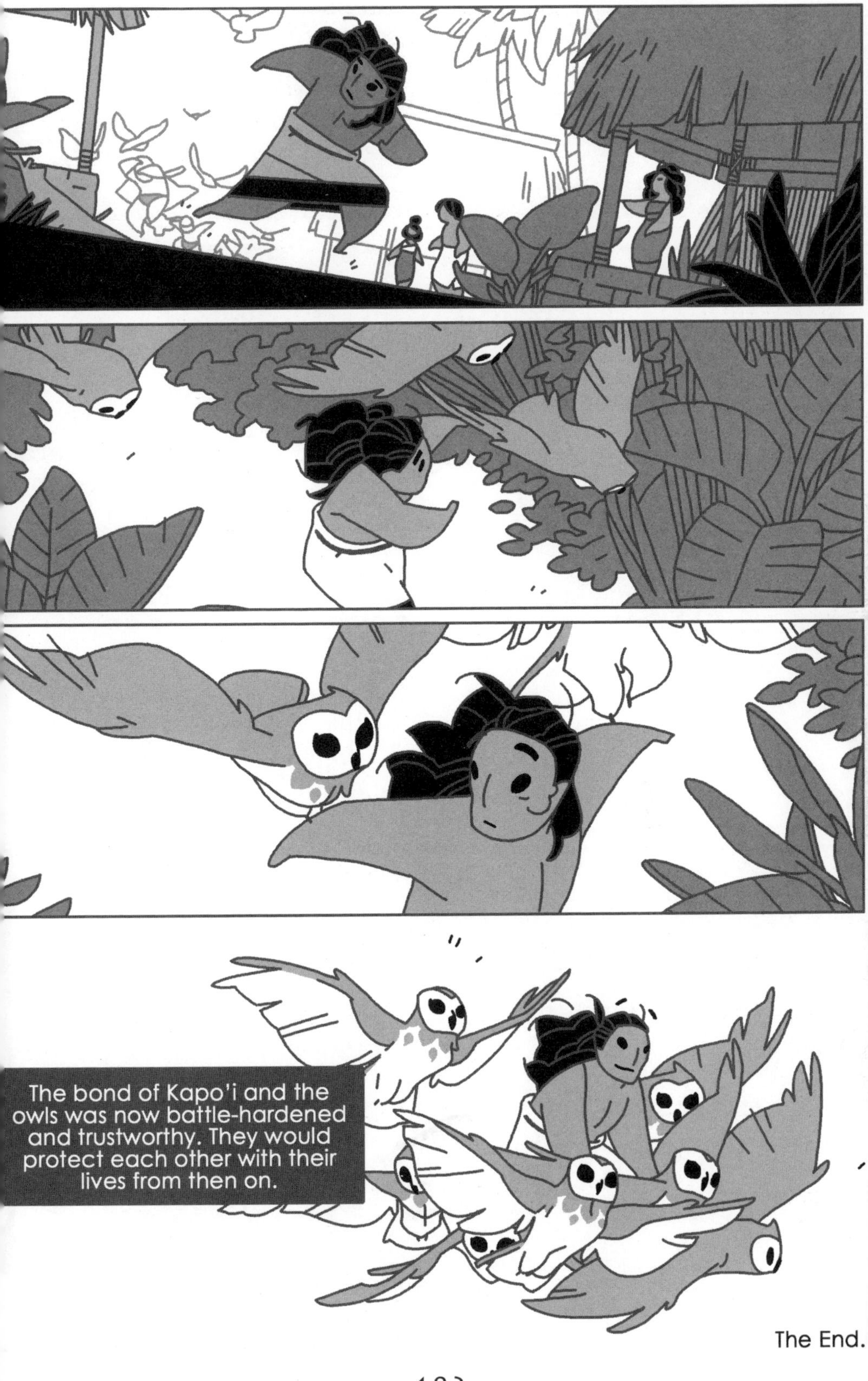
The bond of Kapo'i and the owls was now battle-hardened and trustworthy. They would protect each other with their lives from then on.
The End.

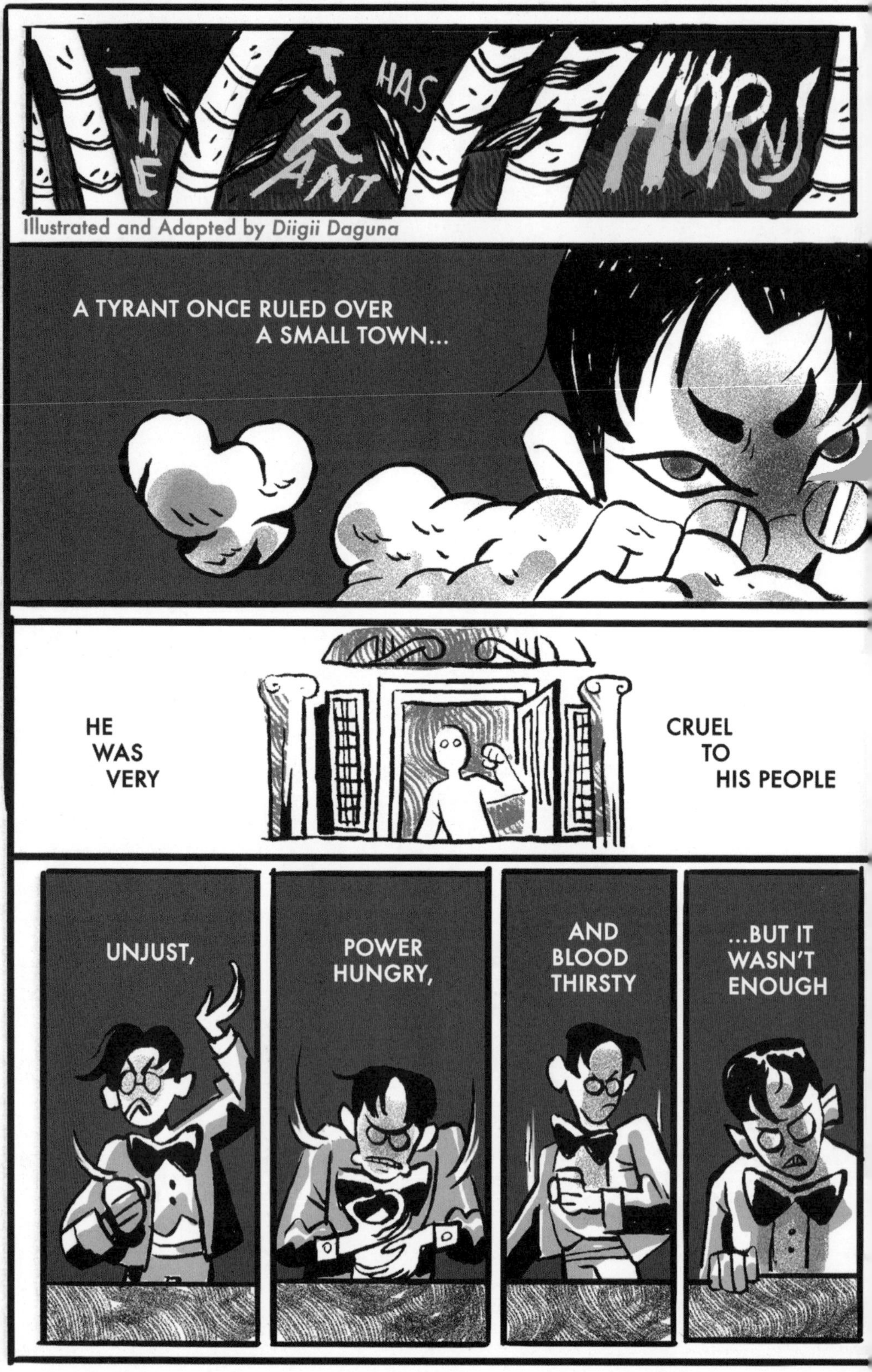

THE TYRANT HAS HORNS
Illustrated and Adapted by Diigii Daguna
A TYRANT ONCE RULED OVER A SMALL TOWN...
HE WAS VERY
CRUEL TO HIS PEOPLE
UNJUST,
POWER HUNGRY,
AND BLOOD THIRSTY
...BUT IT WASN'T ENOUGH

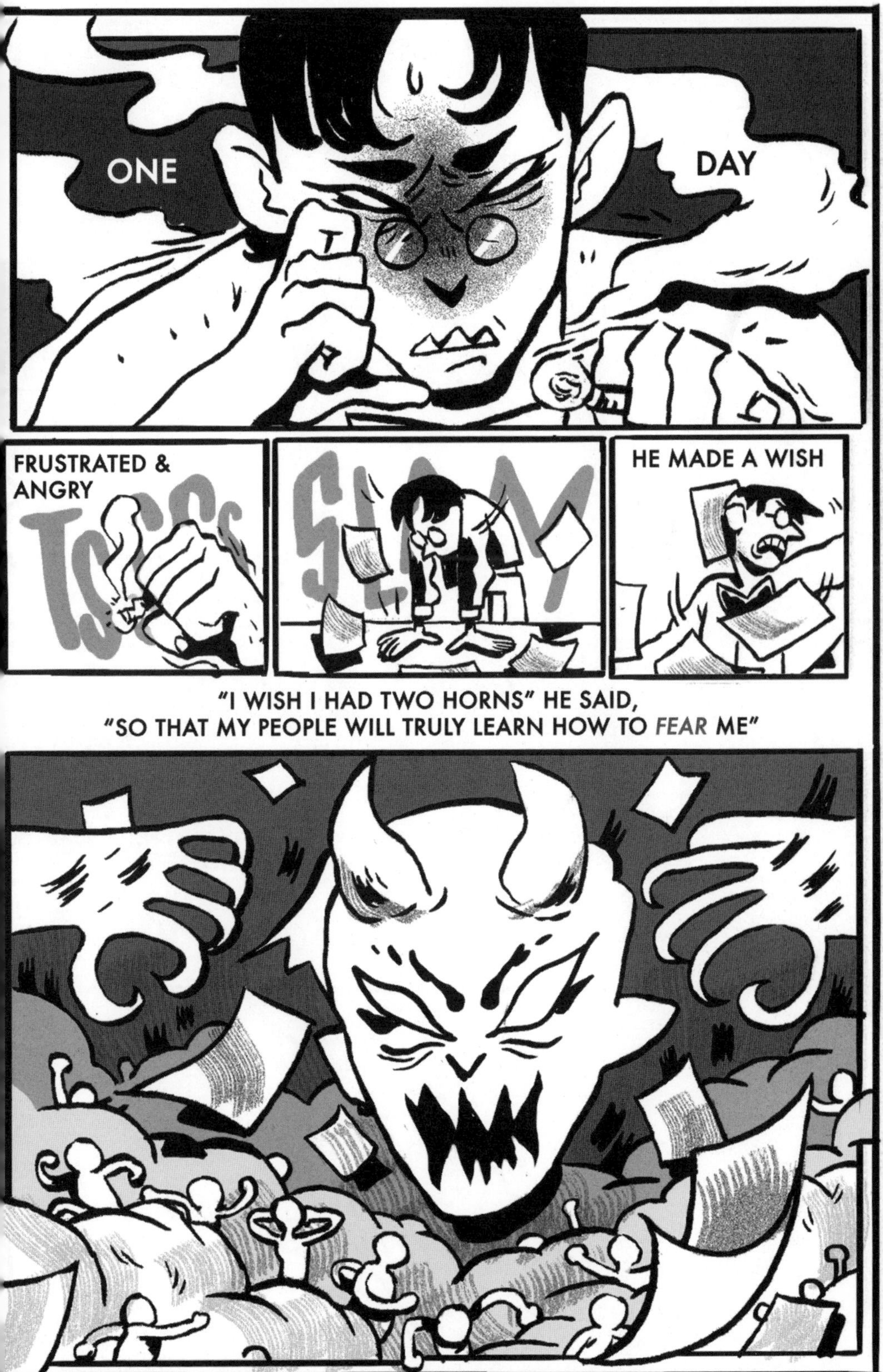
ONE
DAY
FRUSTRATED & ANGRY
HE MADE A WISH
"I WISH I HAD TWO HORNS" HE SAID,
"SO THAT MY PEOPLE WILL TRULY LEARN HOW TO *FEAR* ME"

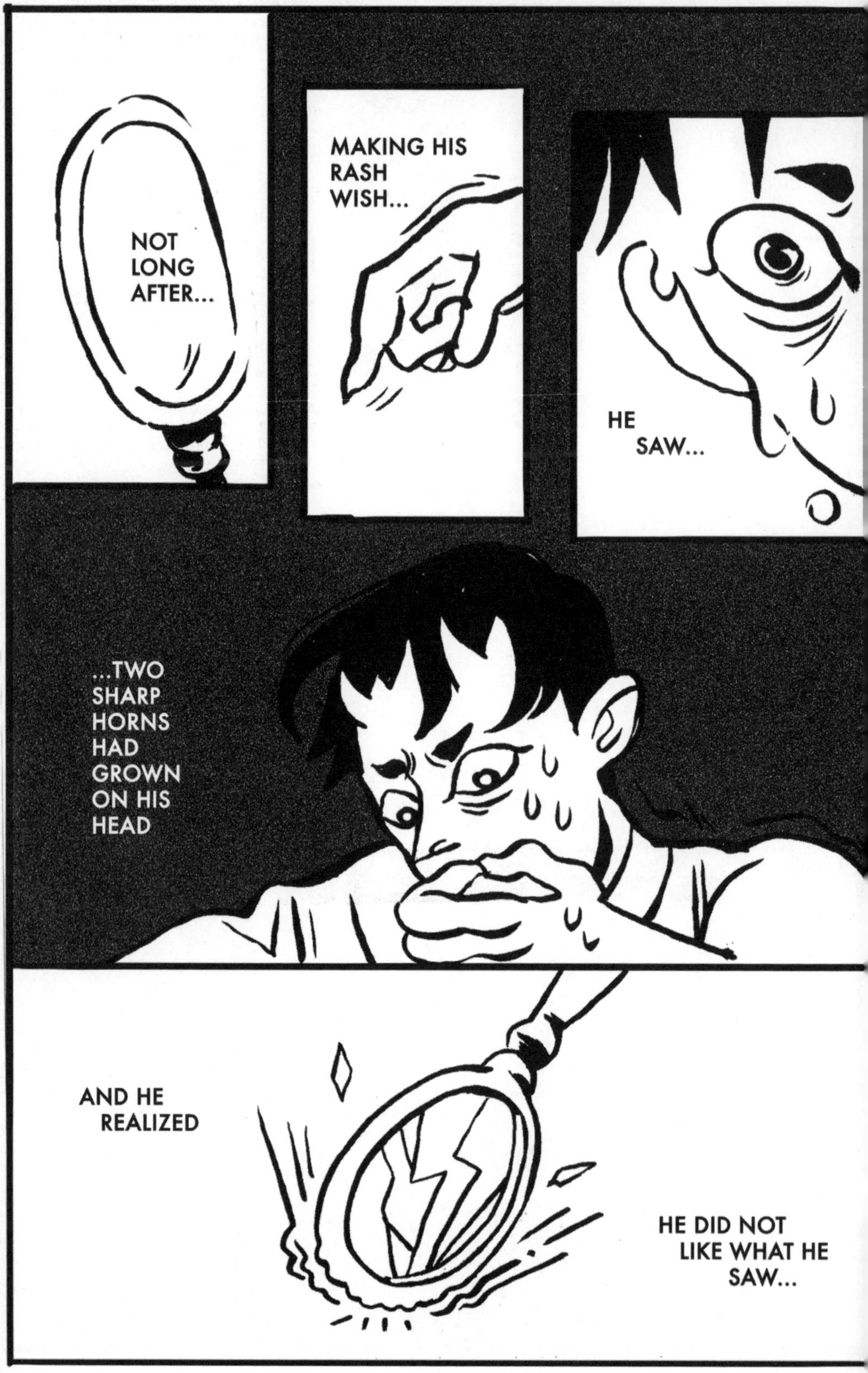

NOT LONG AFTER...
MAKING HIS RASH WISH...
HE SAW...
...TWO SHARP HORNS HAD GROWN ON HIS HEAD
AND HE REALIZED
HE DID NOT LIKE WHAT HE SAW...

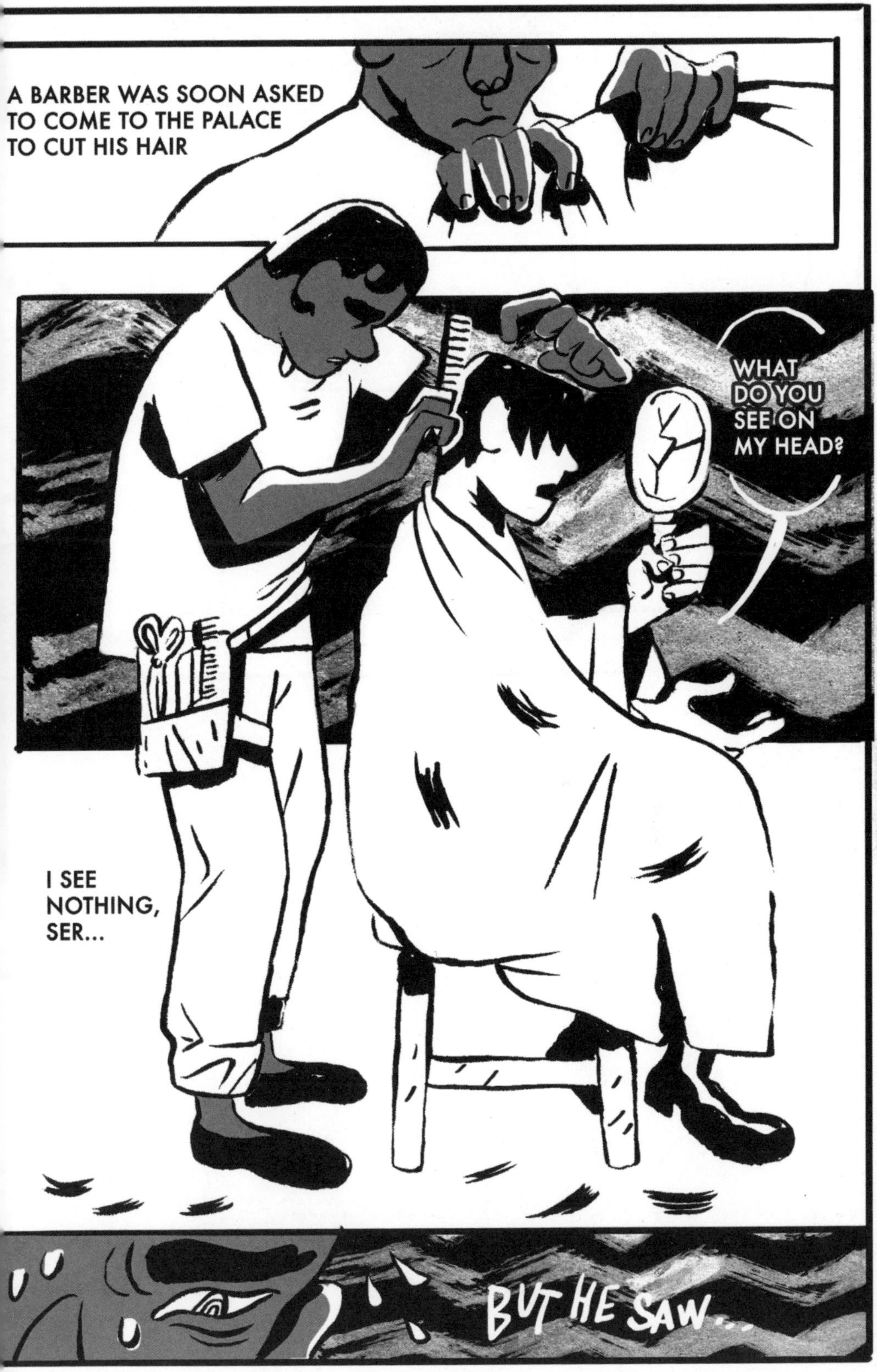
A BARBER WAS SOON ASKED TO COME TO THE PALACE TO CUT HIS HAIR
WHAT DO YOU SEE ON MY HEAD?
I SEE NOTHING, SER...
BUT HE SAW...

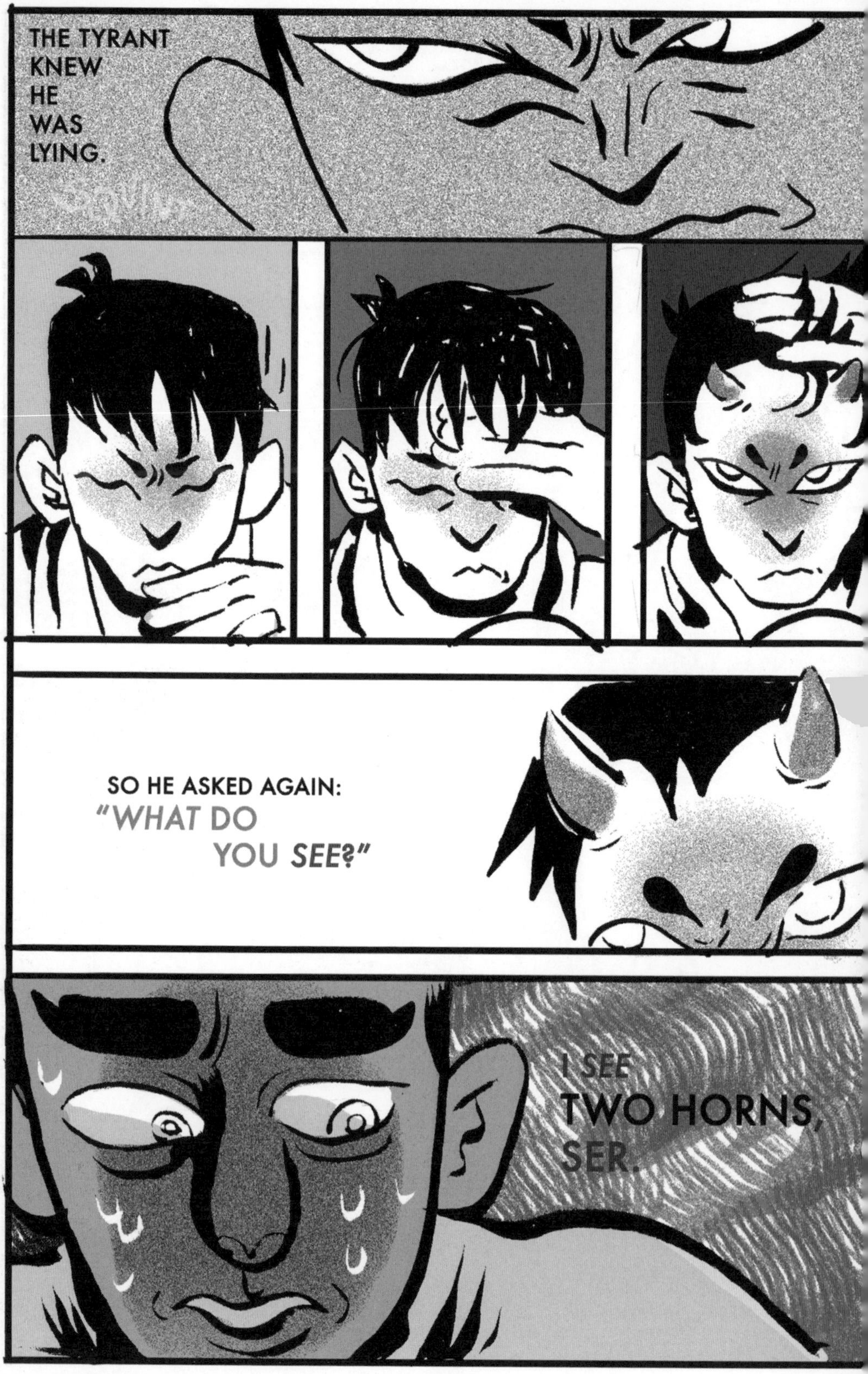

THE TYRANT KNEW HE WAS LYING.
SO HE ASKED AGAIN: "WHAT DO YOU SEE?"
I SEE TWO HORNS, SER.

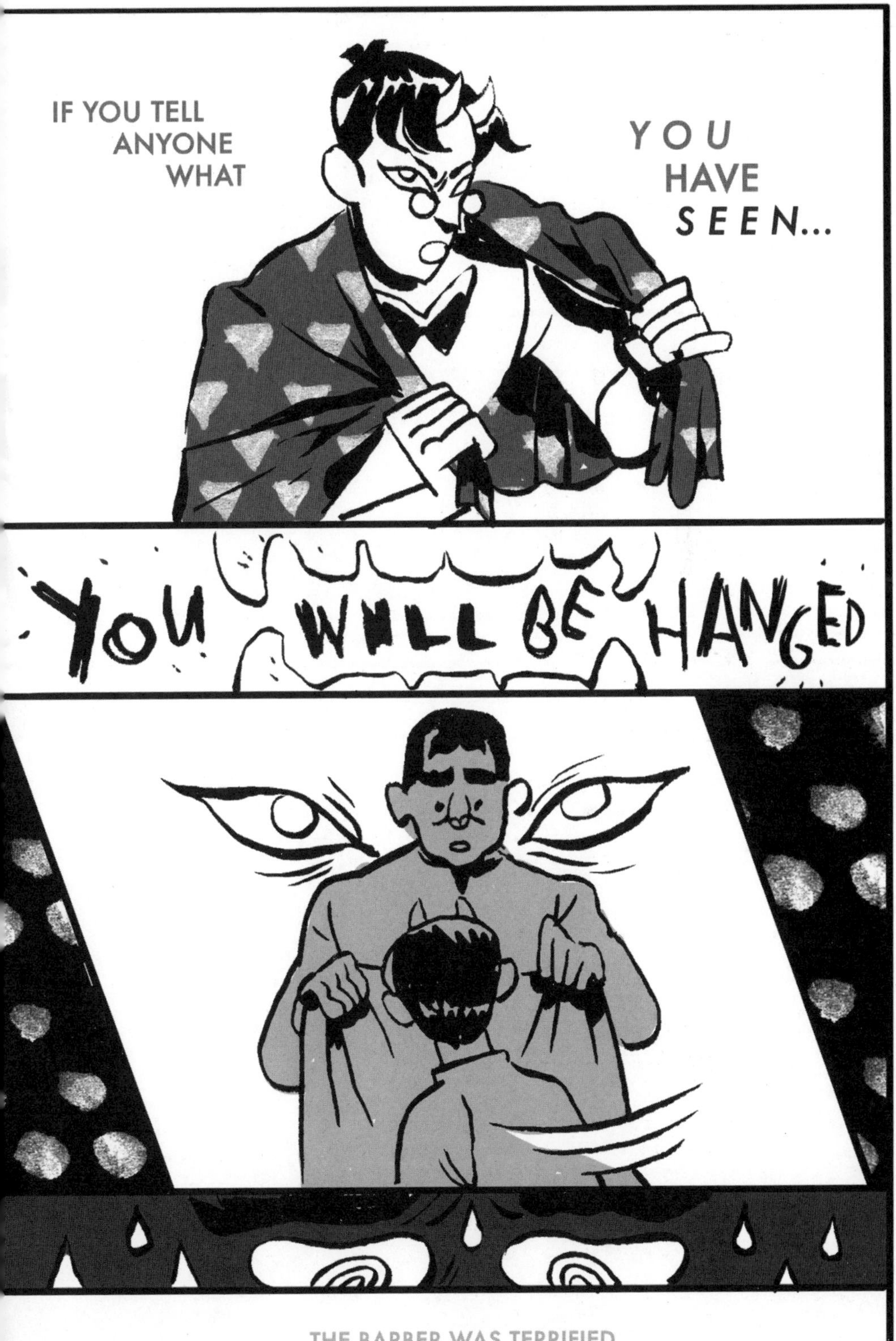
IF YOU TELL ANYONE WHAT
YOU HAVE SEEN...
YOU WILL BE HANGED
THE BARBER WAS TERRIFIED

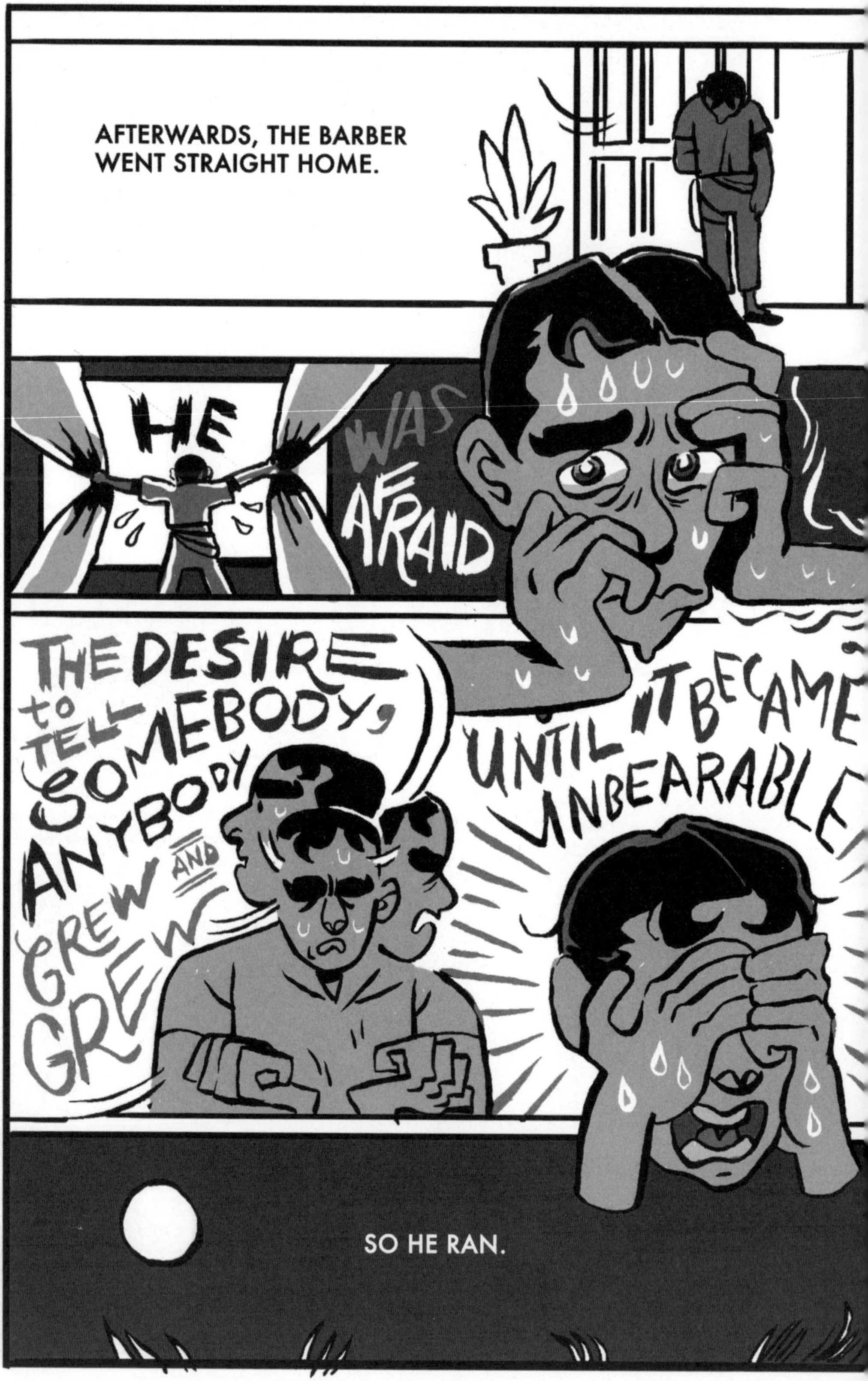
AFTERWARDS, THE BARBER WENT STRAIGHT HOME.
HE
WAS
AFRAID
THE DESIRE to TELL SOMEBODY, ANYBODY GREW AND GREW AND GREW
UNTIL IT BECAME UNBEARABLE
SO HE RAN.

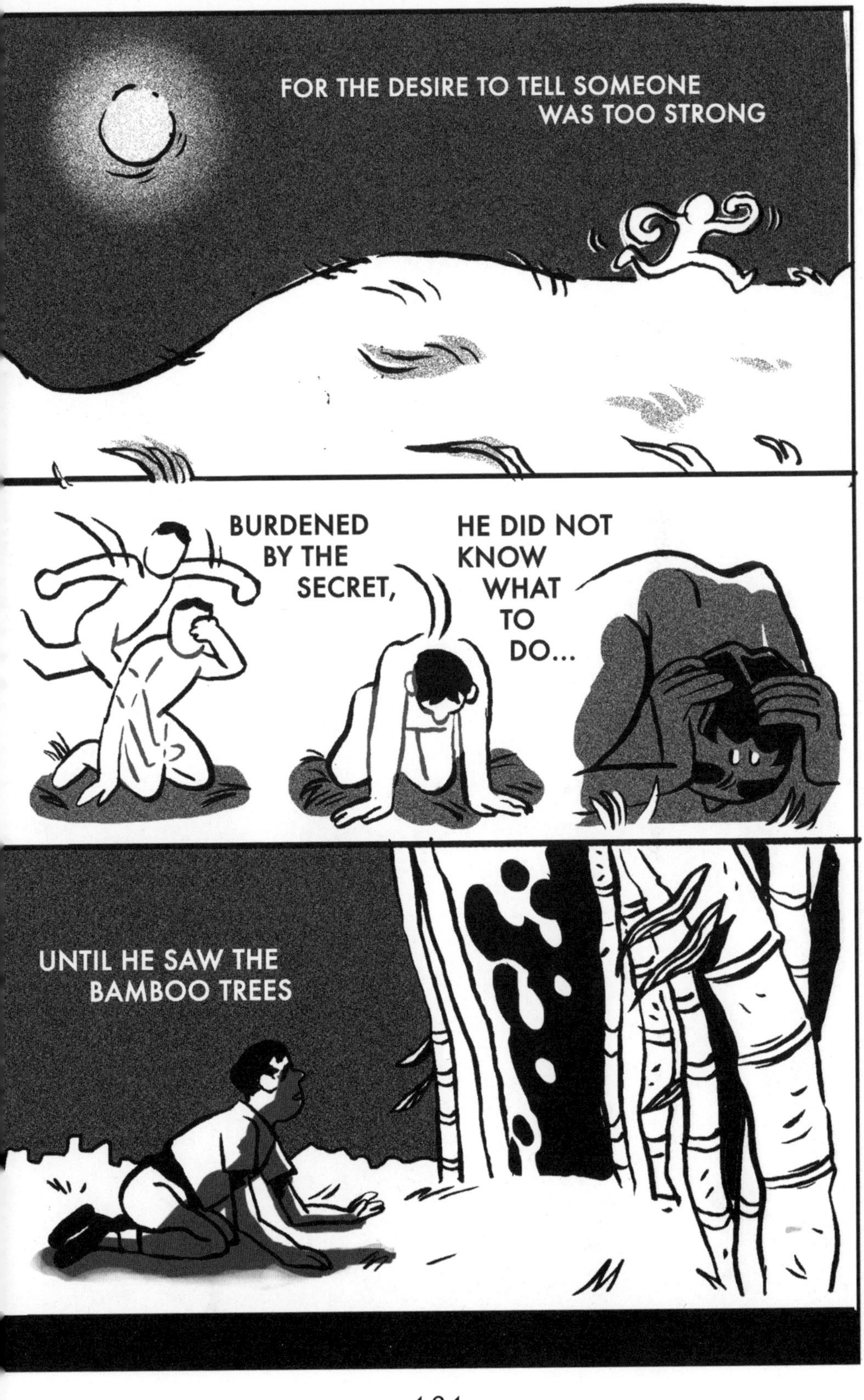
FOR THE DESIRE TO TELL SOMEONE WAS TOO STRONG
BURDENED BY THE SECRET,
HE DID NOT KNOW WHAT TO DO...
UNTIL HE SAW THE BAMBOO TREES

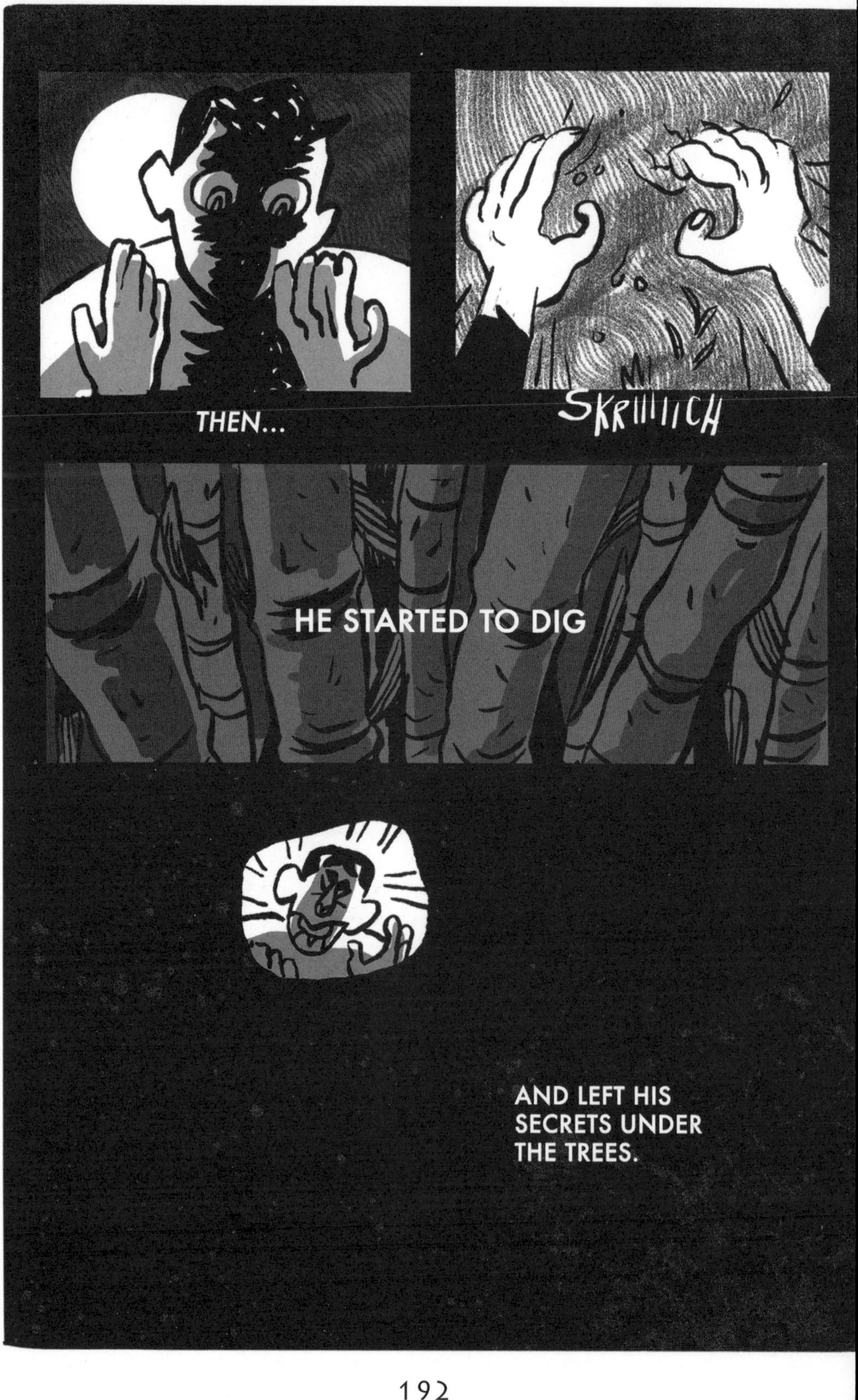
THEN...
SKRIIIIICH
HE STARTED TO DIG
AND LEFT HIS SECRETS UNDER THE TREES.

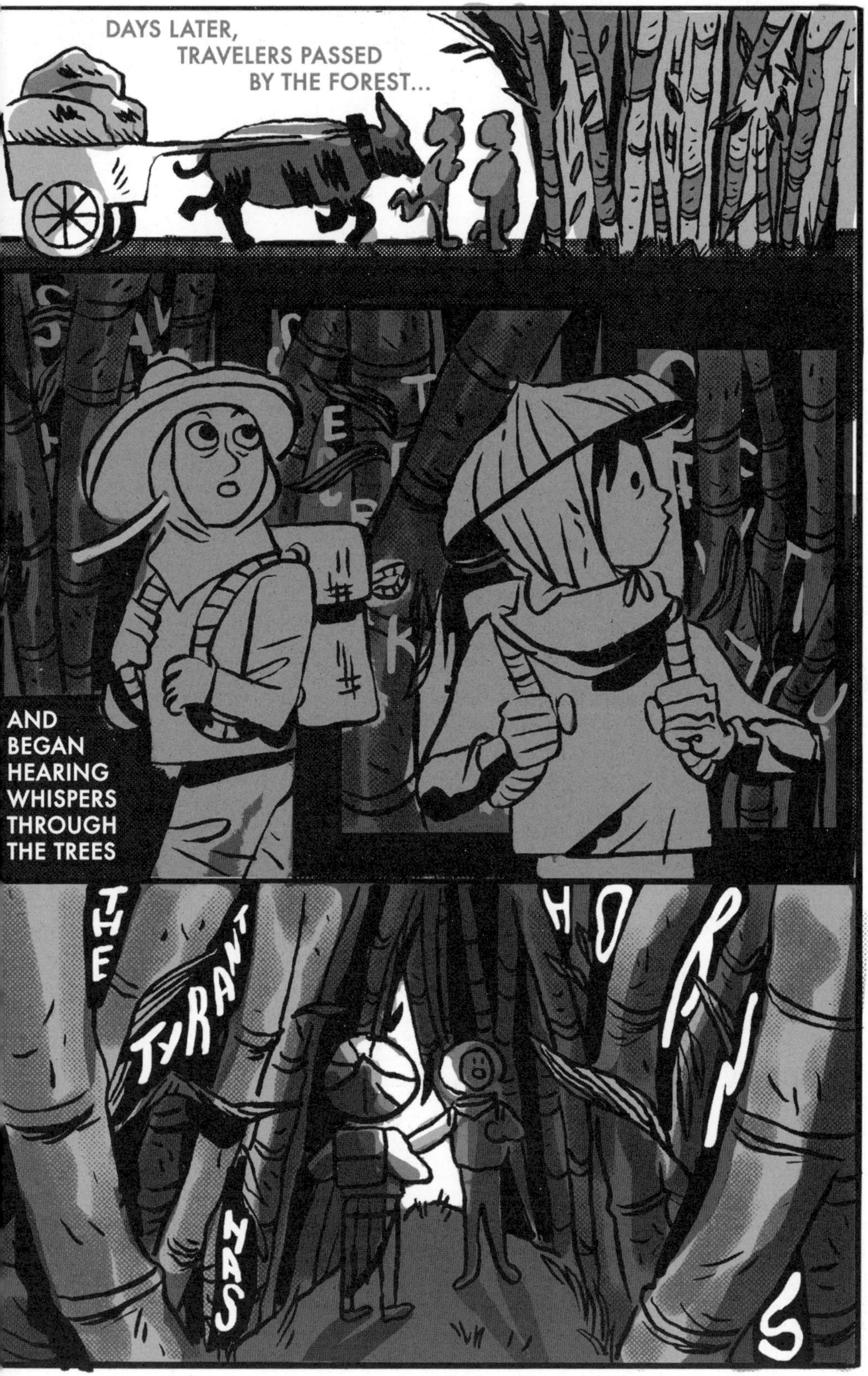
DAYS LATER, TRAVELERS PASSED BY THE FOREST...
AND BEGAN HEARING WHISPERS THROUGH THE TREES
THE TYRANT HAS HORNS

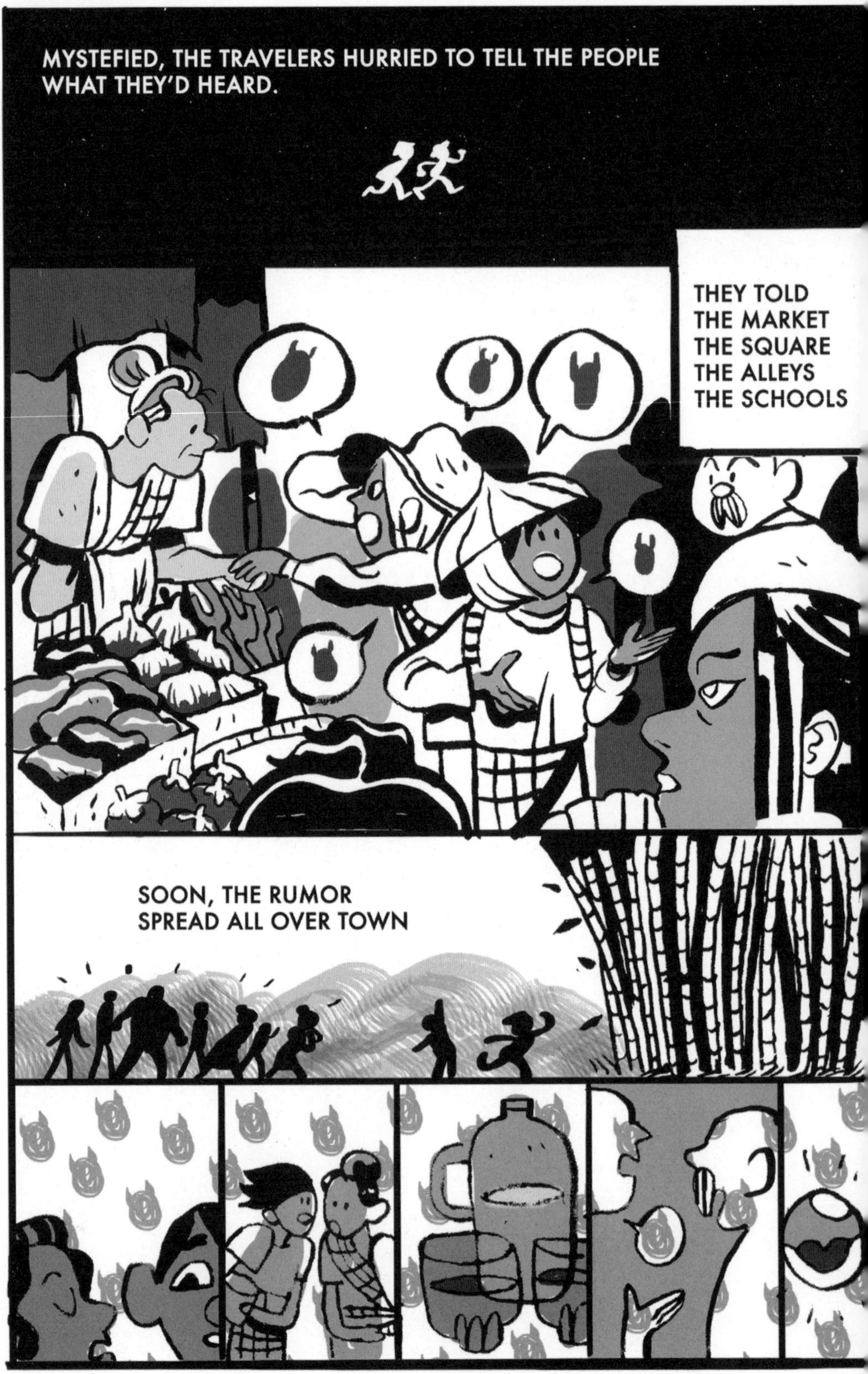
MYSTEFIED, THE TRAVELERS HURRIED TO TELL THE PEOPLE WHAT THEY'D HEARD.
THEY TOLD
THE MARKET
THE SQUARE
THE ALLEYS
THE SCHOOLS
SOON, THE RUMOR
SPREAD ALL OVER TOWN

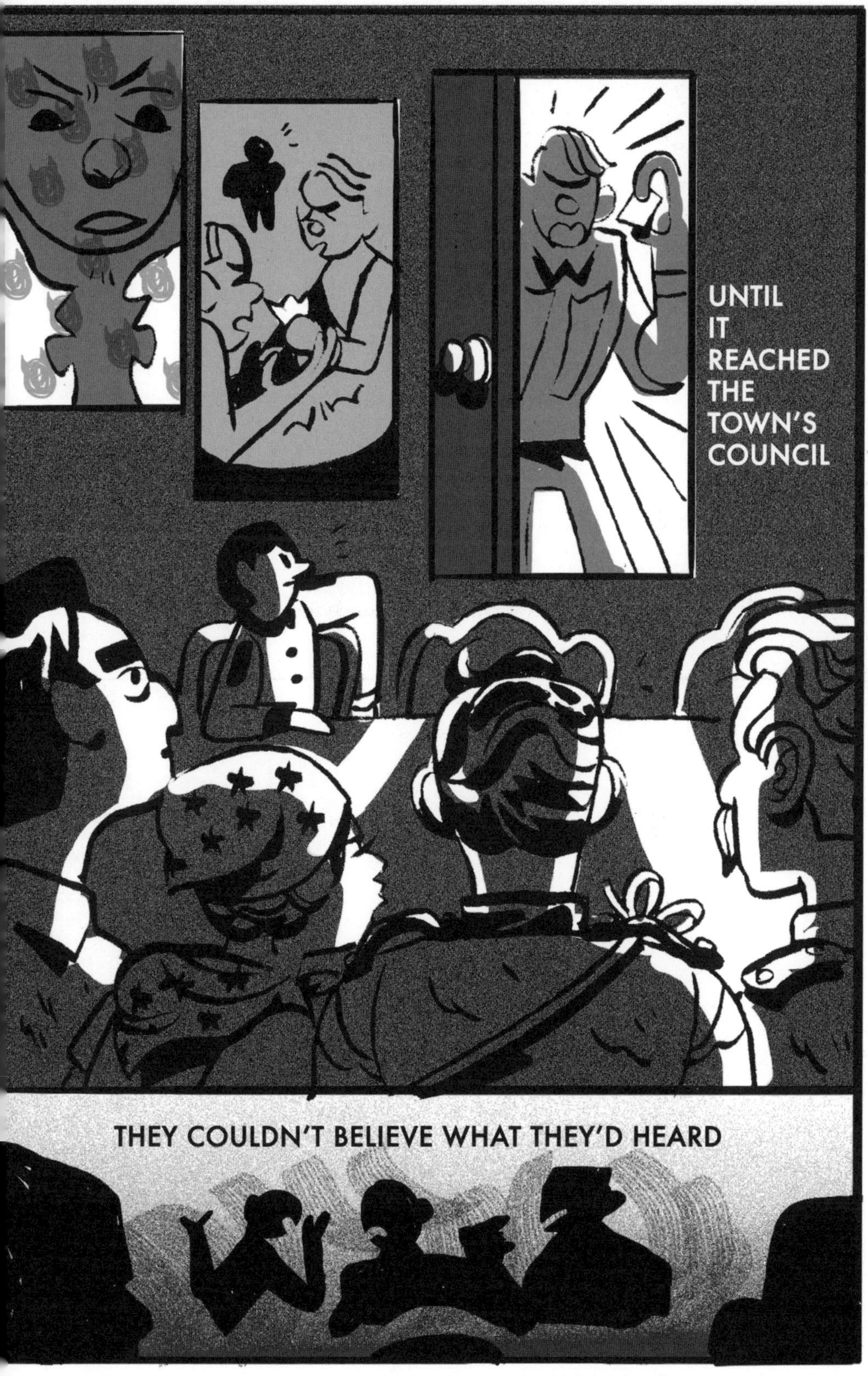
UNTIL IT REACHED THE TOWN'S COUNCIL
THEY COULDN'T BELIEVE WHAT THEY'D HEARD

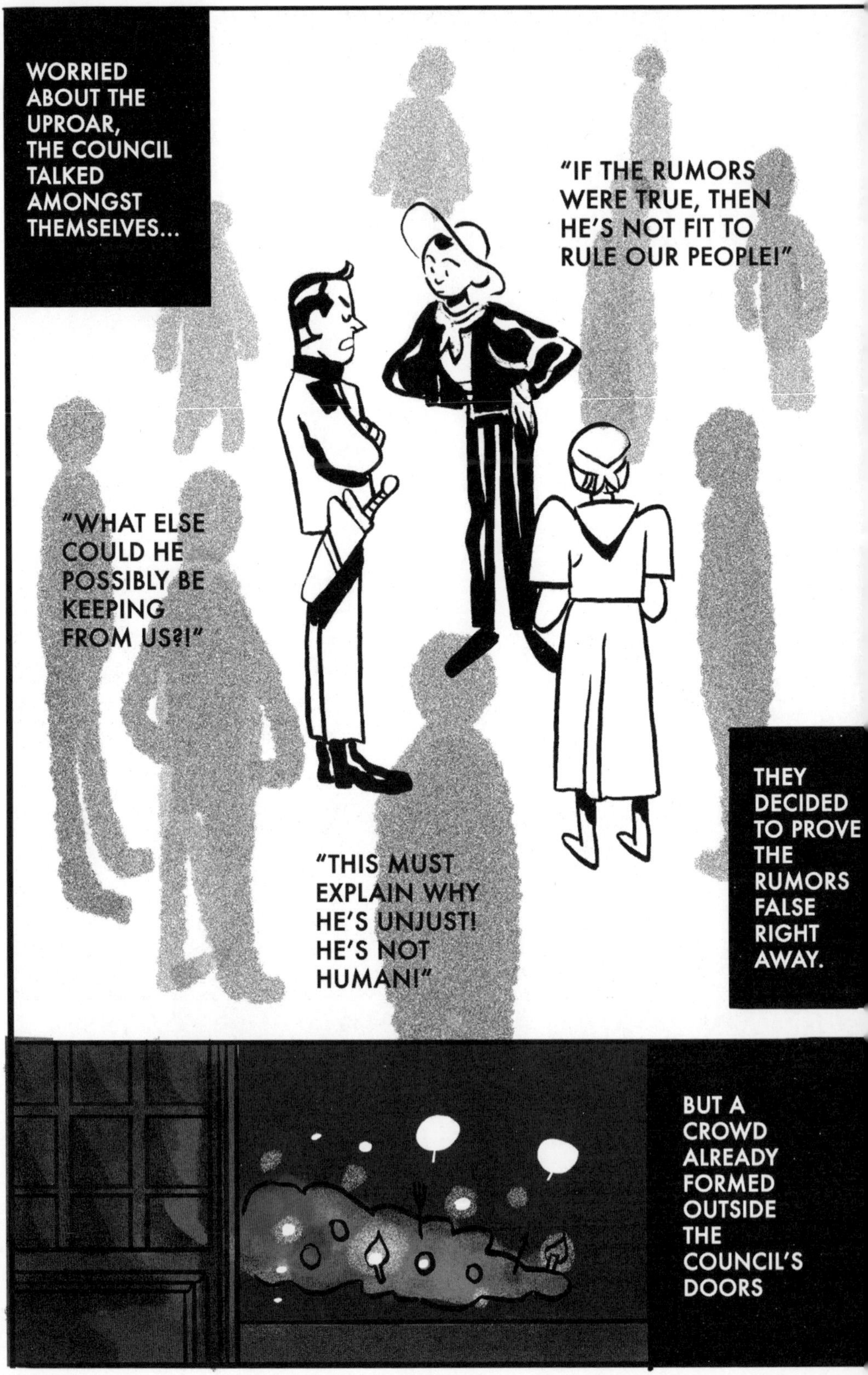
WORRIED ABOUT THE UPROAR, THE COUNCIL TALKED AMONGST THEMSELVES...
"IF THE RUMORS WERE TRUE, THEN HE'S NOT FIT TO RULE OUR PEOPLE!"
"WHAT ELSE COULD HE POSSIBLY BE KEEPING FROM US?!"
"THIS MUST EXPLAIN WHY HE'S UNJUST! HE'S NOT HUMAN!"
THEY DECIDED TO PROVE THE RUMORS FALSE RIGHT AWAY.
BUT A CROWD ALREADY FORMED OUTSIDE THE COUNCIL'S DOORS

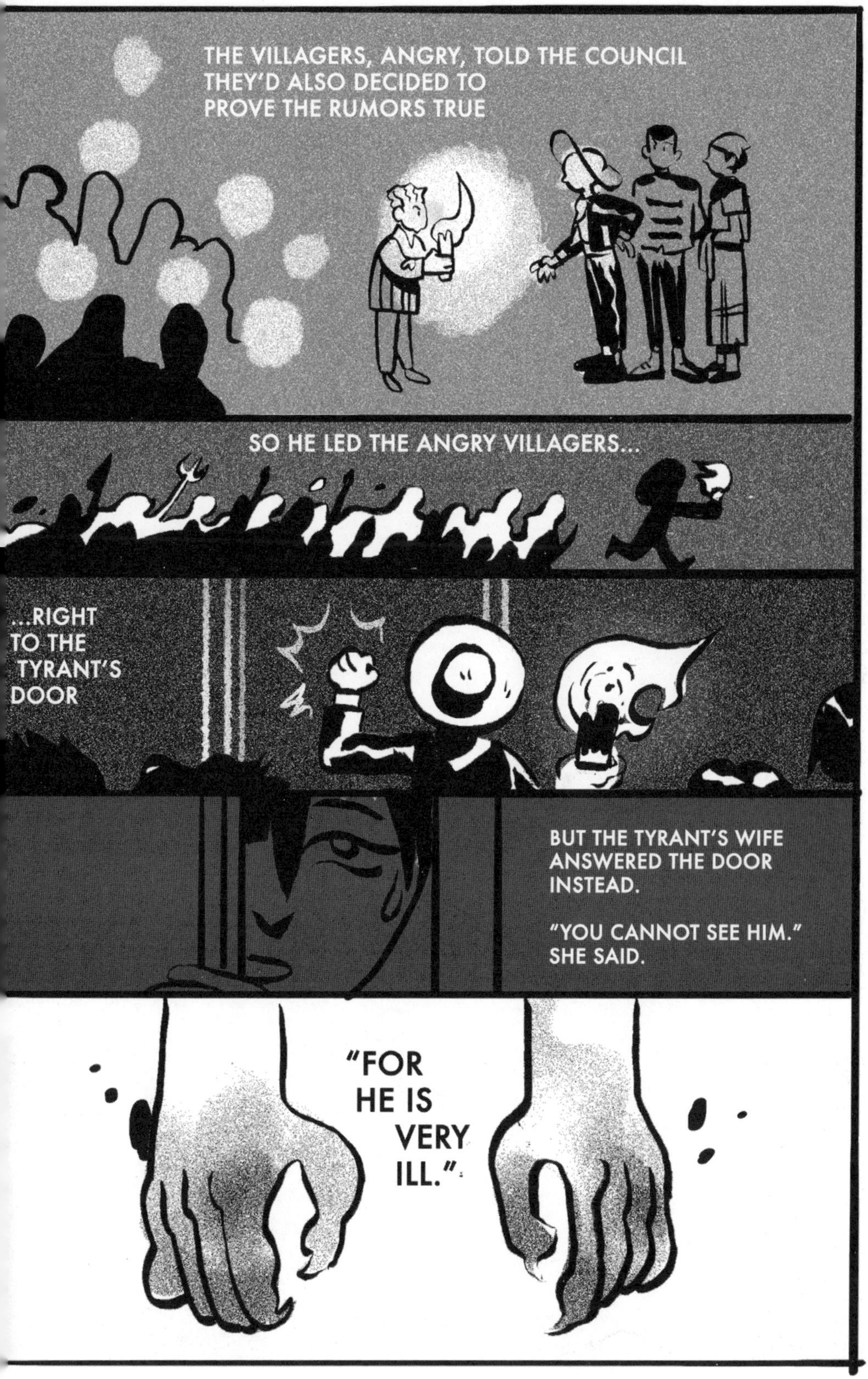
THE VILLAGERS, ANGRY, TOLD THE COUNCIL THEY'D ALSO DECIDED TO PROVE THE RUMORS TRUE
SO HE LED THE ANGRY VILLAGERS...
...RIGHT TO THE TYRANT'S DOOR
BUT THE TYRANT'S WIFE ANSWERED THE DOOR INSTEAD.
"YOU CANNOT SEE HIM." SHE SAID.
"FOR HE IS VERY ILL."

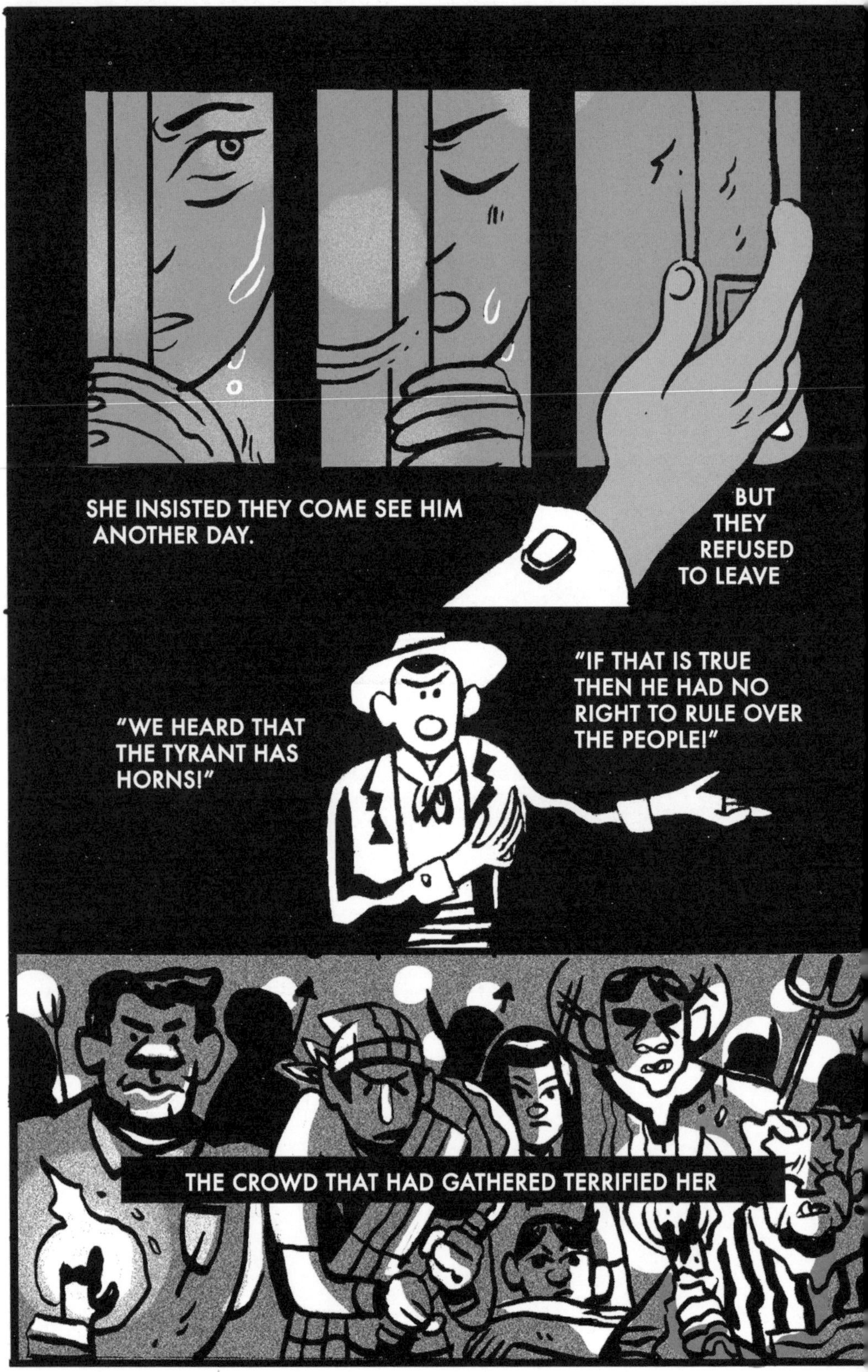
SHE INSISTED THEY COME SEE HIM ANOTHER DAY.
BUT THEY REFUSED TO LEAVE
"WE HEARD THAT THE TYRANT HAS HORNS!"
"IF THAT IS TRUE THEN HE HAD NO RIGHT TO RULE OVER THE PEOPLE!"
THE CROWD THAT HAD GATHERED TERRIFIED HER

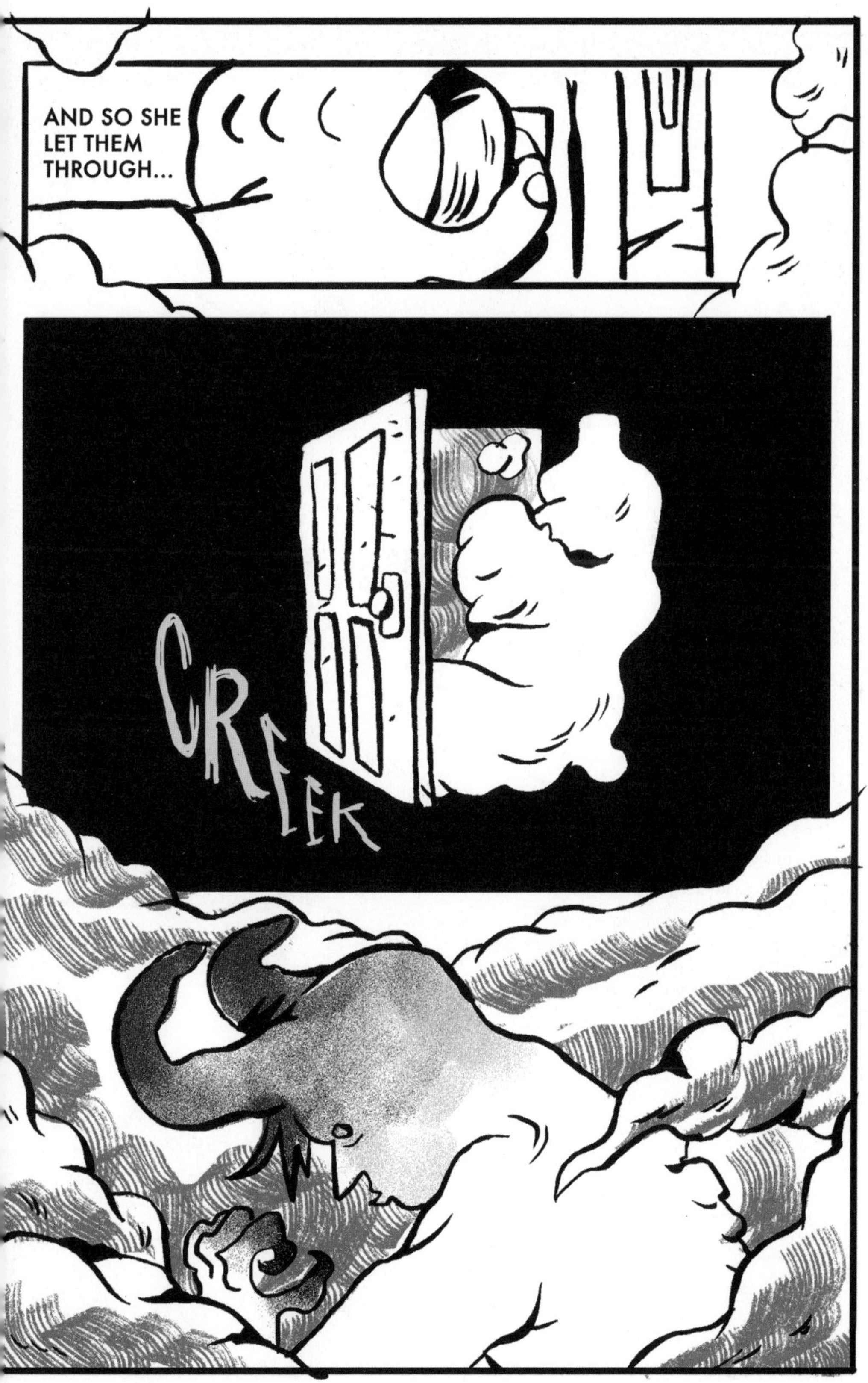
AND SO SHE LET THEM THROUGH...
CREEK

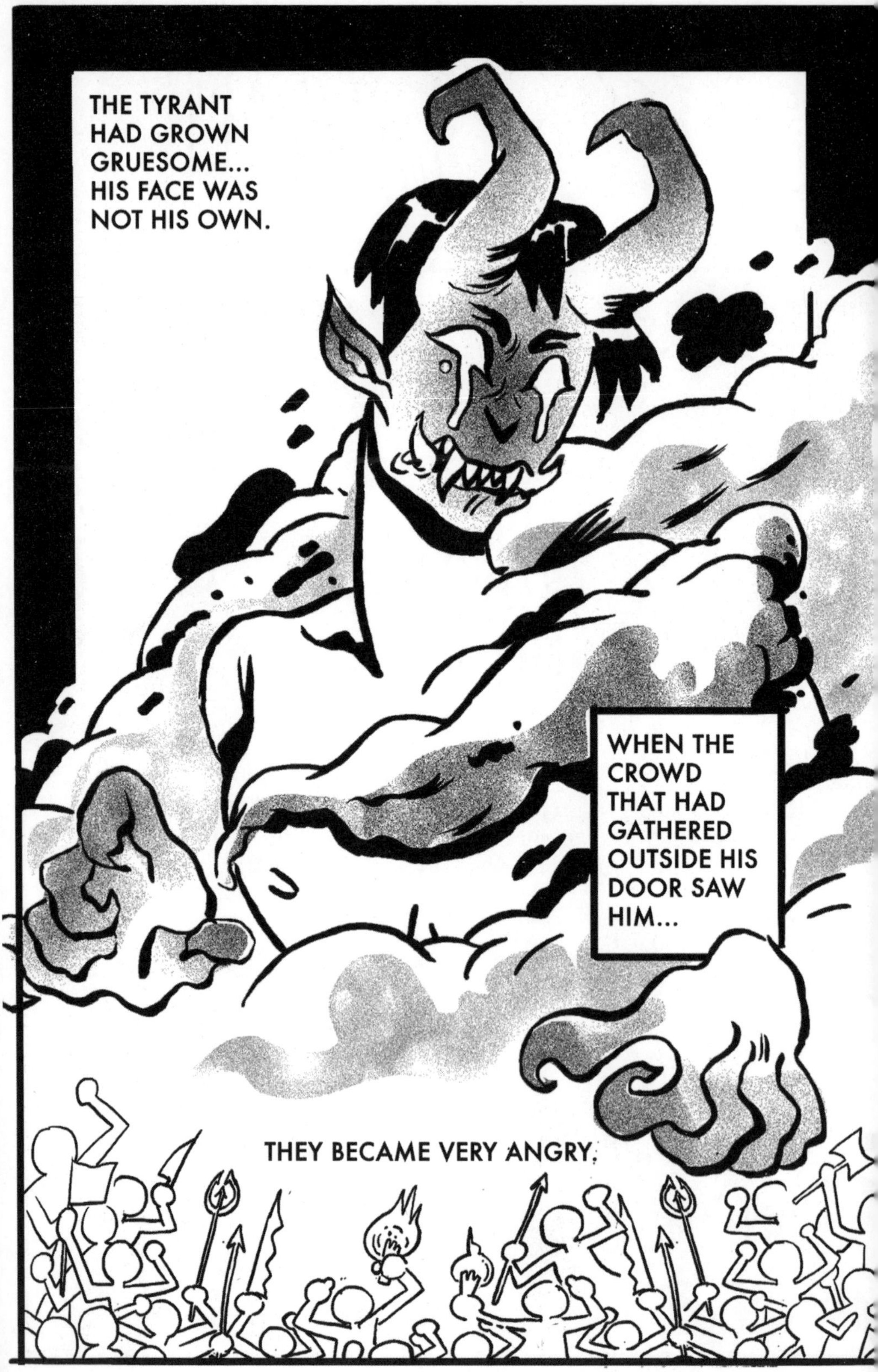
THE TYRANT HAD GROWN GRUESOME... HIS FACE WAS NOT HIS OWN.
WHEN THE CROWD THAT HAD GATHERED OUTSIDE HIS DOOR SAW HIM...
THEY BECAME VERY ANGRY.

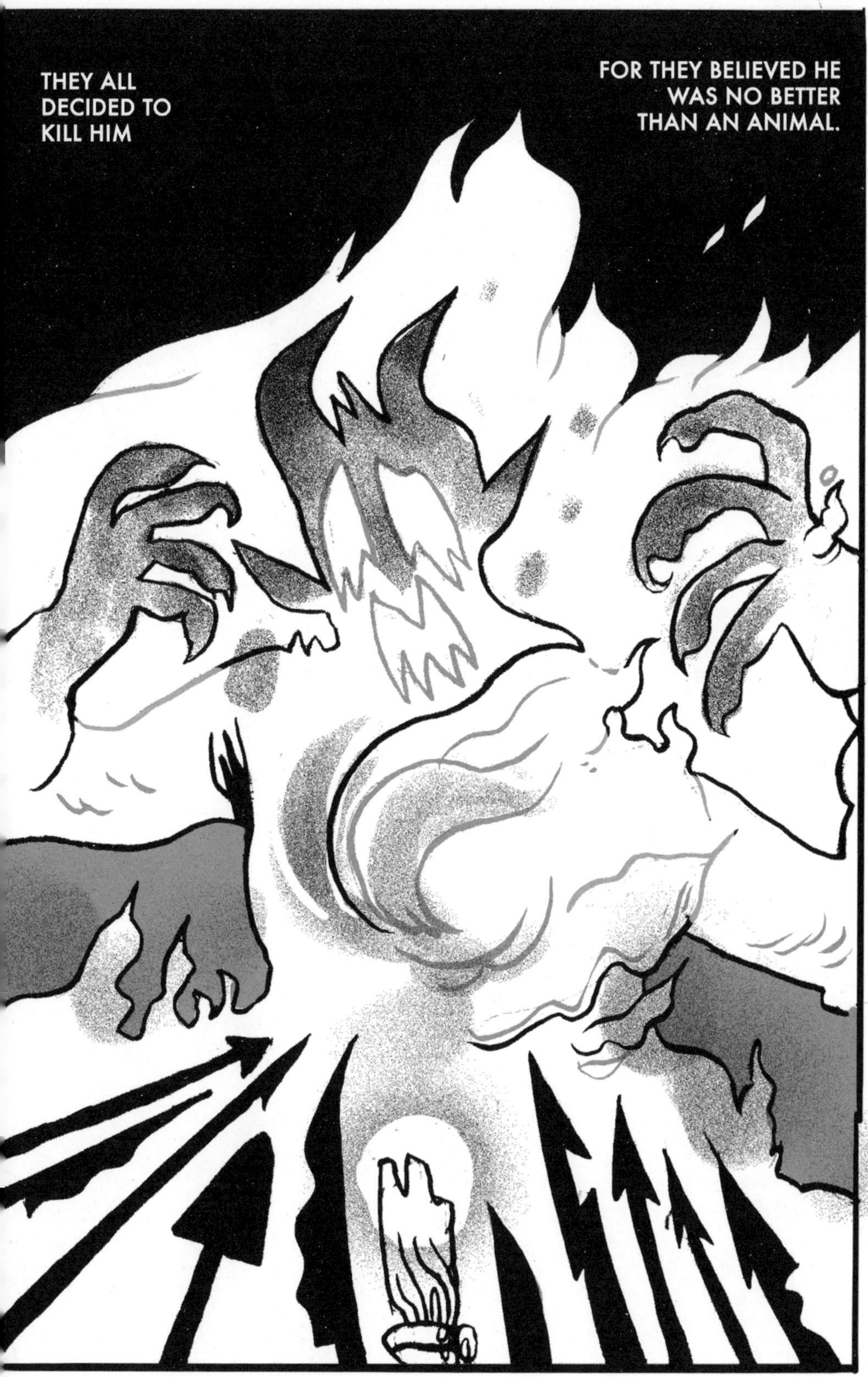
THEY ALL DECIDED TO KILL HIM
FOR THEY BELIEVED HE WAS NO BETTER THAN AN ANIMAL.

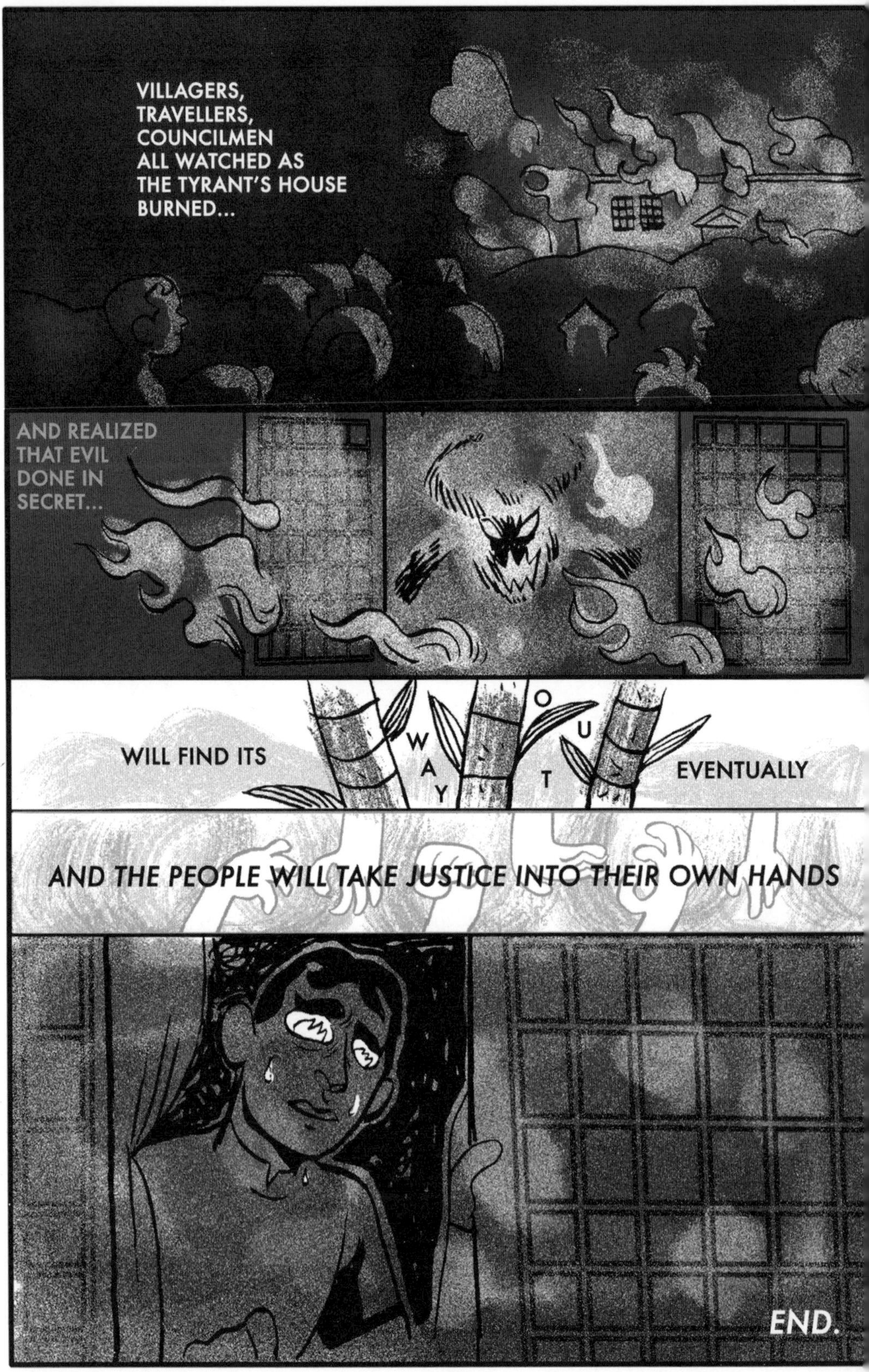
VILLAGERS, TRAVELLERS, COUNCILMEN ALL WATCHED AS THE TYRANT'S HOUSE BURNED...
AND REALIZED THAT EVIL DONE IN SECRET...
WILL FIND ITS
WAY OUT
EVENTUALLY
AND THE PEOPLE WILL TAKE JUSTICE INTO THEIR OWN HANDS
END.

IBALON EPIC

A RETELLING OF BALTOG

AFTER FRAZETTA

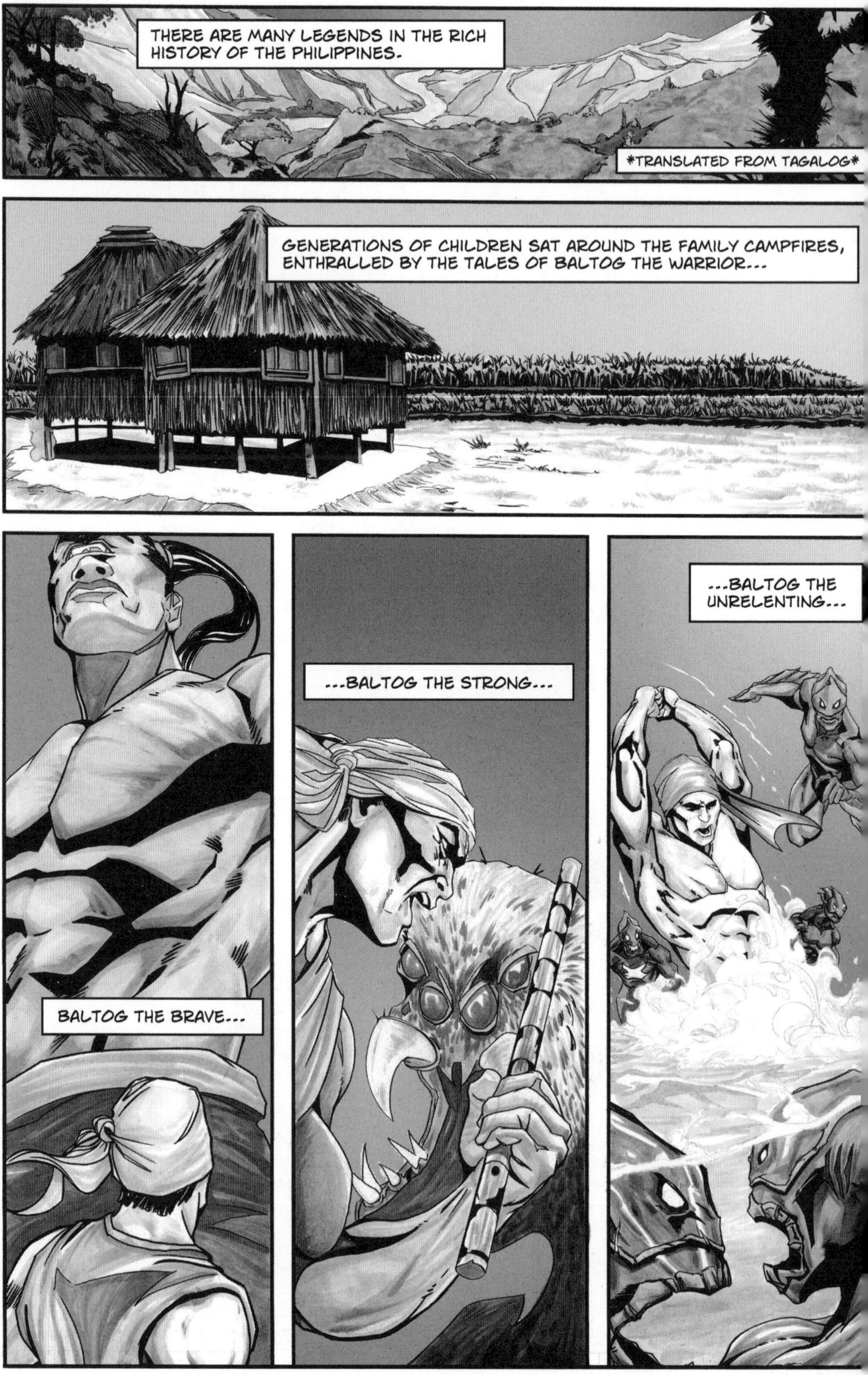
THERE ARE MANY LEGENDS IN THE RICH HISTORY OF THE PHILIPPINES.
TRANSLATED FROM TAGALOG
GENERATIONS OF CHILDREN SAT AROUND THE FAMILY CAMPFIRES, ENTHRALLED BY THE TALES OF BALTOG THE WARRIOR...
BALTOG THE BRAVE...
...BALTOG THE STRONG...
...BALTOG THE UNRELENTING...

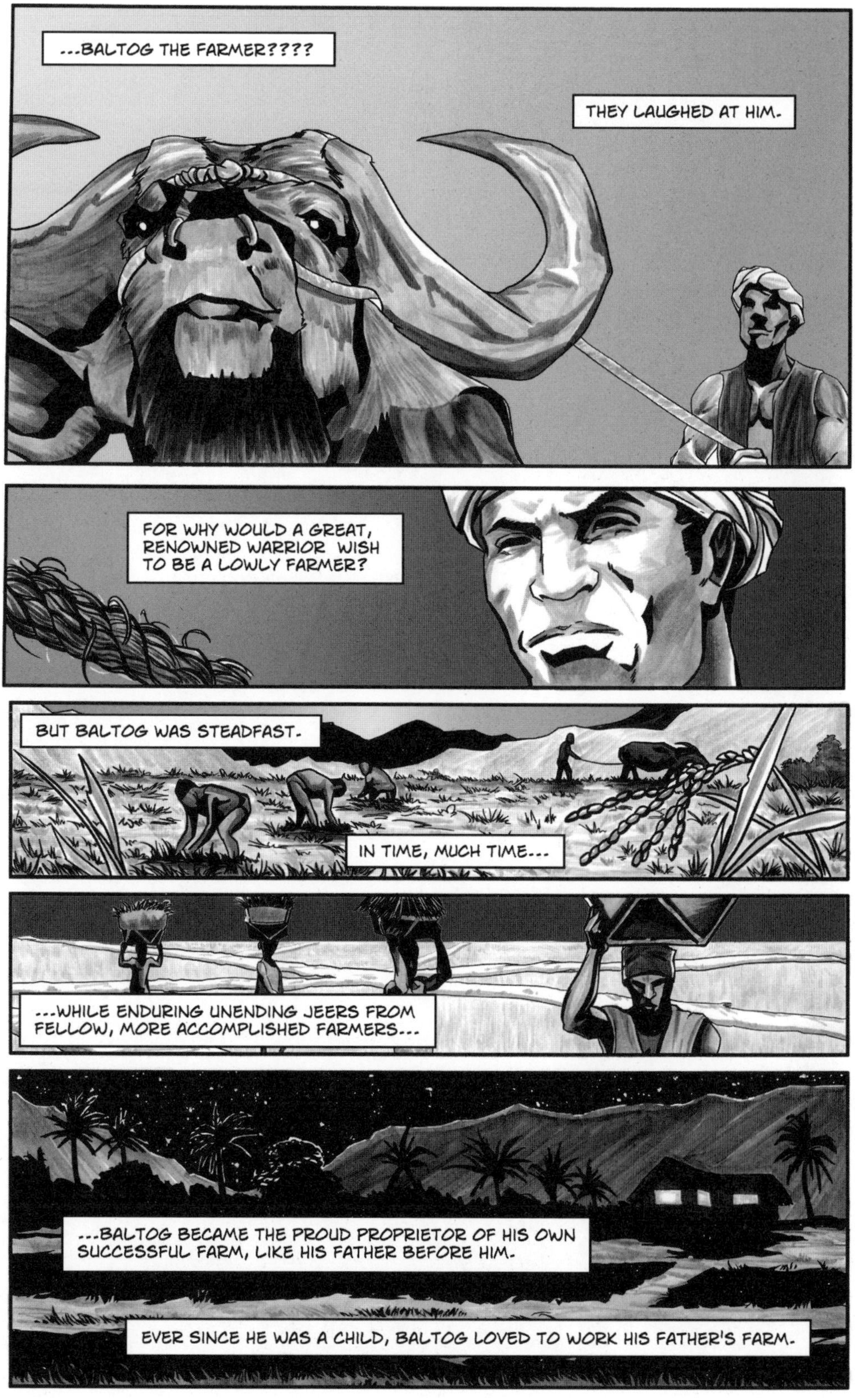
...BALTOG THE FARMER????
THEY LAUGHED AT HIM.
FOR WHY WOULD A GREAT, RENOWNED WARRIOR WISH TO BE A LOWLY FARMER?
BUT BALTOG WAS STEADFAST.
IN TIME, MUCH TIME...
...WHILE ENDURING UNENDING JEERS FROM FELLOW, MORE ACCOMPLISHED FARMERS...
...BALTOG BECAME THE PROUD PROPRIETOR OF HIS OWN SUCCESSFUL FARM, LIKE HIS FATHER BEFORE HIM.
EVER SINCE HE WAS A CHILD, BALTOG LOVED TO WORK HIS FATHER'S FARM.

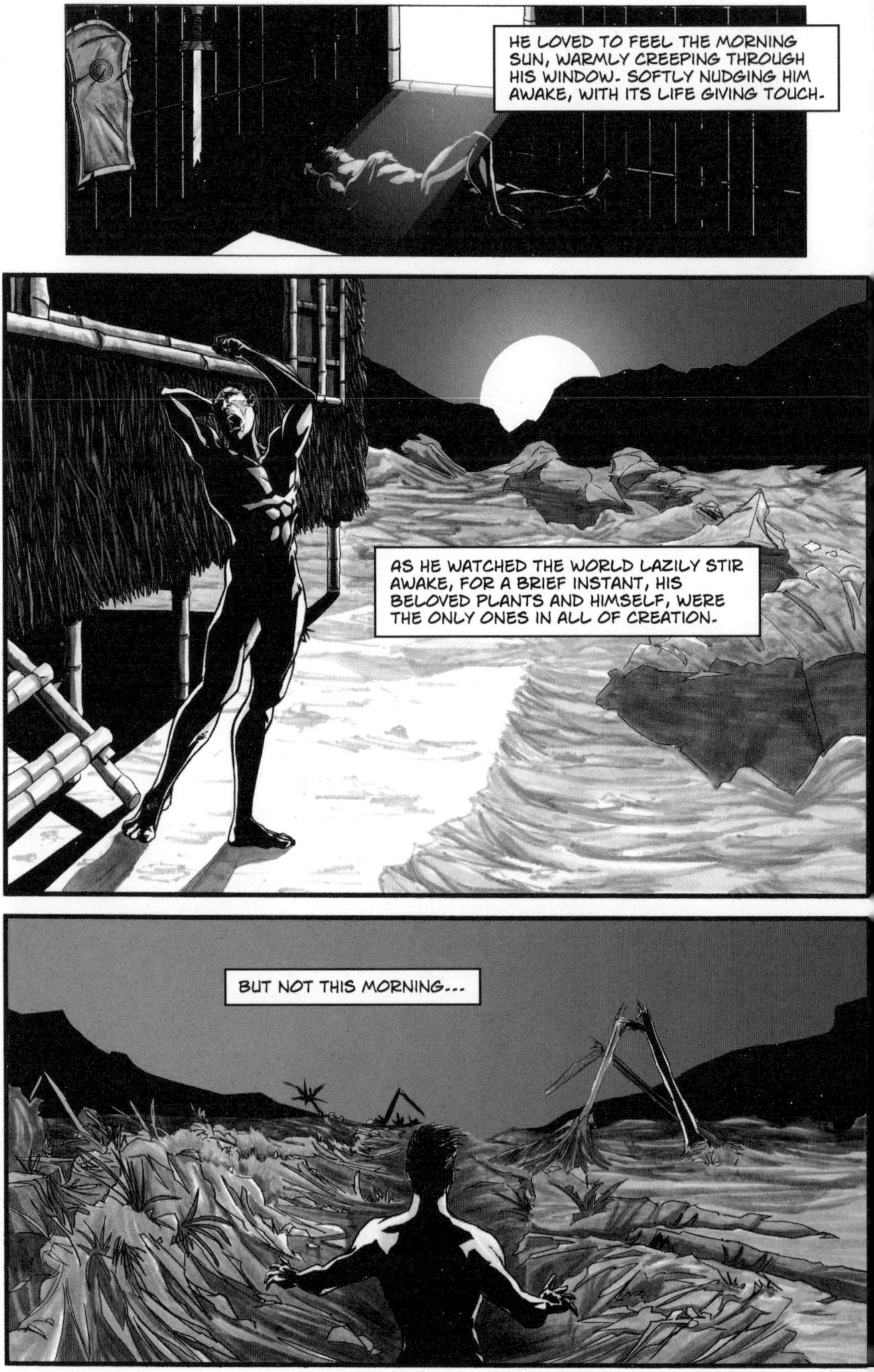
HE LOVED TO FEEL THE MORNING SUN, WARMLY CREEPING THROUGH HIS WINDOW. SOFTLY NUDGING HIM AWAKE, WITH ITS LIFE GIVING TOUCH.
AS HE WATCHED THE WORLD LAZILY STIR AWAKE, FOR A BRIEF INSTANT, HIS BELOVED PLANTS AND HIMSELF, WERE THE ONLY ONES IN ALL OF CREATION.
BUT NOT THIS MORNING...

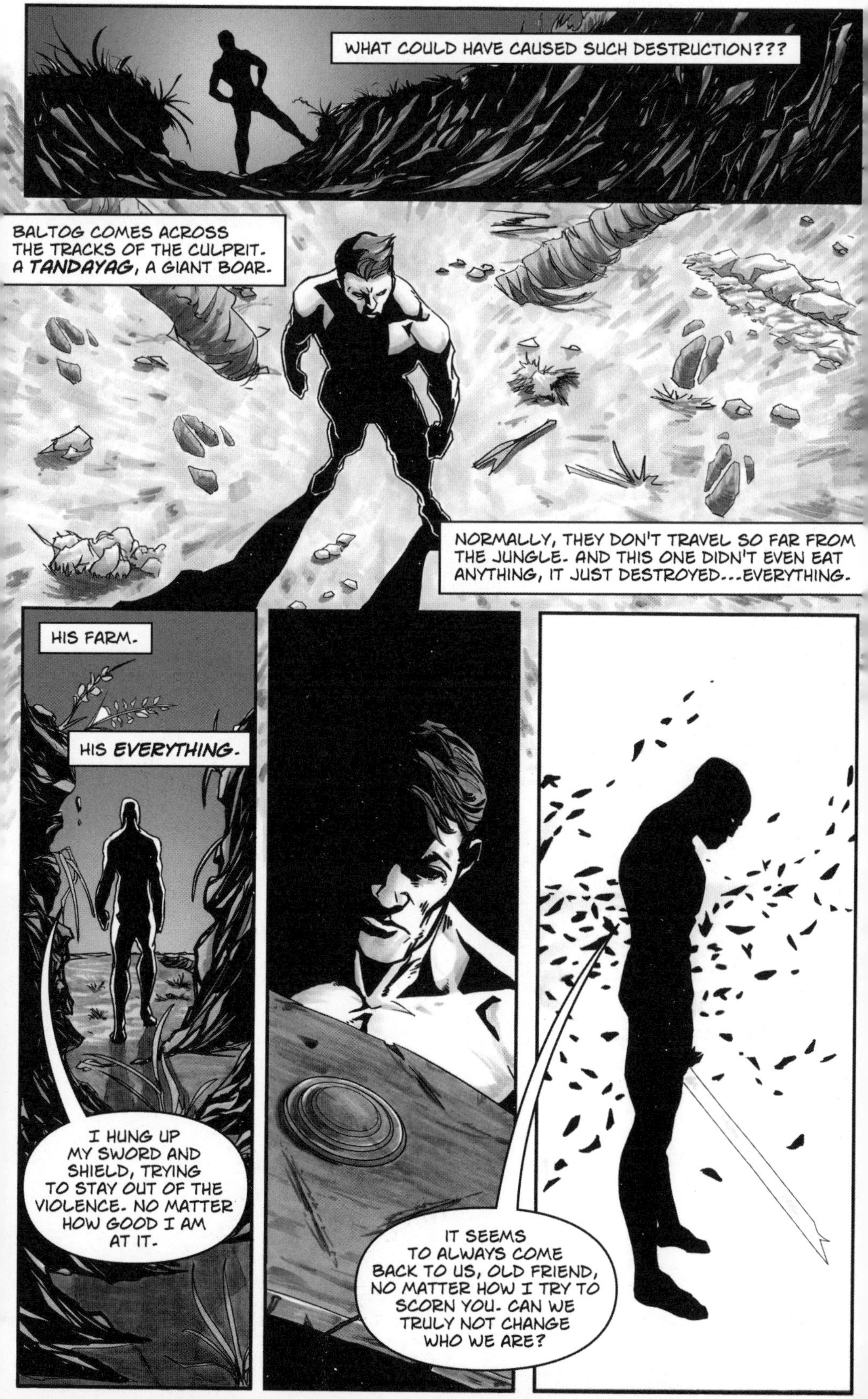

WHAT COULD HAVE CAUSED SUCH DESTRUCTION???
BALTOG COMES ACROSS THE TRACKS OF THE CULPRIT. A *TANDAYAG*, A GIANT BOAR.
NORMALLY, THEY DON'T TRAVEL SO FAR FROM THE JUNGLE. AND THIS ONE DIDN'T EVEN EAT ANYTHING, IT JUST DESTROYED...EVERYTHING.
HIS FARM.
HIS *EVERYTHING*.
I HUNG UP MY SWORD AND SHIELD, TRYING TO STAY OUT OF THE VIOLENCE. NO MATTER HOW GOOD I AM AT IT.
IT SEEMS TO ALWAYS COME BACK TO US, OLD FRIEND, NO MATTER HOW I TRY TO SCORN YOU. CAN WE TRULY NOT CHANGE WHO WE ARE?

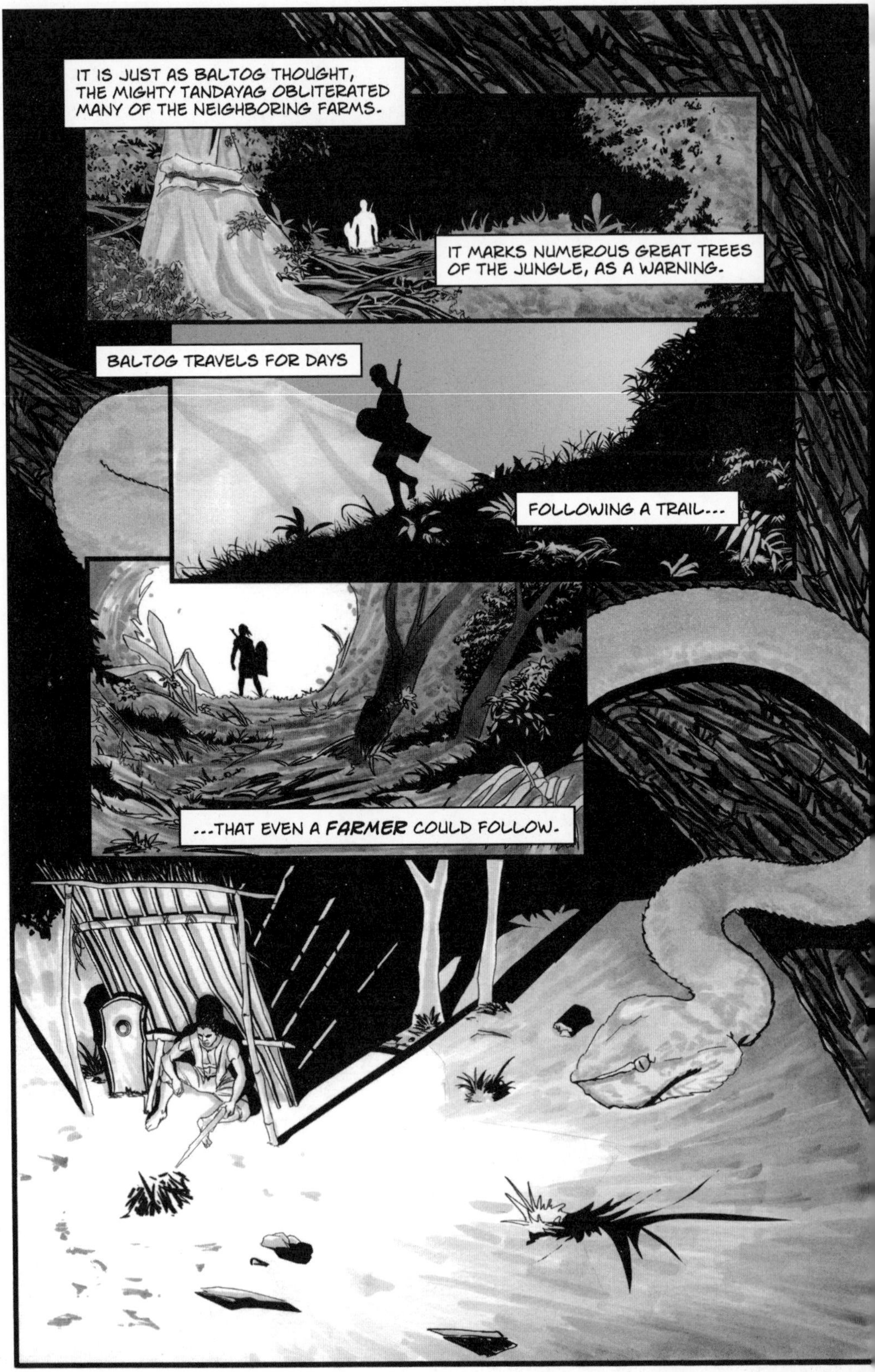
IT IS JUST AS BALTOG THOUGHT, THE MIGHTY TANDAYAG OBLITERATED MANY OF THE NEIGHBORING FARMS.
IT MARKS NUMEROUS GREAT TREES OF THE JUNGLE, AS A WARNING.
BALTOG TRAVELS FOR DAYS
FOLLOWING A TRAIL...
...THAT EVEN A **FARMER** COULD FOLLOW.

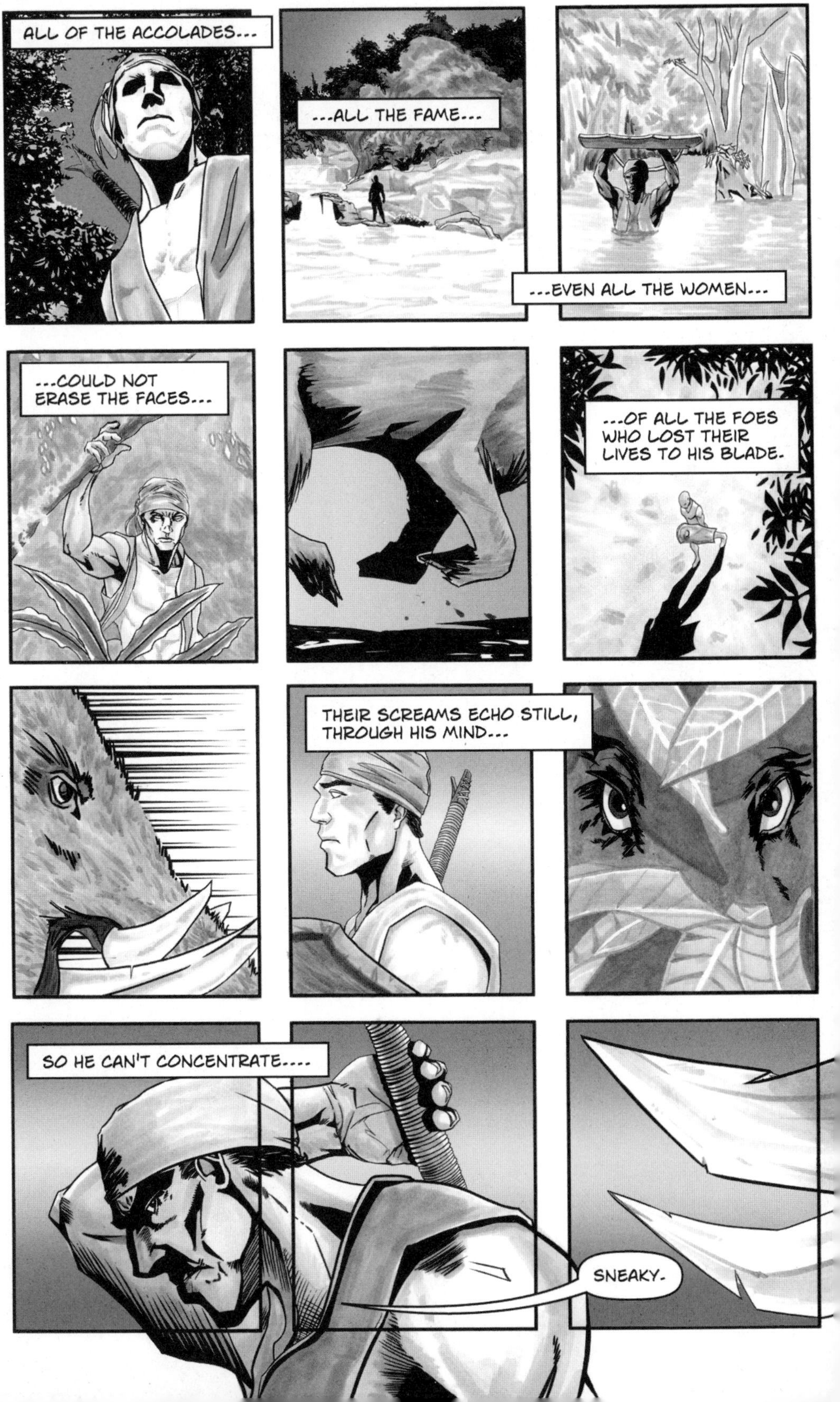
ALL OF THE ACCOLADES...
...ALL THE FAME...
...EVEN ALL THE WOMEN...
...COULD NOT ERASE THE FACES...
...OF ALL THE FOES WHO LOST THEIR LIVES TO HIS BLADE.
THEIR SCREAMS ECHO STILL, THROUGH HIS MIND...
SO HE CAN'T CONCENTRATE....
SNEAKY.

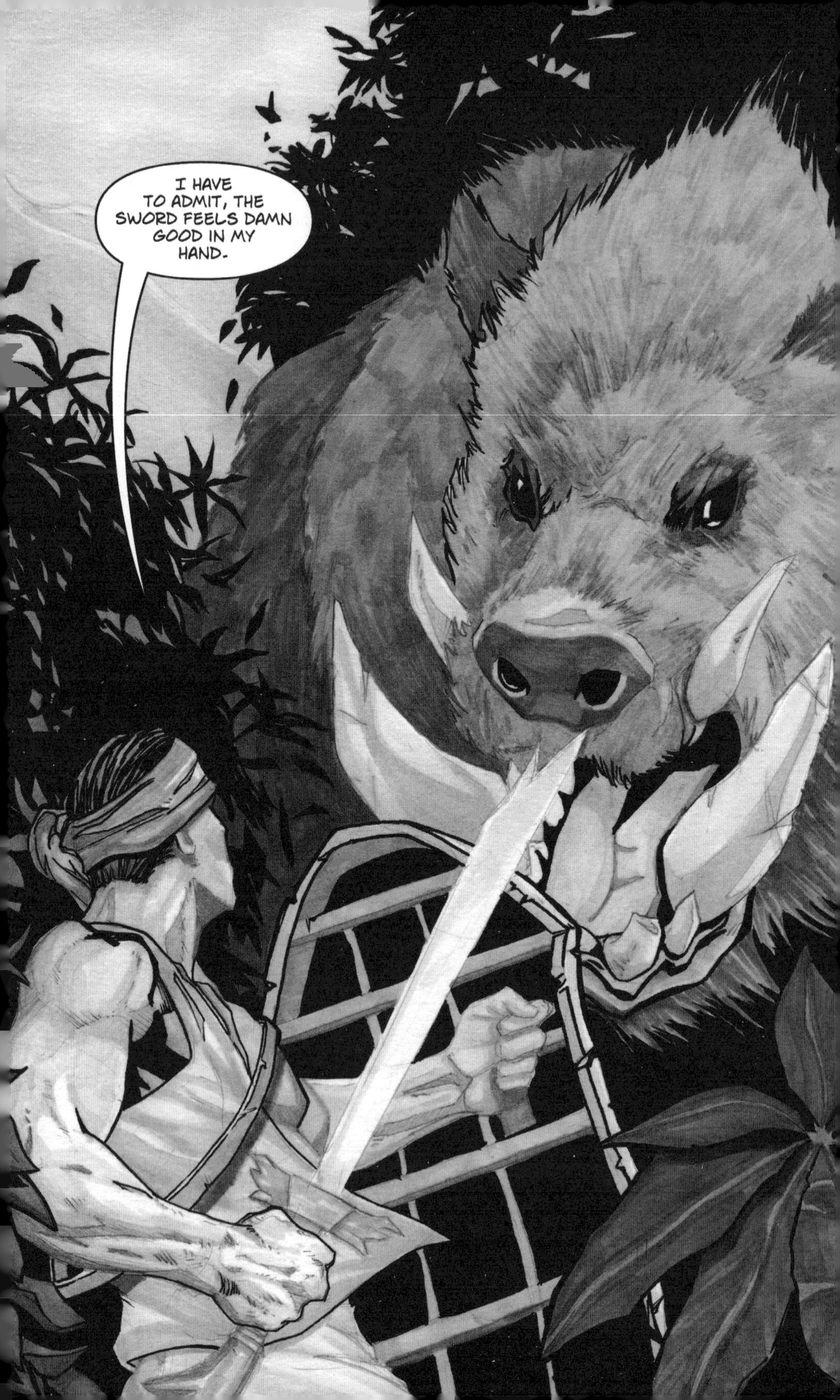
I HAVE TO ADMIT, THE SWORD FEELS DAMN GOOD IN MY HAND.

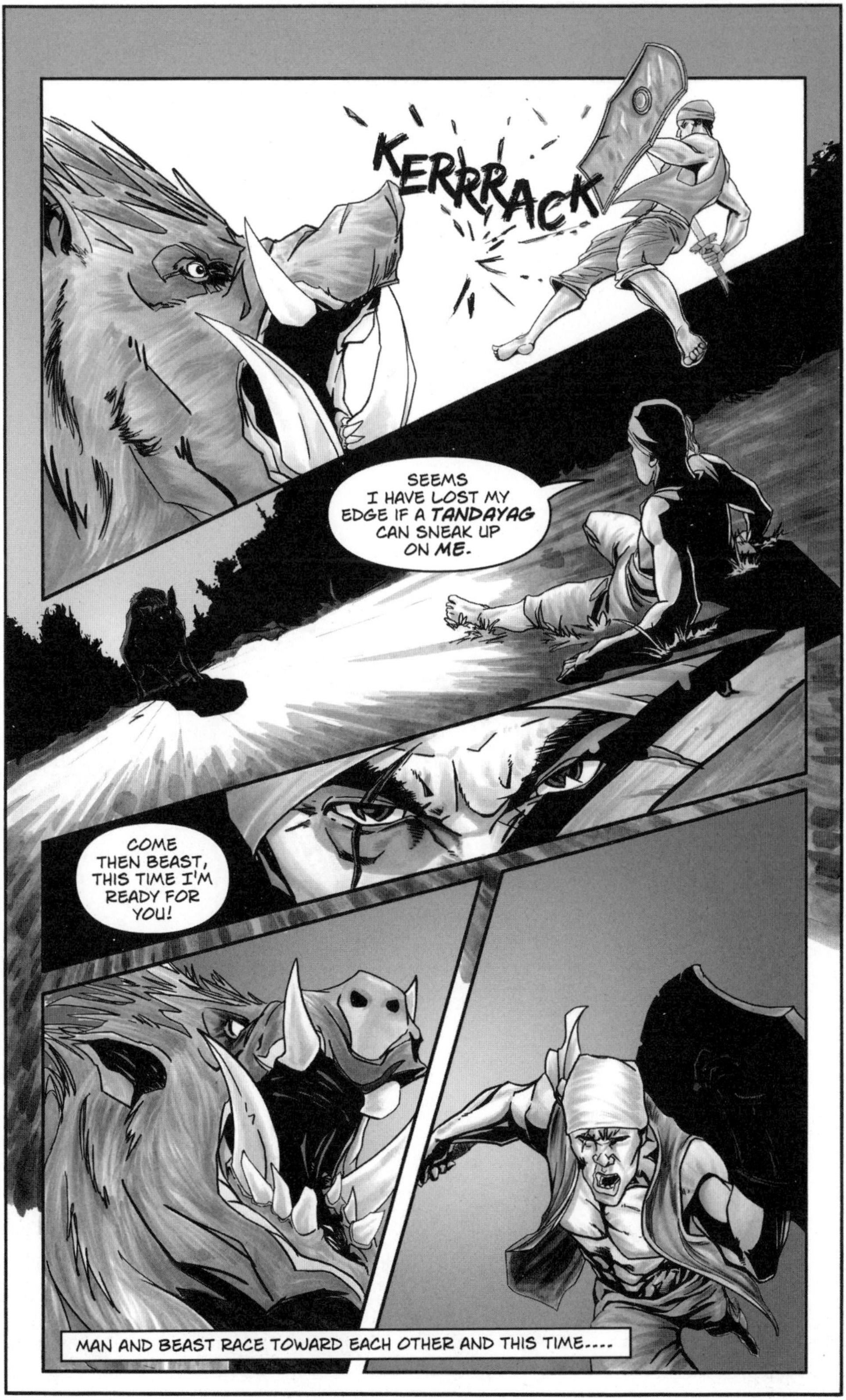
KERRRACK
SEEMS I HAVE LOST MY EDGE IF A TANDAYAG CAN SNEAK UP ON ME.
COME THEN BEAST, THIS TIME I'M READY FOR YOU!
MAN AND BEAST RACE TOWARD EACH OTHER AND THIS TIME....

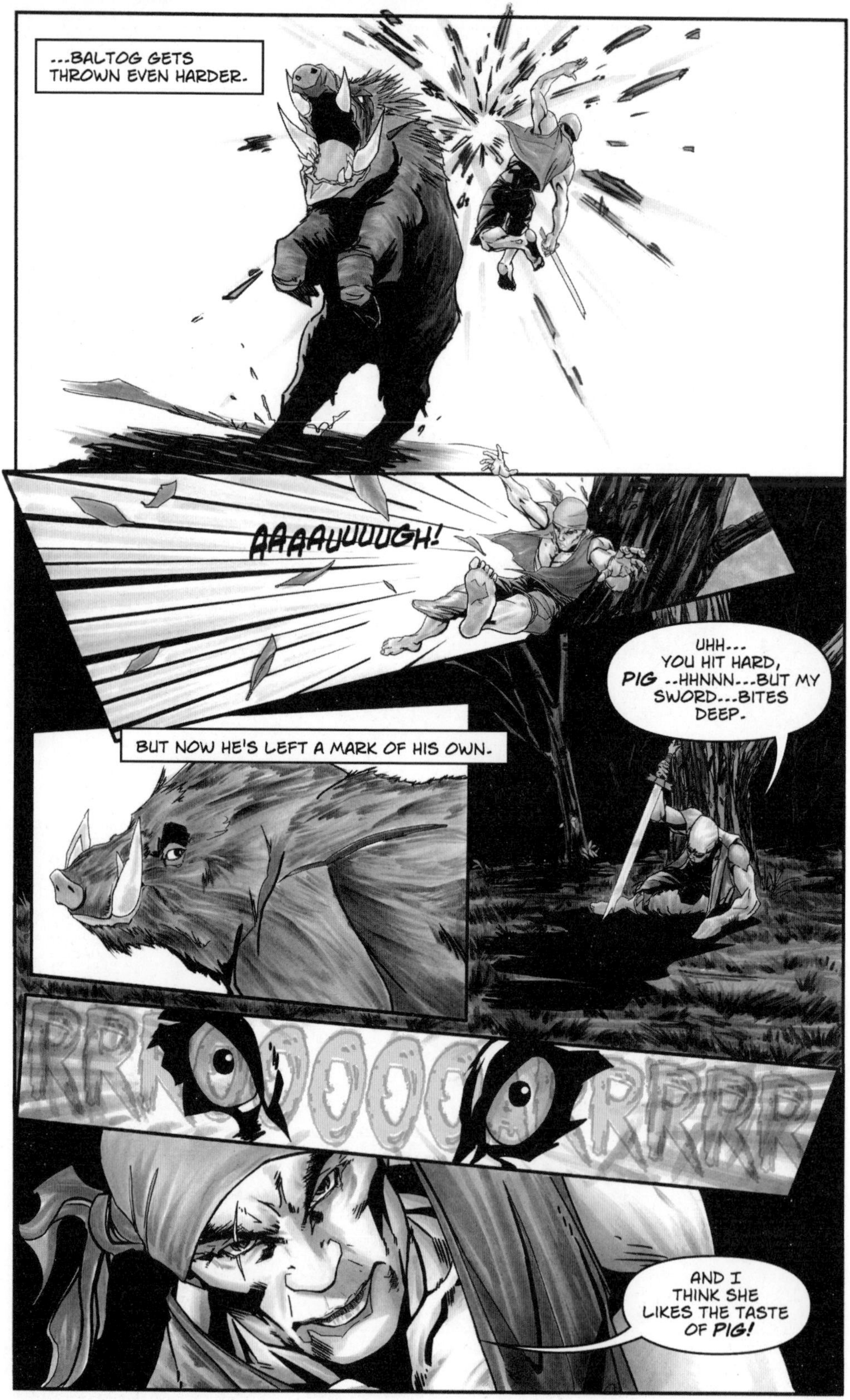
...BALTOG GETS THROWN EVEN HARDER.
AAAAUUUUGH!
UHH... YOU HIT HARD, PIG --HHNNN...BUT MY SWORD...BITES DEEP.
BUT NOW HE'S LEFT A MARK OF HIS OWN.
RRROOOOORRRR
AND I THINK SHE LIKES THE TASTE OF PIG!

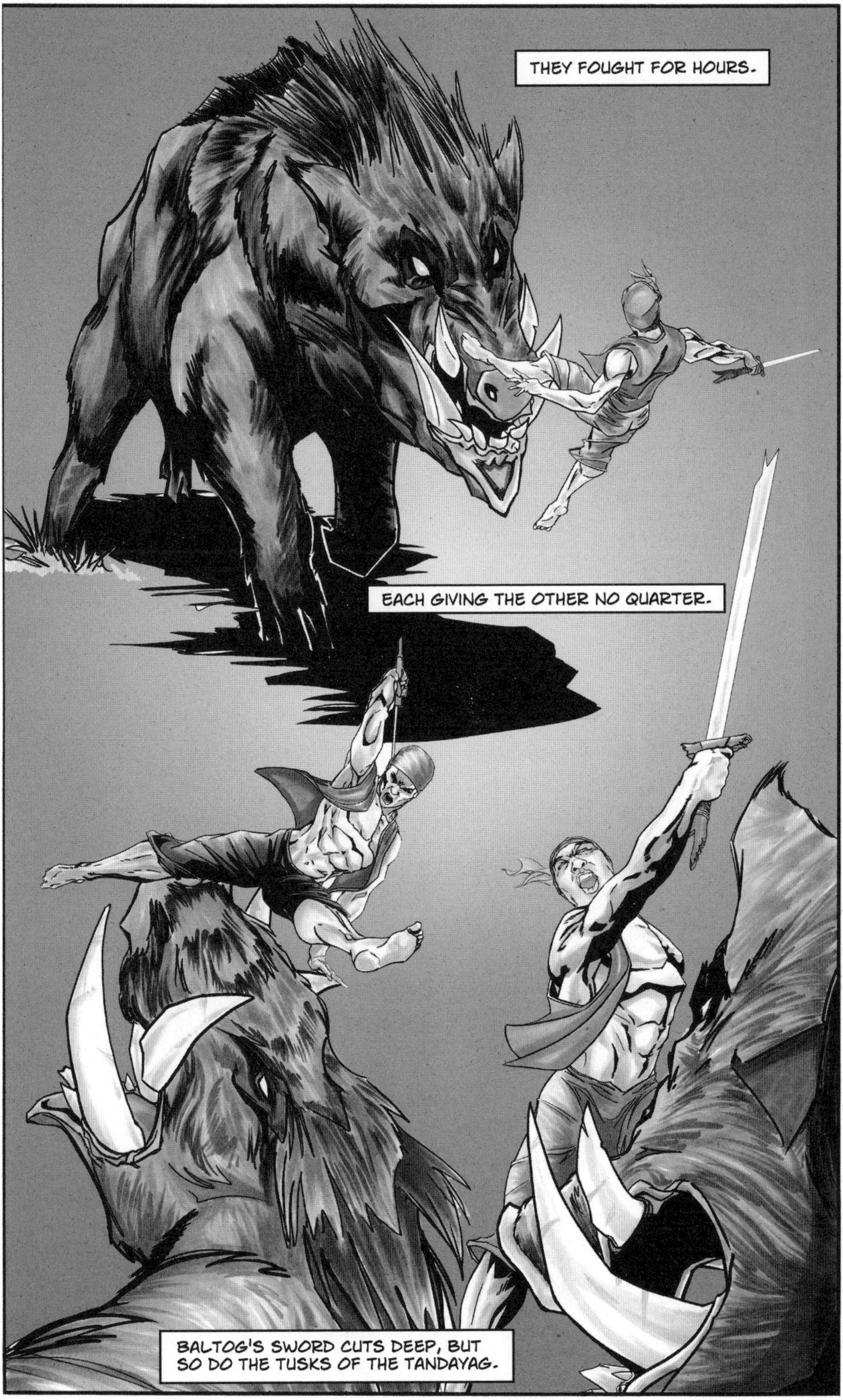
THEY FOUGHT FOR HOURS.
EACH GIVING THE OTHER NO QUARTER.
BALTOG'S SWORD CUTS DEEP, BUT
SO DO THE TUSKS OF THE TANDAYAG.

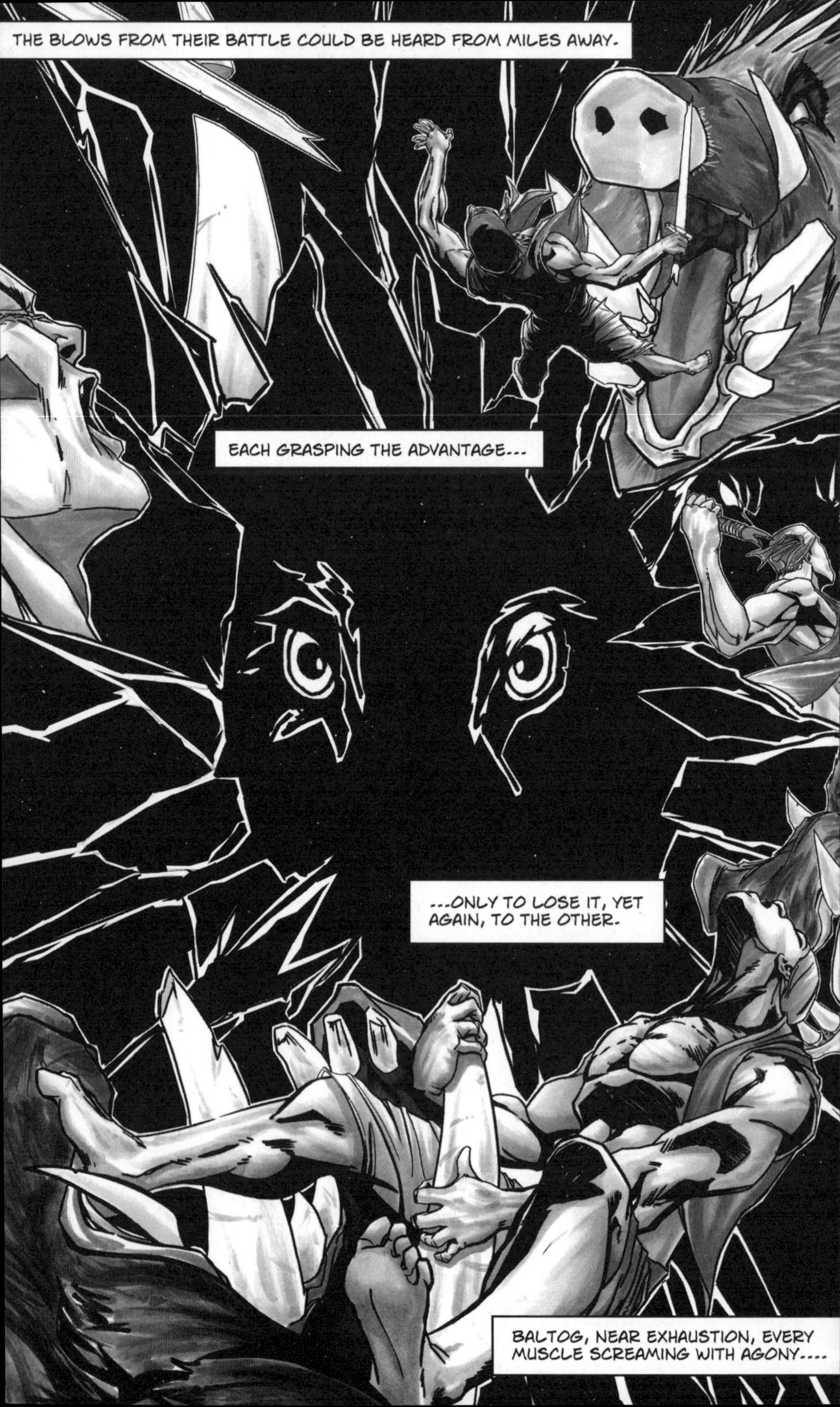
THE BLOWS FROM THEIR BATTLE COULD BE HEARD FROM MILES AWAY.
EACH GRASPING THE ADVANTAGE...
...ONLY TO LOSE IT, YET AGAIN, TO THE OTHER.
BALTOG, NEAR EXHAUSTION, EVERY MUSCLE SCREAMING WITH AGONY....

...UNTIL HE FALLS TO THE DANK, JUNGLE FLOOR.

AS HIS ENEMY LAYS BESIDE HIM...

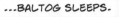
...BALTOG SLEEPS.

ND DOESN'T STIR, FOR THREE LONG DAYS.

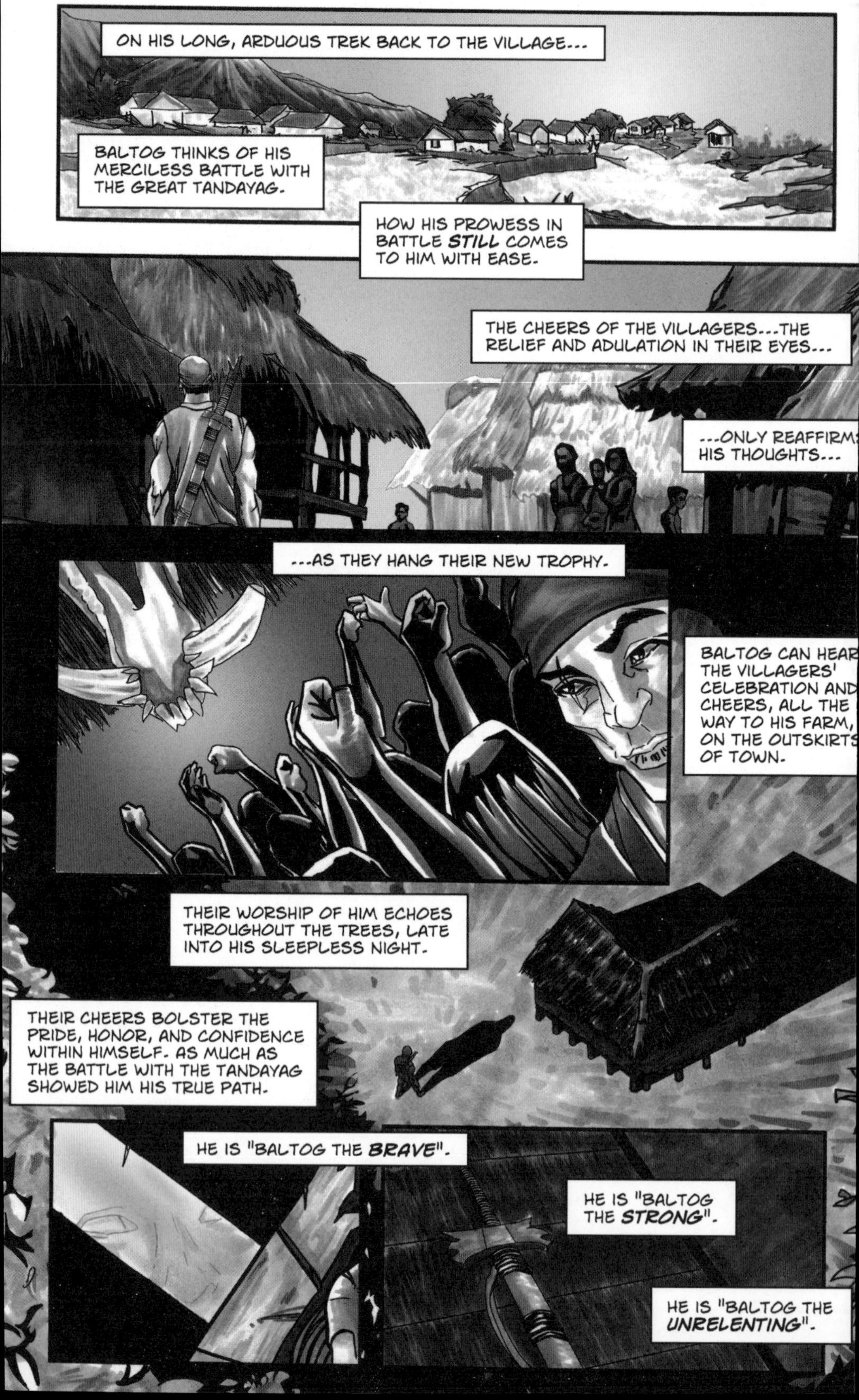
ON HIS LONG, ARDUOUS TREK BACK TO THE VILLAGE...
BALTOG THINKS OF HIS MERCILESS BATTLE WITH THE GREAT TANDAYAG.
HOW HIS PROWESS IN BATTLE *STILL* COMES TO HIM WITH EASE.
THE CHEERS OF THE VILLAGERS...THE RELIEF AND ADULATION IN THEIR EYES...
...ONLY REAFFIRMS HIS THOUGHTS...
...AS THEY HANG THEIR NEW TROPHY.
BALTOG CAN HEAR THE VILLAGERS' CELEBRATION AND CHEERS, ALL THE WAY TO HIS FARM, ON THE OUTSKIRTS OF TOWN.
THEIR WORSHIP OF HIM ECHOES THROUGHOUT THE TREES, LATE INTO HIS SLEEPLESS NIGHT.
THEIR CHEERS BOLSTER THE PRIDE, HONOR, AND CONFIDENCE WITHIN HIMSELF. AS MUCH AS THE BATTLE WITH THE TANDAYAG SHOWED HIM HIS TRUE PATH.
HE IS "BALTOG THE *BRAVE*".
HE IS "BALTOG THE *STRONG*".
HE IS "BALTOG THE *UNRELENTING*".

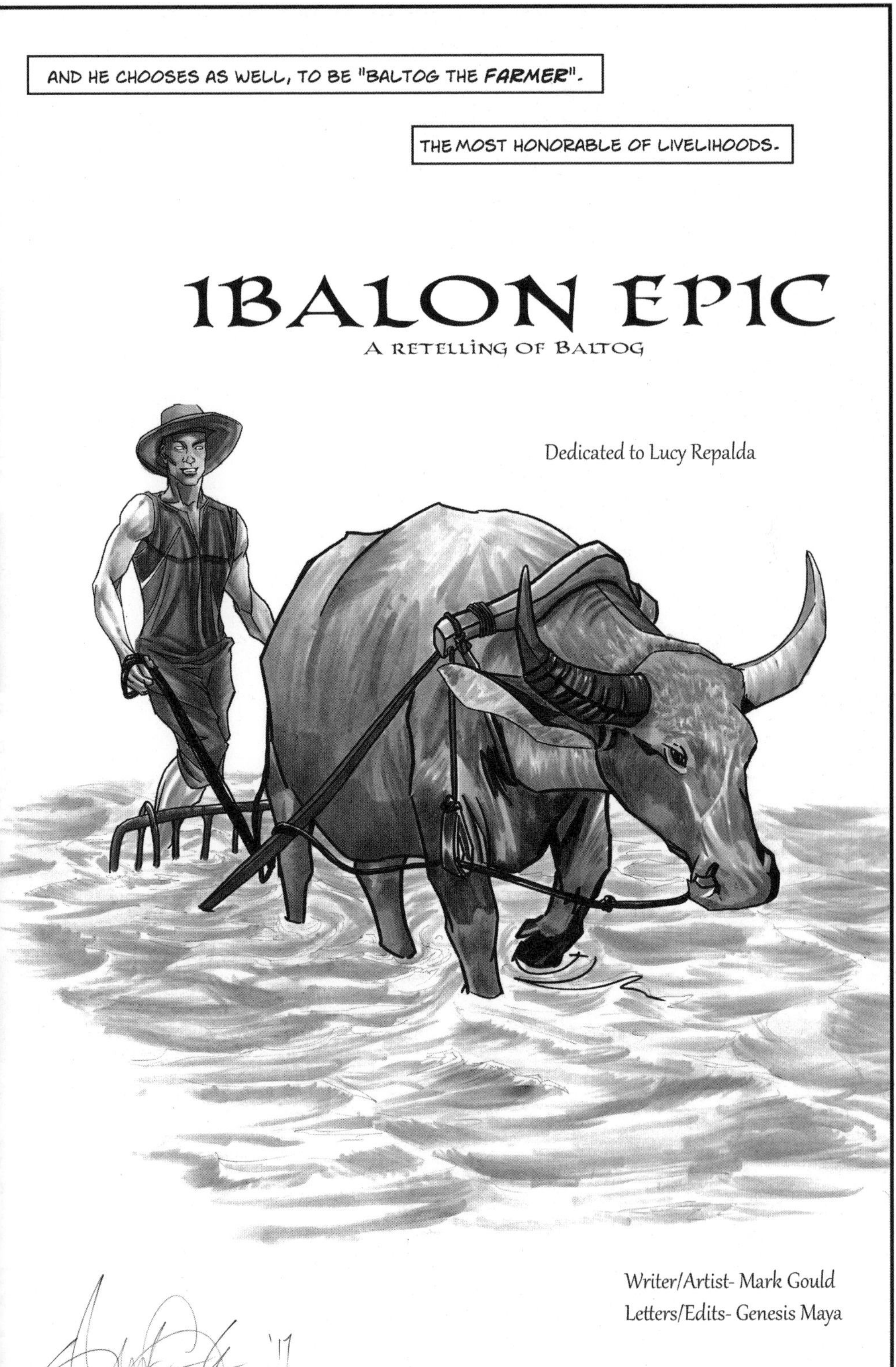
AND HE CHOOSES AS WELL, TO BE "BALTOG THE FARMER".
THE MOST HONORABLE OF LIVELIHOODS.
IBALON EPIC
A RETELLING OF BALTOG
Dedicated to Lucy Repalda
Writer/Artist- Mark Gould
Letters/Edits- Genesis Maya

Left in the Canefields

by Brady Evans

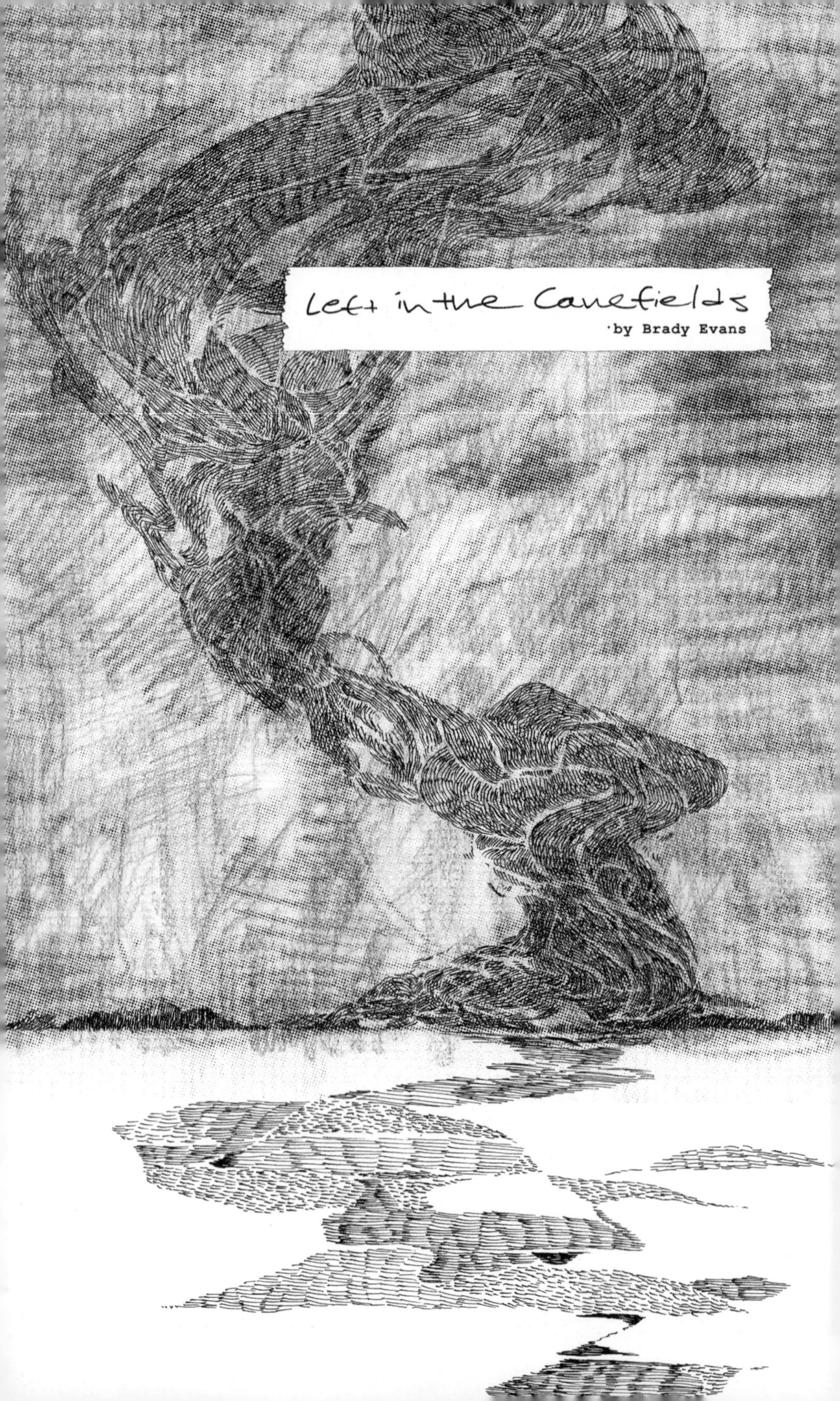

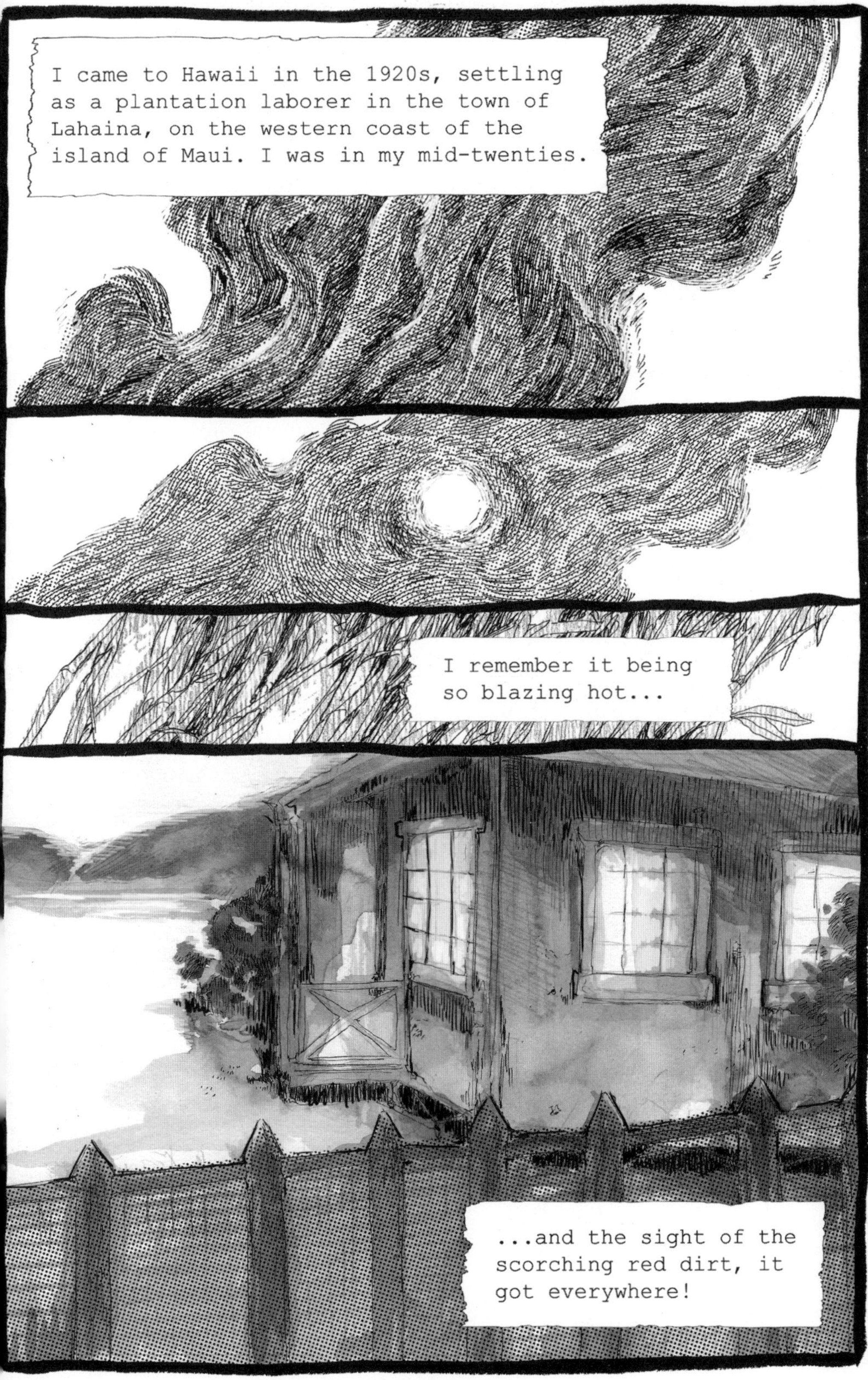
I came to Hawaii in the 1920s, settling as a plantation laborer in the town of Lahaina, on the western coast of the island of Maui. I was in my mid-twenties.
I remember it being so blazing hot...
...and the sight of the scorching red dirt, it got everywhere!

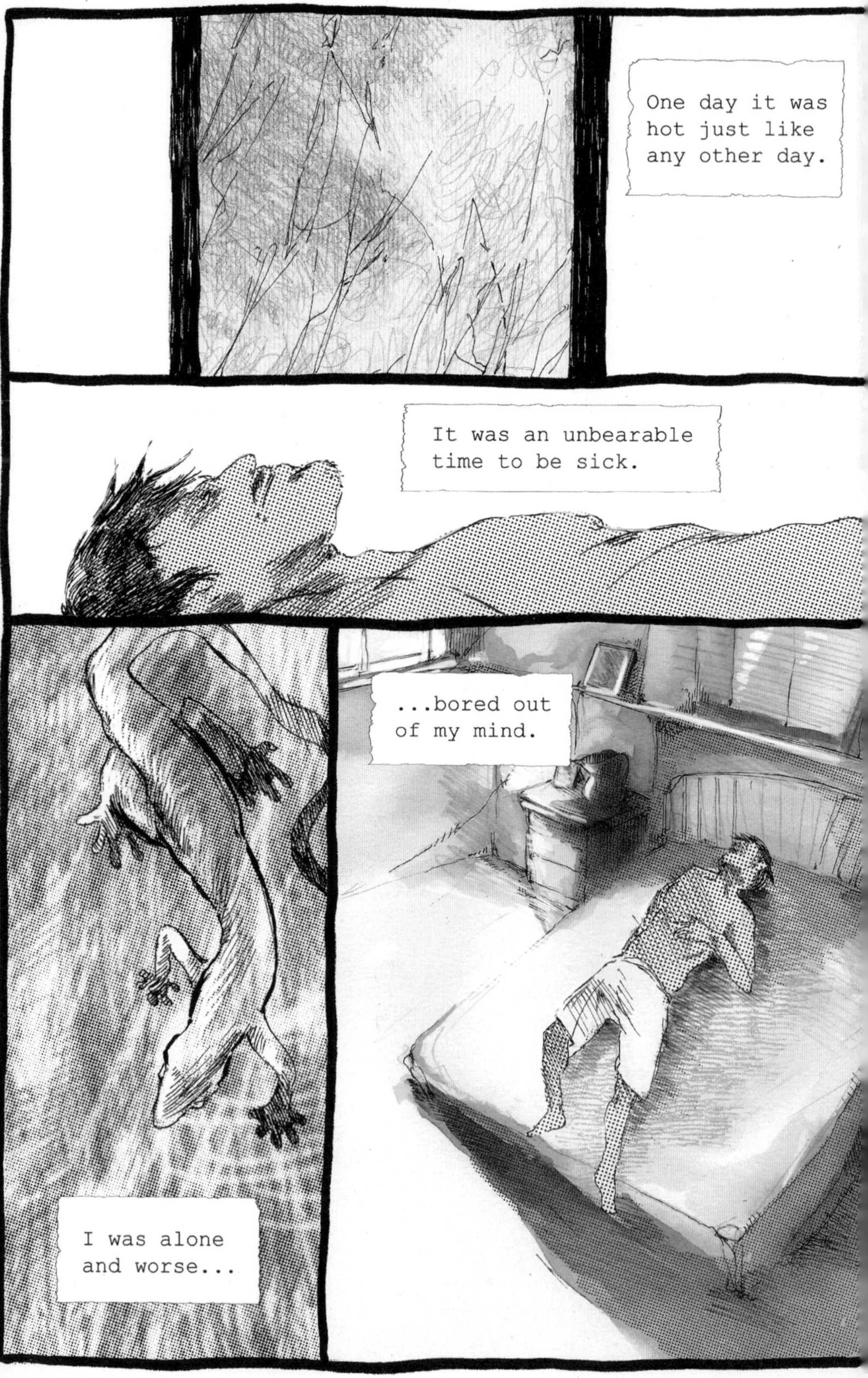
One day it was hot just like any other day.
It was an unbearable time to be sick.
I was alone and worse...
...bored out of my mind.

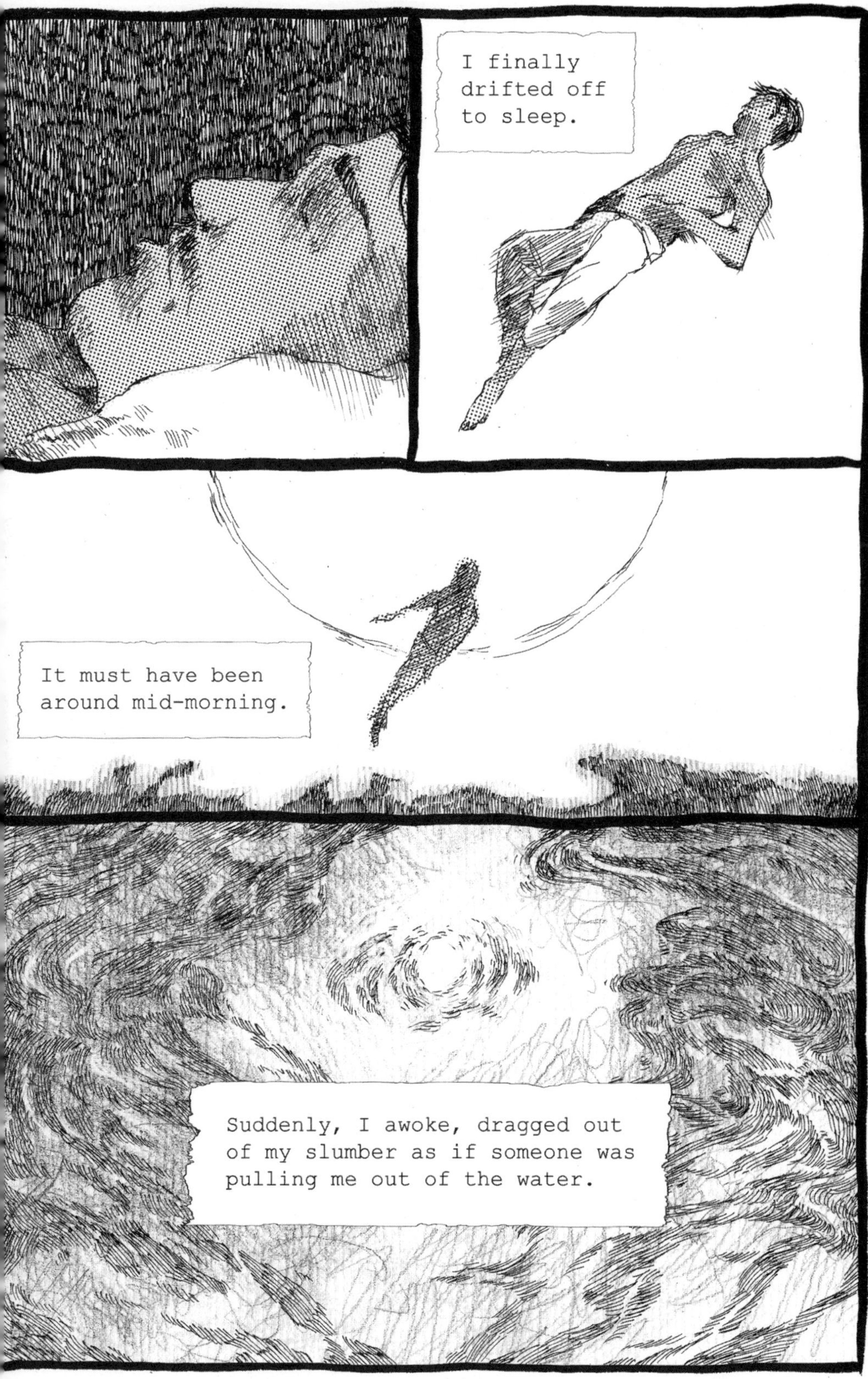
I finally drifted off to sleep.
It must have been around mid-morning.
Suddenly, I awoke, dragged out of my slumber as if someone was pulling me out of the water.

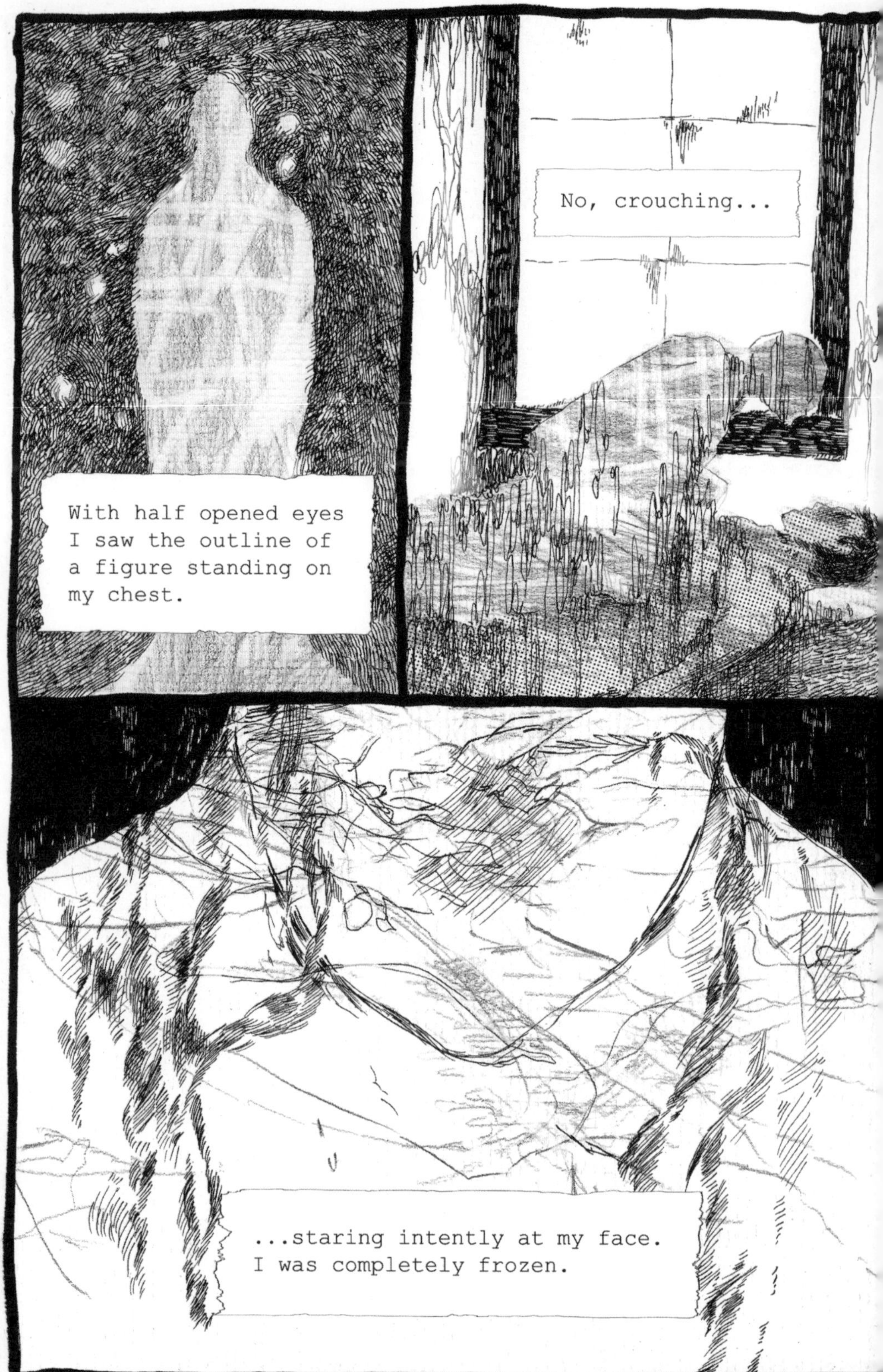
With half opened eyes I saw the outline of a figure standing on my chest.
No, crouching...
...staring intently at my face. I was completely frozen.

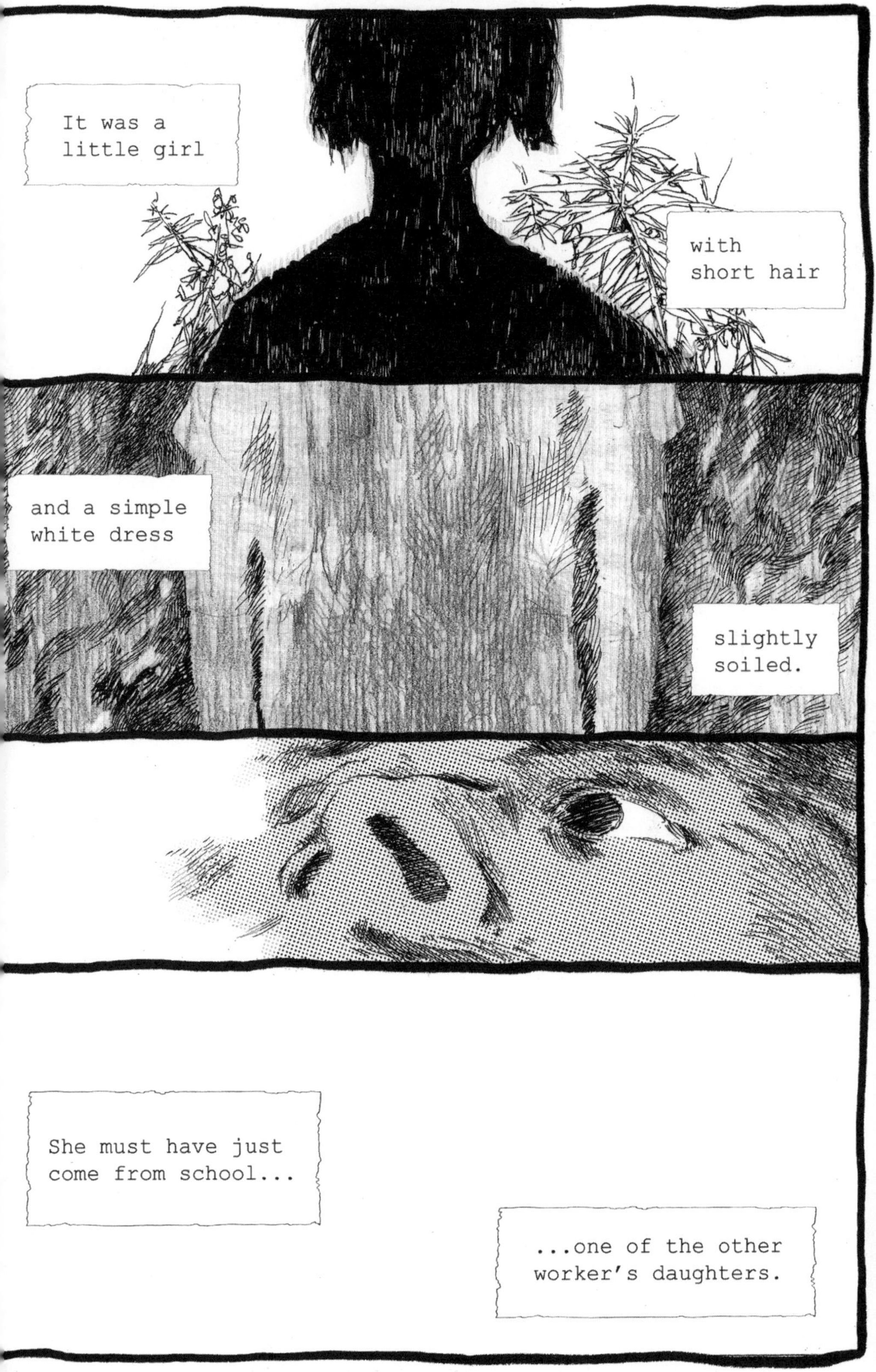
It was a little girl
with short hair
and a simple white dress
slightly soiled.
She must have just come from school...
...one of the other worker's daughters.

She had...no face.

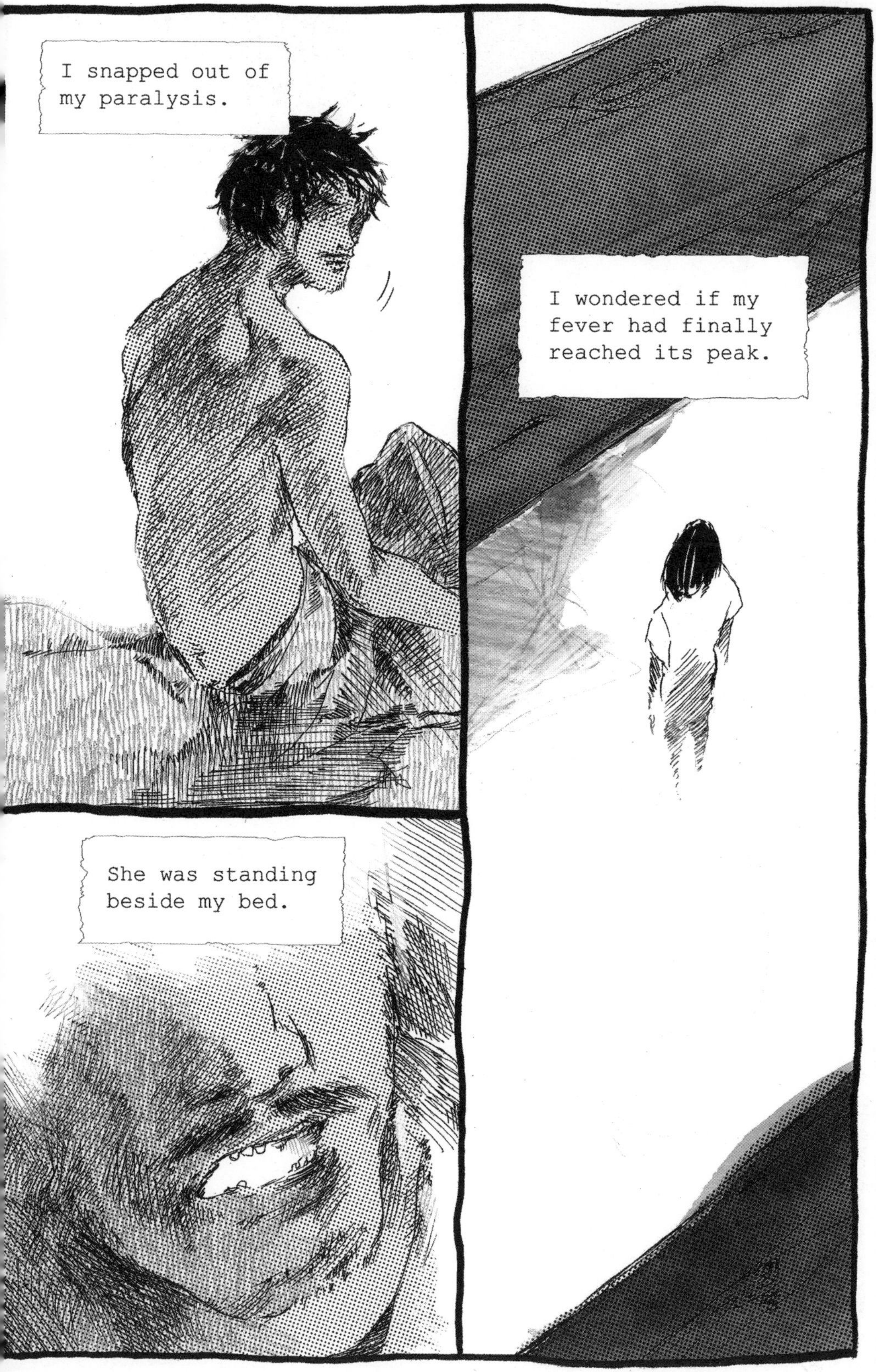
I snapped out of my paralysis.
I wondered if my fever had finally reached its peak.
She was standing beside my bed.

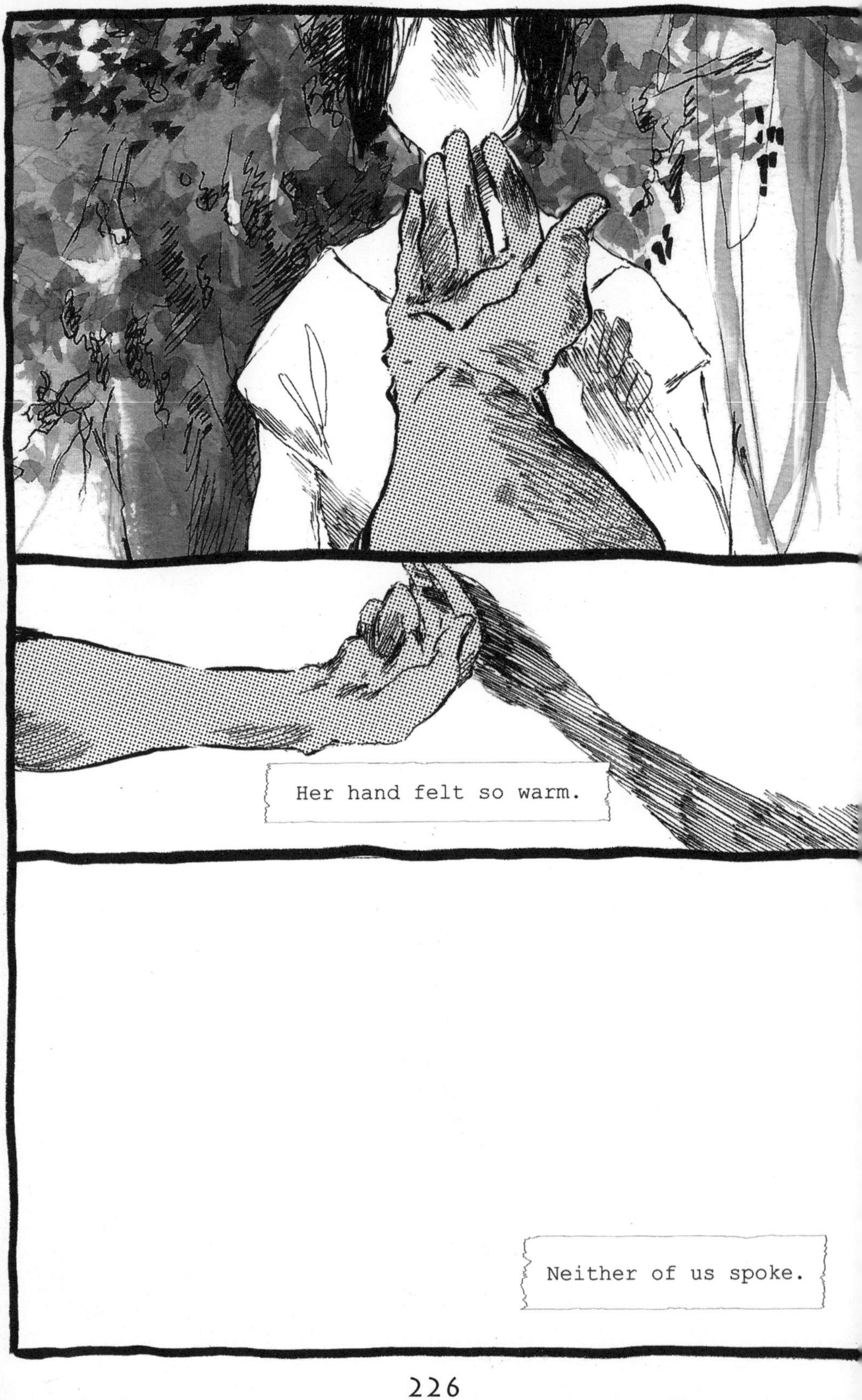
Her hand felt so warm.
Neither of us spoke.

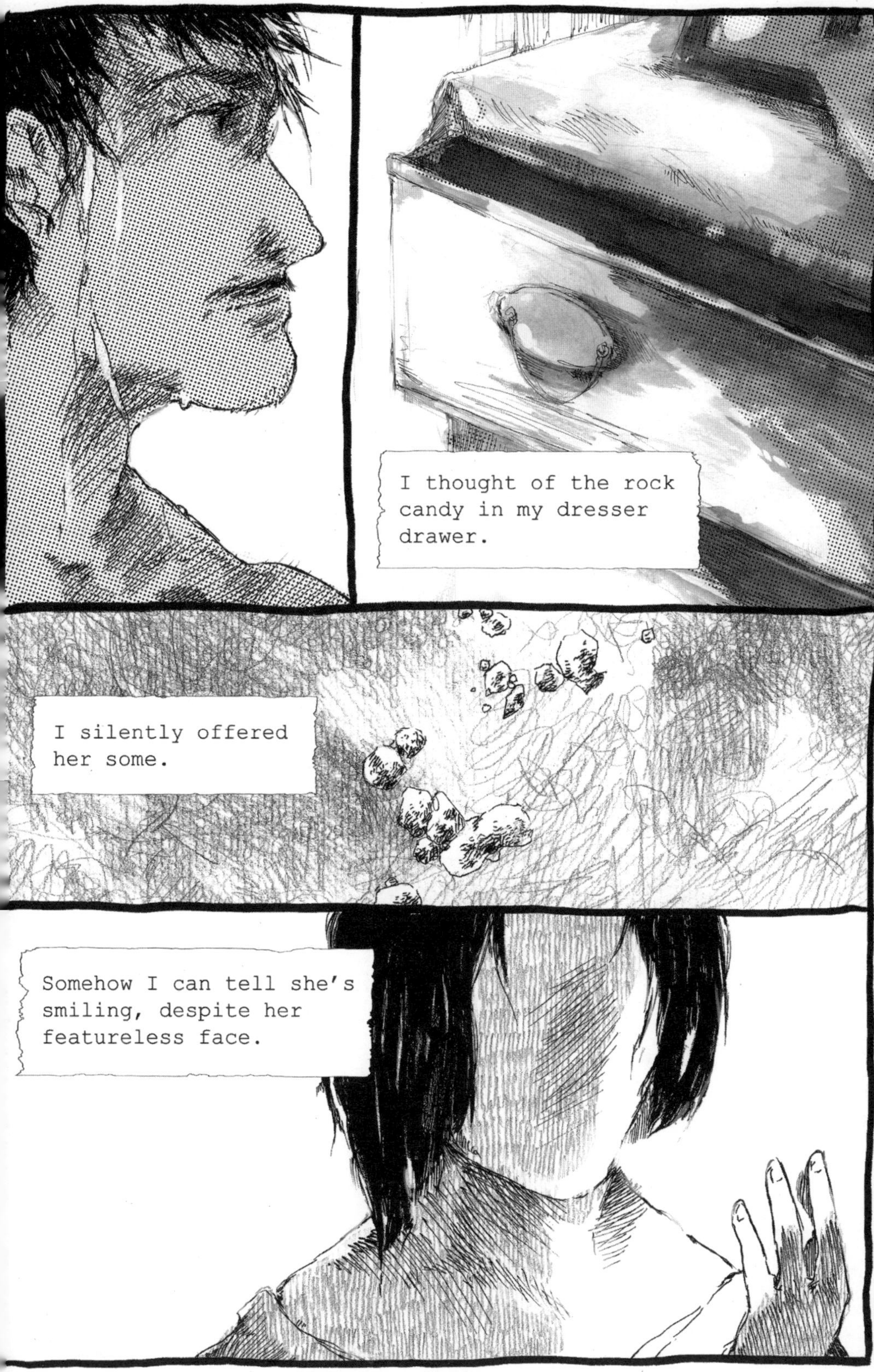
I thought of the rock candy in my dresser drawer.
I silently offered her some.
Somehow I can tell she's smiling, despite her featureless face.

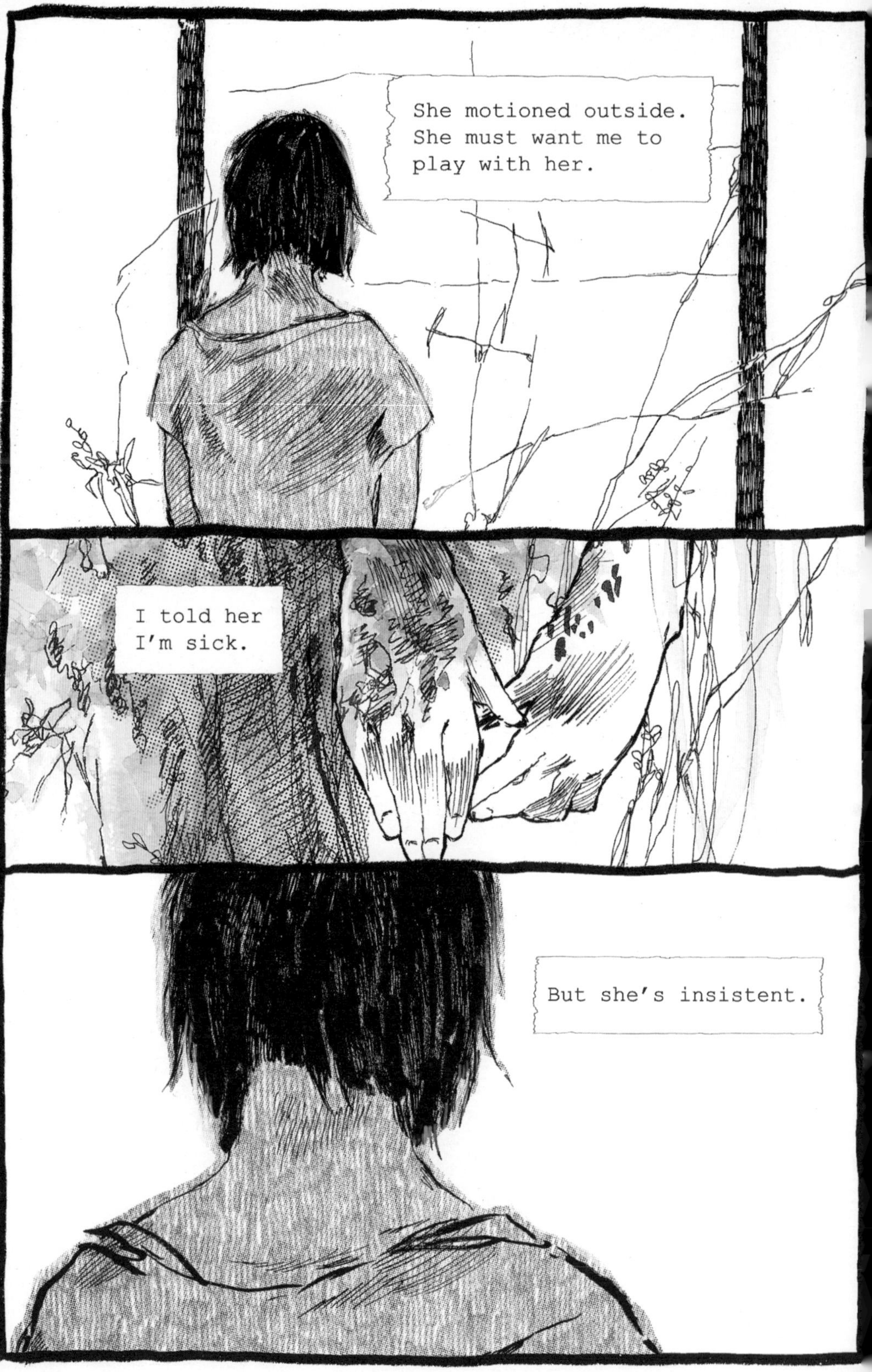
She motioned outside. She must want me to play with her.
I told her I'm sick.
But she's insistent.

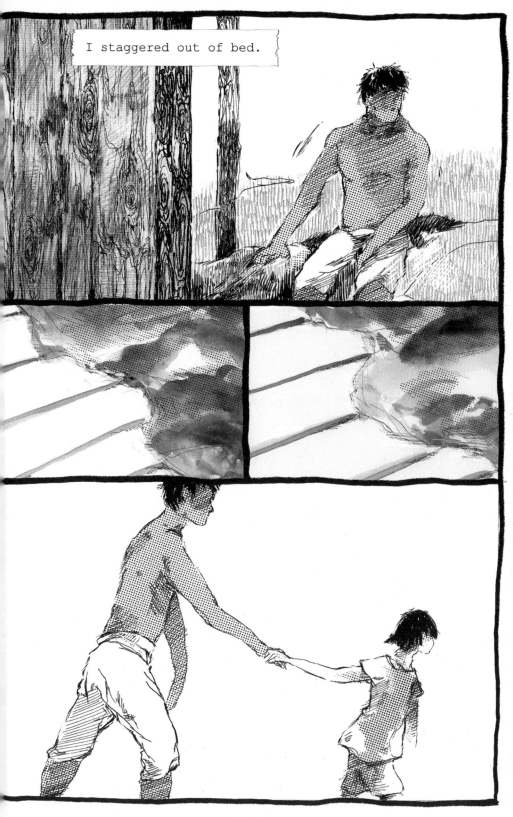

I staggered out of bed.

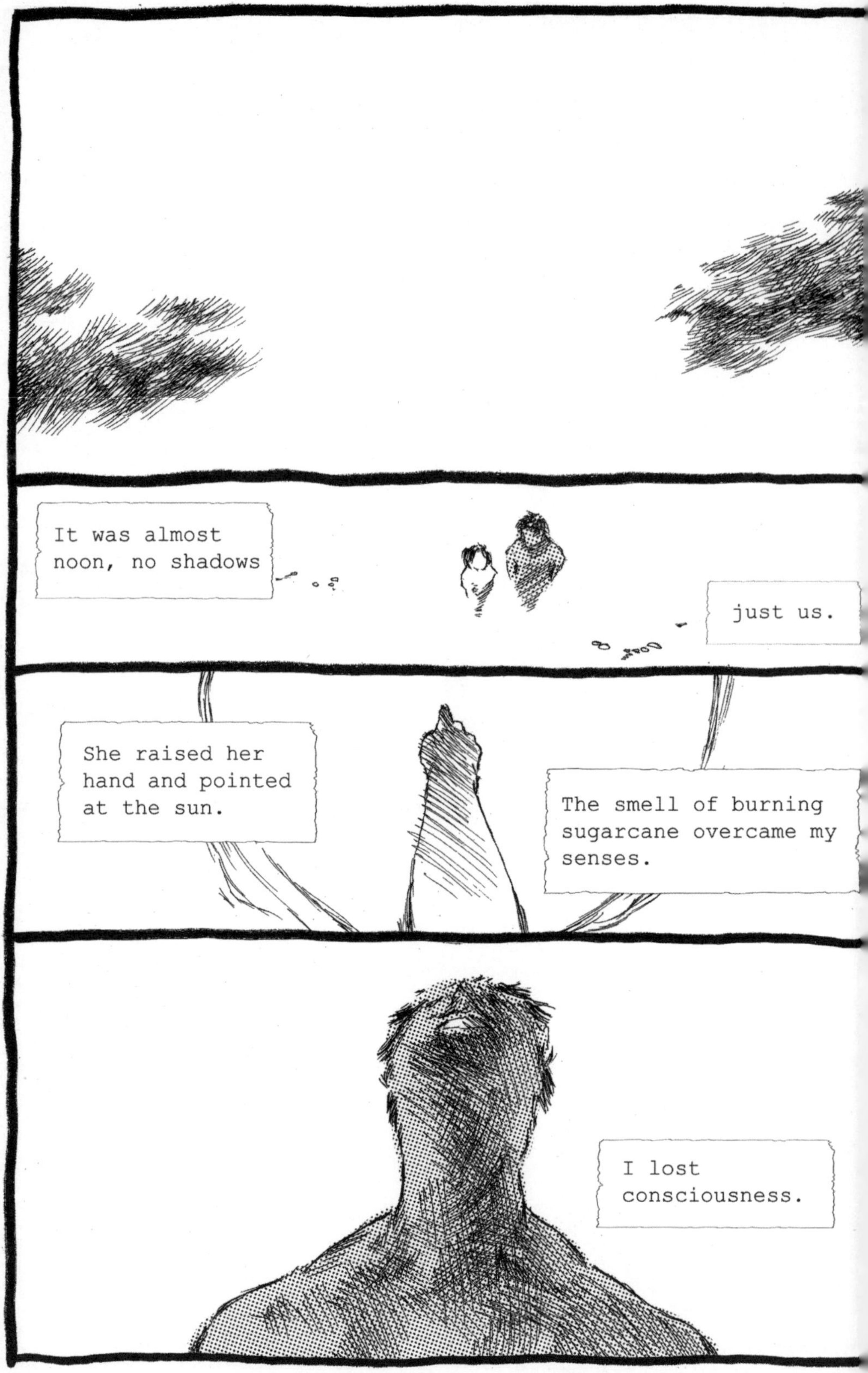
It was almost noon, no shadows
just us.
She raised her hand and pointed at the sun.
The smell of burning sugarcane overcame my senses.
I lost consciousness.

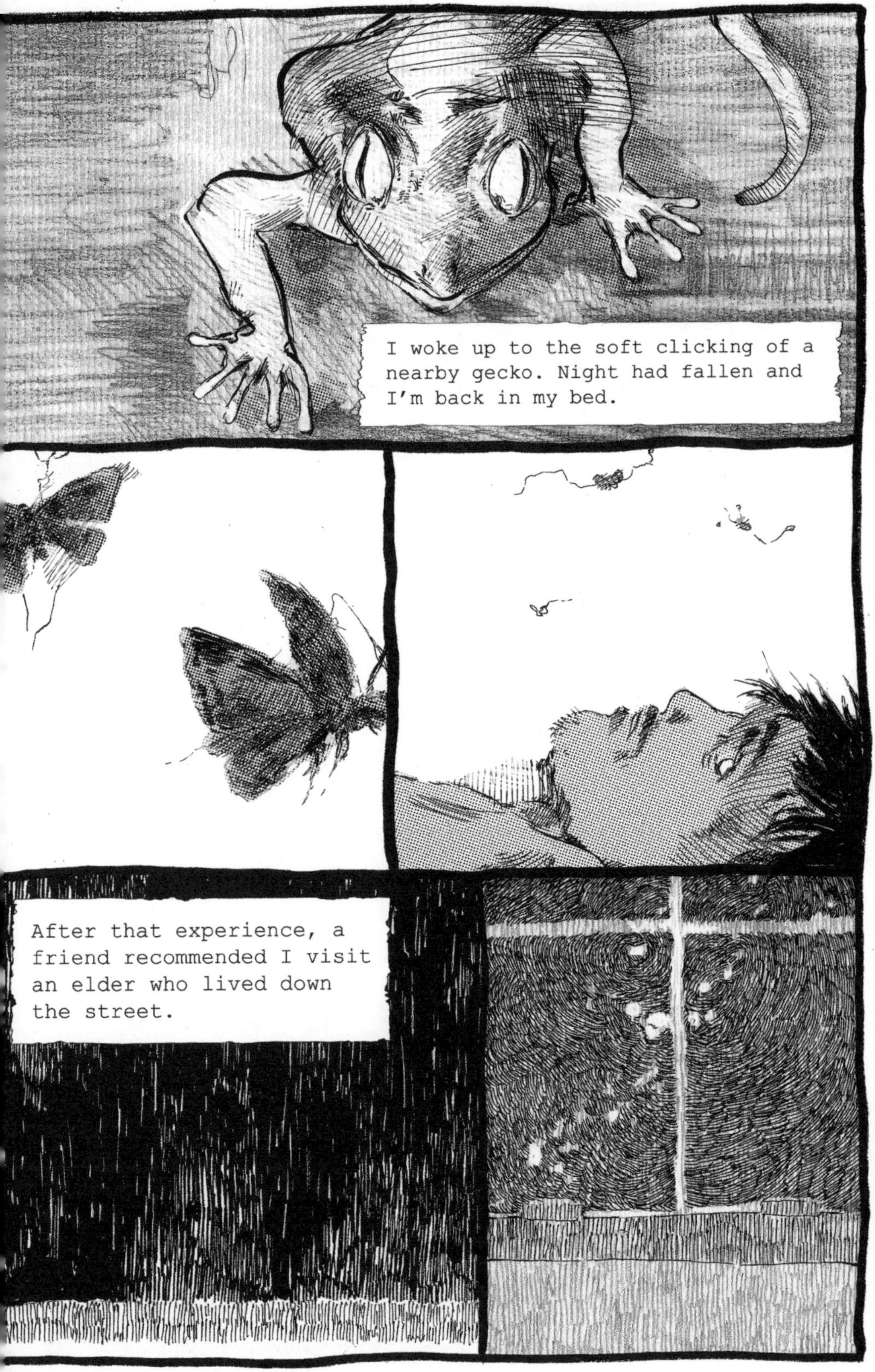
I woke up to the soft clicking of a nearby gecko. Night had fallen and I'm back in my bed.
After that experience, a friend recommended I visit an elder who lived down the street.

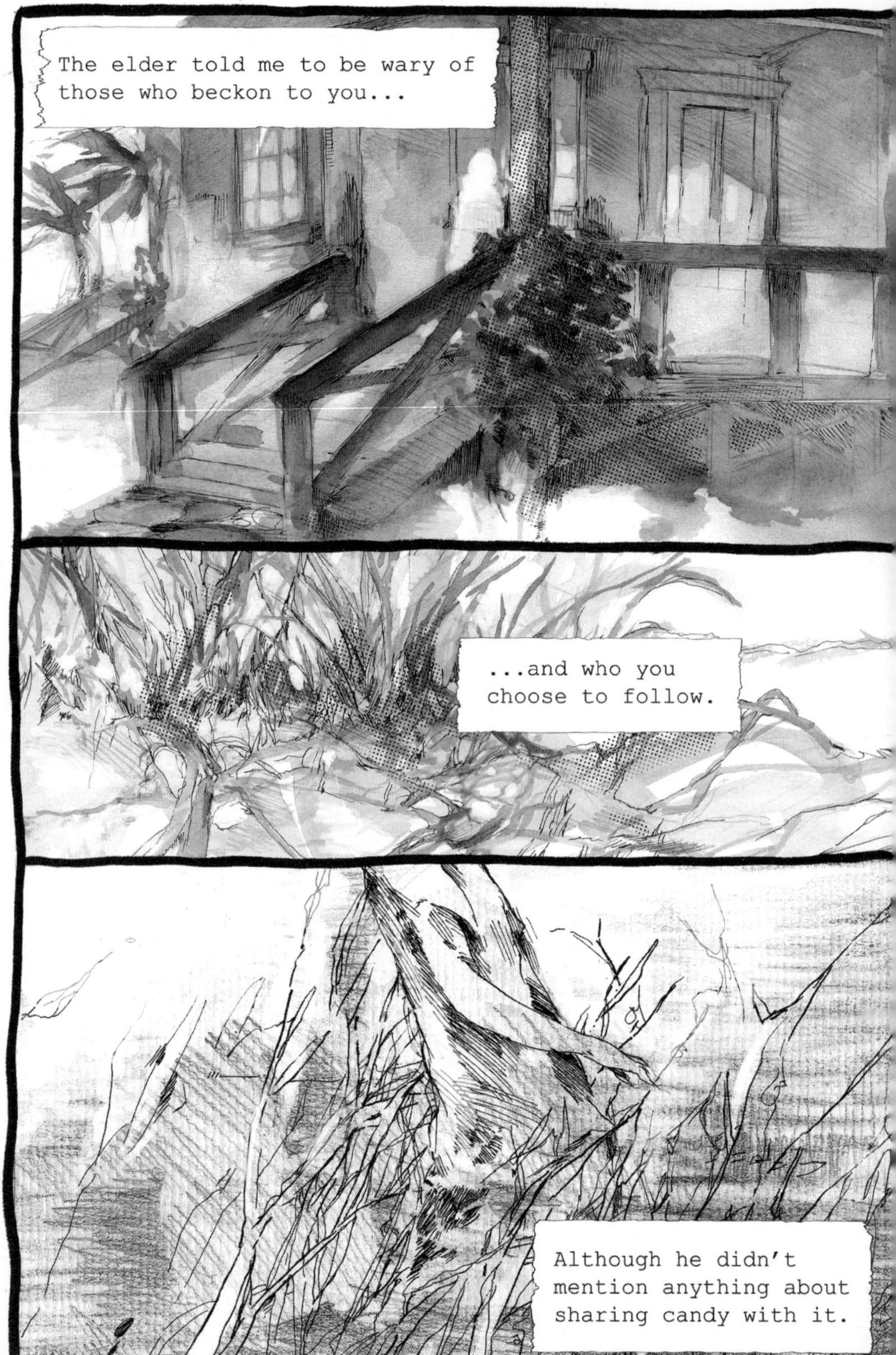
The elder told me to be wary of those who beckon to you...
...and who you choose to follow.
Although he didn't mention anything about sharing candy with it.

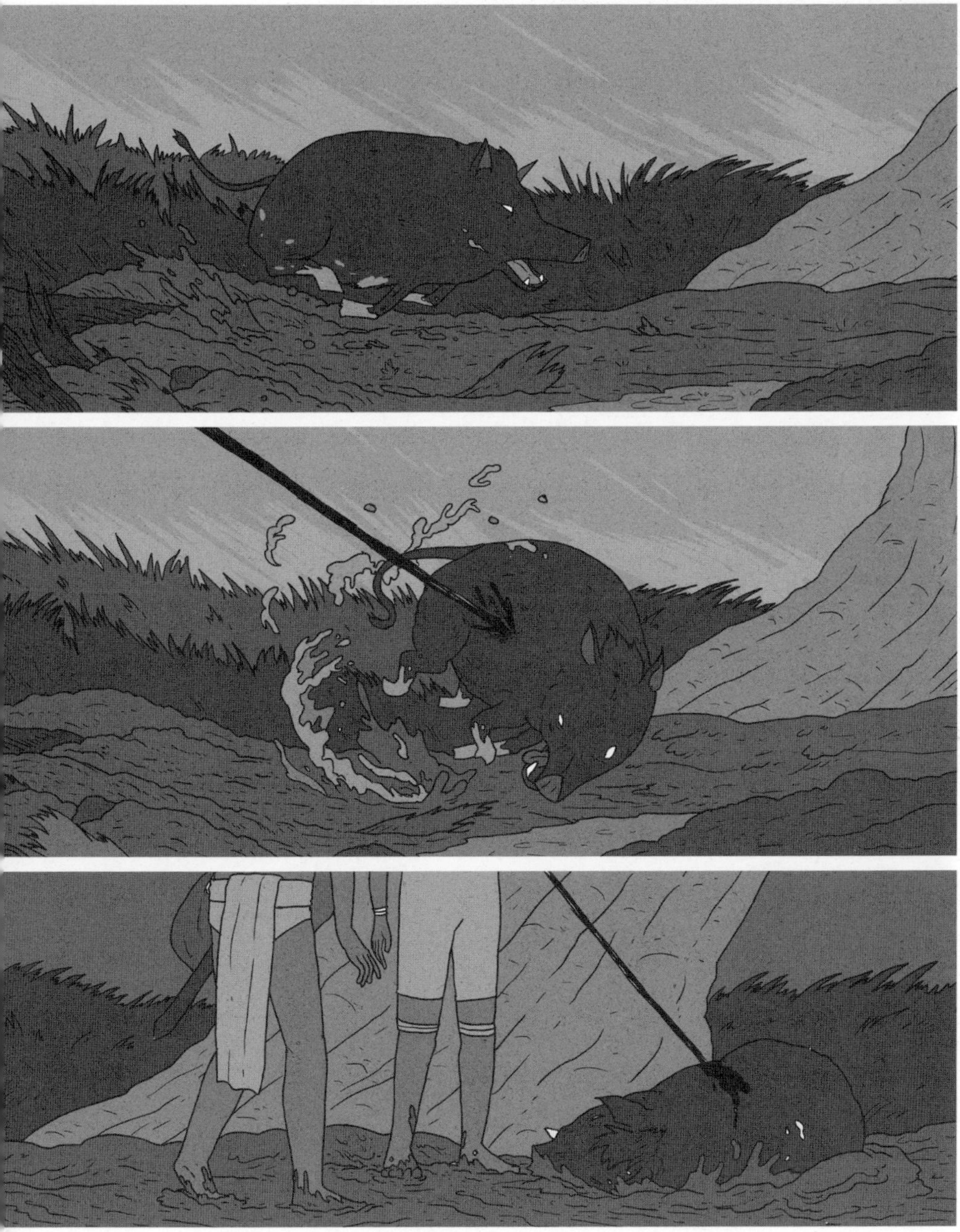

The Alan and The Hunters

by Rob Cham

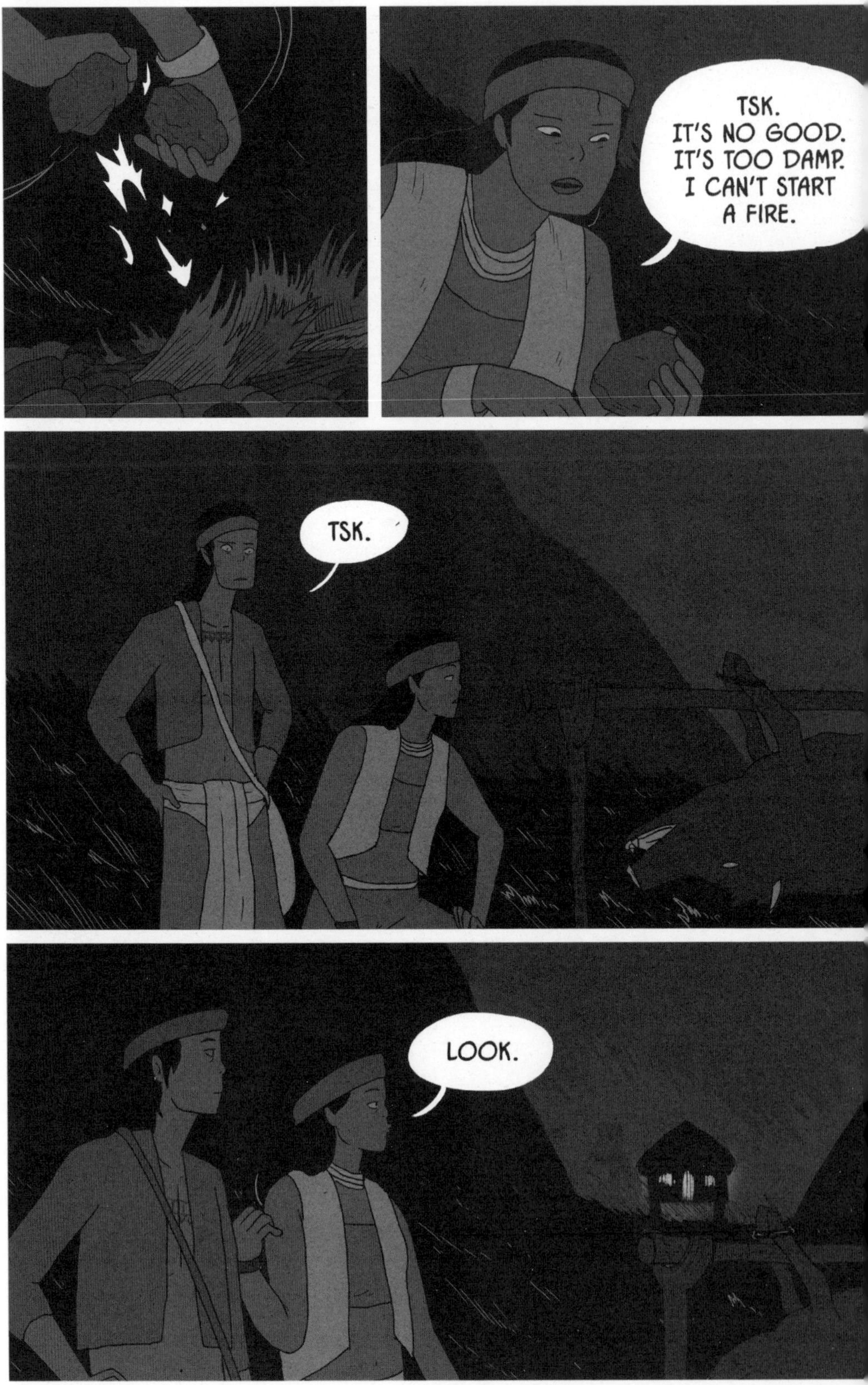
TSK.
IT'S NO GOOD.
IT'S TOO DAMP.
I CAN'T START
A FIRE.
TSK.
LOOK.

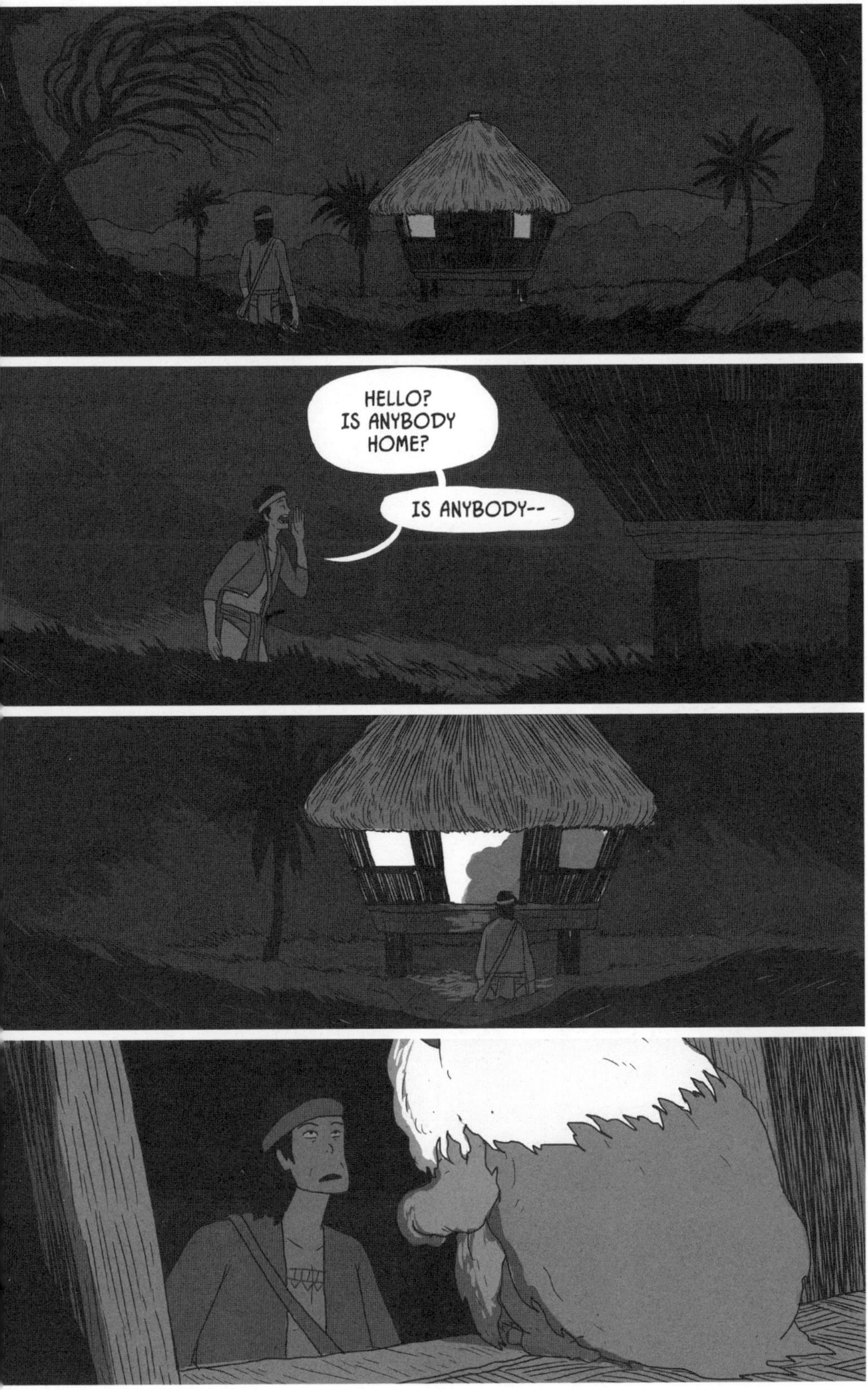
HELLO?
IS ANYBODY
HOME?
IS ANYBODY--

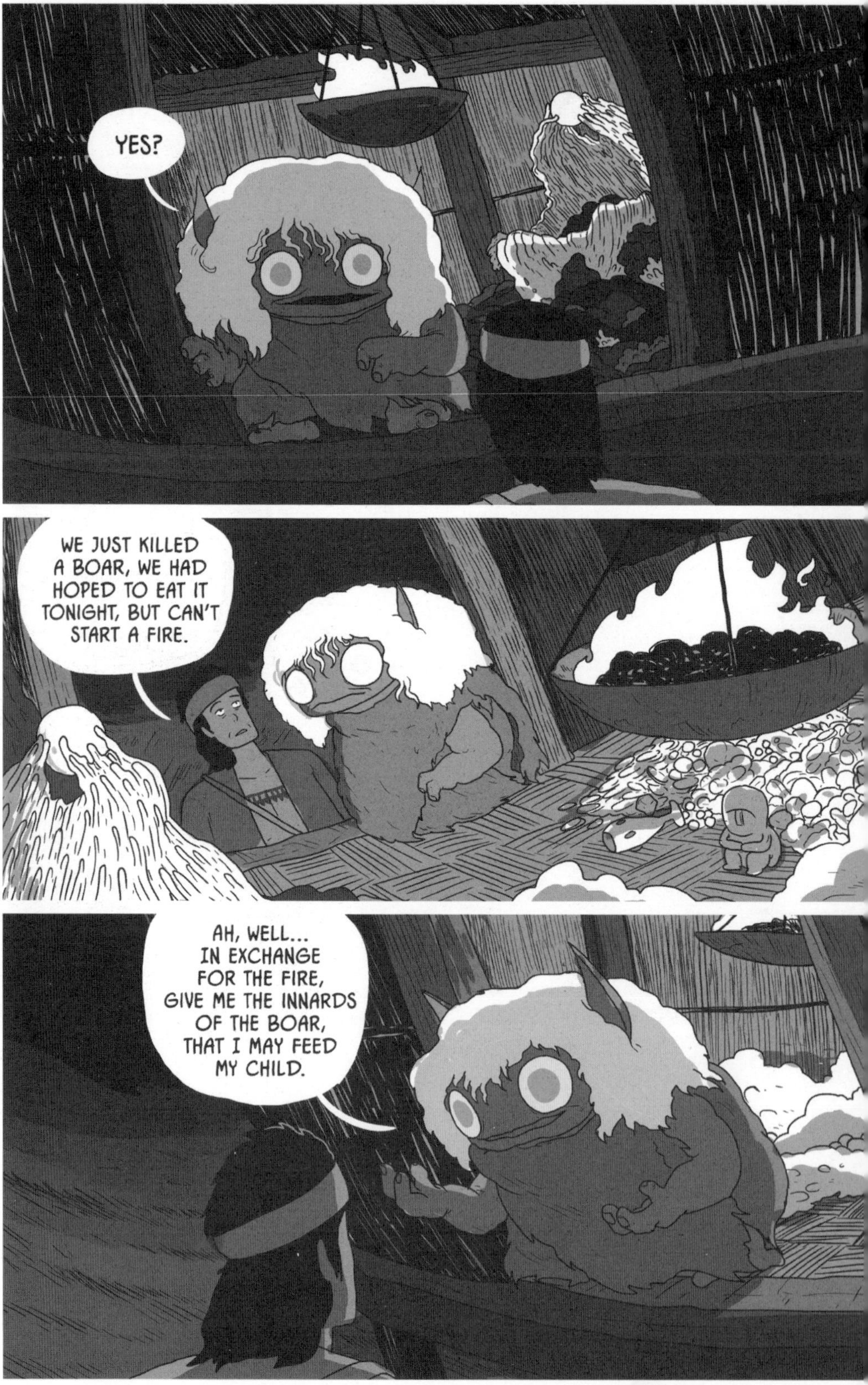
YES?
WE JUST KILLED A BOAR, WE HAD HOPED TO EAT IT TONIGHT, BUT CAN'T START A FIRE.
AH, WELL... IN EXCHANGE FOR THE FIRE, GIVE ME THE INNARDS OF THE BOAR, THAT I MAY FEED MY CHILD.

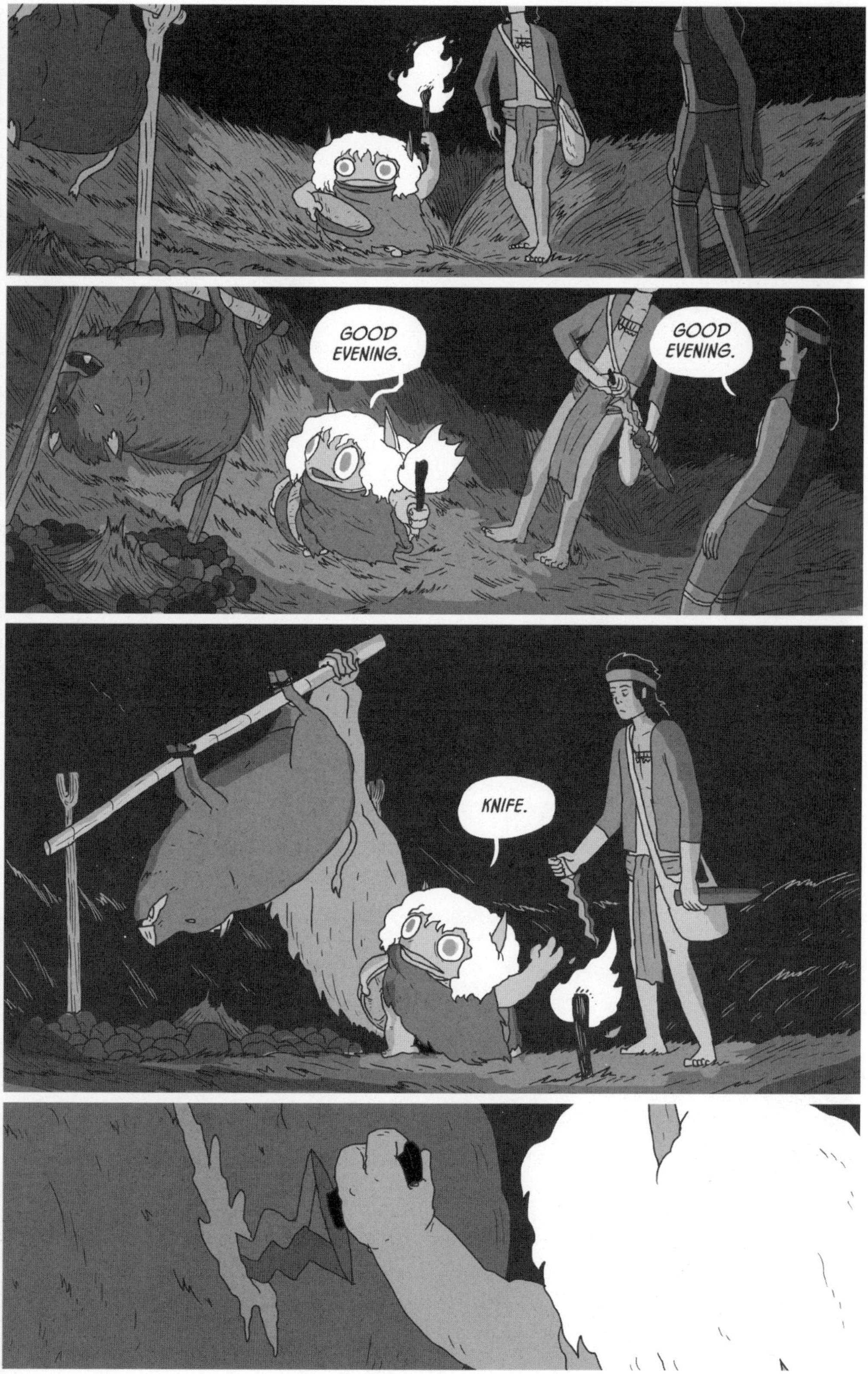
GOOD EVENING.
GOOD EVENING.
KNIFE.

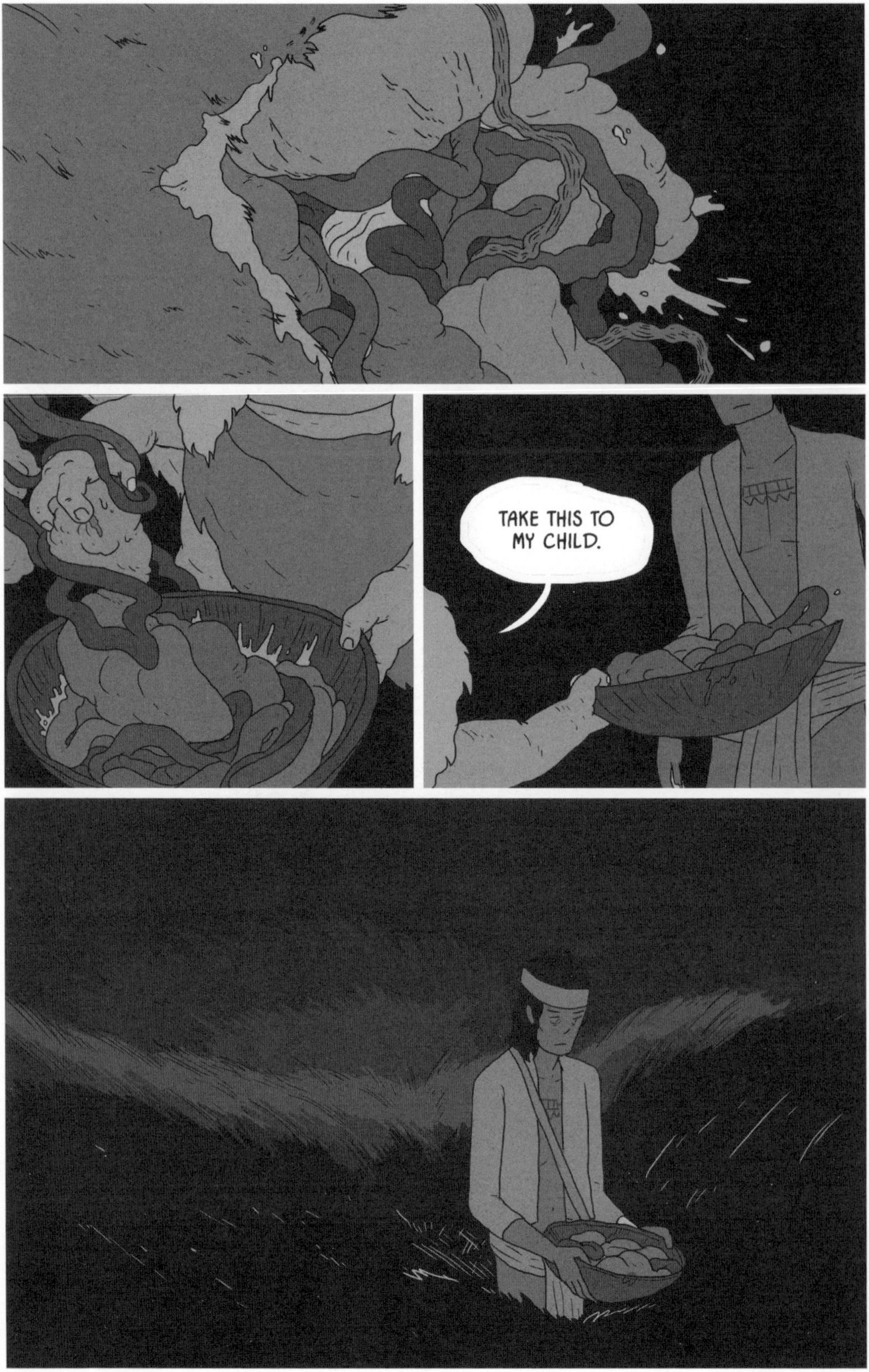
TAKE THIS TO MY CHILD.

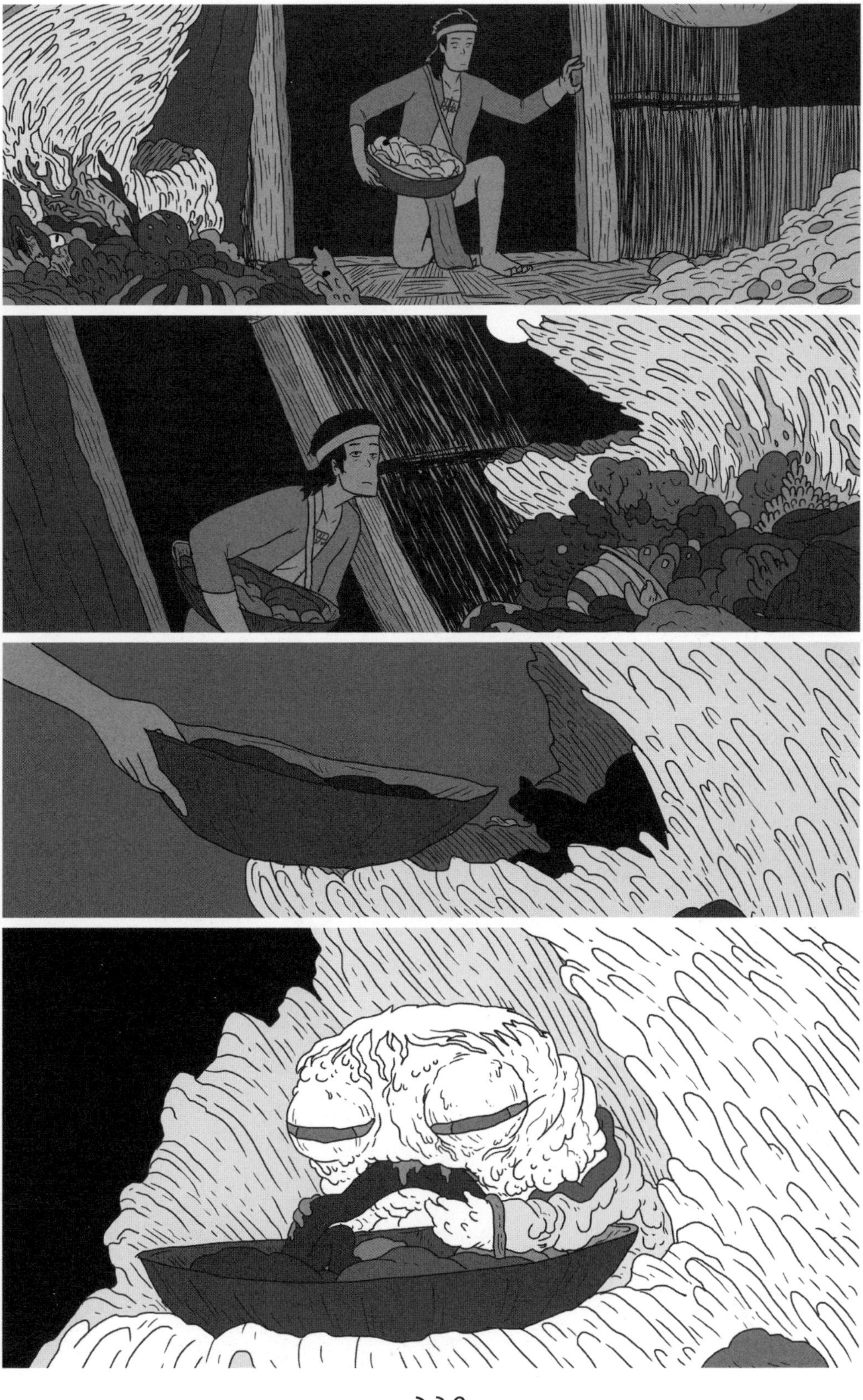

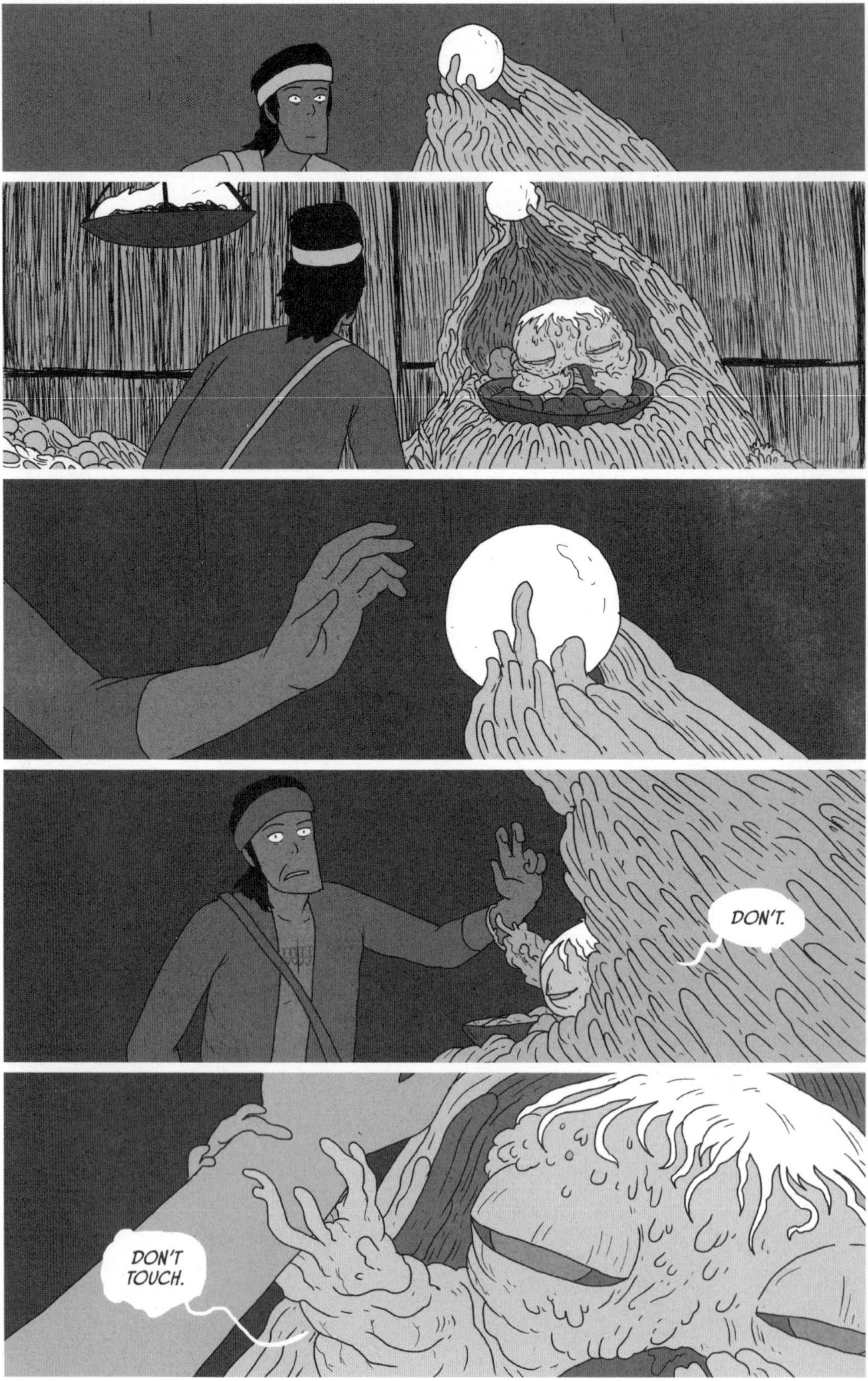
DON'T.
DON'T TOUCH.

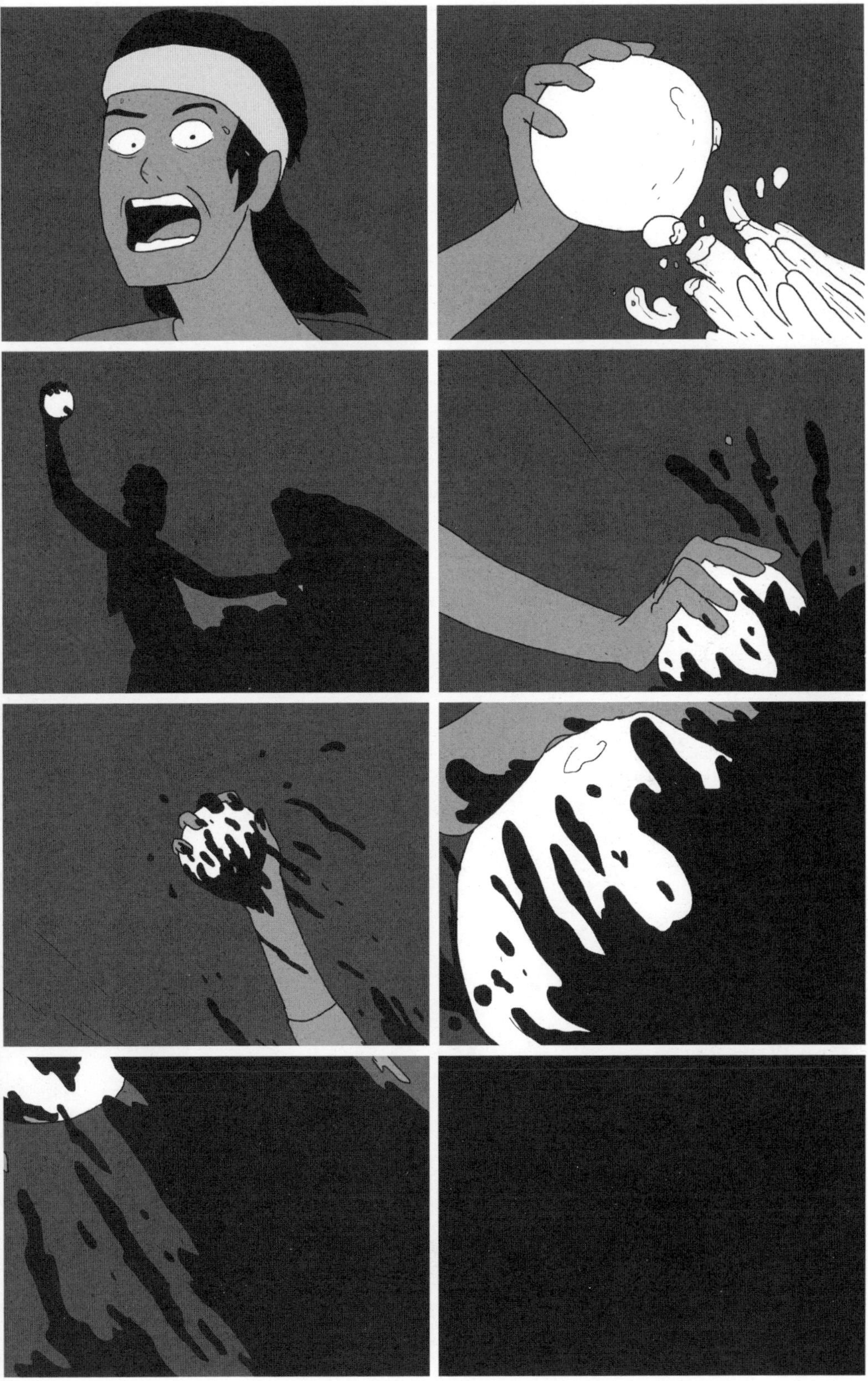

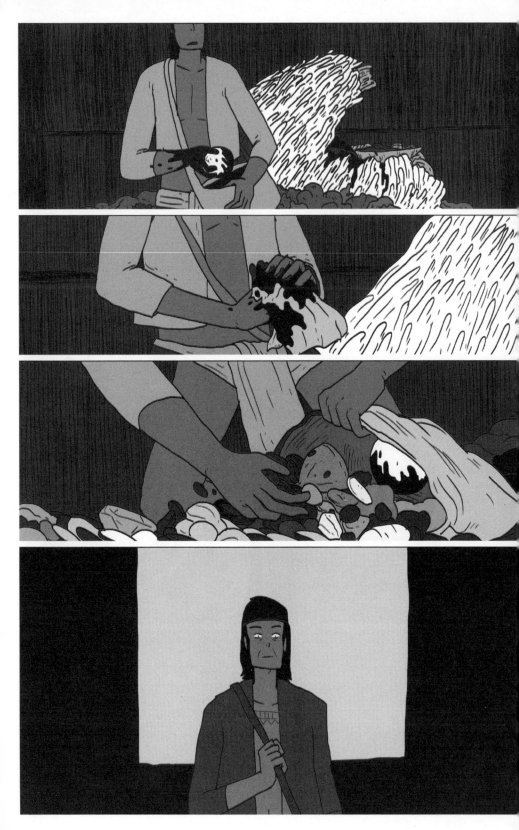

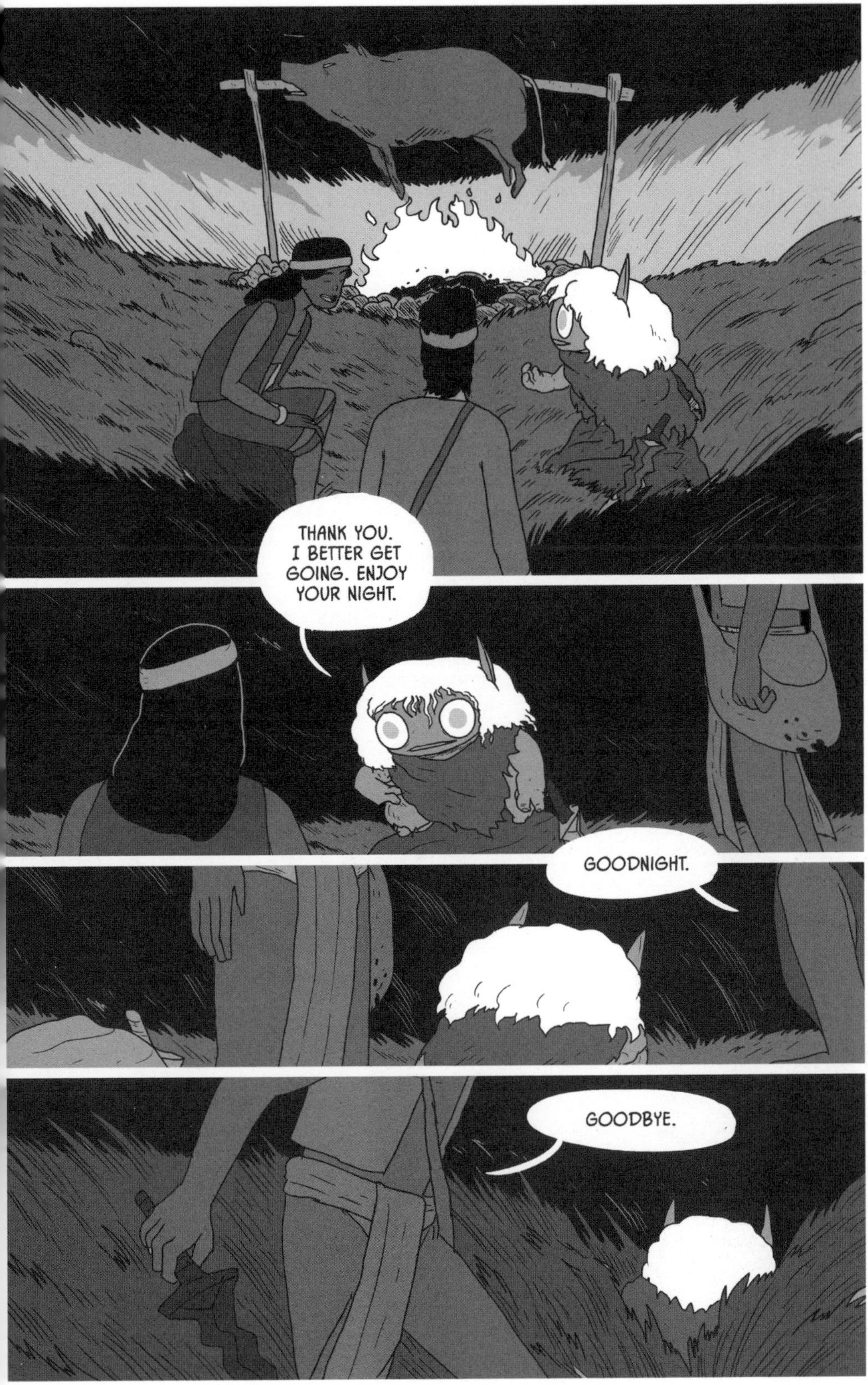
THANK YOU. I BETTER GET GOING. ENJOY YOUR NIGHT.
GOODNIGHT.
GOODBYE.

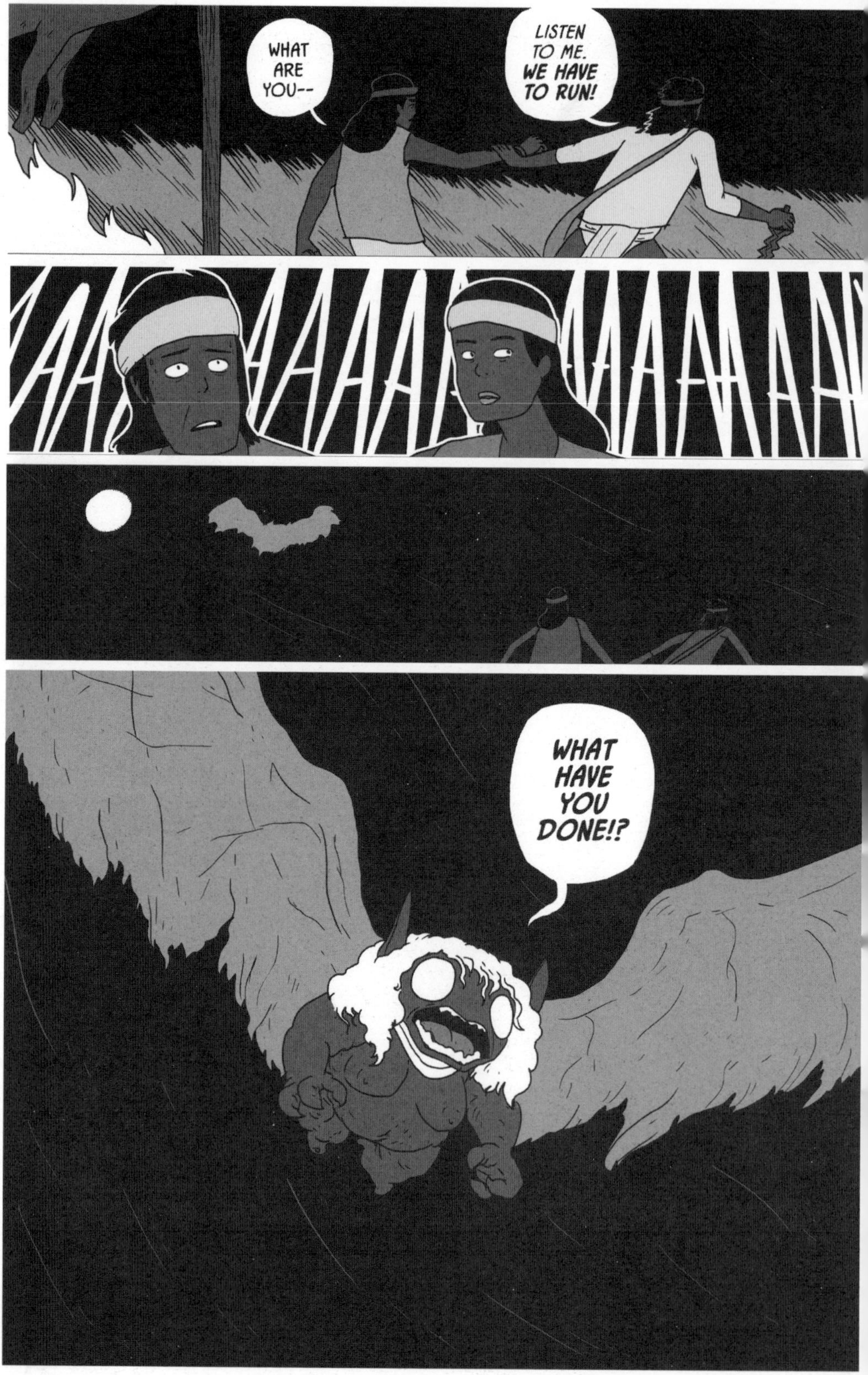
WHAT ARE YOU--
LISTEN TO ME. WE HAVE TO RUN!
AAAAAAAAAAAAAAAAAAAH
WHAT HAVE YOU DONE!?

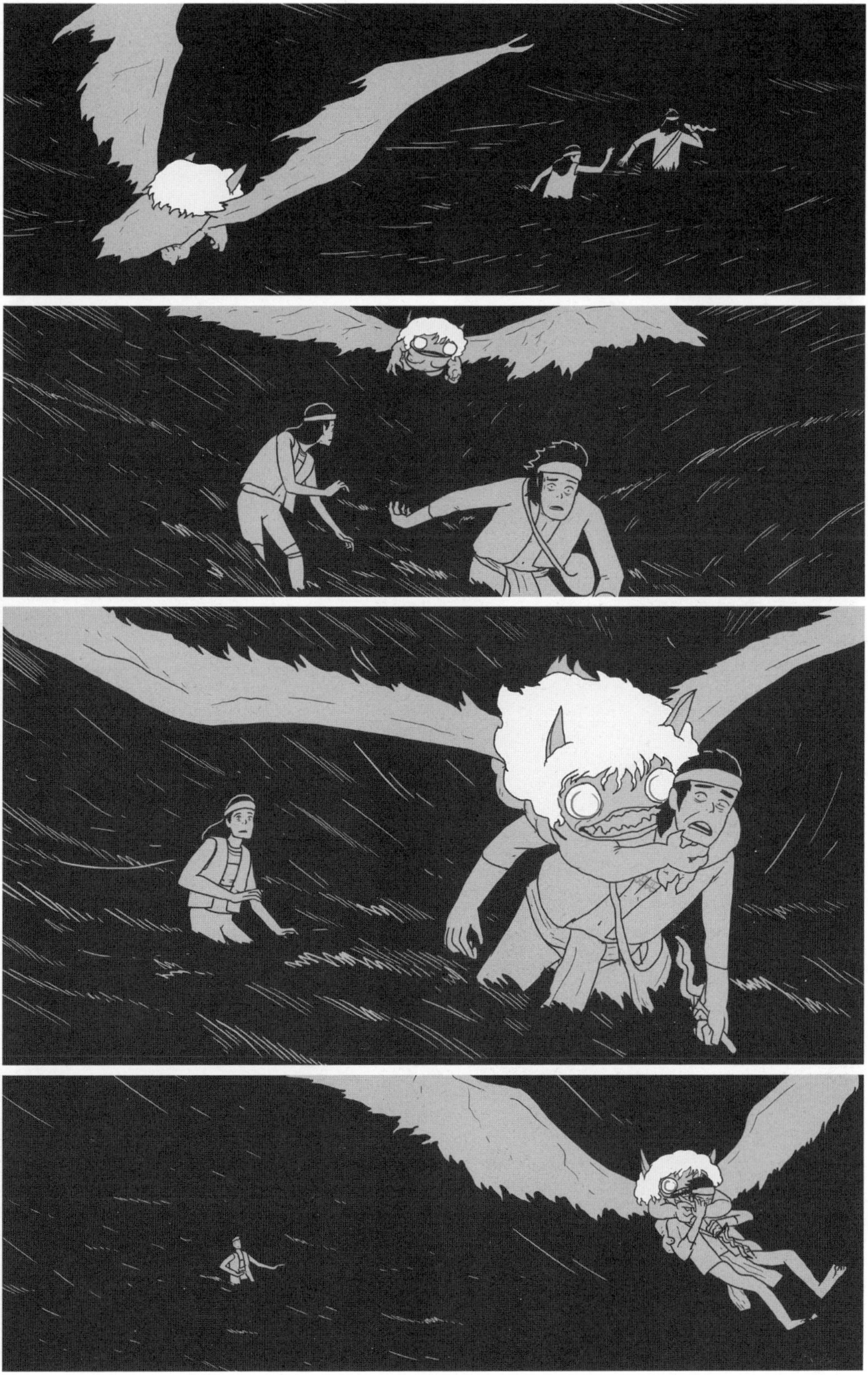

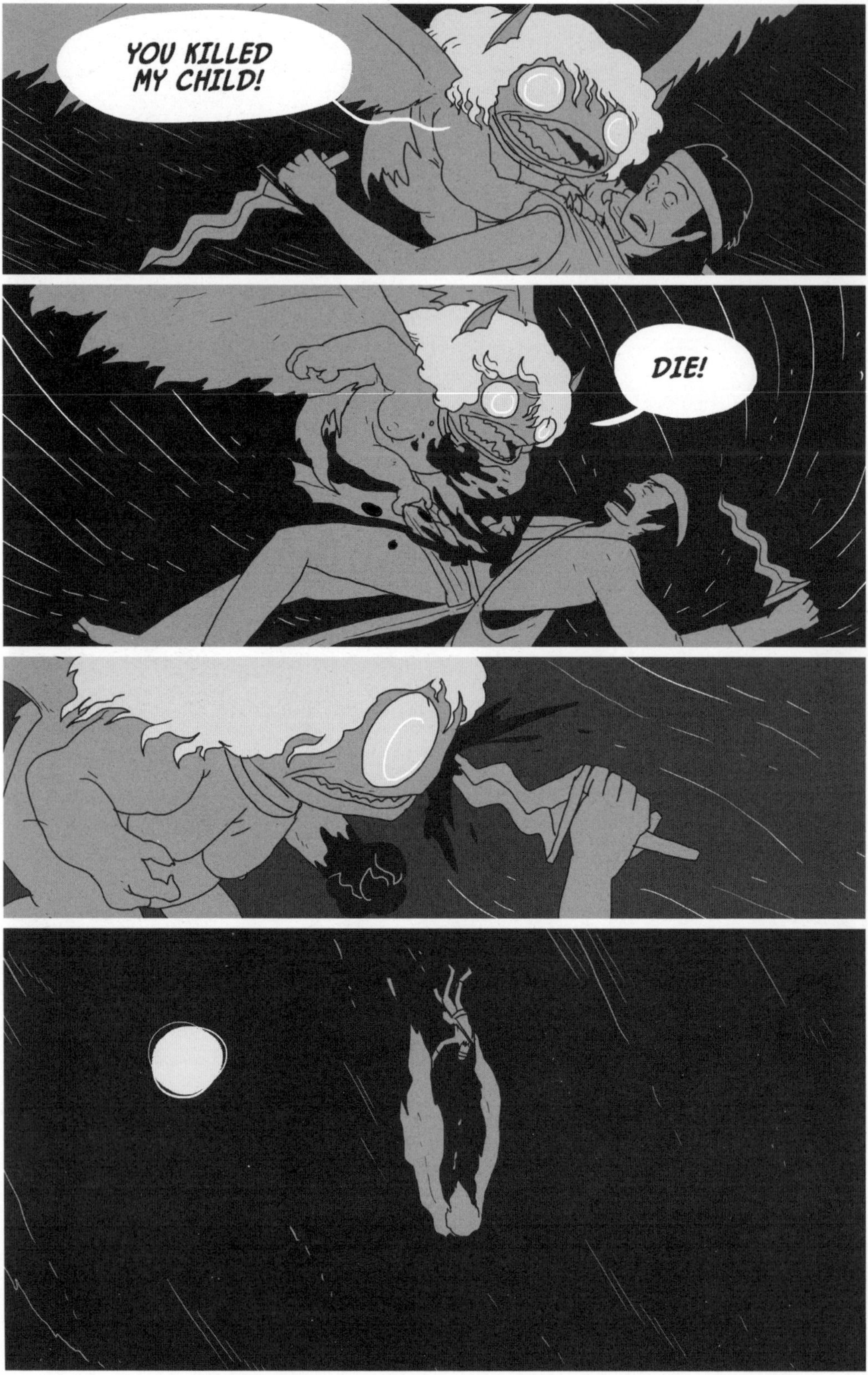
YOU KILLED
MY CHILD!
DIE!

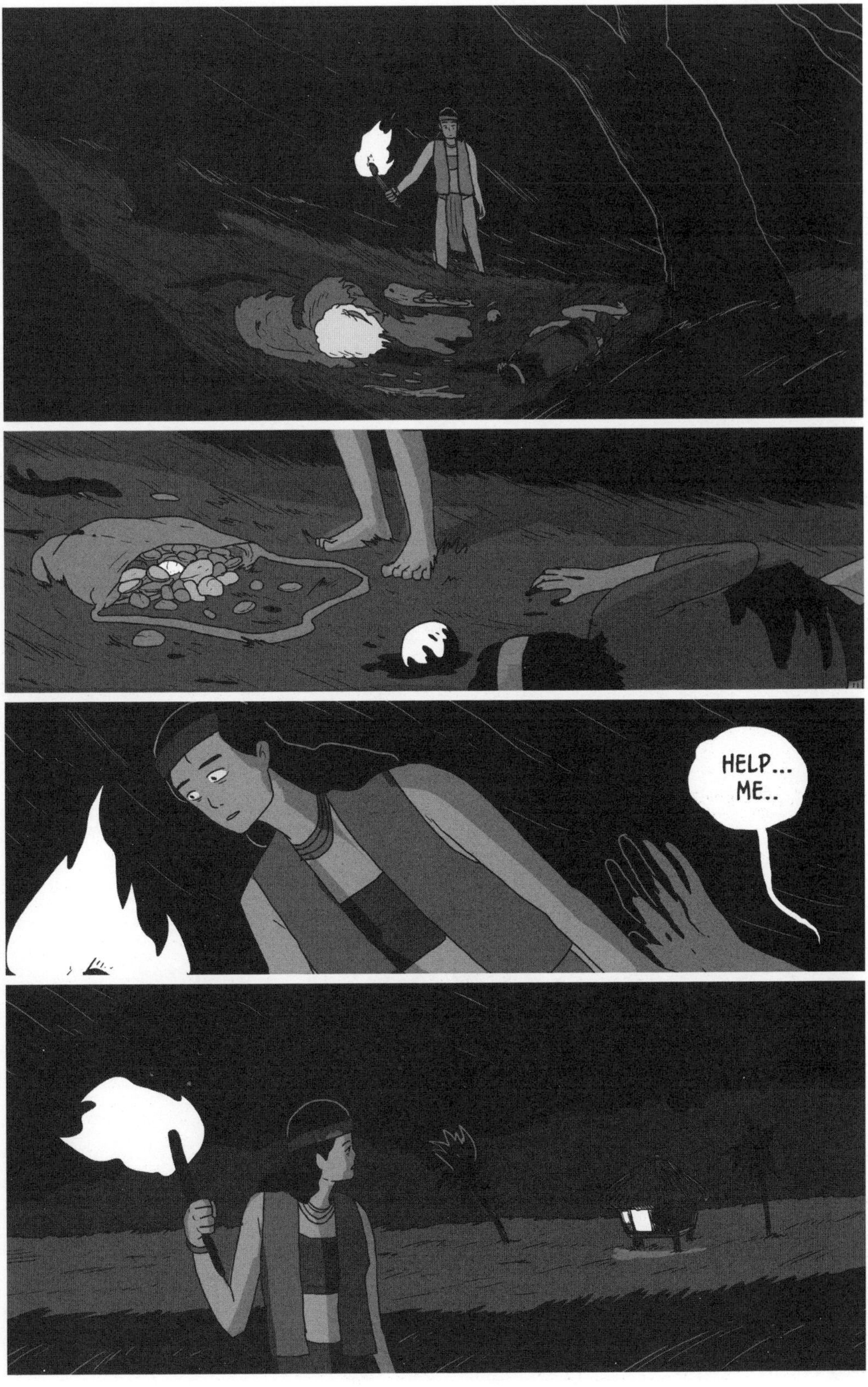
HELP... ME..

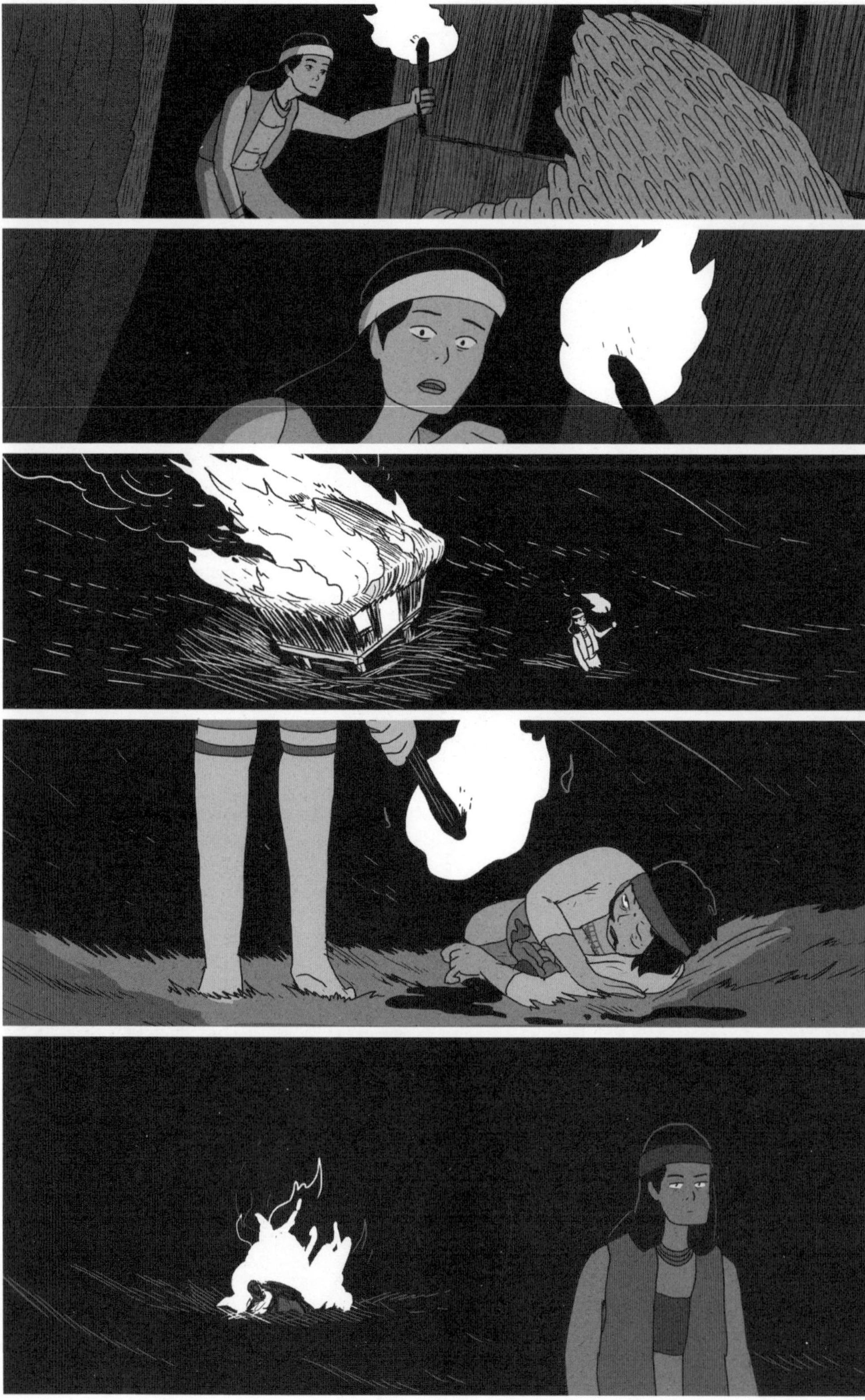

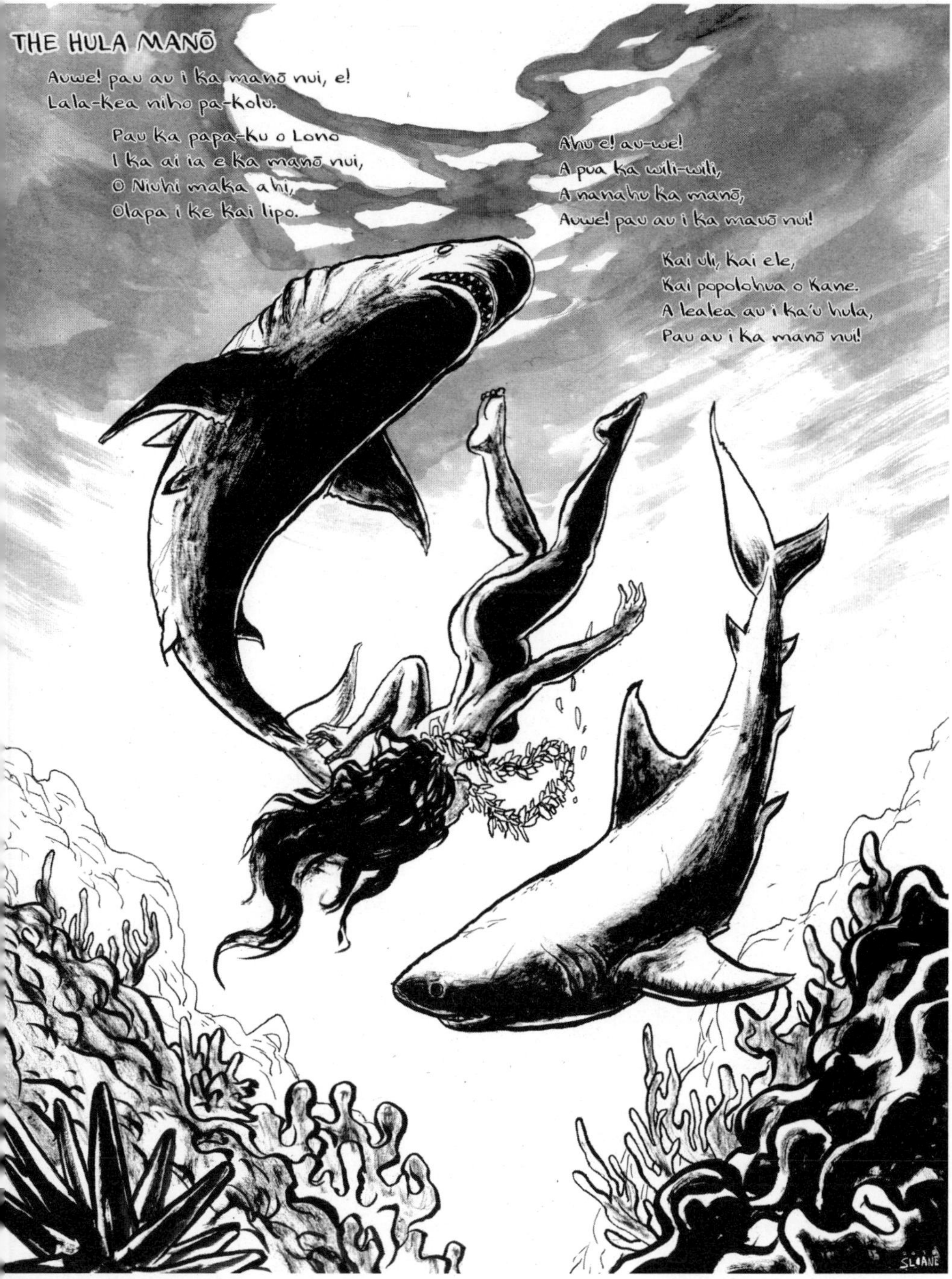
THE HULA MANŌ
Auwe! pau au i ka manō nui, e!
Lala-kea niho pa-kolu.
Pau ka papa-ku o Lono
I ka ai ia e ka manō nui,
O Niuhi maka ahi,
Olapa i ke kai lipo.
Ahu e! au-we!
A pua ka wili-wili,
A nanahu ka manō,
Auwe! pau au i ka mauō nui!
Kai uli, kai ele,
Kai popolohua o Kane.
A lealea au i ka'u hula,
Pau au i ka manō nui!
SLOANE

HE HULA MANŌ BY SLOANE LEONG

ABOUT THE ARTISTS

Kate Ashwin lives in West Yorkshire, England, with her very understanding husband and two fat cats. She has been making webcomics for around 16 years, which is a silly amount of time to be doing anything, but here we are anyway. Her current project is *Widdershins*, a series of Victorian-era adventure stories, which can be read online at widdershinscomic.com.

Jonah Cabudol-Chalker is an emerging illustrator completing his studies at California College of the Arts. He has an interest in storytelling and passion for work that allows him to express his Native Hawaiian culture. *Cautionary Fables and Fairytales: Oceanian Edition* is one of the first published projects he participated in, and his portfolio can be viewed at jonahcc.com.

Rob Cham is an illustrator, comic book creator, and friend. He's released two graphic novels, *Light* (2015) and *Lost* (2016) under Anino Comics. He won the National Book Award for *Light* in 2016 for Best Graphic Fiction (Wordless). You can check out his comics and work at robcham.com and @robcham.

Yiling Changues is an illustrator/artist/painter/graphic designer, living between Paris and Tahiti. From publishing to pattern design, as well as animation, she uses whatever involves drawing, colors and inspiration to express her cultural heritage, exploring the question of multiculturalism, diaspora and cultural heritage. She hopes to connect Contemporary Art and Polynesian Traditional Art, Culture and History, so people worldwide can discover and reclaim their traditions in a modern way.

Paolo Chikiamco writes prose, comics, and interactive fiction. He's the Managing Editor of Studio Salimbal (SalimbalComics.com), a Filipino comics studio. If you liked his story here, he has also edited *Alternative Alamat*, an anthology of stories that re-imagines Philippine mythology. His fiction has been published in anthologies such as *The Sea is Ours* and the *Best of Philippine Speculative Fiction* (2005-2010), and his most popular work is an interactive wrestling novel for Choice of Games called *Slammed!*.

Diigii Daguna is an illustrator and comics artist from Manila, who wishes they can cook as well as they can eat. They live off of brewed coffee, street food, noodles and manga. One of their biggest dreams is to pet every cat.

Brady Evans is an artist and illustrator born, raised, and working in Honolulu, Hawai'i. With a strong interest in manga and other forms of sequential imagery and storytelling, Evans' work is often narrative and explores themes that include death, humor, and our place in the natural and supernatural worlds. Find his work at bradyevans.com

Born and raised on the melting pot that is Oahu, Hawaii, **Mark Gould** was surrounded by many different cultures while growing up and grew to love them all. He tries to share the local culture of acceptance as best he can in his work. You can see more of his art in his book *Native Sons: Ring of Fire* or at facebook.com/nativesonsringoffire

Gen H. is an illustrator, born and raised in Hawaii. She believes that pineapple belongs on pizza.

Nick Iluzada is a designer residing in sunny Los Angeles, California. He draws things for animation and makes photo zines about being kinda Filipino. When he isn't drawing, you can find him lifting heavy objects, geeking out over bags, and scouring LA for the tastiest cheap treats.

DJ Keawekane was born on Oahu, but moved to Hilo as a young child, graduating from Hilo High. He was obssessed with drawing since he was five years old, to the point of getting into trouble for it, though he went on to more practical pursuits at 18. However, in 2002, his spine was broken in three places as a result of a car accident. In the year-long recovery that followed, DJ resumed drawing, eventually creating his own comic book, *Exillion*. firstwatchstudios.com

Sloane Leong is a self-taught cartoonist, artist and writer of Hawaiian, Chinese, Italian, Mexican, Native American and European ancestries. Her work focuses on exploring silenced narratives from her own communities, to connect personally with individuals through storytelling, with an aim to cultivate a kinder, more understanding future. She is currently living near Portland, Oregon.

Nicole Mannino is a freelance comic artist and illustrator who loves bright colors, wonky perspective, monsters, and cute things. She has a passion for lighthearted, feel-good stories, which she explores in her current ongoing comic *This is Not Fiction* (thisisnotfiction.com).

Mariel Maranan is a Filipina-American artist from California who has been drawing since she can remember. Taking inspiration from her family and friends, she aspires to publish her own graphic novel and continue writing stories about hidden worlds and genuine friendships. Currently she collaborates with Rudy Mora on the webcomic *The Red Muscle* (theredmuscle.tumblr.com).

Meredith McClaren does comics. You may have heard of some (*Hinges*, *Hopeless Savages V4*, *Heart in a Box*). She lives in a constant state of exhaustion. Approach with caution.

Kel McDonald has been working in comics for over a decade—most of that time has been spent on her webcomic *Sorcery 101*. More recently, she has organized the *Cautionary Fables and Fairytales* anthology series, while writing and drawing. She has worked on the comic *Buffy: The High School Years*. She recently finished creator-owned series *Misfits of Avalon* for Dark Horse Comics. She's currently working on her self-published series *The City Between*. You can find her work at kelmcdonald.com.

Kim Miranda is a Filipina-American illustrator and comic book artist, who also teaches painting. Her aim is to her use her passion with character design, concept art and visual development as cooperative sibling mediums to create engaging connections between cultures and unique stories. She loves reading about art history, poetry, indigenous world culture, human rights, contemporary painting. Kim also adores growing miniature gardens in her front yard.

Philippine-born artist **Tintin Pantoja** graduated with a BFA in Cartooning and Illustration from the School of Visual Arts NYC, having acquired a love of comics from early exposure to Herge's *TinTin*, *Archie*, and *X-Men*. She has been illustrating comics since 2007. Among her works are adaptations of *Hamlet*, *Pride and Prejudice*, and the educational middlegrade *Manga Math* series. She divides her time in Manila between making comics, caring for her four dogs, and scouting the web for fountain pens. You can see more of her work at tintinpantoja.com.

Iole Marie Rabor is a freelance illustrator and designer living in New York City. She graduated from Virginia Commonwealth University with a BFA in Communication Arts (Illustration/Design) and is currently job/internship hunting, while taking some side classes at the School of Visual Arts and living her life. She enjoys reading and making comics, drawing fanart, watching films, and storyboarding, while one day hoping to learn the art of animation. Iole is a Filipino-American that is very proud of her family, her culture, history, and the superstitions and myths that come from the Philippines as well as other cultures.

Cy Vendivil is a Filipino freelance artist based in Metro Manila who has experience working with cartoons, children's books, and comics. Since 2015, he has produced art for various indie titles like *Mono Kuro*, and *Bravos: Cebu*. His work is at about.me/cyanroll.

Extras

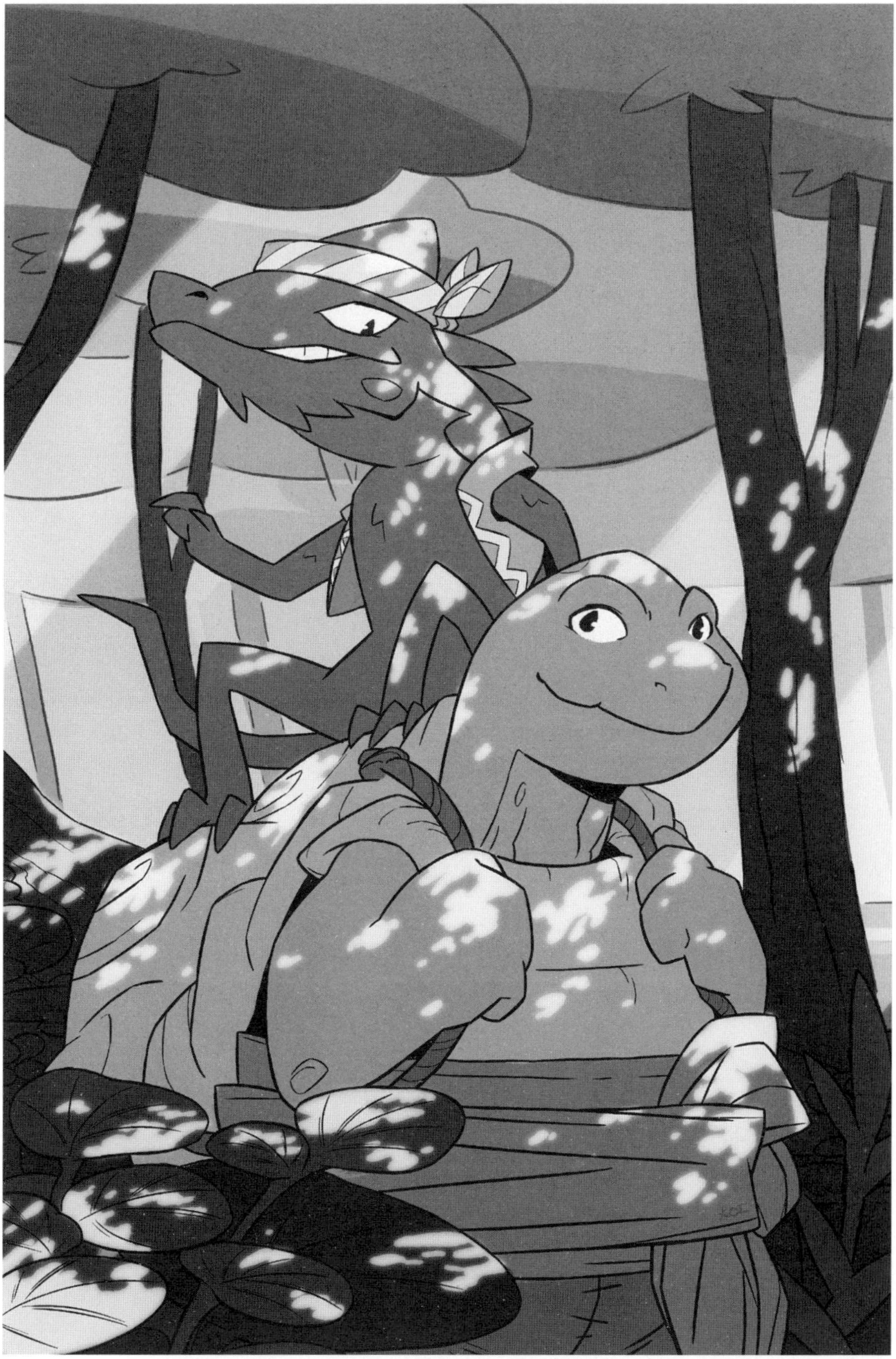

The Turtle and The Lizard
by Koi Carron

Cover Sketches
by Nick Iluzada

Nick Iluzada
Kel McDonald
Iron Circus Edition Cautionary Fables - Oceania
Sketches: 01

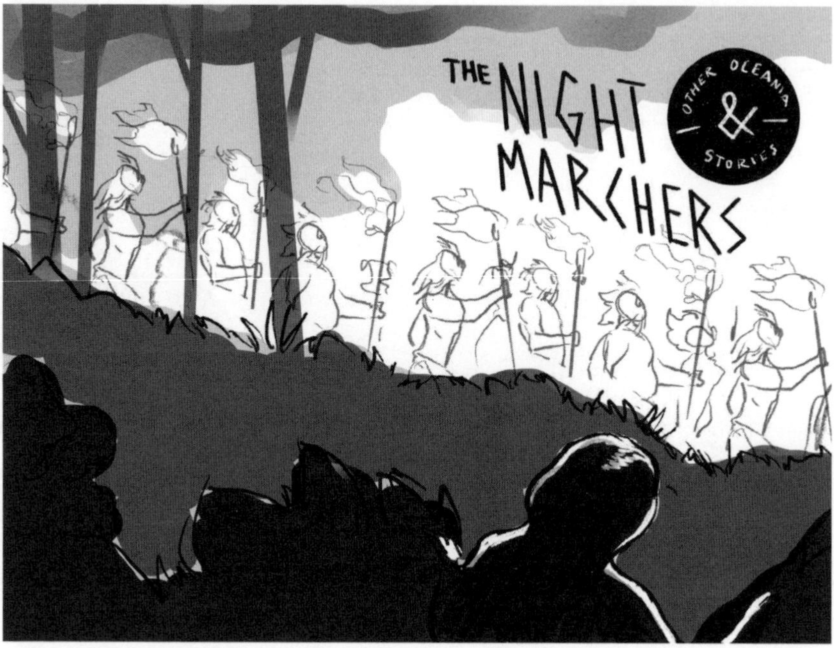

THE NIGHT MARCHERS
& OTHER OCEANIA STORIES

direction 1: scene-driven and more closely related to main narrative

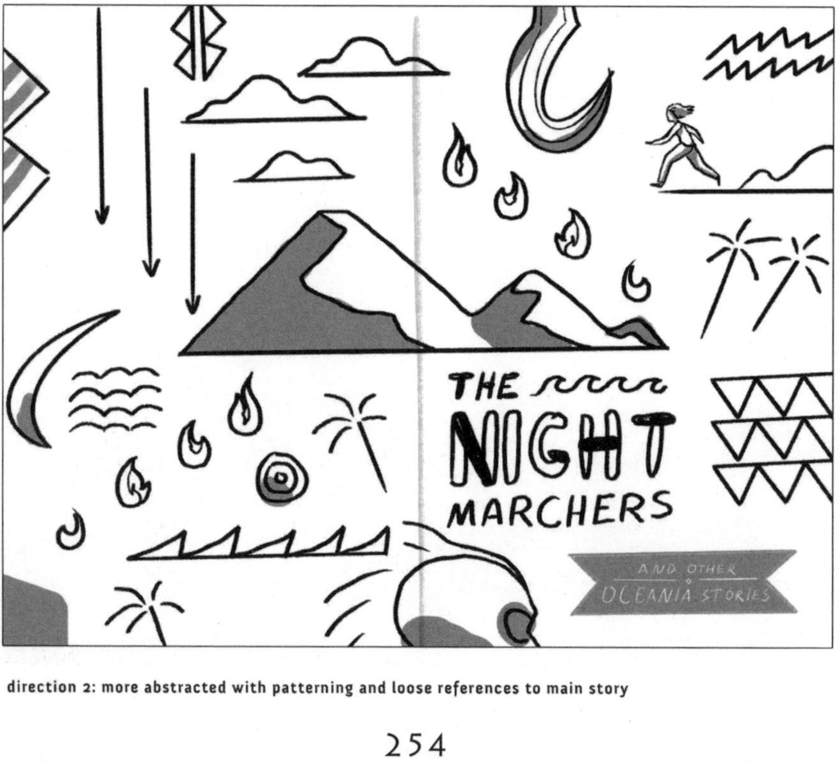

THE NIGHT MARCHERS
AND OTHER OCEANIA STORIES

direction 2: more abstracted with patterning and loose references to main story

Nick Iluzada
Kel McDonald, Sloane Leong, Kate Ashwin
Cautionary Fables and Fairy Tales Cover- sketches

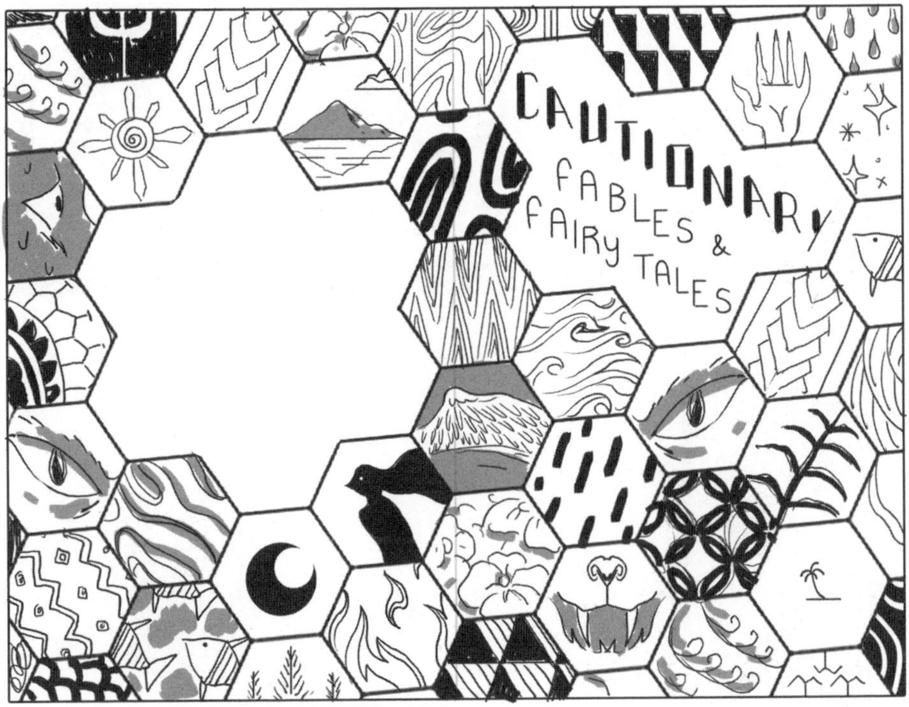
CAUTIONARY
FABLES &
FAIRY TALES

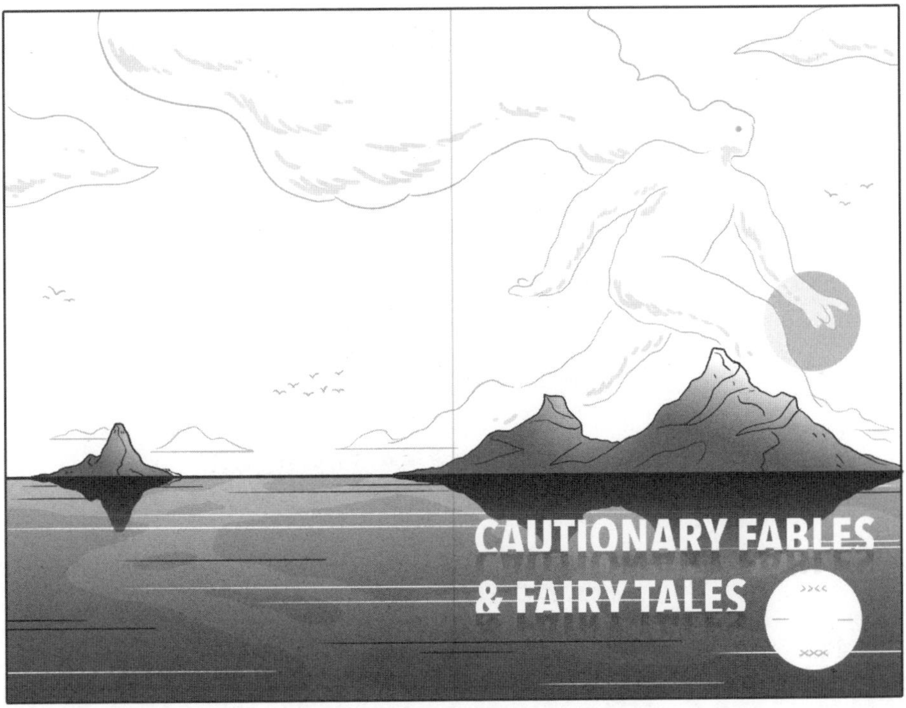
CAUTIONARY FABLES
& FAIRY TALES

EXPLORE THE WORLD WITH

CAUTIONARY FABLES & FAIRYTALES

A CAUTIONARY
FABLES & FAIRYTALES BOOK
THE GIRL WHO MARRIED A SKULL
AND OTHER AFRICAN STORIES

The Girl Who Married a Skull and Other African Stories

TAMAMO THE FOX MAIDEN
AND OTHER ASIAN STORIES

Tamamo the Fox Maiden and Other Asian Stories

The Nixie of the Mill-Pond
and Other European Stories
A CAUTIONARY
FABLES & FAIRYTALES Book

The Nixie of the Mill-Pond and Other European Stories

AVAILABLE NOW AT IRONCIRCUS.COM

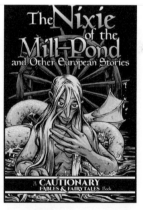